THE CUCKOO

By Leo Carew and available from Wildfire

Under the Northern Sky

The Wolf

The Spider

The Cuckoo

THE CUCKOO

LEO CAREW

WILDFIRE

First published in 2022 by
WILDFIRE
an imprint of HEADLINE PUBLISHING GROUP

Map Illustrations by Tim Peters

1

Cataloguing in Publication Data is available from the British Library

Hardback ISBN 978 1 4722 7312 3
Trade paperback ISBN 978 1 4722 7308 6

Typeset in 11.76/14.56 pt Zapf Elliptical 711 BT by Jouve (UK), Milton Keynes

Printed and bound in Great Britain by Clays Ltd, Elcograf S.p.A.

MIX
Paper from
responsible sources
FSC
www.fsc.org
FSC® C104740

Headline's policy is to use papers that are natural, renewable and recyclable
products and made from wood grown in well-managed forests and other
controlled sources. The logging and manufacturing processes are expected to
conform to the environmental regulations of the country of origin.

HEADLINE PUBLISHING GROUP
an Hachette UK Company
Carmelite House
50 Victoria Embankment
London EC4Y 0DZ

www.headline.co.uk
www.hachette.co.uk

Dedication

For Al, for Soph, and for Ragnar
No surrender

ALBION
Lake Avon
Haskoli
THE BLACK

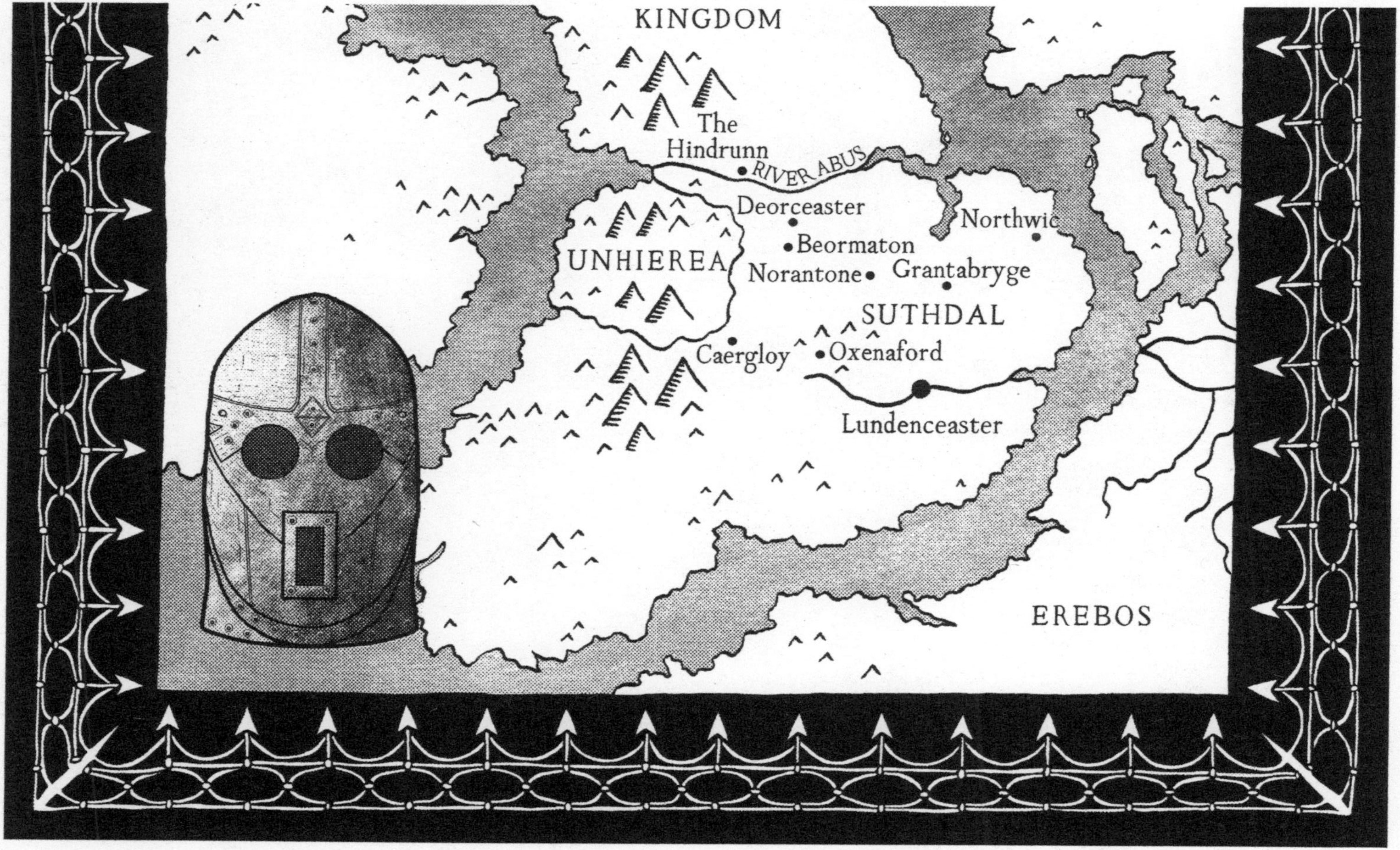
KINGDOM
The Hindrunn
RIVER ABUS
Deorceaster
Northwic
Beormaton
UNHIEREA
Norantone
Grantabryge
SUTHDAL
Caergloy
Oxenaford
Lundenceaster
EREBOS

Contents

Part II – Keturah

Part III – Bellamus

Prologue

Pain.

It riddled Vigtyr like woodworm. His foot had been lanced through, and agony swept up his leg each time he shifted onto it. The wound at his chest gaped like a salamander's mouth whenever he spread his arms. The roots of his teeth burned cold as each breath ran over them, and his eye – whatever was left of his blind, flattened eye – throbbed with each heartbeat.

The man who had done this to him was dead, Vigtyr was sure. He had seen him die; he had struck every blow it had taken to put him down. Limping, spitting and sobbing, he had dragged his body to the camp perimeter and abandoned him there. But it still felt as though he was close: listening for Vigtyr's cries, just behind the canvas of his tent. The dark interior was hot, and filled with Vigtyr's own thoughts, circling him like dogs. He fumbled at the toggles to the entrance and staggered into the night.

A buttercup-yellow moon shone overhead, and to his left, the city of Lundenceaster still burned orange behind its high walls, like a vast cauldron of coals. Campfires flickered around his tent, battered legionaries huddled around them, most of them awake and talking softly.

Vigtyr needed distraction: anything to take him out of his own head. He bent to seal his tent, trying to think what he might do. And a distraction arrived.

From the dark came the sound of hooves and the clink of a harness. He straightened, and turned to see a black horseman riding by. The rider was powerful and straight-backed, but the horse beneath him looked beaten. Even as Vigtyr watched, the beast nearly stumbled to its knees, recovering at the last instant. Legs trembling, it lifted itself once again, and as it did, there was a moment when the rider's face was illuminated by a campfire.

On instinct, Vigtyr retreated into the shadow cast by his tent. 'No,' he hissed, as the rider's face: grim, robust, and instantly recognisable, slid back into shadow. He knew that man, and the sight of him sent one deduction after another tumbling into place. *'No!'*

The man on the horse was Leon Kaldison: a Sacred Guardsman, and a terror. He had been at the haskoli – the mountain school – guarding Lord Roper's surviving brother from an assassin sent by Vigtyr. If Leon was here, it could only be because that task was now unnecessary.

There might be two reasons for that. The first was that the brother was now dead, and so had no need of protection. But that was not it. A man did not flog his mount to exhaustion to deliver bad news to his lord; to announce that he had failed, and the Black Lord's brother had been murdered. But he might if the assassin had been foiled. If he had been caught, interrogated, and given up Vigtyr's name as the traitor working against the Anakim.

Leon had paused to ask directions from the men gathered about the campfire. One of them raised a hand, pointing the guardsman towards Lord Roper's hearth.

Vigtyr swore. He hesitated one moment more, then turned and fled into the night.

An agonised limp was the best he could manage, and while he limped, he thought. If he tried to leave camp, he would be noted by a sentry. When the search began with torches and horses and knives, the sentry would point them exactly in his direction. Some of the Skiritai – the army's rangers – could scent like dogs. They could track in the dark: picking up the most infinitesimal clues by torchlight. He would be dragged from whatever pitiful hiding place he had found, and given over to the monsters of the Kryptea.

The thought was enough to bring Vigtyr to a halt, and he cast about wildly. The camp was huge and the blackness profound. His only chance was to hide here somewhere. With luck, they might assume he had slipped past the perimeter and not search too long within its boundary.

He began to limp once more, veering left and keeping to the corridors of darkness between each hearth. He had no more than moments before this camp erupted, and hissed with each agonising step, limping faster and faster for the northern field hospital. 'Please,' he breathed, passing into the void between the campfires and the hospital. He could hear the faint wailing of the hospital's injured. 'Please, please, please.'

Then came a roar which made Vigtyr flinch: unmistakably his own name, bellowed into the night: 'Vigtyr!' It rang across the camp, a howl of such distorted rage that the voice was unrecognisable. It might have been any one of those who had been close to Pryce, or perhaps Leon, that remorseless hound, even now sniffing him out.

'No,' he gasped. 'No, no, no.'

The shouts behind him were getting louder, and the campsite began to stir. News was spreading that Vigtyr was a spy and a traitor, and that thousands of this army lay dead because of what he had done. There was an ugliness in the aftermath of that assault, and all the fury and venom of fifty thousand men would be turned on Vigtyr.

But for now they were behind him, and Vigtyr was nearing the low, dark mound he had been aiming for.

Bodies. Hundreds of them, unsuccessfully treated in the hospital and piled here to await burial. Before he had even reached the mound, Vigtyr was unbuckling his belt and pulling his tunic over his head. He tossed it aside, stripping not just his clothes, but tearing dressings and bandages off his wounds as well. He must resemble every other corpse on this pile. His half-dozen injuries would be his camouflage, as would the overpowering stench rising from the dead. He fumbled at his boots, tugging them off with a puff of the dried grass he had used as socks. He hurled them aside before realising he had left his sword in his tent. He hesitated, but the shouts at his back were getting closer, and there was no time to find a replacement.

Vigtyr cast one look over his shoulder, and wished he had not. Torches were streaming into the dark, spreading out across the plains and searching the night.

He looked away, swearing under his breath as he took a handful of dirt and rubbed it into the wounds at his foot, chest, neck and eye, so that the fresh blood would look old and congealed. Then he climbed onto the mound of bodies, staggering across the uneven surface to its centre.

It *stank*. He held back a retch, looking back the way he had come to see his clothes scattered on the ground beyond the mound, in what may as well have been a declaration of his presence. *'No, no, no, no, no!'* He scrambled back onto the grass, eyes on the torches bobbing nearer and nearer. He thrust the garments beneath a body, before staggering back onto the mound. He dragged one cold, stiff corpse across his legs and then lay down, pulling another body over his torso. He tried to move a lower leg that was nearby so that it covered his face, but it was stiff, and each time just drifted back to its original resting place.

He was panting much too hard, and would be detected the instant the legionaries arrived. He tried to slow his breathing, but found the force of it overwhelming. Gasping, heart thundering, he stared up at the sickly yellow moon, the noises of pursuit growing.

A gang of legionaries was approaching the mound, in loud discussion which ceased abruptly when they reached his hiding place. Vigtyr heard a noise of disgust, then a voice spoke. 'Surely even *he* wouldn't stoop to this.' There came a few heartbeats of wild hacking, before another voice interrupted.

'Don't,' it said. 'Leave these poor bastards to their rest. The prick is long out of here.'

'We should at least check.'

'Check, then. But no need to mutilate them.'

There came the sounds of several men climbing unevenly onto the mound. Vigtyr kept his eyes open, like most of the other corpses, and tried again to hold his breath. He was trembling faintly, and there seemed nothing he could do to stop it. The legionaries prowled across the bodies, Vigtyr catching sight of a torch above him as one of them came near. It quivered in the corner of his vision, and then swept away.

Two more torches appeared, illuminating their bearers' intent faces, scouring the bodies. They were nearly on top of him, bending down and pulling some of the corpses roughly aside. A wave of pain pulsed up Vigtyr's leg as one of the legionaries trod on his injured foot, forcing it into an extension. He heard the tiniest breath escape his throat, but that, and the brief spasm that crossed his face, were missed in the darkness.

'Let's go,' came the voice again. 'He'll be out past the perimeter.'

The legionaries gave the bodies one last glance, one of them looking right over Vigtyr. But he was looking for the man he remembered from tournaments, subject of scandalous gossip, and thrilling sightings in the street and the mess: Vigtyr the Quick. Vigtyr the Whole. He was not looking for a man with a ruined eye, or an empty, toothless mouth, or a flapping wound in his neck. Vigtyr looked as dead as any of the others, and the legionaries turned away, clambering off the bodies and leaving him alone on the mound.

The voices were retreating, and Vigtyr's thoughts turned to escape. But it seemed impossible. Even if he could make it past the perimeter sentries, he could not think how to cover his trail well enough that the Skiritai would not overhaul him.

He waited there, naked and shivering, for hours. No ideas came to him, grey light tinged the east, and with it came a sense of dread. Dawn was near, and he still had no plan. He ignored the dread for a time, but as the light grew, that became impossible.

Horror clutched him. He had to move. He should run, or perhaps burrow deep into the corpses, and cower inside the mound. Anything but lie here, skin crawling, among bodies who had died because of him. The corpses on top were suffocating and he stirred, half sitting up, fighting his way clear of his cover and no longer caring if he were caught, because he could not stay here.

Then he heard a low growl.

Vigtyr froze, profound footsteps filling the dark. Something was moving towards him. He realised what was happening and very slowly, sank back onto the bodies. The Black Lord must have recruited the Unhieru to the search. The giants were prowling the camp, doing whatever they did to elicit the feeling of awful panic they commanded, and clearly hoping it would flush Vigtyr into the open.

He knew he must not move, but the terror was nearly past endurance, and the beast was thudding closer. The feeling was so visceral that it made his rational decision to stay put seem terribly feeble. It was dread potent enough to kill, drowning the distant whisper in his head that insisted this must pass. *Hold on*, said the voice, buffeted by a wordless swirl of panic. *This will pass, hold on. It will move away, just stay here.*

Words, decisions, thoughts: flimsy things beside the horror making his flesh crawl.

But the dread was fading. The Unhieru was moving past, taking with it that terrible aura. It was not long, just another minute, before it was gone. Vigtyr found he was drenched in cold sweat and trembling violently. He leaned aside and retched as quietly as he could, curling into a knot and closing his eyes.

The night seemed quieter, most of the voices more distant than they had been, and it was nearly dawn. Vigtyr rolled onto his stomach and began to crawl for the edge of the mound, casting about for legionaries. The grass seemed deserted, and he retrieved his clothes, dressed quickly and began to limp for the perimeter. Perhaps there would be somewhere he could slip past.

He spotted a distant party of legionaries, clutching torches and evidently still searching for him, and he swerved away, putting the dawn at his back and heading north-west. This brought him to the line of pickets, standing by braziers and guarding the perimeter of the camp.

They had been tripled. Each brazier burned high, casting long shadows on the ground, the silhouetted figures stirring restlessly. There was no chance of slipping past.

Vigtyr ground to a halt. It was as though the warren in which he was sheltering had just had a ferret fed into the entrance, even now snuffling through the tunnels towards him. He was standing in the middle of a singed wheat-field, and but for the dawn-touched darkness, would be completely exposed.

Nearby was a cluster of trees. It was small, and offered no corridor out of the camp, but the foliage was thick, and hunters seldom thought to look above the ground. He might be able to conceal himself among the branches, and limped towards its cover. Nearest was a high oak, with a hollow above his head that would suffice as a handhold. He latched onto it and pulled, grunting at the pain in his chest, boots scrabbling at the bark until he could snatch out at the lowest branch. That hurt even more, but he caught it and held on, waiting for the agony to subside.

Then a hand seized his ankle.

Vigtyr cried out in shock as he was yanked from his two handholds, crumpling to a heap beside the oak trunk. Pain swept up his leg and he opened his mouth to scream. But the breath died as he felt sharp metal pressed against his neck, and a cold voice hissed in his ear: 'You didn't think everyone looking for you carried torches, did you?' There was soft laughter, three or four voices nearby. 'No noise, now,' warned the cold voice. 'Or I'll open your guts here and now.'

Vigtyr was dragged upright, his hands forced behind his back and bound roughly. He could not resist a groan of pain as the wound at his chest separated again. A rough fist seized his hair and tugged his head backwards. 'Did you not hear what I said? No noise. Save it for when you kneel before our master.'

Vigtyr could not kneel before Roper. He thought wildly of escape, but it was impossible. Even if he could somehow break free of these men, he was too injured to outrun them.

The guards turned him around and propelled him deeper into the trees. Vigtyr tripped over a root almost at once and used his stumble as cover to steal a glance at his captors. There seemed to be three of them walking silently alongside him, another at his back, all masked in black leather. He needed a cover-story: something that explained what he had done, and he began sorting through excuses in his head.

Vigtyr was thinking so intently that he missed several important details about his captors. He did not notice when they steered him away from a distant patrol of legionaries, diverting beside a low hedge and aiming for another knot of trees so that they would not be seen. He did not notice that they had told him to be silent, or think why any Black Legionary would want that. And in the dim light before dawn, he did not even notice that on each of their masks was the imprint of a spread-winged cuckoo.

He knew the master he was about to kneel before. But it was not Roper.

Part I
ROPER

1
The *Wounded* Giant

Over the grass plains surrounding Lundenceaster rose the old sun of a tired summer. Orange light capped the charred fortifications and warmed the backs of two hundred and eleven men, kneeling in prayer before a pile of rubble, which had lately been the city's eastern wall. When they had last knelt, two days before, there had been three hundred of them. But they were used to losing peers. They had prepared for it from their earliest years.

We kneel before thee, Mighty One, mortal flesh in fear and silence, thy servants in deed and spirit. Grant we feel near thee when we lay in earth, receive peace in pain, be freed in death, and cede nought to fear.

The ancient prayers would usually have been the captain's responsibility, but he was missing. Last night, he had charged alone into the darkness and he had not returned.

Instead, the prayers were led by a man kneeling alone before the guardsmen. He was uncomfortably lean: his knuckles and fingers swollen, the tendons at his wrists and elbows tenting the skin, and his cheekbones jutting out beneath steady green eyes. His name was Roper: often now Roper the Daring to his face; sometimes Roper the Restless, or simply Old Mad Dog, behind his back. And at that moment, the guardsmen were paying homage to the ruins that had once been their enemy's greatest settlement.

Lundenceaster was beyond repair. The earth beneath it had charred. The fire that had stormed the previous night had been frightening: a billowing yellow mountain, hot enough to crack stone. From sunset to midnight, a trickle of rats loped clear of the doomed city, and when the gates finally collapsed into embers, a smog the colour of death tumbled from the gatehouse and poisoned the grass beyond.

The city had stood more than a thousand years. Many of its buildings were the remnants of a vast empire that had stretched over these lands in the days before Sutherners spoke Saxon. It had been home, they said, to five hundred thousand people: more by far than existed in the entire Black Kingdom. It would never rise again, and Roper was responsible.

He had marched two hundred miles south, dragging sixty thousand legionaries behind, with the monstrous ambition of subduing a nation. He had travelled a country of warrior-giants, and bargained, flattered and competed until they had agreed to join his quest. He had preserved the army from disease, and driven them on when hunger and thirst threatened to overwhelm them. He had been first of the Anakim over the formidable breach, and into the city behind. And it had been he who had fought through the defences and opened up a path for his men to sack the city.

Mighty One, grant us love in what life to us remains. Grant awareness that this soon will end. Grant swift passage from this world to the other. Keep us thy agents, until we walk with thee.

Roper had become used to being alone. So used to it, that when the prayers finished and the others stood and stretched, he stayed kneeling, head bowed in final prayer.

'Your will is not mocked, Mighty One. May your angels be after Vigtyr the Quick. Hasten our path to his footprints. Hold him until we're on his heels. Then show him your wrath through our hands.'

He carried on for some while, and when finally his prayers were finished and he stood, a hand landed immediately on his shoulder. 'My lord.'

Roper turned, finding a black-haired man in early middle-age, a cloak of rippling bronze feathers over his shoulders. 'Tekoa. Any sign?'

Tekoa looked pale, his eyes only half focused on Roper. 'Nothing. He's vanished.'

'What? No sightings? Is there no sign of a trail?'

'Some sightings, none convincing. No trail. I've got the Skiritai searching out past the perimeter. Perhaps with the light . . .' He shrugged.

'You need to scour the west, he'll probably try and join the Sutherners. How much ground are the rangers covering? He'll use the forests as cover; you've focused there?'

Tekoa looked flatly at Roper, who nodded. 'Of course you have.' There was a pause before Roper turned away slightly. 'Vigtyr,' he murmured, shaking his head. 'What would you do, Tekoa? When we catch him?'

'I?' At the question, Tekoa's familiar scowl lifted. He twisted slightly so that he could prop himself against a boulder at the base of Lundenceaster's breach, and stared at the rising sun, his eyes glassy. He was nearly as lean as Roper, and much paler. 'Sticky-fire is too good for that monster.' He was silent a moment longer. 'Do you know, my lord, I wouldn't kill him.'

'Oh?'

'I would take him north, back to the Hindrunn, and chain him in the street. I would let the subjects heap indignities upon him. Beat him and spit on him, so that he has not a single moment where he does not fear what is to come; not a shred of rest. Let him be degraded into the most pitiful, most diminished human being that has ever existed, so withered and broken over decades of abuse that our children know his name and his deeds, but cannot imagine how something so pathetic ever caused such pain. I would take him to the moment when he begs for death, and then drag his existence on for years. That, I think, for a man like Vigtyr, who craves recognition and status above anyone else, would be the worst we could inflict on him. He gave death to Pryce. We must reserve something worse for him.'

'A good reply,' said Roper. 'So let's get him.'

'You should eat, my lord,' said Tekoa, not looking at him. 'For the first time in months, we have a food surplus. At least for the time being. Let's make the most of it.'

'Later.'

'Now. You look like a broom.'

Roper kicked a stone across the grass, watching it bounce and clatter into the rubble of the breach. 'I suppose. Won't be able to finish the war otherwise.' From the corner of his eye, he saw Tekoa wilt, ever so slightly. It was why Roper now preferred to be alone. 'Come, then.'

The two limped back to camp. Roper's joints were stiff like they had rusted solid, his foot agonising, and his shot calf so sore that Tekoa had to check his stride to stay level with Roper's hobbling.

Dawn had spilt over the plain, glittering off mountains of captured Suthern weapons and armour; warming the heaped corpses; and casting long shadows from the legionaries stumbling back to sleep.

'Any sign of Gray?' Roper asked. The captain had last been seen running into the night, bellowing Vigtyr's name.

'Are you expecting any sign of him?'

'Of course. Why? What do you mean?'

'I mean, what makes you think he's coming back?'

Roper did not reply until Tekoa went on. 'I don't see him returning, not unless he finds Vigtyr.'

'Gray would not surrender to possession,' said Roper after a moment.

Tekoa scoffed. 'Did you not hear him last night? He *has*

surrendered. He's abandoned restraint for grief, the question is whether he recovers.'

A Skiritai officer fell into step with them, reporting they were sweeping the forest like a brush, heading west. 'If he's there, my lord, we'll find him.'

'Thank you, Galir,' said Roper. 'Make speed. He's injured, and will have tried to procure a horse. If he's found one, he has quite a start on you.'

The Skiritai bowed and departed.

Presently, Roper and Tekoa came to their hearth. Beside it was set a fine side of bacon, recovered from Lundenceaster's royal hall. Roper eyed it heavily. 'Give this to the Sacred Guard. They've earned it. What else is there?'

'Beans,' said Tekoa, flatly.

'Beans it is.'

Tekoa arranged for a guardsman to collect the bacon, staring wistfully as it retreated. Roper affected not to notice, setting a pot above the fire and adding beans, dried mushrooms and water. The smell was like a meal in itself and the pair of them ate together in silence. Roper tried to finish the bowl, but was full to the point of nausea after a few mouthfuls. He set it aside, waiting for his appetite to return, and found he could not bear to be still.

'So,' he said. 'We must go west immediately. The Skiritai have already scouted the land in their pursuit of Vigtyr, so we can move fast. We need to finish subduing this country before any resistance can form.'

Tekoa looked up from his bowl, face arranged in complete bewilderment. 'Lord Roper . . . Are you not exhausted?'

'Exhausted?'

Tekoa stared at him a moment longer. 'Perhaps you're not. But I can inform you that your men will not march another step. Have you not seen them? Most have not slept in two days. Before that, they were starving. They have fought, and searched, and salvaged without rest. They have already given you more than I ever thought they could. They would do anything for you: especially after the breach. But be careful what you ask of them. Even if you could coax them onwards today, we'd be in no state to overcome resistance if we encountered it. The only thing to do now is rest.'

The thought of that nearly brought Roper to his feet. *Rest?* The idea was unbearable. His chest felt as though it had a poisoned arrow lodged in its centre, and his heart churned so much that he could not sit with it. But Tekoa was staring at him, and he forced a tone of calm.

'Last night I dispatched eleven heralds to the major cities that have yet to surrender. They'll soon know Lundenceaster is destroyed and their king is dead. We . . . can wait here for their reply. Then be ready to march.'

Tekoa nodded slowly, but was still watching him in consternation. Roper looked down at his bowl, took up a spoonful of food, but before it had made it to his lips, put it down again. He got suddenly to his feet. 'You're right,' he said, turning west. 'The men need rest.'

'Then where are you going?'

'To see Gogmagoc.'

He left Tekoa alone, staring after his retreating back.

It was not far to the Unhieru camp. Between them and the Anakim lay five hundred yards of empty ground, pocked with the scars of old hearths which had been abandoned when the Unhieru arrived. It was the giants' smell that was most disturbing: a sweet reek of urine, which made Roper's hair stand on end, and was nearly overwhelming by the time he reached the edge of the camp.

The Unhieru at the camp periphery were small: barely taller than an Anakim. They were the lower caste of males: brown-eyed, shorter and rangier than their golden-eyed counterparts, and without their great shaggy manes. They were a wretched crew; even lacking fire, and many of them bearing scars and disfigurements. They stirred restlessly as Roper passed, eyeing his limp, his stooped posture, and being ignored in turn.

As he walked further inside the camp, the Unhieru grew

steadily larger and healthier. Here groups of forty or fifty sprawled together around great smouldering bonfires, snoring loudly. They were more relaxed than those on the outskirts, and uninterested in Roper, who hobbled as fast as he was able for ten minutes before he encountered the first females. They were squatter and broader than the males, and largely engaged in raucous conversation. Sitting nearby were the first of the maned males, whom Roper eyed warily. When they were enraged, these people flushed red and lost control so completely that they felt no pain, and could not recall their actions afterwards. And he had felt for himself the profound horror they could elicit in those nearby, and which he had tried to harness to find Vigtyr.

As Roper had suspected, he found Gogmagoc at the centre of things. The giant king was sleeping in a heap of ashen flesh, entwined with two of his wives. High on his back was a puncture wound which went right through him, and bubbled sluggishly with bright red blood. Roper eyed it, wondering that it did not cause the giant greater distress. He walked around to stand in front of Gogmagoc's broad face, skin pocked like the low moon, and undeniably beautiful.

He cleared his throat. 'Lord Gogmagoc.'

Gogmagoc opened eyes of deep honey, resting them on Roper but otherwise giving no sign of wakefulness. His deep breathing rumbled on at the same pace, and his mouth stayed slack and drooling, the saliva stained with blood.

'We need to talk,' said Roper, in Saxon.

'Talk,' mumbled the king. One of his wives shifted beneath him, but kept her eyes closed.

'I have had word,' Roper invented, 'from my scouts in the west, that they have seen the Eoten-Draefend.' Gogmagoc closed his mouth and heaved upright, the vertebrae fastened in his mane rattling. He did not greatly care for the weapons and armour that the Anakim had supplied in return for their alliance. The land they would receive into the bargain was of more interest, but above all, Gogmagoc had only been convinced to join Roper to gain revenge on Garrett Eoten-Draefend: a hybrid warrior famous throughout Albion, mostly for the act of killing Gogmagoc's eldest son. Roper himself wanted Garrett dead nearly as much as Gogmagoc. The hybrid wielded a long-bladed spear, which had been fashioned from an ancient blade belonging to Roper's house; Bright-Shock: the sword that had been in Roper's father's scabbard when he died. Roper still coveted that weapon.

'Eoten-Draefend?' rumbled Gogmagoc. His expression was hard to read at any time, but it seemed to bear a trace of suspicion. 'You told me he was in the city, River-King.'

'I said that was most likely,' said Roper, 'though we did not know. But we hear now he is in the west, with the last remnants of Suthern resistance.'

Gogmagoc regarded him for a long while, a little bloody saliva on his chin. The Unhieru were intelligent, Roper could tell. The reason for the squalor in which they lived, and their lack of architecture and metalwork, was not incapacity, but apathy. Gogmagoc was no fool, and clearly he suspected that he was being manipulated. 'I do not believe you.'

Roper shrugged. 'Believe me or not. I just thought you should know.'

'You thought—' Gogmagoc spluttered to a halt, and began coughing violently. Blood foamed from the hole in his chest and spilt from the wound like a lava flow. At the noise, his wives and a few of the males about the fire stirred, sitting up to stare at their king. After some time, Gogmagoc made a retching sound and ejected a fat, wine-dark clot from his mouth, which slid to the floor like an eel. He shot a glance at the other males, some of them nearly as huge as him, before catching his breath. Roper did not move, waiting for him to resume.

'You thought, River-King, that I would go west and destroy the Suthern men for you.'

'I think it would suit you to go west,' Roper replied. 'You could find Garrett. The Sutherners are in disarray, and you'd make light work of them. You could torch and harvest to your heart's content. Metal, food, sheep, slaves: take what you like.'

Whenever Roper had negotiated with Gogmagoc, he had done it surrounded by Unhieru. He hated it. He felt pathetically feeble in the face of people who respected strength alone.

Gogmagoc sat forward, drawing a few bubbling breaths. 'And if we go west –' he made a brief throwing gesture in Roper's direction – 'where do you go?'

'North. We must pacify the country we came through. The cities we bypassed should surrender now their king and capital have fallen. But my men have worked very hard for a long time, and first they must rest.'

'So we are to destroy the rest of the country,' surmised Gogmagoc, 'and finish this war for you, while you stay. That is why you say the Eoten-Draefend is in the west.'

'I told you because that's what I heard,' Roper insisted. 'But if you think I am lying, what of it? We subdued most of Suthdal while we were waiting for you. My people have paid for the new lands we will share in far more blood than yours: you have your own side of the bargain to uphold. Mopping up the fragments cowering in the west is no great task for you. And when we rule Suthdal from one coast to another, Garrett has nowhere to hide, and he is yours.'

'I will decide,' said Gogmagoc, making a gesture as though flicking Roper away.

'Decide, then,' said Roper, who thought the king would probably refuse out of stubbornness. He glanced at the frothing wound in his chest, a thought occurring to him. 'Your wound.'

'Yes,' said Gogmagoc, in a growl designed to dissuade Roper from further observation.

'It is dangerous,' said Roper, flatly. 'We can treat it for you.'

Gogmagoc gazed at Roper, then glanced once more at the males sitting around the fire behind him. 'How?'

'Clean it,' said Roper. 'Seal it. Stop the air from escaping, stop the blood, stop a fever from setting in. Make it easier for you to breathe.'

Gogmagoc looked away from Roper, shaking his great mane and making the bones rattle. 'Treat, then,' he said, without looking at Roper.

So it was that when Roper walked back into the Anakim encampment, it was with the giant king ambling beside him. Gogmagoc had been hiding how vulnerable he was. Before they reached Roper's hearth, he had to stop twice to cough up mouthfuls of clot. Roper doubted the wound would even have time to kill him. One of the other males would surely do the job faster.

Tekoa was sleeping so soundly by the time they arrived that he was not even woken by Gogmagoc's hacking coughs. Roper told the giant to sit, and summoned the battle surgeons.

While they worked, Roper called over every warrior he saw passing by, inviting them to join their hearth and informing them in genial Anakim that they should stay with him for a moment. By the time the two sides of the wound were sealed with a poultice of yarrow and sphagnum, and bound in linen strips, Gogmagoc was surrounded by thirty or so legionaries, watching the king's treatment curiously.

Roper asked whether Gogmagoc had come to his decision.

Gogmagoc looked at the assembled band, then met Roper's eye briefly before looking away. 'We will go west today,' he replied.

Roper beamed. His men would get the recuperation they so badly needed, while not a moment would be lost hounding the last scraps of Suthern resistance. When they had rested, the legionaries could go north and gather one surrender after another from Suthdal's great towns and cities. After what had happened to Lundenceaster, they should not be difficult to obtain. He wished Gogmagoc good luck. 'I hope you find the Eoten-Draefend, Lord King.'

'I will,' the king replied, rising to his feet.

'And destroy everything you see in the west.'

'I will.'

2
The *Warning*

For three days, the Black Legions camped outside the ruins of Lundenceaster. They ate until full, slept until the sun was high, and when the first petty scuffles broke out, Roper knew it was time to march. Some of the city was still smoking: they had not lost so much time.

Yet still, there was no sign of Gray, and Roper was worried.

He had found the resting unbearable. He had tried to run the camp perimeter each morning, but experiencing unexpected pain, had removed his boot to see his little toe tumbling onto the grass. There was a puncture mark on the boot from a wound he had not noticed on the assault on the city. Running too painful, he had settled for climbing Lundenceaster's breach again and again until exhausted. His wounds knitted, and by the third day, he was equal to running the two miles back to his hearth. There, he found a solitary figure he had not expected.

Roper panted for a moment, his tunic stuck to the sweat on his back, and stared at the man. 'Master Jokul,' he said, sitting heavily and leaning back on his hands. 'I'd offer you tea, but I see you've already helped yourself. Where's everyone else? Tekoa, the legates, the Chief Historian?'

'I thought we should speak alone,' said Jokul in his crisp voice.

'This sounds ominous,' Roper observed.

Jokul nodded very slightly. 'It does not have to be.'

The Master of the Kryptea was slight, cold and fastidious, with eyes pale as windowpanes. He and Roper had clashed from their very first encounter, each hating everything the other represented. To Roper, Jokul was master of an office purpose-built to check his ambitions, and which had previously accomplished this by assassinating Roper's ancestors. To Jokul, Roper was just the latest in a line of potential tyrants, and one too green and too bold to truly understand his actions.

'Then you have me to yourself,' said Roper. 'What've you got to say?'

'You plan to march soon, Lord Roper?' asked Jokul.

'Tomorrow,' said Roper. 'We have rested enough.'

'And where do you plan to go?'

'North,' said Roper. 'The Unhieru are scattering the resistance that remains in the west. We shall go back through the lands we have already flattened and collect surrenders from any city still standing. Suthdal is to be pacified.'

Jokul nodded briefly. 'That is what I suspected. Well then, my lord, here is what I have come to say: cease at once. Under no circumstances are you to do as you have just said.'

Roper looked up at the sky for a heartbeat, eyeing the moon still visible behind the Master. 'And why is that?'

'Because it is a fantasy,' Jokul replied, words emerging in a torrent, much angrier than the conversation seemed to warrant. 'I have watched you drive this army into ever greater depths of despair, to the point where the men who were trapped in Lundenceaster's breach were, by all accounts, ready to die just to make an end of it. Somehow, you pushed them through even that, as lethal as it proved. Impressive, I shall admit. I commend your ability to wring every drop from the men you command. But even to you, it should be obvious that you have spectacularly overreached yourself. This task is *impossible*.'

He glared at Roper, who felt only confusion. 'Why come to

me now?' he asked. 'The battle is all but won. Why would we withdraw when our enemy is on its knees?'

'Because the battle is the easy part,' Jokul shot back. 'You cannot possibly believe we can rule over a nation of millions, for decades, with a few tens of thousands. If you remain for the time required to pacify these lands, there is only one possible result.' He leaned forward and spat one word at Roper: '*Mutiny!* And if not mutiny, then rebellion from the nation you are trying to suppress. And if not that, then our men will fall victim – properly, this time – victim to that dreadful plague that stalks this land and selectively kills Anakim and hybrids. Your quest has reached an end, of sorts. You have destroyed Lundenceaster. A famous achievement, though one that cost us five times as many men as it was worth. But it does allow you to turn back without losing considerable face. You have your revenge for the death of your father and the invasions of last year. Suthdal's king is dead, her capital is dust. The Sutherners are thoroughly cowed, and will take decades to recover, time during which we too can rebuild. But occupying this land is not feasible. So, home is my command to you. End this now, and spare yourself the moment when the legions revolt. You appear confused,' added Jokul, impatiently.

Roper had been glaring at Jokul, and now shook his head. 'Why are you telling me this? You've never extended this courtesy to any of my ancestors. If you mean to stop me, you'll do away with me as you did them. If you're going to assassinate a man, you should do it without putting him on his guard.'

'I'm giving you the chance to turn back before it comes to that, Lord Roper.'

'But I cannot think why, Master.'

Jokul made a great effort to control his temper. 'All other things being equal, it would be better if you survived. If there is a mutiny, the result will be our second civil war in two years. A few legions may stay loyal: those commanded by legates close to you. Whichever side wins, we shall be terribly weakened.' Jokul paused for a moment and then twitched irritably. 'Well then. Is it impossible for you to believe I have some regard for you, Lord Roper? Unlike other tyrants, you genuinely seem to believe you're doing the best for your people. That is why I give you this warning. Turn back – now. Leave this task.'

Roper had been shaking his head throughout this speech, a furious ringing rising in his ears in protestation at this command. He was still so shocked that he could offer only the briefest counter-offensive. 'But I don't believe this. After all we have committed, all we have suffered, we are a hair's breadth from subduing Suthdal, and putting a permanent end to a war that has ravaged our kingdom for centuries. We have come so close, and you want me to abandon this now?'

'But we are not close,' snapped Jokul. 'Nowhere near. You see how defeated the legions are by *kjardautha* – homesickness – already. They barely have the will to fight. Imagine how they will be after decades in the south. They will not tolerate it. Here is where your ability to cajole people into action has reached unchallengeable fact. You ran roughshod over the other factions in the kingdom when you started this war, in secret, giving them no opportunity to object. You allowed my order to be blackmailed and intimidated by your own officers, to prevent us exercising our ancient duty. At every step, I thought the legates themselves would push you back, but you overrode them too, and they let you. Now, I tell you, I will not be moved. Now, the time has come to turn back. Do it yourself, or the Kryptea will depose you, and it will happen nonetheless.'

'Ah!' Roper could not help this furious exclamation, for he finally understood. The Master's concluding rant had exposed his motivations.

Jokul was scared of him.

He might have believed what he said about their task being impossible; about the Sutherners being destined for rebellion, and the legions for mutiny. But in reality, he was trying to restore the Kryptea's status in the Black Kingdom. He feared a lone ruler who was powerful enough to ignore him. He considered Roper too driven, too persuasive, too influential, and wanted him stopped now. And as for the idea that Jokul had offered him a choice out of respect: it almost made Roper laugh. Jokul did not want to depose him because he was still too popular with the legions. He feared that if the Kryptea tried to remove him, it would destroy itself in the process. Even if the institution survived, Jokul himself would almost certainly face a lynch-mob.

Months before, Roper's officers had publicly overruled Jokul and undermined his power. The Master had bided his time, hoping Roper's popularity would diminish sufficiently that he could be removed without consequence. It had not happened, and now he had sought this meeting with Roper alone, in an effort to intimidate him into behaving once more.

Roper bowed his head in dismay. 'You are trading the status of the Kryptea for the security of the kingdom, Master. This has the ring of madness to it.'

'A risk that anyone sane, who is prepared to engage with a madman, must take,' snapped Jokul. 'Heavy investment in a task does not makes it prudent, Lord Roper. And whatever you think of us, the Kryptea is here to stop people like you from making mistakes to which future generations are bound. When the legions march tomorrow, it will be back to the Black Kingdom.'

Roper was thinking as fast as he was able. 'At least grant me a night to consider your request. Then I might be able to find a compromise which satisfies us both.'

Jokul got to his feet, his tea sitting untouched by the fire. 'There will be no deals, Lord Roper. You will address the legions tonight, at Pryce Rubenson's embalming. Thousands will be in attendance. Inform them then that we are going home.' He raised an eyebrow. 'You can be sure it will be a popular announcement.'

In spite of everything, Roper knew that was true. He gazed up at Jokul, suddenly plunged into complete hopelessness. He tried one final objection. 'And what about the Unhieru?'

'What about them?' asked Jokul, flicking a dismissive hand. 'They have already profited from our alliance, and have no investment in your cause. They shall go home the moment they learn that you have.'

Roper smiled bitterly. 'This is what it comes to, then. You help me to secure my throne, and then rule from the shadows, dictating what I can and cannot do. Is that it?'

'You don't have to do as I say, Lord Roper,' replied the Master. 'As you observe, it is your throne. I'm just telling you what will happen if you continue.' He made to turn away and then caught himself. 'Oh, and get a new horse. Your destrier is an extravagance.'

'Zephyr?'

'I assume you know he killed one of his handlers yesterday.'

'An accident,' said Roper.

'Which will happen again. He's dangerous. Good morning, Lord Roper.' Jokul nodded curtly, and turned away, hurrying across the camp with his cloak clutched about his chest.

Roper watched him go. It did not seem feasible that here was where their great task ended: outside the ruins of Lundenceaster, at the whim of this sinewy bureaucrat. That they should finally be defeated not by starvation, armies, or plague, but Jokul, was crueller than Roper could bear.

He got stiffly to his feet and limped towards the field hospital, trying to let what he had just been told sink in. He did not wish to discuss it with anyone. Perhaps Keturah, if she were here. She would be able to snap him from his self-pity and invent some particularly cutting insults for the Master. But his wife was in the north, and the next she would hear from Roper was the herald he would send, bearing news that Pryce was dead, but that her father had returned to the army alive.

Roper wanted distraction and resolved to find it at the field hospital. It was on the far side of camp: a long tent decorated with strips of papery snakeskin. Through the canvas flap came a stinking waft; ferrous blood and something sickly and heady beneath it. Within, the light was like dusk, just after the sun has dipped beneath the horizon, and hundreds of figures lay on bedrolls. It was hard to feel sorry for himself here.

One of the surgeons near fell over himself in his efforts to greet Roper, smiling foolishly. 'May I help you, my lord?'

'I'm just here to see the men, thank you.'

The surgeon sniffed. 'That is handsome of you.' He gestured helplessly around. 'Take your pick, lord.'

Roper sat by the first man, who seemed held together by his bandages. He had lost an arm and the canvas wall behind him was stained mahogany with his blood. 'Your name, brother?'

The man was very pale as he squinted at Roper. 'My lord? Lord Roper?'

'It's me. Roper the Restless, Old Mad Dog, Boy-Roper; whatever you wish. What do I call you?'

'Skafnir, my lord.'

'Out with it, Skafnir, what bravery brought you to this place? And no false modesty, I want to hear every stroke of your sword, every intervention you made, every wound it took to put you down.'

Skafnir began his story, but fell to sobbing almost immediately. 'Sorry, lord,' he muttered.

'No apologies,' Roper commanded. 'Keep going, you can't leave me at that point in the tale.'

Skafnir, who had been alone and frightened since that terrible breach, sobbed his heart out to Roper, who said he would spread the story of his bravery, that he was in awe, and honoured to command such men. Then he moved on to the next man whose eyes were open, hoping to catch Roper and tell his own story. 'Well, brother, that'll be hard to top,' said Roper as he sat down beside the man. 'Be sure to tell me every good thing you did.'

He had moved almost to the end of the hospital when he became aware of a man moving up behind him, searching every injured face on his way past. Roper turned.

'Gray?'

3
The Embalming

Gray stopped abruptly, eyes on Roper. 'I've been worried for you,' said Roper, placing a soft hand on his shoulder. 'Are you all right?'

'I'm fine,' he said. But he looked wild. His face was scratched, his hair dishevelled, and his broken tooth, snapped in the assault on Lundenceaster, gave his face the look of a brawler. But it was his eyes that had altered most. The steady brown gaze, which so typified the captain, was torn somehow, as though the eyes were not quite looking in the same direction. It was as though this most consistent man was terribly drunk.

'Where have you been?'

'Oh . . . I was just . . .'

'Looking for Vigtyr.'

'I thought he might've disguised himself,' said Gray, glancing again at the wounded.

'You've been gone three days,' said Roper. 'We were worried something had happened.'

That seemed to snap Gray back to the present. 'Please don't worry for me, lord. I'm well.' Roper pulled Gray into an embrace. The captain froze briefly, and then returned it.

They broke apart. 'Gray,' said Roper, forcing himself to speak. 'You must be angry with me.'

The captain said nothing.

'You warned me about Vigtyr. And I did not listen.'

'I did, lord,' said Gray, distantly.

'Well I . . . I just wanted to acknowledge that. And apologise. I was wrong. Forgive me. I blame myself.'

Gray took a deep breath. He seemed to be struggling with something. Then he nodded curtly.

Roper wanted to go on. He was doubly guilty, having dispatched Pryce to look for Vigtyr. He had deprived Gray of his greatest friend and confidant through carelessness and arrogance, but feared if he tried to express any of that, he would unravel. So he cast about for something else to say. 'You came back just in time.'

'In time for what?'

'Pryce's farewell.'

By unanimous verdict from the legates, it had been decided Pryce would not be buried. The guardsman had been such a peerless warrior that his armed and armoured remains would instead be preserved, in the Hindrunn's Holy Temple. There he would stand guard until the day the dead rose, when he and the other mummified heroes would be called upon in defence of the living. And what a cohort they would make: each the greatest of a generation, lining up behind the Almighty and his angels, against the massed forces of Catastrophe.

Thousands assembled for the embalming: craning from the shoulders of their peers, or sitting on horseback, or perched on wagons and tree branches to catch a glimpse of the great man as he passed into fable. He was carried at the head of a procession of Sacred Guardsmen, his body resting on a nest of spears, his distinctive ponytail hanging down and lashing the air beneath.

The procession arrived at an altar, where Pryce was laid in front of three legates in their eagle cloaks. A battery of drums began to thunder, and one legate held an eye of woven holly leaves over the corpse, while the other two set to work. They cleaned the skin, sewed and sealed his terrible wounds, and then washed him in aromatic and antiseptic oils. The smell of lemon-balm, myrtle and betony was powerful enough to make Roper, observing from the front of the crowd, lightheaded.

Pryce's belly was sliced open along the midline between his bone plates, and a legate reached into the incision, holding a flint blade. When his hand re-emerged, it clutched the great dark clot of Pryce's liver, which was laid on a fire roaring beside the altar. Before long it was joined by the other organs, and the smell of the oils was overwhelmed by roasting offal. Even Pryce's eyes were removed and replaced with two grey, sea-smooth pebbles. Only the heart was left in his ribs; the empty chest and abdomen packed with sawdust and salt. As the legates began to sew the cavity closed again, the drumming changed, the rhythm condensing and slowing until, with the final stitch, it had become a booming heartbeat.

To this thump, Pryce was outfitted in full battle-rig. Undertunic to hide the incision in his belly, leather tunic with chainmail skirt above. His polished cuirass clamped over his chest, his boots, his grieves, his gauntlets, his sword and helmet strapped into place. Finally, his right hand was bound over his sword hilt, so that the body might dry in the first action that would be required on his waking. Then the two peripheral legates stepped back and Tekoa, face streaked with tears but voice resounding above even the drumming, chanted the Prayer for Preservation. It was written to accompany that percussive heartbeat, and though it was supposed to be intoned by a single voice, Gray, standing at Roper's side, began quietly to sing with Tekoa.

Freeze his eyes, preserve his tongue,
Leave in the heart, replace the lung.
Remove the unclean, retain the bone,
Retain the skin and dry till stone.
Give him a sword, Almighty blessed,
Temper the steel with sins confessed.

Tears sliding down his face, Gray's voice broke at the high note which ended the first line. He took a deep breath and began to sing louder, crying up at the sky. Roper watched him, heart wrenching for his friend, and then joined in. A few around them followed suit, and suddenly the entire assembly was singing.

Accept this warrior dread Almighty,
Preserve his form with fear from his enemy.
With his brave deeds and the love of a friend,
Link body and spirit after his end.
Power his arm with the wingbeat of birds,
Seed his thoughts with ancient words.

It was not just for Pryce. They had all lost friends. They were sick of Suthdal, of hunger, mud, marching and pain. They could finally give voice to that, and the prayer was howled up at the evening sky until Roper's ears rang.

The singing was cut off, and the drumbeat all that remained as the preserved body was lifted into a pale cask of holly. As the lid was hammered into place, the drumming softened abruptly as though it truly had emanated from Pryce's chest, and was now muffled.

The cask was loaded onto a wagon, and Roper stepped forward into a profound silence, the drumming coming to a stop. He hoisted himself onto the wagon and turned to face the expectant crowd. Thousands stared back, faces flushed by the occasion. Roper's own heart began to pound in his ears, and his mouth seemed too dry to speak clearly. Then, unexpectedly, a voice roared out from the mass: 'Hooray for Pryce the Wild, and Lord Roper the Daring!' The legionaries cheered and began to applaud.

Roper was taken aback. Having forced these men on against their will for so long, and so far from home, he had expected a resentful silence. But it seemed that his actions in the breach, and their respect for his unyielding drive, trumped all that.

He raised a hand to stem the applause, but it was some while before order was restored.

'Peers!' Roper bellowed. 'Peers. We gather to bid farewell to one of our very best.' There came another ovation. 'I count it one of the great honours of my young life to have known Pryce Rubenson, and even more, to have numbered him as a friend. With any other man, you might wonder whether it was appropriate to do him the extreme honour of joining those heroes in the Holy Temple. But not, I think, with Pryce the Wild. In any age, a man such as this is special.' Roper allowed silence to fall, and laid a gentle hand on the holly casket, staring down at its lid. 'If only we could preserve every fallen peer this way. If only we could bottle the memory of those who came south on this quest; hold onto some of the energy which they brought with them, and saw us destroy the capital of our great enemy. Today, we do honour to that endeavour. This occasion is not merely for Pryce: it is for all those who came with us. And particularly those we shall leave behind.'

There was a murmur of approval and the crowd applauded once more.

Roper drew a breath. *Peers*, he would say. *Our quest is now at an end. We have done what we came to do. It is time, at last, that we went home.*

But the breath caught in his throat, and he found he could not utter those treacherous words. He stared at them all, and thought of how many they had left in an alien grave. Of how pointless this endeavour would be if they did not now finish it. Of the unborn generations he would betray by retreating, when the most important part was yet to do.

The atmosphere had tautened in the long pause, and Roper took a breath. 'Peers,' he called. 'I am more moved by your endeavours than I can possibly express. The sweat you have shed, the blood you have given, the friends you have lost. Never – *never* – can a Black Lord have been better served by his legions.'

'And never legions better served by their lord!' called a voice, to a roar of support.

Roper was breathing rapidly. 'It has been my honour!' he called, before the hubbub had subsided. He clutched at the Almighty Eye on his tunic. 'To have served you all, and our people at home, is the task I live for. Will you agree with me, then, when I say that we have more to do in the south?'

There was a pause, then murmurs swept across the crowd. Roper raised his hands, and they yielded him the floor once more. 'Our enemy's capital is dust. Their armies are bones in the fields. Their king is a heap of soot-stained gold behind those walls!' he jabbed at Lundenceaster. 'Suthdal is on her knees, and *you* did it!' There were scattered cheers, which he encouraged. '*You* did that. You smashed them in the field, and then again behind their high walls. You took all the punishment they could give, and marched on, through their sick, strange land, until they had nothing left in them. That makes this land *yours*!'

Now the cheers were building, and Roper jumped off the cart to seize a handful of mud. He climbed back up, holding it above his head. 'This is yours!' He hurled it to the ground. 'You bled for it, you paid for it, it's yours, whether you asked for it or not. And we will keep it, until it resembles land fit for an Anakim. We will grow the trees; let the bears, wolves and aurochs flood the south. This land will smell of resin, and elk, and wild rose and juniper. And one day, generations from now, your descendants will find these ruined walls, standing between the trees. And they will remember the ancient generation of heroes who gave them that!' The roar was now deafening, and Roper inflamed it further. 'They'll think,' he bellowed as the noise subsided briefly, 'of the chants and songs about this time, astonished that the Black Kingdom once ended at the Abus. That it was once populated by people with the resolve to make a kingdom which will last forever. They will stand before this body,' Roper thumped his hand on the holly casket once more, 'and think him the greatest of every one in that temple of heroes, because he belonged to *our* generation!' By this time, the legionaries were rocking.

'We shall leave these walls standing!' Roper shouted. 'Because if we did not, no one would believe what you've done! Our children, and their children, for a thousand generations, will have peace because of your sacrifices.

'Today, I had a message from the Kryptea.' Roper himself was in such a trance that he did not see the shocked stir at the front of the crowd as Gray and Tekoa nearly lurched forward to pull him off the wagon. 'I was told to turn back, to take you all back north, or my life would be forfeit. After all you have sacrificed, and all you have achieved, I was commanded to take this army back beyond the Abus, and cower there.'

There was a bellow of rage from the crowd, and it surged forward a little, the legionaries spitting obscenities at the Kryptea.

'For myself, I have no care what they say,' said Roper, waving a hand. 'Pryce the Wild died for our cause: if it comes to it, so shall I!' The noise was frightening. '*Tell* me then! They want us to run from this great responsibility! Is this what we'll do?'

'No!' roared the crowd.

'Onwards, you say? Where next, my peers?'

'*Onwards!*' went the cry.

'Onwards!' Roper bellowed.

'Onwards, onwards, onwards, onwards!' The legions chanted with him, thumping their feet on the ground, the drummers taking up the beat.

'So, shall you promise me, that if I die, you will continue with our task?'

'Yes!'

'Will you promise me, that if I die, so shall the Kryptea?'

'Yes!'

'Here's what we'll do!' Roper's voice was ringing like beaten brass. 'We march north, to Deorceaster, and Northwic, and Oxenaford, and Norantone, and collect their surrenders. Our Unhieru allies are already wasting any opposition that remains in the west. And then, a longer task begins. Some of you will go north, and rest well. You will see your families, tell them what we've done here, and help the historians compose their chants of this famous time. You shall need your strength for when you relieve those of us who will remain, and pacify. We will keep the Sutherners from creating weapons. We will tax their crops, and have years of plenty. And we will begin turning this land; fertile, for all its nakedness, into something our children will be proud to call home. Then our roles will swap. Military service, from hereon, shall include the wilding of the south. Do you approve?'

'*Yes!*'

Roper nodded. 'Yes,' he repeated very quietly. He bowed to the crowd, and then knelt by Pryce's coffin. Before them all, he stooped over the holly boards and kissed their smooth surface. 'Thank you, my friend,' he murmured. 'I know you'd have been with me.' Then he dismounted the wagon, to see Gray and Tekoa's shocked faces.

'Lord,' said Gray. 'What have you done?'

4
What is Coming

Bellamus sat back and admired his handiwork. His hand ached, the parchment before him covered in a shining black scrawl.

From Her Majesty Aramilla, Queen of Suthdal and Protector of the Realm, in Her own hand, to His Royal Highness Karoli, Holy Prince of Frankia, Marobodia and Bretonia,

My Prince, I know You must have heard tell of what has happened in my Kingdom, and to my beloved King. It is with the heaviest heart I write to confirm that Suthdal is overrun. The Black Legions are on the march, have subdued a majority of our nation, and have proven irresistible in the field. They have joined with the wild nomads of Unhierea, and together are rampaging across our country. It will not be long before all Suthdal has been subjugated, and they rule the island of Albion unopposed.

I need not relay how disastrous this would prove, not merely for the brave subjects of Suthdal, but for Erebos as a whole. To have an entirely hostile power off your own shores, free to accrue might and influence unopposed, represents a threat to the whole continent. The new Black Lord has proven a radical and unstable ruler, determined to end Suthern law, and his ambitions – manifest within days of his succeeding the Stone Throne – will surely not end at our white shores.

The Black Kingdom is better understood as a colony of creatures, such as ants, rather than a holy society. Their extreme uniformity, potent technology and physical strength, combined with the resources of all Albion, shall make them difficult to resist. Moreover, they propose to turn our population into serfs, thus liberating their own people from the task of subsistence, and allowing every one of them to train exclusively for war. With our own agricultural techniques employed to feed their legions, there can be no doubt that this new power would have the capacity to become the foremost in all Erebos.

Imagine too, my Prince, the repercussions of this news on your own Alpine Anakim population. If the Black Legions successfully overcome Suthdal, without the Ereboan brotherhood raising voice in protest, it will show other Anakim that they can do likewise. This war will become the first of many, as emboldened Anakim populations look to emulate the Black Kingdom and expand their own borders. The fighting may have begun in Suthdal, but unless it can be stopped here, it shall sweep the continent. We must join together, beneath the sign of the cross, to do battle with the Evil Eye, and crush the Anakim, utterly and without mercy. Should the Black Lord be allowed to triumph, then I fear the balance of power in Erebos will shift decisively to the Eye.

My Prince, I beg for your aid with all my heart. My people are being slaughtered in countless thousands. My beloved husband has been murdered, and our capital burned. I have been forced to the ancient town of Wiltun, but shall not last long in my refuge without your help. Pray do not come yourself – the danger to your Royal Person is too great. But if there is anything you may send in support – soldiers above all – but arms, engineers, steel, food, anything at all – it would be met with my undying gratitude. Assist us in this worthy cause, preserve a holy nation from demonic rule, and you shall surely earn God's blessing, as well as no truer friend than my salvaged kingdom.

There was a time we joined together against the Evil Eye – all holy men, under the banner of the Teuta. You will know better than I the history of that noble endeavour. Our diverse peoples put aside common difference in favour of solidarity and stood against the forces of darkness as long ago as the reign of Chlodowich, and across the ages since. Shades of this ancient alliance were seen last year, when your own mercenaries came to help us subdue the Black Kingdom. Now, we need your help more than ever. I have written to the other rulers of Erebos, and pray that we may find the will and courage to reassemble that ancient brotherhood. The Teuta will march once more beneath the cross. Together, we may halt this disaster.

In fondest fellowship,

A space had been left at the end for Aramilla to add her labyrinthine signature. Bellamus scattered sand over the wet ink, and huffed it dry. 'What do you think?' he asked, offering it to the queen. The two of them sat in a wood-panelled chamber that had once been the Earl Penbro's dining room, and was at that time having Aramilla's own arms – a hawk – painted carefully on the wall behind.

The queen took the parchment and studied it. 'Do we not want King Karoli here? Saying he wouldn't be safe does not imply confidence. He's supposed to be a very great general.'

'Too great,' replied Bellamus. 'Have Karoli here, and we'll swap an Anakim overlord for a Frankish one. We must keep him at arm's length, or having helped liberate these lands he'll concoct some means by which he can keep them.'

'How clever you are,' said the queen, eyes narrowing as she thought. 'But then it's a risk calling on any of these rulers,' and she gestured at the already-completed stack of letters lying beside them, clamped shut with vast wax seals. 'Surely one will try the trick of stealing my kingdom while claiming to save it.'

'One surely will,' Bellamus agreed. 'The trick will be to play them off against one another. If it is not to be themselves who profit most from this coalition, they will want to prevent it being one of their rivals. That would be enough, I trust, to check individual ambitions. But there will undoubtedly be proposals of marriage. I expect one from Karoli. They shall talk of binding two great kingdoms indelibly against the Anakim, but in truth, there are not many wives whose dowry includes a nation.'

'I could be queen of two lands. That thought worries you?' Her hand fell on his arm, one finger toying with his cuff.

'Does it not worry you?' He breezed over the implication of jealousy. 'A queen unopposed at present, but a peripheral figure once more if you marry a king.'

'You cover yourself well, my Upstart.'

'Lord Upstart now, I think you'll find, Majesty.'

She gave her magpie's laugh at that, sitting back. 'You're right. Better lose this kingdom to the Anakim than surrender it willingly to a foreign king.'

It took Bellamus a moment to realise what she had said. He thought of the Black Legions wading through fields of crops; of ruined city walls choked with weeds; of a whole populace born into serfdom, and found that just for an instant, his face wore open contempt. He composed himself. 'We shall see what they reply, and must simply hold on until then.'

'And how are we to hold on, Lord Upstart?'

Lord Upstart sums it up best, Bellamus thought. Born a foreign peasant, he had been driven across Erebos by obscene ambition. A life spent in the shadows, a fascination with the alien, and an uncanny knack for seeing to the heart of a matter, had uniquely equipped him to take on the Anakim. It had also left its mark on his face. One brown eye was blind, and covered by a patch rimmed in gold thread. The grey at his temples had expanded, and every now and then he would flinch as an unexpected noise rubbed at his frayed nerves. But he had profited too, rising to become Lord Safinim: the most powerful man in Suthdal. At any moment, they might be attacked by the Anakim war-machine. It was still the most secure Bellamus had ever felt.

In reply to Aramilla, he gestured at the door. Those nobles who remained in Suthdal had gathered for a *witan* to formulate a plan. Aramilla, to whom the game of power came very naturally, had left them waiting in the hall for some hours already. 'Perhaps the time has come to discuss. They've waited for long enough, I'd think.'

'Your judgement does you credit,' she said, standing in a green silk eruption, and offering her arm. Bellamus stood, taking the arm with a bow. Together, the two entered Earl Penbro's hall. The witan's murmured conversation fell away at the sight of them, a shocked hush descending at the intimacy between a queen and a low-born foreigner. Nobody spoke, however. Aramilla was just the woman to take control of this shaken kingdom, and too powerful for anyone to object.

Bellamus helped her up the stairs onto her throne, and when she sat, she stared about the hall, surveying the witan in imperious silence. It stretched so long that Bellamus began to wonder if she was waiting for someone else to speak. He caught the eye of Stepan, a knight who was his particular friend, and winked.

'You may sit, my lords,' Aramilla decreed, eventually. There was a sigh of relief as the nobles settled themselves on the benches assembled around the hall, and rustled themselves comfortable. 'Let us begin at once. My Lord Widukind.' She called first on a bishop, who stood at his name. 'What forces have we gathered?'

Widukind appeared to have been resurrected from a previous age. His face was gaunt, long, and made to appear longer still by a narrow beard which sprouted to his navel. His hair was grey and wild; his eyes the same. Though he was a bishop, he had spent far more of his life serving an army than serving the church. Bellamus knew he had belonged to some minor

Ereboan kingdom, which had been conquered by the Frankish King Karoli. Widukind was a notorious and effective rabble-rouser, and had led the resistance against Karoli. Every time his army had been routed by Karoli's vastly superior forces, the bishop had somehow produced another as a seasoned street conjurer produces a card. Consequently, it was he who had been given responsibility for mustering Suthern resistance.

'The *fyrd* are gathering,' Widukind began, without bow or honorific to the queen. 'Eight thousand at present, some hundreds more each day. Very few have weapons. With these are six thousand regular warriors, spearmen and men-at-arms.'

'So fourteen thousand in total,' surmised Aramilla, 'less than half of whom are properly armed and trained. You occupy your post, my Lord Widukind, because you have a reputation for magicking armies from nowhere. So how will you improve this tally?'

Widukind trained his eyes on the queen. They were very light, and surrounded by dark rings which gave his glare such an intensity that even Aramilla seemed to blush under his gaze. 'The good soldiers will train the bad. For a . . .' he paused to consider a word, '*motivated* warrior, a plough or a shovel is an adequate weapon when given an edge.'

'Keep a working edge on your tools, my Lord Widukind,' Bellamus interrupted. The hall stiffened slightly at the upstart's commanding tone. 'There is no point trying to beat the Black Legions in the field. Labourers will be more valuable to us than soldiers, for now.'

'Sounds rather defeatist, Safinim,' said another lord, slyly. 'The Black Lord bested you, so he cannot be defeated. Is that it?' There was a rumble of satisfied laughter followed by gleeful muttering as the upstart was put in his place. The speaker, Lord Sutton, ruffled himself contentedly on his bench. He was plump, his beard wispy, his features shrewish.

The lightning bolt beat me, thought Bellamus furiously. *Not Roper. I had him. I know I did.*

Aramilla laughed loudest at Sutton's observation, but was

regarding the shrew-like noble as might an owl. 'What was that, eh, my Lord Sutton?' she asked, still wearing a charming smile. 'Go on, you have some military wisdom to impart?'

The smile fell from Sutton's face and he bowed, clearly hoping to avoid evisceration.

'You are all right to laugh,' said Aramilla, flashing her smile over the witan. 'Sutton speaks from grand experience. You've all heard of his victories, I assume? The most famous, of course, being the legendary fox he duelled over five seasons, vying for control over his chicken coop.'

Nervous laughter took flight, most of it relief that they were not the ones to be singled out by Aramilla.

'He was a wily combatant, but six gamekeepers and a team of hounds, and you were eventually able to get the better of him. Isn't that right, Sutton?' She left a long silence, but Sutton would not reply, and Aramilla went on. 'Then of course there was the campaign against the moles ruining your bowling lawn. That one rumbles on I understand, but I have faith you will prevail eventually.' There was a gentler laugh now, the witan a little uncomfortable. 'In fact, my lord, why are your talents wasted in this hall when *you* should be commanding against the Anakim! My Lord Safinim, is there some theatre in which we could unleash Lord Sutton to bring this war to a swift close?'

Bellamus would have preferred to distance himself from Aramilla's games. 'We shall need to upgrade the fleet, Your Majesty. The Anakim are far less assured at sea, and that's a theatre in which we shall be able to gain a crucial advantage.'

'There, Lord Sutton!' said Aramilla, giving every appearance of delight. 'You can be our grand admiral! At last, somewhere to use *all* of that experience.' Silence stretched in the hall. Bellamus realised he was grimacing, and composed his face. 'Do you accept this very great honour, I bestow upon you, Lord Sutton?' pressed Aramilla mercilessly, toying with her prostrate opponent, like a cat.

Sutton murmured that he should be very pleased.

'Well!' said Aramilla. 'I look forward to observing your progress. Lord Safinim, my apologies. I believe you were speaking?'

Bellamus, far more uncomfortable now than he had been at Sutton's joke, bowed to the queen. 'Thank you, Majesty. I am being realistic, rather than defeatist, my Lord Sutton.' He strode out to occupy the hall's centre. 'We will beat the Anakim, but it will not be by taking them head on. At least, not yet. My noble companions, here is what you must grasp about the Black Lord: he keeps gambling. Many of you have never seen a battlefield, and there is a truth that gets neglected in the stories which make their way back to comfortable parlours and good dinner tables. It is that most generals are exceedingly cautious. They feel their way into battle; at all times trying to avoid committing fully, hoping until the very last minute that the enemy will back down. Fighting is what happens only when there is no choice. And despite their bloodthirsty reputation, this is true for Black Lords more than most. Historically, they have been loath to spend men, and prefer the reputation of their legions to do the fighting.

'I have spent much time as Lord Roper's prisoner, and he is different. He needs conflict as a herring needs salt water. Since arriving in this court, I have heard him described as the Wolf, many times. Roper is not the Wolf. The Wolf is whatever stands behind him. Whatever drives him, and makes the horror of a battlefield seem mild compared to turning around and facing it. He will not back down, and I'm afraid what you must grasp, too, my lords, is that Roper's army is now just like him. His men have become accustomed to swallowing their fear and committing so hard that healthier and less desperate soldiers are appalled to stand against them. Anyone who takes the field against even half that army, commanded by that man, will leave it first.

'So no, we will not line up against the legions with sharpened shovels and hoes, and untested men. We will hold them off, and wait for the inevitable result of such a voracious king commanding such a limited pool of soldiers. They will burn themselves up, and our job here is to make sure they burn up before Suthdal does.' Bellamus turned back to Widukind. 'Please bear this in mind when you are recruiting, my Lord Bishop. We need labourers before soldiers.'

Widukind looked blankly at Bellamus, and it was Aramilla who broke the silence.

'My Lord Widukind is a man of very few words. A believer in actions instead. I hear your Abbio are riding now, looking for further reinforcements?'

The bishop inclined his head gravely. The Abbio were his personal guard, who had chosen to go into exile with him, rather than remain on mainland Erebos. To join this elite cavalry band, they had to imitate Widukind's ascetic lifestyle. The bishop ate no meat, and abstained shoes, alcohol, fire and bathing.

Aramilla seemed curiously taken with the bishop. 'My Lord Widukind cuts an impressive figure, does he not?' she observed. 'He and Lord Safinim alone do not disappoint me.'

She began to interrogate Lord Penbro over their food supplies, so coldly that Bellamus did not want to watch. He looked away, and spotted a messenger hovering by the door, attempting to catch his eye. He glanced at Aramilla and hastened to join him. 'My lord,' the messenger murmured, bowing. 'There's an Anakim outside who has been asking to see you.'

Bellamus leaned towards the messenger, thinking he had not heard him. 'An *Anakim*?'

The messenger nodded.

'Speaking Saxon? Did he say his name?'

'He did, but I struggle to repeat it, lord. He is quite hard to understand.'

'You'd better bring him to me. Not here,' he caught the messenger's arm as he bowed and made to turn away. 'Bring him to my chambers.' He glanced once more at the unfortunate Lord Penbro, who was to be interrogated for a while longer, before slipping out of the hall and into his own chambers. These were immediately beside the queen's and very nearly as large. He had no possessions with which to fill them: the only furniture was a desk, a chair, and a bed in one corner with a chest at the end. He sat behind the desk, staring at the wood-panelled wall. He was considering having some arms designed for himself, now he was a lord, and painting them on that wall. Aramilla had given him a spider brooch once, and that seemed as good a symbol as any.

Footsteps in the corridor outside announced a pair of royal guards, who entered in front of the largest Anakim Bellamus had ever seen. He was a hideous wretch, pale and thin, with a ruined eye, sunken lips and a number of inflamed scars. Two more retainers entered behind him, and reduced the Anakim to his knees. He was still significantly taller than the seated Bellamus. 'My lord,' he said, bowing his head.

'Your name?' Bellamus replied.

The name, when supplied, was such a mess of sibilance that Bellamus could make no sense of it. This creature had evidently lost his teeth recently, and produced more in the way of saliva than sensible words. 'I am your servant, lord,' the Anakim explained clumsily, staring down at the floor. 'I—'

'Let's speak Anakim,' Bellamus interjected. 'Who are you?'

The creature repeated its name. 'I was an informant of yours for months,' he explained, a little more clearly now that he was speaking his native tongue. 'I wrote you letters, on the movements of the Black Legions. I . . .' He stopped abruptly and wiped some of the spittle from his chin, stealing a look up at Bellamus. 'We have met before. We spoke, you remember? In my tent, when you were the Black Lord's prisoner. I . . . that is, I *tried*, to organise your rescue.'

Bellamus leaned forward incredulously. *Vigtyr*, he remembered. What terrible fortune had befallen this man since they had last met? Now Bellamus knew who he was, he recognised him, but only barely. 'Yes . . . Yes, I recall now. I am lucky to be alive at all after that attempted rescue, Vigtyr.'

'I tried, lord,' said the huge man, dipping his head.

'What brings you here?'

'I had hoped, with the services I have done you over the

years, my lord, that there might be a place for me here. In the court, perhaps. As an adviser?'

Bellamus blinked at the absurdity of this request, and then laughed, gazing at this broken figure with his comical speech. 'I take it you are no longer welcome with the Black Legions?'

Vigtyr hesitated, and Bellamus nodded to himself.

'I don't think so, I'm afraid,' he said, standing, and thinking he should return to the witan. Vigtyr stirred suddenly, but Bellamus forestalled him with a shake of his head, not meeting his eye, and already on his way out. 'In honesty, I'm doing you a favour, Vigtyr. The final decision of what happens to you would rest with the queen, and I fear you would be an amusement to her. I thank you for some of your services. Others, I could have done without.' He was at the door, when Vigtyr called desperately from behind him. 'But I have news, my lord!'

'I'm sure,' said Bellamus, not pausing.

'Word on the enemy. You are all in terrible danger! Please, lord. They'll kill me if you don't hear me out!'

Bellamus paused, and then turned back to Vigtyr. 'Who will kill you?'

'The Kryptea, my lord. They helped me escape, they brought me here. But if you send me out so soon, they'll know I failed!'

Bellamus considered Vigtyr for a moment. 'I think desperate men say desperate things, Vigtyr. If you are quite certain you have something to say to me now, I'll listen. I'll take you in, and you'll stay here until we know whether you spoke the truth or not. If it transpires you were lying to advance your own cause, then you will be very severely punished.' Bellamus shrugged. 'However, it may be that you misspoke, and have nothing to say, in which case I shall leave, and you shall be released.' He met Vigtyr's eyes, unblinking. 'So, are you quite certain that you have something to tell me?'

'Certain, lord,' said Vigtyr, with such vehemence that a great loop of saliva dribbled off his chin.

'Go on.'

When Bellamus slid back into the witan a few minutes later, his face was grave. Another lord was droning on about the fortifications surrounding Wiltun, and when he was finished, Aramilla maintained an expression of detached surprise. 'Understand me now, my lords, all of you shall have to do better. The threat we are facing is vast, and urgent. Our time before the Anakim arrive is *precious*, and I need more from you all. Take your lead from Lord Safinim,' she said, inclining her head in his direction. 'Finally then, what news of the enemy, my lord?'

Bellamus ignored the resentful stares directed against him, taking a few steps out into the middle of the hall. He was still not quite certain whether to trust Vigtyr's report, but instinct told him the wretch was in earnest. 'My lords, I must be blunt. The news is grim.'

'You assured us,' Lord Sutton spoke suddenly, still purple-faced after the humiliation from Aramilla, 'only a few days ago, *Lord* Safinim, that the Black Legions were spent, and needed to recuperate before they could march against us. You said we would have time to build a resistance. And now it seems the news is grim?' Sutton looked about the hall, trying to force his features into an expression of sarcastic surprise, but failing to display anything but indignation. 'Could it be that you have at last disappointed, like the rest of us?'

There was soft laughter at these words. It was as close as the nobles would come to defying Aramilla.

Bellamus merely nodded. 'And I was right. The legions are indeed too weary to march. They remain at Lundenceaster. However, I have good reason to believe that their Unhieru allies, who are far better rested, are already marching on Wiltun.'

There was silence as that news settled over the hall, the anger draining from Sutton's face.

'How many are there, my lord?' asked Lord Wulfheard.

Bellamus paused, wondering if there was some way he could soften this blow, and realised the silence was just making things worse. 'Ten thousand.'

The witan was too stunned to respond. All except Aramilla, who asked: 'How long do we have, Lord Safinim?'

'They will be here in three days,' said Bellamus.

There was a heartbeat's stillness, then a fierce muttering swept around the hall. Aramilla looked faintly surprised but also rather excited. Bellamus thought she must be the most anarchic monarch ever to have occupied the throne.

'Calm yourself, my lords,' said Wulfheard, standing amidst the hubbub and raising his hands. 'Calm, calm. So often you seem to have a plan, Lord Safinim. What now?'

'I am considering,' said Bellamus.

Widukind's sombre voice came next. 'You must put your faith in God. We are His right hand in this land, and shall not fail.'

'You are indeed the last word in suicidal ideology, bishop,' called Lord Nerven: a gruff noble of past fashions and crumbling halls, with a haughty consistency which made him well respected, nonetheless. 'Your blind belief will doubtless stand us in good stead when the Unhieru arrive.' He too got stiffly to his feet. 'My land borders theirs, and let me tell you, gentlemen, we may as well pick a fight with the gods. Giants. Bigger even than the Anakim, less civilised, with a leader still more barbarous. And if Lord Safinim is to be believed, they have now been armoured by the Anakim's own forges, so as to be near impregnable. Our men are neither properly trained, nor equipped.' He shook his head, looking about the hall. 'You take my advice. The only sensible thing to do is get out of the way.'

'Sit down, my lord,' said Aramilla calmly. Nerven hesitated but was a man too in love with tradition to defy his monarch. He sat reluctantly. 'We've been over this,' the queen went on. 'We are here to fight, not flee for Erebos. All you should take from Lord Safinim's news is how urgent your task has become. We shall spend day and night in preparations, and meet again tomorrow afternoon. By then, you will each have better news for me.'

5
The Barrel and Nails

As the witan dispersed, Bellamus threaded his way through the crowd towards Stepan, who stood head and shoulders above the throng. He found himself passing by Bishop Widukind. For an instant, he caught his pale eyes, deep-set and surrounded by dark rings. With it came a waft of his scent, nothing like the scent of a man. It was fresh, like wild mint. A little damp and musty too, like moss. There was a hint of the raw flesh of a mushroom, and the sap of a silver birch, and a waving carpet of heather. In fact to Bellamus, whose time in the mountains remained the starkest of his life, Widukind's scent was like nothing so much as the smell of cold.

He nodded at Widukind, who gave no sign that he had even recognised Bellamus as a man, and passed on. It was better treatment than Bellamus received from the rest of the nobles. His lowly birth and the queen's special favour, had so far resulted only in resentment from the rest of the court.

'Odd character, isn't he?' said Stepan. He had come to meet Bellamus, and followed his gaze to the departing bishop.

'I rather like him,' said Bellamus. 'Most of us do what we want and justify it later. He lives by his convictions. An unusually principled man.'

'Principled is a gentle term for Widukind.'

'What would you call him?'

'Fanatical.'

'We will need fanatics in the next few days.'

'So you say. What makes you so confident the Unhieru are coming this way?'

'I'll show you,' said Bellamus. He led Stepan back into his chamber, where Vigtyr was still kneeling, held by the four guardsmen. Stepan stopped abruptly at the sight of the wrecked Anakim, who screwed his head unnaturally far round to get a view of them in his good eye.

'I've . . . have I not seen this one before?' asked Stepan.

'You may well have done,' said Bellamus, sitting on his bed. 'He came to Seaton's camp to try and get me rescued, when we were outside Deorceaster.'

'Yes,' said Stepan, studying the captive. 'In happier days for him, though. Remind me of your name?'

Vigtyr tried to speak again, but Bellamus gestured for him to be quiet. 'Vigtyr. He can't speak Saxon very clearly, but says he was smuggled out of the Anakim camp and into our lands. When he was cut loose, he was told to relay the news that the Unhieru were marching. All ten thousand of them, with their axes and chainmail, heading this way.'

'You believe him?'

Bellamus looked down at Vigtyr. 'I do, as a matter of fact. And it's what I would do, if I were in Roper's boots.'

'Then what on earth are we going to do?'

'I don't know yet,' said Bellamus. 'But there's always a way out.'

'But like what?'

'I'm thinking.'

Both men kept an unhappy silence, observing Vigtyr with knitted brows. Bellamus was trying to think of something reassuring to say when the door opened once more and Aramilla swept in. She saw Vigtyr and stopped in her tracks. 'Great God. What is this?'

'Vigtyr, here, has defected to our side, and brought the news of the Unhieru.' Bellamus glanced at Vigtyr. 'He'd like to be an adviser at court.'

Aramilla smiled suddenly, her eyes narrowing. 'An adviser? Yes . . . Why not?' She gave Vigtyr a look of amusement. Vigtyr leapt at her words like a trout for a fly, and scrambled into a kneeling-up position from which he could very nearly look her in the eye.

'I can serve, Majesty,' he spluttered in Saxon. Bellamus grimaced as he made a mess of the words once again, and Aramilla's smile widened.

'I'm sure you could tell even Lord Safinim here a thing or two about your kind,' she observed.

'I hope so, Majesty,' said Vigtyr, spilling more saliva.

'Well then, we'll have to find you some clothes befitting your new position,' said the queen, beaming. The Anakim were a direct people, but perhaps it would not have been obvious even to a Sutherner in Vigtyr's position that Aramilla was mocking him. 'You'll understand if we keep these men with you, for now,' she added, indicating the guardsmen. 'For your protection too, of course. I think my court would be a little shocked to see an Anakim walking around unsupervised.'

'Of course, Majesty.'

'He can have room in the servants' quarters for now,' said Aramilla, gesturing to the guards. 'See him there now.'

'Thank you, Majesty, thank you!' said Vigtyr, bowing clumsily from the floor.

Bellamus and Stepan exchanged a glance, the knight biting his lip, as Vigtyr was led out. Aramilla turned on them, snorting. 'A proper court should have a fool, and he'd be marvellously appropriate, would he not? Good morning, Sir Stepan,' she added, smiling pleasantly at the knight.

'Good morning, Majesty.'

When it came to people, Aramilla missed nothing, and must have decided to ignore his disapproving tone. 'The Unhieru, then,' she said lightly, turning to Bellamus. 'What are we to do?'

'I was just going to suggest to Stepan here, that we might talk on it for a while. See what we can come up with.'

'Do that,' she agreed, waving a hand generously. 'I'm going to walk with Cathryn. She says there's a man in town with a goshawk that's the most superb hunter. Let me know what you come up with, won't you, Lord Upstart?'

When she had gone, Stepan said: 'Does Her Majesty genuinely have no fear? Or does she not understand?'

'I think it may be a little of both,' said Bellamus. 'There has not been enough consequence in her life for her to truly believe bad news will affect her. In an Unhieru advance, all she hears is a break from a life she finds boring. But us, my friend? We're men of action. So what are we going to do about it?'

'Ah,' Stepan hesitated. He looked around for somewhere to sit, and then realising that Bellamus's spartan quarters offered nothing but the bed, resigned himself to standing. 'If I'm being honest, Captain . . .'

Bellamus just waited, not the faintest idea what Stepan might be about to suggest.

'I wasn't . . . *really* hoping to discuss the Unhieru. I'm not sure . . . I'm not sure I plan to be here to fight them, either.'

'Why's that?' asked Bellamus.

'Well. As you know I've wanted to secure my household – my wife, my dogs, my servants – for some time now. They're all further north, in Anakim-held territories. I've no idea what's happened to any of them. I haven't been able to get a message to them for . . . months. They probably think I'm dead, killed at Lundenceaster or by some Anakim head-hunting patrol. I need to get them, Captain. I need them here.' He and Bellamus looked at one another. The knight was playing with a silver charm about his neck, biting his lip again. 'I want to go now. Today.'

'My friend,' said Bellamus, shaking his head. 'Of course you do. Of course. But . . . you can't travel there alone. This country is in *turmoil*. Even if you don't hit a Black Legion out foraging and end up being skinned alive, the roads are infested with brigands. If you try and go today, your family won't just believe you're dead. You actually will be.'

'Well,' said the knight slowly, 'that's true. But I'd hoped you might lend me some men. Just a few – twenty, maybe – enough to keep the brigands at bay and protect my household on the way back.'

Bellamus took a breath, faltering at the look of hope on his friend's countenance. He shook his head. 'Stepan . . . Why would you want your household here? This is probably the most dangerous place in Albion.' Bellamus gave an incredulous laugh. 'We're about to get stomped on by ten thousand giants! Forgive me, but wouldn't they be better off in the north? At least the Anakim-controlled lands are stable.'

'There's no safety anywhere, Captain,' said Stepan. 'I'm not sure we know which bits of the country are more dangerous any more. I'm not sure it even makes sense to try and choose between them, we could be struck down anywhere, at any time. At least this way, we'd be together.'

Bellamus found he could not look the knight in the eye, and though he felt like a coward, he addressed his next words at his rug. 'Brother . . . we're about to be overrun. We're talking about arming the fyrd with hoes and ploughs to fight chain-mailed Unhieru. I can't spend twenty good men on a ride across country, who wouldn't be back before the Unhieru started battering at the walls.'

'Don't worry,' said Stepan quickly, and Bellamus could see his embarrassment at having asked. 'I knew it would be difficult. But better to know.'

'Any other time,' said Bellamus, just as quickly. 'It's just now . . . if we hold on to this town, it'll be with our fingernails. But soon, I promise. The moment we've got half an inch of breathing room, you shall have a full company, riding under the queen's banner.'

'Don't worry,' Stepan insisted. 'And you're right, I can't go alone. I wouldn't make it. Let's talk about the Unhieru.'

Lubricated with a flagon of ale and a length of good blood

sausage, they talked through the afternoon and into the night, but few sensible ideas came to them. Stepan noted that the Unhieru had no horses, and were therefore relatively ponderous. 'Maybe Widukind could distract them with the Abbio,' he suggested. 'Lead them in circles.'

More likely the Unhieru would just ignore such a meagre force and carry on, Bellamus thought, but they had come up with so little that even this was not to be sniffed at.

They went to quiz Vigtyr in his quarters as to precisely what deal Roper had struck with the Unhieru. The Anakim turncoat could do no more than describe their original negotiations in Unhierea, though he also mentioned that Gogmagoc had since been injured.

Bellamus retired to bed that night, wondering how he could possibly stand before the witan with such feeble schemes to hide behind.

The morning felt like the first day of autumn. The light was different, and the air newly cool and fresh, until a maid arrived to kindle the hearth in his chambers. To an Anakim, this was *The Dying*. The flies, and fungus and mould which had time to take hold over the growing months, and might otherwise replicate until they choked all Albion, would be destroyed. The earth was refreshed, and winter wiped the slate for the new year.

And as surely as a reckoning was coming for the summer insects, it felt as though the same was coming for the Sutherners in Albion. The Unhieru would arrive the next day.

No inspiration had arrived during the night, and though Bellamus sat at his desk with paper and quill until mid-morning, he had little to report when Stepan knocked at his door and asked if he had made any progress.

'I was thinking about something Vigtyr said last night,' said Bellamus, laying down his quill. 'Seems as though if Gogmagoc were dead, the alliance with the Anakim would be forfeit. He's already injured: maybe we could lay an ambush and finish him off?'

Stepan made a noncommittal noise. 'Possibly. Are our men up to it?'

'Almost certainly not,' said Bellamus, bitterly. Even with well-trained men, an ambush was fiendishly difficult to organise. 'It depends where Gogmagoc is travelling. If he's at the van, or an edge of the column, the Abbio might be able to plunge in and do the business before they're wiped out.'

'No worse than any of our other plans,' Stepan observed. 'And if anyone could pull it off, it'd be Widukind. He's quite the fellow, isn't he?'

'I thought you said he was a fanatic.'

'Oh, he's definitely that,' said Stepan comfortably. 'But I got friendly with one of the Abbio lads this morning, told me all about the bishop's teachings.'

'Oh?' murmured Bellamus, looking back at his paper.

'A man of almost complete silence, apparently. He thinks it's better to say nothing at all if you can. His big line is that words are worth nothing because they're so cheap, and only actions are worth paying attention to because they're so costly.'

'Well he certainly lives by that principle. There aren't many people whose actions have been more costly than Widukind's.'

'I was asking how he raises his armies so fast,' Stepan went on blithely, settling himself on Bellamus's oaken chest. 'His lads talk about him like he pisses fine wine. They say he's the closest to God that any man has been, and can heal the sick.'

Bellamus looked up. 'Heal the sick?'

'They've seen it!' protested Stepan, sensing the scorn in Bellamus's voice.

Bellamus laughed and rolled his eyes. 'Stepan . . .' he muttered, smiling in spite of himself.

'I'm not the only one gullible enough to have swallowed that tale,' the knight insisted. 'Widukind's with the queen as we speak. She asked him to come and pray with her.'

Bellamus snorted. 'God, he's become another vogue in court,' he said. 'Widukind is unique, and a little wild, and all those men in there –' he jerked his head at the wall, through which lay the court – 'who've never seen anything wilder than their own archery range, mistake that wildness for power of some sort. They're so keen to be elevated above the common man, sporting the latest ideas and fashions, that it makes them absurdly vulnerable when something new appears.'

Stepan raised his eyebrows at this bitter outburst. 'But you like him, don't you?'

'I like his principles,' said Bellamus curtly. 'I like his dedication. They make him forceful. But I don't believe his hocus pocus. Now come, we need a solution. I have to go into court this afternoon to explain how we survive the Unhieru.'

Stepan shrugged. 'In all honesty, Captain, I think retreat is our best option. At first sight of those monsters in full battle-rig, axes fit to fell an oak, the fyrd are going to hurl down their weapons and sprint for whichever gate offers the best chance of escape. And the regulars won't last much longer. If we can even persuade them to engage the Unhieru, the fight'll be exceptionally brief. With the forces we have here, we can't hold them.'

'But we can't retreat,' said Bellamus. 'This has to be the place we defend, there is no pulling back.'

Stepan observed him thoughtfully. 'Is this to do with the project you've had the fyrd working on? I've seen them coming and going at every hour, so muck-covered it's like they're wrestling pigs. What have you got them doing?'

'I'll tell you soon,' Bellamus assured him. 'But for now . . . the fewer people who know, the better. The witan will think it's mad if they find out before the time is right. I have to show them it's possible before they know it's happening.'

Stepan raised his eyebrows. 'So what *are* you to tell the witan?'

Bellamus wished he knew. When he stood before the queen and assembled nobles that afternoon, confidence was his only shield. He explained how they would ambush and kill the weakened Gogmagoc, causing the Unhieru mob to fall apart. And if that did not work, they would set traps before the walls to dishearten their enemy, who would be lost without Anakim expertise in fortress-breaking. He told them this was their last chance, and that with their queen and the famous Bishop Widukind inspiring resistance, the fyrd would hold off even the Unhieru.

But he had no faith in this plan, and nor did the court. As they traipsed from the room, even Bellamus's enemies were downcast. Scorn him they might, but they had wanted him to show how they could win.

It was a brittle evening at Penbro Hall, with arguments erupting in parlours and kitchens. Aramilla seemed the only one unburdened by thoughts of the next day. She breezed the corridors in high humour, calling on every lord, and Bellamus most of all, to talk fashions, autumn fruits, Widukind and Vigtyr. 'What I want to know is,' she declared to Bellamus, perched on the edge of his bed, 'how did these Kryptea people get old Vigtyr out of the Anakim camp?'

'In a wagon with a false bed,' Bellamus replied. 'They smuggled him here, told him the Unhieru were coming and said they'd wait to make sure we were preparing for their arrival. If we weren't, they would know Vigtyr had failed, and come to punish him.'

'Do you suppose the old rogue was lying? If the Unhieru are due tomorrow, then why haven't our scouts sighted them yet?'

'I wish he were lying, Majesty,' said Bellamus heavily. 'I will be expecting them in the afternoon.'

'But do you trust him? Why would these Kryptea people work against the Black Kingdom?'

'They work *for* the Black Kingdom, but against the Black Lord. They thought their kingdom would be better off without involving itself in Suthdal, and without Roper on the Stone Throne. Now usually they'd have executed him, but at the moment they are not popular, and the Black Lord very much is. So their only option was to work against him in secret, and hope to turn public opinion against him.'

'So that is why they protected this Vigtyr creature.'

'Precisely. The Black Legions only recently discovered Vigtyr's treachery, and the Kryptea helped him escape them, again as a means of undermining Roper. That's why I'd be surprised if the information about the Unhieru was wrong. Helping us fits with the objectives of both Vigtyr and the Kryptea.'

Aramilla gave every impression of being thrilled at this news. 'Marvellous! I've still not seen a giant. I'll be able to watch from the walls as you beat them back, Lord Upstart.'

Her confidence was so out of place that Bellamus found it alarming. More than anything, it underlined that the defence of this city lay on his shoulders. Long after Aramilla retired to bed, he was still scheming in the pool of yellow light spilt by a large oil lamp. He was so focused on his work that he only realised it was dawn when the distant tolling of church bells penetrated the walls. He raised his head for a moment, staring at the lightening window. 'Heaven help us.'

He tried to write a warning order to be pinned around the marketplace, but found his hand was shaking so badly he had to dictate instead. 'When you come back,' he told the scribe as he left to distribute the copies, 'bring wine.'

The market was closed. The streets drained. Even the filthy labourers, working on Bellamus's secret project, ceased to traipse in and out of the gate, which was shut, barred, and materials for a barricade set out in readiness.

Bellamus waited and drank through the morning, and then went up to stand on the battlements with the queen in the afternoon. Together they inspected the rolling fields about Wiltun, but no mass of Unhieru warriors darkened the pasture.

'They're terribly slow,' Aramilla observed. She had taken to a wardrobe of ivory gowns inlaid with silver and trimmed with fur, and now sported an incarnation so pale and glittering that it was as though Bellamus was accompanied by a vast icicle. 'What's keeping them?'

'I'll not question it, Majesty,' Bellamus replied. 'Another day's preparation is exceptionally welcome.'

But the Unhieru did not arrive the next day either. Nor the day after that.

Repeatedly, Bellamus was summoned to the queen's chambers to report. Was there any word? What was the delay? He had no answers, and three days after the Unhieru had been expected, Aramilla lost patience.

'That Vigtyr creature has sold us out!'

'I doubt it, Majesty,' said Bellamus. He was tired of making these reports and had no wish to further interrogate the wretched Vigtyr. 'I see nothing he'd gain from that lie. If we have been misled, it'll be because the Kryptea lied to him.'

Aramilla waved a hand. 'Who cares where the information came from? Vigtyr should be made an example of. Come, I want to speak with him.' She latched onto Bellamus's arm and led him to Vigtyr's chamber, all the while expressing her very great admiration for the Lord Upstart, her gratitude that they should have him organising their defences, her disbelief that he should have been a commoner in his homeland. 'How lordly your bearing is,' she declared, sizing him up as they walked. 'There must be noble blood in there somewhere. Surely the get of an illicit liaison, my dear Bellamus. A bastard child of royalty perhaps.'

Bellamus doubted it.

They found Vigtyr in his chamber. He was under guard from two royal retainers, who showed them through the door. They found a dingy wood-panelled room, and Vigtyr scrambling up in bed, where he seemed to have been dozing. At the sight of them, he slid off the bed and into a deep bow. 'Majesty. My lord.'

'Kneel, blackguard,' snapped Aramilla. Vigtyr dropped to his knees at once. The guards crowded in behind them and Aramilla paced around the room until she stood behind Vigtyr. Even on his knees, he was barely half a head shorter than she was. 'We have taken you in, Anakim,' she said coldly. 'We've fed and sheltered you. We even spoke of favouring you, against the judgement of all at court. And now it seems you were lying to us.'

Vigtyr raised his head and met Bellamus's eye briefly. 'My lady?' he murmured.

'Where are the Unhieru?'

Vigtyr's eyes widened. 'Are they not here?' he gabbled in Saxon. 'I assure you, my lady, they were coming. Or at least, I was told they were coming.'

'Or perhaps you intended to frighten us from our capital? Perhaps you were sent simply to rot morale?'

'No, no, I swear, my lady!' Vigtyr was immediately close to panic. He shut his eyes tight. 'I promise, they told me. The Kryptea told me they were heading this way!'

'And they said the Unhieru would come in three days?' demanded the queen.

'Yes.'

'And yet here we are, rogue,' Aramilla spoke to Vigtyr once more. 'A week since you arrived, and still no sign of them.' Vigtyr seemed to be holding his breath as Aramilla stood over him. For his part, Bellamus did not feel entirely safe. They had two armed guards, and Vigtyr might be injured, but he was desperate. 'Confess to your lie now, and things will be easier for you. You still stand by your story?'

Vigtyr nodded frantically.

'Then you better hope the Unhieru are here by tomorrow. If they're not . . . Well there's a hill leading down the main road and into the market. It's long and steep, and at the bottom is a statue commemorating the last time we rebuffed the Black Legions from these walls. We'll put you in a barrel. We'll hammer fifty nails in through the sides. And then we'll roll you down that hill.' Bellamus was gazing at Aramilla in horror. 'We'll see what your story is then.' She winked at Bellamus, and walked around Vigtyr, heading for the door. 'Think about the barrel, rogue,' she said on her way out. Bellamus followed, shutting the door on Vigtyr's wide eyes.

'Leave him to stew overnight,' said Aramilla. 'We'll see if he's changed his story by the morning.'

Bellamus said nothing. Immediately after the queen had

gone, he summoned a scout. 'I want a dozen of you to go out as far as you can today. A gold sovereign for whichever one of you finds me the Unhieru.'

The scout was back to claim his sovereign in the afternoon. The Unhieru had ground to a halt on the road to Wiltun, just twenty-five miles away. For whatever reason, there was something delaying their assault.

This at least exonerated Vigtyr, and Bellamus went to tell him so he would be spared a night considering the inside of a barrel. But the waiting was wearing at Bellamus, and once back in his room he called again for wine. The evening disappeared in a haze, and shortly before midnight, Stepan came to find him. There was no knock, the knight opening the door without introduction. 'Knew you wouldn't be asleep,' he said, seeing Bellamus sat at his desk, three oil lamps lighting a parchment before him. 'What've you got there?'

Stepan was carrying a candle of his own, and advanced to peer down at Bellamus's handiwork.

'Ah,' said Bellamus, shuffling some papers over the top of it. 'Just a drawing of the town. Contingencies for when the Unhieru arrive, streets we could barricade, houses we can bring down to funnel them into traps, that sort of thing.'

Stepan nodded. 'So we're ready?'

'Ready?' Bellamus gave a short laugh. 'We'll never be ready. But this is the closest we'll get. At least until support starts arriving from Erebos.' He shook his head bitterly. 'Really, old friend, this is desperate. Unless the Unhieru give us another fortnight, they'll walk through our defences.'

'We haven't got another fortnight,' said Stepan, gently.

Bellamus looked up, the knight's tone sobering him like a pail of water.

'I've just been up on the battlements,' Stepan reported. 'They're here, Captain.'

6
Uprising

Bellamus and Stepan sat together on Wiltun's battlements, watching the lights of a distant army. They had dipped again into the Earl Penbro's ample wine cellar, and Bellamus now passed an earthenware jug of exceptional vintage to Stepan. 'How d'you rate our chances?' asked the knight, taking a swig. 'For tomorrow?'

'We'll do what we can,' said Bellamus tiredly. 'And when it doesn't work, take ship for Frankia.'

Stepan chuckled. 'Not as bad as that, surely?'

Bellamus shrugged. 'We'll see. But either way, we should survive. I'll have some horses waiting, and we can quit one of the far gates once the Unhieru are through the walls. They have no cavalry, we should be fine.'

'But what about all those contingencies?' asked Stepan. 'The barricades you were planning, the houses you'll bring down?'

'Really, my friend? Those are to stop our men running away, to make them think there's a plan. They won't delay our enemy. You remember that shipment of Unhieru chainmail we intercepted? It was an inch thick. We don't have a single weapon that can penetrate that.'

Stepan cleared his throat, but made no reply.

Bellamus took the jug. 'You know my great regret about losing this war?'

Stepan glanced at him. 'Have we lost it?'

Bellamus just raised his eyebrows.

'Go on,' said Stepan.

'That I'll never see the Hindrunn. How I wanted to walk the streets of the Anakim capital. I have a feeling that five hundred yards over those cobbles would tell me more than every interview I ever conducted.'

'Doubtless.' They watched the fires twinkling from afar. 'I'm not sure I can just flee tomorrow, Captain, if the Unhieru get through. All the poor souls of this town facing that menace alone. I'm not sure my honour would allow it.'

Bellamus nodded thoughtfully. 'That is noble. But I fear either your honour will survive or you will. This is not the war for it.'

There seemed no point trying to sleep and instead they talked. They spoke of misadventures and fights in their youth, friends they had lost, and the change they had seen. Then the topic turned to home, and Stepan sobbed his sorry heart out. Even numbed by the drink, Bellamus could barely listen to his cries. He did not want to be reminded that the Unhieru had taken so long to arrive, Stepan would have had ample time to take a cavalry troop north and return with his household.

They stayed on the wall until birds heralded the dawn and the distant fires were outshone. The Unhieru must have started marching in the dark, for the light revealed a swarm darkening the far hills.

The church bells began to toll, calling the fyrd to the walls. They arrived still filthy from construction work, clutching splitting mauls and wearing three tunics instead of armour. They crowded behind the gate and waited in silence, as in threes and fours, they were reinforced by the townsfolk. Blacksmiths wielding hammers, butchers with huge cleavers, others carrying hunting bows. At first they were met with pats on the back, then growing cheers as each new arrival joined the throng. The crowd worked themselves into a fury like a hive of bees, and even Bellamus, sour-headed and cynical, found his defeatism tested. They were brave, they were angry, and he dared hope they might stand against the Unhieru after all.

Then the regulars arrived. Men-at-arms in shining plate armour clutching halberds. At their head marched the wizened Lord Nerven in an antique, rust-speckled breastplate, helmet clutched under one arm so the crowds could see his face. They roared at the sight of him, reaching out to rap on his armour and even tousling the old man's white hair. He climbed the walls to stand beside Bellamus, greeting him with a nod. Bellamus could not help but grin.

'Good to have you here, Lord Nerven.'

'Lord Safinim. You speak like a noble. Let's see if you fight like one.'

Stepan burst out laughing. 'He's about to disappoint you, my lord.'

A fresh wave of cheering was building at their backs, and Bellamus turned to see a new procession carving through the crowds. It was Widukind, barefoot as ever and clutching an ugly, pocked mace, more like a hafted meteorite than any metalwork Bellamus had seen before. He walked at the head of the Abbio, usually a cavalry unit but now dismounted. They were armed with spears, a bright pennant dripping from each haft, and steel wings sprouted from their helmets. They filed up the steps to take up stations either side of the gates, as eerily silent as Widukind.

Stepan nudged Bellamus, glee in his eyes. 'Come on, Captain. It's going to be a good show.'

Bellamus grinned back. The mood was irresistible.

'And they're smaller than I expected,' said Stepan cheerfully. He was watching the van of the approaching army, marching in loose order and spilling over the sides of the road to Wiltun's main gate.

Bellamus frowned. They did look small. And though he

was sure the Unhieru used no cavalry, there appeared to be half a dozen mounted soldiers at the head of the army.

Lord Nerven turned to address the crowd below him. 'This town has never fallen to the Black Legions!' he called. 'It's never fallen to the Unhieru! It won't today!'

'I think he's right,' muttered Bellamus over the cheers.

'That's the spirit!'

Bellamus shook his head. 'These aren't the Unhieru.'

The closer this army came, the more human their proportions seemed. They still appeared huge, but not Unhieru huge.

'By thunder,' murmured Stepan. 'It's the Black Lord.'

'The Black Lord rides under a Silver Wolf,' said Bellamus. 'Not whatever that banner is.'

Held above the horsemen was a strange flag of some sort: oddly shaped and oddly textured, like a large irregular blanket of leather.

'Great God,' murmured Stepan, observing the banner. 'That's a skin, isn't it?'

It was: an unfolded human figure, its arms held wide at the top by a frame, the horrid flat legs dangling beneath.

'I think so,' said Bellamus. 'And look: they want to talk.'

A gentle breeze was stirring the white flag that hung alongside the flayed skin.

'But who are they?' said Stepan.

Bellamus had a suspicion that he knew. 'Horses,' he said to an aide. 'Bring us horses.'

They had barricaded the gates, and had to clear away the boards, barrels and sacks that had been heaped against them before they could be heaved open. Bellamus left Widukind to command the walls, and rode out with Nerven on one side and Stepan on the other. 'Shut the gates behind us,' he warned.

From ground level, standing in front of the walls of Wiltun, the central horseman was shockingly familiar. 'Surely not,' said Stepan in disbelief. 'No. That villain?'

It was Garrett.

Garrett Eoten-Draefend: hybrid warrior and one-time bodyguard to King Osbert, whom he had abandoned to ride with Bellamus and have his fill of terrorising the Anakim. It had not taken long for him to abandon his new master too, taking Bellamus's specialist household warriors, the Thingalith, with him. And now he was grinning at his old comrades, and riding at the head of his own army.

His fever-yellow eyes scoured the Abbio arrayed on the walls, and came to rest on the gate creaking shut behind Bellamus. 'Is this any way to greet an old friend?' he asked, as Bellamus came within earshot.

Bellamus had nearly forgotten how shocking Garrett's appearance was. His nose had been cut off, stranding two tall nostrils in the middle of his face. His hair was a bright blond shock, and at his side was strapped a long-bladed spear, the tip sheathed in Anakim leather.

'A lot has changed since we last saw each other,' said Bellamus pleasantly, drawing up before him. 'You'll remember Sir Stepan, and this here is the Lord Nerven. And as for your companions . . . you seem to have accrued an army.'

Bellamus was craning his head to look at the men assembled behind, who were quite as shocking as Garrett himself. There were thousands of them, all hazel-rod thin, many carrying half-healed wounds, all standing unnaturally still and silent. They carried spears so long they were very nearly pikes, and wore a mix of mail and rough armour-plating coloured like terracotta. All had the same yellow eyes as their master.

Bellamus raised an eyebrow at that. *Slaves.*

It was an army of Anakim-Sutherner hybrids, commonly held in bondage near the border with the Black Kingdom, but scarcely ever encountered this far south. Garrett, a hybrid himself, must have liberated them from across the north, and brought them here. That was why they stood so still, and spoke so little: each had been trained from their earliest years to attract as little attention as possible.

'How many of you are there?' asked Bellamus.

'Four thousand,' Garrett supplied.

'Nearly your own legion. Have they all got arms and armour?'

'All of them. Nearly a thousand with Anakim bone plates. The rest have chainmail.'

That information was perhaps the most startling of all, but Bellamus kept his face impassive. 'And formed exclusively of slaves, it seems? I fear this will be interpreted as an uprising, Garrett. And that makes you an extremely dangerous rebel.'

'I only rebel against the Anakim,' said Garrett. 'Every one of my men was freed from territory controlled by the Black Legions.'

'*Your* men, though?' Bellamus clarified, politely. 'I am aware of no authority that might permit you to raise an army.'

Garrett gave an unhinged laugh. 'Having an army is my authority to raise one.'

Bellamus could not help but agree with that. He glanced at the tradition-bound Nerven, who was staring at Garrett in disgust.

'And I don't recall you having much in the way of authority when I rode with you,' added the hybrid.

Bellamus found himself agreeing with that too, and abandoned that line of enquiry. 'What are you doing here, Garrett?'

'I have come to fight the Black Legions, of course.'

'So you'll surrender your army to the crown?'

Garrett shook his head with a grin that made his face irresistibly skull-like. 'We will resist the Anakim better if we join forces. That is why I am here. But I claimed these men from Anakim-held lands. They are *mine*.'

'Still slaves, then,' Bellamus observed.

'Slaves by choice,' Garrett replied, shrugging. 'Like the rest of us.'

Bellamus looked down and fiddled with his reins. 'The trouble is, Garrett, that having been slaves beneath the Sutherners, your men might understandably feel a certain animosity towards our own. How do we know they will fight with us, and not against us?'

'The Black Legions are slaughtering every hybrid they encounter. Compared to the strength of their feelings about the Anakim, my men don't care about yours at all. And they are loyal to me. And my desire is to do to the Anakim what they are trying to do to us.'

This was the first Bellamus had heard of legionaries massacring hybrids, and he wondered if it was true. More likely Garrett, who uniquely hated and resented the Anakim, was using that story to motivate his men. Bellamus suspected it would not be enough to keep these soldiers in line. Hybrids were notoriously unstable, as Bellamus had discovered when he had tried to fight alongside Garrett before, and paid for it with an eye.

The use of hybrid soldiers was a risk which might pay off handsomely, however. They were nearly as tall and strong as the Anakim, and possessed a freakish capacity for endurance. Reluctant as he was to ally himself with such forces, and with this man, they were desperate.

'Very well, then,' he said, nodding at Garrett. 'I shall return to the queen and tell her the Eoten-Draefend is at her disposal.'

'Lord Eoten-Draefend,' Garrett interjected. 'That is what I shall be called, if you want assistance from my army. How similar we are, Lord Safinim. And I am grateful to you for showing Albion how a low-born man might rise.'

From the corner of his eye, Bellamus spotted Lord Nerven turning very slowly to examine him. By countenancing an alliance with a slave uprising, Bellamus was already confirming Nerven's worst fears that the upstart, having come from the masses, was committed to obliterating the social order. But now that Garrett – a reviled and mistrusted hybrid – was demanding admission to the nobility, Nerven might take his chances with the Anakim. Above all, Bellamus could not be seen endorsing such a man.

'As we're old comrades, I fear you shall always be Garrett to me,' Bellamus replied lightly. 'What of the *Thingalith*? The men of mine who you took with you when you left?'

'Mine,' said Garrett.

'You might return them to me, as a sign of good faith,' Bellamus observed.

'You might refer to me as *lord*,' said Garrett shrugging.

'So where are you to make camp?' Bellamus asked, half turning away.

'The town, of course,' said Garrett with an obscene grin.

'I doubt the residents would look kindly on that,' said Bellamus.

'I should think not!' exploded Nerven.

Garrett turned his yellow eyes on the old lord with a look of sly resentment. For his part, though over sixty and more than a foot shorter than Garrett, Nerven returned his glare coldly. Bellamus felt sweat break out on his palms.

Stepan cleared his throat. 'I think the town must be reserved for soldiers sworn to the crown,' he said diplomatically.

Garrett looked away from Nerven. 'If you're quite certain of that, then we shall take up residence in the old fort, at Searoburgh.'

'We are *quite* certain,' said Nerven vehemently. He was looking at Garrett with an expression of utmost hatred.

'I will report your arrival to the queen,' said Bellamus hastily. 'And look to find you there to liaise further. Good morning, Garrett.'

Clicking his tongue, he rode deliberately in front of Nerven so that the moment between he and Garrett was broken, and then turned back for the gate. He was relieved to hear the old lord's horse fall in behind his.

'A rebellion!' said Stepan, once they were beyond earshot. 'There'll be trouble from that gang.'

'There's been trouble already,' said Bellamus. 'Three thousand sets of chainmail! He can only have robbed those from our own side. What a villain, but I suppose you have to hand it to him. He's certainly taken advantage of the chaos.'

'He seems to be modelling himself on you,' Stepan observed.

There was uncomfortable truth in that, and Bellamus did

not reply. Instead he watched Nerven spur past them, lips pursed and looking resolutely ahead.

'This won't do my standing at court any favours,' breathed Bellamus watching him go.

'Come now,' said Stepan cheerfully. 'This is good news, Captain! Unreliable they may be, but that's an extra four thousand fully armed and armoured warriors. We're up to eighteen. With Wiltun's defences, perhaps that's enough for us to hold out against the Unhieru?'

Bellamus was watching the gates being hauled open for Lord Nerven, a frown on his face. 'No . . . No we're not there yet. But . . . maybe we don't have to be.'

'My lord has had an idea,' said Stepan comfortably. 'At last.'

A giddy relief was descending on Bellamus, like cool water over his head and neck. 'An idea? Well that's all it is, but . . .' Suddenly he could not contain himself and he laughed wildly. 'We *could* do this, Stepan. Old Garrett, eh? We could hold this town!'

7

Brother

Keturah's bags were full, her horse saddled, and it was time to go. The assassin sent to kill Roper's brother was dead, his master had been unmasked, and at last, she could leave the mountain academy and prioritise the child stirring in her belly. It was best born in the safety of the Hindrunn, with an attending midwife. Above all, she prayed it would not come while she was on the road: while bears and wolves prowled the trees, ears pricked for vulnerable cries.

She guided her horse out of the courtyard, raising a hand in farewell to the watching tutors, and set her eyes on the far mountains and the cotton clouds pricked on their summits. She joined the path leading down to the lake, but had barely made it past the far longhouse when she caught sight of a crouching figure: back against the silvered pine boards, head cradled in his hands.

She twitched the reins, curbing towards him and drawing her horse to a halt. 'Hello, Ormur.'

Roper's young brother raised his head to reveal a face so blotched by old bruises that it was the colour of beaten egg.

'What happened to you?'

'Thrashing,' he muttered, dropping his eyes politely.

'What for?'

'Insolence.'

Keturah tutted. 'The tutors said you have been exceedingly rebellious.'

Ormur paused, and then nodded, as if to say that was a fair assessment.

'Why?'

The boy shrugged.

'They said you'd been fighting too.' He did not answer, but Keturah knew the truth of it from his scabbed knuckles. She sighed. 'Do you have any friends here, Ormur?'

The boy shook his head. 'Not any more.'

Keturah tutted once again, turning to the mountains momentarily, and then back to the shrunken figure before her. If he stayed here alone, haunted by the ghost of his brother, his assassin, and his treacherous Master, she was not sure he would survive. She had rarely seen a figure so wretched. 'Perhaps your time here has run its course.'

He shook his head. 'Not for another year. Not until I've completed the Trial.'

'Don't be a fool, like most here you will leave without completing that absurd test. I guarantee it: you're coming south with me.' She had just decided.

Ormur was sufficiently baffled that the wretched expression cleared from his face. 'South? Where?'

'Enough questions,' said Keturah sternly. 'From now on, you will travel south as my servant, deferring to me in all things. There is to be no more insolence, and no more fighting. You will keep my horse, cook my meals and, most importantly, be my company and entertainment on this long road. I will call you brother, will keep you fed, and show you how the world turns beyond these mountains. I will be at your side whenever you call, and spit on the bones of anyone who hurts you. From this day forth, we stand back to back, until one of us lies dead. Then the other shall drink to their memory, or avenge them if necessary. Well, do you understand?'

Ormur just stared at her mutely.

'Now go and get your things, while I see to your departure.'

'I own nothing.'

'Then wait here for me.'

When she delivered her proposal, imperiously and from horseback, to the tutors, they did not much object. She was, after all, wife to the Black Lord, and had arrived from nowhere to rid the school of the assassin that had plagued it for months. They just looked at each other and shrugged. Before they had time to respond properly she had turned away, declaring the matter settled. Only then did one of them call a cheerful 'Good luck!' after her.

She returned to Ormur, still crouched behind the longhouse, but now wearing an expression of puzzlement. She held out her hand, and he hesitated for a moment, looking up at her. Then he took it and she helped him into the saddle behind her. 'We're going to the Hindrunn, brother. Have you ever seen it before?'

'Never, my lady.'

Keturah huffed. 'For goodness sake, Ormur. I am *Miss Keturah* until I have given birth. If you're going to be deferential, at least do it accurately.'

'Yes, my lady.'

Keturah snorted.

They were nearly at the lake before she added that there was one further service she might require. 'If I go into labour whilst we're still on the road, you must stay away. It is the most disastrous bad luck to have a male present at the birth, so you will just have to prowl around and fight off the predators.'

Ormur, evidently unable to tell if she was joking, made no reply. They rode south, descending clear of the snows gathering once more in the passes, and into the treeline. The boy was exceedingly quiet. She supposed he had never seen a young woman before, and was not sure how to speak to her. There were none in the mountain school where he had trained, and nor would he have encountered one for another five years of education.

Keturah, for her part, tested her companion with a range of

jokes. 'Imagine not seeing a woman until you're seventeen,' she pondered. 'It's a wonder more of you don't just detonate when you get into the Hindrunn.'

But it was not until the bruising on his face had faded that she first broke him, with a comment to the effect that Leon would have walked on all fours, had he not needed a hand free to hold his sword. It elicited a guilty chuckle from Ormur, who had resented Leon almost as much as the assassin he had been sent to catch. Thereafter, though he still spoke little, he laughed much more easily.

'Did you enjoy your life in the mountains, brother?'

'Yes, my lady.'

'Which parts?'

'All of them.'

Keturah tutted. 'Come now, you can't have enjoyed all of them. You were thrashed often enough. Did you enjoy your thrashings?'

'No, my lady.'

'There! So which other bits did you not enjoy?'

Ormur shrugged, and Keturah came to suspect the boy truly had no personality. What he liked or did not like had been irrelevant in his young life so far: he'd merely had to obey. Or maybe his tongue was still held by grief. Either way, there was no sign of the hostility and insolence familiar to the tutors at the haskoli.

'You will thaw to me eventually, brother.'

'Yes, my lady.'

'Try not to make it sound so dutiful.'

'I was ordered to defer to you in all things.'

Keturah laughed delightedly. 'Why! Was that a joke?'

One morning, riding one of the Anakim roads that twisted through the forests like a root, they found their path blocked by a fresh landslide. The entire hillside had been swept away, and the road stoppered by a mass of mud and uprooted trees like the nest of a thunderbird. 'Looks like we're going the long way round.'

'We could go over it,' suggested Ormur.

'Ormur versus the landslide,' mused Keturah, turning their horse around. 'Sounds like a proverb.' They retraced their tracks for half a day and took a new turning. The road they found themselves on had once been well-travelled, but the encroaching forest had now narrowed it to little more than the width of their horse. Brambles dragged at their knees and moths fluttered low in the sunbeams.

Presently, the road began to climb. 'It's paved,' noted Ormur, staring down at the even stones on which their horse's shoes clacked and sparked.

'Naturally,' said Keturah. 'This was once the kingdom's major road.'

'*This?*' There was a silence as Ormur inspected the choked path. 'Why? Where does it go?'

'You'll see soon enough.' Instinctively, Keturah rested a hand on her stirring belly. This ancient road was famous, and she had longed to walk it since she was a child. Now, she feared it would cost her an extra two days she could not afford. Then she berated herself. When had she become so fretful?

'Why is it not used any more?'

'Well, it does climb rather steeply,' said Keturah. 'And I'm afraid people are said to disappear near here.' Ormur did not reply. 'Pay it no mind, Ormur,' she told the space over her shoulder. 'The Black Kingdom is full of such legends.'

The trees began to thin, and low beams of sunlight were shining into their faces by the time they came upon an aged stone archway. The road passed through it, while on either side stretched stone walls, half-hidden beneath a torrent of ivy.

'Strange cave,' said Ormur.

'This is a gate, brother, built by our ancestors.' Keturah paused their horse to stare up at the ancient stonework. 'This was our capital, in the old days. Myrklettur.' The silence at her back was sceptical and Keturah laughed. 'Look.' She indicated the walls.

'At the cliffs?'

'Not cliffs, Ormur: walls.'

The boy stayed silent and Keturah creaked around in the saddle to look at him. 'You don't believe me, do you?' His life had so far been spent in low dwellings of timber and thatch, and it seemed huge constructions of stone were beyond his comprehension.

'I do,' said the boy, unconvincingly.

'You will. Seems a shame to gallop through an ancient monument, don't you think? We'll stay inside tonight.'

'I thought you said people disappeared near here.'

Keturah just laughed. 'I see that's been on your mind.'

They trotted into the shadow of the gatehouse. The ancient stones had been carved so perfectly and laid so tightly that there was no sign of either mortar or moss between them. The walls stood as they always had, except that the top had been smoothed and rounded by centuries of wind.

Within, they found a plain of lumpen grass. The ancient streets and buildings had been buried and overgrown, so that it looked the work of subterranean dwarves. Centuries of wind-blown earth had heaped against the insides of the walls, so that from where Keturah stood, the old fortress seemed to nestle in a dish of emerald, which dazzled in the last of the day.

She dismounted, leaving Ormur to rummage in the saddle-bags and hobble the horse while she walked the grass slope up to the ancient battlements. Myrklettur had been built on a flat-topped mountain, and with the crenellations almost completely eroded, she found herself standing on the edge of a high cliff. Beneath her toes was a drop some hundreds of feet, and the canopy of the Black Kingdom stretched to the horizon like a verdant bank of clouds.

She heard Ormur climbing the bank behind her. 'No wonder they abandoned it,' she said. 'Imagine trying to get enough water up here to sustain a city.'

Ormur did not reply.

She watched the sun dropping behind the trees until it

strained her eyes. There had been much satisfying about today, but still she felt unsettled. Now she considered it, she realised she had for months.

'Well . . .' she said. 'At least we shall be safe from the wild animals up here. Shall we make some food?'

Still, there came no reply. She glanced over her shoulder, turned on the spot, and found that she was alone on the ancient wall. 'Ormur?' She could see their horse where she had left it, hobbled now at the ankles and the saddlebags stacked neatly beside it, but there was no sign of the boy.

'Ormur?'

Where usually the horse would have started grazing, its head was up and its ears twitching vigilantly.

She descended back into the long shadows of the old town, calling for the boy. It was cold away from the sun, and without the vantage point of the walls, she found herself wandering through a maze. She searched the old streets, at first striding, then breaking into a trot. 'Ormur!'

At the far side of the lumpen town was another huge wall, broken by a tall passageway bored into the stone. That was where she found Ormur. He stood with his back to her, staring into the black inkwell of the passage. 'There you are,' said Keturah, coming to stand by him. 'I thought you might've been snatched by something.'

There was a cold breeze coming from the passage. Beneath her feet, the flagstones were worn smooth by a million footsteps, and the tunnel walls were carved with spikey symbols, which put her in mind of the Suthern writing. Keturah had the strongest impression that standing in the gloom, just out of sight, was a person.

'Come, brother,' she said, taking his arm and pulling him gently away before he could express a desire to go in. 'I'd thought we'd spend the night here, but our poor horse looks uncomfortable without any tree cover. Maybe we should go through, and into the forest.'

'I think we should,' said Ormur, quickly.

They turned away and walked back to the horse in silence. Keturah reattached the saddlebags and Ormur removed the hobbles. The sky had turned to sapphire, and without a word being said, they both knew they were racing the night. They mounted and fled the old fortress at a trot, passing through a gate at the far side and down, back into the forest.

It took some while beside a cheerful fire to banish the sense they had felt as they left: that of something pursuing them out of the fortress. Ormur was staring down at a hare, caught that morning and roasting over the fire. 'Is the Hindrunn like that?' he asked.

'Not at all,' said Keturah. 'The Hindrunn is full of people and feels alive.'

'I didn't like that place.'

What surprised Keturah was how much she wanted to agree with the boy, but she thought one of them should be practical. 'It's behind us now. The next place on our road will be home.' How she missed it.

'Your home.'

'Yours too. You can stay with me, in the Black Lord's quarters.'

At that, Ormur seemed to brighten, perhaps imagining his brother's quarters more expansive than in reality. Keturah decided not to spoil his mood.

'Is the Black Lord popular?' asked Ormur.

Keturah laughed. 'Popular? Depends who you ask. To his soldiers, yes, absolutely. To the rest of the kingdom? Well . . . they probably respect him, even if they don't like him.'

'Do you love him?' asked the boy artlessly.

Keturah raised an eyebrow at this new impudence. 'Certainly.'

'How do you know?'

'Is this for your arrival in the Hindrunn?' she asked. 'You want to know what love feels like so you don't declare it to the first poor girl who crosses your path?'

'I just wondered,' he mumbled.

The boy seemed in earnest, and she considered his question. 'Most people appear to shrink as you get closer,' she said eventually. 'You get past their witty and charming exterior and they do something to disappoint you. You love someone if they get larger as you get closer. If their imperfections, as they betray them one after another, only seem to add to them. Do you understand?'

Ormur shook his head.

'You will.'

8
The Statue

It was on a crisp morning some three days later that Keturah was finally able to declare: 'Well, there you go, brother.'

They had emerged from the forest and onto the grass ocean that surrounded the Hindrunn. The trees for miles around had been cleared so that the fortress's bronze cannons had a clear line of sight, and from this distance it looked like a small mountain. Ormur, laying eyes on it for the first time, went very quiet, and nothing Keturah said could coax him into speech. That did not stop her. 'You see those shining circles, above the gate? They're for focusing a white light of lime and gas on invaders, both to dazzle and to illuminate if they try and attack at night. If an invader makes it through the gate, they'll wish they hadn't. There are holes in the gatehouse roof through which boiling oil can be poured down on them.'

The boy evidently did not know what to believe any more.

It was only when they passed into this tunnel of boiling oil, boring through the gatehouse, that Ormur said quietly: 'It's like Myrklettur.'

'Nonsense. Once we're through, you'll see.'

But when they emerged onto the cobbled streets of the outermost district, it was Keturah's turn for disbelief. 'Great heavens,' she declared, a look of revulsion on her face. 'How hideous!'

'Who is *that*?' asked Ormur, staring at the new statue standing directly before them.

'Ormur, don't look,' said Keturah, covering the boy's eyes. 'Spare yourself.'

Ormur removed Keturah's hands from his eyes and inspected the figure. 'Who's it supposed to be?'

Even stranger than refusing to believe in the Hindrunn, it seemed extraordinary to Keturah that the boy did not recognise this most famous figure. He had been Roper's great rival for the Stone Throne: the Captain of the Sacred Guard, and the Black Kingdom's foremost warrior, until Pryce had hacked his body to pieces on top of Harstathur. But of course, Ormur would never have seen Uvoren the Mighty in the flesh. 'His name was Uvoren Ymerson,' said Keturah, scowling at the figure.

'*That* is Uvoren?'

Keturah did not reply. She felt a sudden foreboding. Someone had erected this statue so that it was the first thing anyone saw when entering the stone heart of the Black Kingdom. That was not good news, and nor were the bundles of herbs and copper offerings left at its fired clay feet.

The statue had real hair set into its head and metal armour covering its cracked orange flesh. It was highly stylised, little resembling real human proportions: twice the size of any living man, with the shoulders very broad, the arms held wide in a stiff spread-eagle, the hands huge and lumpen, and the face entirely blank. It was clearly Uvoren, though. There was an Almighty Eye over his right shoulder; a replica of Marrow-Hunter – the captain's famous war hammer – in its fired clay hand, and something skilfully Uvorenish in its stance and posture.

'What's it doing here?' asked Ormur.

Keturah did not answer, having no further desire to look upon the likeness of their old enemy. She clicked her tongue and they rode onwards. Bystanders halted what they were doing to stare as they went by, and Keturah fancied there was something hostile in those looks.

She wanted to find one of her friends and discover more, and soon encountered an old ally by the name of Sigurasta. Small, pale and plump, Sigurasta dropped the sack of wool she was carrying, and assessed Keturah from head to toe with a look of disbelief.

'*Keturah!* It is remarkable you would show your face here. But I suppose face is one thing you always had.'

Keturah observed Sigurasta haughtily to give herself a little time to think. 'You've lost me, my dear.'

'Oh,' said Sigurasta, bristling now. 'So you and your over-excitable husband take the legions permanently abroad, without so much as the opportunity to say goodbye, and now that they are defeated by ruin and starvation, thought to just crawl back here? You thought those of us left to carry on were just fine with that, I should imagine.'

Keturah stirred. 'Ruin and starvation?'

'You're a poor liar, Keturah. You have been with the army. You know what has befallen it.'

'But I haven't been,' said Keturah, gesturing at Ormur behind her. 'Not for many weeks. I went north to Lake Avon. Come now, there's been word on the army?'

Sigurasta looked triumphant. 'Plague has all but wiped them out, with those few who remain, starving and mired in central Suthdal.'

Keturah had been leaning towards Sigurasta, and now straightened. Though she could not be certain, those sounded like lies. 'What would you know about any of this?' She heard the anger in her own voice and tried to suppress it. 'The plague struck while I was there. The army survived it. And when I left, the army had just triumphed in the field, and was marching for Lundenceaster. Whatever else happened, I am quite certain they made it there.'

Sigurasta evidently had no desire to surrender her righteous indignation. 'Hogwash, Keturah. You've been playing politics with our men. The details will not redeem you.'

A few bystanders had stopped to listen, and began heckling Keturah, pointing accusatory fingers up at her.

Keturah felt another flare of fury. The whole fortress was evidently gripped by possession – that cardinal sin, where emotion overwhelms clarity. The subjects of the Black Kingdom were discouraged from venting rage, jealousy or grief: because emotions are contagious. Left to their own devices, a crowd was perfectly capable of whipping itself into a mob, based on nothing but wildfire supposition. People in such a mood, Keturah knew, would not be troubled by the truth: that last she had seen, the army was intact.

'So, you people here,' Keturah called over the top of the jeering – a measure of quiet falling as some tried to listen. 'You no longer cheer victories over the Sutherners? You would rather that Uvoren had inherited the throne? If your view is that he would not have marched on Suthdal, I agree – he refused even to defend us from the Suthern invaders last year!'

'Liar!' came a shout. 'It was *your husband* who ruled then, and prevented us marching!'

'How nice for you, that you've returned to birth your child in safety!' added Sigurasta, pointing at Keturah's swollen belly. 'While our sons fall on alien soil!'

There was a roaring in Keturah's ears now. 'You know nothing!' she bellowed. 'How you even have an opinion on this is beyond me!' But now she could not hear her own words over the jeering. Impotent in the face of their hysteria, she jerked the horse about and rode away, panting with rage as mocking cries followed them down the street. Heads started appearing in the windows above, looking down curiously to see the source of the commotion. 'Stick your heads back in,' she spat under her breath.

Ormur was frowning. 'So that's what the statue means,' he said. 'That Lord Roper is so unpopular, people would rather Uvoren had won the contest for the Stone Throne.'

It was her turn for silence now as she fought to overcome

her rage. 'Almost,' she said eventually. 'What it really means is that those fools are being manipulated. Roper should've taken steps to avoid this. *I* should've told him. Every minor skirmish, and every pace marched south, we should've sent a herald north to proclaim it a magnificent triumph. As it is, someone has been working against us while our backs were turned. And I bet I know who.'

'Who?'

Keturah felt as though her jaw were clamped shut, and Ormur had to ask again before she would answer. 'There were two legates left behind when we went south. They were the ones who'd have made most trouble if they'd come with us. The first is named Skallagrim, of the Gillamoor. He's a reluctant old fart, but harmless. The second is Tore, one of Uvoren's childhood friends, who despises Roper. He commands half the fighting men left in the kingdom, and that makes him powerful. He will have lobbied for the statue, and Old Skallagrim isn't dynamic enough to stand against him.' Keturah was breathing hard through her nose. 'But we'll convince him to take it down. We just need to wait for the right moment.'

'Which will be when?'

'When I've delivered this child.' She rested a hand on her belly. 'If it's healthy, and especially if it's a boy, my position will become rather more secure. In any case, there is no need to act at once.'

But that assertion was tested on arrival at the Central Keep. Standing guard over the entrance were a pair of Dunoon legionaries: Tore's men, since he had been stripped of the Greyhazel the year before. So certain was Keturah that they would not let them through, that she did not bother to take the horse to the stable and instead left it with Ormur, climbing the steps alone.

As feared, the legionaries stepped in front of her before she could cross the threshold into the keep. 'No further,' said one of them.

Keturah had already decided this was not a battle worth fighting, and mustered a smile. 'Perhaps you'd tell me where to find your master? There seems to have been a misunderstanding.'

'No misunderstanding,' said the legionary. 'Your husband is a public enemy. I'd no sooner let you into the keep than the King of Suthdal.'

Keturah gave her practised laugh. 'Now really. When did a legate acquire the power to declare *anyone* a public enemy? And now you're telling me the Black Lady isn't welcome in her own keep?'

'You're no lady,' said the legionary, truthfully. 'Be gone.'

Keturah shrugged and turned away, affecting carelessness. She was shaken, though. First Sigurasta, now this. Did she have any allies remaining? Or would they all have disavowed her? And her baby, due any time now – would she need to deliver that alone?

Her head was slightly bowed as she descended the steps, taking the reins Ormur offered without a word. 'Where now?' asked the boy, as she hauled herself into the saddle. He did not seem worried, clearly assuming Keturah would handle this.

She raised her eyebrows in imitation of her usual sardonic fashion, but she did not want to ride back through those streets and through that vicious jeering. 'My father's house,' she declared after a pause. 'Come on.'

As Keturah had feared, when they left the honeycomb of stone surrounding the keep, some of those who had jeered them before were still standing there. Among them was Sigurasta, who now pointed at the returning Keturah. 'Too humble for the keep, now, Keturah? You'll have to live like the rest of us!' A dozen people who had come with her began to hiss, attracting the attention of others nearby who came to add to the scorn.

Keturah did not acknowledge them, all her attention spent suppressing a boiling rage. The crowd did not just let her pass, instead keeping pace alongside them, forming a forty-strong guard of dishonour. The faces staring up at her were terribly animated, spitting curses and jabbing fingers like knives. They were largely women, the men being either away with Roper, or serving in Tore and Skallagrim's overworked legions.

'Shall we move faster, my lady?' Ormur called over the jeers.

'What? Have we done something wrong, Ormur? Don't give them a single inch.' But she had no idea how to react to this ferocity. She noticed her left hand was shielding her belly, and dropped it to her side.

'My lady!' There was a warning note in Ormur's voice. A strange fixity had come into the faces staring up at her, as each individual fed off the rage around them and surrendered their identity to the mob. Their horse had started dancing and snorting as though swarmed with wasps, and the crowd, more than sixty now and screaming, began to press very close.

A hand clutched at her boot and she withdrew it sharply, accidentally kicking the horse. The panicked beast lunged forward and those nearest shrank back, opening up a channel before them. The horse lurched into a gallop, in which Keturah's only choice was to hold on grimly or be hurled onto the cobbles. Ormur's fingers crushed into her shoulders and they jostled clear of the crowd and clattered round a corner.

They were going the wrong way and Keturah fought to regain control of the horse, dragging at the reins and telling it furiously that it would receive a terrible thrashing if it did not stop at once. It was not until they had streaked through the gate to the bakers' district that she finally succeeded in bringing the beast to a halt. For a moment, she and Ormur just panted.

'Savages,' she spat, chest still heaving. 'Barbarians!'

'Did you see their faces?' asked Ormur. 'I've never seen people look like that.'

'A first insight for you, Ormur,' she said acidly, 'into why possession is such a sin.'

Keturah disguised her short hair and distinctive profile with a cowl, and turned the horse back towards Tekoa's house.

Neither of them spoke again before dismounting in front of the familiar oak door. Keturah tugged on the cord which lifted the latch and leaned into the wood, but it did not budge.

'The boards must have swollen,' said Ormur.

'It's barred,' Keturah snapped, then felt immediately ashamed. 'You may not have encountered that in the haskoli,' she added, more gently.

'The people here bar their doors?'

'Not usually. But things are changing.' She looked up and down the street, noticing a few curious onlookers staring from the far end. 'We need to find another way in.'

Keturah looked up at the large glassless windows above. The stones of the wall were laid very tight, with few obvious holds. Even if she gave Ormur a boost, she could not see how he would climb the final six feet.

A grating noise from behind the door made her take a pace backwards. It swung inwards, and was swallowed by a dark pool of shadows behind. From this gloom appeared a flashing sword, followed by the armoured figure which held it.

'Miss Keturah?' The sword was lowered at once.

'Oh, Harald, bless you!' She stumbled over the threshold and embraced the legionary.

'By the storm, what are you doing here?' Harald had been Tekoa's retainer since Keturah was a baby, and had clearly been left in charge of the premises while the legate was away. He was stocky, and short enough that their embrace pressed his face into Keturah's shoulder. They broke apart and he looked up at her, with a countenance that might be callous if she were not so familiar with it.

'Come in, girl, come. Don't linger out there.' Harald stepped aside. 'The boy is with you, is he?'

'This is Roper's younger brother,' Keturah explained, pulling back her cowl and leading the way into the living quarters. She heard the boy yield his name behind her, and the sound of Harald barring the door once more.

Entering the familiar parlour felt like piloting into the calm waters of port following a tempest. A fire was slumbering in the hearth, casting orange light over the great tapestry on the far wall and making a black kettle hung above steam. Pulled up next to it was a chair, in which Tekoa had sat so often. The whole room smelt of the pine tar he used to wash, and Keturah rested a hand on the back of the chair. 'If only you were here,' she murmured. It was only recently that she seemed to have lost her blind optimism that the plague which had infested her father's legion would have spared him.

Harald followed her in. She thought he would ply them with questions, but instead he just stared into her face for some while with an expression of horror. For the first time she considered how careworn she must look, after fighting and travelling and starving for so many months. Abruptly he shook himself, banked the fire and drew up an extra chair for Ormur. 'Sit, both of you.' He vanished, and returned some while later with two goblets of steaming elderberry wine. 'You'll need that,' he said. 'Food's on the way.'

'Harald, I'm perfectly capable—' but Harald had gone. Keturah sipped the wine and felt warmth spread to her toes. She shot a glance at Ormur, who had taken a gulp and started coughing violently. 'Ever had wine, Ormur?'

The boy shook his head, eyes watering.

'The treats that lie before you.'

When Harald reappeared, he was holding two plates laden with cold ham and warm bread. 'Really, Harald,' said Keturah, sternly accepting the plate. 'We are hardly at death's door.'

'You look like you need it. And it's the very least I can do,' he added quietly, and she knew he too was thinking of Tekoa.

'You heard about my father?' She tried to sound carefree, but found she could not hold his eye. She looked away to sip at the wine again.

'Yes, Miss Keturah. I heard.'

'Perhaps not everything?' Keturah suggested. 'I do not know for sure that he was claimed by plague.'

Harald, who had been piling more wood on the fire, froze.

He straightened up and turned to face her. 'I heard he was dead.'

Keturah looked back at him, and at the word *dead* found she was fighting back tears. 'He might be.'

'But not definitely?'

'The sickness was thick among the Skiritai. Tekoa took the whole legion into exile to let it run its course, and spare the rest of the army. I haven't heard from them since.'

Harald gawped at her, and Keturah thought how it must have been for this loyal man to wait here alone, certain his master was dead. She was amazed that he had stayed. Eventually he sniffed grimly. 'Just like the legate to put the army first. Much good it did them.'

'But it did, Harald. The army was intact when I left. I don't know what you've heard, but the sickness was contained with the Skiritai.'

'When did you leave?'

'A few weeks ago.'

'No,' said Harald abruptly. 'I heard the whole force had succumbed! Truly?'

'Truly,' Keturah confirmed. 'They were marching to Lundenceaster, last I saw. But what has been going on here?' she demanded, sitting forward now and resting cup and plate on the floor. 'Where are these rumours coming from? Why is there a ghastly statue of Uvoren behind the gatehouse? And *why* is Roper now a public enemy?'

'Oh!' Harald made a violent shooing gesture, as if to say *Do not speak to me of that!* 'It has been awful since you left, Miss Keturah. Skallagrim was named regent, but it was like putting a sheep in charge of a wolfpack, and Tore soon saw him off. The Gillamoor were sent to work on the canal, Skallagrim went with them, and hasn't been able to find an excuse to come back. Tore's been plotting ever since, though he didn't put up the statue.'

'No, I suppose that would've been too obvious,' said Keturah. 'Who did it at his request?'

'Vinjar Kristvinson,' said Harald, naming one of Uvoren's old allies, and Sigurasta's husband, who had been toppled in Roper's efforts to secure his throne.

'*Vinjar!*' said Keturah. 'He was disgraced long ago! What authority would he possibly have for that?'

'He's now Master of the Hindrunn,' said Harald.

Keturah's lip curled involuntarily. 'There is no such post.'

'There is now. The Ephors created it.'

'The Ephors are thick with Tore?'

Harald, never politically minded, shrugged, and Keturah shook her head and answered her own question. 'Of course, they'd have been slighted by Roper launching an invasion without their permission. So Vinjar was exonerated.'

Harald nodded. 'He appeared in one of the honeypots and made a speech in his defence. It was good,' he admitted. 'And the Ephor ruled that the evidence against him had been fabricated by Lord Roper.'

'Which it wasn't,' said Keturah, angrily, though this news at least explained why Sigurasta, Vinjar's wife, had reacted so ferociously to Keturah. She was trying to convince herself that he had been innocent of the crime that brought him down: adultery.

Harald shrugged again. 'I think they planned the whole thing. Once Vinjar had been cleared, he turned to the crowd and said that the story – that Uvoren had tried to take command at Harstathur and nearly lost the battle – was a fabrication, and that when Pryce killed him it had been nothing other than murder. It whipped the crowd into a frenzy; folk have been saying for a long while that it was wrong to obliterate his body.' And there, Keturah agreed. By destroying Uvoren's corpse, Pryce had denied his soul its chance on the Winter Road: the great traverse, which all Anakim must navigate to reach the Otherworld. Instead, Uvoren had been condemned to a tortured, earthly existence and to the many who venerated Uvoren as a hero, that had been exceedingly harsh. 'So it was decreed that Pryce should be arrested, and that Lord Roper should appear before the Ephors when he returned,' Harald finished.

'And what were the charges against Roper?'

'Corruption, for bringing down Uvoren and his allies, and a separate charge that he'd exceeded his mandate in Suthdal.'

Keturah cursed herself bitterly. With all their attention tied up in the south, their enemies had been plotting at home. Had she not told Roper, all those months before, that he did not think through the consequences of his actions at home? And she had fallen into the same trap, allowing herself to become equally blinded by the campaign, and forget their civil enemies. She should have foreseen all of this. 'And the statue?'

'Just a few days after the Ephors decreed Lord Roper should appear before them, a herald arrived with news that his army had been struck down by plague, and the survivors were starving in Suthdal. Lord Tekoa was said to be dead, and the army on the verge of mutiny.'

'And then?'

'Well, after that . . . all the talk was that Uvoren should have taken the throne instead. Roper's campaign was declared illegal, and he was made a public enemy. That old villain Uvoren has been venerated ever since. It's become a cult, and Vinjar made himself wildly popular by having the statue made.'

Keturah was silent a moment, and then threw herself back in the chair. 'No wonder the crowd was so vicious.'

Harald narrowed his eyes furiously. 'Who was vicious to you?'

Keturah jerked her head to say that it did not matter, and picked up the wine once more. 'I rather suspect all Tore's plotting will be in vain,' she observed. 'The army is completely loyal to Roper. When he comes back with fifty thousand men, I don't think even the Ephors will be too keen to cross-examine him for corruption. The legions would riot. But this will not do. I am barred from the Central Keep, and will be heckled if I set foot outside the house! And that statue!' She stamped her foot. 'I want that down.'

'There's nothing you can do, Miss Keturah,' said Harald, gently. 'We can't have you trapped in this house, we should get you out of the fortress.'

'I think not,' said Keturah indignantly. As much as she had been shaken by the vitriol of the crowd, her pride was also wounded. Roper's uncanny abilities in the field were far superior to his statecraft. Keturah had taken that responsibility as her own and could not bear the idea that Roper might return from a campaign in which he had spent everything, to find the Hindrunn had turned against him. 'I shall not be chased from my home by the effigy of the monster who poisoned me and tried to assassinate my husband,' she declared. 'I'll fix this.'

Harald shook his head in dismay. 'Miss Keturah. Please! Tore rules these streets, and will do anything to get at your husband. If you stay here, you are in terrible danger!' Despite her defiance, the look in his eye plucked between her ribs: desperate concern and fear which nearly brought tears welling to the surface. She had grown up with this man as her caretaker: played with him when her father was away; confided in him when her mother had lost her mind. 'Please,' Harald said, crossing to her. He knelt in front of her chair, clasping her hands in his own.

'Don't,' Keturah commanded, looking away from him.

He turned over her hands and stared, appalled, at the ill-healed wounds on her palms. They were deep cuts from an enemy halberd which she had seized in her desperation, fighting for her life in a canvas tent. 'You must have seen terrible things in the south. And your father . . . I miss him every day.'

'Harald!'

'I can't bear it, Miss Keturah. You walk through that door alone, half-starved, terribly scarred.' The world before Keturah was blurring, and she could feel her breaths turning to hiccoughs. She did not want to look at the marks on her hands, and tried to revert to fury at how feeble she now seemed. 'And I know, girl. I've been there, in the fighting. And afterwards you're just relieved to survive, but when you get back, and there's nobody left who saw it with you, or understands what it was like, and it isolates you on top of everything—'

And she broke. All that had been bubbling beneath the surface for months: Tekoa's exile, the threat of plague and pressure of starvation when carrying her first child, what had happened in that blood-washed tent and the appalling destruction of Hafdis's body; all of that erupted past her iron control. She howled, leaning into Harald, who put his arms round her shoulders and held her. Ormur was by her side too, one hand on her back and looking down in some confusion.

'We must get you out,' said Harald, one hand on the back of her head. 'You are not safe here.'

It was the strangest sensation. She had never understood before that she might not be able to stop herself from crying. Always it had been a conscious choice in whether or not to let go, but on this occasion, there was no restraining it. And perhaps for the first time ever, it felt a release. So she let it come, sobbing into Harald, simultaneously shocked and relieved by what was happening.

At last she composed herself, leaning back to offer the legionary a watery smile. 'I'm going nowhere, Harald. I will *not* be driven from my home by a memory. I will see that statue smashed.'

'It isn't worth it.'

'It is, Harald. If I start running now, when shall I stop? I won't ever live in fear. It's no good resolving that in future: it's a decision I must take now, or not at all. But as I seem to be at some risk, perhaps you'd perform me a service tomorrow?'

'Anything.'

'Ask Tore if he will guarantee my safety for a parlay. I have some things to say to him.'

'I will.'

Keturah beamed and pressed the familiar birthmark behind Harald's ear, as she had when she was a child. She turned to the neglected plate of ham and bread, and tried to show it proper appreciation.

That night, she showed Ormur into Tekoa's room, the bed made with woollen blankets and a small fire in the hearth for light rather than warmth. She bade him goodnight, but the boy barely registered it, gaping around the stone chamber in disbelief as she closed the door. Outside, she found Harald waiting for her. 'The boy seems a bit overwhelmed,' Keturah observed.

'I know. He's extremely loyal to you, Miss Keturah. He said you'd trapped the man who killed his twin brother.'

Keturah smiled wearily. 'Indeed.'

'That's a story I shall need to hear tomorrow. Why did you bring him back from the mountains?'

'He's soon for the berjasti anyway,' said Keturah. 'And I thought he needed to get out of that school. He was haunted up there; his brother killed, along with two of those who were sent to protect him. He just needed to escape that place. He's already ahead of his peers in everything important: he is best served now by some time in which he can digest the last few months.'

Harald admired her a few moments. 'What a woman you've returned,' he said.

'It is quite wonderful to see you again, old friend,' said Keturah.

They embraced and said goodnight, Keturah returning to the familiar bed she had occupied before her marriage. The blankets smelt of her childhood and the horsehair mattress was almost euphorically comfortable after months sleeping rough. She had meant to consider how she would defeat Tore, but was claimed within moments by a deep and dreamless sleep.

By the time she woke next morning, Harald had already left on her behalf. She rose, marvelling to find herself in her own home. Even the cold stone steps down to the parlour were a familiar joy. There, she found Ormur sitting by the fire, and they took tea and toasted bread while they waited for Harald.

It was mid-morning by the time they heard his thundering

on the door. Ormur rose to unbar it. 'Check who it is first, Ormur,' Keturah called after him. 'It wouldn't take much deduction from Tore to work out where we've fled.'

She heard the boy call through the door, and then froze when an unfamiliar voice replied. She did not catch the words, but Ormur had begun to remove the locking bar. Keturah scrambled after him and knocked his hand away. 'Don't,' she whispered. 'What did he say?'

'That he was a herald, sent by Lord Roper,' Ormur replied, voice low as hers.

Keturah narrowed her eyes. 'I fear very much he has been sent by Tore.'

'Tore?'

'He may have captured Harald,' whispered Keturah. 'And . . . questioned him. Go upstairs and look out of the window. If you're seen, say that nobody else is in.'

Ormur disappeared upstairs, and the voice came again through the boards of the door. 'I'm looking for Keturah Tekoasdottir.'

Keturah stayed silent, and Ormur was soon back downstairs, now armed with a poker. 'Just one man I could see,' hissed the boy. 'But he looked rough.'

Keturah deliberated. It could be a trap – indeed, it seemed most likely that it was – but a locked door would not stop Tore getting to her if he was determined.

'Thank you, Ormur,' she said, speaking normally now. 'We may as well face whoever it is. Put that thing down,' she added, but Ormur held the poker resolutely before him. Keturah lifted the locking bar, and stepped back, pulling the door with her.

The man who stood on the threshold did indeed look rough, with a squashed brawler's nose and a massive, round-shouldered physique. He wore the herald's crest though: a diamond-profiled owl. Perversely, Keturah found the man's appearance convincing. If this was a disguise, it was an exceptionally feeble one. Tore would surely have avoided this bruiser at all costs if he had truly wished to fool her.

The bruiser bowed to Keturah. 'The Black Lady, I presume. I am Virtanen Lanterison, a herald lately with your husband's forces in Suthdal. May I come in? The news I carry is not yet for everyone's ears.'

Keturah stepped back to show him in. 'I suppose you'd better. Tea, Virtanen?'

'Well that would be extremely welcome, it has been a long journey.' He stepped over the threshold, nearly wedging his bulk into the doorway. He followed Keturah into the parlour in a muscular waddle, taking a seat at her invitation, while she fetched a birch-bark cup and a sprig of pine. She was breathing fast. Whether or not this man was who he claimed, things were about to change. She noticed Ormur was still hovering just out of sight from the parlour, clutching his poker.

'A long journey indeed to deliver such news, sir. When did you last see the army?'

'Six days since, my lady.' Keturah unhooked the kettle and steeped the pine needles in steaming water. Virtanen leaned forward to accept the cup. 'Thank you.' He toasted her briefly before sitting back. 'My lady, my news is extensive and I must be blunt, not all of it is good.'

Keturah took a cup of her own and sat opposite Virtanen. 'We will get to it. First, what was the situation when you left?'

'Context is all,' he acknowledged, inclining his head once more. 'The army had just taken Lundenceaster.'

Suddenly, there seemed no doubt that this man spoke the truth. A wave of relief swept Keturah, so palpable that it felt as though someone had tipped cold water over her head. She gasped, and closed her eyes briefly. *Well done, my love.* She looked back at Virtanen and toasted him. 'So not all of your news is ill, sir,' she said softly. 'Come now, at what cost?'

'Two legions lost,' Virtanen admitted, and Keturah recoiled. That was a dreadful price to pay. *Ten thousand men!* She ought to have expected it, she knew. The city had been packed with defenders, and Roper's army had been weak.

But the herald was trying to catch her eye with an expression which said, *Brace yourself.* It seemed he was not finished. 'And among them,' he said gently, 'your cousin, Pryce Rubenson.'

'Pryce?' said Keturah blankly. The sprinter took terrible risks in battle, but his death was still incomprehensible. A man whose will seemed one of the laws of nature: where anything was possible in his presence, and you had the impression that whatever he desired, the world would accommodate it. She and Pryce had not been close: their characters too unyielding to rub along easily, and he too proud to have much of a relationship with anyone except Gray. Nonetheless, they were family, and Keturah felt some certainty leave her at the news that he was dead. A world without him was a flatter place. 'Someone who burned so bright was never going to last,' she said. 'Did anyone see him fall?'

Virtanen shook his head sadly. 'My very great condolences, lady. It is as you say: brilliance is fleeting.' Despite his appearance, the herald was clearly a man of diplomacy. 'But while there were plenty of witnesses to his bravery during the battle, I'm afraid there were none to his death. He actually survived the breach, and was killed very soon after by Vigtyr the Quick.'

'Vigtyr!' hissed Keturah. 'The army knows? That he's a traitor?'

'They know. Leon Kaldison arrived with that news just a few hours after Pryce had died.'

Now that was cruel; that Leon should have been so close to rescuing the situation. She thought of the journey she had taken to the haskoli, and wondered if she could have travelled a bit faster, and arrived a day earlier. What difference might that have made?

She looked bleakly at Virtanen, suddenly exhausted by the tidings he had brought. 'I hope I can lift some of your despair,' he said with a small smile. 'It is my pleasure to report to you that Legate Tekoa is alive. He has returned to the army, and was safe and well six days ago. The plague has been vanquished from the Skiritai.'

She raised a hand to cover her eyes. This was too much. She

had felt mighty relief at the news Lundenceaster was taken, but that paled in comparison with this. She was shaking, tears overwhelming her once more. Everything had become raw and cool and sweet. It felt as though some pustule within had suddenly burst, and a tension went out of her.

There was a splattering noise, and Virtanen suddenly stood. 'My lady.'

'Careless, I'm sorry.' She must have spilt her tea. Keturah glanced at her cup, but it was full. She sat forward, and cleared her eyes to see a great puddle shining on the floor beneath her chair. For a moment, she could not think how it had got there.

Then she realised. Her waters had broken.

The child was coming.

9
Built From Bones

'What have you done?' shouted Gray.

Roper could barely hear him over the noise of the legions erupting around them. 'I have *done*,' he said, flushed himself and breathing hard, 'what I have always said I will do. I have done what I had to.'

'You have made a weapon of their grief,' said Tekoa, gazing at the legionaries who were now roaring like bison. He did not sound angry, or appalled: just shocked.

'You have possessed the whole lot of them,' added Gray.

'Jokul will *kill* you!'

'Let him!' snarled Roper. 'If anything happens to me now, the Kryptea go down too. I swore, before this campaign had even begun, that I would break Jokul someday. I swore the child that Keturah carries, *your* grandchild,' he added to Tekoa, 'would live outside the Kryptea's shadow. If they kill me, then I have achieved not one, but two of my life's great tasks here in the south. It seems a good trade to me.'

This was no place to talk further. Gray clearly feared immediate Kryptean vengeance and began bellowing for the Sacred Guard. They assembled in heartbeats and clamped round the party as completely as an oyster shell. And not just the guard. Sensing the danger, regular legionaries swarmed around them too, determined to escort Roper clear of the crowd. He heard Leon snarling for one legionary to step back, only to be met with the reply: 'I'm going nowhere.' Half an hour before, these men had been desperate to go home.

Over the heads of the crowd Roper could see an eddy of violent jostling and shoving. Jokul stood at the centre of this activity, a score of men keeping him safe from the attentions of the crowd. His defenders wore no uniform, but perhaps for the first time, members of the Kryptea had been forced to show themselves in the open.

'Leon,' called Roper, pointing at the knot. 'Mark those men. This is not an opportunity we'll get again.'

'I see them,' said the guardsman, pushing his way towards the group.

Jokul seemed to be trying to push away his defenders, snarling that they were betraying themselves and they should leave him to the crowd. Then he spotted Roper and raised a finger to point at him. 'Tyrant!' he shouted. 'Tyrant! Now you have truly revealed yourself. I will make you regret this, Roper Kynortasson!'

Roper shook his head. 'You can't!' he called back.

'I *will*!' Jokul's face was suddenly flushed and quivering as, for the first time that Roper had ever seen, he lost control. 'Do you hear me, Lord Roper? I *will*!'

Roper turned away, borne towards his hearth on a tide of protective legionaries. It had never been his intention to endanger Jokul personally. That was why he had not mentioned him by name. The Master had shown his claws and Roper had bared his teeth.

Roper reached his hearth and the Sacred Guard, along with the volunteers from the crowd, set up a cordon around him and his generals. The Chief Historian, Frathi, was already waiting by the fire, and on her face was a look of disdain such as Roper had never seen. 'To think I helped put a tyrant on the Stone Throne,' she said.

'That word seems cheap today,' said Roper. 'In my place,

you would have allowed yourself to be blackmailed, and scuttled back north would you, my lady? The future of our people held hostage, and this kingdom ruled from the shadows by a band of murderers?'

'I would have allowed them their say, certainly,' she replied. 'I did not really expect someone of your age to understand, but I thought that at least your advisers would know better.' She regarded Gray and Tekoa.

'We had no idea he was going to commit political arson,' Tekoa snarled back at her.

'My Lord Roper chose to do that himself,' Gray agreed.

'And it was no mistake,' Roper interjected. 'Either I have blocked the Kryptea, and shown them the limitations of their own power. Or they will kill me, and at last that band of assassins will be uprooted from the country, as they have long deserved. Either way, the conquest of Suthdal continues, and I leave a legacy for whoever rules after me, and for unborn generations. I have achieved exactly what I hoped.'

'You fool,' said Frathi coldly. 'The institutions of the Black Kingdom are built from bones. Each was born when so many of our subjects had died that we decided it could not go on. That process has honed our society into a potent survival machine. You cannot see the utility of our customs because you have never seen the world without them. That does not mean they are not working. You have just cast aside the wisdom of your ancestors like a cloak you do not need on a summer's day. Observe the line of Black Lords before their formation and after. There is a dramatic improvement in their behaviour once they were accountable with their lives, which is no coincidence. Our institutions are built from bones and you took a hatchet to them today.'

'Not all laws stay relevant,' said Roper, stubbornly. 'Our ancestors could not foresee the world we live in today.'

'What has changed, Lord Roper?' Frathi demanded. 'If you think the circumstances you face today have never arisen before, you have not looked. I shall give you one thing, however. You are the most compelling man for many generations to have sat upon the Stone Throne. Your command over the legions already made you unusually powerful, at an unusually young age. And now you have lifted the only restraint standing between you and tyranny.'

'That word again,' said Roper, coldly. 'Power corrupts, is that it? You think that I'll now begin executing and persecuting those who displease me, just because I can?'

'Power does not corrupt, as the crude reading of history goes,' decreed Frathi. 'Power *unmasks.* When you are free to do as you wish, without repercussion, we see who you really are. And already, I have seen that you refuse to be guided by your advisers, that you are prepared to trample anything that inhibits you. You have ignored all the other offices, factions and councils in the kingdom, and unilaterally commenced this campaign, spending sixteen thousand legionaries in the process. And now you have irreparably upset the delicate balance which exists between Kryptea and Black Lord.'

'Good,' said Roper, holding her gaze, though her words made him nauseous. The last thing he wanted to think about was the men dead on his orders. 'You should have greater faith in our objective.'

The Chief Historian cast her eyes heavenwards. 'Tell me, Lord Roper, how much do you know about swords?'

Roper said nothing, just watching her.

'Could you make one?'

Roper shrugged. 'Perhaps.'

The Chief Historian nodded. 'Or something which resembled one, for a bit. But would you know how to quench it so that it didn't shatter from being too hard, or fail from being too soft? Could you balance it so it didn't exhaust your arm?' She looked at him. 'Would you know where to dig for ore, how to mine it, refine it, combine it in the right proportions to produce Unthank-silver?'

Roper shrugged again. 'I don't see your point.'

'Well the answer is no. You use one every day. It's a simple object, which you think you understand. Yet of the bucket's worth of knowledge required to produce one, you have but a drop. The same is true of every single decision you make; because you are a mortal being, and cannot possibly know enough to alter something as complex as a nation without the unintended consequences spilling into the future like a torrent.'

Roper watched her flatly. 'But you know better, do you?'

She gave a half-nod. 'A little. Because I know history, as much as can possibly be accommodated in a human mind. I know where we have come from, and so which direction the path is heading in. You are lost in the fog, clutching onto a lion's tail you believe to be a bullrush. As its last act, that lion will destroy the fanatic who currently occupies the Stone Throne. The Kryptea will kill you. And I shall support them.'

Roper blinked, and then nearly laughed at the absurdity of that statement. But he greatly respected Frathi, and in the face of her certainty, his confidence diminished. 'I think your faith in them may be misplaced,' he observed. 'It took them months to find Bellamus. And they never even discovered Vigtyr.'

The historian frowned at this, cocking her head a little. 'But can you really have misunderstood so completely?' she asked. 'They knew where Bellamus was from the beginning. Their information, and when they give it to you, is the only way you left them to wield their power. And not only did they know about Vigtyr, they shielded him.'

'I don't believe you,' said Roper abruptly.

'That has always been your problem,' Frathi observed dismissively. 'Really, Lord Roper, I thought you understood this game and had just decided not to play.'

'What would possess them to keep secret the location of our foremost enemy, and the identity of our foremost traitor?' Roper demanded.

'They foresaw what we all should have: you are dangerous. Your own officers blocked the Kryptea's usual means of exercising authority, and they saw in Bellamus and Vigtyr a way to turn you back without the extreme loss of life that occurred at this city. They only turned the spymaster over to you when it became clear he was developing a weapon to use against the legions.'

'Well, aren't we fortunate the act of retrieving Bellamus didn't unleash the weapon,' said Tekoa sarcastically.

Frathi shrugged a single shoulder. 'They did not know it was a plague. They hoped to intervene before it had been developed. Like you, Lord Roper, they knew a little but not enough.'

But Roper was ahead of Tekoa. He had understood about the weapon; had already realised that the legionaries murdered during the campaign by the Kryptea had not been meant to target the Suthern spies, as Jokul had claimed, but to demoralise his men, and increase the pressure on Roper to turn back. He had moved on to other matters. 'And you, lady,' he said, quite softly. 'You went to defend Bellamus when our encampment was raided outside Deorceaster. You wanted him kept alive so he could be used against us. You knew, too.'

Frathi paused, but did not flinch. 'I knew.'

Roper looked down at the ground, smiling bitterly. 'I was warned the Academy and Kryptea were entwined. Clearly, I had not taken that seriously enough.' He looked up at Frathi. 'Well, my lady, as it seems you've been standing against us all along, I think it's best you depart this army.'

'Or what, Lord Roper?' demanded Frathi, feet rooted to the earth. 'What happens now, if I incur your displeasure?'

'I shall not harm you,' said Roper, 'but neither am I prepared to defend you. And when word gets out about the stance you have taken in all this, I would think your safety will be in considerable doubt.'

Frathi nodded. She did not seem perturbed. 'And you two?' she demanded, gaze swinging from Tekoa to Gray. 'Will you continue to support this man as he dismantles the kingdom we have served our entire lives?'

'Certainly, I shall avenge myself on anyone who threatens him,' said Gray. 'Until this moment, lady, I thought that I would kill anyone I found to have aided Vigtyr. It seems I was wrong about that. But I agree with Lord Roper. Your aims and this army's clearly do not align.'

'The Sacred Guard,' grunted Frathi. 'A pack of dogs. And you, legate?'

'I by no means support every action Lord Roper has taken,' said Tekoa. 'But how appropriate that the symbol of the Academy is the Angel of Madness. Your silence on Vigtyr resulted in the death of my nephew. Fuck off, my lady.'

Frathi was not offended. 'As I feared. You shall both fall with him.' She was about to turn away, then glanced once more at Roper.

'So shall He whom Kryptea defy,
Be cast down, nether Temple stones,
And body bound in Kungargrav,
With walls for doors and windows of stone.
Punished past pain and desperation,
Despotic Black Lord lingers alone,
Soul sentenced and mind tormented,
Till shall hell seem sweet sanctuary,
And blackness beauty past paradise.

'The Chant of the Kryptean Pact, now forgotten it seems. Perhaps I should have reminded you of it earlier. But you should believe the Master when he says he will make you regret this.' She turned on her heel, and was gone, striding across the camp. The crowds parted swiftly before her, unaware that she had just declared against their lord.

In her wake was a bitter silence. They watched as she retrieved her black stallion, took a little food for the road, and trotted out of the camp, heading north. It was Roper who started moving first, piling fresh wood on the fire.

'Onwards,' he said.

Whether the Kryptea came or not, they would march on tomorrow. Seven cities remained defiant. The pacification of Suthdal had begun.

10
Submission

When Roper retired to bed the night after Pryce's embalming, it was with Sacred Guardsmen slumbering around him. He tried to dismiss them, but they would not go. With them, remained twenty of the legionaries who had leapt to Roper's side in the aftermath of his speech, and they conversed with the guardsmen in low murmurs as they took turns at watch.

Roper barely slept. The scurrying of mice became dark figures scuttling in the dark, and each crack from the fire brought him lurching from sleep. In the end, he decided that his best distraction would be to thank the men who stood on guard for him. As he rose, he heard Leon stand and fall in behind him. 'Your names, peers,' said Roper to the first trio of volunteer guardsmen.

They beamed to be addressed by him. 'Rethin, lord,' said the first, as Roper took each of their hands in turn.

'Yngvar, lord.'

'Sakeus, lord.'

'Sakeus,' said Roper, frowning. 'We've fought side by side, have we not? I remember your face.'

'That's right, lord,' replied the legionary. The warmth was stained into his face, eyes hung in a spider's web of creases and twinkles. 'At Githru. You dismounted and joined in with the Fair Islanders.'

'I remember. You lost your sword I think.'

Sakeus was nodding eagerly.

'And then – I must surely have fabricated this – you took off your helmet and used it to beat a Sutherner over the head?' The legionaries laughed at this evidently familiar tale.

'That's right, lord.' He nudged the men next to him. 'I told the boys I got to fight beside Lord Roper, and ended up hammering a man to death with my hat.'

Roper laughed in earnest at that.

'The look you gave me, lord. You were being assaulted by some devil with a spear, but kept taking your glass off him and staring at me, as though you couldn't believe it.'

'I couldn't, especially because I remember you had a long knife in your belt. I was wondering what sort of man takes off his helmet when he has a real weapon to hand.'

'An *extremely* stressed one,' said Yngvar.

'It worked, didn't it, lord?' Sakeus insisted.

'Against all odds, it did.'

'He was probably just pretending,' said Rethin, who had the fierce, unshakeable eyes of a hawk but the grin of a child. 'Thought the fight had already got out of hand and wanted no further part in it.'

'This guy is furious – he's hitting me with his bloody hat.'

Leon cleared his throat and Roper, grinning, raised his hands. 'We should probably keep it down boys, the others are trying to sleep. But I wanted to thank you all. It means everything to see you here.'

All three bowed. 'Sleep well, my lord. If the Kryptea come, we'll turn them around again.'

Roper moved on, thanking each group before attempting sleep once more. But he could not stop thinking about those men surrounding Jokul: his first sight of Kryptean agents, who had appeared to protect the Master as though conjured from the earth.

Dawn came as it always had, and Roper was there to see it. At last, they could begin pacifying Suthdal, and the army packed up and marched north. The day was filled with autumn light the colour of straw, and a fresh breeze blew dust up the road. Roper rode Zephyr, and mounted beside him were Gray, Tekoa, Leon and Randolph: the remnants of his close war council. They were all that remained, with Leon a recent addition. Pryce was dead. Sturla Karson, legate of Ramnea's Own, was dead too. The Chief Historian had abandoned them, and as a result of their confrontation, the Battle Historian had been estranged. Keturah, most valued of all, was in the north.

'My friends,' Roper began, haltingly. 'I am greatly touched by the loyalty shown me thus far. But . . . but I can't have armed men standing over me all hours of the day and night. The only shield on which I can rely is this campaign being more popular than killing me would be.'

'No mistakes then,' said Tekoa. 'The legions' faith in this campaign will stall when we stop making progress, so that is what must not happen. We gain surrender from one city after another and if we do, you will outlast Jokul. If he delays too long, then he proves himself powerless. Let's make sure we give him that time.'

Roper clung to those words: perhaps there was still hope he would survive this. He was sure it had been right to confront them in the open, but whatever he told the others, he did not want to die. Out loud, he observed: 'Nevertheless, we should prepare for the worst. What happens in the event of my death?'

Tekoa spoke again. 'It depends on whether Keturah has a healthy child, and particularly a son. In that instance, if you were deposed, then it should be possible for her to take your place as regent, until my grandchild was old enough to rule. And that would give Keturah twenty years on the throne. Now, you know better than I: would she continue the fight for Suthdal?'

'She would,' said Roper, without hesitation. 'But could she, if the Kryptea are committed to forcing us back north? It seems a waste to lay down my own life if she is next in line for the executioner's block.'

Gray spoke for the first time that day. 'If the Kryptea come for you, I think popular opinion will favour us rooting them out most thoroughly,' he said, to a noise of violent assent from Leon. 'We should be able to protect her.'

'Good. And if our child does not survive?'

There was a pause. 'You could rule, legate,' suggested Randolph, looking to Tekoa.

'Obviously,' said Tekoa dismissively. 'But the Stone Throne is not a comfortable seat.'

Randolph was grinning. 'Fortunately I don't think anyone here expected a modest response.'

'I have nothing to be modest about.'

'Too much like hard work for you?'

'Too likely to get murdered. As my son-in-law here so ably proves, it is a supremely thankless task.'

'But you are the grand old rooster,' Randolph pressed. 'Everyone would expect you to crow and settle yourself at the top of the coop, and if you didn't, there'd be chaos. A bunch of lesser men scrapping and pecking at one another, maybe for years. The case could be made that it's your duty to take over.'

'I have no interest in what you think my duty is,' said Tekoa loftily.

'It'll be my brother,' said Roper, firmly. 'Maintaining Jormunrekur rule would be the easiest way to avoid conflict. If the Vidarr took over, the Lothbroks would be incensed, and vice versa. The status quo is the answer here.' Managing the rivalry of the kingdom's three great houses – Jormunrekur, Vidarr and Lothbrok – had been nearly as great a challenge as sacking Lundenceaster.

'Ormur is a boy,' said Tekoa. 'What makes you think he'd continue the conquest of Suthdal?'

'I daresay you could keep an eye on that, Old Rooster.'

Tekoa brooded. 'I could, I suppose. Very well.'

'Good. These then, are my wishes in front of all you witnesses. If I fall, bury me in armour and appoint Keturah as regent until either my heir, or Ormur comes of age.'

So the future of the Black Kingdom was decided, and they rode in silence for a moment.

'Why would you want to be buried in that armour?' said Tekoa, eventually. 'I've seen brothel-masters with greater integrity than that cheese-plate.'

Roper looked down at his pocked and patched breastplate. 'It does its job.'

'Not for long. I'll commission you some. I have an armourer who thinks he can make a full cuirass of Unthank-silver. A gift, in honour of your conquest of Lundenceaster.'

'That's kind of you,' said Roper, a little embarrassed. 'Though I'm still struggling with the last gift you gave me.' He patted Zephyr's neck gently. 'I fear . . . it may be time to give him up.' The vast iron destrier still tolerated Roper as his rider, but was beginning to rebel when handled by anyone else. As Jokul had pointed out, he had kicked one of his handlers to death, and the others dreaded coming near him.

Tekoa eyed the horse, which had been produced in his stables and given to Roper as a wedding present. 'We wanted to create the nastiest war-mount we could. He's got wild horse in him, from Trawden. It was the best bloodline we could find for size and strength but . . . perhaps the temperament is not quite right. In a few generations, maybe we'll have something more biddable.'

Roper knotted his fingers into Zephyr's mane. He and the horse had fought together on desperate battlefields, and he was one of the best allies Roper had. There had never been any indication he might pose a threat to his master, but it could not be proper to ask his handlers to risk their lives in keeping him. Still, Roper could not bear to part with him just yet. He was still young: perhaps he would learn discipline.

*

It was a journey of fifty miles north to reach Grantabryge. They had left it untaken on their forced march south, as Roper had aimed to bring the conquest to a head before they were defeated by starvation. It was surrounded by a flat, saturated country of marsh and fen, and the legions travelled on causeways above wind-rustled reeds and mirky waters stirring with pike.

They arrived singing, arranging themselves fifty-thousand strong around the city's palisade wall in a manoeuvre that took an entire day to complete, while Roper waited in front of the main gate on Zephyr. With the Jormunrekur banner of the Silver Wolf over one shoulder, the Almighty Eye of the Sacred Guard over the other, it was not long before they were received by the plump and harried-looking mayor, who named himself Gunnwaerd.

He listened in silence to Roper's demands, and then shrugged helplessly. 'I don't seem to have a choice.'

'You have the same choice they had at Lundenceaster, and at Lincylene, and outside Deorceaster. I think they would now all agree they chose wrong.'

They harvested the food, the arms, the armour. For three days, the legions worked to topple and burn the walls. At first they were alone, but by the third morning some of the braver townsfolk came to watch in curious silence as their palisade was dismantled. Roper encouraged the legionaries to grant some of their bread to the watching townsfolk (who had baked it, after all). A very few accepted, and when these did not fall grievously ill, a great queue formed to receive the blessing of the Black Legions.

'This is our greatest victory of the campaign,' Roper told Tekoa. 'We needed one city to submit early to show we can be generous masters. It will encourage the others to do the same.'

'We should leave our mark as well,' replied the legate. 'They must not forget who now rules them.'

Roper approved of this suggestion. 'Flatten their grand church? We could raise a temple to the Almighty in its place.'

Tekoa rolled his eyes in a gesture irresistibly like his daughter. 'Good lord, it's like having a goose on the throne. Quite exceptional at waddling mindlessly to war, less impressive when pressed on matters of policy.'

Roper gave him a sour look. 'What would you do?'

'Send in the legions with instructions to choose a building each and carve one handprint into it. You do not offend their god, their life is no less comfortable. But wherever they go, they never forget whose city this is.'

Roper resisted only briefly to irritate Tekoa. The next day, fifty thousand Anakim prints had laid claim to the city. Roper went further, returning the food supplies to the nobles and the clergy, and so depriving any resistance of leaders around which to assemble. By the time they left, the legions were wandering unarmed through the city streets and were tolerated without protest.

The mayor, Gunnwaerd, made the mistake of swearing undying friendship, the smile fading from his face when Roper accepted his offer and suggested he travel with the army.

'I'd merely slow you down, lord, I'm quite certain.'

'No, it would be good to have a Sutherner to advocate on our behalf.'

'But the show you made in coming here was so impressive, I could add nothing to that.'

Tekoa had overheard. 'Gunnwaerd, your choice is quite simple,' he said genially. 'You may come with us in one piece, or remain in several.'

With Gunnwaerd, they took a score of hostages to further ensure the good behaviour of the city's elite, and marched on, for Northwic. Roper walked in the ranks with his legionaries, staring wistfully overhead at the wedges of ducks and geese fleeing south. 'Think your lot could get hold of some of those, Sakeus?'

Sakeus and the score of men who had volunteered to defend Roper from the Kryptea had been adopted as honorary guardsmen, and still travelled with them.

'Yes!' said Tekoa, delighted. 'Duck! We've heard much of your abilities as a huntsman, Sakeus. Do your arrows fly as fast as your words?'

'Arrows, my lord?' asked Sakeus. 'One hunts duck with a net. I fear I have none.'

'We have some,' said Roper. 'In the baggage train. How many can we expect? One between a pair of guardsmen?'

'You believe you're teasing me, my lords,' said the legionary. 'But if we stop before dark so I can lay some decoys on the water, you may expect one per pair, and more.'

Glee flashed across the group. Fresh meat seemed an impossible thing just then; for weeks the only meat that had passed their lips had been dried hare, dried fox and occasional salted venison. 'I think we'd better get Sakeus his net,' said Roper. Sakeus was excused marching on his own two feet to sit on the back of a wagon and fashion his 'decoys': blocks of wood with feathers bound to the back. Then he rode ahead to the evening's campsite in anticipation of their arrival.

The van of the column arrived two hours later. Roper helped his men assemble the camp, and then sat with his companions by the fire, waiting for Sakeus to return. 'Duck is the finest meat of all,' declared Tekoa, as though this were a known fact.

'Give me a venison back-cut,' said Leon.

Tekoa tutted. 'Too lean and tastes of iron. I would permit dissent for pork.'

'Really, Tekoa,' said Roper. 'I had no idea you adored greasy meat so much. Light your hair and I believe you'd burn like a candle.'

'It's the diet of a bear gaining weight for the winter,' agreed Leon dismissively.

'Where do you stand, Gray?' asked Roper. The captain always had to be invited into the conversation now.

'Mutton, in fact, lord,' he replied. 'I agree, pork is too greasy. Though I make special exception for crackling.'

'Just for crackling?' expostulated Tekoa. 'What about bacon?'

'Bacon, too.' This seemed almost always to be their evening conversation. Dreams of when this was all over: the food they would eat, the bed they would lie in, the woman they would lie in it with.

'Duck, as ordered, my lords,' said a voice from the dark. Sakeus had approached in complete silence, and with a flourish dropped a heap of broken feathers by their hearth. He bowed and made to depart.

'Wait, Sakeus; wait one moment,' called Roper. 'This duck is most unusual.'

'Lord?'

'I've never seen one before with one leg and one wing.'

The legionary was grinning. 'Hunting was harder than expected, lord. I tend to bigger game, so I've had to spread them out a little.'

'Are you quite sure it's even a duck?' asked Tekoa, peering at it. 'It may lately have been a robin.'

'Definitely duck, my lords.'

'I thank you, Sakeus,' said Roper. 'I didn't truly think you'd manage to get anything. You have enough for yourselves, I trust?'

'Of course, he does,' said Tekoa, gesturing at the bird. 'We're dining off his scraps.'

Pryce had loved duck, Roper remembered. He thought of the guardsman often; his long ponytail lashing behind him as he ran, his hard gaze and unexpected moments of tenderness.

They reached the city of Northwic the next day, which at first would not even receive Roper. They left him waiting in front of the gates until darkness fell, and despite the objections of a visibly wilting Tekoa, Roper stayed there on horseback through the night, furnished with food and hot drinks by the sentries. When the dawn came, it illuminated the Black Lord standing just where he had been the night before. There he stayed until midday, but still there came no response.

Roper swore softly, heart sinking at the massacre that

would be required if the city refused to yield. 'Idiots,' he said vehemently, staring at the watchmen visible above the palisade. 'You stupid, stupid bastards. Just submit, you bloody fools.' Surely they should have learned by now.

'What do you command, lord?' asked Gray.

Roper blew out a breath, turning Zephyr away from the walls. 'Start constructing siege works about the city. And ask Gunnwaerd to use some of his writing and make a message for them. They have until tomorrow morning to surrender.'

But Gunnwaerd could not even get close enough to deliver the message. Roper watched him try three times to approach the gates, driven back on each occasion by volleys of arrows. 'No . . .' he breathed. 'You fools.'

They began building ladders and rams to go with the earthworks now being constructed around Northwic's walls. But by the time darkness had fallen, they had barely started either, and that was how it should stay, thought Roper. This was a waste of their time, and the Kryptea would be waiting for the slightest indication that the campaign had faltered.

So it was that after dark, Roper gathered together the Sacred Guard and addressed them from atop a wagon bed. 'Peers: we go tonight. You have an hour to ready yourselves, then meet me back here. No need for plate armour or torches. Just bring yourselves and a sharp sword, and cover any exposed skin with dark clothes.'

There was no moon.

Shortly after midnight, Roper and Gray led the three hundred pattering into the dark. The sentries silhouetted on the walls ahead were militiamen, warmed by large flickering braziers. Had they been more experienced, they might have known that a large fire atop a wall will ruin your night-vision, but cast very little light on the ground beneath. They might have known that a moonless night requires exceptional and intensive vigilance against attack. They might have realised that an opposing army building siege weapons and fortifications does not necessarily intend to use them.

The Sacred Guard had covered their hands and arms, and ran with faces cast down so that the braziers above would not reflect off their bright skin. Roper selected a lightly defended spot near the gate, and his men were soon spread silently beneath the walls. Gray was on Roper's right, Leon on his left, all guardsmen equipped with grapples. Roper looked up at the wall's dark bulk, estimating it at twenty feet. 'On my lead,' he hissed, and tossed his grapple. It hooked over the battlements on his second attempt, and he began hauling himself up swiftly and silently, Leon soon catching up on his own rope.

Roper thrust his head over the battlement and to his astonishment, found a sentry standing directly behind it, staring back at him in equal shock. The man had clearly seen the grapple, and approached in dull silence, wondering what was happening. For three heartbeats, they looked each other full in the face. 'Hey!' shouted the man, lowering a spear at Roper, who ducked back below the battlement. He nearly let go of the rope, and in his efforts to clutch on, ended up with his face pressed into the palisade, knuckles trapped painfully between the taught rope and the wood.

But he had distracted the sentry, and from the corner of his eye he could see Leon scrambling over the wall. There came the rasp of a sword being drawn above Roper, who pulled himself back over the top to see Leon dismissing the spear jabbed at him, and booting the sentry off the wall. He fell with a cry and a crash on the cobbles below, and Roper was on the fire step with Leon, Cold-Edge in his hand.

It was all starting so slowly. The militiamen knew the basic facts: that they were guarding this wall, and that there was a chance they would have to defend it. But they had no insight into the intensity of war. A battle, as they imagined it, would not start with something as innocuous as two unarmoured men standing on their fire step. There were no senior officers present, nobody was quite sure who was in charge, and most of the sentries just stared at Roper and Leon, as if trying to confirm who they were before reacting.

They were already too late.

A dozen grapples had clattered over the battlements, while Roper and Leon charged for the gatehouse. A sentry stood in Roper's path, spear levelled and shield raised. He was waiting for the onrushing Roper to attack first, which was a mistake. The Black Lord was more than a foot taller than him, and made of the denser stuff that constitutes an Anakim. Roper stepped one way then the other, evading the spear. Then he crashed into his shield, barging the man clean off the wall. He cried out as he fell, hitting the ground with a crunch.

Roper tore along the fire step, heads appearing over the battlements on his right. Still, everything remained incongruously silent. Only a few nearby militiamen had realised they were facing an assault, and most were too cowed to do anything other than freeze as Sacred Guardsmen swarmed over the battlements, bringing an intensity in stark contrast to Northwic's defenders.

One more defender stood between Roper and the gatehouse. He jabbed a spear at Roper, who again manoeuvred so that the man's shield was between them. He seized its cold iron rim and pulled it forward to expose his enemy's body to Cold-Edge. He raised the sword, which was enough to persuade the defender to rip his arm from the shield grips and hurl himself off the wall, preferring the drop to being stabbed. He toppled aside and Roper flung the shield after him, the gatehouse now exposed.

Leon swept past him, plunging through the door that led into the gatehouse tower, Roper on his heels. By the time he was inside, another defender was already tumbling down the stairs; Leon bounding after the clattering Sutherner who shed a grieve, a helmet, a dagger and his shield before smashing into the wall at the base of the tower stairs. Leon ignored him, plunging past the stupefied guard and exiting the tower at ground level, by the gates. Roper streaked after him. Outside, five or six defenders were charging from the left, one of them limping heavily and clearly only recently recovered from falling off the wall. 'I've got them,' shouted Leon. 'Get the gates!'

Roper seized another guardsman. 'Hartvig! Help me!'

Leon and a dozen others were holding back the defenders, while Roper and Hartvig heaved at the two huge locking bars that held the gate. They came away one after another, the second hardly out of the way before the gates were blasted open by a rush of Ramnea's Own legionaries, waiting on the far side. Roper was pressed into the wall of the gatehouse as they charged past him, torches bobbing as they flooded the streets.

'Done,' spat Roper, and it was. The shocked defenders were suddenly outnumbered and outclassed, and those assaulting the Sacred Guard discarded shields and weapons and pelted away from the walls. Roper hollered that the Guard should not pursue, but stay at the gatehouse. They were unarmoured, and there was no sense risking them now the city was won. They gathered above the gates, and watched as fires began to break out on either side of Northwic's main road.

At Lundenceaster, they had paid for entrance in so much blood that retribution seemed, if not right, then in some way natural: part of the same order as what happens when a wild animal is provoked. Here, they had crossed the walls without losing a life, but faint wails and screams were already ringing across the city. Figures began to scuttle from distant streets, like insects from a burning log, and half a dozen houses had started billowing with thick smoke. 'Idiots,' Roper repeated, bitterly.

But they had arrived at this policy to preserve as many as possible, on both sides. If other cities heard that Northwic had resisted and been spared nonetheless, this war might drag on for decades. The legionaries turned a blind eye to those escaping Northwic's western gate, but officially nobody was spared. By dawn, even the cathedral was smashed to a heap of rubble.

Two cities were pacified.

Four remained.

11
The Barleymen

The night after Garrett's army occupied the old fortress at Searoburgh, those who had belonged to Bellamus's old unit, the Thingalith, began to defect. Within three days, so many had appeared in Wiltun that they formed a little encampment in the town square, sheltering beneath cloaks they had strung up in a small yew grove. Bellamus and Stepan took a barrel of ale to greet their old comrades, and were received like royalty. A ham was produced from somewhere, along with bottles of corrosive-smelling spirit, and they settled about the fire to talk.

'How was life in the hybrid's army, lads?' asked Stepan.

There were so many tales that none was finished properly.

'He's a maniac,' one began.

'As soon as the hybrids outnumbered us, they started treating us like slaves.'

'They stole our weapons and armour—'

'We've just been serfs.'

'And starving! They live off *nothing*.'

'Remember Dunwulf? He tried to take his armour back and he got hacked to bits.'

'They sound excellent fellows,' said Stepan. He and Dunwulf had loathed each other.

'Not just Dunwulf, though,' said another man. 'Four or five of us gone now.' There were nods from the forty or so gathered about the fire. 'If we'd had somewhere to go, we'd have deserted months ago. Some did. Three tried to run, what, six weeks ago? Garrett tracked them down and flayed them alive.'

'He keeps their skins as rugs in his tent.'

Bellamus was revolted. So, it seemed, was Stepan: 'That dog needs putting down. Glad you boys got out of there.'

'It's marvellous to have you back,' agreed Bellamus, toasting them all. In return, he was offered a swig from one of the noxious bottles of spirit, which burned his lips like they had been scrubbed with sand.

'You get used to it,' observed the Thingman who had offered the drink, as Bellamus spluttered and spat. '*Lifsin*, they call it. This is what Garrett's army runs on. They are always drunk.'

'Every one of them is addicted,' said another. 'It's turned them into a force of barley-harvesters. They seize it from defenceless towns and distil it into *lifsin*. Two months ago, they ran dry and sacked a town for supplies.'

'What?' asked Bellamus, shocked.

'Radcot. They stormed it, plundered the drink and the barley, and burned anything they didn't smash. I truly think that army has done more damage than the Anakim invasion. At least the Anakim have a plan. The Barleymen just prowl around, looking for enough drink to keep them sedated.'

'Barleymen? That's what you call them?' asked Bellamus.

'That's all there is to them,' said the Thingman, shaking his head. 'They're fiends. They'll do anything for *lifsin*, and Garrett makes sure they have it. So they do *whatever* he asks.'

'Well, that's not the only reason,' said another Thingman. 'When Garrett freed each man, he let them kill their old master.'

'I bet I know how,' said Stepan.

'Flayed alive,' murmured Bellamus.

Here, Garrett seemed to have taken after Bellamus once again. When raising the Thingalith, Bellamus had bonded them by fostering the belief of otherness; a sense that they were all outlaws together, who had each other and nobody else. Garrett had taken that tribalism to the extreme, with anyone outside the Barleymen simply a source of leather. At any other time, this uprising would be one of the most dangerous that Suthdal had faced. If they could defeat the Anakim together, Bellamus knew he would have to beat Garrett soon after.

'How many Thingalith are left with the Barleymen?' he asked.

'Sixty or so,' came the answer. 'Poor bastards. Now there's so many of us gone, I can't imagine how they'll get out. Garrett will be keeping an eye on them.'

Bellamus had had enough, and steered the conversation into happier waters. 'Well, you're free, my friends. What have you done since finding yourself in a proper town?'

As they had no money, the answer was very little.

When they had finished the ale, Bellamus stood and held up his purse, clinking with gold. 'You're still my men?' he asked.

'Always, lord,' said Diethaad, one of his old lieutenants.

Bellamus left them the purse, and he and Stepan walked together back to Penbro Hall.

'If we could gather the final sixty Thingalith, it would be magnificent,' said Stepan.

'We were quite a band, weren't we? I can't believe so many stayed together after Brimstream. If we can get those final sixty back, it would take us over a hundred and fifty: enough to rebuild the unit, I should think.'

Stepan flashed a glance at Bellamus. He cleared his throat and then seemed to think better of it, looking ahead. Eventually he said: 'Enough to go and fetch my household? They're good riders all,' he added hurriedly, 'and maybe the canniest band in Albion – more than a match for the road-wolves. I know we can't spare any riders, Captain, but I'm so frightened.'

Bellamus turned to look and was shocked and embarrassed to see tears in his friend's eyes.

'I know the Unhieru are coming, but I'm so frightened that

if we wait any longer, I'll be too late. Please, my friend. All those stories of what the Barleymen have been doing in the north; I couldn't stop thinking: *What if they passed my estate?* I know Ede isn't much safer down here, but I just want us to be together, whatever happens. You've lived on the edge for such a long time, it seems you can just accept that Suthdal may be finished any day now. I can't. I need to go, with or without the Thingalith.' Stepan cuffed at the tears sliding into his beard and took a steadying breath.

Bellamus was appalled. Had he really become so callous, that this resilient, ebullient man was reduced to tears? 'Go, my friend,' he said, shaking his head. 'Take any Thingalith you want, and bring your household back here. That is the very least I owe you.'

And to his further embarrassment, these words only served to make Stepan weep harder. He stopped Bellamus to enfold him in a great embrace, and sobbed into his shoulder.

'I'm sorry, Stepan,' said Bellamus, returning the embrace. 'I should have let you go earlier. I can only plead . . . I've had a lot on my mind.'

'I know, Captain, of course. Don't think I don't know. You can't . . . You can't come with me, I suppose?'

'There I must disappoint you, brother,' said Bellamus as the two broke apart. 'I am needed here. You and the Thingalith together can handle anything that might come up; I can't think what I'd add. When will you leave?'

'Tomorrow,' said Stepan, sniffing as they resumed their walk back to the hall. 'I'll see if any more escape from Garrett tonight, and then go. I'll be quick, I promise. You'll have the men back before you need them.'

Bellamus doubted that.

They hurried back to Penbro Hall, and another witan to discuss the Unhieru. Sitting with the council, they found an unexpected figure.

Vigtyr.

The enormous Anakim was dressed in harlequin's robes,

clearly tailor-made for him from materials which would have been out of fashion forty years ago, and yet still comically small. The hems reached only his bare mid-calf, and stopped far short of his wrists. He sat uncomfortably on a bench near the queen, and at the sight of him, Bellamus froze. This man, in these clothes, was here as entertainment.

'Lord Safinim,' said Aramilla, seated on her throne at the hall's head and beaming in welcome. 'Come and sit on my right. You with him, Sir Stepan, I know how highly he values your presence.'

Bellamus went to sit on the bench on Aramilla's right, Stepan settling next to him.

'I know you have a plan, my lord, though we shall hear first from our new adviser here.' Aramilla gestured towards Vigtyr. 'Vittles, was it?'

Vigtyr stood quickly, face reddening as a chuckle swept the hall. 'Vigtyr, Your Majesty.'

As ever, his Saxon was poor and the words imprecise through his broken teeth, so that his own name emerged as 'Bigpyr'. The laughter intensified at his mangled pronunciation, and Vigtyr went redder still, casting around the room with such self-consciousness that Bellamus could hardly watch. This, he knew, was the position Vigtyr had been desperate for, along with the status and respect he had imagined would accompany it.

'And I understand you know much of the Unhieru, Big-Pair, having helped negotiate the alliance between Gogmagoc and the Black Lord.'

The Anakim were less subtle than the Sutherners, and alone in that hall, it seemed Vigtyr could not hear the undercurrent of mockery in the queen's words.

'Tell us what we can expect from the barbarians,' Aramilla continued.

Vigtyr looked pleased and important to have been so courteously addressed. 'They are physically extremely strong, my lady.'

'She's not a lady, she's a Majesty!' interrupted one of the lords, and the hall hooted with laughter.

They're not really laughing at Vigtyr, Bellamus thought. The Anakim was a vent for their fear at the approaching Unhieru, and their resentment at how Aramilla had so far toyed with them all.

'They are physically strong.' Vigtyr tried to go on above the merriment, a tremor rendering his voice still less impressive. 'And they are dressed in Anakim mail—'

At this the laughter redoubled, for Vigtyr's pronunciation had rendered 'mail' into the Saxon word for 'grapes'. He carried on, but barely anyone was listening above the hilarity. By the time Vigtyr abruptly curtailed his speech and sat down, some of the nobles were in tears of mirth.

Aramilla was beaming around the witan, sharing confiding glances here and there. 'Lord Safinim,' she said, 'did you understand enough to translate?'

Bellamus looked unhappily at Vigtyr, still towering above those sitting to either side. 'I understood perfectly, Your Majesty.'

'Well, you are a specialist,' the queen observed. She raised a careless hand to restore the room to order. 'But we must look to the long-term as well, my councillors. It shall be no use surviving the Unhieru if we have not planned beyond them, and there is good news. Our pleas for help have received answers from across Erebos. Many of the nations that once comprised the *Teuta* – an ancient alliance against the Anakim – have responded already with offers of gold and men. Thirteen thousand trained spearmen are already waiting for us across the sea, and with them a war treasury to keep our army fed for months. My Lord Sutton, what progress have you made with our naval forces? If we are to receive the aid we hope from Erebos, we shall need ships.'

Sutton stood, the grin at Vigtyr's humiliation still on his shrewish features, and fidgeting with impatience to deliver word of his successes to the court. 'Good news, Majesty,' he said, with a bow. 'With the men you placed under my command after the last witan, I was able to seize all cargo ships at Portmuthe. We can use them for supplies or to ferry troops, as Your Majesty wishes.'

'What?' said Bellamus, before anyone could react. 'You've acted already?'

'Indeed I have, Lord Safinim.' Sutton was preening, clearly mistaking Bellamus's surprise for admiration at how swiftly he had achieved this feat.

Bellamus sighed. 'Forgive me, my lord, but that was not wise. Seize every boat at Portmuthe, and no merchant will openly stop in one of our ports again. Why would they, if they are to have their livelihoods seized? Our supplies will dry up, and the navy you have begun will grow no further, unless you build ships from scratch.' He stared calmly back at the furious Sutton. 'Which takes years. And a fortune. And expertise we do not possess,' he finished, damningly.

The queen tutted at Sutton's incompetence, and leaned towards Bellamus. 'How would you do it, my Lord Safinim?'

Bellamus wished she would not show such blatant favouritism before the court, but he was irritated by Sutton's blunder. 'I should start by releasing the ships you have taken, Sutton, and pay handsome compensation to any you requisition in future. Then we borrow ships from foreign powers. The Frankish navy is formidable, as are their shipwrights. Long-term we shall learn from their expertise and build our own, but for now we rely on trade to keep our army supplied. We need our merchantmen more than our fleet.'

Aramilla was amused, and broke in again. 'Really, my lords. Must Safinim perform all your roles? At least, Lord Sutton, your plan made more sense than the talk of armoured grapes to which we were just subjected.'

The hall laughed once more, and Sutton was allowed to chuckle as he sat back down, his slip excused.

Bellamus supposed that what Aramilla was doing was skilful, in its own way. Her tongue was a lash, and the tragic, conspicuous figure of Vigtyr was a promise: that however low her court might feel, there would always be one beneath them.

Bellamus stood before the laughter had subsided, bowing to the queen and assuming her permission to speak. 'My lords . . .' He raised a hand for quiet. 'My lords may not know, but it was Vigtyr here who brought the news of the Unhieru approach. Our scouts validated his account.' He gazed at them all flatly, watching the smiles slip. 'They are not moving at present. But they could conclude their march here in a day.' He gave Sutton a curt nod. 'There is no room for errors now.'

The grey-haired Nerven stirred suddenly. He was wearing an old-fashioned closed-neck jerkin, which along with his plum complexion, made it look as though his throat was being crushed. 'It was days ago that I first felt besieged, Safinim,' he shouted, 'as a rebel army – once comrades of yours – approached our gate!'

There came a full-throated jeer from the witan. Everyone had heard that Garrett's army was comprised of slaves, and that their leader had once ridden with Bellamus. Fingers were pointed in his direction from all sides as the court found this excuse to turn on him. Bellamus raised his hands for silence, but it did not come. They were not prepared to yield to him and contrived to turn the jeer into a roar with gales of knowing laughter. Bellamus looked to Aramilla, who could have silenced this room with a single slim finger. But she was sat back against her throne, a sly smile on her lips.

Bellamus was forced to wait minutes until the court quietened, and even then was interrupted by occasional cries of: 'Traitor!'

'Peasant!'

'Upstart!'

'The Eoten-Draefend and I diverged a long time ago.' He suffered another chorus of mocking laughter before he could go on. 'As this court will recall, he once guarded His Majesty King Osbert. Men with nobler blood than I have employed that hybrid's services.' Some of the chatter fell away at that.

'And he may be our only chance of survival. The Unhieru could arrive at any hour, and Garrett is the key to defeating them.' Bellamus reached onto the bench behind him and picked up a sheaf of papers which he held high, for everyone to see. 'Time is short, and we must use it as best we can. Your Majesty. My lords. For your approval, I lay out the plan to stop the Unhieru. And defeat the Black Lord.'

'So that's what you've been up to,' murmured Stepan as they threaded their way out of the hall and into the corridor outside with a throng of other nobles. 'Well done. It's the best plan we've got.'

'May well come to nothing though,' said Bellamus. 'If the Unhieru head this way, everything comes to an end anyway. If Wiltun falls, Stepan, don't bother bringing your household back south. The ports will be desperate, and the ships either rammed or gone. The most stable places in Suthdal will be those already firmly under Anakim control. Whatever the witan thinks, the Black Lord doesn't want us all dead: ultimately, he just wants us to leave. Head to the lands around Lincylene, wait for the dust to settle, and your time to escape will come. You would be far better avoiding the first desperate rush after Wiltun is destroyed.' Stepan was nodding, and Bellamus pursed his lips. 'I just wish . . . I'd given you a chance to do this sooner.'

'You had no choice, Captain. I wish you could come with me, though I know you have no choice about that either.'

Bellamus was distracted, for Vigtyr was being led up the corridor towards him by half a dozen royal guards. The huge Anakim was trying to catch his eye, and Bellamus studiously ignoring him, until Vigtyr suddenly lunged for his arm. Bellamus was dragged violently round to face him, and there was a sudden flurry as the guards escorting Vigtyr panicked. Their halberd blades condensed on the Anakim like a closing mantrap.

'Please, my lord,' said Vigtyr, trying to lean away from the sharp edges thrust at his eyes and throat. 'I hoped you might be able to find me some better-fitting clothes.'

'I can't help you, I'm afraid,' said Bellamus, trying to shake his arm free. It would not come, however, and Bellamus could feel the flesh beneath Vigtyr's grip beginning to tingle for lack of blood.

'Release him,' snapped a guard, but Vigtyr was desperate.

'I am not being treated with dignity,' he hissed, now in Anakim.

Suddenly, Stepan had produced a knife which he held at Vigtyr's wrist. 'Open your hand, friend, or I'll cut it off.'

'This is not the way to win allies, Vigtyr,' said Bellamus calmly.

Vigtyr let go, and the guards barged him against the wood-panelled wall. 'Perhaps we could meet somewhere more private, then?' Vigtyr called over their heads, as Bellamus started down the corridor once more.

'Not now,' called Bellamus, over his shoulder. 'Not ever,' he breathed once they were out of earshot.

'I feel for the wretch, in some ways,' said Stepan.

'He shouldn't have come here,' Bellamus replied. 'He was deluded if he imagined he'd be a respected adviser at court.'

Bellamus knew how it felt to be an outsider in a room bursting with titles, but he had bigger problems than the turncoat's wellbeing.

Stepan was not the only one to congratulate Bellamus on his plan. Alone in his chamber that evening, he was sealing some orders for Garrett when there came a knock at the door.

'Come!' He looked up to see Aramilla peering into the room. 'Your Majesty,' he said, getting to his feet.

She waved him down. 'So it all comes down to tomorrow,' she observed, sliding into the room and closing the door. Her pupils were very wide. 'Do you think the plan will work?'

Bellamus sat, and she came to perch on the edge of his desk.

No, said the weight in his chest. *I do not think it will work.*

'Who knows?' he replied lightly. 'Does it matter, just now? It's the best we've got.'

'Indeed it is,' she said, giving his cheek a quick caress. 'And bravo for it. Though if it's a success, my wait to see one of the Unhieru continues.'

Bellamus struggled to keep the disbelief from his face. For a moment, he had thought she was frightened, like him: like any sane person would be. But this crisis was somehow still exciting to her. 'Whatever happens, I'm certain you will see one before long, Majesty.'

'The Anakim were stranger than I ever expected. You did not tell me about their posture. How they watch and hear everything, and have so much focus and composure.'

'Hard to render those things in words,' he said. He was tired, and wanted only to finish his work, and sleep.

'You're right. I can't think how I'd describe that to someone. In form, they're not so strange. Bigger; more rugged perhaps. But the real difference is in their manner.'

'I suppose I noticed that when I first met one, but had forgotten.'

'Frightening though, isn't it?' she went on. 'At first, anyway. I felt like a child that's meeting an adult for the first time.'

'That's a good way of putting it.'

'Though what a wretch, that Vigtyr fellow is!' She gave her magpie's laugh. 'Do you suppose he's realised his position, yet?'

'I think it became clear today.'

'We'll make it clearer. Come, my Upstart,' she added, taking his hand and getting to her feet. 'I shan't be able to sleep tonight. Come and keep me company.'

Bellamus forced a smile, allowing himself to be pulled to his feet. 'Your servant, Majesty.'

Bellamus had deserted the queen's chambers by first light to see Stepan's departure. The streets of Wiltun were already packed. Soldiers lounged on every corner, gambling, drinking and harassing the passers-by, while refugees continued to pour in from the surrounding lands, waiting outside the gates until they opened with the dawn and they could spill inside.

The Thingalith mustered behind Wiltun's main gate while the refugees passed. They had grown overnight to a company of one hundred and ten. Leaving their armour behind for speed, they had taken only a little food for when the road did not provide. Bellamus watched them jealously. He might be more secure, more influential, and more comfortable as Lord Safinim, but he missed the outlaw's freedom; that of a horse, a band of companions, and no master.

And he watched Stepan, mounting a grey horse, clad in his richest knightly clothes: hopelessly impractical for the journey, but worn nonetheless so he could greet his wife properly after so many months. His face, usually so solid and cheerful, seemed frayed, and he fingered a charm hanging around his neck as the Thingalith rose up on their steeds about him. He caught Bellamus's eye then, and forced a smile in imitation of his usual cheer. He raised a hand in farewell, then gestured to his company. 'This way, boys!' he called, nudging his horse towards the city gate, the Thingalith falling in behind him.

Bellamus looked down. In his hand was a bundle of sealed orders to be delivered urgently to Garrett. If they did not work, then there really was no hope. What happened to Wiltun would happen whether he was present or not. And he thought about what Stepan had said about facing risk in any event, but wanting to be together for it. He knew who he would rather die next to, if it came to it.

He looked up. 'Stepan! Wait!'

12
The Outlaws

A chalk and flint track took Bellamus and Stepan north. Bellamus would accompany the party as far as Garrett's camp at Searoburgh to deliver the orders, and then return to Wiltun, while Stepan continued to his estate. A low autumn sun trailed long shadows from their horses, hooves, and Stepan was still gushing that Bellamus had joined them.

'I can't say how much I appreciate it, Captain, I really can't,' he declared again, left hand playing absently with the charm around his neck. 'I'm just sad I shan't be able to show you around the estate. We put in quite a few apple trees last year, and we may have a modest yield from them. We tried to make cider before, but it was rough stuff. The new trees are said to be good for cider though, so I'm hopeful we may have a better batch this year, something fit for Her Majesty. She'll be angry, eh, that you've left on the day the Unhieru are due to arrive?'

'I'll only be gone a couple of days,' said Bellamus. 'I left her a note explaining. But all our plans are now in place, and if they don't work? Then there won't be anyone left to complain that I left.'

'But don't you think it will look like you thought you might fail, and have just fled the city?'

Bellamus nodded. 'It may well. But I am in a bind with Her Majesty as it is, and I can't say I care too much.'

'A bind? Is that why you spend so much time in her chambers?'

Bellamus smiled thinly. 'I'm not sure I have much choice in that.'

'You poor soul. Forced to share a bed with a beautiful queen.'

'Beautiful, it's true. But the Anakim have a word for someone like her: an *unga*. A person whose company I enjoy, but who I do not like. In fact, I don't believe it would be too strong to say I hate her.'

Stepan raised his eyebrows, squinting as the road carried them directly towards the orange sun. 'I can't say I'm Her Majesty's most devoted servant, but it's not much like you to hate anything. You're usually more measured.'

'I suppose I could tolerate her if she were just nasty, but it's her moments of charm which make me despise her. She has so much capacity for intimacy and humour. Her whole character is built around making you think she's on your side, and you're somehow special to her, before she humiliates you publicly. Everyone knows what a snake she can be, but she is confiding and witty until you think maybe she's changed. You lower your defences, get comfortable in her company, and then she bites you again.'

'This is a poisonous assessment indeed!' said Stepan comfortably. 'She seems remarkably consistent towards you, though.'

'More so, these days. I seem to be her favourite at present, but that has isolated me from everyone else at court. They are her outdoor hounds, and I am her favoured lap dog, who must fetch and wag my tail to maintain my place beneath her table. The court despises me for it. And I can't help but agree with them.'

'Better to stay on the right side of someone like that,' said Stepan, firmly. 'You'll need to be in her good graces to win this war.' Bellamus did not reply. It suddenly seemed he had revealed too much. He was not on this road because he hated Aramilla, but because he hated being her instrument, held so close to her person, his own freedoms and responsibilities curtailed.

They cantered uphill, through the tall beech forest that surrounded the causeway to Searoburgh. Bellamus kept glancing at the brown leaves on the ground, at the bushes spattered with berries, and thinking that they did not have to delay the Anakim for long before the campaigning season was over. Three times they passed groups of rough-looking men; evidently brigands, who would have attacked them had they been less capable. Road-wolves, Stepan called them, and indeed, their behaviour was hard to distinguish from a pack.

Presently, they came within sight of Searoburgh, once an ancient fortress, now little more than a wooded hill, gouged with concentric rings of steep banks and ditches that had been half-eaten by tree roots. It did not seem wise to approach with a force almost entirely comprised of Garrett's deserters, so Bellamus and Stepan left their companions behind and approached alone.

Bellamus had never thought of the old fort as particularly intimidating, but when he spied the first of Garrett's company standing between the trees, he was suddenly uncomfortable. There were four of them, guarding the ridges either side of the narrow causeway that led into the fort. They were lean, dressed in plates of repurposed Anakim bone armour, and standing so unnaturally still that Bellamus wondered at first if they might be totems dressed up as scarecrows.

'And look.' Stepan pointed to the fort's outermost bank. Among the trees, and standing quite as still, dozens of solitary figures stared down at them, each leaning on a long spear like a staff. 'Thank God we didn't let the maniac inside the city.'

They rode up the causeway in silence, and when they were at last inside the fort and able to see behind its high ridges, the pair of them ground to a halt. 'What on earth,' muttered Stepan.

Between the trees, they could see hundreds of men, almost

all supine and strangely motionless. They lay wrapped in patched and holed cloaks, still wet with the morning dew. Some had terrible wounds: dark slashes of rotten flesh about which crows were gathering. Every now and then, one of the birds would peck experimentally, and the figure would stir briefly until its tormentor hopped back, cocked its head, and then advanced once more. There were no fires.

'Sleeping off the *lifsin*?' murmured Stepan.

Bellamus nodded ahead, at a lean figure approaching on horseback. The nag stank of saddle-sores and tottered forward on trembling limbs little more than bone, while the man astride it was in scarcely better condition. He stopped before Bellamus and Stepan and regarded them through jaundiced eyes.

'I'm here to see the Eoten-Draefend,' said Bellamus.

'Lord Eoten-Draefend is busy,' said the hybrid tonelessly. 'You will have to wait.'

'No time,' said Bellamus. He reached into a saddlebag and produced a sealed envelope, which he held forward. 'See to it that your master gets that. Tell him it's from Lord Safinim.'

'I know who you are,' said the hybrid, taking the letter. Without another word, he turned and rode back the way he had come.

'I'm relieved we didn't have to talk to him,' murmured Bellamus as they descended the track out of the fortress.

'I wonder if his men can even fight,' said Stepan. 'The whole lot of them look like a stiff breeze might knock them flat.'

'For now, we don't need them to fight,' said Bellamus. 'They've been slaves all their lives, and we need them to do what they do best: labour.'

They had reached the road where their ways would part. The pair turned to each other, and Stepan grinned. 'I shan't forget this, Captain.'

'Godspeed, my friend,' said Bellamus, surprising himself, for he was not a religious man. He held out a hand, and Stepan grasped it. 'See you back in Wiltun.'

'If it still stands,' said Stepan with a wink. He turned, raising a hand to the fifty Thingalith who would accompany him. Bellamus watched them clatter down the road before he turned for home. He suddenly found himself irritable, and did not want to talk, but one of the youngest Thingalith, Agnolo, would not be dissuaded. 'Took your gold to a tavern last night, lord,' he said cheerfully.

'Astonishing.'

'You came up. Lord One Eye, the villagers call you.'

Bellamus looked at the young Thingman, intrigued in spite of himself. 'Is that so?'

'There's a lot of rumours! Some were saying you've got a tongue like quicksilver, and are our only hope of repelling the Anakim.'

'How sensible they sound.'

Agnolo grinned. 'Some others disagreed. They said you've placed the queen under an enchantment and are in cahoots with Grendel.'

Bellamus frowned. 'Grendel?'

'The Black Lord,' said Agnolo. 'Everyone calls him Grendel now, have done for a while.'

'Why *Grendel*?'

Agnolo looked confused, then brightened. 'I forgot you didn't grow up here, lord. Grendel is an old monster from a folk tale. Everyone hears it in the crib. He ruled Albion from sea to sea, in the days when it was young and full of shadows. Until some hero came along to stop him.'

Bellamus considered this. 'And how did this hero defeat Grendel?'

'It was fairly straightforward. He pulled his arm off.'

'Interesting. I'll try it on Roper next time I shake his hand. What else did they say about Lord One Eye? Handsome, I expect.'

Agnolo laughed. 'A crusty drunk, was the consensus.'

There was not much of the day left, and Bellamus did not spy the city walls again until the following afternoon.

They still stood. He had almost convinced himself that in his two days on the road, the Unhieru would have reduced the capital to a midden. Perhaps there would yet be time for his plan to work. Perhaps it was already working.

Returning to his quarters, and heartened to find no stern messenger demanding he explain his absence to the queen, Bellamus resumed his duties with a fervour. The hinges on his door squealed at all hours as he was attended by engineers, ambassadors, smiths, soldiers, farmers and clergy. The Unhieru still did not come, and nor did a royal summons.

And whether it was the long silence from the queen, or Stepan's absence, or the unrelenting threat of armoured giants bearing down on a city relying on him for defence, Bellamus found he was not sleeping. There was always more to do, and it was easier to do it than lie still. Soon after that, he discovered that if he drank his wine from a water mug, he received fewer comments. He never quite escaped the hope that the next person revealed by the door might be Stepan, returned from his mission.

It was some days later, descending from Wiltun's main gatehouse, that he slipped. The steps were worn, something slid beneath his heel and he was on his backside, clattering rapidly to the base of the wall. There he lay, inspecting himself for the pain of a break or sprain. He seemed unscathed, yet still he could not move. He stared up at the clouds above, feeling nothing. He could not bring himself to stand, until a voice cried: 'Lord Slip-Up! I mean, Upstart! Do you need a hand, sir? Here, here!'

Rough hands were grasping at his tunic. A man was bending over him, dressed in a jerkin bearing Aramilla's swooping hawk and jostling him roughly.

'Off!' Bellamus expostulated. 'Off me, now!'

'Ah!' The man sprang back and Bellamus swung upright, glaring at him. He was thin as a barley stalk, with a balding crown and a face alive with anarchy the like of which Bellamus had not even seen on Aramilla's cold features.

'There's been a misunderstanding, lord,' said the man. 'It looked like you needed help! But I'm truly sorry, clearly not. Perhaps your old friend, Chance, will help you up? Certainly she helped you down there. She, and the contents of the Earl Penbro's wine cellar.'

Bellamus bristled at that. He cast around, hoping for a pair of his Thingalith to set upon this scoundrel, but they were alone. He eyed the man before him.

'You're Her Majesty's new buffoon.'

Diethaad had mentioned him. Aramilla had met him in a monastery, found him amusing and brought him to court. It had been years since the Suthern monarch had had a buffoon, King Osbert having executed the last for unkindness. They were traditionally outside the hierarchy of nobility, one of their primary functions being to tell powerful lords and ladies truths they would otherwise never hear. Worrying Bellamus like a terrier was perfectly within his remit.

Bellamus got to his feet as steadily as he was able and pulled his jerkin straight. 'Your name?' he demanded.

'Sommers, my lord,' replied the man, staring back with eyes of guileless blue. 'Just Sommers. No need for titles or honorifics, I am as humble now as you once were. Shall be again, I daresay, unless you return to favour with Her Majesty.'

Bellamus froze. 'Eh? What do you mean by that?'

'Oh, nothing, nothing,' said Sommers happily, turning half away. 'Though it seems to me you used to appear at court rather more often. I understand you and the queen were once very close.'

Bellamus scrutinised him at those words, but the buffoon looked entirely serene. 'I've been busy,' he said.

Sommers nodded and beamed at him. 'That must be it,' he said simply. To his surprise, Bellamus found he had to look away first.

'Make no mistake, Sommers,' he managed eventually. 'Ancient tradition may protect what you say, but lay hands on me again, and you'll regret it.'

Sommers just laughed at that and turned his back on Bellamus. 'See you at court soon then, eh, Safinim? I and all your other friends will be looking for you.'

Bellamus watched the buffoon leave, sweat trickling down his back. He had noticed Aramilla's silence – of course he had. But at first, when he had feared a summons and a reprimand for departing without permission, it had seemed merciful. And now it had stretched into something more callous. He imagined the whispered conversations behind his back; of declining influence and enemies comparing schemes.

How he *hated* that buffoon.

Bellamus stalked back to his quarters, paced across them for a full half-hour, and then went to present himself to the queen. *She was busy*, came the reply from her royal retainer. *She would not see him.*

'Tell her I am at her disposal, will you?'

The retainer stared at him blankly. Bellamus backed away, receiving not so much as a murmured, *lord*.

It was another five days before Aramilla called for him: a summons to justify the huge sums he was drawing from the treasury. They met at one of the vast construction sites swarming with Barleymen, and central to Bellamus's plan for defeating their enemy. Aramilla arrived in a gown of star-pricked cream, the barefoot Bishop Widukind walking beside her, and a royal train at her back.

It was a day so overcast that the heavens seemed to weigh over the earth, pressing the colour from leaf and garment. Aramilla did not even meet Bellamus's eye, instead strolling past him and climbing a high burial mound, making observations to the silent Bishop Widukind. Bellamus fell in behind them, standing clear as they surveyed the construction site.

'There is a long way to go, is there not, my Lord Bishop? I hope your prayers will hasten their progress.'

Aramilla went on without the slightest input from Widukind, leaving Bellamus unattended for so long that he began to wonder if she expected some extravagant gesture of apology.

Finally she turned to Widukind and beamed at him, taking his gnarled root of a hand between her own. 'I do find your silence so inspiring my Lord Bishop. There is no denying you are particularly favoured with grace. Pray for me?' The bishop knelt before the queen and brushed his lips over her hand. Then he stood to leave, eyes snagging briefly on Bellamus before he departed as silently as he had come.

Bellamus took the vacant place beside the queen, who continued studying the construction site beneath them. 'Safinim,' she observed distantly. 'At last, you wait on your queen.'

Bellamus knelt beside her and took her hand. 'I have been remiss, Majesty. Forgive me. There were things I had to see to.'

She slipped her fingers from his. 'Indeed?'

'I . . .' He hesitated. 'Well, yes. It was only to deliver orders to the Eoten-Draefend in your service, Majesty. Though I should not have left the town, and for that, I can only beg your pardon.'

She gave him that familiar appraisal from the corner of her eye. 'In my service, was this? Then what are the stories I hear of you going for a day-ride with a companion?'

Bellamus hesitated. Still, she had not invited him to stand. 'That was a happy coincidence, Majesty. I assure you my main purpose was to ensure Garrett knew his task perfectly. It is of utmost importance.' He was suddenly fervently grateful that only he and Stepan had been present for the interaction at Searoburgh.

'I think you felt your duty to a knight exceeded your duty to your queen.'

'No, Majesty, by no means. I suppose I did not think they were at odds.'

She turned to face him properly, looking down at him flatly. 'We were facing invasion from the Unhieru, and you, the mastermind of our defence, felt you were not required for two days?'

The answer Bellamus had ready fell short of this comment. 'I did not think the defences required my presence on the battlements, Majesty, but forgive me. I was wrong to leave.' *I wasn't wrong,* he thought. *We're still here, aren't we? Is the town not still standing?*

'I'm hearing more excuses than I should like, Safinim,' she declared. She took a pace back and inspected him. 'Perhaps if you're unwilling to take responsibility for this mistake, I should find a warmaster who will?'

Bellamus stirred. 'Majesty? If I have given the impression that I do not take responsibility for this then that is another mistake. I do. Utterly. I am at your service and will perform whatever penance is required.'

'How could you make up for it?' She shrugged, then gestured dismissively at the work beneath them. 'How delayed was all this work by your absence? By your drunkenness since?'

He flushed, saying nothing.

'You have been selfish, Safinim. You have cared too much for your own affairs, and not enough for my kingdom.'

Bellamus bowed his head, in part to hide his rage. 'Truly, Majesty. I am determined to make it up to you, by any means possible.'

He raised his eyes to hers, and she stared back expressionless. 'Impossible, unfortunately. Have my construction works finished in time to be of some use. Good day, Safinim.' She turned on her heel and strode down the hill, retainers and ladies falling in behind her.

That night, Bellamus strode his quarters, knotting his fingers as he wondered whether to leave this doomed endeavour. If there were no personal rewards for him, then why take the risk of standing against the Black Lord?

He did not sleep, and by dawn he had half resolved to flee with a few trusted Thingalith, when a knock at the door nearly shocked Bellamus off his feet. 'Who is it?' he demanded, half expecting royal guards.

'Diethaad, lord,' came the voice from outside. 'Beg pardon, I didn't mean to intrude. I saw your lamps were still lit . . .'

Bellamus strode to the door and pulled it open to reveal the new captain of the Thingalith, whom he had left riding north with Stepan. The pair of them looked at one another for a moment, and Bellamus could tell at once he was here for nothing good.

'Come in.' He held the door open for Diethaad and then closed it and leaned against the inside, eyeing his captain, who stood awkwardly in the centre of the room. 'Well, Diethaad? What's this about?'

'My lord . . .' Diethaad cleared his throat and straightened. The man seemed to be sweating, and kept tugging at his cloak. 'We can't find Sir Stepan.'

'Explain yourself.' Bellamus knew his tone was harsh, but was too fraught to care much just then. He strode around the Thingman to make a reflexive grasp for a mug of wine.

'He rode off, lord, after we found his estate.'

Bellamus watched him carefully over the rim of his cup. 'Why?' he asked, when he had drained it.

Diethaad shifted once more. 'The . . . the Barleymen had got there first.'

'Garrett's men had been to Stepan's estate?'

The captain's silence was answer enough.

'And?'

Diethaad shook his head helplessly.

'What did you find, Diethaad? What happened?'

'Everything, lord,' he breathed. 'They'd destroyed everything.'

Bellamus sagged, slumping wretchedly onto his bed. 'His wife?'

Diethaad looked pale.

'His servants? His dogs?'

Diethaad was shaking his head, but not to disagree. 'All of it.'

'How long ago?' he asked. *Please. Please let it be weeks.*

'A week, perhaps, lord. It must've been just before they came to Wiltun.'

Bellamus dropped his head in his hands. So they could

have stopped it. If he had given Stepan the men when he had asked, his household would still be alive.

'We went to the estate, lord,' Diethaad gabbled on, 'and found a woman – I think it must've been his wife – hanged from an apple tree. And Sir Stepan, he saw and . . . he was roaring, and then he fled. He rode off, and we never caught up with him.'

Something had suddenly occurred to Bellamus. He glanced up at Diethaad, taking in his shifting feet and knotted hands as though for the first time. 'But you knew all this already, Diethaad,' he said quietly. 'You must've been there, when the Barleymen were.'

Diethaad made no reply. He just stared at Bellamus.

'You all must've been. You must've realised that you were on the road to the estate you'd just plundered.'

'We didn't do anything, lord,' he objected defensively. 'It was Garrett's men! We were there, yes, but we didn't know whose estate it was, and we couldn't stop them! We had nothing to do with it!'

Bellamus scrutinised him. 'That is hard to believe, captain, when you have tried to deceive me. You told me this story as though you had not been there when the estate was destroyed.'

Diethaad just shook his head, teeth gritted. 'We had no choice, lord,' he muttered. 'Garrett was in charge. We couldn't very well refuse.'

Bellamus watched the Thingman dispassionately for a moment. 'Don't ever lie to me again, Diethaad,' he said, quite calmly. 'Now get out of my sight.'

Diethaad bowed hastily and turned on his heel, scrabbling at the door for some while before he was able to lift the catch. Bellamus ignored him. He was already on his feet, preparing to march on Stepan's house.

It was not far across the town, lit smoke-blue by the dawn. When he reached it and hammered on the door, a bleary-eyed servant answered him. 'Stepan!' Bellamus demanded. 'Sir Stepan, is he here?'

The servant replied that Stepan had returned a full two days before, but was not at home to visitors.

'Tell him who it is,' Bellamus insisted. It took much persuasion, but eventually the servant relented, and disappeared to find his master. When he came back, he seemed almost angry.

'Sir Stepan is not seeing guests!' he declared, and slammed the door in Bellamus's face.

13
Arrival

Keturah chose to give birth in Tekoa's chamber. 'I believe what I have missed most is his look of horror. I look forward to seeing it when I tell him.'

She waddled upstairs, followed by Ormur and the herald Virtanen. Boy and man gathered all the blankets in the house so that Keturah could lean against them and sit comfortably in the bed.

'Brother, come here . . .' Keturah paused for a moment and closed her eyes, finally exhaling softly as a contraction passed. 'I have Virtanen here to help me with anything I can't do myself. But staunch though your company is, I'd rather not do this without someone who's got a little experience. I need a midwife. Think you can find one who'll come for the wife of a public enemy?'

'I . . .' Ormur knew nothing about this fortress. He had never been here before, and his only experience of the streets was wholly hostile. Where he might find a midwife, he had not the faintest idea. 'Yes. Will you be all right without me?' He eyed Virtanen, still a rough-looking stranger, despite his diplomatic air.

Keturah laughed and gave him a wink. 'I'll survive, Ormur. Virtanen may not. Get help quickly, for his sake.'

Virtanen was rolling up his sleeves gravely. 'I hope to have the honour of heralding the birth of the Black Lord and Lady's child.'

'Go, Ormur. A triple knock when you come back, so we know it's you.'

Ormur fled down the stairs and into the street, hearing Virtanen follow and replace the locking bar behind him. *Where is Harald in all this?* The legionary had been absent a long while.

Ormur looked left and right, utterly lost in this stone warren. He picked a direction at random and started running. He was three streets away, four, five, and then decided to ask for help. 'A midwife,' he demanded of a passing woman. She was plump, a goose clutched beneath one arm and a hand clamped around its beak to prevent the bird honking. It still emitted a low hiss like steam escaping a pot. 'I need a midwife.'

The woman blinked to see a boy of his years on the streets, unsupervised. His shaven head marked him as the lowest of the Black Kingdom's occupants. 'Where have you escaped from, boy?'

'My sister, who needs a midwife,' said Ormur flatly. 'Where are they?'

The woman raised her eyebrows. 'I don't know what you're playing at boy, but off with you.'

Ormur was irrationally incensed. Could this obstructive woman not see this was an emergency? He made to move past her, and then turned back to the goose's feathered rear protruding from beneath her arm. He gave it a shove, and the bird burst free with a battery of percussive wingbeats, ripping its beak clear of the woman's hand and honking furiously. Ormur was already running onwards, leaving behind the sounds of the woman swearing and the goose hissing in triumph.

He had an idea that scene would not endear others to him, and turned a corner before asking another woman: this one slight, and shorter than he was, with arresting ice-blue eyes. 'Midwife! I need a midwife, where are they?'

She regarded him coldly. 'Is that how you address a peer, boy? Eyes down.'

Ormur had no idea how he was supposed to tell she was a full peer, but dropped his eyes. 'Please, lady.'

'I don't know what you're doing here. Are these the guttersnipes being produced by the haskoli these days?' She continued to glare at him, and Ormur was on the verge of bursting clear of his submissive stance. There was no time for any of this. 'You'll find the midwives in the inner district. A low building, opposite the Holy Temple.'

Ormur kept his eyes down. 'How will I know the temple?'

'What do you call me, boy?'

'How will I know the temple, lady?'

The woman gave a reluctant snort. 'Such temerity! It almost deserves a reward. The Holy Temple you shall recognise by the Dead Legionaries standing around it. That building,' she pointed, 'above the walls, is the Central Keep. Keep walking towards it and you shan't miss the temple. Off you go now.'

Ormur ran, feet slapping on the stone cobbles. He soon hit one of those impossibly huge curtain walls and skirted around its base. He had come to suspect that he was making no progress whatsoever when he found an open gate, and plunged through, emerging into a fresh district. He ran on, the soles of his feet numb and tingling from the unyielding cobbles.

Everywhere stood the creatures absent from his life so far: women – laughing in clusters of three and four, driving small herds of dark sheep, carrying wares over their shoulder or on a hip, scrubbing garments in the gardens which bordered each stone house. He ran what must have been two miles and saw just four men; two pairs of patrolling legionaries. He supposed the others were all south, with his brother.

The Holy Temple was indeed obvious when he found it. An upturned cauldron of lead and rock, guarded by cadaverous heroes, each sheltered beneath its own stone alcove, and watching through a pair of blank stone eyes. There were several buildings opposite, and Ormur again turned to one of these busy and unhelpful passers-by. 'The midwives, lady?'

The woman pointed to a building like a miniature of the temple, with a spiral-shelled turtle carved over the door. Ormur attempted to follow her finger inside, but behind him came a shriek. 'What are you doing?' He froze, turning back to the woman. 'You can't set foot in there, boy, you'll pollute the whole place!'

'Well then how am I supposed to get a midwife?' he demanded.

The woman scowled at him. 'Perhaps I should have let you go and endure the vinegar-whip thrashing that would have resulted. Wait here, you ignoramus.'

She swept past him and beneath the stone turtle, passing out of sight. Ormur hopped with impatience, glaring around and settling on the dried corpses. Despite the urgency of his errand, they were fascinating.

He glanced quickly after the vanished woman, and then approached one of the alcoves, craning his neck to try and see how this long-dead warrior was supported, armour and all. But as far as he could see, it was standing by some residual strength in its long-dead limbs. Its dry hand was gripping a sword, ready to draw it from the sheath, and Ormur gaped at it. Imbedded in the hilt was a ring: one of those gifted from Black Lord to Sacred Guardsman to symbolise mutual obligation, and symbolise too, everything that Ormur had been taught to value from his earliest years. Duty, discipline, courage, service, sacrifice, selflessness. He reached out a hand to finger the pommel, and received a stinging blow to the side of his head.

'Ah!' he cried out, knocked half off his feet. He looked left and saw a woman, hand drawn back to strike again.

'Oaf!' she snarled, clouting him again and making his head spin. 'You do not touch! That ancestor is two-score your value, even in death! Approach on your knees or not at all, and do not ever presume to touch sacred flesh again!'

Ormur scuttled back, trying to avoid being struck once

more and giving the woman a snarl. So many rules in this stone complex! He knew that at the end of their time in the berjasti, the young *nemandis* were inducted into life in the Hindrunn, given a tour of its streets and told its history and customs. Now he could see why: his every interaction seemed to offend some ancient custom or institution.

The woman was still threatening him with her palm, and he muttered apologies until she left him with a lingering glare. He looked back at the corpse, but was sufficiently chastened not to approach once more.

'Boy!' A hand fell on his shoulder, and Ormur flinched. But it was merely the woman who had gone to fetch his midwife. She jerked her head at the young woman standing next to her, dressed in a robe with that spiral turtle on her chest.

'Well?'

'My sister,' Ormur explained. 'She's giving birth, now!'

'Has she had a child before?' asked the midwife. She had a brusque and competent air.

'I don't think so.'

'I don't think so, *lady*.'

'Is there anyone here who isn't called lady?'

'Not to you,' said the midwife, calmly. 'Not merely a *haskolin*, but one who doesn't know if his own sister has given birth before?'

Ormur shook his head. 'Please, lady, I don't know. I don't think so, we must hurry!'

'Have her waters broken yet?'

'There was a mess.'

'That's it. How long ago?'

'An hour and a half?' guessed the boy.

The midwife nodded. 'If it's her first, we should be in good time. Lead on, boy.'

Ormur did, drawing the midwife back to Tekoa's house. He made no mention that she was coming to facilitate the birth of a baby that would be criminal as soon as it opened its mouth to bawl.

Just before reaching Tekoa's household, the midwife began to slow. Her eyes were darting around the street, and finally settled on the door that was their destination. 'Wait, wait, boy. Who is your sister?'

'Come and see, lady,' he tried.

'No, I don't think so. Am I going to assist in the birth of the Black Lord's child?'

It seemed word of Keturah's arrival had spread through the fortress already.

'Does it matter?'

'It certainly does. I cannot assist a public enemy in any way.'

Ormur was by the door, ready to knock for entrance. 'This isn't a public enemy, it's just a baby.'

'*His* baby. Lord Roper is not to be given shelter, fire, water or food until he has stood trial, by Ephorian mandate.'

'And which of water, shelter, fire or food is this?'

The midwife scowled. 'I cannot help.'

'Is your duty not sacred, lady?'

She narrowed her eyes. 'And how would a bald-headed adolescent know that?'

'Everything's sacred here.'

'Impertinent,' said the midwife dismissively, turning away. 'Wish Miss Keturah good luck in becoming a subject.'

Ormur glared after her retreating shoulders, and then knocked on the door three times. When the locking bar had been scraped back, it was Harald who stood behind it. 'Boy!' He leaned out and looked up and down the street, evidently disappointed. 'No midwife?'

'There she goes,' said Ormur, bitterly.

'She wouldn't help?'

'Not when she found out who.'

'Hold the door,' said Harald. He ran down the street after the midwife, Ormur watching as he beseeched her, evidently becoming steadily more desperate. She was resolute, however, and eventually Harald was forced to retreat. 'Inside,' he muttered, following Ormur and barring the door once more. A shriek pierced the gloom; harsh enough to make Harald flinch.

'Keturah!' Ormur shouted. There came no reply, and he lunged forward to run up the stairs, but a hand had gripped his shoulder and jerked him round.

'No boy!' hissed Harald. 'A male presence at the birth would invite disaster.'

'Is that how you've excused your cowardice?' snapped Ormur, and suddenly he was pinned up against the wall by his throat. He was almost picked off the floor by the pressure of it, his vision blurring as tears flooded his eyes and he fought for breath.

A voice hissed very close to his ear. 'I would die for that girl. Do not *ever* imply otherwise. Do you understand me, you half-laid turd?'

Ormur spluttered as close to assent as he could manage, and after another couple of heartbeats to ensure the message had sunk in, he was released. He managed to stay on his feet, but felt suddenly shaky and took several paces back from the legionary, who was pointing into the parlour.

'Get in there.'

Ormur did, scurrying round the corner to find Virtanen on the edge of a seat by the fire, hands resting on his thighs as though about to spring to his feet. 'She banished us half an hour ago,' said Harald, following him in. 'If we go upstairs, we as good as doom her child. We only go if she calls for help. Until then, she's on her own.'

Ormur glared at Harald. He wanted to shout that she would never call for help, especially if she thought it would kill her child. But the legionary was still bristling, daring Ormur to disobey, and the boy had the good sense to stay quiet.

'No midwife?' said Virtanen. His fingers were drumming on his knees.

'She wouldn't come when she found out whose child it was,'

said Harald, joining his hands behind his back and beginning to pace the parlour. 'Got right up to the house, and turned back.'

'The mood in this fortress . . .' Virtanen made a despairing gesture. 'Utter possession.'

'I have heard endlessly of the Hindrunn,' raged Ormur, 'and I have never been to a worse place. *Stupid* rules and customs, and everyone so unhelpful!'

Virtanen and Harald exchanged a glance, but otherwise did not reply to this outburst. There came another extended groan from upstairs, and everyone went still. Ormur took a breath to shout an enquiry up to Keturah, but Harald cut him off. 'She's better saving the energy it would take to reassure you. Sit down, boy, and don't say anything.'

Ormur stayed stubbornly on his feet. 'I'm not sitting until you do.'

There came a jerk at his neck, and Ormur was hurled into a chair. Virtanen had leaned forward, seized him by the back of the neck and now pinned him to the seat with a hand on his chest. 'I'm sure you've had your fair share of thrashings in the haskoli,' said the herald. 'But one more word, and I will deliver the worst you have ever experienced.'

Harald was seething at him, and Keturah cried out again from upstairs. This room seemed on the verge of combustion, and it was all Ormur could do to fold his arms and stay silent. Virtanen released him and sat down, while Harald, his face very white, set to pacing once more across the parlour.

Frightful noises invaded the room. Keturah would give an extended howl, making all three of them freeze until it had subsided into a relieved moan.

'What happened with the legate?' asked Virtanen, eventually. 'Did you manage to speak to Tore?'

Harald was silent, craning his neck and listening upstairs, but they could hear nothing. 'He said that she was welcome to come and see him in public,' Harald said finally, head still cocked and listening intently for sounds from upstairs, 'but he could not guarantee her safety. *The people deserve to hear her explanation*, he said.'

Virtanen tutted. 'Clever, clever. Of course she can't do that, the crowds would shout her down. So he can claim he offered to see her, and is on the side of the public, and she looks like a coward for refusing.'

'Well, matters should change somewhat when Lord Roper gets home with fifty thousand loyal men,' said Harald.

'Do not expect that any time soon,' said Virtanen. 'His plan was to stay in the south and pacify it.'

At these words, Harald turned his full attention to Virtanen for the first time. 'But that'll take years!'

'Decades. And if Tore strengthens his grip on the Black Kingdom, I fear it is more than plausible we shall end up with two rival Anakim nations. One below the Abus, ruled by Lord Roper, and one above, under Tore.'

'Then Keturah has to leave,' murmured Harald. 'She cannot stay.'

'But she will stay,' said Ormur, to general disregard.

There came another cry from upstairs. When it had abated, Harald said quietly that he was going to put food and water outside her door, in case she needed it. By the time he was back, the windows had darkened, and the main source of light was the lazy flickering from the hearth. They lit candles, and Harald produced some hard-boiled eggs, which nobody had the stomach for. The fire burned low, and the only sound in the parlour until midnight was Keturah's groaning, getting slowly fainter.

'She's getting weaker,' Virtanen murmured.

Ormur stood to insist they went to see her, when there came muffled cheers from the street outside. For a moment, all three listened as the crackle of distant applause came through the door. Then Harald took Ormur's wrist and dragged him towards the door. 'Go and see what that is,' he said, removing the locking bar.

He clearly wanted rid of Ormur who, if he was not to see Keturah, was only too glad to oblige. Harald held the door open and he slipped out into the cold night. There was frost glittering on the cobbles, the air was milky, and at the end of the street to Ormur's right, he could just see the silhouette of a crowd. They were undoubtedly the source of the applause, lining a road that ran perpendicular to his own, and watching something Ormur could not see.

Ormur slid along the street, following the crowd as it started shuffling along the road, chattering excitedly and processing in the direction of the Central Keep. Ormur fell into step with them, and every now and then caught a glimpse of the figure they were following: tall, cloaked and astride a black stallion. Whoever this person was, the crowd seemed to be providing a guard of honour, and more subjects were falling into step as word of the important arrival spread.

They passed through two gates, and Ormur could just make out a distant chant coming from the front of the procession: *'Call them home! Call them home! Call them home!'* None of the crowd carried lights, and the atmosphere was excitable and volatile, the people beside Ormur shielded both by the dark and their numbers.

They reached the steps of the Central Keep, where the rider at the centre of this commotion dismounted and began to climb the steps. Word had evidently preceded the mob, because a stocky figure was descending to greet the rider; cloak billowing at his back and arms held wide in a picture of munificence. Legionaries carrying torches were flooding down the steps on either side, casting flickering light over the higher figure's cloak, which was rippling and shimmering in the gloom. It was a liquid-bronze tapestry of eagle feathers: a badge of office that even Ormur recognised. The higher figure must be Legate Tore.

The figure climbing to meet him had swept back her dark hood to reveal herself as a steel-haired, sharp-boned woman, whose identity Ormur could only guess at. When the two finally stood level, they embraced, Tore gripping her arms after they had broken apart, beaming at her and evidently making expressions of great welcome. Then he took her hand and raised it over his head in a symbol of unity, turning to face the crowd. They burst into applause, so rapturous that they did not notice how quickly the woman snatched her hand back. To his credit, Tore recovered well, beginning to applaud generously with the crowd. The steel-haired woman ignored him, raising her palms for silence until eventually the crowd was in rapt attention.

'Peers, I am recently returned from campaign with the Black Lord's army!' Her voice was emotionless, but undeniably authoritative. 'In good conscience, I cannot work with a leader who so lightly discards the other sacred voices of the kingdom.'

Tore led the next round of applause, holding his hands ostentatiously high and nodding his head.

'Before I departed, the Master of the Kryptea, as is his ancient duty, met with Lord Roper, and insisted that he return the army to the Black Kingdom. I regret that Lord Roper not only refused, he publicly denounced the Kryptea in order to intimidate them. His intention is to keep the legionaries beyond the Abus for decades in order—' she was forced to stop and wait for the crowd to stop baying. 'In order to subdue Suthdal completely! Until he has stood before the Ephors, and submitted to the sound judgement of these ancient streets, then I no longer follow Lord Roper.'

The crowd cheered, and began chanting again '*Call them home! Call them home!*' In the tumult, Ormur took the opportunity to slide closer to the front. The steel-haired woman was fixing Tore with a look that patently indicated he should not try and embrace her again, and which was succeeding in keeping him at arm's length. At the front of the crowd, Ormur could just make out the crest on her robes: an angel with giant eyes and long, spidery fingers.

Tore started a speech of his own, and Ormur slid back

through the crowds to deliver this news to Tekoa's house. He had left them far behind before the distant chanting restarted, rendered this time as: *'U-vor-en! U-vor-en!'*

The streets were freezing and empty for his return, and when he knocked at the door he was readmitted at once by Harald. 'Thank the thunder, I should never have sent you,' he said, standing back and beckoning him in. 'I'm sorry boy, we should have just ignored it, you were gone a long while.'

'Did you see anything?' asked Virtanen, clearly less concerned by Ormur's extended absence.

Ormur explained, pausing every now and then for the respectful moment they seemed to have agreed whenever Keturah groaned feebly from upstairs.

'Describe this woman,' said Virtanen, when he had finished his account.

'Old, tall, bony face. She had black robes with the Angel of Madness stitched into them.'

Virtanen and Harald looked at each other. 'The Chief Historian,' said Virtanen.

Harald swore softly.

'What?' asked Ormur. 'This is bad news?'

'Most certainly,' said Virtanen. 'With the Chief Historian onside, our enemies have been strengthened dramatically.'

'Why?'

'She has influence,' said Virtanen. 'A most respected woman, at the head of our most ancient and honoured institution. And at the moment, with Tore trying to win public opinion, influence is what matters.'

'And she commands soldiers, lad,' said Harald.

Ormur was sceptical. 'Which soldiers?'

'The berserkers ultimately answer to her. There's only a few thousand of them, but they terrify almost everyone. If she and Roper have fallen out, and the historians have departed the army, then the berserkers will be following her up the road any day now.'

'So two legions and the berserkers now defend the fortress,' said Harald. 'More than enough to make a fight of it, if Tore decides to keep Roper out. It would be true—'

There came a scream from upstairs; louder than any Keturah had emitted for hours, which dragged on and on in an agonised shriek of effort. She was dying, Ormur was quite certain. He lurched forward but was seized once more by Harald, and he struggled as the scream rang through the parlour.

'Get off me!' He was twisting and tugging against Harald's hand on his wrist. Keturah's howl faded away, and in desperation, Ormur turned back on Harald like a snake and sank his teeth into the back of his hand. Harald bellowed and snatched his hand away, and Ormur was released, sprinting up the stairs.

'Boy!' came the roar at his back, but this had gone too far. Ormur hurtled round two corners, past Keturah's untouched food and water outside the door, and into Tekoa's chambers.

The room stank of blood, piss, and other fluids Ormur could not name. Keturah was lying back on the bed, hair ragged with sweat and her face dripping with it. Or some was sweat, and some tears, for she was sobbing, head bent over the writhing thing cradled in her arms. The bed was flushed crimson, and Keturah was trembling minutely in every limb, her hands bloody. Ormur nearly looked away, because she was completely naked, but before he did so, one disturbing sight caught his eye. The child; the baby in her arms, was being fed upon by a giant and repulsive snake; its head buried in the baby's guts, and a twisted, moonlight body running back between Keturah's legs.

'Shit, shit!' he said, as the baby started to bawl. 'What do I do? Keturah! What do I do!'

But Keturah was laughing. She threw her head back and crowed manically at the ceiling, cheeks flushed, the rest of her ashen. Harald pelted in behind Ormur, face like slate, and took in the scene.

'Harald!' Ormur exclaimed, pointing at the snake.

'It's the baby's cord you idiot,' said Harald, cuffing Ormur gently around the head. But he was grinning quite as insanely as Keturah. He quickly stooped for one of the discarded blankets and covered her nakedness. She still did not care, holding that strange, squirming, bawling creature in shaking arms, shoulders heaving as she gazed down at it. 'The babe's well?' asked Harald, tentatively.

'Him?' She could barely speak through exhaustion and joy and relief. 'Yes, but he had the easy job.'

'He?'

'He,' said Keturah. She bent over her son, and bawled with him.

14
The Old Tongue

Keturah had not really known what to expect from childbirth. She had heard vague anecdotes, of course, but when caught in the throes of a natural process like a tempest-driven sea, none of the half-remembered advice occurred to her.

The contractions consumed her as though she were a great rope, twisted and twisted under waves of extreme pressure, wrung like a rag until she was sure she must tear, or her insides spill out altogether. It would build, coil, crush and then subside just a little: each trough nothing more than a moment to breathe, and a cruel reminder of how sweet life was without pain. Then she would begin to twist again. An overwhelming urge to push came over her, which she kept at bay, clinging to some half-forgotten words from long ago, that if she pushed too early she would exhaust herself before the time was right. When she could hold on no longer, and surrendered to the urge, the labour seized her like a current and she was compelled onwards, pushing and pushing on hands and knees like an animal. She thought she was blocked, broken, exhausted, until some shocking final will had come over her and she screamed, knowing it was now, or die.

And then a calm, quite as dramatic as the storm before. She

uncoiled, the tension falling off her, her breath easy, the sweat cool on her skin. She did not care about her nakedness, nor even the great scarlet stain on the bed, because there was a baby. It was nearly dawn and she could hear birds singing outside. It was done.

She had done it alone. Suddenly, she did not want the men to crowd this room with their expressions of concern and congratulation. It was between her and her baby, whom she scooped up, all the strength stretched from her limbs, and cradled.

Ormur arrived a few heartbeats later, and she could see him struggling with himself to remain. He tolerated the smell and the strange moonlight-bodied snake, but when she experienced another sudden contraction and expelled what seemed to be the tangled roots at the end of the infant's cord, his look of horror brought her to hysterical laughter.

'What, Ormur?'

The boy suggested, a touch prickly, that someone should have explained babies grew like marrow-plants; on the end of a twisted vine, with visceral purple roots. 'Is this one . . .' he paused, but went on under the closest she could manage to an encouraging smile. 'Is it not ripe? Seems like the roots shouldn't have come out with it.'

Keturah cried laughing, too giddy to restrain herself even in the face of Ormur's flushed countenance.

Harald and Virtanen had more legitimate concerns, eyeing the spreading pool of blood on her sheets, but Keturah found she did not much care. The baby quietened, and even consented to feed, while Harald severed its tough cord with some difficulty.

'There, Ormur, seems you were right,' she observed gravely. 'Very unripe indeed.'

When she next checked beneath her blanket, she was able to report the bleeding had stopped. Harald looked near to fainting. He laughed, ruffled Ormur's hair, and then gave the boy a vehement hug. He bestowed the same upon Virtanen and looked close to following suit with Keturah, before he thought better of it and skipped from the room. He returned, humming merrily, with a plate of cheese and toasted flat-cakes for her.

She asked for a little time alone.

They jostled out, hushing and beaming, and Keturah cradled the baby, sinking down in her filthy bed and managing just a mouthful of cheese before she was asleep.

She was woken by the baby's crying, with no idea how long she had slept. It was still light through the window, and a half-eaten lump of cheese lay beside her. She fed the baby, and then it seemed time to wash, dress and totter down the stairs to join the others. They ushered her into a seat, laid tributes of wine, fruit leather, blood sausage, ham, and bread until she could barely be approached without upsetting some dish or other. Then they crowded round, chattering and casting a partisan eye over the heir to the Stone Throne.

'Calm as his father already.'

'Has an intelligent face, doesn't he?'

'And eyes just like yours, Lady Keturah. Vivid green.'

Keturah thrilled to hear her new title. 'I only wish I could celebrate with people outside the house,' she sighed.

This observation was followed by a strange silence. Harald glanced at Virtanen and cleared his throat. 'Well, now, we have news too, girl.' He told her of the Chief Historian's arrival the previous night.

At first Keturah shrugged off this account, looking back down at the baby for a time. Then she said: 'Well that's a blow.' Her giddy relief was suddenly gone, and she felt all the exhaustion of her labour. She looked up to try and give Harald a smile and a reflexive jest. 'He denounced the Kryptea, eh? That's the last time anyone tries to back Roper into a corner.'

But fear had sprung from nowhere. If someone had told her that the Kryptea would give Roper a choice between his life being forfeit, or retreat, she knew he would have chosen the former. How he could survive those murderers, she could not imagine. This baby, sleeping peacefully in her arms, might even now be fatherless.

There was a taut silence, before Harald patted her awkwardly on the shoulder. 'I'm sorry girl, I should have told you later. And now I've made you cry.' He knelt down beside her, putting an arm over the back of her chair.

'No, no, Harald, don't be absurd. I'm just exhausted.' Tears were splashing onto the baby's swaddling and she sniffed irritably. She was a new mother, despised by this fortress, resisting a powerful enemy, and now here was the news that her husband was either dead, or soon would be. 'Stupid man,' she muttered. She brushed at the tears, but they kept coming, and the baby stirred and began to cry. She tried to hush him but he would not be still, so she just held him close and they cried together.

It was Virtanen who broke the uncomfortable silence. 'Lord Roper has survived worse than this, my lady,' he said. 'Circumstances bend to accommodate that man. Why, you don't know the half of what happened in Lundenceaster's breach! If he made it through that, he can survive the Kryptea. There's a lucky star above him.'

Keturah did not believe any of that. If Pryce could die, so could Roper. In any case, she did not want to entertain the hope that he might survive the Kryptea, and then have to face the reality that they had done to him what they did to everyone else who defied them.

She jerked her head up suddenly, wiping away her tears, shelving the grief for later. Turning to Harald she said, 'Don't worry, old friend. I had to know. I suppose . . .' she took a deep breath and nodded to herself a few moments. 'I suppose this just underlines the importance of clearing Roper's name here. If we're not too late, it'll make it that much harder for the Kryptea to act.'

'What? No, girl, don't be stupid.'

'Yes, Harald,' Keturah insisted. 'I'm quite out of people to fight my battles for me, and besides that was never much my style.'

'But the Chief Historian is with Tore now,' Harald persisted. 'Frathi is one of the most esteemed people in the kingdom! Perhaps you could have won a contest with the legate but it's hard to think how you could outmanoeuvre her as well.'

'Well, indeed,' said Keturah. She looked down a moment. 'But what do I have to lose? If I let things play out here, I've lost my home, my husband, my friends, and any chance this baby has of a secure life. We'll be exiled. If I leave, I bring exile upon myself. At least by fighting, I've got a chance. And imagine how it would look to abandon the fortress now. It would be as good as an admission of Roper's guilt, and my involvement in it. We must cut the head off that narrative at once.'

Harald seemed to be panicking. 'Virtanen,' he appealed. 'Tell her.'

The herald tucked his sausage-like thumbs into his belt and exhaled thoughtfully. 'Harald certainly has your best interests at heart, my lady, and I fear he may be right. Forget those things you mentioned: stay, and the mob may turn ugly. You may be trapped here, in isolation, which is no life for anyone. In the very best-case scenario, your choice boils down to this: survive within the fortress, or live outside it.'

'There,' said Harald. 'Virtanen always knows how to put it. What do you say to that?'

'I think people often mistake good phrasing for good advice,' she replied briefly.

'Keturah, please—'

'It's no use, Harald. My mind is made up. And besides . . . Tore has given me an invitation to meet publicly, has he not? I should accept it.'

'Why? What for?'

'A showcase trial,' Keturah declared. 'A public contest, where we clear Roper's name and bring his enemies to heel.'

'What is to be on trial?' asked Virtanen.

'Roper's campaign. And Uvoren's record. And Tore's treachery, and the right of the Ephors to declare the Black Lord a public enemy. I'll advocate to have Uvoren's loathsome statue reduced to smithereens, and we'll interrogate the whole damned tale.'

If she did not immediately set a date for this public trial, Keturah knew that she might never feel prepared for it. That same day, she dispatched Harald with word that in one month, Tore should meet her on the steps of the Central Keep, and each would make their case. 'Let him know that the Ephors are invited to hear what I've got to say as well, Harald.'

When Harald returned, it was with the news that Tore had been visibly thrown by her request. 'Safe to say he didn't expect that, though when he'd recovered he seemed very pleased by it.'

'Let him be pleased. If he underestimates me, more fool him.'

'Keturah—'

'I really have never known a man who wastes as much breath as you, Harald,' Keturah interrupted, before he could try and dissuade her once again. 'If you care for my safety, the best thing you can do now is help me prepare.'

She would not begin immediately, however. She was sore and exhausted, and besides, the baby needed constant attention. It also needed a name: something appropriate for an heir to the Stone Throne. Something too, which would do honour to Roper, if he ever got to meet the child. Ormur had become Keturah's most constant companion since the birth, and on the second day she asked: 'How would you feel if I named the baby Numa? After your brother.'

Ormur stiffened and inspected the baby cautiously. 'I would be very honoured.'

'Numa he is, then.'

From that moment, Ormur behaved towards the baby as might a dog. He would sit with his back against Keturah's chair, making regular checks on the peaceful child while Keturah slept off her exhaustion. *Feburk* – the week of drenching mists – passed, and when it had slipped to *Ghoppip* – the week mistletoe berries arrive, Keturah was ready to begin.

'The problem,' she opined to Harald and Virtanen, stretching her legs in the parlour while Ormur cradled the baby, 'is political, rather than legal. The Ephors have never mandated against a Black Lord before: previously the Kryptea have got to him first. Every day they are exploring the limits of their power, and if we can shift public opinion back towards Roper, they will at once –' she snapped her fingers – 'find that power does not extend as far as they hoped. On such unsteady ground, they shall not rule against overwhelming public opinion. Therefore, that is the position we must put them in. Win the crowd, and the statue will fall. Win the crowd, and they will realise they do not have the authority to summon the Black Lord before them.'

'The crowd are well against us,' Harald objected. 'How do we turn them?'

'The trial will only be part of it. I once had a lot of friends in this fortress, and I doubt all of them have deserted me: I shall set them to work. As for the trial, some research is in order, I think. I'll go to the Academy and see what I can dig up.'

Virtanen cleared his throat politely. 'Remember Frathi is now your enemy. You plan to just stroll into her domain and harvest information to undermine her?'

'Why, yes, I do.'

'That might be seen as antagonistic,' he said mildly.

Keturah made a sceptical noise. 'My enemy she may be, but Frathi is a woman of principle. She believes in the Academy too much to prevent me using it, even if it will be to defeat her.'

'And you're sure about that?'

'Well, let's find out.'

Eight days after Numa's birth, Keturah stepped onto the streets of the Hindrunn once more. Even with a hood low over her face, crossing the threshold for the first time since her arrival was daunting. She found she was shaking, her fear made worse by the knowledge that a previous version of her would have shaken off the discomfort, and stridden onto the deserted cobbles. Harald was at her back, sword concealed beneath his cloak, and he offered his arm and an encouraging smile.

Together they went to seek out Keturah's old allies, she aware of a painful tugging as she drifted further from Numa. He had been left with Ormur, who had a cup of her milk into which he could dip a rag and let the baby suckle.

First, they called on one of her oldest friends from the freyi: Kaiho Larikkasdottir. They had been drifting apart until last year, when Kaiho's husband had been imprisoned. His name was Urthr Uvorenson, and he had been convicted in a purge of Roper's enemies. Keturah had called on her old friend to offer some words of comfort, and express the hope that all was well between them. In fact, Kaiho had been greatly relieved to be rid of Urthr, whom she had hated and been pressured into marrying. His imprisonment had been a welcome excuse to divorce him with her honour intact, and she and Keturah had caught up as old friends.

But hammering on Kaiho's door now, Keturah was uncertain of her reception. She had thought Sigurasta was a friend, and she had publicly shamed her. She felt absurdly grateful when Harald rested a hand on her shoulder and gave it a gentle squeeze.

The door before them opened to reveal a dark-haired woman with pocked cheeks and black, melancholic eyes. At the sight of the hooded Keturah her mouth formed a perfect O, and she gripped on to the edge of the door. 'What are you doing here?'

'I had hoped,' Keturah felt slightly breathless and cleared her throat, 'that I might come in, and we could talk?'

Kaiho half hid herself behind the door's edge and pushed it a few inches closed. 'No, I'm sorry, Keturah, I don't think so.'

'Kaiho, you aren't going to close the door on me. I need your help.'

But Kaiho did close the door: hard. Keturah affected a careless smile at Harald and knocked at the boards again. 'Kaiho? Come now, you aren't just going to leave me standing on the street. Kaiho?'

There was no response.

Keturah turned away and hovered in the street for a few moments, not sure what to do.

'Let's try another,' Harald suggested.

'Of course. I was just trying to think who.'

She led Harald to the house of Alvilda, another old ally who lived nearby. Widowed young, Alvilda was only fifty-two but already led a prestigious deep history cell in the Academy. Her door was answered by a legionary, who raised an eyebrow to see Keturah.

'Good morning. Would you tell Lady Alvilda that Keturah Tekoasdottir has come to see her?'

'I shall see if she's available,' the legionary allowed. He shut the door and when he reappeared a few moments later, he was shaking his head. 'Lady Alvilda is not available at present.'

'Perhaps you might ask her to call on me when she is?' Keturah suggested, but the legionary was still shaking his head.

'Quite impossible, I'm afraid.' He shut the door.

Keturah was not sure her battered confidence could take another rejection, but nor was she accustomed to giving up, and she proposed to Harald that they approach one final ally. Talva Radburnsdottir was a notorious gossip, and the subject of many rumours herself. Keturah had heard that most of her information was acquired by going to bed with potential sources. She would associate with anyone, so long as they had juicy stories for her to feast on, and if Keturah had any asset in abundance at that moment, it was stories.

But Talva's door was opened by a woman whom Keturah recognised by sight but could not name. 'Oh, Keturah,' said this woman, raising her eyebrows so high they were in danger of unmooring from her forehead and floating off altogether. She gave a surprised laugh. 'You're here to see Talva, I suppose. She's not in, I'm afraid.'

That claim was undermined when Talva's raucous and unmistakable laugh rattled through the hallway. Keturah looked flatly at the woman before her. 'Perhaps you'd tell her I called.'

'If you would really like,' said the woman, widening her eyes to indicate how desperate she thought that would be. She shut the door in Keturah's face.

Keturah turned away frowning. She tried not to imagine word of her visit being relayed to the parlour, and Talva's savage tongue gleefully lacerating the friendless Keturah.

'Well, never mind, Harald. We'll keep trying tomorrow, shall we? I'm not sure my confidence is up to much more of that today. Let's go to the Academy and see what we can uncover there.'

But when she crossed the narrow stone bridge into the Academy and went to witness her first chant, Keturah could barely absorb the words. Her mind fled to her waiting infant, and whether Ormur was managing. Or whether she might stumble into the Chief Historian and be ejected. Or to Talva, salaciously sharing a hundred hoarded and embellished stories about Keturah to a parlour full of women, cackling like fighting magpies.

But there was no encounter with Frathi. She was tolerated until the historians departed to go running, when she emerged into the evening dark to find Harald still waiting for her. He winked. 'Home, my lady?'

'Home, old friend.'

They found Ormur and Numa asleep together by the fire, the cup of milk empty beside them. The scene was so peaceable that Keturah felt a spike of jealousy.

She retired to bed, promising herself she would try to recruit some allies again tomorrow. But it was a fractious night for Numa, Keturah slept badly, and could not face the inevitable rejection that would come. She would do it the next day, she told herself. And so she kept telling herself, day after day.

For two weeks, Virtanen accompanied Keturah to the Academy. Unlike Harald, he came in with her to conduct his own research, so that they could compare findings on the return journey.

'I did wonder whether a line on Lord Rokkvi's occupation of Lundenceaster might be fruitful,' he observed one evening. The streets were grey with mist, a few stars glinting through the fog overhead, and the herald kept his voice low so they would not be overheard by the three legionaries passing the other way. 'And how he was lauded, where Roper has been tried, defied, and decried. You know – *Where has that fighting spirit gone, my subjects? Was courage the preserve of our grandparents' generation?* – that sort of thing.' The herald had a knack for turning a phrase, and had already supplied Keturah with a number of devastating lines that helped build her confidence.

Just as he finished speaking, there came a horrible scream from a side street, and Keturah flinched violently, flattening herself against Virtanen and clutching his arm. She swivelled the herald around to face this threat – a fox. It skipped out of the mist, round a corner and was swallowed again.

'Vermin,' said Keturah, releasing Virtanen's arm with an apologetic pat. 'Everywhere at the moment it seems.'

Virtanen muttered his agreement, and they walked on. 'Perhaps you should allow me to deliver this speech, my lady,' he suggested gently.

Keturah felt herself blush. 'I was just startled, Virtanen.'

'Of course. But you are taking on a great deal, and I've been addressing public audiences my whole life. It might be safer for me to make a public appearance on your behalf.'

'These words must come from my own mouth, Virtanen. Any fear on my part will look like guilt, or lack of confidence in our cause. I cannot skulk behind a herald.'

'I know your mind is set, my lady, but this plan is exceedingly dangerous.'

Keturah shrugged. 'It's war.'

'Then at least permit me to help you train for it. You'll need to be in fine voice for the trial to come.'

Keturah was sceptical of this, but when they reached Tekoa's house, Virtanen gave her a modest demonstration of his own powers. His voice was rich and resonant, perfectly pitched and clear, even when Numa's howls were echoing from the parlour's stone walls. This much, Keturah had observed already, but he then shocked her by manhandling her mood. Just by using wordless exclamations, he forced her emotions first one way, then another. A low breathless groan would induce swirling fear in her guts and chest. A prolonged, harsh ticking, and she became aware of a growing anger boiling within her. And then he was producing the softest mewing which brought sudden tears to her eyes, and, rather unexpectedly, an embarrassing spill of milk beneath her tunic. He finished totally unflustered, and for the first time she sensed how that power was at work in his every utterance, making his tone as compelling as his words. For his final demonstration, he stunned Keturah into silence by 'hurling' his voice at a small bell placed on the other side of the parlour, and setting it ringing. Keturah demanded he repeat this several times before she was satisfied that it truly chimed to the herald's voice alone.

'You learned all this through training?'

'Years of it. We will not have so long, of course. Not to master the finer skills. But plenty long enough to make a difference.'

It was clear what a weapon a voice like that might be, so Keturah added morning and evening training with Virtanen to their daily trips to the Academy. First, came control of breathing. 'All else is built on that,' the herald reported. 'There is no sense progressing until you have mastered it.'

She was given exercises three times a day, learning to calm herself with long exhalations, becoming aware of the rhythm of her breath, and how to hold it for first one minute, then two. Then came voice exercises, to put force behind her words and make them resonate in the stone parlour. He decreed that this was where they should focus their efforts before the trial. But Keturah wanted more and she pleaded and cajoled until he agreed to teach her a little of those wordless incantations that he used to alter emotions.

'What you are doing,' he told her, 'is learning to speak the Old Tongue. It is older than the mountains: the first language that any of us spoke, long before words. It is understood by anything with ears, and anyone with a throat can speak it too, but only in extremis. Unless, of course, you have trained. Words are our modern language, and fine things they are: elegant and exact, but they are not as powerful as the Old Tongue. Your babe speaks it better than most adults. Cause him pain, and he will make a noise which chimes at your heart and sets it ringing. The Unhieru, I am told, speak it very well, or at least the unpleasant bits of it. Have you heard death, Lady Keturah?'

She thought of Hafdis's blood-curdling scream, just before she had died in Vigtyr's tent. 'Yes,' she said quietly. Even the memory of that sound made her coil in on herself. She would never forget.

'Then you have heard the Old Tongue spoken in earnest. That fox we saw the other night spoke it too. It comes in fear, in extreme grief and joy and exhaustion. But to utter it when calm is a matter of utmost control. And when you have that, you can add hints of it to your words. You will be a sorcerer, speaking spells others find near impossible to resist. Come, let us begin with your babe.'

By trial and error and intense focus, they worked together on calming Numa, and soothing the infant's cries just by noise. But after nearly a week, it seemed she had made no progress whatsoever. 'That is why I thought it would be a waste of your energies,' said Virtanen, as Numa kept howling and Keturah abandoned her efforts at the Old Tongue and tried feeding him instead. 'This skill takes years. You must satisfy yourself with the journey, and then you may eventually arrive at some sort of destination.' Virtanen smiled apologetically. His eyes were always kindly, but Keturah was not sure she had seen him smile before. It was unbalanced, warping his nose and nearly concealing his black eyes; at once the ugliest and most disarming smile she had seen.

Virtanen glanced out of the window and back at Numa, who was feeding greedily. They would usually have left for the Academy by now, and the day was threatening to get away from them.

'Why don't you go and get started, Virtanen?' said Keturah.

'I shouldn't like to leave you to walk alone, Lady Keturah.'

'My confidence is far better than it was,' Keturah replied. 'And Numa looks as though he intends to be here for some time. Go, I'll catch you up.'

Virtanen excused himself gratefully, while she settled Numa, leaving him once again in Ormur's care.

She took to the streets alone for the first time since re-entering the fortress. At once, she seemed burdened by stares she had not noticed before. She resolved that she was being over-fearful, but when the stares had become mutterings and jabbing fingers, it became apparent there had been something in the herald's imposing bulk that had sheltered her.

She felt her pace quicken and tried to control her breathing as Virtanen had taught, throwing a glance over her shoulder. She saw that she was now being trailed down the street by six women strung out in a crescent. They stared back at her, saying nothing and keeping pace in ominous silence.

Keturah snapped her head back to the front. *Control*, she thought. C*ontrol your breath, just as you've done so often.* But she was already near running, and when she next looked back at the group behind, it was a crowd of twenty.

Without a word, or so much as a taunt, the first apple was hurled. It struck her on the shoulder, sharp and painful. The rest of the crowd began to follow suit, pelting her in determined, menacing silence. Keturah tried to turn back to them, holding up a hand to ward off the barrage and hoping to reason with them, but was struck in the face. She was blinded, her eyes streaming, unable to see her attackers as one projectile after another pummelled her flesh. She opened her mouth to plead, but had barely made a sound before she was struck in the lip and her mouth filled with the iron taste of blood.

Her confidence crumbled, and though she was closer to the Academy than Tekoa's house, she knew where she would rather be trapped. She ran, squinting through blurred eyes, the mob still silent as she pelted down a side street, twisting away from the hands she imagined grasping after her.

She did not look back until she was hammering on Tekoa's door. Harald took a painfully long time to answer, and when he did she stumbled inside to be greeted by the sound of Numa crying.

'Keturah? What's happened?'

She could not answer. She simply lay prone behind the door, panting and shaking, until Harald barred it once more. The crowd had frightened her, her child's tears gnawed at her, but above all else, she was devastated by how weak she seemed to have become.

'Are you all right, girl?'

Some youthful elasticity had gone out of her, and the strength that had played such a part in her identity seemed to have deserted her.

'I'm fine, Harald,' she mumbled into the floor. How on earth would she stay calm enough to publicly confront Tore, when she could not even manage a half-hour journey across the Hindrunn? 'Fine,' she repeated, pushing herself onto her knees. 'I should go and see to Numa.' She stood, avoiding Harald's gaze and went into the parlour.

Virtanen reappeared shortly after noon to discover what had become of Keturah and found her sitting by the fire, Numa still bawling in her arms. He appraised her for a moment. 'Felt like a day off?'

She fancied she could hear the disappointment in his voice, though he was evidently trying to be sympathetic.

'Something like that,' she murmured.

'That is not the voice we practised,' he observed, sitting opposite her.

She tried to make a joke of it, imitating the resonant voice they had worked on together, but it came out embittered rather than humorous.

He raised his eyebrows briefly, turning his massive presence away from her and towards the hearth. 'Have you given up?'

'I can't give up.'

'But you have.'

She did not reply. She knew she was sounding like a spoilt child, and resented herself for it, but still could not summon the energy to answer convincingly, or explain what had happened on her way to join him.

'Two choices, then,' said Virtanen, stretching out his legs before the fire and brooding at it. 'You let me take on Tore, on your behalf. That would certainly be safer than facing the mob. Or you forget this, and we get you out of the fortress.'

A spike of anger lent some vehemence to her reply. 'I said I wouldn't leave the fortress, and I stick by that.' Numa was still crying, and she suddenly wanted to shout at the baby. 'But . . . I want this to work. And it seems more likely that will be achieved with you as the mouthpiece, rather than me.'

'That is a wise decision,' said the herald.

Keturah's first feeling was relief at a weight lifted. But it was not long before she became aware of a subtle nausea; the sense that she had just taken a step closer to her own disintegration. She had never backed down from anything in her life before.

But this is too much, she thought. *There is no shame in recognising that. You are a mother for the first time: exhausted, friendless and frayed. Heal now, and perhaps you can come back later.* She had seen friends of hers take decisions like this at every stage, and despised them for it. Now here she was, bowing to her own shredded nerves.

Numa had stopped crying, and casting around for signs, she took that to mean she had taken the right decision. 'I'll still help you plan, Virtanen. I'm up to that.'

'I'd be glad of it,' he said, a little dutifully.

'Back at it tomorrow,' she said bracingly, getting to her feet. 'Ormur, would you take Numa for a moment?'

She took the stairs to Tekoa's chamber. There, she slumped against the wall beside the high window, and slid down into a crouch. She shivered, pulling the neck of her tunic closed, and stared vacantly at her knees.

She had never hated herself before.

15
The Riot

'Stick close, boy.'

'Why?'

'Because you're a target, that's why. Your brother has many enemies, and they will use you to get at him.'

'I survived the haskoli.'

'Enough impudence. Be silent now.'

Ormur glared at Harald, and was ignored in turn. Keturah had badgered both parties into visiting the market together, and they now walked streets the grey of an oyster shell in silence. There was a quality in the light and air that made it feel like winter, every figure tottering by now tightly wrapped in cloaks.

'This way.' With a hand on the boy's shoulder, Harald guided him to the right, into a circle of stalls thronged with people and pearly with misted breath.

'I don't have to stay with you, I can go and buy something,' said Ormur. 'Then we can go home.'

'Nobody will trade with you,' said Harald. 'Just watch and learn.'

'How are we paying?'

'Labour.'

'Labour?'

'We promise them some work in future, and they give us what we need.'

'So we could take what we need, and then never do the work?'

'If you did that, people would very quickly stop trading with you.'

Ormur pondered this. 'How do you have time to work for others? Aren't you busy?'

'Enough questions. Over here.'

They edged around two women arguing over some manky pigs, and Ormur was shrieked at when he nearly tripped over a basket. Harald seized his shoulder, apologising to the owner who now bellowed that it contained a venomous snake that might have killed him, and dragged him hard towards a cheese stall. Harald and the stallholder exchanged pleasantries and offers, and Ormur did not really pay attention until he noticed the woman at the stall sizing him up. 'Two weeks?' she suggested.

'Done,' said Harald.

Ormur suddenly realised what was happening. 'Is it *my* labour you're trading?'

'You're damned well not just hanging around the house,' replied Harald, not taking his eyes from a large wheel of cheese being wrapped in cloth before him.

Ormur fumed. 'And two weeks of my work is worth one block of cheese?'

'I'm surprised too,' said Harald, thrusting the enormous cheese at him and dragging him away. 'Let's go before she realises she's been ripped off.'

Ormur followed from one stall to the next as his future was bartered away for nails, firewood, and a linen-wrapped ham. 'You don't have much luck haggling,' he observed from behind the cheese.

'I'm better at it when it's my own time I'm selling.'

Harald seemed distracted, and Ormur followed his gaze into the crowd. A sense of purpose had come over the people before them, every face turned away and looking at something Ormur could not see. He tried to push his way forward and investigate, but Harald kept him still. 'Don't leave my side, boy,' he said, quite gently.

There was cheering and wild applause coming from the centre of the crowd. Then came words, so forceful and emphatic that it was less like a voice and more like an instrument of brass and leather. Ormur could sense the tone, but not make out the words. 'I can't see,' he declared, tipping the cheese onto Harald's boots. Harald, his own arms filled with ham and a bag full of nails, swore and attempted to rescue the cheese, while Ormur took the opportunity to barge into the crowd. At his back came a volley of curses from Harald, and the people around him hissed and tutted as he pushed past. One woman even belted him around the head with something heavy, but he ignored her, burrowing into the packed bodies until he was standing at the front.

He found that the crowd had encircled a group of three men. One was the eagle-cloaked legate, Tore, who possessed that fearsome voice Ormur had heard, and was even now red in the face as he continued some declamation. The other two looked – there was no other word for it – nasty. It was as though Tore stood between two particularly vicious dogs. Both were large-framed and lean, with sunburnt skin and arrogant, hostile faces. They stared above the crowd, haughty and disdainful as the legate raised their arms into the air.

'The *injustices* of Roper's reign are being reversed at last, and it is not a moment too soon!'

For a fortress primarily filled with women, there were a disproportionate number of men in this crowd. They did not merely cheer at Tore's declarations: it was a more forbidding noise, like a pride of lions, which stood Ormur's hair on end. Tore gesticulated like a wild conductor, coaxing the roar into a crescendo, and Ormur felt a prickle of fear for the first time. Tore let the noise fade and then continued.

'He thought he would get away with it! He thought he could

trample on us all, and we would lie down and take it! Today we send a message, which travels all the way to Suthdal: We are not to be ignored or sacrificed at the altar of his ambition! Those he—' Tore paused and held up his hands to dampen the roars that had greeted his words. 'Those he crushed will rise up! The time has come for a correction! Why, he still has friends in this fortress who dare show their faces in public! That should not be – they should know shame and fear, to be associated with such a tyrant! May all trace of him in this fortress be *extirpated*!'

Now bands of the crowd were peeling away and pushing their way out of the market circle, booming and chanting. There came a crash as someone upended one of the stalls, its shocked owner backing away with hands over her mouth as fruit tumbled and bounced across the cobbles. The man responsible held the table aloft, while two others had found wooden beams which they beat against its surface as a drum. There were more crashes as more stalls were capsized, and then Ormur's head cracked open.

He was suddenly on the cobbles, a high-pitched whine in his ears, his vision foggy and the images overlapping. 'You idiot,' said a voice above him as something heavy thumped onto his chest. 'If you run off again, I'll bloody kill you. Now get up. Get up, or I'll leave you here to die.' It was Harald. Ormur was too dazed to stand unaided and the legionary seized him by the scruff of his neck and hauled him upright. 'Take that ham, or next time I'll use it to knock you out. We need to get out of here. Right now.'

Uv-or-en! was the cry as the crowd began to stampede. Ormur could not see much. He had just enough awareness to hold onto the knuckle of ham with one hand, as Harald crushed the other with a talon and dragged him through the throng. He was shoving and swearing to create a path, Ormur trailing in his wake. Blurred, snatched images were filtering through his stupefied head: a flaming cloth someone was whirling about their head; one woman taking another two arm in arm and shepherding them out of the market; the cheese stall being reduced to splinters and the wares rolling into one of the stone-bedded streams running out of the market. Then came an image of unusual clarity. It was Tore, standing very still, as the mob whirled about him. There was a smile on his face, which fascinated Ormur, even in his confusion. It was sly, and excited, and most of all, it was ominous.

Then Harald gave his hand another jerk and Tore disappeared behind a group of chanting women. Ormur felt sick, but some clarity was returning, and he realised for the first time that there were people grasping at Harald. The legionary had dropped the cheese and was knocking them aside with his free hand, his other still clamped onto Ormur.

Somehow, he fought them both clear of the mob. He spat some words over Ormur's head, which the boy did not register, but stopped their pursuers in their tracks. Then they were out of the market circle and hurrying down a backstreet, Ormur stumbling in his efforts to keep up.

Only now did the boy have time to realise how frightened he was. They pelted round one corner, then another, and another, running easier than it ever had been before. There was a shout behind them, and over his shoulder Ormur caught a glimpse of three men dashing after them.

'Drop it you fool, and run!'

Harald knocked the ham out of his hand and they were now sprinting in earnest. Behind them, the slapping of feet grew louder as the men gained on them. Ormur could hear their harsh breath and one of them crying: 'Grab him! Grab him!'

'Go!' Harald said something Ormur did not catch and gave him a final shove, which almost knocked him over. He stumbled, just keeping his feet and on the verge of toppling forward for an impossibly long time. Finally, he regained his balance and was able to accelerate. It seemed the shouts and the footsteps were receding, and he kept fighting and fighting his waning stamina.

The door to Tekoa's house was in sight, and it kept him

going until he petered into a walk a few feet away, gasping and spluttering. He hammered at the boards, turned to rebuke Harald for pushing him, turned again, but could not see the legionary. He looked back the way he had come, but there was no sign of him. Their pursuers were gone too, but he could still hear the roaring crowd. There was distant drumming and a noise like a heaving ocean. What was it Harald had said, just before he pushed him? He had not understood at the time, but looking back it might have been: *I'll catch you up*. He surely had not stayed to fight off their pursuers.

There came a scraping as the locking bar was pulled back, and the front door swung inwards to reveal Keturah. Numa was clamped to her chest by a sling and she stepped back to give him room. 'Get inside.'

'Harald!' Ormur did not move.

Keturah glanced out at the street. 'Where is he?'

'I don't know. I think he stayed!'

'Stayed where? Ormur, what's happened?'

'There's a riot, they were looking for allies of Lord Roper—'

'Just get inside, Ormur.'

In the parlour, Ormur explained what had happened, finishing with a blurted: 'But, Harald!'

'Yes.' Keturah was pacing before the fire, staring down at the flagstones. 'What did you think he said? "Don't wait for me"?'

'"I'll catch you up."'

'You're sure?'

'No.'

'But that's what you think he said?'

'I think so.'

Keturah pursed her lips. Ormur was desperately aware of each passing heartbeat with Harald out on those streets. This was his fault, and he needed to make amends. The muted roar of the crowds carried into the parlour. It seemed to be growing louder. 'We can't go anywhere, Ormur,' said Keturah at last. She was very pale.

'We can't just leave Harald on the streets!'

She directed that green glare at him for the first time, and he had to look away. 'We must. We would both be torn apart as soon as the mob set eyes on us.'

'Where's Virtanen?'

'The Academy. Almighty, I hope he doesn't try and come back through this.'

Some of the noises coming through the stonework were inhuman: like violent retching, and growing louder and louder was that drumming.

Ormur had no insight into how hard it was for Keturah to shelter inside while Harald remained on the streets. There was a time she would have known that plunging into that chaos was insanity. Now, however, she was tormented by the decision. Would she have gone out to face them before her confidence had broken? Was this another sign of her backing down, and her inevitable descent into the shell of the woman she had been?

Ormur did not press the issue, too engulfed in his own guilt. They sat in silence as frightening noises penetrated the parlour and darkness fell outside. At one point, there came a crash from upstairs. They armed themselves with a fireside implement apiece and climbed to Tekoa's room. There they found an uprooted cobble had been hurled through the window and smashed a water jug on the table. Keturah put a finger to her lips, and they backed out of the room just as there came the smash of a second cobble bouncing off the outer wall. They watched from the shelter of the corridor as six stones in total made it inside. They landed with frightening force, though most did no damage beyond chipping the stone floor.

They retreated down the stairs, where at any moment Keturah expected an assault to be made on the front door. Crashes and yells reverberated from outside, and at one point an impact shook the entire room. That woke Numa, who alone had managed to sleep, and set him bawling. Keturah tried again those noises Virtanen had taught her, crooning low and soft to soothe her son. And for the first time the baby hushed. He stirred a moment more, then fell back into sleep.

Keturah glanced at Ormur. 'You're mastering it,' said the boy.

'I've been trying so long, it was bound to happen once by coincidence.'

In the pause, they could hear a piercing scream from the street.

'Who were the two men at the centre of the riot?' asked Ormur.

'They sound like Unndor and Urthr Uvorenson.'

'Uvoren's sons? So what did Tore mean about wrongs being righted?'

'They were both disgraced on charges of rape and cowardice to destabilise Uvoren. Like Vinjar, he wants them exonerated. Until today, I would have said that bringing them close was a miscalculation. Both were guilty as a fox caught in a chicken coop. It was well known, just nobody had ever brought all the witnesses together. Though tonight suggests he hasn't miscalculated at all. Clearly the people are now prepared to forgive anyone working against Roper.' She considered briefly. 'But the crowd was mostly men, you say?'

'Yes.'

'Probably Lothbrok goons then,' she grunted. 'Men from Uvoren – and Tore's – house. They'll have been instructed to cause trouble and make it seem as though support is more widespread than it is.' She sighed. 'He's trying to make it impossible for anyone to publicly oppose him. It may be too dangerous even for Virtanen to speak now.'

Outside, the mob stoked itself up. Peers who preached duty and restraint discovered the heady power of moving as part of a crowd, before which an individual could only kneel and pray for clemency. They discovered that violence, if free from consequence, was a thrill. Drunk on their own inexorability, they declared death to anyone who stood against them. Especially Keturah Tekoasdottir, wife to the Black Lord.

Ormur and Keturah sat in silence until there seemed a sliver of dawn beneath the front door. Keturah glanced at it. 'Sounds as though things have settled down a little out there.'

A hammering at the door made them both jump. 'Keturah!' hissed a voice. 'Lady Keturah, it's me! Quickly, I beg!'

'Virtanen,' said Keturah. 'Ormur, let him in.'

The boy obeyed, and returned with the herald at his back, looking shaken but unhurt.

'Virtanen, you're well?' Keturah was on her feet, still cradling Numa.

He stopped before them. 'I am, my lady. Quite well, thank you.' He took a deep breath. 'But I regret, I carry appalling news.'

There was a silence. 'Harald?'

Virtanen nodded, and Keturah sank slowly back into her seat. The room before her was blurring. She heard Ormur turn and stamp upstairs. 'You saw? Or heard?'

The herald prepared her with a look. 'His body is on display,' he said, gently.

The tears were splattering down her cheeks. 'How?'

Virtanen hesitated. 'Hanged, my lady. He's been laid at the feet of Uvoren's statue.'

Keturah broke down and wept.

She felt entirely responsible. Harald had died because he was associated with her. Not only that, but she had insisted he take Ormur with him yesterday and he had died preserving the boy. That precious man, who had protected and watched over her, hanged by a furious mob. And if she had left the fortress, as they had all begged her to do? Surely he would still be alive.

Quietly, Virtanen settled himself opposite her. 'I am sorry, my lady. How I admired him, even from our brief acquaintance.'

She tried to smile at Virtanen. 'Thank the Almighty you're back. How did you survive?'

'I was in the Academy when the rioting broke out. Bless those berserkers, they may be utterly mad, but they are at least independent, and nobody would dare cross them. Even the most incensed members of the crowd turned away at the sight of the squad guarding the bridge into the pyramid.'

Keturah had not really heard. She was staring down at Numa, sleeping in her arms. *What do we do now?* Tore had turned the streets into such a hostile place that it felt they could not possibly counter him in public. She did not see how he could be defeated.

Virtanen seemed of the same opinion. 'We can see how things change, my lady,' he said slowly. 'Perhaps it would be prudent to wait for the streets to settle a little anyway. But our priority must now be to preserve your safety.'

Keturah did not reply. Virtanen's words made her feel a complete failure.

It seemed a time for action rather than grief, but there was nothing to be done. Nothing until mid-morning, when there came a hammering at the door.

'Allow me,' said Virtanen. He had been pacing the parlour and went upstairs to look out of the window. He clattered back down at once. 'It's the boy!' he hissed.

Keturah rose with a jolt. 'Who? Ormur?'

But Virtanen was at the door already, Keturah hurrying to join him, just as he hauled it back to reveal Ormur standing with a woman. There was something large and dark at their feet, which at first Keturah did not register properly. She was too shocked that the boy had somehow got outside the house and now seemed to have returned with this woman, whom she recognised. Kaiho Larikkasdottir: the first of the old allies she had tried to recruit. Keturah was so shocked to see her that she took a pace back. Numa seemed to feel the tension in her arms and began crying again.

'Lady Keturah,' said Kaiho, giving a little bow. She hesitated, and then gestured down at the dark mass at their feet. 'May I come in?'

Only then did Keturah register what Ormur and Kaiho had brought with them.

Harald's body.

Virtanen glanced at Keturah, who was still too shocked to respond, and then seized one of Harald's limp arms. 'Quickly.'

They carried him inside and arranged him on the table in the parlour, where they had a moment of silence. Keturah had seen the corpse of a friend all too recently, but Harald's was worse. He was naked, and part-burnt. The density and savagery of the injuries was such that she only recognised him by the familiar birthmark behind his ear.

She suddenly turned to Ormur and delivered a hard smack about his head. 'You fool! What were you thinking, going after his body?'

Ormur straightened slowly from the weight of her blow and did not take his eyes off Harald.

'Answer when I ask you a question.'

'I was thinking he did more for me.'

'A poor way to repay him,' snapped Keturah.

'You climbed out of the window?' asked Virtanen.

'Dropped. I didn't want to leave the door unbarred.'

Numa was still crying, and Keturah distractedly made that crooning noise again. Even she did not notice that the baby instantly fell quiet. She stared at Harald, swallowing her nausea and hoping he had been dead long before most of the wounds were inflicted. When she turned to Kaiho, the other woman could meet her eye only briefly. 'And you. What drags you over our threshold?'

'I saw Ormur here, trying to drag Harald away from the statue. I wanted to help.'

'That is novel from you indeed,' Keturah observed.

Kaiho raised her hands helplessly. 'Keturah, please. I'm sorry about turning you away before. I wished I hadn't, but really, there was no choice.'

'No choice?' asked Keturah. She spoke softly, but the weakness that had consumed her lately was overwhelmed with more rage than she had ever experienced. 'No choice? Your choice was the simplest imaginable. Possession versus courage. A mob or the truth. Law or *murder*!' She lashed out and smacked Harald's cold shoulder with her hand.

'How could I have known it would end like this?' Kaiho protested.

'How could you not, you fool! You think possession is a sin just because it is unseemly? It is lethal!'

'You're certainly showing fine restraint now,' Kaiho replied sullenly.

A silence fell over the room like a gale-driven blizzard. Keturah let it build until Kaiho had to turn her face away and shield it from the glare. 'May you show as much restraint if you are ever unfortunate enough to find yourself in these circumstances.'

Kaiho was still staring at the floor. 'I did not think it would come to this.' Keturah was pitiless and Kaiho had to go on, or face that horrible silence. 'I did not see the mob going as far as murder, or Urthr being welcomed back. Whatever Lord Roper did—'

'*Nothing*, you imbecile!' Keturah interrupted.

'He is better than Tore,' Kaiho finished. 'Tore is a liar.'

Keturah wanted to drown Kaiho in acid truths. For her foolishness, her betrayal, her complicity in Harald's death and Keturah's humiliation. In the end, it was not her own restraint that held her back, but something personal in the way Kaiho had said the word *liar*. 'Has he lied to you?'

Kaiho's dark, melancholy eyes never seemed to move, as though they could only look straight out from her face, which was still pointed at Keturah's feet. 'He has lied to everyone.'

'But what did he say to *you*?'

Kaiho stood very still, hands folded in front of her. 'He promised me Urthr would never return.'

Keturah took a calming breath. 'And why would he promise anything to you?'

Kaiho voice was very small as she replied. 'We were very close.'

Keturah felt as though she were freezing to death, only to

see a tiny yellow flame stir in the tinder-pile before her. 'Were you intimate with the legate?'

Kaiho did not deny it. Instead, she turned her face up towards Keturah at last.

Virtanen was looking between Kaiho and Keturah. 'I apologise, I don't know you, Lady . . .?'

'Just Miss Kaiho,' she muttered.

'Miss Kaiho. I'm sorry to ask, but you seem sympathetic to our current situation. I admit we're balanced on a boat's gunwale. If you have indeed been intimate with Legate Tore, is it something you might admit in public?'

Kaiho took a deep breath. 'That is why I'm here,' she said quietly.

An extra-marital relationship might sometimes be sanctioned by the Ephors for the purposes of reproduction. Children were of paramount importance to their diminishing society, and if a union had failed to produce any, then both parties might try their luck with different partners, raising the resultant offspring within their marriage. However, such a relationship would never be permitted for someone like Tore, who already had children with his wife. For him it was not merely illegal, but an indelible stain on character.

'Do you have any proof?' asked Keturah brutally.

'If necessary.'

'It shouldn't be,' said Virtanen, reassuringly. He was more prepared to compromise than Keturah, who wanted revenge for the man now lying lacerated before her. 'If you can prove it, we can simply use that as leverage over Tore. If he wants to rule, he can't be seen to have had an affair.' Virtanen laughed suddenly. 'We can force him to withdraw!'

'Withdraw?' asked Kaiho. 'From what?'

'We are preparing a public trial, to have Uvoren's statue removed,' Virtanen explained.

'He might withdraw, but that won't be enough,' said Keturah, flatly. 'The people in this fortress are utterly possessed and want blood. Even if Tore steps back from the trial, Frathi wouldn't, and the people are too enraged to pull back from the brink. You played your part in that, did you not, Kaiho?'

'I never supported the mob's actions.'

'But you did! When you stood by, refused to help, and even had an affair with the architect of this madness. It's only now it's come to this,' and she gestured furiously at Harald's body, 'and Urthr Uvorenson, your horrid husband—'

'*Former* husband!'

'—has come home, that you've realised which side you were supporting.'

Kaiho gave an exasperated huff. 'Keturah, *everyone* believed Tore! Everyone said Roper had lost the army, why would I believe any different?'

'Why would you believe evil stories about someone when the only source is their sworn enemy?' retorted Keturah, stamping her foot. 'Why did you give a smear of goose shit for the thoughts of a possessed mob? What are you if you don't stand by your own convictions?'

Kaiho was pink in the face. She tossed her hair, and visibly tried to calm herself. 'I am not the only one who will have thought differently after last night. What happened in the market changed things.'

'So, who else has seen the truth staring them in the face?'

'I will go and find out,' Kaiho allowed. 'But I've placed myself in your hands, now, have I not? Isn't that enough of a sign that I'm with you? But . . . if we can use the information about Tore without it becoming public,' she glanced at Virtanen. 'It would be better for me.'

'Oh, don't worry about that,' said the herald heartily. 'I'm sure we can wring some handsome concessions out of him if we agree to keep this quiet.'

'We'll see,' said Keturah brusquely. 'The streets were on fire last night. I want to do some burning too.'

'So I see,' said Kaiho. 'I will bring you allies. Enough to drown out that Lothbrọk mob.'

'Thousands then?' Keturah asked coldly.

'Stop testing me, Keturah.'

'Is testing you unfair, Kaiho?'

Kaiho resumed her dead-eyed stare at the floor, her cheeks still flushed. 'I should go before I'm seen here. I'll find recruits, I swear.'

Virtanen showed her out, barring the door behind her. 'Don't be too hard on her, my lady,' he began as he re-entered the parlour.

Keturah forestalled him without looking up. 'Virtanen, I'm very grateful for all you've done for us, but not another word.' There was not another word. 'And you,' she said, turning to Ormur. She glared at him for a moment, and he stared back with eyes lifeless as a pair of painted eggs. 'Well done. I am proud to have an idiot like you for a brother.'

Virtanen had taken no offence at Keturah's tone. He cracked his knuckles. 'I'm going to the Academy,' he said cheerfully. 'By the Almighty, we have our chance.'

'I'm coming,' said Keturah.

Virtanen froze. 'My lady . . .'

'Not another word. Ormur, you'll care for Numa?'

The weakness was gone. Keturah had room only for rage.

The streets leading to the Academy seemed frozen, as though last night's violence had shocked them into stillness. Everywhere was wreckage, of people as well as things. Harald had been one victim among dozens that they saw. Many of the cobbles had been ripped out of the road like missing teeth, and branches torn off the low hawthorn trees hanging over the street. There were even bodies in the clear waters surrounding the Academy: visible as greenish blurs, their outlines swimming fifty feet below.

'The berserkers were called into action after all,' Keturah observed savagely.

'They were the calmest people in the fortress last night. I imagine the riot looked gentle compared to some of the things they get up to.'

They bid each other farewell at the entrance, each going to make separate enquiries. Keturah's took her to the apex of the pyramid, nearly the full length of the great Time-Passage, which the historians used as a memory aid. She was usually fascinated by the carvings etched along the walls, but was so focused this day that she did not notice them. In fact, walking an increasingly tight spiral, she very nearly collided with the Chief Historian coming the other way.

Keturah blinked and stepped back at the sight of Frathi, fearing she was about to be ejected. Frathi showed no surprise whatsoever.

'Tekoasdottir. I heard you had been visiting.'

'Heard from whom, your Kryptean goons?' She had not meant to sound so aggressive.

Frathi looked a little surprised and gave her one-shouldered shrug. 'Yes. Among others.' That admission chilled Keturah. 'Apparently you plan to combat me in public advocacy.' Being too secure for ostentatious emotion, Frathi was not scornful or amused. She appeared mildly interested, as though a neighbour had directed her attention towards their new roof.

'You?' asked Keturah.

'Certainly if you propose what I hear, then I shall join the legate in opposing you. You are doing your researches, I assume.'

'It would be foolish not to.' She did not reveal it would be Virtanen speaking against Frathi. Best to wrongfoot their opposition however they could, and Frathi might prepare differently if she thought she were facing an untested speaker.

'The foolishness would be trying to defend Lord Roper's actions. Leave it, Lady Keturah. Even if you could succeed, your position will be one of extreme isolation. Lord Roper cannot survive.'

Keturah flushed, and her tears, closer to the surface than ever after Harald's death, nearly sprang forth once again. 'I am committed to what is right, lady. I am surprised you would defend a statue of Uvoren, though. You had no great love for him.'

'We both know that is not the true debate.'

'Is it not? In that case, you might find yourself ill-prepared for what I have to say.'

'A risk I shall take,' said the historian. 'I am glad to see you well after last night's violence. That was unseemly.'

'That is who you have allied yourself to.'

'I would befriend worse against your husband.'

That felt like a stinging blow across the face.

Frathi nodded and walked past Keturah, calling over her shoulder: 'I trust your new child is well.'

That encounter was a relief, in some ways. It was as Keturah had thought: Frathi was more institution than woman, and had no regard for any personal feelings that might have caused her to bar Keturah from the Academy. In what remained of the day, Keturah sat through twenty chants, making mental notes of precedents and narratives, which she compared with Virtanen on the walk back.

'Look,' Virtanen diverted the conversation, gesturing at the passers-by who now stared at them curiously, but did not harass them. 'The game has been reset. After last night, nobody's sure what's normal any more. Show enough face, and we may be able to dictate the new rules.'

Keturah remembered the words of Sigurasta when she had first returned to the fortress. *Face is one thing you always had.* She would need it now.

That evening, she, Virtanen and Ormur carried firewood into the streets, using their own store as well as the wreckage that strewed the cobbles. In the last of the sun before it disappeared beneath the houses to either side, they built a pyre in the middle of the thoroughfare and laid Harald on top. He had been well known and well liked, and at the sight of his body, their neighbours began to emerge. By the time Keturah touched a flaming linen spill to the mass of shavings and splinters at the base of the pyre, a crowd of two-score had blocked each side of the street. The flames were low and dark; greenish smoke pouring from the damp fuel as the crowd looked on. Keturah observed the faces: sombre and reverential. The flames crackled higher and she took a breath. The first lines of the 'Hymn for the Departed' came out as a croak, but Ormur's voice joined her own, and Virtanen's an instant later. And the crowd began to murmur with them.

Numa, clutched in Keturah's arms, started to wail. Again, she made that noise Virtanen had taught, and again, the child hushed. Her throat was tightening, her vision melting. The words became a howl. Virtanen placed a massive hand on her back and she finished the chant crying in the Old Tongue until her throat tore. She turned furiously to meet the now-watching crowd. Some looked abashed. A dozen or so bowed to Keturah, and then, piece by piece, they dispersed.

All except one; a woman with a hood covering her face, who stepped forward.

'Good evening, Kaiho,' croaked Keturah, turning back to the pyre, the heat now so fierce she had to take a step back and shield Numa beneath her cloak.

'Good evening, my lady,' said Kaiho. 'As promised, I've found you some allies.'

'Very good,' said Keturah, eyes following the sparks howling up into the dusk. 'I am grateful. Has Talva agreed to help?'

'Not yet. I am hopeful she will come round, in time.'

'She will, when she sees that all of her friends have. So go away, and recruit me some others.'

16
Grendel

Bellamus left Stepan's house primarily relieved that his friend had made it home on his own. It was understandable he should be upset, and Bellamus himself was sick with guilt. But objectively he did not think he had done so much wrong, and the next day sent Stepan a letter, suggesting they go for a ride. It was returned unopened.

Undeterred, the next day he marched again on Stepan's house armed with wine, ginger and a pie still warm from the kitchen ovens, but his advance was ignored. After an hour of increasingly fraught exchanges with the servant manning the door, Bellamus was forced to turn and trudge home. There, he sat on his bed for more than an hour, simply staring at the wall. He only moved when a royal retainer arrived with a summons to the queen.

Sudden fear banished his guilt. He had allowed himself to become distracted, and remembering the queen's wrath, thought he should have ridden for Portmuthe while he had the chance. He was left with little choice but to follow the retainer to Aramilla's chambers.

He was shown inside, half expecting a death warrant, or a ceremony in which he would be stripped of his title, but instead found her smiling pleasantly at the sight of him.

'The Lord Upstart returns,' she declared, gesturing him in. Then she raised her eyebrows. 'You look troubled, my lord.'

Bellamus glanced about the quarters, looking for armed men, or watching nobles, but it seemed to be just the two of them. 'Just some ill news, Majesty. Of no consequence.'

'Nonsense, Safinim. What is it?'

Bellamus did not trust her good nature, but feared showing his surprise might frighten it away. He told her about Stepan's mission to retrieve his family, and what he had found.

'That's who you were helping? Sir Stepan, the knight? Tall and blond? Well let us have him at court, to take his mind off things. He always seemed most agreeable.'

Bellamus was stunned. This was the last reaction he had expected. 'I'm sure that would be appreciated.'

'The least I can do for a friend of yours.'

'I don't think he sees it that way any more.'

'Oh, hogwash, you did what you could for him. He'll realise you had no choice, soon enough. He and the rest of Suthdal are in your debt. Warriors specialist in Anakim fighting are flooding off the transport ships, thanks to your good judgement. And my reputation, of course,' she added.

There was no reference to her previous displeasure. She bade him sit and summoned breakfast, and Bellamus, once he understood he was not to be punished, found himself giddy with it, laughing riotously at her comments, and even tried to express enthusiasm for her summoning Stepan, despite his unease at how that gesture would be received.

The knight appeared in court the next day, a wreck of a man. His face had changed inconceivably, as though he had withdrawn from it. Before, blue eyes had glared out beneath a stern brow, wry and playful and sceptical. Now they were dull, and hesitant, and lost. It was as though he had reverted to some child-like state, where he had become a bit part in the drama of Suthdal, instead of the protagonist of his own tale.

He knelt before Aramilla's throne, carefully avoiding having to acknowledge Bellamus. 'Majesty,' he rasped.

'Rise, dear sir, rise. Any friend of Lord Safinim's is a friend of the court.'

Stepan stiffened at this, but said nothing.

'I wished to tell you, sir, that you can rely on us absolutely. Anything we can do to relieve the distress you must feel, shall be done.'

'Majesty,' he said hoarsely, meeting the queen's eyes fleetingly before he bowed once more. 'Will justice be done? Will those men responsible for what happened to my wife, my household, be brought to judgement?'

'Who did you have in mind, sir?'

'Garrett. Him and his bunch of wild men. Worse than brigands, Majesty. Worse than the Anakim and fighting beneath our banner, alongside good men.'

Aramilla glanced across at Bellamus. 'What say you, Lord Safinim? Can we have Garrett here on trial?'

Bellamus felt the colour drain from his face. She knew perfectly well they could not. Though a volatile ally, everything depended on the hybrid. Less than anything could they afford to alienate him. 'We're already making the Eoten-Draefend and his men toil in penitence, Majesty,' he murmured. 'They have a great deal to repay.'

Stepan's lip curled at this, but Aramilla seemed to think it would satisfy him. 'There, sir, Lord Safinim has it in hand.' She stood, motioning Stepan up, and in a display of extraordinary favouritism offered her arm. Stepan looked at it unwillingly, seeming to fear that by taking it he might trade-in the chance to punish his household's murderers. But he could hardly refuse. 'Sir Stepan and I are going to tour the grounds,' the queen announced to the court, as he gripped her arm stiffly. She beamed at him, leaning conspiratorially close and beginning to whisper as she led him out into the gardens.

'I don't know why I bothered,' huffed Aramilla, when she came back in to find Bellamus afterwards. 'Still moping and swearing vengeance on Garrett, the man can't be helped. Still, we'll keep him at court. It'll show I keep my word.'

'Good idea,' murmured Bellamus. This was the kind of work the queen engaged in while he supervised the defence of Suthdal. She barely glanced at the alliances he brokered, the money he poured into armour and fortifications, the ships being laid down, the constant stream of potent spirit delivered to Searoburgh, or the soldiers joining their cause from Erebos, each with a unique list of demands from the princes who supplied them.

Bellamus abstained all but necessary company, and though he felt exhausted, found he lay wide awake in bed each night, too hot for bedclothes. He took to long baths at night, which he would spend plucking absently at the hairs on his own chest, removing them one by one.

And sometimes he found himself standing at the end of the corridor that led to Vigtyr's quarters, his guts heavy, staring at the guards outside the door at the far end. He ought to sleep, but instead was taking uncertain steps closer to that door, ignoring the curious guards. 'Excuse me,' he murmured, raising a fist and knocking gently. Without waiting for a response he opened the door and peered around, stepping into the pitch-darkness beyond.

'Vigtyr?'

'Who's there?' came the sibilant voice in Anakim.

'Lord Safinim.' Bellamus stepped back outside and took the oil lamp hanging on a wall bracket so that he could see the turncoat. A tide of warm light revealed Vigtyr sat up in bed, blanket around his waist so that the ugly wound at his chest was exposed.

'Why are you here?' he asked, suspiciously. He did not seem to have been asleep.

Bellamus leaned against the wall, unsure as to the answer himself. 'I came to see if there was anything I could do for you.'

Vigtyr's eyes were narrowed to dark slits. 'Why?'

'In light of services you have rendered us . . . I feel you deserve better than your current condition.' Bellamus shrugged and cast about. 'Some proper quarters perhaps. This room is much too small for you.'

'That would be welcome,' said Vigtyr cautiously.

'And what else?'

Vigtyr watched Bellamus for some time before replying. 'I find, Lord Safinim, that I wish to fight. That is what I want now. I hear your people have great tournaments, in front of crowds. I'd like to partake in those.'

Bellamus raised his eyebrows at this request. He had expected Vigtyr to ask for some proper food, or better clothes, or female company. 'I will see what I can organise.'

There seemed no more to discuss with the Anakim, so he nodded and began backing out of the room.

The lamplight began to fade from Vigtyr's baffled countenance. 'Thank you, lord,' he said softly.

Bellamus nodded, and left him to the darkness. He could not make things right with Stepan. But that was not the only source of the great pool of guilt which seemed to have swallowed him up.

'You want Vigtyr to fight in a tournament?' asked Aramilla, when Bellamus broached this with her. It was noon the following day, and they walked Wiltun's battlements beneath a buoyant sky, Aramilla wearing the uniform of ivory and silver which she had adopted as her own.

'I worry we'll put off other informants, Majesty,' said Bellamus. 'If they cannot come here and be well-treated, it will make future spies think twice about helping us.'

'But he'd smash everyone, wouldn't he? That wouldn't go down well with the court. It wouldn't seem fair.'

Bellamus shrugged. 'We can see.'

'Well, if you think it will help, I grant you can move him to larger quarters,' she decreed. 'But I'm against this tournament business. Allow him to fight against nobles and it makes him their moral equals. Perhaps we could have him fight some beasts. A bear or a bull?'

'Never mind,' said Bellamus quickly. 'You're right, it's impossible.'

'It would be entertaining though,' she said, narrowing her eyes at the thought.

'Should you like to see how our workmen are progressing, Majesty?' Bellamus put in. 'I think you'll find yourself well satisfied.'

She glanced at him, amused by his distraction techniques. 'Not again. Old Grendel still suspects nothing of our plans?'

He blinked at those words. 'Where did you hear that name, Majesty?'

'What, Grendel?' She gave her magpie's rattle. 'You've forgotten your common roots, Lord Upstart. Everyone calls him Grendel now.'

'We should abstain,' said Bellamus, firmly.

She looked at him as though he had just spat on the stones. 'Is that so?' she replied, dangerously.

'We must not hand him such an easy victory,' Bellamus insisted. 'We must not call him *The Wolf*, or *Grendel*, or refer to his troops as devils or anything else. They are men. We will defeat them only if we think of them as men.'

She raised a pale eyebrow, and then latched onto his arm once more. 'You do keep me entertained, Lord Upstart. Your thoughts are always unique. How long until your grand plans are ready?'

'A month,' said Bellamus. 'If I can buy one more month, I believe we can hold them back. One month is all we need.'

17
Talva Radburnsdottir

Now when Keturah walked to the Academy, she did so with such an air of disdain that she was not harassed. There she would witness thirty or forty chants per day, Numa in her lap, hushing him with those soothing noises taught by Virtanen. Often they did not work, though she was coming to suspect that meant the babe required either feeding or changing.

Sometimes it felt as though order was returning to her life. Then she would remember that trial in the offing: rolling closer like a ship with foreign-cut sails. The thought made her palms prickle, and the week before, it was all that filled her head. She would spend long nights lying awake in her room, hot even with the woollen blankets kicked back.

The day before the trial, Virtanen entered the parlour to see Keturah calming Numa. He watched with interest and then nodded his approval. 'The Old Tongue. And unusually fast, my lady.'

Keturah shrugged at the herald and then inspected him more closely. He stood on the balls of his feet, leaning forward like a heron awaiting the moment a plump trout strays within range. 'You're bursting to tell me something, Virtanen. Out with it.'

Virtanen beamed and sat in one of the chairs with a flourish. 'Tore has withdrawn.'

'Has he?' Keturah supposed this was good news, though for weeks now she had been more worried by the Chief Historian.

'He did not look comfortable at the revelation that Kaiho is prepared to talk, and has decided he would rather save himself that embarrassment. I shall face only Frathi,' he concluded happily.

'Good then,' said Keturah, who had found this statement irritating for reasons she could not place. 'Anything else?'

'Kaiho reports the Chief Historian intends to use Unndor and Urthr as witnesses. She's been preparing them, so they can be cross-examined for evidence of Roper's abuse of the courts.'

'Come now, surely not,' said Keturah. 'That would be too easy.'

Kaiho had done exactly as Keturah requested, calling in every favour and friend she had in the fortress. Many had been desperate to help, distancing themselves from the Lothbrok mob who had proven so unruly. But most valuable of all would be Talva, that notorious gossip whose great pleasure it was to accrue power by bedding as much of the fortress as possible. Above all, Keturah wanted what she knew. Nothing seemed as likely to even the odds for them before the trial began, but so far she had proven stubbornly resistant.

Keturah got to her feet and began pacing the parlour. 'The key to this,' she said, brushing aside Virtanen's news like shavings on a workshop floor, 'will be the illusion of public consensus. The Ephors have no precedents for something like this to guide them: they will not dare go against the crowd when it has proven so volatile. Win over the crowd, and the Ephors will follow.'

'My lady, you can be sure the crowd will be stuffed with Lothbroks, as it was in the marketplace riot. Tore is trying to make it look as though the whole Hindrunn is on his side, when really it is the biddable, and a handful of thugs driving them.'

'Precisely,' said Keturah. 'That is why we need as many allies as possible to drown out his unsavoury coalition.'

'Almost every man left in this fortress,' said Virtanen carefully, 'is one of Tore's legionaries. On your side it shall be almost exclusively women. I would be trying to convince wives and mothers to go up against soldiers.'

'To be frank, Virtanen, I don't think you know what this fortress is like when the legions are away,' she replied. 'Men are largely irrelevant. This is our fortress. We own most of the property, occupy most of the remaining positions of power, and the prospect of mass derision is enough to stop those legionaries using the only weapon available to them: crude physical strength. In fact,' she said grimly, 'I should like nothing more than if they try. Imagine how quickly Tore would fall if his legionaries were to become violent against the women of the fortress.'

'It is a brave plan,' murmured Virtanen.

'Keep your gloomy euphemisms to yourself. Winning the crowd is quite achievable; Frathi is too straight for such games. She will address her arguments to the Ephors, and you will outflank her.'

'I'm not sure,' said Virtanen. 'A crowd quickly forgets. The Ephors less so. As it is our side bringing the case against Uvoren's statue, I shall go first, and Frathi, speaking for the defence, will go second. A case targeting the emotions of the crowd would be better suited to the concluding spot, after the prosecution has fired its shot and been forgotten.'

'Perhaps. Not an option though. We are bringing the case, we can't speak second. And with the Ephors out to punish Roper for his purge, they won't rule against Frathi unless they're forced to. And only the crowd can force that.'

They spent the day practising Virtanen's arguments, Keturah playing Frathi's part and interrupting with objections and counter-blows. She felt itchy, striding the parlour faster than ever, Numa laughing as he was borne along as on a tide of white water.

'May I give you some advice, my lady?' Virtanen asked, stopping her with two gentle hands.

'I don't believe in advice, Virtanen,' she said, avoiding his eye. 'You never know when you're speaking to someone desperate enough to take it.'

'Nonetheless, my lady, you seem nervous. We are committed now. We must simply do our best.'

'It is not nerves, Virtanen. As always, the worst of it is indecision.'

'You wonder if we should quit the fortress?'

'Heavens, no,' said Keturah, looking at him fiercely. 'No . . . Virtanen, I must be the one to speak. At the trial, it must come from me. I am the Black Lady. I am the one Uvoren poisoned. I cannot hide behind you.'

The herald showed no surprise, but he looked at her carefully, as though assessing her sobriety. 'As you say, you are the Black Lady, whereas I am just a mouthpiece. If I stand up there, and lose, they will let me walk away. You know what happens if you do it?'

Keturah met his eye. She ran over all they had prepared in her head, testing her knowledge of the arguments. She toyed with the words: *You're right. You'd do it better than I* and found they repulsed her. Neither did she believe them. 'I do,' she said firmly.

Virtanen gave his crooked, brawler's smile. 'I'll admit, I've never practised these arguments as though I'd actually deliver them myself.'

So they rehearsed, and time slipped through Keturah's fingers. Ormur kept hold of the fractious Numa, and occasionally fortified their staged debates with roasted burdock, dried mutton and elderberry wine. Even so, both became prickly as the day wore on. 'Do not make the mistake of succumbing to emotion,' Virtanen advised. 'You'll enchant those already on your side, but alienate the undecided.'

'I am angry though,' said Keturah. 'I want these idiots to know how stupid they've been.'

'Naturally. But they might come to the conclusion that you're unbalanced, rather than that they're foolish.'

Keturah narrowed her eyes, but was interrupted by a hammering at the door.

'Allow me,' said Virtanen. He disappeared, but it was not he who led the way back into the room.

Instead, there came two women. The first was blonde-haired, with eyes the blue of daylight. At the sight of Keturah, she narrowed her eyes in something close to a smile. Keturah raised her hands to her mouth. 'Sigrid?' It seemed so unlikely she was here that Keturah almost did not recognise her old friend. Then she crossed the parlour and embraced her, leaning her head into her shoulder. 'My friend!' They broke apart, Keturah still reeling from her appearance. 'What are you doing here?'

'All the historians left the army when Frathi did,' said Sigrid, beaming. 'She rode ahead, the rest of us travelled north with Pryce's Convoy. But who have we here?' she asked, approaching Ormur and the bundle treasured in his arms. 'Don't deprive me Keturah, who is *this*?'

'Of course, you've not met,' said Keturah proudly. 'May I introduce Numa Roperson?'

Sigrid asked the solemn permission of Ormur, and then scooped the baby up in her arms. She cooed and babbled at it, while Keturah turned to the woman who had followed Sigrid into the parlour.

'Talva,' she observed, raising her eyebrows. 'I had rather given up on your coming to visit us.'

At the eleventh hour, Talva Radburnsdottir had crossed their threshold. She was red-haired, her teeth yellowish, her profile rather square and more usually described as handsome, than beautiful. Nevertheless, there was a pleasing lack of self-consciousness in her manner, as though she relished showing herself off. It reminded Keturah of how she had once felt.

'It's always such fun to see you, my love,' she replied. 'You needn't have worried.'

'Or perhaps Sigrid here persuaded you.'

'She's a persuasive character,' said Talva. She did not seem prepared to engage, and Keturah turned back to Sigrid.

'What did you mean, "Pryce's Convoy"?'

Sigrid looked up. 'You heard about Pryce?'

'About his death.'

'Yes. And his embalming?'

Keturah was stunned. 'They embalmed him?' It was a once-in-a-generation honour, but if she had thought about it, she supposed she might have expected it. It had not occurred to her that it might be done to someone she had known.

'They did. We brought his body back here. We were to put it beside the temple, but I fear we could not do that safely. The mood is ugly.'

'Well, indeed. So where is he now?'

'Our house,' said Sigrid. 'I couldn't think of anywhere else it would be safe.'

With the rehabilitation of Uvoren, Pryce was a more controversial figure than he had been. It was he who had executed the captain, in an act now viewed as murder. If his body were found at Sigrid's house, it would place her in great danger.

Keturah turned back to Talva. 'Well out with it,' she said, too frayed for games. 'You surely aren't here for a social call. Will you declare for our side?'

Talva looked a little deflated by this brusqueness. Her attention slipped off Keturah, past Sigrid and the babbling Numa, and diverted to a wooden globe, nestling in a cradle. Talva caressed it briefly and moved on to a tapestry hung on the wall: a vast serpent, devouring the roots of a tree. 'I don't know that my declaring for any side will make a difference,' she said distantly.

'She'll help,' said Sigrid, not looking up from Numa. 'Won't you, Talva?'

Talva shrugged, regarding Keturah as though it were she being aloof. 'I know some people who could.'

Keturah just looked at her flatly.

'Two of those who are passing judgement tomorrow,' prompted Sigrid, nodding pointedly at Talva.

Keturah took a breath. 'You know something which would compromise two of the Ephors?'

Talva shrugged, her expression mild.

Keturah was suspicious. 'How?'

'The usual way.'

Keturah grinned in spite of herself. 'You old wildcat.'

Talva raised her eyebrows and fell into a seat by the fire. She glanced at Virtanen, now standing by the parlour door, and gave the herald a frank assessment, from boots worn to suede, up to his flattened nose and swollen ears. For the first time that Keturah had seen, Virtanen looked bashful, and was averting his eyes.

'How long ago?' Keturah pressed. 'The youngest is a hundred and fifty. And badly weathered at that.'

'Well, not so long,' said Talva, still looking at Virtanen. 'I doubt they'd have been so pleased to betray their wives in the days that they had more options. Men love validation, Keturah.' She moved and spoke, Keturah thought, as though slightly drunk, but that was just her way.

Keturah sat opposite her, and Talva finally looked away from the herald. Relieved, Virtanen seemed to assume he was dismissed and ushered Ormur from the room.

'Come back soon,' Talva called after him.

Keturah snapped her fingers to draw Talva's attention back to her. 'So I take it this isn't common knowledge.'

'No,' said Talva.

'Which two?'

'Sentur. Valkin.'

'And you think they would be resistant to that information becoming public?'

'Don't you?' Both were married.

'I do, rather,' said Keturah. She pondered. 'What do you want for it?'

Talva still looked a little unwilling, and Sigrid came to stand next to her. 'She wants you to beat Tore.'

Talva shrugged, and then added suddenly, 'Well, beat him, and then, as a favour, destroy Urthr Uvorenson.'

'Destroy . . .' repeated Keturah, looking at Talva. She displayed her emotions so openly that many considered her to be indulgent, and un-Anakim, but Keturah had never seen her angry before. Yet there it was: fury, from the foundations of her face.

'Just make sure that whatever happens, that man cannot return to polite society.'

Keturah watched Talva intently. 'You've never really been one for polite society, my dear.' Talva looked suddenly pleased and the two of them shared a grin. 'Destroying Urthr would be my pleasure,' said Keturah. 'I'm quite certain we have a deal there. But how to use this new leverage?'

Talva seemed more engaged now and threw a glance at the ceiling as if to say that was obvious. 'Ask them to rule in your favour.'

'Two of five Ephors, not a majority,' said Keturah thoughtfully. 'So a wasted shot, unless we can get the crowd on our side. And if we do that, we've won anyway.' She thought a moment longer and then snapped her fingers. 'I have it. Would you pay a visit to your two old lovers this afternoon, my dear?'

18
Keturah's Army

Keturah did not sleep the night before the trial. She and Virtanen skittered about the parlour, spending quite as much time brewing hot drinks and staring silently at the floor as they did polishing their arguments.

'You have a natural poise,' Virtanen observed. 'I think when you're feeling anxious it doesn't show like you think it does.'

'I never get anxious,' Keturah declared, and immediately felt a fool. That was pathetically transparent, and she knew she had only said it for Virtanen's benefit. She felt herself blushing and neither of them spoke for some time afterwards.

Dawn, when it came, made Keturah think she would be sick. Her stomach seemed to have a fire lit beneath it, boiling away the contents. Worst of all was the knowledge that she could simply hand this responsibility to Virtanen, and watch him execute it with his usual aplomb.

The herald, who had spent the final two hours dozing in a chair, awoke suddenly and caught sight of the dusty light beneath the front door. 'Time has stolen a march on me. Are you ready, my lady?'

She took a deep breath. 'Who ever is?'

The two of them put on their cloaks, Keturah lingering on the feel of it for any distraction. Ormur, who was to stay and take care of Numa, watched them in silence. Virtanen smiled encouragingly at Keturah, she nodded back, and they stepped outside.

There was a crowd waiting for them. The street was crammed with people, almost all of them women clutching iron pots and wooden spoons, though some men stood with them. At the front were Sigrid, Kaiho and Talva, who stepped forward to greet her.

'Three cheers for the Black Lady!' declared Talva, and the crowd clattered into life, beating pots with spoons. In spite of everything, that made Keturah beam. She embraced Sigrid first, and then the other two, before she acknowledged the crowd. She was tall enough to see over most, and could see the party was some two-hundred strong. She had hoped for more.

'Thank you, peers, thank you all for coming,' she called. 'Come. There is nothing to hold us here. To the keep!'

The procession set off. The iron pots rang as they passed through each district, so that they sounded like a parade. Talva, relishing the spotlight as Keturah could not, began a war-hymn which was taken up by the rest. Keturah found herself joining in, and at the noise, hundreds of heads were thrust from their windows to stare into the streets. Many just watched the parade pass by, but others, sensing something historic, rushed out to swell their ranks.

'Come join Keturah's army!' Talva shouted, doing an entirely passable impression of a lictor.

For the first time since she had returned, Keturah felt she commanded these streets, and the momentum of their little column grew apace. By the time their band reached the Central Keep, clanking, singing and cheering, Keturah could see no end to those gathered behind her. Of those she could see, almost none were familiar; doubtless many here only for the spectacle. She could not yet count on their support, but still thought this must be how Roper felt, riding Zephyr at the head of his legions.

Roper. She wanted to retch, but doing this felt easier knowing she was helping him. *For you, my love.*

A platform had been constructed on the steps of the keep, twenty feet above a crowd of rough-looking men who had gathered beneath it. They turned to her and hissed, but Virtanen's voice slashed through them like a cannonball. 'Stand aside you dogs! Aside, move there!' They kept hissing, but jostled back to allow a path to the front. Keturah's crowd pushed in, forcing the path wider. As she had hoped, the Lothbrok supporters were not prepared to be rough against a party of women, and her own followers matched Tore's for volume. But following behind her came a growing mob of the undeclared. They were the ones she would have to convince.

Virtanen took the cloak from her shoulders, then turned her head to face him with a soft hand on her cheek, before clasping her hand warmly in his massive paws. 'You are ready, my lady.' The smile she returned felt tremulous. She squeezed his hand in response but was already looking up at that platform. Heart thudding, she began to climb the stairs.

As she emerged above the crowd, it erupted at the sight of her, making her legs tremble like grass stalks in a gale. The platform was rough-split chestnut, which sang like thrushes when she stepped onto it. Already waiting were the Chief Historian and the five Ephors in their eagle-feather cloaks, kneeling at the back and talking between themselves. The Chief Historian raised an eyebrow at the vast entourage Keturah had brought with her, and Keturah was surprised to find she could look the tall historian in the eye. 'What sort of contest is this to be, Tekoasdottir?' asked Frathi, inscrutable as ever.

'That is up to us, lady,' said Keturah, civilly, but she could not tell if Frathi had heard as the crowd beneath them boiled over. They were roaring, the Lothbroks vying with Keturah's entourage for control of the soundscape. Her lungs were pumping like she had hiccoughs and the people beneath stirred and heaved.

One of the Ephors, Sentur, stood and moved to the front of the platform, raising his hands. The crowd quietened, but still murmured and called restlessly.

'Peers!' bellowed the Ephor. 'You here are witnesses to an ancient and sacred tradition. You are the many eyes of the Almighty here, present to ensure we conduct ourselves in a manner befitting his servants and his kingdom. I remind you to behave as such.' He left a pause to test the impatient crowd, which they were barely equal to. 'We deliberate on the statue of Uvoren the Mighty, lately constructed at the entrance to the fortress . . .' Sentur was forced to pause as a mixed cheer and hiss erupted at the mention of Uvoren's name. He adopted a posture which suggested that the crowd had let itself down and waited for silence to resume. '*Against*: Lady Keturah Tekoasdottir, who alleges the statue is unlawfully constructed. *In favour*: Lady Frathi Akisdottir, who declares it legal.' The Ephor paused, and Keturah held her breath. 'The trial shall last two days. As the statue was constructed without permission being sought in the first instance, Lady Frathi shall be obliged to make the case for it on the first day.'

A great stirring came over the crowd and Keturah felt a flood of relief wash over her. 'Almighty bless Talva,' she murmured, the blessing drowned even to her own ears by a shout of anger which Keturah was sure belonged to Tore, standing somewhere in the mass below. The advantage, as all knew, lay in speaking second: the position traditionally occupied by the defence. This was how they had spent Talva's unique influence: framing Keturah as the defender, who would have the last word.

Frathi was unmoved by this news. She merely gave her single-shouldered shrug, as if to say justice would be done either way, and it would be done in her favour.

'Lady Frathi will speak today,' the Ephor continued, and Keturah thought she could hear anger in his voice. 'On the second day, Lady Keturah will speak against the statue. And when she is finished, we shall deliver our judgement.'

The Ephor turned aside and nodded curtly at Frathi, gesturing her forward. Then he nodded at Keturah and together they retired to the back of the platform, Keturah kneeling like the Ephors as she watched the old historian step forward. For perhaps the first time that Keturah had ever seen, Frathi looked amused. She raised her hands.

'My lords,' she began.

19
Frathi's Case

It was an autumn day to die on. Frathi stood above a heaving human tide, a cornflower sky behind. 'My lords,' she inclined her head to the Ephors. 'My peers,' she looked out over the crowd beneath. 'We gather today not to discuss a statue.' She dismissed this with her hand. 'But what this statue represents, and whether we were right to install it. I shall tell you what it is: a symbol that we will not acquiesce to the wishes of a tyrant. One who slaughters esteemed peers without trial, dismantles our ancient institutions, spends our menfolk as freely as acorns after harvest and bends an entire kingdom to his ambitions.'

She cut an impressive figure, lean, tall and fierce; the platform beneath a mere serving dish on which she was the centrepiece, offered up to the crowds.

'Roper Kynortasson spirited away your men for a decades-long undertaking, which he had you believe was a summer raid. This much is certain. Today, I shall prove to you that he has done worse. I shall prove that he ordered Uvoren the Mighty hacked to bits, so that his soul will travel the earth in torment from that day until the last. I shall show you that he twisted the courts in order to secure his own throne last year. And I watched with my own eyes as he dismantled the final check on his power, and turned his legionaries against the ancient institution of the Kryptea.'

'So you say!' called Keturah sceptically.

Frathi froze as though Keturah had thrown something. Then she turned jerkily so she could see Keturah, who suddenly knew she had made an error. 'Indeed I do. But since you doubt me, Lady Keturah, why don't we call upon another witness who was present? One who I'm sure you'll agree has the most impeccable character. The herald who has worked with you – Virtanen, I believe he's called – perhaps he'd agree to testify? I see him there,' Frathi pointed down at the audience, who recoiled from where Virtanen stood so that he was suddenly alone in a clearing. With a single imperious finger, Frathi beckoned him up to the platform. 'Come, sir. Let us go no further before we've established the truth of this.'

Keturah cursed herself. If she were to win this, she would need to pick her battles. It was a blunder to have allowed Frathi this opportunity to strengthen her own case.

Stiffly, Virtanen ascended the steps to the platform, observing Frathi as though she were a cannon on which the fuse was fizzing. The crowd sensed its own part in this and had tensed like a predator, frozen and straining with attention.

'I name you Virtanen Lanterison, a senior peer in the guild of heralds,' Frathi began, striding across the split grain of the platform.

'Correct.' It was as close as Keturah had ever heard to a mumble from Virtanen.

'And by the ancient traditions of your esteemed order, you are bound to speak the truth absolutely.'

'Yes.'

'Describe to us the speech made at the embalming ceremony for Pryce the Wild – one of the thousands lost at Lundenceaster. In particular, we wish to hear what Lord Roper said with regard to the Kryptea.'

'In fact, Pryce Rubenson did not die during the successful

sacking of Suthdal's capital,' said Virtanen suavely. 'He was killed shortly after.'

'Indeed,' said Frathi, giving the crowd an amused glance at this prevarication. 'We shall get to that, I assure you. Now, to the matter at hand, sir. Please describe the speech.'

Virtanen looked at her unhappily. *Lie*, thought Keturah, desperately hoping Virtanen would save her from her own blunder. *Just lie*.

'As I recall, Lord Roper revealed to the army that the Kryptea had ordered him to turn back and bring the legions home.'

'And what was the effect of this address on the legions?'

'I should imagine it affected each differently.' The beast beneath them – the crowd – let out a low hiss of frustration. Keturah sensed the neutrals begin to align with Frathi for the first time. Virtanen had to tell the truth.

'Yet I'm sure you'll agree there was a general mood in the aftermath,' said Frathi, watching the herald play into her hands. 'Please describe it.'

Virtanen was trapped. 'Generally speaking,' he allowed, 'the legions were emboldened to remain in the south.'

'And how did they behave towards the Kryptea?'

Virtanen hesitated. 'There was some anger towards them.'

'And did you witness physical hostility from the legions towards the Master of the Kryptea, Jokul, in the wake of this address?'

'I did,' said Virtanen stiffly. The crowd began to murmur and Virtanen suddenly boomed in his herald's voice: 'Though the Master was unharmed!'

'And in your truthful opinion,' Frathi shot back, 'was this the effect that Lord Roper had intended his speech to have? To create hostility between the legions and the Kryptea?'

'I cannot speak to Lord Roper's motivations, my lady.'

The beast before the platform began to stir. 'Shame!' someone shouted, and there was a swell of approval.

'Thank you, Virtanen,' said Frathi with a trace of satisfaction. 'That is all for now.' Red-faced and furious, Virtanen began to descend the steps. Frathi inclined her head at Keturah. 'I trust that satisfies you, Lady Keturah.'

Keturah did not reply. She had learned this first thing about her tradition-bound opponent: she was not above a little theatre.

'Let us waste no more time,' Frathi declared, striding back across the platform. 'It is beyond doubt Lord Roper turned the army against the Kryptea. This is in contradiction to the wisdom of our ancestors, who deemed that office an essential check on the Black Lord's ambitions. But which side does historical narrative support? Our young Black Lord? Or the wisdom of our ancestors? Six occupants of the Stone Throne have been executed at Kryptean hands . . .'

Not to mention hundreds of innocents, Keturah thought. She knew that before her shaky opening she would have said that out loud. Now she was too uncertain.

All of history was at Frathi's fingertips, and she launched into a narrative which, in spite of herself, Keturah found compelling. She made it seem unarguable that the Kryptea performed the very function for which it had been formed, frightening the otherwise untouchable Black Lords into ruling justly.

'The common objection to this, of course,' she said at one point, 'is that the noble office of Ephors already fills this role. They can declare a Black Lord outlaw, and summon him before the court for punishment. This, people say, means there is no need for the Kryptea. But as we have seen over and over, the Ephors cannot control a man who commands legions. Much as they might try, they are public officials, whom the Black Lord can intimidate with his superior military power, or ignore, or simply murder.

'The Kryptea, by contrast, are anonymous. They live entirely in the shadows, excepting the Master, who allows them a public face. They are immune to the blunt power invested in the Stone Throne. They are essential, and Lord Roper knows this. That is why he has chosen to tear them down.'

It was a murderously effective opening battery from Frathi. Keturah threw a glance at the five Ephors and saw them nodding vigorously at each point. The inclusion of how impotent their office was against the Black Lord's legions was well-judged. Their fear would make them harsh.

The crowd was growing restless, with occasional shouts and angry exclamations floating up to the platform, which Frathi inflamed expertly. 'Six tyrants the Kryptea have executed, but the need would have been many more had it not been for the band of assassins, which the Black Lord could feel scrutinising his every move. They have been our shield from the first day the cuckoo spread its wings.'

When she finished, the morning was in its adolescence, and Frathi called for a break. Tore's legionaries infiltrated the crowd with skins of tart elderberry wine and hot flatbreads; a gesture Keturah could not afford herself.

Frathi was impatient to continue, allowing the crowd just quarter of an hour to buzz and chew before she was upright once more and waving a hand for their attention. 'Come, come, come, let us examine the record of the outlawed Roper Kynortasson, and what treatment he deserves from us. I call my second witness; the Master of the Hindrunn, Vinjar Kristvinson.'

Keturah scowled as the portly Vinjar hauled his false title onto the platform. There he was interviewed civilly, Frathi thanking the Master for having taken the time to appear at the trial.

It was the Master's pleasure.

The whole fortress was grateful, Frathi was sure, that he continued to serve so diligently after his wrongful disgrace last year. How had that come about?

Vinjar recalled his shock at being accused of adultery by a woman with whom he had a casual acquaintance, nothing more.

Keturah watched Vinjar sweat on the sun-blasted platform. He looked dreadful: the transition from prison-ship to bloated opulence making him puffy and berry-red. He concluded with the significant observation that many of Uvoren's closest friends had faced trial around the time of his disgrace.

'Your own wife condemned you!' Keturah interrupted impatiently.

'Lady Keturah, either make your objections in the proper fashion or be silent,' called Valkin, a senior Ephor.

'We will come to Sigurasta in good time,' said Frathi, waving a hand. 'I have a more pressing question. The Master of the Hindrunn reminds us that many of Uvoren's closest allies were dragged down last year. Too many to be coincidence. So who was responsible? Who was it who condemned Vinjar? Who abused the courts for their own ends, and made a mockery of the Ephors?' She left the question hanging, before nodding brusquely to herself. 'I call my next witness, Aslaug Yversdottir!'

A slight figure was ushered onto the stage: a cringing, crouching woman who kept her eyes fixed on Frathi so as to avoid acknowledging the watching crowd. She had black hair and dark blue eyes set tight to the sides of a narrow nose.

'Now unfortunately,' said Frathi by way of introduction, 'Ukalek Aktalsdottir, the woman with whom Vinjar was accused of adultery, died earlier this year.'

Keturah rolled her eyes. 'That's convenient!' The crowd gave a surprised hoot of laughter.

Frathi overrode this noise. 'But here we have Lady Aslaug, who can shed some light on this situation. Please tell us – and speak loudly so all can hear – of the exchange you witnessed between Ukalek and the notorious traitor – Vigtyr the Quick.'

That was the first time Vigtyr's name had been spoken that day, and it shot through the crowd like a crack through ice. There was an interval, somewhere between a silence and a collective inhalation, before a fierce muttering swept the throng.

Vigtyr. They all knew of his treachery by now. Had Roper's disgrace not hung over the fortress, it would have been all anyone talked about. He had been famous, and well-regarded, and a fortress-favourite for appointment to the Sacred Guard. Then flashing over the Hindrunn like a summer blaze had come the news that he was that worst of things: a traitor, consorting with their great enemy, Bellamus of Safinim. Most people, it transpired, had never liked him anyway. He had seemed *off*: a little distant, a little catty. It was no wonder none of his marriages had lasted.

Frathi galloped through the interrogation. Aslaug had been a maid in Ukalek's household for two years when she had seen her mistress receive a visitor she knew by reputation: Vigtyr the Quick. He had come to her during the day and ordered that she was to accuse Vinjar – then Councillor for Agriculture – of adultery.

'And why would Ukalek acquiesce to this request of Vigtyr's?' demanded Frathi, so fiercely that Aslaug was visibly cowed. 'If it was untrue, why would it be in her interest to appear before the Ephors and testify against a respected peer?'

Aslaug hesitated and then mumbled a reply inaudible even to Keturah, kneeling just yards away.

'Speak up!' Frathi snapped. 'The whole fortress must hear. Why did Ukalek yield to Vigtyr?'

'The traitor had some leverage over her,' Aslaug murmured. 'She was in his debt somehow, and he was blackmailing her.'

Keturah stood now, making her first formal interruption. Irritably, Valkin allowed her to speak. 'Be quick about it, Lady Keturah.'

'I shall, my lord. I just wanted to know why Aslaug here had held her tongue until now. She claims to have discerned the mechanism by which a councillor was fraudulently accused and convicted – yet for more than a year, she said nothing.'

Aslaug did not reply. She merely watched Keturah tremulously until, exasperated, Keturah called, 'You're supposed to answer, Aslaug. Why have you only come forward now?'

Aslaug glanced at Frathi and licked her lips. 'Vigtyr,' she muttered. 'I was scared of Vigtyr. He knew I'd seen them talk.

If anyone had found out about his threat, he'd have known it was me. I'd have been killed.'

Frathi shrugged. 'Even from this brief interview, it should not be hard to believe Aslaug was as cowed as she describes,' she observed brutally. The crowd was not really interested in Keturah's objection. They itched to hear more about Vigtyr, and Frathi indulged them.

Aslaug was dismissed, and the next witness was Vinjar's wife, Sigurasta. Through a stream of tears, Sigurasta choked that she had been forced to testify against her husband, who could never have done as he was accused.

'And who forced you to speak against your own husband?'

Vigtyr.

Again, that name was uttered, and this time there came a low hiss from the crowd. Keturah felt an iron-clad foreboding settle upon her. It was obvious where Frathi was taking this.

Next to stand upon the platform and protest their innocence were Unndor and Urthr, accused of rape and cowardice. More witnesses were produced, exceedingly dubious to Keturah's eye but prepared to tell the crowds exactly what they wanted to hear. Who had fabricated the evidence against these two brave legionaries?

Vigtyr.

More witnesses appeared, linking Vigtyr with the immolation of Baldwin, who had been an old and influential friend of Uvoren's.

'We have learned,' said Frathi, striding across the platform as the last of the witnesses were ushered away, 'that last year, the courts faced a terrible abuse. Uvoren's closest allies were targeted unjustly, each of them torn down and their lives destroyed at the hands of Vigtyr the Quick. It must be obvious that the purpose of these baseless attacks was to undermine Uvoren, and evidently they were successful. When Uvoren was at last executed at Harstathur – hacked to bits without trial, as any number of witnesses will attest – no one spoke out in his defence. Who, then, benefited from the ruin and death of the Captain of the Sacred Guard?' Frathi left that question hanging in the air, and the crowd stared up in rapt attention. They would all be thinking of the same man. Sweat slid down Keturah's back.

'I call my final witness,' said Frathi in a much softer voice than she had used so far that day. 'Sindri Steinnson!'

This final witness was familiar not just to Keturah, but to the whole crowd. Sindri was a blacksmith, famous throughout the kingdom. He was short, stout and powerful, his hair tied in a flamboyant high ponytail, which was a horrendous breach of etiquette. The high ponytail was reserved for lords and Sacred Guardsmen, and by sporting one in public, Sindri was declaring himself a lord among smiths. However, this assessment was so undeniably accurate that his hairstyle had at first been tolerated, and was now celebrated. Only a figure so unapologetic could carry it off, but that was Sindri. Irascible, self-indulgent, judgemental and wildly talented, he stood over the crowd, quite unabashed by their attention, an arresting figure for his strength of body and character.

Frathi moved to the back of the platform and when she returned, was holding something long and narrow, wrapped in cloth. She unfurled it brusquely and cast the cloth aside, holding the object above the audience. It was a sheathed sword, the handle of which shone like silk in the late afternoon sun.

'I name you Sindri Steinnson,' said Frathi, still holding the sword aloft and not looking at the blacksmith.

'Correct.'

'And for those unfamiliar with your work, what is your profession?'

'I make the finest swords in the world,' he said frankly.

'And this sword I am holding now, whose handiwork is this?'

'Mine.'

'And can we be certain of that?'

'You can be certain because it's peerless,' said Sindri. 'But if you need further proof, you will observe my maker's mark at the base of the blade. The Antlered Man.'

Frathi crossed the platform and held the sword hilt out to one of the Ephors. 'Perhaps you'd confirm this for those too far to see, my lord.'

The Ephor drew the blade by six inches and nodded, sliding it back into the scabbard. 'It bears the mark.'

'Undeniably the work of Sindri, then,' said Frathi, returning to occupy the centre of the platform. 'Do you recall forging this sword, sir?'

'Of course.'

'How's that? You must've forged thousands of swords. How is it that you remember this one so clearly?'

Sindri held out a hand, gazing at the weapon as though it were a dog being coaxed back to an old master. Frathi yielded it to him and with a flourish, Sindri drew the sword so that it flashed over the stage. There was unmistakable artistry in its profile, the alloy clean as a shard of ice. But it was the handle that the blacksmith directed them towards, gripping the blade between two fingers so that the dark blanks riveted to the tang were visible. 'This is rosewood,' he declared. 'When milled and oiled as I have here, its properties are exceptional. It will never warp or crack, and time will have no more effect on it than on the blade itself. The wood is exceedingly strong and dense. Its grain is so straight and free from knots that it is able to transmit energy into the blade as cleanly as a whip. Couple that with an alloy pure as a mountain spring, and you have an edge that will cut wood like fruit, and shatter all but the best swords that it comes up against. It is flawless. The tool of a master swordsman, and just twice in my life have I made a sword with a rosewood handle. I should not forget it.'

'Why?' pressed the Chief Historian. 'If it is as fine as you say, why have you only produced such a sword twice?'

'Rosewood is not native to Albion, nor even Erebos. It comes from the furthest corners of the earth and bringing it here is prohibitively expensive.'

'And such an unusually fine sword, with such a handle, must take weeks to make?'

'Months.'

'So this is surely a work of commission? You would only stand such expense if you were assured of a buyer at the end.'

'Of course. I made it at the instruction of Lord Roper Kynortasson.'

There came a gasp from the crowd, and then a muttering ran from one end to the other. Dread was stealing over Keturah. She felt as if that name, from that man, were her own death sentence.

Frathi held up an imperious hand but otherwise did not acknowledge the disturbance. 'Lord Roper famously uses the weapon Cold-Edge. Why did he need another of such quality? What did he do with it?'

'This sword was named Warspite. And it hung at the belt of Vigtyr the Quick.'

Frathi kept the crowd silent with her hand to indicate she was not yet done. 'So, Lord Roper gave one of the finest blades you have ever produced to Vigtyr the Quick. What service could possibly have merited such a gift?'

'An exceptionally great one,' observed the smith.

Frathi turned away, walking deliberately across the stage. 'Peers, this is no casual gift from lord to subject. This is payment; remuneration for the man who secured his throne and reduced a great enemy to his knees.' She raised her hands to the sky, planted her feet on the platform, and in the tones of a vulture, she cried: 'Is he not guilty?'

As the crowd began to roar, Keturah kept her face composed and crossed her arms, as though what Frathi said were amusing and interesting. But it was all she could do not to flee from the stage. The crowd was seething and spitting, and she could see Virtanen being jostled violently for even his minor association with Roper.

Frathi was still declaiming above the noise. 'Lord Roper worked alongside the vilest criminal imaginable in Vigtyr the

Quick!' she cried. 'Together, they manipulated the courts into bringing down Uvoren, one of the great heroes of our generation! Twice winner of the Prize of Valour, Captain of the Sacred Guard! Peers, Lord Roper speaks pretty words: it is why his legionaries follow him so willingly.'

Keturah bristled at that. It was *not*. The legionaries followed because Roper was decisive, and brave, and did all he asked of them and more.

'He claims to be a servant to this realm. But if you want to know what a man believes – what he truly believes – don't ask him. Watch him. Watch what he does. Tell me, is it he who serves this kingdom? Or the kingdom who serves him? Are the Kryptea unaccountable and corrupt, or are they a necessary check on the ambitions of a tyrant? Was Uvoren justly executed for crimes against the kingdom, or was he murdered by a ruler without conscience?' The crowd was baying, and Frathi could barely be heard now.

'Lord Roper has done all this, and more. If that is not worth outlawry, I do not know what is. If that is not worth rehabilitating our unjustly murdered hero Uvoren, then I do not know what is. The statue remains!' Frathi lowered a quivering finger at Keturah and looked her full in the face. 'And Lord Roper dies!'

20
Rangalist

Roper had taken one half of the army, Tekoa the other, and they besieged one city after another. Next to fall had been Norantone.

Roper arrived at the city and issued an ultimatum, which at first the city resisted. But they had come prepared for this, and showed Norantone what had happened to Northwic's defenders. Using broad fabric slings, they tossed mouldering Suthern heads into the streets for two and a half hours. Before they were even done, the gates were dragged half-open and then abandoned. No white flag was raised. No herald came out to invite Roper inside. They did not want the smallest interaction with the Anakim.

Onwards.

They ripped down the walls and marched for Beormaton. A herald arrived from Tekoa's army reporting that Theodford had surrendered and he was besieging Oxenaford. He did not know how long they would take to submit.

Roper nodded. 'My compliments to the legate. Carry on.'

The herald hesitated, realised that was Roper's full message, bowed and wheeled his horse around. Gray, Leon and two of the legionaries who had attached themselves to the Sacred Guard, walked alongside Roper, and started laughing as soon as the messenger was out of earshot.

'Economical, lord,' said Yngvar, one of the score of legionaries who had volunteered to defend Roper from the Kryptea. They had stayed with him ever since, adopted as honorary guardsmen and now known ironically as the Belated Guard.

'Tekoa isn't a dog,' said Roper. 'That herald wasn't sent in the vain hope I'd return him with a pat on the head. He's just keeping me informed.'

Gray cleared his throat. 'I can't think of anyone who would enjoy a compliment more than Tekoa,' he demurred.

'Well he bloody well didn't get one there,' said Yngvar.

Roper tutted. 'Thank you, Gray. If you want one from me, you should take a new protégé. Leon's had one for weeks. Don't deny some promising warrior your mentorship.'

Gray gave a strained smile. He seemed exceptionally reluctant to fill the role which had once been occupied by Pryce. 'I know. Just give me a while.'

'I'll take the post,' said Sakeus, another Belated Guardsman.

'Not on offer for you.'

'Why not? Did I not volunteer to protect my lord against the Kryptea?'

'One of them would actually have to turn up for you to earn a spot in the Sacred Guard,' growled Leon. Roper smiled, though was too touched by the Belated Guard's actions to take anything away from them.

'Gray can keep a close eye on you at Beormaton,' suggested Roper. 'Perhaps you'll get the chance to show your courage there.'

The city was two days away, and they rode in silence for a time.

'I was thinking about it last night,' said Roper thoughtfully, 'and I don't believe I've taken off my boots for a week. You men?'

'Now you mention it,' said Sakeus, 'I don't think I have for three days. We've been moving too fast.'

'Gray?'

Gray looked mildly appalled. 'I take mine off every night unless we're sleeping near the enemy.'

'We are in enemy lands.'

'An enemy who has no army.'

'True. Leon? How long for you?'

'Three weeks.'

'Bloody hell!'

'Maybe I'll take them off tonight,' the guardsman allowed.

'Who sleeps next to Leon?' asked Roper. 'Yngvar, is it you?'

'Not any more.'

'Leon,' said Roper firmly, 'tonight before sleep, you and I shall find a stream, remove our boots and wash our feet.'

When they arrived at Beormaton, it was with fresh dried grass stuffed in both their boots, and the promise that neither of them would ever leave it so long again to refresh their footwear. Long before they reached the city, they could see the gates were open. Outside hovered a noble and effusive welcoming committee who had come out to greet Roper on foot and clutching gifts. Roper mounted Zephyr for the occasion and rode forward to meet them.

'My liege,' said the most highly decorated of them. He prostrated himself before Roper, pushing forward the small chest he carried with the desperation of a man trying to placate a dragon with his firstborn.

'With so little spine, will he even be able to straighten up?' murmured Yngvar, in incomprehensible Anakim.

'You speak Saxon, my Lord King?' asked the nobleman, carefully focusing on Zephyr's ankles and avoiding Roper's eye.

'Yes.'

'How excellent. Welcome, my lord, to your city of Beormaton. I am Adalbert, Mayor here and if I may be so bold, your own representative.'

The proffered chest, when Leon had snatched it up and cracked it open suspiciously, turned out to hold one of those artless Suthern tapestries, depicting a tussle between some shadowed beast and a brightly armoured Sutherner. It was bordered with gold thread and inlaid with jewels for the beast's eyes, and must have been worth a fortune.

Roper cast an eye over the nobles behind Adalbert, each of whom had similarly knelt and offered gifts, though some wore expressions of revulsion at their mayor's fawning display. Roper himself was more inclined to punish such invertebrate behaviour than reward it, but knew he should honour those who surrendered, as much as punish those who resisted.

He dismounted, raised Adalbert up and told him that he and his people would be rewarded for succumbing so wisely. 'Keep your food,' he told the mayor, walking towards the city gates with one arm over his shoulder. Leon spoiled the comradely atmosphere by walking behind them with his sword drawn, keeping so close that he kept treading on Adalbert's heels. 'We will destroy these walls, of course, but you live under our protection now, and so have no need for walls. A gift of land for all of you here, in return for your beautiful presents. Five hundred acres each from the pastures surrounding Northwic. Tell me, are there any nobles who did not see fit to come and greet us here?'

'One or two, my lord.'

'Perhaps you'd tell Leon, here, where he can find them?' suggested Roper, indicating the guardsman. 'Then you can divide their land between you as well.'

'Certainly, my lord,' replied the mayor with a clumsy bow.

Over the next two days, they destroyed the walls, and Leon paid a visit to each of the men named by Adalbert. Thus were all those most resistant to Anakim rule (as well, Roper suspected, as several of Adalbert's personal enemies) destroyed. Roper hesitated in none of this. There was no question of mercy, and no time to regret. They were so close now. If Tekoa was successful in capturing Oxenaford, then suddenly, there was only one major city left.

Roper turned his eye to Deorceaster. 'Do you see how close we are, brothers?' he called out to his men on the morning they began their last march. 'Do you see how nearly done we are with our great task? What now?'

'Onwards!' they bellowed, well familiar with his constant refrain.

'What was that? Where next?'

'Onwards!'

Roper mounted Zephyr, treasuring each use of this horse, which he feared very much he would have to surrender. He rode up and down the column, haranguing his men to make haste, give it all and give it now, and use this last effort to ensure their names echoed through the Academy forever. They were delayed by a strange scene, which was nearly concluded by the time Roper happened upon it.

He could hear jeering and shouting up ahead, and raked Zephyr forward, guardsmen clattering after him. They came upon a seething crowd with drawn swords, their ire directed at a smaller band, which they had surrounded. The second group had also drawn swords, and at their centre was Jokul. His pale face was splashed crimson with blood from a split eyebrow, but still he snarled contempt at the larger group: Ramnea's Own legionaries, who seemed on the verge of losing control and butchering Jokul, and the protective knot of Kryptean agents who surrounded him. Three men lay on the floor already, all Krypteans and all bleeding, though from fists, boots and pommels rather than blades.

'Steady, steady!' called Roper as he arrived. 'What's this, peers? Who ordered you to break ranks?' There was a tiny pause after these words, which Roper seized. 'Well? Answer me!'

'You encouraged this savagery, Lord Roper!' howled Jokul. 'Don't try and distance yourself from it now!'

'We won't march with that bloody traitor, lord!' bellowed a lictor, jabbing a finger at Jokul. 'Him or his mob of poisonous weevils!'

'You will do as you are told,' said Roper harshly. 'Back into the column!'

Nobody moved. Roper rode forward and forced Zephyr between the two groups. Everyone backed away from the horse at once. 'Jokul's office is performing its ancient role,' said

Roper. 'I am performing mine. Sheath your swords.' He glared at the lictor who had called out until, eventually, the man obeyed. Reluctantly, those around him did the same. 'Onwards, men. We have no time for distractions, least of all from within. To Deorceaster.'

Slowly, the legionaries filtered back into ranks, their section of the column stuttering forward once more. Roper turned back to Jokul, the blood on his face red as strawberry.

'Well done, Lord Roper,' said Jokul, bitterly. 'You've turned the whole army against us.'

'No,' said Roper mildly. 'You did that.'

'You're responsible for this, you tyrant.'

'That word seems very cheap these days. You can't march with my men, Master. For your own safety.'

'Exile then.' Jokul looked up at him with fury, which Roper had expected, and something else which he had not. Triumph, was it? There was a look in his eye that Roper did not like, as though the Master knew something he did not. 'You're no different, Lord Roper. Each of your ancestors has cited "safety", when beginning their abuses.'

Roper rode away without replying, doing nothing to stop each of the Sacred Guardsmen spitting at Jokul as they passed.

That night, nearly embracing a fire glowing like the winter sun, and listening to the legionaries singing in the dark, Roper felt euphoria creeping over him. Jokul could not touch him. The men loved him too much. All he needed was an excuse to disband the Kryptea altogether, and he would have fulfilled the promise he had once made to Keturah, that he would break that backstabbing institution. And even greater than that, Suthdal was on its knees. He had gambled, and won. Those two great impossibilities had been achieved, and one had allowed the other.

When he finally laid eyes on the palisade wall of Deorceaster and saw that the gates were shut, it seemed the smallest of hurdles. They would open for him. One way or another, they would open.

'Surround the walls.'

'I know the routine,' said Gray, the sinking sun shining in his brown eyes.

'I wouldn't mind going out with a battle,' said Roper. 'Seems a shame for such an historic campaign to sputter out.'

'It would be more of a shame to die just before going home. The men will follow Roper the Daring anywhere, but let's try and finish this without bloodshed.'

That was unusually firm intervention from Gray.

'Was there a little fear behind those words, brother?' asked Roper, trying to sound mild.

'There was, my lord.'

'What of your quest?' Roper was always fascinated to hear whether Gray made any progress towards his ultimate goal: that of transcending the fear of death, and living without fear.

'I remain on the path, lord. I find that Pryce's death . . . I find I care less, since then.'

Roper reached across the gap between their horses and gripped Gray's wrist. 'Please take a new protégé. Whoever it is needs your wisdom, but I think you need someone to fill that gap, too.'

'I will,' Gray promised.

'But you're right, of course,' said Roper. 'No fighting unless we have to, eh? Though let's not let the Sutherners know that. As far as they're concerned, it should look as though you're my dogs, slavering for a scrap, and I can barely hold onto the leash.'

They had besieged this city before they had taken Lundenceaster, and even fought a battle about its walls. It seemed an apt place to end this campaign. When he slept, Roper dreamed of Deorceaster's streets. Awake, he fantasised about their defences, and how he would beat them. By the end of the first day, he had a dozen strategies. By the end of the second, a score. And at the beginning of the third, Leon tapped him on the shoulder and said: 'Trouble.' He was pointing over Roper's shoulder.

Roper turned. There was a familiar figure crossing the campsite, though one so unexpected that Roper could not immediately place him. *What on earth?*

It was Tekoa, ploughing directly for them. He sent a cooking pot spinning out of his path with a vicious kick, half-boiled oats slopping across the grass. The legate should have been nowhere near here, and with his arrival came a sudden foreboding.

'Legate?' Roper called out. 'What brings you here?' His tone made it sound as though Tekoa was unwelcome, which he was. Roper did not want to hear whatever news had brought him here in person.

Tekoa drew a quivering finger like a knife, which he levelled at Roper. 'What brings me here?' he bellowed. 'Do you truly not know?'

'Calm,' said Roper, raising his hands. 'Just explain.'

'I've explained,' said Tekoa, coming to a halt before him. 'With half a dozen heralds, none of whom have been returned, I've explained over and over.'

'I've received none of them,' said Roper. 'Just tell me from the beginning.'

Tekoa opened his mouth, but was evidently given pause by the news that his heralds had not got through. 'We've found the Unhieru,' he said abruptly.

'I trust they've started an extremely large fire,' said Roper.

Tekoa nodded. 'Imagine if, instead, we found them just five leagues from my army at Oxenaford.' There was a pause. 'Imagine that on hearing this news, you visited Gogmagoc and learned that they hadn't been to Wiltun and left already; they *never even arrived*.'

Roper was aware of the sensation of subsiding, as though the earth beneath his feet were slumping. 'No.'

'Yes,' hissed Tekoa. 'Yes! Yes! Yes!'

'Why?' Roper's heart was thumping. They had to move, then and there. If the Unhieru had never reached Wiltun, then the heart of Suthern resistance was still untouched, and had been allowed weeks to prepare. Roper had been wasting his time in the north, while their enemy marshalled in the south.

Tekoa was about to reply when Roper cut him off. 'Never mind,' he said. *The Kryptea*, he thought. *Jokul. Does he know about this?* If he did, it might be his excuse to assassinate Roper at last. If this campaign was faltering, then so would the popularity that was his only shield. 'Right.' His boot tapped the ground, thumb and forefinger pinching together convulsively. 'Right. We go *now*.'

'This city—' Gray began.

'Is totally worthless. Force march south, right now.'

There was a heartbeat's pause while Roper stared at them all, incredulous that nobody was moving. Then, like some clockwork monster on which the tiniest of levers has been pressed, the army juddered into life.

Leon turned away. 'Well?' he roared at the curious knot of guardsmen who had watched Tekoa's arrival. 'One bloody hour! Prepare yourselves! Move out! Force march! Move out!' They scattered, Leon stalking behind and still bellowing at the top of his voice.

Gray sprinted in the opposite direction. Where he was going, Roper had no idea until a distant drum rattled into life: the raging tattoo of an emergency rally, played during surprise attack. The entire army was on its feet already, prepared to do something even if they were not yet sure what. Then the femur trumpets began to skirl: an incessant, harpy war cry that started soldiers moving involuntarily.

Into this aimless chaos strode Roper, Tekoa and Leon. 'Now! Now! Now! We march in one hour, prepare yourselves!'

'Where?' Randolph shouted back.

'South!' replied Roper.

'Will there be fighting?'

'This is an army!' bellowed Tekoa. 'What do you think, you idiot?'

Music is the Old Tongue speaking pleasant words. The trumpets and drums together, screeching like the vultures of the

Winter Road itself, produced its opposite. *Rangalist*, the Anakim called it: *anti-music*. The Old Tongue invoking urgency, horror and fear. The Sutherners were unpractised at this. Though they did use the Old Tongue in their own way, for them it was a pastime and an indulgence, targeted at pleasure and catharsis.

But to the Anakim, music was just one edge of a powerful tool, and the other was *rangalist*. Sometimes the occasion demanded a rainstorm of iron shards; the bubbling of underwater thunder, or the shrugging of a mountain. Horrible sounds, which made sitting still quite impossible, or could appal an enemy army, or bind men together with a common dread.

Everything was rolled in, packed up, tied together and snuffed out. The lictors prowled among the legionaries, helping or hollering as their mood dictated.

'We're in the wrong place!' bellowed Roper. 'Move, legionaries, move! Pendeen, Ramnea's Own, Ulpha, Fair Isle! Guardsmen, Sacred and Belated! Move!'

They did. In half an hour, the van had lurched forward, the Skiritai groping the landscape ahead. By the hour's end, the whole army had shuddered into life, following their rangers, the baggage train left in the dust to catch up.

It was midday. They marched until the moon shone in their eyes, and then the ruby sun once more. And they kept marching.

21
The Wall

'So what the bloody hell happened?' muttered Roper. He and Tekoa walked together at the front of the column, setting an impossible pace as rain began to spit.

'Gogmagoc was dethroned,' said Tekoa. 'With his wound he was vulnerable for the first time in decades, and it took no time for a new king to take control. He had no treaty with you, no desire to fight where Suthdal was most heavily defended, so he just *sat* there. They all did, plundering and pillaging, getting fat and drunk, seven leagues short of Wiltun.'

Roper swore softly. 'Where did you hear this? You went to visit the new king?'

'I went myself, yes, but by the time I got there, Gogmagoc was back in control.'

'How?'

'He recovered. There was no fighting on either occasion. He just declared he wanted the throne back and his rival knew he couldn't beat him at full strength, and surrendered.'

'So Gogmagoc regained control, what? Two weeks ago? How did he end up five leagues from you?'

'Now things get harder,' said Tekoa grimly. 'Even while I was treating with Gogmagoc, the Eoten-Draefend appeared.'

Roper pursed his lips. Garrett Eoten-Draefend, whom Roper

wanted dead, and Gogmagoc even more so. He thought he knew where the tale went from here.

'He was riding with a band of light cavalry, who had winged helmets. They hovered as close to the north side of the Unhieru camp as they dared, peppering them with arrows, obviously trying to lure them into pursuit, and the idiots had no choice but to follow. Gogmagoc has been chasing him across Suthdal, miles from Wiltun.'

'Gogmagoc is no fool,' said Roper. 'He must know he's being baited.'

'He knows. He doesn't care. He views Garrett as his true reward for joining us. He made me promise to come north and see you, and demand you send cavalry to pin Garrett down. He can't catch Garrett himself, though he's tried ambushes and even bribing Sutherners to work with him.'

Gogmagoc isn't a fool, thought Roper. *But I am*. He could not believe how stupid he had been. *Of course* he should have sent mounted troops with the Unhieru! He should have sent bowmen too, so they could not be tormented in this way. The Unhieru were too slow to operate unsupported, and he should have foreseen that. He supposed he had, at the back of his mind, but that knowledge had been outweighed by the dread at leaving any of his men in Unhieru company. He swore, and then bitterly swore again. He had blundered.

'So you plan to march on Wiltun?' pressed Tekoa.

'Yes.'

'Will you see Gogmagoc?'

'No. I'll send cavalry to capture Garrett, take him down to Wiltun and tell Gogmagoc I'll hand him over if he destroys the town.'

'He's not in the mood to be antagonised,' Tekoa warned.

'Do I look in the mood to be antagonised, Tekoa?'

Unusually, the legate stayed silent.

On the road ahead, they could see a knot of figures. Roper studiously avoided eye contact with any of them, while they stared at him in naked hostility. They moved off the road to avoid a collision, and the two groups passed one another in silence. Just as they were about to round a bend, Roper threw a glance back at the pale-faced figure who stood at the centre of the other group. Jokul was staring back at him and their eyes met for a moment.

'You exiled them?' said Tekoa.

'Ramnea's Own did.'

Sakeus, walking behind Roper, made an obscene gesture at Jokul, and the Sacred Guard began to hiss as they passed.

'I see. And how do you think Jokul will react to our turn south?'

'Not well, I should imagine, Tekoa. In fact I think he knew about this.'

Tekoa glanced at Roper.

'What do you suppose happened to your heralds?' asked Roper. He remembered the look of sly triumph in Jokul's eye as he had been banished from the army. 'I think he knew before any of us, and has been keeping it from us. It's lucky you came yourself. Now, as much as I value your presence here, I value it more in command of the other half of the army. Return to them for me, and I'll meet you at Wiltun. How soon can you make it?'

'Four days.'

'If you push?'

'That is pushing, and ambitious. Four days.'

Roper reached out and grasped his hand. 'We'll meet you there.'

Tekoa narrowed his eyes, as if to say that four days would be difficult for his half of the army, and absurd for Roper's. But then he simply shrugged helplessly. 'Four days. Until then.'

And what, wondered Roper as he watched Tekoa float back through the ranks in search of his horse, *will we find when we arrive? The Sutherners haven't just delayed us for no reason. They wanted time. But for what?*

Roper found out what Bellamus had been preparing a few days later, though he did not realise when he first encountered it. He was at the van of the column, leading the march on foot, when one of the Skiritai officers came to him on horseback. 'The road up ahead is blocked, lord.'

'Clear it,' Roper replied. 'You have all the manpower you can use.'

'It's flooded, lord.'

Roper blinked. 'There hasn't been any rain.'

'Sorry, lord.'

'Don't apologise, show me.'

They rode on ahead, hooves clattering on the stones of the road. They were following the trail of the Black Cavalry Corps, which had been sent out to find Garrett, and it smelt powerfully of the dung they had left behind.

It was not long before Roper could see the road ahead of them descend into a valley and disappear into flat, tawny floodwaters.

'The nearest alternative path is quite a detour, lord,' came the voice of the Skiritai behind Roper, who had ridden close to the waters and was inspecting them with a frown. 'Lord? Which way?'

Roper did not reply. He did not know what he was looking at. All that was clear to him was that this path should not be flooded. These old roads seldom did, and there had been nowhere near enough rain to change that.

'Lord?'

'We'll cut across country. The wagons can go by road, we march as the crow flies. But I want you to explore this flood. Tell me where it's come from and what's on the other side.'

Twenty scouts went out, each with a swift horse, and the first of their reports came in that afternoon. The valley had been flooded by a diverted river, pouring through the valley wall which had been hacked away like a chipped rim of pottery. Then came another scout, who had encountered an unfamiliar chain of forts, perched high up on hills and ridges. The valleys between them had been dammed and flooded, and Roper saw them for himself the next day as the army was forced to skirt around them: steep banks crowned in palisade walls, a few defenders looking down at them curiously, aware they were perfectly safe behind their flooded defences.

And they were forced to change course again the next day, when they came to a river; unnaturally swollen, and impassable without boats or bridges. It was only when one of the Skiritai pointed out the walls of Wiltun on the far side that they realised this was the Wylie: usually a body of gentle glass, now a torrent. This corner of Suthdal had been upended so completely that it was as though Wiltun had been picked up and placed in an entirely new country of Bellamus's own invention.

'Send the Skiritai along the edge,' said Roper in a flat voice. 'Find out how far the defences go in both directions.'

He did not need the report which came back. The line they had encountered at the flooded valley, followed past the chain of forts and into the swollen Wylie, stretched from one coast to the other. This was what Bellamus had done with his time. Where there had been valleys, there was now water. Where hills, there were forts. Ridges became walls, passes were sealed by landslide and dams reared across every moving body of water. Some sections bristled with waiting siege bows, catapults, primed avalanches and trebuchets. Some sections had no defences, but those were the ones that did not need them. By adapting the landscape, a corner of Albion now stood behind some of the most fearsome defences Roper had ever seen.

Bellamus, he thought. *You said you'd had enough of this.*

'Did you see any way through?' he asked Aledas, the Skiritai officer who had led the investigation.

'No.'

Roper, Gray and Tekoa stared down at the stick-map Aledas had whittled for them.

'Boats?' suggested Tekoa. Aledas had found the legate stranded further up the line of defences. His half of the army had hit the same flooded valley as Roper's, and turned the other way in an effort to find a way past the defences. 'The rivers are so swollen we could sail up them from the sea.'

'There is a Suthern fleet at the coast,' said Aledas.

'How many?'

'We counted fifty-five ships.'

'So the sea is theirs.'

'Until we can scrape together a fleet to challenge them,' said Roper.

Gray let out a soft breath. 'I know you are used to confounding those who tell you *No*, my lord, but please don't waste your time there. A fleet is not like an army. A ship's crew can only become proficient with experience at sea, and the Sutherners will not allow us that. And we simply do not have the knowledge to build ships that can compete with theirs.'

'We could buy Suthern ships and crews,' said Roper, stubbornly.

'Even if we had the resources, or the will, who on Erebos would trade with us?'

'Well, the alternative seems to be giving up,' Roper observed.

Gray did not reply.

'There must be a way through,' he continued. 'There must. I'm going to ride south-east, and you ride north-west, Tekoa. We'll both find the weakest portion of the line we can and come back here to decide where we'll break it.'

Silence greeted this plan and Roper, frustrated by the general defeatism, gave an instinctive stamp of his foot. '*Onwards*.'

He took the Sacred Guard, and because they still refused to leave his side, the volunteers of the Belated Guard came too. He was grateful for the extra numbers. He had not seen the Kryptea since they had passed them on the road back south, but Roper thought of them almost constantly. They would not have let him escape.

They rode along the Wylie Lines, as the fortifications were becoming known, their progress slow and frustrating. The fortifications were new, so of course no road traversed them. They squelched over marshes, and ripped through dense bracken and brambles, their formation spreading out further and further as his party's stamina waned. At one point Roper realised that his nearest companion was Leon, three hundred yards behind him and nearly out of sight.

Roper did not wait.

He drove Zephyr further ahead, his mood growing darker with each passing league. He could see no way through the defences that did not look suicidal, and knew that Tekoa would be finding the same in the other direction. He fumed to himself that Gogmagoc had failed so badly, that the resolve of his companions had wilted already, that Gray was still indulging his melancholic blame of Roper. He spurred Zephyr on until late afternoon, when suddenly the ground dropped away and he found himself standing on top of a great white cliff. The sea roared and sucked beneath him. Roper was looking across the foaming waves to the shadow of Erebos on the horizon.

He looked at that distant land for a moment, then laid a palm on Zephyr's neck and swung himself out of the saddle. 'You idiot,' he muttered.

Here was the edge of Albion: the island he had come so close to securing. He let go of Zephyr's bridle, the huge horse reversing from the edge of the cliff and ambling away to graze. Stiffly, Roper lowered himself to the grass and sat with his legs hanging over the drop, staring desolately out over the gunpowder sea. Anchored some leagues down the coast, he could see the prickly shapes of the fleet Aledas had promised.

'This is your fault, you fool,' he murmured. He did not see how he could convince his men to brave the defences he had just seen. His popularity was about to crash, and the Kryptea would smell blood.

'There you are, lord.'

Roper had not even heard the hoof beats of Gray's horse.

'Don't ride off again,' came Leon's gruff voice.

'Well . . .' said Gray, when the only response was the boom of waves beneath them, 'at least here's proof Blacklaw now stretches from one end of Albion to the other. For the first time ever.' Still Roper said nothing, and a gentle hand was laid on his shoulder. 'Come, my lord. You haven't eaten all day. We need food, then we can plan where we go from here.'

Roper allowed himself to be pulled upright, body overcome with stiffness and heavy fatigue. Gray and Leon led him back to Zephyr, whom Roper stroked absently. 'Hard times, old friend,' he murmured. The horse just snorted hot breath into his palm and rubbed its head against his shoulder. He pulled himself into the saddle, and they rode a mile inland to a shady woodland. On the way they met the score of Belated Guardsmen, including Rethin, Sakeus and Yngvar. 'Still with me?' asked Roper, giving a tight smile. 'You're more reliable than the actual guard.'

'Still here, lord.'

Together they entered the trees and kindled a fire beneath the canopy. Leon returned holding a corner of his cloak like a basket, filled with birch-cloud fungus which he cut up and began to boil for tea. Gray produced some fruit leather which he pressed on Roper. It was hawthorn and lingon; chewy and tart and a source of strength before Roper had even swallowed it.

'We've got something for you, lord,' said Rethin.

Chewing on the fruit leather, Roper looked up and had to blink at the sight before him. He tried to clear his head with a shake, but suddenly he could not move at all, because there was a blade held at his throat.

'I did tell you, lord,' came Sakeus's voice in his ear, hot and breathless with rage. 'I did tell you I hunt bigger game.'

Gray and Leon had frozen too, each with a pair of sword-tips pricking their necks. Every blade was matt black.

Roper let out a tired breath, the truth sinking in. 'I take it your Master briefed you,' he surmised, 'in case I tried to denounce the Kryptea at Pryce's embalming?'

'You didn't really think he'd be out-thought so easily,' said Rethin.

All along, these men had been Kryptean. After his speech

at Pryce's embalming, they had reacted immediately, knowing it was the last chance they could get anywhere near Roper. Then they had waited weeks for the moment he left the Sacred Guard behind. For the moment when the army's momentum faltered, and they could murder him, and hope the legionaries tolerated it. He had to admire their patience, and their forethought. He had been out-manoeuvred.

'I suppose it was optimistic,' he replied. 'And where is Jokul?'

'Not far, don't worry. You're going to see him now. On your feet, tyrant.'

Roper stood carefully, trying to move as predictably as possible.

'Good, my lord. Finally you do as you're told,' crooned Sakeus in his ear.

Roper could feel the rage pulsing off him, brewing for weeks and given vent at last.

Gray was trying to meet his eye imploringly. He threw a glance down at Ramnea, his sword unattended by the fire, and then back at Roper with a question on his face. Roper smiled and shook his head a fraction.

'Don't be a fool, Captain,' said Rethin, following his gaze, sword held at Gray's throat. 'Nobody else need die now. Just be still. There will be wiser Black Lords for you to defend.'

'Wiser?' said Gray. 'You mean ones who will share power with parasites like you?'

'I mean those who won't drive our kingdom to ruin,' he replied. 'You and Guardsman Leon can stay here, with Yngvar, Inhaf, Sunhi and me. Sakeus and the others will take Roper to see Jokul. After an hour or so, when they're finished, you'll be released unharmed. You have my word.'

'Fuck your word,' said Leon.

'It's the best you've got just now.'

Sakeus began to drag Roper backwards, and Gray stirred suddenly against his captors.

'My lord!'

'Don't, brother,' said Roper, giving a fleeting smile as he was pulled away. 'There's a lot left to do, and you are needed. Don't throw away your life here.'

Leon stirred violently but was kept still by the swords held at his neck. Gray gave a little moan of frustration.

'Keep still, stupid dog,' muttered Rethin.

'Just hold on,' Gray implored. 'I'll find a way.' Roper was being dragged back through the trees, and their eyes met one last time. 'Serving you has been my honour, lord!'

Roper smiled at his captain and placed a hand over his heart. Then he was yanked backwards by Sakeus. The Kryptea closed ranks around him, and he disappeared behind a dozen figures wielding matt-black swords. Roper was bundled into a saddle as five more Krypteans gathered up the reins of every remaining horse.

The Black Lord was spirited away, between the trunks, into the gloom.

22
Keturah's Case

'We must leave. Tonight. If you go back before that crowd and try to defend the Black Lord . . . I fear they won't let you.'

Keturah did not argue. She could not think what to say.

Night had fallen and she, Virtanen, Ormur and Numa were together in the parlour of Tekoa's house. The fire was blazing in the grate and all was quiet outside. Even so, Keturah would have been surprised if she saw the dawn. After the case Frathi had just made; after the mood she had elicited from the crowd and the months of rumours turning the fortress against Roper, they surely would not be left in peace.

'Remember what I said about not taking advice, Virtanen?' she said eventually, in a small voice. 'If I abandon this now, the knowledge that I didn't even try will torture me forever.'

'For a time,' he said. He crossed the room to kneel before her and held out his hands. She placed her own in his; warm and unexpectedly wonderful. 'For a time,' he repeated. 'But over the years the regret will fade. You'll realise discretion is the better part of valour. How much you'd have lost if you'd stayed. You'd make your peace with it, and be glad you trusted to the road.'

Keturah left her hands lingering in his, the feel of it so

charged it made her heart thump. She was unaware of Ormur staring wide-eyed at them.

'I've been places, my lady. A herald's life takes you far away. There's an island, across the sea, halfway to the Otherworld. Beautiful, cold, and the ground smokes and trembles. It is empty. The place for a fresh start, where no one and nothing could reach you. You could go there. You could go anywhere, for however long, and I'll come with you. Just leave tonight. Please.'

She was not sure what was being proposed any more, but suddenly she became aware of Ormur, mouth hanging open and Numa clutched in his arms.

There came a roar from outside and she withdrew her hands suddenly. Feet were pounding in the street and, avoiding Virtanen's eyes, she crossed to the door and pressed her ear against it.

'Keturah!'

She jumped back as a voice she knew shouted through the boards.

'Keturah!'

Reckless with shame, she unbarred the door to reveal Sigrid standing on the threshold, a hood covering her bright-blonde hair, white-blue eyes shining out beneath.

'Oh, my dear!' Keturah fell into an embrace with her. Sigrid felt stiff in her arms, and when Keturah opened her eyes to look over her shoulder, she saw the street behind was filled with enormous, lumpen figures.

Berserkers. Fifty of them, prowling the cobbles like animals, covered in white warpaint with a shocking red map of arteries painted on top.

'I come bearing a message from Frathi,' said Sigrid. Keturah stepped back to see her face. 'She has sent these men to guard your house tonight. She says you are safe, and she will see justice done.'

Keturah observed the berserkers bleakly. 'My dear,' she murmured. 'Am I being protected, or detained?'

Sigrid pursed her lips. 'I fear it is both.'

The news that she was a prisoner made Keturah oddly calm. Now the choice had been taken away, there seemed less to worry about. 'I see. You'll stay here tonight, Sigrid? You'd be an enormous comfort to me.'

Sigrid held up a bag of supplies that had been clutched at her side. 'That's what I'd hoped.'

Keturah squeezed her shoulder gratefully and stood back to let her inside. Sigrid greeted Ormur and Virtanen, paid her compliments to the sleeping Numa, and began to unload lavender, comfrey and camomile for tea; a skin of elderberry wine sweetened with honey, and cakes of salmon, lingon and lemon from her bag. They warmed them all by the fire, Keturah surprised to find tears pricking her eyes at these homely comforts.

Virtanen seemed to have understood that leaving was now out of the question and hovered awkwardly, while Sigrid talked calmly and clearly of how the fortress had received the first day of the trial. 'There's a bit of a stir,' she acknowledged, 'and might've been some unrest, except Frathi sent out the berserkers and that's frightened off even Tore's legionaries. Things always look bad after one side has had a full day to make their case. We must simply prepare for tomorrow.'

Sigrid's calm pricked the bubble of fear that had swollen within the parlour. The wine numbed Keturah enough that she could stomach a few restorative salmon-cakes, and then they sipped tea together. Sleeping was out of the question for any of them. The berserkers were roaring outside and in any case, wakeful moments now seemed very precious.

'I didn't expect to feel so hopeless this evening,' Keturah admitted. 'Our case is dead and buried, and it still will be when I've finished speaking tomorrow. It'll be like painting a smile on a cadaver.'

Sigrid did not laugh. 'That is a surrender hiding behind a joke.'

Keturah was stung. 'I don't surrender,' she said, reflexively.

'No,' said Sigrid. 'I know. I was in that tent with you.'

Keturah had met those daylight eyes over a floor of corpses. In darker moments than this, they had been the last lights shining.

'You're right,' muttered Keturah. 'I don't know why I seem to have made a habit of it lately. But I haven't felt like the person I was since that day.'

'Why would you? A horrifying day.'

'But you seem unchanged by it.'

Sigrid shrugged. 'I had you there with me.'

Keturah looked away. 'Bless you,' she muttered.

'And I didn't have to leave immediately afterwards, like you, to end up in a new place with new people. I spent the next weeks with Gray, who was also there. We didn't even talk about it. It was just enough to be with someone who knew what it was like.'

That resonated with Keturah. 'You think that's right? It's not the event itself, but whether you can share it and be . . . understood?'

'You know it is. You've spoken to me before about how Lord Roper suffered from his lonely position. The confident person you remember being wasn't just you: it was you magnified by the people who loved you.'

Keturah shook her head. 'I feel like a fool.'

'Better now than in front of the crowd tomorrow.'

Keturah did not want to stand before them: the idea of winning this case was ludicrous. But Sigrid was right, the only choice now was to commit. 'It'll be worth going up there if only to get revenge on Sigurasta,' she muttered. 'Does that wretched woman ever stop bawling?'

'As good a means of motivation as any other,' Sigrid observed. 'What else do you want to say?'

Keturah stared into her cup. 'I want all the kingdom to know Uvoren was a monster,' she said quietly, 'not fit to have his bones turned into broth, let alone honoured as a statue.' She was silent a moment. 'I want to show Urthr to be the rapist I know him to be, who should be locked behind bars until the key has rusted to dust. I want to show Vinjar couldn't empty a chamber pot properly, let alone master the Hindrunn. I want that thug Tore to have the head twisted from his shoulders like a cork from a wineskin.' She was no longer muttering. 'I want to finish the work Roper started, and show this kingdom that the Kryptea are a gangrenous limb we should sacrifice at the next moment possible, before it rots the whole lot of us from the inside. And I want every last one of them to know they should be grateful to my husband; get down on their hands and knees, kiss the earth and thank him for risking and giving everything to save the unborn children they are ignoring.'

She caught Virtanen's eye and he looked away abruptly, and then found Sigrid's steady gaze. 'I also want to hear you say all that,' Sigrid said.

Though it was dark, it seemed their best course was to go to the platform and wait for the morning. They donned cloaks against the chill and stepped outside, Sigrid informing the berserkers where they were going so confidently that it brooked no argument. They walked unharried through the streets, the berserkers rustling alongside them, the moon overhead like a monstrous silver egg nestled in soft clouds.

As though it was the site of their last stand, they laid claim to the platform, stationing a wall of berserker flesh before them. Dawn came, then the first people. Any inclined to mock Keturah were silent in the face of the painted berserkers. The first group arrived and fell into a silence which they gave to the second group, the contagion spreading as more arrived. And by the time Frathi and the Ephors had appeared magisterially, even their presence was not enough to spark the crowd, who just waited.

The Ephors ascended the platform and settled behind her, Keturah feeling the collective attention of the crowd staring up at her. Her veins were filled with lightning and her mouth paper-dry. She glanced at Sigrid, now standing on the platform behind her, and Virtanen next to her.

Yesterday, the Chief Historian had given the crowd what

they wanted: scandals and stories of Vigtyr. *I'll give them more. I'll give them a show.* 'Sigrid,' she murmured, stepping close to her. She whispered in her ear and saw Sigrid's eyes widen. She nodded and darted off the platform. Keturah watched her go, then she turned back to the crowd.

'Let us begin,' she declared, in the voice Virtanen had taught, 'by retracing some of the ground my esteemed opponent covered yesterday. I call Urthr Uvorenson as witness.'

The deathly silence prevailed as Urthr made his surly way onto the platform, flanked by two guards. Keturah stood before him appraisingly, trying to make him conscious of the attention that roared past them both. Then she began to stride across the platform, controlling each step carefully so nobody would see her shaking. 'We've discussed this once already, Urthr, so we can be brief. I count half a dozen accusations of rape. Tell us, what is the truth of this?'

Urthr gave her a contemptuous look. 'Lies.'

'But you said yesterday you did bed them,' said Keturah.

'And yet it wasn't rape.'

'So these women – six of them – slept with you *willingly*?' Keturah pitched her incredulity just right. The crowd gave a theatrical hum of scepticism, and then laughed at its own cleverness. Keturah shared a knowing look with them and then appraised Urthr in some confusion. Eventually, with a note of bafflement in her voice, she observed: 'I suppose it must have been your charm?'

The crowd laughed again, but Frathi was on her feet. 'Don't be shy, Lady Keturah. Are you accusing the witness of being ugly? That is not a crime, and suggests that there is not much substance to your case.'

'Not ugly, though I beg you to keep interruptions to a minimum, my lady, I really want to spend as little time in his company as possible.' The crowd hooted at this rejoinder, but Keturah was striding across the platform, her face serious. 'It is certainly no crime to be ugly. But it grows hard to see how there are so many voluntary candidates to share his bed. You madam!' Keturah pointed at a woman in the audience. 'Would you?'

The woman shrank at this sudden attention, and shook her head vigorously. The crowd grew a little nervous that the attention might fall on them, but Keturah could see the next woman along gazing back at her frankly and picked her out. 'And what about you, my lady?'

'Not if he was glazed in honey!' The audience loved that, and so did Keturah.

'And dare I ask, sir?' Keturah winked at one of the legionaries guarding Urthr, who played along by pretending to consider his captive, and then delivering a grave shake of his head.

By now, Urthr was purple in the face and the crowd thoroughly enjoying this game. Part of the reason it worked was that Urthr was not pitifully ugly; with eyes like two weevil holes drilled through a door, his character stood out on his face.

However base she knew it to be, Keturah was intoxicated. The Chief Historian had come with a formidable arsenal of knowledge and arguments, and Keturah was playing her at a wholly different game. She would show Frathi how to win a crowd.

Keturah suddenly changed her posture, straightening up and fixing her gaze on the Ephors. 'I call the witnesses.' A deathly hush fell over the crowd as seven women, dressed in mourning black at Keturah's direction, filed onto the stage. The crowd knew the time for humour was done.

Keturah arranged them on the far side of the platform from Urthr, and bowed as she approached the first. 'You, my lady. Did this man,' she pointed across the platform, 'force himself on you?'

The woman looked at Urthr calmly. 'He did.' The scene was all the more powerful when contrasted against the humour which had preceded it.

Keturah went to the next woman. 'Did this man force himself on you?'

Tears were running down her cheeks, but the answer was unequivocal. 'He did.'

The Chief Historian had spoken of theories and conspiracies: paper arguments beside witnesses like these.

Six times, those two damning words were uttered in the most convincing terms possible. The seventh woman she came to was Kaiho, Urthr's former wife. 'And you, Kaiho Larikkasdottir. You were married to this man. Do you believe him capable of such violation?'

Kaiho looked at Urthr with complete hatred. 'I know it.'

Urthr snapped. 'You bitch!' he shrieked. 'You pathetic bitch! You weak, poisonous—'

'Remove him!' called Keturah, her voice trained by Virtanen to carry over Urthr's howls. He was dragged off the stage, and before the muttering of the crowd could build too far, Keturah pointed a vengeful finger at the Ephors. 'And you permitted him back into the fortress, before his conviction was overturned. I pray your judgement is sounder than it seems here.'

Heartened by this early performance, Keturah's supporters in the crowd found their voice and gave a low hiss. A few of the Ephors shifted in embarrassment.

'I call my next witness, Unndor Uvorenson.'

As Unndor was ushered onto the stage, Keturah felt a sudden weariness. She threw up her hands. 'Must we really go through all this again?'

Her supporters jeered angrily.

'We should, we should. Let us show better judgement than the Ephors, my friends. Let us put this to bed.'

Up onto the stage came witnesses to reaffirm the charges of cowardice that had seen Unndor struck from his legion. Damning tales, repeated and corroborated, of a man who dirtied his sword by striking at men already engaged in combat, and then shrank behind the flesh of braver friends when an enemy came forward calling for revenge. Who drank longest from the skulls at the victory feast, and declared to one man after another that they were lucky he had been there to save them.

'And how is it, to fight beside such a man?' Keturah asked one particularly grizzled lictor.

'Poison,' replied the lictor. 'It saps the morale of the whole century.'

Unlike Urthr, Unndor did not go down fighting. He shrank before these tales and when the lictor cast a disgusted gaze over him, Unndor could only look down in shame.

'Vigtyr is gone and disgraced,' said Keturah. 'He wields no more influence here, so who now will my opponent claim has forced these witnesses to speak?' Keturah looked at Frathi, who observed her coolly in reply. 'Or could it be they speak at their own behest, just as they did last time?'

Urthr had been convicted by women, his brother by men, and the combination was effective. It seemed particularly damning that Uvoren's allies had sinned so grievously in both spheres of life. Keturah had him led off the stage, making an aside to the crowd as he went. 'In summary, you will agree: these men were correctly tried and punished. There was no abuse of the courts.' She shrugged and seemed about to turn away when she added carelessly, 'And I would ask only what sort of man raises two such morally bankrupt sons. The sort of man we should be building a statue to honour?' She waved a hand. 'Let us move on.'

She next called on Sigurasta, who slouched onto the stage with a reluctance Keturah found extremely pleasing. 'Any of you who were at the *Master of the Hindrunn*'s' – she invested Vinjar's title with all the pomposity it deserved – 'original conviction will know that one of the most vehement condemnations came from his own wife, Sigurasta here. She bawled on that occasion quite as much as she did yesterday. Now Old Onion-Eyes has altered her story completely.'

The crowd laughed knowingly, for Sigurasta was famous for using her tears as a weapon.

'So what caused you to change your mind, Sigurasta? That

farcical villain Vigtyr again, is it, who holds so many strings that we're all his puppets?'

'Well, yes, it was,' said Sigurasta, flushing scarlet. 'I was *forced* to testify against my husband.'

'Well, you gave the information quite freely to me, in private, long before you gave it to the court, but never mind that, eh, Sigurasta? I'm sure that was at Vigtyr's instruction as well.'

'I have no idea what you're talking about,' replied the witness.

'You forget so much!' said Keturah, delightedly. 'Tell me, did you also forget that by lying to the court first time round, that you have brought the death penalty upon yourself?' Sigurasta froze. 'That is the usual punishment, is it not, my lords?' Keturah asked of the Ephors. 'Knowingly lying beneath the Almighty Eye, even when under duress, is usually punished with roasting I believe.'

She let the idea of cooking a person alive with the focused light of a dozen great concave mirrors sink in.

'Generally speaking, yes,' acknowledged Valkin.

'You will be pursuing this, I'm sure.'

'We shall.'

Perhaps Sigurasta had assumed her husband's new title would protect her, or that the Ephors would overlook her change in testimony in their quest to condemn Roper, for now her eyes were huge and brimming once more.

'Surely not *more* tears, Sigurasta?' said Keturah to a jeer from the crowds.

'I didn't,' Sigurasta spluttered, glancing at Frathi, who did not come to her aid. 'I haven't—'

'What was that, Sigurasta?' asked Keturah. 'The story changes again, I see. Did you lie to the court, or not?'

'No!'

'But you have presented two different versions of events, at two different courts.'

Sigurasta said nothing. She just threw another desperate glance at Frathi.

'I should tell the truth, if I were you. Did your husband commit adultery, or not?'

'I'm . . . I'm not sure.' Sigurasta was sobbing now. 'Please, I'm not sure. He might've. It's possible. I've told the truth. I was threatened by Vigtyr, but he might've.'

The crowd let out a noise of disgust and Keturah threw back her head and laughed. 'Do we believe this witness?' she asked.

'No!' roared the crowd.

'I'm not sure there is any more to be gained here. Lead her away.'

Sigurasta screamed as she was dragged off stage, and Keturah almost felt sorry for the fool. 'My opponent seems to have constructed a case out of feathers and straw. One good puff and the whole thing collapses.'

This time, there came no laughter. *So you're still on her side, are you?*

'There are compelling aspects to it, let nobody say I do not acknowledge its merits. Why, we should expect the Chief Historian to have a multitude of examples from the past at her disposal to support her point. Did she not provide us with those? And yet –' Keturah paused and looked down at the stage, walking deliberately across it so that it seemed she only reluctantly disagreed with the kingdom's foremost historian – 'she doesn't actually know whether the Kryptea are a force for good. She can't. None of us can. Because history is at the Kryptea's mercy. There is an ancient concordat between those assassins and the Academy, little known but hugely significant. The Kryptea extended their role to protect the Academy, who in return allowed them to edit any chants that referenced their work. *Any* information that relates to them – *any at all* – is likely a work of Kryptean imagination.'

There was a stir at this, but Keturah continued to pace the stage. 'You will note the Chief Historian does not object, because this is information contained within the walls of the Academy itself. "*So came Kryptea to couple with Academy; so that both stand together in thick balustrade against Black Lord.*" The very institution Frathi represents is committed to upholding this band of assassins. Is that not true, my lady?' she addressed Frathi.

'Do not look to me to make your case for you, Tekoasdottir,' she replied.

'And yet you would contradict me if I were lying. The Kryptea control our very past. They police the Black Lord, and so they control our future as well. Their power and influence is infinite – they are worse than a rogue Black Lord could ever be. How can *that* be a proportionate response to tyranny? At great risk to his own safety, Lord Roper attempted to root them out. My opponent would have you believe that was a crime. Was it? Or was it the ultimate public service? Was it not an attempt to recapture this kingdom's soul?

'Frathi will have you believe that lives have been saved by the shadow of the Kryptea, which has scared Black Lords into ruling more justly. What about the thousands dead at Kryptean hands that we don't know about, because the information has been eradicated? What about the fear we all feel, watching our words, afraid that they might be overheard by a Kryptean informant? I would pay for that in blood. That is why I stand before you now, denouncing them in public. My husband risked death to weaken them, and I do the same. Cast off their suffocating shackles. Let us be the people who stand toe to toe with tyrants, not look over our shoulders for faceless murderers!'

They were wavering, she could tell. All of them felt that fear, of having the wrong words overheard and facing Kryptean vengeance. But she needed more than that. If the Ephors were to come down in her favour, she needed the crowd so emphatically on her side that they could not be overruled.

And beneath her, she could see a procession parting the crowds: Sigrid, returning at the head of twenty berserkers, who carried between them a great pale casket of holly wood. Keturah beckoned them forward. 'I would like to finish today by showing you all something. Bring up the coffin!'

Carried up onto the stage by half a dozen berserkers came the wooden sarcophagus, which they deposited in the centre. 'Stand it up, please,' said Keturah in that herald's voice, and they tilted it onto one end.

Keturah herself took up a spike and began to wrench at the nails holding the lid shut. The crowd waited in complete stillness, now desperate to see what she had to show them. She could feel her own anger, and no small amount of fear at what she might find beneath these boards, as she ripped and wrenched at one side, loosening it. She attacked the other, the nails protesting as they were uprooted until with a final squeak, the lid was hauled away and crashed forward onto the platform, followed by a rush of feathers.

There came a great groan from the crowd and a long gasp like a million pebbles scrambling after a retreating tide. Then a roar of adulation nearly swept Keturah off her feet. She staggered back to appraise the body at a few paces. 'Hello, cousin,' she said softly.

Before them again stood Pryce the Wild, his flesh stiff, his eyes a little open to reveal two blank grey stones, his teeth bared in a slight grimace. He was quite as intimidating as he had been in life.

Keturah raised her hands and gesticulated towards the coffin. Obediently, the crowd began to applaud. 'Let us cut away the fat, and come to the issue at hand!' she cried. 'Yes, my husband went further than expected in the south. But when did the people of the Black Kingdom grow tired of victory? I left the army a couple of months ago, and they were marching on the Suthern capital. They had taken Lincylene! They had destroyed Suthdal's army in the field! And whatever you may've heard, they were not vanquished by plague! They cut the contagion out and have since taken Northwic,' she raised one finger. 'They have taken Oxenaford!' She began counting off cities. 'Norantone! Grantabryge!' The crowd began to cheer along with each point she made. 'And Lundenceaster! The Suthern capital is now *ash*, never to rise again!'

The noise was frightening, and she had to stop for some while to let the crowd calm.

'Yes, many have died! Among them this man, my cousin. That is the price of glory, and security, paid by every generation before us. But the whole purpose of this campaign is that we can at last settle that debt. Subdue Suthdal, and we bring to an end the constant erosion of our people! We secure our own future in perpetuity. We make a sacrifice today, which will be repaid a thousand-fold to our descendants. If that is not the definition of wisdom, what is? If there is ever a period when that does not define our people, then we are lost!

'Peers! Peers, I amend my motion. I do not simply want the statue of Uvoren removed. I want it replaced by this body. May it stand forever as a symbol of who we are; what we sacrificed, and why.' Just as the Chief Historian had done the day before, Keturah planted her feet and raised her hands above her head. 'Are you not with me?'

It seemed the most reasonable proposition in the world, and a matter of utmost patriotism. Who could deny her? As the crowd began to bay Pryce's name, Keturah at last stepped back and accepted a drink of water from Virtanen.

'Bravo, my lady.' He had to bellow, and still she could barely hear him. 'Are you going to make the last point we talked about?'

'I believe so.'

'Be gentle.'

Keturah turned back to the crowd now feverishly chanting Pryce's name. She could not resist the flash of revulsion that came over her own countenance. These people would have murdered her last night, given the chance.

She held up her hand, and after a time they let her speak. 'Let us not forget that we were all of us taken in by this. I am quite sure my opponent and I are on common ground, when I say that the violence seen on these streets in recent weeks is unprecedented.' Keturah glanced at Frathi, who inclined her head graciously.

'Undeniably.'

'How would you judge it, my lady?'

Frathi examined Keturah frankly. 'Appalling.'

'I agree wholeheartedly,' said Keturah, turning back to them. 'These unmoored emotions are not the behaviour of full peers and subjects of the Black Kingdom. They are the preserve of the Sutherner.' She paused. 'That is not us. It never has been. We now have a choice. Which kingdom do we want to be? His?' And she pointed at Tore, standing beneath her. 'Or his?' She swung her arm towards Pryce's embalmed remains. She shrugged and looked at the Ephors. 'Finished.'

As she walked to the back of the platform, the crowd began to applaud. By criticising them at the last, she risked losing them altogether. But she thought that at their core, they would agree with her. The frenzy whipped up by Tore ran contrary to a far stronger, far deeper instinct.

She sat, and the Ephors huddled together like a mass of crows. She heard Tore begin a chant of *'U-vor-en!'* which was immediately drowned out by *'Pryce! Pryce! Pryce!'* It built and swelled, some of the Ephors casting angry looks towards the crowd as they struggled to comprehend each other over the din.

At last, Valken nodded to his fellow Ephors and stood. The crowd bayed at the sight of him and he had to hold his hand aloft for minutes before he could be heard.

'The court has weighed the persuasive cases put forward by both sides. We find Uvoren's statue was unlawfully constructed—'

'No!' came Tore's bellow.

'And should be replaced with the remains of Pryce the Wild. Lord Roper must still answer before the court for all he has done, but shall do so as Black Lord, and not an outlaw.'

Valken bowed, the crowd thundering its approval. Keturah ignored them. She crossed the platform to Frathi and bowed before her opponent.

'My lady. After the chaos that has gripped this fortress, it seems to me more important than ever that there should be respect between two adversaries. It was an honour to share this platform with you.'

Frathi stood, and held Vigtyr's sword, Warspite, out before her. 'Well spoke, Lady Keturah. The Black Lord paid for this. It should be yours, I think.'

Keturah took the sword, and the pair of them bowed to one another. She found Sigrid and Virtanen standing behind her and embraced them. Ormur had scurried up onto the platform, and she held the sword out to the boy. 'Here,' she said. 'One of the best ever made. Unlike Vigtyr, I've no doubt you'll be the warrior worthy of it.' Ormur accepted it mutely, open-mouthed.

Keturah did not wait for a response, turning back to the crowds and raising her arms. 'Who will carry the coffin with me?'

The platform faced instant invasion, dozens swarming forward to take Pryce's sarcophagus and carry it jerkily down the steps. Keturah followed it. 'May I borrow this?' she asked one of the berserkers on the way down, holding a hand out for his axe.

He stared at her expressionlessly, and when she regarded him unwaveringly, he unhooked the axe and handed it over. It was vastly heavier than she expected, so that it felt as though the head was about to tip her forward. She promised to return it and fell in behind Pryce's sarcophagus. Together they piled through one district after another, until they arrived at Uvoren's statue before the Great Gate.

Keturah was breathing hard. She felt that rage again as she looked up at the blank countenance of her old enemy. 'It's better than you deserve, you villain.' She drew back the axe and someone yelled for everyone to stand back. Then she swung it with all her might at the statue's terracotta knees. They folded into shards with a tinkling crunch, the statue dropping six inches into its own ankles. Then it tipped forward. The crowd scrambled out of the way, and with a pure note, Uvoren the Mighty hit the ground and shattered.

23
The Cliffs

It was just the six of them left. Gray and Leon, and the four Krypteans: Yngvar, Rethin, Inhaf and Sunhi. Gray and Leon's swords, Ramnea and Silence, lay by the fire. They might as well be lodged in the forest canopy, for all the guardsmen would be able to reach them. Leon was staring transparently at his own, and Rethin had seen.

'Try, if you like,' he said encouragingly. 'I've not killed a Sacred Guardsman before.'

'You couldn't kill a mangy fox, brother,' said Leon without moving his eyes.

Gray was thinking hard. This was not the time for a rash attack: the two of them were Roper's only hope of survival. The Sacred Guard had been well spread out on the journey here and were not likely to arrive in time. Gray and Leon had to leave this clearing alive and expedite their journey here. Or one of them did.

'Do you really think you could kill a Sacred Guardsman?' Gray asked Rethin, trying surreptitiously to look around the clearing. The fire was still burning brightly, the pot of birch-cloud tea bubbling in the flames. Their own weapons might be out of reach, but the Kryptea each carried two matt-black blades. They were infamous weapons, said to be so poisonous that even a shallow cut could kill a man in hours. Each agent held one, the other sheathed at their belts. Gray just needed a moment; just a single heartbeat when they were distracted. 'Not with your faithless backstabbing. I mean; man to man, when your enemy knows you're coming. Like a warrior.'

'Like a fool.'

Gray laughed hollowly. 'I thought not.' *As soon as I move, they'll kill Leon. How do I warn him?* 'Why would you spare us?' Gray went on. 'The only reason I can think of is that you're scared. You suspect the army will destroy you for taking the Black Lord, and are trying to avoid stirring up more anger.' Rethin did not reply, and sensing weakness, Gray dug deeper. 'Even a year ago, the Kryptea would never have done that. You'd have killed us both and damn the consequences. Even you don't have confidence in what you do any more.'

'It must be hard, being where you are, Captain,' Rethin replied mildly. 'Knowing that the Sacred Guard have been bested once again, and the tyrant you wait on has been consigned to history. Again. The Guard's martial reputation must be one of the least deserved in Erebos.'

'By contrast, you have earned yours completely. Pure backstabbers, not a shred of honour or courage to share between you. What I want to know is, how many of you hoped to be appointed to the Sacred Guard, and were only seduced by the Kryptea when you found out you didn't make the cut?'

Rethin seemed to stiffen slightly. 'You won't provoke me,' he said, voice still calm. 'I waited until Roper Kynortasson had almost brought disaster upon us. I can wait a little longer.'

I can't.

Gray ducked. His body twisted and his left hand snatched at the hilt of Inhaf's sword, which he caught by his fingertips. He lunged towards the fire, pulling the matt-black blade with him, unable to see how the assassins were reacting. Every nerve in his back was alive to the moment steel might dig into the skin, and he contorted himself like a cut snake, dodging swords he anticipated but could not see. He trod right in the fire and raked back with his heel, sending embers and brands spitting at Leon and the two agents who guarded him. There was a bellow of pain at his back, and Gray's foot upset the pot of tea onto the embers in an eruption of steam. Gray twisted around, sword raised, trying to prepare himself and ignore the feeling that he had already come further than he had any right.

Somehow, Leon had forced his way free of his two guards. He had no weapon, and was backing away as they advanced on him, swords outstretched. Gray had a sword, but was outnumbered two to one, Rethin and Sunhi stalking closer with their own weapons held forward. 'That was slippery, Captain,' said Rethin, amused.

Gray looked over Suhni's shoulder, widened his eyes and nodded vehemently.

Sunhi could not help himself. Gray seemed to be at a safe distance, and the bluff was so convincing that just for a moment, Sunhi thought he was signalling to Leon. He cast the swiftest of glances over his shoulder, and Gray had started lunging before he had even known the Kryptean would take the bait. He was a long way back, Gray at the very limit of his range, just managing to score a red line on his forearm.

Sunhi's head snapped back to Gray, a look of surprise on his face, but the captain was already moving, scrambling away from Rethin, who had not fallen for the bluff and launched a riposte at the captain. Gray's feet moved automatically to place Sunhi between himself and Rethin.

Gray's eyes were on the cut dribbling scarlet down Sunhi's arm, and the Kryptean followed his gaze, registering the wound for the first time. He swore, taking an involuntary pace backwards and jerking the wound up to his eyes, panic in his face. He stepped back again, tangling with Rethin, who was trying to get to Gray. Sunhi could retreat no further, was distracted and shocked, and Gray lunged off his back foot, black shortsword again at the very edge of its range but finding the centre of Sunhi's chest. It struck the tough ligaments between his bone plates, and Gray felt the tip stall for an instant. Then it broke through, between the bone plates and into the great artery which ran in front of the spine.

At once, Sunhi's face went the colour of fog. He staggered, swayed slightly, and then collapsed forward as Rethin thrust him out of the way. Gray retreated, stealing a glance to his left, where Leon had picked up a branch and was using it to parry stabbing blows from his two attackers, backing further and further from Gray. Leon needed a weapon. Their longswords lay abandoned by the fire. Get either of them into Leon's hand, Grey knew, and the fight was over.

'Leon, towards me!' Gray shouted, deflecting a lunge from Rethin. The blow took a chip out of Gray's sword the size of a birch leaf. The matt-black steel was exceptionally hard and brittle, and evidently not forged for extended duels. Rethin had drawn his second sword and now assaulted Gray with one in each hand. Gray defended with clear eyes, deflecting, dodging and stepping, but unable to launch a counter-attack. He was technically better than Rethin, but the Kryptean's two swords were a substantial and frightening advantage. The rumour that these swords were poisoned was true, Gray knew. Sunhi's horror at even a minor wound showed that, and Rethin was slashing at him as though harvesting grass, looking for no more than a scratch, which would condemn Gray to an agonising death.

There were desperate noises. Panting breath, the scrape and scuff of boots and leaves, little grunts of effort. Gray could not get past those two blades without sustaining a fatal wound, but neither could he just defend. Leon surely would not last long with just a branch, and with each moment they delayed, Roper was closer to death. They were his only hope of survival. If they died, Roper died too. If they won too slowly, still, Roper died.

There was only one thing Gray could think to do. He kept retreating, stepping carefully backwards and slowly drawing Rethin around so that it was Gray who stood closer to the fire.

Leon was trying to do the same, though with less success against his two attackers.

Rethin suddenly redoubled his attack. He launched a half-lunge, checked and then lunged again, forcing Gray to take several rapid paces backwards. His heel snagged on a root and he was suddenly stumbling, losing his balance as Rethin surged after him like a falcon. One of his swords lashed out, coming so close to Gray's shoulder that it snagged in the material of his tunic. Gray leaned back further still, falling out of control, certain he would topple to the earth until he slammed into a thick birch tree and his fall came to an abrupt halt.

But Gray had trained his entire life to focus; to master fear, and panic, and by sheer habit, his thoughts remained unclouded. He pretended to be still off-balance, sliding to one side of the tree, tempting Rethin after him, and then pulling abruptly back to centre. Rethin's right sword had been inches from piercing his cheek, and instead jarred off the bark of the birch. He was over-extended by his lunge, and Gray took that swift moment to manoeuvre the tree half between them, so that its woody bulk defended his left-hand side like a shield.

Still, Rethin had the intensity of a stalking cat, eyes burning into each scrap of Gray's skin on which he might land any cut at all. He made a hard slash at Gray's exposed right. Gray parried, and the two swords met with a dull clunk. Gray's blade snapped, a spike of brittle black steel toppling away from the rest and leaving less than half a sword in his hand. Without pause, he drew back his arm and hurled it at Rethin.

He turned and ran before he saw whether it had struck home. Rethin yelled behind him, out of rage or pain Gray had no idea, just sprinting hard and blind for the two longswords that lay by the fire. 'Leon! Leon! Leon!' he was bellowing, diving for the nearer sword. Gray arrived on all fours, desperate as a wounded dog, snatching up Silence along with a handful of twigs and eroded leaves. Rethin's footsteps were pounding up behind him, and he flashed a glance – all he had time for – at Leon grappling with his two opponents just yards away.

'Leon!' There were no choices left, and Gray drew back his arm and hurled the sword, scabbard and all.

Silence cartwheeled through the air, belt still attached to the scabbard, the heavy buckle on the end swinging wildly. Leon had heard Gray's bellow, knew what he had planned. He thrust his chipped branch hard at his two opponents to buy a heartbeat, and lashed out with a desperate hand.

As if conjuring her from nothing, Leon snatched Silence from the air, sweeping off the sheath in the same movement. Gray unleashed an involuntary scream of triumph as Leon parried a blow with the sheath clutched in his left hand. With his right, he brought Silence down in a huge overhead slash at Yngvar. The Kryptean raised his sword to block, but the black blade smashed like glass beneath Leon's blow. Without losing a fraction of its speed, Silence travelled on like a meteor and cut off Yngvar's arm and half his shoulder.

Gray saw none of this. Rethin's footsteps were almost upon him, and he rolled aside, right hand clasping Ramnea as he did so. He stood and turned, sword rasping clear of its scabbard and launching a huge slash at the onrushing Rethin, who did not have time to stop. Ramnea carved across his chest, shattering one of the black swords and stopping him in his tracks. The wound was not fatal, but that realisation brought Gray a savage pleasure. For an instant, his desperation turned into vicious triumph. He forgot how little time they had and knew nothing but a fierce desire to wound; to inflict as much pain as possible on his enemy. His range now far exceeded Rethin's and he propelled Ramnea's tip into his traitorous face.

It struck home and Rethin's head snapped back, a cheekbone shattered by the blow. The Kryptean howled, his two swords – one broken and the other whole – flailing incoherently as Gray drew back Ramnea and drove it as hard as he could into Rethin's chest. It smashed into the left side, through the bone plates and into the wall of his heart.

'Bastard,' Gray snarled.

Rethin staggered backwards and then stumbled to his knees, eyes still locked on Gray with the utmost intensity. Gray met that falcon's gaze, now with a huge, black puncture wound beneath his left eye. 'I wish I could inflict the pain you deserve.'

Then Rethin's broken sword wafted up, almost lazily. Like a leaf burned on the fire until only its weightless skeleton remains and floats up on a current of hot air, the sword drifted towards Gray's left hand and scored a deep cut on his palm. 'Ah!' Gray recoiled too late. Ramnea stayed lodged in Rethin's heart, and the Kryptean capsized, dead, onto the forest floor. Gray held the cut hand up to his face, just as Sunhi had done, a horrible roar of fear in his ears. 'Shit.'

It could not be poisoned. He stared in numb denial, looking for some indication that it was just the scratch it appeared. Then the cut began to burn so hot he half expected smoke to pour from between the two lips of skin.

A hand seized his own. He looked up dumbly to see it was Leon, who dragged him by the wrist, six feet to an ash tree. Gray threw a dazed glance at the two decapitated corpses Leon had left behind, and then down at Silence, covered in blood. 'Leon?'

The guardsman pinned Gray's left hand high up against the tree, and drew back the blood-covered sword like a butcher with a cleaver. 'Hold still,' was all he said.

There was enough of a fire left smouldering that, once Leon had scraped the embers together and blown them back to a red fever, they could quench the pulsing stump of Gray's wrist. There was pain, but the cauterising was too fast and too surreal to be agonising. Leon withdrew the charred, smoking lump where heartbeats before had been Gray's left hand, and began to bind it with scraps of Rethin's cloak.

'Stop,' said Gray, trying to push him away. 'Stop, Leon.'

Leon just pinned him down irritably. 'You need this or you'll die, you idiot.'

'I know. I'll do it, get off me!' He managed to fight hard enough that Leon was temporarily dislodged. 'Get the Guard, Leon. Don't wait for me, go and get as many as you can, as fast as possible. Stop it, you fool, listen to me. Jokul won't be alone, we need at least a score, more if you can get them.'

Leon took one moment to satisfy himself that Gray was thinking clearly, and then stood up. 'You'll wait here?' he asked, wiping his sword on Yngvar's body.

'I'll try and find Roper, maybe I can guide you to him. But don't look for me, look for Roper, and if I can help, so much the better.'

Leon was already striding away, sword sheathed at his side. 'I'll not fail,' he called over his shoulder, breaking into a trot.

Gray had no idea how he would catch up to a mounted party of Krypteans when he himself was on foot and badly weakened. He could see the great splash of blood on the tree trunk where Leon had struck off his hand, and standing felt beyond him. *Roper*, said a voice in his head. *He needs you. You have to go now.* 'On your feet then, Gray,' he said aloud.

He rolled onto his one good hand and knees, and a wave of nausea swept over him, his vision shimmering into white. He tried to stand, but there was no strength in his legs and he collapsed back to the ground. Despite Leon's swift actions, some of that poison must have made it past his wrist.

He started crawling towards one of the water-skins lying next to a decapitated Kryptean body. 'Come on,' he muttered. Water would help with the blood loss. He uncorked it and took a long draught, surprised to find it was not water at all. It tasted salty and bitter, and he swallowed one harsh mouthful after another until the whole skin was drained and he felt sick.

He threw it aside and clutched a second skin, catching his breath for a few moments before he tried again to stand. Fog blew across his vision at once and he seemed to weigh nothing at all for a moment, so that he could barely tell if he were standing or lying. He waited for the sensation to pass, but though a little colour came back to the world, he felt no steadier on his feet. 'Onwards,' he mumbled to himself, thinking of Roper. *Onwards.*

He crashed between the trees, managing just a dozen paces before he stumbled back onto his knees. *Come on! Come on!* He could not stand, so for twenty feet, he crawled. Even that felt like hauling himself hand over hand up a rope.

How he was to find the Kryptea like this, he had no idea. *Would that have stopped Roper?* It would not. Gray staggered back up, trying to walk again, charred wrist held in at his chest. He did what his master would have done and just placed one foot before the other, desperate, hopeful, resolute. Whenever he reached out to steady himself, his right hand sparked and tingled with each touch. Like a man at the extremes of drunkenness, Gray followed a thoughtless star, which led him out of the forest.

It was only when he reached its edge, just a hundred yards from where he had lost his hand, that he first realised he had left Ramnea by the fire. *No matter,* he thought. *You can't wield it anyway. Onwards.*

He squinted at an outcrop of rock fifty yards away, and told himself he just had to make it there. *Just reach the rock. For Roper, just get to the rock.* He arrived, took a bitter drink from the water-skin at his side, and found another target: this one a stump just forty feet away. *Better,* he thought. The rock had felt too far.

It seemed as though there was a veil between his body and his mind: everything strangely distant and faint, and his sense of time eroded so that every footstep seemed to take an age. He set one target after another, and when he had managed half a dozen, he leaned on the last, a rotting fence post, so he could look back the way he had come. The treeline from which he had emerged was a little over a hundred yards away. He had barely travelled any distance at all and gave a soft moan. *My king. Please, please just hold on. I'm coming.*

But perhaps he was walking more easily now, and he

thought his vision was a little clearer. Whatever was in those Kryptean water-skins seemed to be doing him some good, and he leaned against the post, sucking greedily until the second was empty. *Good. You'll be stronger now. Keep going.*

He did, over gentle hills, the sea on his right, simply trusting the instinct that said he was moving towards Roper and not away from him. He was definitely growing stronger. He could almost see clearly now and enough awareness of his body had returned that he could feel the throbbing of his burnt wrist. He was beginning to register what had happened, too. 'Idiot,' he whispered. 'Why did you let them stay? Why would you let anyone except a guardsman anywhere near him? Stupid. *Stupid. Stupid. Stupid.*'

The sun was low behind him. He was so busy cursing himself that when he crested a hill, he did not immediately realise there were figures in the shallow valley below him. He blundered on, heavy head drooping, until he looked up and saw them. Men with lanky shadows, arranged in a circle some two hundred yards away.

Gray dropped at once, swarming behind a rocky outcrop from which he peered at these figures. Their horses were tethered nearby and they made a circle around two central silhouettes. One stood: small, lean and wrapped against the wind. In front of him knelt a prisoner: bigger, wearing a familiar cloak, which flashed with embroidered lightning in the wind.

Roper! They were not yet too late.

Gray rolled onto his back and thought. He needed to get to high ground: somewhere Leon would be able to see him. Feverishly, he began to crawl back the way he had come, slithering over the crest of the hill, aware that their time must be nearly up. A little way back in the direction he had come, Gray spotted a rise. If he ran up it, he thought he might be invisible to the Kryptea, but visible to Leon's party if they came this way from the forest.

Gray stood once more and began a feeble trot towards the

hill. He was exhausted: his mouth dry, his tongue swollen, his legs rusted solid. He cast a glance over his shoulder to check the Kryptea had not followed, and saw instead a group of horsemen half a mile inland.

'Leon!' He almost shouted, but the Kryptea were more likely to hear than Leon was. Frantically, he waved his arms over his head. They were too far from the sea and had already passed Gray. On their current path, they would pass the Kryptea too.

Gray reversed a little higher up the hill, still flapping his arms madly as the horsemen passed on. He swore, panic giving him strength as he made it to the summit and kept waving, silhouetted now against the evening sky.

One of them must have seen him. The whole group wheeled and began to gallop in his direction, clods of dark earth flying up in their wake. The Kryptea stood between Gray and the horsemen: as long as they came towards his hill they would stumble upon the scene. Leon seemed to have brought about twenty men. There were perhaps thirty Kryptea: it might be enough, if Leon was bold and fast.

Gray began to drop down the hill, losing sight of the guardsmen and running for the crest where he had first sighted his enemy. He could not see them yet, but the galloping hooves of Leon's party rumbled across the still evening. If he could hear them, so could the Kryptea. *Shit. What if they kill Roper now?* 'Hold on, brother. Hold on!'

When he crested the ridge, the Kryptea were scuttling like woodlice beneath an upturned log. They must have heard Leon's approaching riders and split, the majority mustering together around their horses, half a dozen others running in the opposite direction: towards the sea. The slight figure of Jokul hurried alongside them, and they were dragging with them a tall silhouette, who flailed and struggled against the many hands pulling him onward.

'Roper!' Gray found he was able to sprint and plunged into the valley, towards the smaller group, just as Leon's guardsmen thundered over a rise and roared the charge. The Kryptean horsemen shouted in return and began a counter-charge, perhaps hoping to hold off the guard and give the smaller group long enough to finish what they had come for.

'My lord! Roper!' Gray was still four hundred yards short of the Krypteans: there was nothing he could do.

Suddenly the tall figure broke free of the hands clutching him and for a brief, glorious moment, he outstripped them, opening up a gap between him and his pursuers. Then a Kryptean agent dived after him and took a swipe at his ankle, knocking his sprinting legs together so that they tangled and he was down once more. The shadowed figures were on him at once, pulling him upright, straining and wrestling, all just yards from the cliff edge. Gray had never run so fast, horrible, horrible fear propelling his legs, desperate to reach his king. 'Roper!'

Still, he had not given up. He was straining and wrestling, fighting with fists, feet, fingernails, teeth as he was dragged within six feet, three, his heels sliding on the grass as four men bore him towards the edge.

'No! Roper!'

They heaved him over.

He did not cry out as he fell. In silence he twisted, snatching at one of the Krypteans and seizing his wrist. The assassin was tugged forward, overbalanced, and with a shriek, toppled off with him. Together, the two of them plummeted.

'No! No!' Gray was running as hard as he could. Some of the guardsmen had broken through the Kryptean horsemen and were riding towards the splinter group.

They were too late. They were all too late.

Gray arrived after half a dozen mounted guardsmen. Every Kryptean had their arms high in a gesture of surrender, all except Jokul, who snarled like a polecat as they came near. 'It's over!' he seethed. 'It's done! We are operating within ancient law. Stand down, all of you. You have no right to interfere in Kryptean business.'

Gray ignored him, pulling up panting before the edge of the cliff. He looked down.

A hundred feet beneath, two bodies lay broken on the rocks. Neither one moved as the swell washed over them, its retreating edge crimson. Everything behind Gray seemed quiet. He just watched as the two bodies were picked up by the surf, and sucked out into the sea. Gray was not sure which was Roper, and which the Kryptean agent. About twenty feet from the shore, both sank beneath the wrought-iron waves. Gray watched a long time, but neither resurfaced. The sea's small waves remained even and unbroken, like a vast wrinkled cloth.

24
Possession

Gray felt numb. He did not believe. It could not be true.

He turned around to see that everyone – Leon was there, Jokul, equal numbers of guardsmen and Krypteans – had been staring at his back. They watched him, both sides waiting on his assessment for what should happen next. Rage began to swell within him.

'Kill them,' he said, indicating the Kryptean assassins. 'Keep him.' He pointed at Jokul.

It was the order Leon had been waiting for. He stepped forward and buried Silence into a Kryptean back. The tip burst out of his chest and the man arched away, screaming, but Leon just pushed him over and hacked at the agent next to him. There was suddenly a fierce scrabbling as Krypteans sought weapons or retreat, but they were chopped down as though it were a farmyard cull. One was even booted off the cliff, falling with a shriek filled with horror and fear. Jokul just watched, perhaps a mite paler than usual, his arms pinioned by a guardsman.

Behind him, the Sacred Guardsmen who had captured the Kryptean horsemen saw what was happening and began to execute their prisoners. There were screams, swearing and the occasional clash of steel as one of the Kryptea found a weapon and was overwhelmed.

One horseman spurred clear of the mass, two guardsmen urging their own mounts after him. The Kryptean seemed the faster, and was drawing away from his pursuers. One guardsman hurled his sword end over end at the assassin. The handle struck him on the back and though the man was knocked forward, it bounced off.

Dimly, Gray recognised the silhouette of Sakeus: one of the original Belated Guard, close to Roper, who had betrayed him so badly. 'Get him!' he bellowed. 'Get him!'

But Sakeus was escaping. The last Gray saw of him he was cresting a far hill and disappearing out of sight. The two guardsmen still gave chase, but were now fifty yards behind.

Gray turned to Jokul, who was staring tight-lipped at this scene. 'We'll catch him. But you're the unlucky one. We'll go back to the army. You'll point out every last Kryptean agent. And if at first you refuse, you will suffer until you do.'

'I don't know them,' said Jokul, coldly. 'I knew their officers, and each officer alone knew the identity of his agents. You have just killed the only people who could've told you what you want to know.'

Gray leaned towards Jokul and looked him full in the face. 'I'm glad if you won't talk yet,' he said. 'I prefer it this way.'

Some of the guardsmen walked the site, dismembering the Krypteans and scattering their pieces to prolong their agony into the next life. Special attention was paid to the 'Belated Guard', for their false friendship to Roper. Gray kept looking at the distant hill for some sign of the guardsmen returning with Sakeus, but there was nothing.

Jokul was bound, pressed to the ground, and then kicked unconscious. On his person, they found Cold-Edge, the sword tucked naked through his belt.

It took them three days to recover the scabbard. Eventually it washed ashore, strapped to the remains of its master's body.

Gray rode back to the army, guardsmen in tow. There was a kind of fever on him, and in days to come, he would not properly be able to recall what had happened next. They ignored the challenges of the sentries, breached sacred custom by trampling their horses through the sleeping and cooking areas of the Greyhazel, and did not slow until they had found Tekoa, at the centre of the legions.

Gray dismounted, severed wrist held in at his chest, Tekoa's eyes on him. 'Captain,' he said. 'You've found a way through?' Then he spied the stump of Gray's hand. 'By the ocean. What *happened*?'

'Gather the legates,' said Gray. 'Immediately.'

'Why?'

'The Black Lord has been slain.'

Tekoa froze. He looked at the men behind Gray in case they might give this away as a joke, but they stared back stony-faced.

'Roper . . .' Still, he seemed to be waiting for Gray to contradict him, but the captain made neither word nor gesture. 'Roper is dead?'

Gray nodded. 'Gather the legates.'

'How? Safinim?'

Gray jerked his head and a guardsman rode forward with a bound figure laid over his saddle. He heaved it onto the ground at Tekoa's feet.

Tekoa looked expressionlessly down at Jokul for a moment. He shared a glance with Gray. Then he started stamping on Jokul's head. Teeth gritted, emitting small grunts of effort and rage, nobody stepped in until the legate had ground to a halt, panting hard. He spat on Jokul, who had not uttered a sound, and responded only by moving one arm listlessly.

They gathered the legates, and meanwhile, word was flashing from ear to ear. The legions started murmuring, and a hissing began to rise from the ranks. The Kryptea had struck. Roper – *their* Roper – was murdered. The Belated Guard had been assassins, and the army was laced through with traitors.

Before the legates had even concluded their meeting, restless bands of soldiers began to approach, demanding instruction. It took longer to send them away than it did for more groups to appear, and soon a crowd was building. Soon after, the Sacred Guard were forced to draw swords in defence of Jokul, who would otherwise have been pulled to string by the assembling legionaries. The legates knew they needed a plan for what to do with Jokul, how to find the rest of the Kryptea, and what to do thereafter. But the noise and unrest around them rose to such a pitch that they abandoned the meeting without even appointing a leader.

It was Gray who had been closest to Roper in life and death, and therefore he who appeared to command what came next.

By nightfall, the bands of soldiers were manhandling comrades to lay before the captain and denounce as members of the Kryptea. Even through his grief and his rage, Gray recognised that not all of these men, perhaps not even most of them, could be Kryptean. They seemed to be the unpopular men from each century, or the most unhappy.

But surrounded by the buzzing, railing legionaries, Gray could not send them away. And as the mood spread, he forgot that he had wanted to. The prisoners were shown to Jokul, who still refused to say anything.

The fires were built up high, and highest of all was the bonfire by which they held the Master of the Kryptea. He thrashed, he begged, he pleaded and threatened as each prisoner was laid before him. Gray presided over the maelstrom, surrounded by queues of legionaries who had assembled without a word of order.

There was no regaining control. The officers had joined with the men, and most were in favour of this upswelling of revenge. The Sutherners were forgotten, and the army began to swarm.

It was days before Gray remembered to do the job which should have been his first priority. At last a herald was summoned and given a message to relay to Keturah.

My Lady. It is my sacred duty to inform you the Black Lord has died for the kingdom. Long live the Black Lady.

25
The Queen of Albion

Aramilla had been there to watch the Anakim turn away from the Wylie Lines, and had immediately announced a feast. 'Good news has been exceedingly short,' she declared. 'Our victories must be celebrated. And no half-measures. I won't have this be a mean reminder that we are a diminished nation, taking an interlude between battles. I want a celebration to restore faith in Suthdal.'

Bellamus did not agree: the war was far from won, and this did not seem the time to relax, or divert the funds donated by their allies into a banquet. But the people of Wiltun were with the queen, and dragged tables out into the streets, hung ribbons and wreaths from posts, fences and doors, and then engaged in the serious business of getting drunk.

Bellamus rode through these celebrations on his way to the queen's feast, and when the revellers spotted him and gave a raucous cheer, even he could not resist the mood. He raised a stern hand in recognition, spoiling the effect by grinning foolishly. The townsfolk were singing, and straw effigies of Grendel, grotesquely exaggerated in size and craggy Anakim features, burned on street corners and market squares, filling the air with bonfire smoke.

Bellamus had come from a royal tournament laid on by the

queen, and joining the queue to Penbro Hall alone, he listened in to the merry dissection of each blow struck and contest fought. It was chilly, the first sting of rain in the air, and the open doors, leaking torchlight and the promise of a warm seat and hot food, glowed like the gates to heaven. Distantly, a choir was chanting in plainsong, and intoxicating wafts of roasted meat and baking pastry drifted out to the waiting nobles.

At the entrance were set bowls of orange-scented water, and Bellamus found himself washing his hands alongside the Bishop Widukind. 'Are you managing to enjoy yourself, Bishop?'

Widukind shook his head, observing a troop of jugglers in flat contempt.

'You disapprove?'

'Of indulgence, yes.'

It had been so long since Bellamus had heard Widukind speak that he had nearly forgotten his voice: measured, and dry as a shed leaf. 'And why's that? You don't think we should be rebuilding confidence and restoring our energies?'

Widukind trained his dark-ringed eyes on Bellamus. 'The wine you drink, Lord Safinim. Do you find that restores your energies?'

Bellamus recoiled slightly, feeling his face redden in the gloom. The bishop inclined his head as if to say that had not been personal, before drying his hands and passing on.

'God keep me from being sat next to him tonight,' murmured a voice in Bellamus's ear. He looked right to find he had been joined by a figure he did not recognise: a bearded lord, perhaps six inches shorter than Bellamus himself, but with the solidity and poise of a bear. 'You'll be the famous Lord Safinim,' this beast observed, leaning forward to grasp Bellamus by the elbows. 'What a pleasure, I've heard so much, and though I'm hardly worth hearing about, I daresay the queen's famous spy-master will know all there is to know about me.' The man stood back, beaming and inviting Bellamus's assessment. He spoke with an unfamiliar accent, wafted the scent of lilies with each airy gesture, and bore a crossed broadsword and sceptre on his breast.

'You are the Lord Ruden,' said Bellamus, with a bow.

'Yes, yes,' said Ruden, twinkling and gesturing at the other nobles, 'but come, any one of these pigeons would have known as much. What else have you heard?'

Bellamus would usually have dismissed this enquiry with a deft remark, but perhaps because he felt so friendless at court, or perhaps because Ruden's attention was so flattering, he found himself considering his noble companion. 'The Lord Ruden of Oche, favourite cousin of His Imperial Majesty the Emperor Karoli, arrived at Portmuthe just three days ago on the *Ruach*. In the hold were a large number of extremely heavy chests, which clink when tipped over. Following in your wake, a corps of twenty thousand armoured halberdiers, specially trained and experienced in fighting the Karantaji Anakim. And behind them, a band of *cataphracts*, which I understand are cavalry of some sort.'

Ruden was still beaming and nodding at this inventory, and Bellamus went on.

'Most of the nobility here are new to you, but I believe you and the Bishop Widukind are already well acquainted. Acting on the emperor's orders, it is you who flattened not one, but two of Widukind's rebellions. Naturally, the bishop despises you for that. You've thirteen children that I know of, four legitimate from your well-regarded wife, Otgiva, and one, if rumours are to be believed, with the emperor's own sister, which may explain why such an esteemed nobleman was sent to this embattled isle.' Ruden's eyebrows had risen, but he was still smiling. 'There are other stories, of course, but the sun has barely set, and we may get to those later.'

Ruden threw back his head and laughed. 'Lord Safinim! Just as I'd imagined, and charmingly frank. I gather we are to sit next to one another. Shall we? It sounds as though there's much to discuss.'

They were indeed sat together, comparing notes on court gossip over the chattering of the hall, and ignoring the tumblers spinning between the tables. They broke off for Widukind to say grace, and then the trumpeters heralded a first course of roasted swan. Each bird arrived to a swell of harpstrings, armoured with foil helmets and lances like knights.

'How marvellous,' said Ruden, observing the birds.

'Our feast is to be in the Frankish fashion, in honour of your master, my Lord Ruden,' Aramilla declared. She was sitting on Ruden's other side so that he occupied her right. 'I believe a dozen courses is customary?'

Ruden hesitated and then took a sip of wine. 'For an occasion such as this, a dozen would be about right,' he replied, toasting the queen.

The swans were carved at the table and Bellamus was specially favoured with his own trencher. Most of his table shared one between two or three, and at the lower tables, most of the courses were not served at all. The diners there subsisted on bread and ale, providing a raucous backdrop to their conversation.

But Bellamus's eye was set on one conspicuous figure, towering above the rest. Vigtyr sat in silence, staring down at the bread and ale cradled between his forearms.

Ruden had followed his gaze. 'I gather he triumphed over the hybrid,' he murmured. 'It sounds like quite a fight.'

'It was.'

Bellamus had organised it. He had begged the queen for a slot in the tournament, and she had granted a window between the beasts and the men for Vigtyr to fight the only champion who would deign to face him: Garrett.

'Ultimately though?' said Bellamus, shrugging and taking a sip of wine. 'Ultimately, Vigtyr was far superior. Garrett was better armed and armoured, but Vigtyr was never really troubled.'

'Vigtyr, is it? . . . I hear he nearly killed the other.'

'Nearly,' said Bellamus, who wished he had.

That was his abiding memory of the fight. Not Vigtyr's skill or Garrett's savagery, or the sparks thrown off by the weapons, or the awed gasps of the crowd. It was the moment Vigtyr had twisted the spear from Garrett's hands and knocked him to the ground with a shoulder. Garrett going down in a puff of fine sand, and Vigtyr leaning over him, cutting the strap from his helmet and tearing it off his head. Then the crowd had fallen still as Vigtyr raised his sword, staring down at his supine rival. His face was surprisingly calm. For half a minute, the two looked at one another, and the silence held. *Do it now,* Bellamus had breathed. *Do it!* But at last Vigtyr tossed his sword aside, and walked away. Garrett was left bruised in the sand, as bewildered as any in the crowd.

Vigtyr's prize had been the lowliest seat of the evening: at the bottom table, near the doors and the cold night beyond.

A minstrel was singing over the harps, and Ruden tapped Bellamus on the shoulder. 'This is the tale of your great victory over the Black Lord, is it not?'

'It has changed somewhat from my recollection,' said Bellamus, amused and pulling his eyes from Vigtyr. 'It was the old Black Lord we were fighting, not Roper. And I don't recall the sun being quite so bright.' Quite the reverse. It had been a miserable day, the ground chewed and watered into a marsh. Arrows spitting from an iron sky, everything cold and damp.

The song was a piece of propaganda composed at the queen's instruction, and Bellamus was one of the very few remaining witnesses to that campaign.

'Do we have this right, my Lord Ruden?' the queen asked. 'For the Frankish style, I mean?' She was pointing at the servants, now bearing forth a platter of porpoise, planked in bread trenchers to look like a boat, resting on a blue sea of cloth and crewed by three roasted piglets.

'Quite magnificent, Majesty,' Ruden replied, as his own trencher was set before him.

The queen ate barely any of her portion, instead letting it sit for a time before sending it down to one of the lower tables. There it was received with a great cheer and many toasts to

Her Majesty. One trencher was sent directly to Vigtyr. Bellamus watched the shock on his face as he received it, standing clumsily to raise a toast to the queen. She beamed at him and inclined her head in return.

Bellamus felt such a swell of pity for Vigtyr that he almost missed the open door behind him and the messenger standing there. He stepped into the candlelight, gleaming with fresh rain, eyes darting about the hall before he spotted Bellamus and began to scurry for the High Table. It was Diethaad.

The reeve intercepted him, but Bellamus found he was on his feet and bellowing that he should be let through. Diethaad flashed a look of sly triumph at the reeve and jumped up to the platform on which their table was raised, remembering a hasty bow as he arrived before the queen.

'One of Lord Safinim's men,' she said, toasting him with her goblet. 'I recognise you, sir, though I'm not sure I recall your name. Rise, and welcome. What brings you here on this damp night?'

'Your Majesty,' Diethaad glanced at Bellamus, who gave a tiny nod. Diethaad's eyes were wide. 'The Black Lord is dead.'

Everyone within earshot had been straining to hear what news this strange herald bore, and at those words, silence swept across the table like a candle blown out by a draught. Bellamus could suddenly hear the rain pouring off the thatch, and a lonely harpist plucking at his strings. 'Grendel?' asked the queen faintly.

'You're sure?' Bellamus blurted.

Diethaad nodded vehemently. 'He's dead, Lord. Killed by their Kryptea. Thrown off a cliff.'

Half the hall had fallen silent by now, waiting for the news Diethaad must have delivered.

Then the queen stood in a rustle of silk and raised her arms to the hall. 'Grendel is dead!' she called.

All eyes turned to her and the last of the conversation died. Bellamus glanced swiftly at Vigtyr, and saw his mouth was hanging open.

'The Black Lord has been slain!' the queen declared into the silence. 'Grendel is dead!'

There was a heartbeat, then came uproar. The hall leapt to its feet with a bellow of triumph, the contents of each goblet hurled above the table in a crimson spray and spattering back down on the noble banqueters. A great rumble of thunder swept beneath them as feet began to stamp. Half the guests were embracing, half with their arms raised. Then some lord began to bellow: 'Hail the Queen! Hail the Queen!'

It was taken up in a moment until the hall was roaring as one: 'Hail! Hail! Hail!'

Bellamus looked to Aramilla and found her gazing out over her guests, chin raised and face triumphant. She let them cheer a long time before raising her hand for silence. Still the banqueters, drunk and eager for her blessing, tried to outdo themselves and be the last to cease chanting. In the end, Bellamus and Ruden had to bellow for silence.

'Dear friends,' she called, 'you will remember this night! Our great foe is dead. With Grendel gone, this war has shifted. You will remember this as the night that the war swung in our favour! May no one doubt the quality of your leadership. I have turned the fortunes of this kingdom around, in the direst of circumstances. Our greatest enemy is gone, and at my right hand in this was our support from Erebos, and from Frankia most of all.' She indicated Ruden, who knelt, took her hand and kissed it. 'And my warmaster: the Lord Safinim.' The noise fell away somewhat at Bellamus's name, but the queen would not be dissuaded. 'His influence in this triumph is second only to my own. His judgement has been impeccable, and he has proven his worth ten times over.' She turned to Bellamus and held out her hand. Bellamus too knelt to kiss it. 'Name me queen of Albion,' she breathed. Bellamus looked up at her, and found her face possessed by a savage joy. 'Declare me rightful queen of the island.' Her voice was too low for anyone else to hear. 'Do it now.'

Bellamus hesitated, but what could he do? He got to his

feet and snatched his goblet. 'This is the rightful queen of all Albion!' he declared. 'To the Queen of Albion!'

'The Queen of Albion!' bellowed the hall, and they drank. Aramilla was flushed, but nodded soberly as this great title was laid before her. Ruden stood, doubtless intending to add his own praise, but was drowned out by a song which Bellamus had not heard before, rising up from the lower tables.

On the Winter's coldest night,
When the moon is high,
The Anakim come riding forth,
The Black Lord thund'ring by!
Grendel-O, Grendel-O,
His bones are made of stone!
Grendel-O, Grendel-O,
He's riding for your throne!

His eyes are ice, his tongue is forked,
His shadow walks alone,
He'll take your child, he'll take your cows,
So gather close your own!
Grendel-O, Grendel-O,
Don't step out your door!
Grendel-O, Grendel-O,
He takes them, rich or poor!

Ruden turned to Bellamus, took his hand and shook it warmly. 'I should think congratulations are in order. Bravo, Safinim. Bravo, sir.'

Then the grey-haired Lord Nerven got to his feet and marched over to Bellamus so that he too could offer him his hand. Bellamus stood and took it, smiling weakly.

'We owe you a debt, Safinim,' said the old lord gruffly, before turning and stomping back to his seat. Other lords were leaning forward and raising their goblets to him, and Bellamus nodded back, toasting them in return and trying to look pleased.

The song still pealed out from the lower tables, and a servant set another dish before Bellamus. It was a subtlety of frumenty: an intermediate course of barley-stew, with cinnamon sprinkled on top through a stencil of the queen's coat of arms. He was grateful for the opportunity to look away from his well-wishers, and stared down at the steaming dish, an odd emptiness in his chest.

Roper Kynortasson had been his enemy, and it did not seem an exaggeration to suppose he had been the greatest threat of this era. No other Black Lord had had his combination of drive, and vision, and the popularity to compel his kingdom into obedience. There was certainly some part of Bellamus that felt a weight lifted at the knowledge they were no longer facing his leadership.

But Bellamus had not imagined him dying. Not yet. That did not seem possible. That someone like Roper could succumb to something as common and dirty as assassination was almost a disappointment. One of the great figures of the age was cheapened, and he had deserved better. He had deserved to meet his end in the cataclysmic duel for Albion, which Bellamus had assumed was their shared fate. Not stabbed in the back by men wearing black.

Bellamus tried to take a spoonful of the frumenty, but found he could not raise it to his lips.

He had been robbed. Of a man he had feared, and respected, and yes, admired. Of a nemesis, the like of which he knew he would never find again. Of a touchstone, to measure himself against and inspire him to more. And of the great task he had set himself: defeat the Black Lord.

It was done. He would finish this banquet, and return alone to his quarters. And what then?

ALBION
Stjornava
Lake Avon
Haskoli
THE BLACK

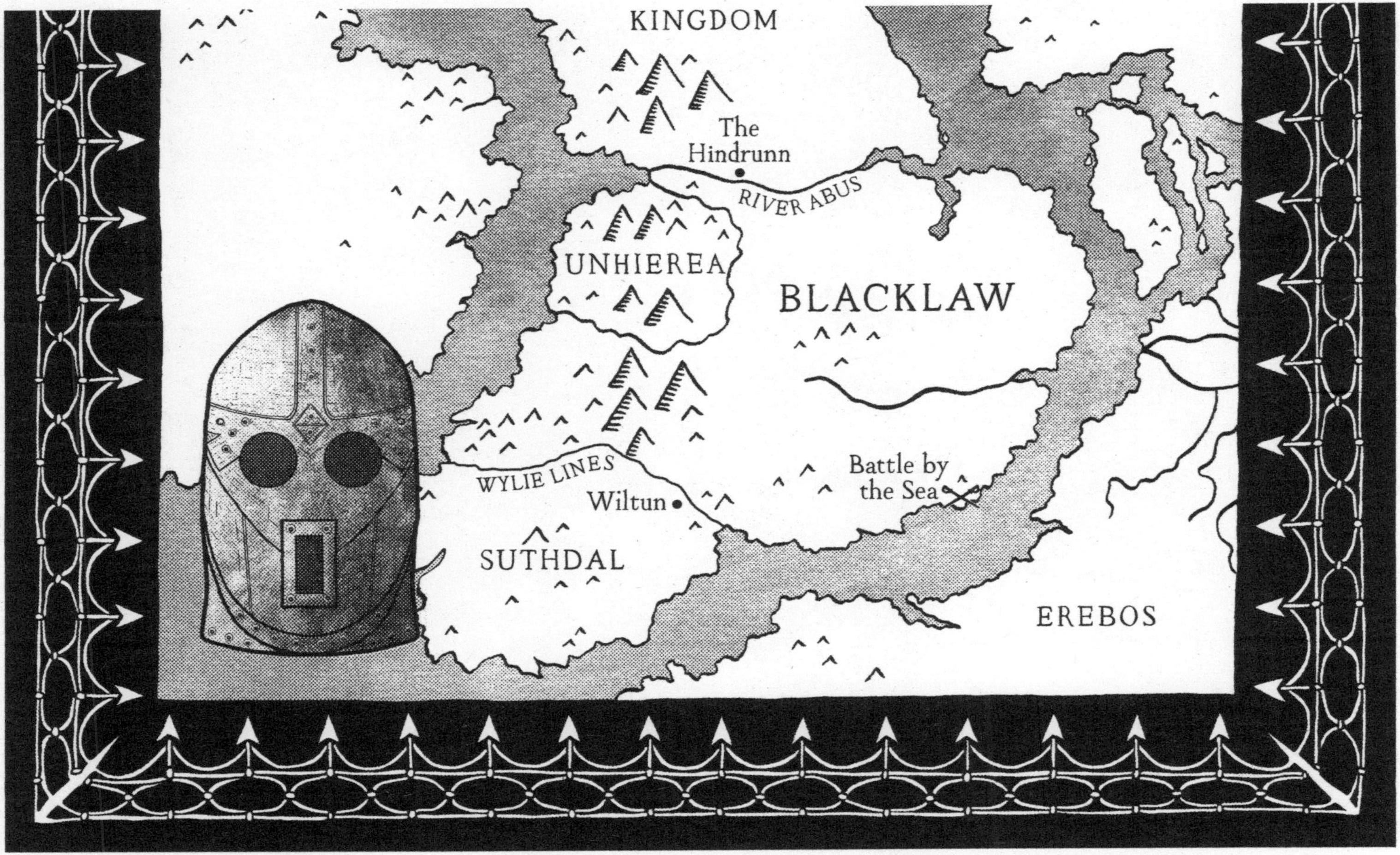
KINGDOM
The Hindrunn
RIVER ABUS
UNHIEREA
BLACKLAW
WYLIE LINES
Wiltun
Battle by the Sea
SUTHDAL
EREBOS

Part II
KETURAH

26
The Crossing

Darkness. Darkness as if the sun had been stamped out. Keturah could hear the waves gushing on the sand, but could barely make out Tekoa, standing at her side. 'This endeavour is doomed,' he said, hopelessly.

'Being pessimistic won't help.'

'Realistic,' he insisted.

'The word pessimists use to hide their blushes,' she snapped.

There came a pause, and she could tell her father's lip would be curling. 'I have a word for you too.'

'Spare yourself,' she said. 'I know which one you'll choose.'

'I might surprise you.'

She sighed. 'Was it *delusional*?'

He laughed softly to himself. 'So you did know.'

On the far side of this channel were reinforcements: thousands of them, volunteered by Anakim kingdoms who had read the tides, and seen that whoever won the battle for Albion would hold an unassailable advantage in the war for Erebos. But the Sutherners were inexorable at sea, and getting those soldiers here was reckoned impossible.

For three months, their allies had marched back and forth, seeking a rendezvous with the Anakim fleet so that they could cross the water. And for three months, their small fleet had been shadowed by a much larger Suthern flotilla, always allowing just enough space that they might be tempted to collect the waiting allies. But the trap was obvious. No sooner would the reinforcing Anakim embark, then the Sutherners would descend on them. Their precious reinforcements would be committed to the deep, and the inconvenience of ever having to fight them on land neatly circumvented.

But tonight, the army would cross the water.

On the beach with Keturah and Tekoa were thousands of dark legionaries, stood in crews beside every rowing boat and barge they had been able to muster. And on the far side of twelve miles of water, lay the coast of Yawland, where their reinforcements waited. The Teutan fleet was trailing them, as ever, but had put in at the natural harbour of Sothaefen for the night. Or they should have put in at Sothaefen. It was the obvious place to go, as long as they had not noticed the contingent of Anakim soldiers left hiding nearby. In the dark of this moonless night, they would slide aboard the Teutan ships, scupper those at the entrance to the harbour, and trap the whole fleet inside.

That was the plan, at any rate, and the first they would know of its success would be when the transport hulks slid into the shallows. The packed beach waited in silence, but for the waves and a corncrake buzzing at their backs.

'You couldn't get me on a ship,' said Tekoa. 'Not for a Prize of Valour.'

'Nor me,' murmured Keturah. 'Virtanen's crossed the sea before though, and wants to do it again.'

'Well, he's a lunatic.'

'Seems rich from you, Father,' she observed, but her father did not laugh.

'I like that herald,' he replied after a time. 'But really, Daughter. You must know the rumours about the pair of you.'

'You waste your breath.'

'Do you swear there is nothing between you?'

'I swear you're wasting your breath.'

'For goodness' sake,' growled Tekoa. 'Marry again, Daughter. To secure this kingdom—'

'To secure the kingdom,' Keturah interrupted. 'Numa must rule. Anyone I marry will want an heir of their own, and suddenly Numa will be a threat to that. A marriage would be not only a betrayal of Roper, but of our son.'

Tekoa was silent for a while, and Keturah could tell there was more he wanted to say.

'To marry would be a betrayal of Roper,' he muttered finally, evidently trying not to be overheard on the quiet beach, 'but whatever is between you and the herald is not?'

Keturah felt herself flush again in the dark. 'There is *nothing* between us. I don't ever want to talk about that again.'

She was spared her father's response, for without warning, the horizon began to flash as though a dozen miniature dawns were bursting and dying, flickering in the space between sea and cloud. Keturah took a breath, covering her mouth with a hand, and Tekoa spoke gently once more. 'What do you say now, my optimist?'

The flashes were the cannon which riddled the Teutan dogfish as they began to erupt. The plan had failed, and the Teutan fleet had escaped the harbour.

'Pray!' Keturah commanded as the distant rumbling reached their ears like far-off thunder.

'Never trust the Aalanders,' said Tekoa darkly, as more cannon began to flicker above the horizon.

'But if the Teuta have engaged,' Keturah murmured, 'then surely our fleet has collected the reinforcements? Otherwise why would they be firing on them?'

Tekoa threw her a sceptical glance. 'More optimism, I fear, Daughter.'

'We should be ready,' Keturah decreed. 'Go!' she cried to the beach at large. 'Our ships are coming and there is little time! You must be ready to unload them!'

At her order, the silent legionaries on the beach began to scrape rowboats and barges down the sand, sliding them into the water. The oars began to plop as they rowed out into the shallows, and behind them, braziers on the beach were kindled to give the distant transport ships a landing site to aim for.

And almost at once, a light replied in the darkness. At first Keturah wondered if it were a star, but it grew stronger, gliding through the black as steadily as a planet navigating the heavens.

'I'll be damned,' said Tekoa faintly, for it was the bow lamp of an enormous ship, far ahead of the Teutan cannon still flickering on the horizon.

It slid closer until touched by the light of the braziers: a tarred, slab-sided mass, the bulwarks fitted with nets crammed with foreign Anakim soldiers. The ship had once been a prison hulk, but the Black Kingdom was now too lean to afford convicts. The prisoners this boat had once held had been pardoned, and now formed their own half-legion.

That decision, Keturah had been told in no uncertain terms, was the beginning of the end. By restoring the subjectcy of the prisoners, Keturah had debased the unyielding code on which the Black Kingdom stood. Why should anyone stand in the battle-line, or give up their children for the good of the kingdom, now that everything it represented had been degraded? Keturah understood that argument. She agreed and regretted unleashing the prisoners, regretted the four legates who had resigned their commissions when they had heard her plans. But she had no choice. The Black Kingdom was not what it had been, and there seemed no clearer sign of that than the ungainly hulk rolling in the waves, the flashes of a pursuing navy growing brighter behind it.

'Well?'

Keturah jumped as Tekoa's voice exploded next to her. He was suddenly striding towards the sea and the boats waiting just beyond the breakers. 'What are you waiting for, you bunch of ponderous jellyfish? The breeze isn't going to blow you over there! Move, you stupid bastards! There is no time, get the men off that hulk!'

The little flotilla splashed into motion, flocking towards the hulk like herring around a whale.

'What did you think you were doing there?' Tekoa was now prowling up the shore, bellowing as the boats bumped into the side of the hulk and began to fill with clamouring allied soldiers. 'This isn't a fishing trip! You are not out for the exercise, or the sea breeze! Get those men onto the shore!'

It was heartbeats before the first rowboats pulled away heavily, so swamped with allied soldiers that their gunwales sat precariously close to the water.

And more transport hulks were gliding into view now, attracted like moths to the fires on the beach.

'I don't know what's happened,' muttered Tekoa, resuming his place beside Keturah. 'But if we can get the boats unloaded before the dogfish arrive, we may yet avoid disaster.'

Keturah did not reply. A few rowboats were already scraping into the sands and spilling the first of their allies onto the beach. They were Karantaji Anakim: mountain people, dressed in thick robes with scale-mail beneath, clutching longbows and curved slashing swords. Among them was a man whose robes were trimmed with fur, whom they helped carefully onto the sands. He looked around slowly, entirely lacking the urgency the moment demanded, and when he spotted Keturah, began to plod in her direction.

'Lady Keturah?' he said solemnly, giving a slight bow. 'I am King Drava.'

The Anakim shared a common tongue, but Drava's dialect was so lyrical that Keturah took some while to unravel his words.

'Welcome indeed, Lord King,' Keturah replied, hardly able to restrain her impatience. 'What's happened? How is it that you are being pursued by the Teutan fleet?'

Drava carried the air of a man eaten from within by terrible secrets, such that Keturah was at first certain he must have witnessed some terrible calamity. 'The Aalanders scuppered much of the Suthern fleet while we were embarking. But some escaped the harbour and pursued us.'

'Have all of the reinforcements made it onto the transports?'

Drava shook his head slowly, and shrugged, as if to say he did not know.

'We've not a moment to lose,' said Keturah. 'Might I suggest your soldiers help unload the rowboats as they come in?'

Drava considered this solemnly, then turned and walked back to the waves where he himself took up a post, waiting to receive an overburdened rowboat.

'Blow me down,' muttered Tekoa, glancing amused at Keturah. 'Surprised the miserable bastard didn't just walk into the sea and drown himself.'

No sooner had he spoken then there came a series of flashes like lightning, so bright that Keturah had to throw up a hand to shield her eyes from the glare. Two heartbeats later came the shocking roar of cannon, and then the sea burst into spray. Flecks of it landed on Keturah's face, and before her eyes one of the laden rowboats was blown to smithereens, its passengers thrown cartwheeling into the water.

Tekoa swore viciously. Now that it had fired, they could see the pale smudge of a dogfish's sail, floating some way beyond the nearest Anakim transports. It had trailed the transport ships in the dark, waiting until it was close enough to reveal its devastating first broadside.

At the boom of the guns, the Karantaji Anakim who had been milling on the beach flinched, and then began to pelt for the shelter of the sand dunes inland.

'Cowards!' roared Tekoa. 'Cowards! Our task grows more urgent, not less! Stay and help! Help unload the boats!'

'Don't you dare address my men like that!' An officer was striding over to Tekoa, face seething by the light of the nearest brazier.

Tekoa was in no mood to be interrupted. 'Why aren't you

doing it?' he hollered back. 'They run while your king waits in the shallows, helping unload. Are you just going to leave him? Tell me, I beg you, what is the delay here?'

'The delay—'

Tekoa blasted over the top of him. 'Cowardice, what else could it be? In spite of his example, you tuck your tail between your legs and leave him to stand alone!'

'You dare,' muttered the officer. 'Drava will hear about this.'

'Oh, I'll make sure he does, you rancid fart! I'll make sure he knows about his officer with a backbone made of butter and all the inclination to follow his lord of a pet rat. Don't just stand there gawping like a landed fish, lad, *piss off*. I'm done with you.'

The officer backed away furiously, but unwilling to endure another savaging, he turned and joined in with the unloading. Some of the rowboats were capsizing as the surf grew near the shore, and men were required to steady the boats while they were emptied, and then turned around to collect the next load.

Lit by the torches proliferating on the beach, the sand was crawling with shadowed figures. Dozens of Anakim ships, some familiar from the Black Kingdom, some low-slung allied designs like floating slippers, had dropped anchors off shore, while the rowboats and barges swarmed around them. And behind this chaos, the Teutan broadsides were growing closer and more accurate, with the first cannonballs smashing into the beach and throwing up grit that stung Keturah's cheeks.

Tekoa was prowling the shoreline, ignoring the fountains of sand, gunpowder flashes lighting the grim sneer on his face. Most of the unloaded soldiers were pelting away from the water to take cover in the dunes, but he collared one after another, swearing at them, shoving them back towards the shore to help as the next wave of boats came in.

It was such chaos that Keturah saw one boat ram into another, capsizing it and spilling a dozen soldiers into the water, where they sank without trace. 'Idiots! Watch where you're going!' she cried, stamping her foot, but Tekoa, passing by, placed a hand on her shoulder.

'That wasn't an accident,' he said quietly.

He was right. Dimly visible, cutting through the water, was the long profile of a ballinger: a Teutan ramming ship, propelled by a bank of oars, which travelled in support of the dogfish. They carried no cannon, but could spit arrows from their high foredeck and would wreak havoc among the little rowing boats. Now that Keturah listened, she could hear the rhythmic barking of the ballinger's helmsman, directing the oars as the ship turned about, searching for a new target.

Even Keturah had to admit, the Teutan fleet was a thing of beauty. It was the one theatre where the Anakim were outmatched. Lord Safinim knew that, and had lavished foreign gold and nous upon it. Unlike their land forces, the fleet did not rely on the aristocracy for deployment: it had professional-class seamen and officers, and the result was before them: towering dogfish, their crews trained to blast out shot at fearsome speed. Balingers, scuttling like ants over the water, oarsmen and helmsman integrated as head and hands. Each vessel was clean and tarred, the sails white and not greened by mould like the Anakim ships.

For now there seemed just the one ballinger among their rowboats, which continued to spill men onto the shore. Another hulk from the Black Kingdom had barged into the shallows, and Keturah saw that its deck was crammed with horses. They began to plunge over the edge, a flood of them whinnying shrilly and splashing into the water, their riders clinging around their necks so as not to sink. Soon the sea was thick with paddling horses, heads held above the waves, eyes rolled back, making for the beach.

Keturah was so distracted by this that she nearly missed the four nearest boats arriving with no men, but piled high with barrels instead, which their crews began carefully unloading onto the beach.

'No supplies!' Tekoa howled. 'Men only you idiots! Leave the bloody barrels!'

The unloading soldiers – Karantaji from their thick robes – paused. 'They're not supplies, lord,' one of them offered.

'Then what are they?'

'Katata!'

Keturah did not recognise the word, and nor, evidently, did Tekoa, who threw up his hands.

'Throw those on the beach and go back for men! If you return with barrels again, I will see that they're dropped on you from a great bloody height!'

But going back would be a dangerous task, as Keturah counted half-a-dozen ballingers now cruising among the rowboats, seeking those crowded with men which they could capsize and drown. There were no combat ships among the Anakim transport fleet, and it was an unequal fight. Still Keturah saw one rowboat with a whip-thin legionary standing in the prow, gathering his courage to leap onto the stern of a passing ballinger. His comrades in the boat were trying to dissuade him, and he left it nearly too late before launching at the ship, missing a wild snatch at the gunwale, but managing instead to clutch onto the steering oar.

'No!' Keturah found she was running down the beach, dodging retreating soldiers to stand at the water's edge. 'You fool!'

The ballinger's helmsman felt the legionary's weight dragging on his oar and looked to see the lone Anakim pulling himself from the water hand over hand. He had disturbed the ship's trajectory, and instead of hitting the crammed rowboat at which it had been aimed, it cruised past, the helmsman fighting to straighten his steering oar. He swore at the legionary, who had now latched onto the gunwale and was pulling himself aboard.

Suddenly, the helmsman had produced an axe, which he hacked down at the sodden legionary. The Anakim twisted aside, and the axe-head thumped into the gunwale. Then the legionary seized the helmsman's hand and pulled him close, enfolding him as a spider would a struggling fly, dragging him over the edge of his own ship and into the water. The helmsman tried to grasp his attacker, but the legionary shook him off, clambering onto the ship, a glittering sword sweeping from the scabbard at his belt as though conjured from the night.

The ship's longbowmen had seen the invader, and two arrows hissed past him, a third striking his chest. Keturah knew from the way it toppled aside that it had not penetrated his bone armour, and the legionary was barely delayed before he stood among the oarsmen.

Keturah could see little in the gloom but the sword carving through the crew rowing at their benches. As oars were abandoned and the ship slowed, the boat from which the legionary had jumped caught up with the stern, and another dozen men boarded to help their comrade.

'Bloody fool,' muttered Keturah, half in admiration, as the Anakim swept the ballinger, the oarsmen unarmed, trapped in their benches, and culled like poultry. The longbowmen at the prow could no longer fire for fear of hitting their own men, and when it became clear the boarders would not be stopped, began to leap overboard, black heads bobbing in the water among the paddling horses.

And now the Anakim had possession of the Teutan ship. The whip-thin legionary who had initiated it all had taken the steering oar, and was bringing the ship alongside another rowboat crammed with Anakim allies. They clambered over the sides, tipping the bodies of the oarsmen into the water and taking their places at the rowing benches. The ballinger began to heave forward, aiming for a Teutan ship pursuing one of the rowboats.

Keturah lost sight of it as a ponderous transport hulk obscured her view. The ship had emptied its belly, and set off towards the two closest dogfish. They were engulfed in pallid smoke and flashing hellishly, producing most of the shot that pulverised their landing. The hulk carried no weapons, and Keturah watched, stupefied by the crew's bravery, as it closed in on the dogfish, blocking their line of fire. Unable to see past its tarred sides, the weight of fire hitting the waters suddenly relented, and the dogfish turned their fury on the lone hulk, trying to blast it apart. Beams and splinters burst from its deck, but it continued cruising towards them, sail pocked by cannonballs, just three crewmen visible on its deck, holding its course.

'Heroes!' Tekoa was bellowing. 'Bloody heroes! Almighty bless you all!'

The men on the beach had seen too, and roared their approval as each new rowboat spilled fresh reinforcements onto the sands. At their backs, the captured ballinger was roaming the waters like a sheepdog, forcing Teutan ships away from the last of the laden rowboats heaving for the beach.

The transport hulk bearing the fury of two dogfish alone was trembling and fracturing, until finally it was reduced to pinnacles of splintered wood. It began to sink beneath the waves, just as the captured ballinger scraped into the beach, its crew jumping overboard, whooping in a most un-legionary-like way. Last off was the whip-thin legionary who had held the steering oar.

He saw Keturah striding towards him, and grinned at her. She slapped him.

'You fool. Don't ever let me see you do something so stupid again.'

'No, my lady.'

'I mean it. One more episode like that and I'll send you back north.'

'I shan't, my lady.'

'You're a poor liar, Ormur,' said Tekoa, stalking past.

Over Ormur's shoulder, Keturah saw another half-dozen dogfish closing in on the shore, their silhouettes broadening ominously as they bared their gunports. Then they disappeared in powder-smoke, flashing as though embroiled in their own thundercloud.

'Run!' Keturah grabbed Ormur and pulled him up towards

the dunes as the beach erupted. They fled, laughing, as thunder swept over them and sand spurted up in huge plumes, more cannonballs shrieking overhead.

They sheltered behind the ridge, where they were cheered by thousands of waiting allies. Keturah embraced first Tekoa, then Ormur. She knew they ought not to celebrate. They were running for their lives, and hundreds had been lost to the sea. But today felt like a victory snatched from defeat, and that was a precious thing these days. Nobody knew if they might see it again.

27
The Giant and the Fool

It was early, Bellamus and the queen breakfasting in Wiltun's great timber hall, alone but for a pair of servants. In the years since Roper's death, it was Bellamus who had aged the worse. His hair was now completely grey, his face lined and gaunt from wine, and the strain of marshalling the competing interests of princes across Erebos.

Aramilla was still golden-haired, but thinner than she had been, her cheeks a little sharper. 'I've been considering peace envoys,' she told him, as careless as ever. They were picking their way through one of the strange cuisines introduced to court by the allies recruited to defeat the Anakim. Bellamus preferred bread and wine for breakfast and found the many dishes of light pastry, crusted with pistachio and flavoured with oranges and honey, infuriatingly insubstantial.

'Envoys? To the Anakim?' He looked to see if she were joking.

'Of course. This war is getting tiresome, and now we are so mighty I'm certain they'd return some of Suthdal.'

'As we are so mighty, Majesty, we could retake it all.'

She laughed as though he were being flippant. 'You've been trying that for years.'

'And our enemy is nearly spent!' Bellamus realised he had

raised his voice slightly and swiftly turned his attention back to the pastry before him, hoping she had not noticed. But of course she had.

Aramilla sat back to regard him with amusement. 'Nearly spent,' she said thoughtfully. 'That's an interesting assessment, my Lord Safinim.' She paused, toying with her pastry. 'From you, particularly.' She looked up at him. 'I heard a story, a few days ago.'

Bellamus could not look at her. *Of course* she had known. She was just saving his punishment for the right moment.

'It didn't seem plausible, I must admit,' she went on. 'Because surely something as significant as an army of thousands of Anakim allies slipping past our fleet and landing in Blacklaw couldn't have been allowed to happen?'

'Majesty—'

'*Surely*,' she went on, holding up a hand to silence him, 'my spymaster would have known such a landing was about to take place, and we'd have been ready for it?' She stared at him with eyes like chips of ice. It was only when he opened his mouth to respond that she went on. 'Do you not stand when making excuses before your queen?'

Bellamus hesitated. Then he pushed back his chair and got to his feet. He wanted to resist, but knew it would only make things worse. There was a ringing in his ears as he prepared his defence. 'Majesty, I've tried to explain before—'

'This is my fault, is it, Safinim?'

'No, Majesty.'

'Oh, but I'm not listening to you? Is that why this happened?'

'No, Majesty.'

'So why is something which was clearly months in the planning, and involved *thousands* of Anakim, not in your ability to detect? Or did you, in fact, know about this scheme and resolve to let it happen?'

Bellamus was briefly rendered silent by that. 'Why would I, Majesty?'

'I don't know, Safinim,' she said, still very calm. 'Really, I'm just thinking how such an appalling lapse could have come about. Perhaps war suits you? You have grown very rich from it, have you not? You have that fine house above the city, and many warriors and servants, all won from your specialist knowledge of the Anakim. Perhaps with your comfortable status, you are not now as hungry or as honest as you were? Maybe it would sharpen your mind if I took those things away.'

Bellamus was silent.

'Do you not see fit to provide your queen with an explanation?'

'I . . .' She was staring at him, and he knew what she was waiting for was some sign that he was resisting her. 'I had no idea, Majesty. I failed, and for that, I cannot express my regret strongly enough.'

'You mean to tell me this was not deliberate?' she clarified. 'That this thing happened purely through incompetence?'

Bellamus felt his battered pride stir once more, and shut his eyes briefly before replying. 'Yes, Majesty.' But he had let his resentment show on his face, and that was a mistake.

'Eh? Say that again, Safinim, why did this happen?'

'I didn't know, Majesty.'

Aramilla looked at the servants, inviting them to bear witness. 'And why not?'

Bellamus met her gaze, smarting. And then he shook his head. 'Anakim spies are harder to come by than they were.'

'You must be distracted,' she declared. 'All that land, and your large household, and your many titles and soldiers. They must be hard to manage. Is that why you now serve me so ill?'

She did not want an answer, he knew. It was best just to be mute and let this punishment resolve.

'Should you not kneel when you are a supplicant to a queen?'

She had only just told him to stand. Bellamus chewed on the corner of his lip, and then stepped around the table and dropped heavily to his knees. He bowed his head. 'I am truly sorry, Majesty. I have failed you.'

'Then why did you not tell me? Why was I left to discover this from a common messenger? Why did my warlord not come and tell me himself of what had happened?'

He gritted his teeth. He did not blame himself for the crossing: since the eradication of the Kryptea, keeping spies in the Anakim army was nearly impossible. He had a handful of informants, who supplied rumours of dubious significance and veracity. But he should have told her, and the honest reason he had not was that he had feared this encounter. Nobody wanted to break bad news to the queen. Bellamus knew that if he had the will, he could make such expressions of sorrow, regret and loyalty that she would be amused and placated, and invite him back to the table. But he could not bring himself to do it.

'I beg your forgiveness, Majesty. My spy network is not what it was . . . I had not appreciated how much it owed to factions within the Black Kingdom working against the Stone Throne. But . . . I believe I'm still invaluable to your person in helping defeat the Anakim.'

'Did you hear what I said?' she asked in a tone of disappointment. 'You propose war again. Truly, I begin to see how it suits you. And the way in which you make others suffer for your ambitions.'

Bellamus took a fortifying breath and said nothing. Aramilla turned back to her pastry in silence. Bellamus remained on his knees for some minutes, head bowed.

'Sit back in your chair, Safinim,' said Aramilla coldly. He resumed his chair in silence and stared at his plate, wanting only wine. 'Tomorrow, you will send out envoys to the Black Lady,' she said in a tone of quiet disappointment.

It was a few moments before Bellamus could bring himself to acknowledge this.

'Majesty.'

He was desperate to be dismissed, but she kept him there,

toying with her breakfast in unhappy silence. He wanted to tell her that envoys were quite impossible, that their Teutan allies had not sent armies across the sea to *talk* to the Anakim. Keturah's forces were still far weaker than theirs, even with her reinforcements. But to say any of that would be to suffer Aramilla's displeasure again.

'Send me Vigtyr,' she said eventually. Bellamus looked up from his plate to see the queen giving him a final look of disappointment to let him know this did not mean he was forgiven.

A servant soon returned with Vigtyr and his escort of six royal guardsmen. He was trailed, as ever, by the buffoon, Sommers.

Nothing that Bellamus had ever encountered made him more uncomfortable than Vigtyr. Just being in the Anakim's presence was enough to simultaneously frighten and depress him. Years of being made to fight animals and criminals had layered scars over his exposed flesh and deadened his eyes. He wore a wire muzzle which kept his jaw nearly completely shut; a legacy of the day in this hall when he had been so demented as to bite Lord Offring. He was not permitted to cut his hair, which now hung nearly to his waist. The worst part of it all was the queen was the only person Vigtyr seemed to trust.

'Ah, Vigtyr! So good to see you,' she greeted him.

'Majesty,' Vigtyr tipped forward, bowing as though broken at the waist. Bellamus had a sudden urge to kill Vigtyr, just to end his torment.

'I was hoping you'd entertain us with one of your battle stories Vigtyr,' said Aramilla.

'I worry you've heard them all, Majesty.'

When Vigtyr started to speak, Sommers the buffoon made a loud farting noise, drowning out his words. Vigtyr raised his voice, but between the wire muzzle and the tormenting Sommers, was barely audible.

'Perhaps you'd allow me to go past the lines to fight? Then I might tell Your Majesty some new tales.'

Aramilla was trying not to laugh. 'I'll think about it, Vigtyr, though I'm sure you're not out of stories yet. Tell us the one about the duel in the tent again.'

Vigtyr let out a long breath. 'Yes, Your Majesty. Perhaps you could order your buffoon to refrain from his noises? It is quite distracting.'

Aramilla smiled kindly and shook her head. 'One of the essential roles of the buffoon, I fear, is to keep us all humble. Sommers is outside our hierarchy here, and I could no more silence him than prevent the wind from blowing.'

Vigtyr gave Sommers a look which made Bellamus glance at the royal retainers. Then he began to recount the story in a voice flat as a puddle. 'Well . . . this was against the Anakim hero Pryce the Wild . . .' He was immediately drowned out by farting. Vigtyr persisted for a few heartbeats, then turned on Sommers and made a wild snatch at the buffoon. Sommers skipped out of reach, still farting loudly as Vigtyr scrambled after him. But he was slowed by scar tissue and half-healed fractures, and Sommers was swift.

Aramilla had tears of mirth rolling down her face as the two sprinted around the hall. Sommers managed to position a long oak table between them and they tore around it like a fox and a goose. So desperate was Vigtyr for revenge that he seized a bench and swung it over the table top at Sommers on the other side. The buffoon was a skilful acrobat and ducked once, twice, three times, farting whenever the bench sailed over his head. Though cruel and vicious, it was also brave, thought Bellamus. If Vigtyr caught Sommers he would kill him.

Finally Vigtyr sputtered to a halt, out of breath and drooling through his wire muzzle, the bench sagging in his hands. Sommers moved temptingly close once more and performed a grotesque imitation of Vigtyr's breathing to try and goad him back into a chase.

'That's enough, Sommers,' said Bellamus quietly.

'Ah, my Lord Upstart feels it so acutely!' The buffoon turned on Bellamus. 'Reminds you of your lowly childhood, I expect, my lord?'

'Enough,' he repeated.

'*Enough!* You are so restrained, my lord, so abstemious. Except when it comes to other men's lives and the gold of the treasury. Then of course there's the wine, enough to bankrupt a lesser lord.'

'Now, now, Sommers, you've more worthy targets than my Lord Safinim,' said Aramilla, smiling gently. 'Why don't you see to those envoys, Safinim?'

Bellamus paused only to offer a half-bow to Aramilla before he was striding from the hall, determinedly avoiding the eye of Vigtyr as he went past. 'Peace envoys,' he muttered. '*Peace!*'

Behind him, he heard Sommers resume his farting noises.

Bellamus ignored the guards outside his quarters, bursting through the door and pressing it closed behind him. Then he slumped, head bowed, and rubbed at the blind eye beneath its patch. He stood there for a moment, slowly exploring the eye, and then shook himself, crossing to a stand by the window at the room's far end. There he poured a cup of wine, draining it immediately. He poured another, and took it to the edge of his bed where he sat, slowly sipping at it.

I should run, he thought.

He hated his life. He had done for years, and could even trace the exact moment it had happened. It was the day he had been named *Lord Safinim*, and shackled to this unstable queen. That had seemed his great victory: the moment he assumed his rightful place with the powerful and influential in Erebos. But in retrospect, all it seemed to have given him was something he was not prepared to sacrifice. And that had cost him his freedom. Being anywhere near Aramilla made him miserable, but could he discard all he had gained just to escape her?

I should, he thought furiously. *I should burn it all and go back to the road.* He imagined the queen's reaction when he left, and how it would feel to shed that mass of responsibility.

But the road seemed very vulnerable. He would be at the mercy of outlaws and brigands, and he could not imagine how he had once navigated it so confidently. The man who had led the resistance against the invading Anakim from an outlaw town seemed to be from a different lifetime.

That man, he thought, would have delighted at defying Aramilla. Not for an instant would he have considered sending peace envoys to the Anakim. Bellamus snorted to himself, taking another draught from his cup. *Peace*. Now was not the time for peace. No. They were just about ready for the battle, to which this road had always led.

He stared into the dark surface of the cup. Then he stood, gathering ink, quill and parchment on his desk, and began to scratch out a note to Diethaad.

There would be no peace.

28
Gravedogs

'Brother?' Gray stood from a low fire, looking hopefully towards the figure approaching through the shadow. Leon walked wearily, eyes meeting Gray's but making no reply. It was an ashen dusk, ushered in prematurely by the thick clouds hanging over the camp.

'Brother, what news?'

'Found him,' said Leon.

'No!'

Leon was grinning, his arms open, and Gray joined him in an embrace, the two thumping one another on the back. 'Found him,' Leon repeated, tiredly. They broke apart, beaming at one another. Leon had been on the road for six days, but looked fresher than Gray. The captain was bloodied, grimed and bruised. They both held onto one another for a moment's support. 'At least I think it's him.'

'Where? Alive still?'

'Alive. Living alone, near Ravenscar. In a cave above the sea. They say there's a nomad comes there every winter. They don't know where he goes in the summer, but he arrives in *Arbaru* and stays until spring.'

'What makes you think it's him?'

'Sounded like him.'

Gray cast about the encampment, looking for some sign of the season. *Arbaru* was the week the deer began to roar, but no deer lived here. This land was so ravaged that the only way of telling the week was the angle of the sun in the sky. 'I don't even know how far away *Arbaru* is.'

'Next week. It's *Brombr*.' The week of ripe blackberries.

'So you had to come back before he arrived?'

Leon nodded and gripped Gray once more. 'The pleasure of finishing him will be yours. You'll make sure?'

'You know I will.'

They helped each other down to sit beside the fire. Gray produced a skin of birch wine and they drank, not bothering to remove their boots.

'You'll tell me how he dies?' asked Leon.

'Every detail.'

'Take your time for me. And Roper.'

Gray did not reply to that. 'If we get him now,' he said softly. 'After *seven years* . . .'

'The Almighty is not mocked. Sakeus may be the very last of them. Kill him and we've finished what we started.'

Gray nodded in weary satisfaction.

'A scrap today?' asked Leon, looking over his battered captain.

Gray nodded. 'You missed another show from Ormur.'

'What now?'

'Scooped up old Arne Kurstason when he got chewed up and spat out by the Abbio. Ormur ran in, knocked a horseman out of his saddle, slung Arne over his shoulders and carried him out.'

'Boy's already got a Prize of Valour. What else is he after? He's going to kill himself,' Leon observed.

'Maybe. But he's got grit. And this isn't just once or twice now. He does this every time.'

Leon said nothing, squeezing out a mouthful from the skin which he swilled absently. 'You could finally take a protégé,' he said at last.

'Not Ormur.'

'That's what you say about everyone. There's always an excuse, and I'm sick of it. You admire the boy, and I've had enough of you punishing yourself for something most people barely remember. If it was ever understandable, it's not any more. This is just self-indulgence.'

Gray raised his eyebrows. 'You may be right.'

'So, do something about it. You chase down every other flaw in your character like it's slapped your mother. Go and get this one.'

'I have thought about a protégé. But not Ormur. If I put him in the guard, he'll not last six months. I don't want to watch that. I don't want to be responsible for it.'

'The boy's going to get himself killed regardless of what you decide. Give him the Eye now, then at least he'll be remembered for it. He deserves it. Has done for a year. Don't deny him that because you can't bear to watch.'

'Even for you this is unusually forthright, Leon.'

'Well I'm right, aren't I? And you always talk about honouring Lord Roper's memory. You know how much it would have pleased him to see his brother being mentored by you.'

Gray did not reply this time, frowning slightly.

'I'm tired,' said Leon, by way of moderation. He brooded into the fire. 'In fact, I'm bloody sick of this whole thing. Last place I want to be is back here, instead of staying north and finishing off Sakeus.'

'It comes across. Come with me when I leave next week, we can finish him together.'

'I can't go back yet,' grumbled Leon. 'My wife would be furious if I reappeared so quickly, she bloody hates me.'

Gray laughed, a broken-toothed, brawler's grin cracking his filthy face. 'So does everyone else, that's why I'm trying to send you away again.'

There came another laugh through the dark. This one desperate and cruel, and immediately taken up by half a dozen other voices.

The smile faded from Gray's face.

'Is nowhere safe from these bastards?' muttered Leon, holding out a hand for the wineskin.

The laughter was coming from somewhere in the near gloom. A dozen voices pitched in deranged hysteria. Both guardsmen laid a hand on their swords, sitting up and peering into a treeline coloured like smoke, forty yards away. There was a flash of something green. Then the noise subsided into a repressed chuckle, like someone trying desperately to hold back peals of mirth. But there was no more movement and eventually the laughter died away.

They waited in tense silence, but the laughter did not return, and presently the two men sat back against their packs. 'I hate them,' said Leon. 'Why aren't they scared of us?'

'I suppose they don't know us yet.' Gray stared into the trees a moment longer. 'Shall we go and find Ormur, then?'

'You've come round?'

'That case was hard to ignore. And if I'm going to Ravenscar, it'd be good for him to be there too and see the end of this. Come on.' He got stiffly to his feet, resting, hands on knees for some while before straightening up. Leon stayed seated, watching him wearily until Gray held out his hand to pull him upright. 'Come on, brother.'

They walked across the camp together. The ground was mud, like most of where they fought these days. So often were the borderlands between Blacklaw and Suthdal turned over by feet and hooves that it seldom had time to put out shoots. And yet it was some of the most fertile soil in the world, fed on a constant diet of blood and carrion. This was a *hoof-camp*, a place so close to the constant enemy raids that the legions were ready to move at any moment, and did not bother to unpack anything more than the evening's rations. Fires were few and far between, singing discouraged in case it drew unwelcome attention, and fresh food forbidden in case it attracted that manic laughter. Perhaps the hoof-camps were why things seemed so hopeless now. Nobody was clear exactly when, or even why, but sometime over the past few years, the feeling that this was a war they could win had faded like ink left in the sun.

The Sutherners – or the Teuta, as their pan-Ereboan alliance was known – had sheltered behind the Wylie Lines for years, while men, money and expertise flooded their lands. When Tekoa had inherited the legions, they had attempted to break through at half a dozen of the locations that seemed weakest. But with Roper dead, the heart had gone from the army, and every attempt had ended in disaster. Their choices were to sit before the lines, and suffer endless raids, or else surrender all they had gained to the Teuta. Their enemy avoided pitched battles: they were not yet ready for that, and still did not have the confidence to confront the legions on a massed battlefield. Instead they had eroded the Anakim, one raid at a time; nibbling at their morale, their numbers, their fitness. The general opinion was that the time was drawing near when the Teuta would be ready to emerge from behind their defences. Their army would be strong enough, the legions sufficiently weakened, that they could fight to reclaim Blacklaw – the land that had once been theirs, now under the control of the legions. But until then, they continued to raid, to scratch, to erode. And the legionaries took it in turns to suffer that fate, spending six-month rotations below the Abus, four months to heal in the north.

Ormur was camped with his legion, the Greyhazel, not far from the guard. When Gray and Leon found him, he was fast asleep, so exhausted he had not even removed his filthy cuirass. He was nineteen, his face still a boy's, but a fresh cut oozing crimson above his eyebrow. A dozen others sat around the fire, muttering and sharing a pot of hoosh. Gray and Leon stopped before the legionaries, who stiffened and began to climb to attention before Gray ordered them to stay seated.

'Good evening, peers,' he said, looking down at the sleeping Ormur for a moment. 'More bravery from our young friend here today, I hear,' he observed.

'You're not taking him away from us, are you, sir?' asked the man sat next to the sleeping boy.

'Don't you think he's earned it?'

There was silence at that. 'The Sacred Guard's taking lads now then?'

'I'd say he's long proven himself a man,' said Gray, mildly. 'But it's up to him. He may turn us down, if he wishes.'

The legionary looked down at Ormur, still in the sleep of the dead. 'You'll look after him, sir?'

'I'll offer him a place as my protégé. If he accepts, I'll keep an eye on him, as best I'm able.'

Still there was reluctance. 'Well . . . I wouldn't give him up for anything less than the honour of being Captain Gray's protégé. That's what he deserves.'

'The honour would be mine. But let us talk to him. He can decide.'

The legionary looked wistfully down at Ormur and nudged him with his foot. The lad did not stir. 'Boy.' He shook his shoulder and Ormur raised his head heavily. 'You've got visitors.'

Ormur looked up and saw Gray and Leon standing over him. He tried to rise but his armour was too heavy and he only made it halfway before dropping onto hands and knees.

'Slowly, slowly, Ormur,' said Gray. 'You've exerted yourself enough today.'

The boy staggered upright, nearly Gray's own height, and they looked each other in the eye. He looked profoundly weary, trying to muster the energy to stand to attention but hardly focused on Gray.

'Come with me,' said Gray. Leon was already stamping away. 'Let's talk.' Ormur fell into step with him and they walked to the camp perimeter in Leon's wake. 'We've heard a lot about your bravery, Ormur,' said Gray as they drew away from his hearth. 'Seen a lot too. It strikes us as the right sort of bravery; borne from a desire to preserve your peers, rather than win glory. You are a bit hot-headed though. We feel you can be a better servant if you show more self-restraint.'

Ormur was looking down at the ground, occasionally half tripping over his own feet. 'If I thought more about what I was doing, sir, I don't think I'd do it.'

'Why not?'

Social interaction always seemed uncomfortable to Ormur, with no conversation quite as excruciating as talking about himself. 'I would be too frightened,' he mumbled. 'I know I need to move fast when the moment comes, or I wouldn't go at all.'

'But you do go, unlike most people. You risk a great deal, Ormur. Have you no self-value at all?'

'I don't know, sir.'

'Well we value you. We can teach you to show that self-restraint, and be a soldier as well as a warrior. We do not usually invite such young legionaries into the guard – I shall have to ask the Battle Historian, I'm not sure it's been done before. But these are strange times, and there's no denying you've proven yourself.' Ormur was silent and Gray realised he did not want to assume any part of this great honour. He needed an explicit invitation. 'Will you become a Sacred Guardsman as my protégé?'

Hooves filled the evening as a band of horsemen clattered into camp. Everyone stiffened and gazed at the shadowed figures, but it was the heavy cavalry of the Black Kingdom, calling to each other as they dismounted and hobbled their beasts. Gray gave Ormur a moment, and then prompted him.

'I don't think I'm ready for that, sir.'

'I'm telling you that you are. Don't contradict me, Ormur.'

'And what about my century, sir? I would not like to leave them behind.'

'We are taking you where we feel you can do the most good. Save the most lives and serve your kingdom best. Your century will miss you, no doubt. But we'd miss you more.'

They came to a rocky outcrop where Leon had already taken up residence, sword flashing as he fidgeted with it. Gray motioned to the boy and they sat side by side on the rock, staring into the pitch treeline. 'I am honoured by the offer, sir,' said Ormur stiffly. 'But I am not ready.'

Gray frowned. 'I don't usually have to persuade guardsmen to accept.'

'I think my century needs me. And I think you've made a mistake.'

Gray felt a surge of irritation at this humility. He did not want to take any protégé, let alone this one, whom he cared for already and who seemed destined to throw his life away before he reached his twenties. And now he was going to have to try and talk him into it.

'Stop being so bloody modest and take the Eye,' barked Leon.

Ormur stiffened, awkwardness replaced at once by a bristling ferocity. Gray hushed Leon, trying to stay calm and looking for the right words. 'I don't want to have to convince you that there's been no mistake. I know what bravery looks like. I know what fear feels like; I am reminded every day. I've watched guardsmen die begging for their mothers, and others who rolled their eyes and told me to stop fussing. In short, Ormur, in one hundred and thirty years on the battlefield, I've seen it all. You have seen more than you should have at your age, but you're still a lad. We have much to learn from each other, but in this you are mistaken. You are ready.'

'But you only watch me from afar,' said Ormur, becoming prickly now. 'Sir,' he added hastily. 'You *don't* know. I'm not like you. I can't follow Pryce the Wild. I'm not like Lord Roper.'

Gray exhaled in frustration. It felt like talking to an irreverent son. It felt, he realised, like talking to Pryce in the early days of their partnership. But at that time Gray had had more energy to break him in. 'You think Lord Roper was ever as assured as he looked?'

'More than me, sir. I grew up with him. He was my brother.'

Gray rested his head in his hands briefly. 'Mine as well.' He was so tired. He did not want this conversation. 'I don't really want you as my protégé, Ormur. I don't want anyone, you least of all.'

Ormur looked horrified. 'Sorry,' he said helplessly.

Gray opened his mouth to say *Forget it*: to brush it off. Then he would stand up, walk away into the dark and they could both get on with their lives. But Leon was right, he had let this weakness lie for far too long. 'The reason I don't want you, Ormur, is because you remind me too much of Lord Roper. Forgive me for being short. The whole purpose of my life was to protect him, and it was on my watch that the Kryptea got through.'

Ormur had gone very stiff, like someone at the extremes of cold. 'Sir, could I . . . Would you tell me about it? I only ask,' he went on in a rush, 'as I've heard a dozen different accounts and would like to know what truly happened to him. You were there. I should like to hear what truly became of my brother.'

Leon had stopped fidgeting.

Gray did not like talking about this either. Another weakness in his character. When had he stopped confronting them? He told Ormur the story and when he had finished he said: 'So now you know. For years there have been false versions flying around, which people are pleased to discuss in front of me. Not once have I bothered correcting these falsehoods, because all of them agree on the highest truth of it. Lord Roper died fighting, and he died bravely. When the Kryptea took him away, and he must've known he was facing his end, his last action was to smile at me.'

'And when you found his body . . .' said Ormur, hesitating, as though worried he were going too far. 'Did he suffer? D'you think he lived past the fall?'

Gray did not seem to mind the question. 'It's impossible to tell, Ormur. He'd been in the water three days and was all chewed up, there wasn't much left to go on. But I saw the fall, and I don't believe anyone would have been conscious past that.'

Ormur seemed to ponder this. 'But then . . . I can see why you wouldn't want me, sir . . . That is, I'm nothing like Lord

Roper, but if I remind you of him . . . Well, why have you not taken any protégé? Because nobody could ever replace Pryce the Wild?'

'Is that what people say, Ormur?'

'It is, sir.'

Gray nodded. 'I think that was true once. I resisted for a few months, while I was grieving. Selfishly. I just wanted to do honour to Pryce and show him that he couldn't be replaced so easily. But I always planned to take another, it's just . . .' On the verge of saying it out loud, he realised how weak it sounded. He should have addressed this long before now. 'After Roper died . . .' he glanced at Leon, who sat uncharacteristically still. 'We went after the Kryptea. I had promised revenge, you see, Ormur. Back when Roper was alive, I warned Jokul. I told him that if the Kryptea targeted this Black Lord, I would make sure they did not survive it. Forget the others they had killed, those were in the past. Perhaps they were tyrants, perhaps they deserved it. But this Black Lord was mine. The Kryptea were not to touch him. And when they did, I cut them out, root and branch.'

'How?'

Gray shook his head. 'You must've heard, Ormur. People must talk about it. On my orders, the Sacred Guard tortured information out of every man we suspected. We tore that army to scraps and hounded out even the faintest whiff of Kryptean influence. Hundreds were executed, without trial, based on the accusations of desperate, screaming men.'

There came a burst of manic laughter from the trees. All three of them paused to see if it came closer.

'You surely had no choice, sir, if you wanted to find out who was in the Kryptea,' Ormur proffered when the noise had died away. 'And now we're rid of them. If there were innocents who died, it doesn't mean you didn't do the right thing.'

'Perhaps. But I didn't do it because it was the right thing.'

'Revenge,' said Ormur quietly.

Gray nodded. 'Possession.'

'I'm certain I'd have done the same in your situation, sir. Any guardsman would.'

'Let us not justify it, Ormur,' said Gray. 'At my orders, men had their ears pulled off, and their fingers peeled. And after that we'd stake them out in the sun, salt their wounds and allow the flies to fill them with maggots. I did some of it myself, willingly. What do *I* have to teach anyone about discipline or courage or self-restraint? I was tested, and failed. And the whole guard partook, on my orders. So I cannot blame you if you don't want to join us, or be my protégé.'

'I accept, sir, if the offer is still open,' said Ormur abruptly.

'Don't accept because you're worried about causing offence,' said Gray.

Most legionaries revelled in what he and the guard had done, and it appalled him. The time after Roper's death had been dark, chaotic and turbulent, but one thing had become immediately clear to everyone. The Kryptea were evil. Why they had been tolerated so long was a mystery, and Gray was horrified to find himself celebrated for the worst thing he had ever done. *Kryptea-Killer*, he was called sometimes, though these days it was always behind his back.

'You're both idiots,' snapped Leon. 'Let's stop this absurd dance. Ormur you are now Gray's protégé in the Sacred Guard. We've got armour which'll fit you. The initiation will be when we're back in the lines, and you'll receive your pommel-ring from the Black Lady on your next rotation north. Ask your questions now.'

Ormur looked lost. 'Do I camp with the Guard now?'

'Are you a guardsman?'

Ormur glanced at Gray. 'Am I—'

'Yes!' bellowed Leon. 'And if you're a guardsman, then where do you camp?' He gave Ormur a look of pure incredulity.

'With the Guard?'

Leon looked at Gray. 'He's sharp. Any real questions, boy?'

'Don't call me *boy*.' Ormur's tone shifted so abruptly to ice that Gray snorted.

Leon observed him darkly. 'I'm looking forward to your initiation.' He stood, bowed curtly to Gray and left the two of them alone. Alone, but for the suppressed laughter coming from the treeline.

'There's more gravedogs than ever,' said Ormur.

'Many more.'

'Where did they come from?'

'Unhierea. I've heard Gogmagoc call them *hyenas*.' Though they kept watching, none of the gravedogs broke cover. 'My first lesson as your mentor,' Gray went on quietly. 'Of all people, try not to antagonise Leon. He could make life very difficult for you.'

'As difficult as he would if I let him run roughshod over me?'

'He is a warrior, not a bully. Don't fall out with him.'

Ormur looked sceptical of this advice. 'So what now, sir?'

'Now, you are my protégé, so I am not *sir* any more, not to you.' Gray took a deep breath. 'As for what we do: bring your things here, we'll initiate you in the next few days. And then . . . Then we're going north. There's something I need your help with.'

'What's that, sir?'

'As thoroughly as I tried, there is one member of the Kryptea to my certain knowledge who survived. Sakeus Ketilson. One of the Belated Guard: the core group who betrayed Roper. He escaped on the day of his murder and hasn't been seen since. Leon believes he has found his winter hiding place. So we're going to find him there, and snuff out the last traces of the Kryptea.'

29
Sakeus

Ormur never wanted to think again of the initiation. Try as he might, his head rang to the words of his oath.

I submit my flesh to Almighty Will, and to my monarch devote my skill. I choose the hardest road so others need not, shall be first to fight and last to stop.

I renounce all claims on a life my own, renounce my blood, renounce my bone, those I love and those I've known. I choose a sacred path of wrath and sweat, and choose to fears and hopes forget. I will not break faith, nor deal in lies; will finish the job my lord supplies. I renounce property and freedom, I need no rest, nor recognition. I am the living blade, the debt repaid, and decree obeyed. I'm the honest word, the cry unheard; avenger lord and dark abroad, the mountain rain, the chosen pain; the hand that stayed and heart unswayed. I am a soul that needs no body, a fire that casts no light, a squire to the battle-angels, I'm God's hand in every fight.

I give all that I am to the Holy Eye and live this day till my last in Sacred Sight.

With them would come the memory of that night.

Led ignorant through the dark to a freezing meltwater river. Around him, torchlight and shaded figures. More standing half out of the water, waiting as he hesitated on the river's bank. *Trust us*, Gray's voice had said.

Trust us.

Then cold, stealing through his ribs, swirling past his ears, pressing against his throat. Hands holding him down in the dark and total possession as he thrashed and fought to breathe. The cold had gone first, then the dark, then last, the desperate urge to breathe.

He had awoken choking, back on the banks of the river, firm hands on his chest and a roaring around him as he was born for the second time in his life.

Gray walked next to him now, less real than his waking memory. It was a blustery morning, the air heavy with the moisture hurled down during the night, which made their boots squelch and slide as they climbed a grass bank.

'Do men ever die? During the initiation?'

'They all die. You died.'

'Well, yes. But are there any you cannot get back?'

'Some things it's best not to talk about, my young friend.'

When it was done, when he sat shocked and shivering, a wolf-fur round his shoulders and his new companions plying him with wine and spirit, he could hardly think. The cold was swallowed in euphoria, and the world around him pure symmetry. Every man there, who had brought him back to life, been there with him, and done it themselves in their time, was a brother. It was cruel, what they had done to him, and brutal. And at first he had bridled and feared until he had been half-forced into the water.

But walking now, with Gray, there was no denying that life had not been the same since. He did not feel like the man who had gone beneath that water.

'How is it that I remember the words to the oath at the first time of hearing?'

'The shock makes you remember. Those words are burned into your brain forever. Try and renounce them if you like. Try taking your life back. They'd haunt you to your dying day.'

They were drawing near the coast, and Ormur could hear a distant roaring. 'What is that noise?'

'Have you never heard the sea at storm, Ormur?'

Then they were over the rise, and there it stretched: the most furious thing Ormur had ever seen, heaving water-blows at the cliff beneath them.

Gray looked at him and grinned. 'You surrender your freedom when you join the Sacred Guard. In reality, we get more of it than almost anyone else.'

No part of Ormur's life had been spent by the sea, but it compelled him immediately. It was energetic, and orientating.

'Come,' said Gray, hitching the pack on his shoulders and turning left along the clifftop. 'The cave's to our north.'

Ormur fell in behind his mentor. 'Will he be there?'

'He should be. Unless he knows we're coming.'

'What then?'

'He'd run if he's sensible. Try and ambush us if he's feeling foolish.'

They walked in silence a moment, and presently Ormur became aware of a thin trace of smoke rising from the cliffside, perhaps a mile ahead.

'Looks like he's in,' said Gray, comfortably. 'Got that fine weapon of yours to hand?'

Ormur clutched reflexively at the rosewood handle of Warspite, strapped over his back. He pulled it a little way clear to make sure it moved easily, but they saw no one until they had descended onto a pebble beach before the cliffs. In front of them was a steep slope of stones, which led up to the entrance of a cave, raised some twenty feet above the beach. At the mouth of the cave, a small fire was crackling with fresh driftwood.

'Sword,' said Gray calmly, drawing his own. They began to climb the pebbles up to the cave's mouth. 'He'll hear us coming on this.'

Ormur pulled Warspite clear of the sheath, he and Gray labouring up together in a rattle of sliding stones. He half expected a figure to appear above them and begin pelting them with rocks, but perhaps the sea covered the sound of their approach, for they made it to the fire without interruption. They could now see into the cave, which was unexpectedly homely. The floor was covered in rush matting, with fish traps and lobster pots piled neatly along one edge. On the other side were racks of drying fish and carefully stacked supplies. A fish broth was simmering in a blackened pot at the edge of the fire, and it smelled rich and fragrant with samphire.

Further back into the cave, a man sat cross-legged, mending a net. His clothes were frayed, his face lined by the hard life of an exile, and his long hair tied back in a ponytail. At the sound of their approach, his calloused fingers fell still, and he looked up at the two guardsmen darkening his entrance.

'You've done well from the life of an exile, Sakeus,' said Gray, walking slowly into the cave, night falling within as he blotted out the light. 'As well as one can, at any rate.'

Ormur was at his side, regarding this man, who he had expected to be gaunt, black-eyed, and ferocious. But the lined face before him was one of natural warmth, though wary as the two guardsmen trod his matting.

Sakeus put down the net and sat back a little, watching them approach. 'Thought you'd find me eventually. I'd heard rumours about a warrior here a few weeks ago. Should've listened to them.'

'Leon,' said Gray. 'He found you.'

Sakeus nodded. 'He would.' His chest was rising and falling rapidly. He watched them approach, then cast a look over his shoulder, but found no escape there. He turned back to them, and Ormur saw a flash of wild fear in his eyes. 'Just do what you've come to do. I completed my life's work years ago, and robbed yours in the process. I should've died then truth be told, but the will to carry on is very strong.'

'You bought yourself seven years' respite,' said Gray,

treading closer. The captain seemed at ease, though Ormur was certain this moment was about to burst into violence. 'But should probably have done the job yourself, somewhere you wouldn't have been found. You'd have had your chance on the Winter Road, for all the good it would've done you. Now we've found you, and we'll see your body destroyed.'

It seemed that something inexorable was crushing Sakeus, who was wilting visibly before them. 'I take solace in knowing that whatever happens to me will be better than the circle of hell Roper inhabits. There's a special one reserved for tyrants.'

'I doubt it,' said Gray.

'Your ignorance, not mine,' said Sakeus. '*Punished past pain and desperation*,' he quoted.

> '*Despotic Black Lord lingers alone,*
> *Soul sentenced and mind tormented,*
> *Till shall hell seem sweet sanctuary,*
> *And blackness beauty past paradise.*'

Gray was unmoved. 'You've turned to heresy to justify your perverted order?'

'I believe those words. More than I believe in any of your precious battle-angels. He has doomed us all and is now paying the price.'

For the first time, Gray seemed angry. He was just feet away from the exile now, and raised Ramnea, holding her tip beneath Sakeus's throat. 'You will never have seen this man, Ormur, and nor will you know the name of Sakeus Ketilson. But this is the last of the infamous Belated Guard, whose betrayal of Roper was coldest and most intimate.'

Sakeus's fear was making him cruel. 'I won, Gray. You can't take that from me, no matter what you do to my body. And I've heard what you did to my comrades when they were still alive. Nor will that avail you. We won. Roper's gone.'

Gray looked down at him. 'You won. But that was the old game, and for the past seven years, we've been playing a new one. You've lived in poverty and exile, glancing over your shoulder for those footsteps climbing the pebbles to your cave. You knew what you'd done would catch up with you. And I'm almost sorry to end your wretched years. What you deserve is to linger here, in fear and loneliness, the seagulls the only voices to break your isolation.'

Sakeus's defiance was crumbling. He shook his head, and glanced at Ormur, who would never forget the haunted flash of those eyes. 'Please. Just get this over with.'

'He was brave,' said Ormur, quietly. The cave was at their backs, the fire at its entrance still crackling merrily, and the pebbles shifting beneath their feet as they trod the path they had come.

'He was tired,' said Gray.

Ormur was silent a long time. 'But even tired,' he said. 'To face your death, just kneeling there? I couldn't do that.'

Gray nodded to himself and they trudged the pebbles together for a while. 'There's something I need you to understand, Ormur. Will you humour me, for a moment?'

Ormur mumbled that Gray was his mentor, too embarrassed to admit he would have listened to anything he had to say at any time.

'It's not that death isn't bad. It is, because mortal existence is grace. Look around you. Smell the sea, listen to it. The earth is made of pleasure. Some days it's near paradise, and the days it's not are what make those good days so exquisite. It is the contrast which heightens your joy, and death is the ultimate contrast. Carry in your heart the knowledge that some day soon, all this will be over, and it will be so sweet you can hardly bear it.' Gray looked at his protégé, walking alongside him. 'I think when you *believe* that, when you truly live it, then you can be grateful for it. You can even anticipate it.'

'Death!'

'Yes, Ormur,' said Gray firmly. 'Because when suffering is set in its proper context, it becomes as new and pleasurable as everything else in this world. Your fear will fascinate you, and you will love it. And I know nothing more alien or fearful than dying. I want to know what it feels like to be there, staring it in the face. And that's how you *have* to live, with the knowledge that death is essential, otherwise by trying to avoid it, you will shrink your life to nothing! You will be Sakeus, in that cave, listless and exhausted.

'That is one of the truths of the initiation you have just undergone. It seems barbaric and cruel, and yes, it is dangerous. But you have just died, and come through it a better man. You are a step closer to intimacy with your own end, to breaking it into something compelling rather than dreadful. You now live a little less burdened than you were before and are a fragment nearer to living the truth: that discomfort should be a signal to walk towards something, not away.

'And that, by the way, is exactly what Roper did. You know, Ormur, I sometimes think that as lauded as he is, he doesn't get enough credit. He saw death in its proper perspective, and didn't let it turn him away from the great task he knew had to be done. He understood suffering, and you know how you can tell? Because that's how he lived. Never trust what someone says if they're not living it. They don't believe it, in their heart. Actions are the words of your soul. Roper lived it. He believed every moment of what he did, and that's why his men loved and followed him. And that's how I know he's not living in hell, because hell could not contain a man like that. If you arrived there by living what you believed, it would not be hell. You would understand that it's the price for doing what you knew to be right. Find what you believe in, Ormur, and pursue it to the end of the earth.' Gray fell silent.

Ormur wanted both to save his mentor the feeling that he had said too much, and to move on from this topic. 'What were those lines he quoted?' he asked eventually.

'Sakeus? Leleain poetry, from the sounds of it. Bombastic stuff. One of the old forms in the Academy, from a bygone era. It was familiar though. I think I'd heard it before somewhere.'

'I don't remember anything about a hell set aside for tyrannical Black Lords.'

'Don't regard it, Ormur. Invented to satisfy their deranged ideology. Sakeus has suffered more over the past seven years than Roper has.'

Ormur dwelt a great deal on Sakeus's end. That look in his eye, simultaneously fearful and exhausted. They were three days' walk from the Hindrunn, and much of it he spent in wretched empathy, imagining the terror of kneeling before two enemies with drawn swords, knowing absolutely that your time on earth was about to end.

It was on his mind when he went to sleep that night, a fire hissing beside them. When he woke the next morning with a leaden feeling in his guts, he could tell he had dreamed of it. It was a clear dawn in the forest, frost on the undergrowth and mist rising from a distant stream. Gray was sitting by the fire, watching him.

'I'm amazed you managed to sleep on that rock.'

Ormur sat up, looking back at the piece of granite protruding into his bed. 'I didn't notice it.'

'You're a hard man, Ormur. These days a tuft of grass is enough to have me waking with a cricked neck. Even dreams were enough to keep me up last night.'

Ormur shuffled the cooking pot, filled with water the night before, to the fire's edge. 'What did you dream of?'

'The Chief Historian, strangely.'

'More of a nightmare then.' He was terrified of Frathi.

'Well, quite. But she had some interesting things to say. Remember that poetry from Sakeus, yesterday? I've remembered where I heard it before. Frathi quoted it to Roper the day she left the army. There was a bit more to it than got spouted yesterday. I can't remember the details, but it was from the "Chant of the Kryptean Pac", as I recall.'

'Do you remember anything else?'

'Not really.'

Ormur tutted. 'Old age.'

Gray snorted. 'You snake. What else do you want to know?'

'If Roper is suffering.'

Gray's smile faded. 'You're thinking about what I said yesterday. About death.'

'I suppose so.'

'Well . . . we're going back to the Hindrunn, my young protégé. You can go to the Academy and see what Sakeus was talking about.'

'I'd sooner stay in the forests,' said Ormur.

'But you need your pommel-ring from Lady Keturah before you are a full Sacred Guardsman,' said Gray. 'And besides, things are changing. The Hindrunn is the place to be if we want to be involved.'

'Involved in what?'

Gray shrugged. 'There's been talk. Infantry massing behind the Wylie Lines. Most of the Teutan forces withdrawn from Blacklaw, and their fleet has been seen flooding Suthdal with supplies. There may be something brewing.'

'What? What would that mean?'

Gray shrugged again. 'Battle.'

Ormur's heart sang to hear that word. '*Battle?* Will there be a battle?'

'There's been one on the horizon for years,' said Gray. 'Though Safinim has avoided it so far. Maybe he's changed his mind.'

Pitched battles were a thing of the heroic past. Ormur had been in more skirmishes and raids than he could count, but never seen a full battle-line: the banners, the drums, the hymns. Glorious cavalry supporting the wings, arrows soaring overhead, the officers haranguing their men. Awe-inspiring, Gray had called it, and Ormur knew nobody more considered with his words than the captain.

Suddenly, they could not get back to the Hindrunn fast enough.

30
Lord Ruden

'Safinim!' Ruden clapped both hands on Bellamus's shoulders in a blow that made his head reverberate. The great Frankish lord had swollen over his years in Albion, and was now solid as a carthorse. 'The Thingalith have been east of the lines I hear. You must wish you were with them, my friend.'

It was early evening, and in drips and flurries Aramilla's council of allies was assembling in Wiltun's great hall. Only half a dozen had so far arrived, and Bellamus was acutely conscious of how Ruden's voice carried across the hall to Aramilla, and how she looked up at this news, gazing at the pair of them.

'Certainly it's more exciting than court, my lord,' said Bellamus mildly.

Ruden seemed to sense Aramilla's gaze on them and turned in a sweeping of bear furs to stride over and kneel before the queen.

'Majesty,' he murmured, taking her proffered hand. 'As ever, my prince sends his most intimate wishes. He feels sure a meeting with you would be immensely profitable.'

Aramilla looked amused. 'Profitable for whom, Lord Ruden?'

'Ha! I wrote to him of your wit only yesterday, Majesty.' Ruden gave a little bow. 'He declares his powerful intrigue at my reports, and his great honour to have his men fighting alongside your own.'

'His Imperial Majesty certainly has my respect and gratitude, Lord Ruden, though how much of that is merely the representation his servant provides, it is hard to say.'

The compliment slid off Ruden like honey from a spoon. He gave his easy laugh and raised a finger to waggle before the queen. 'I fear we are all your servants now, Majesty.'

Bellamus watched this exchange fearing quite the opposite. The number of Frankish soldiers in Albion had swollen over the years, from the original twenty thousand to fifty thousand now. Ruden had become his own force in this land, one whom even Aramilla would think twice before crossing. Nobody said it out loud: Ruden was too charming, and besides was trailed by the influence of Emperor Karoli like a pitch shadow. But it always seemed to be Ruden who set the agenda now: whose words were so mild and so rarely defied.

The remainder of the allied council filled the room and assumed their places at the long table. Representatives from Occitanie, Frankia, Iberia, Autaria, Hatusa and Skaane, filling in around Ruden. Bishop Widukind chose a place ostentatiously far from Ruden, among Suthdal's noblemen. Lord Melcombe had died the previous winter from an ague, and the aged Lord Penbro some years before from a sweating sickness. Otherwise the court was unchanged from when this campaign had first started, all those years before. Even the arch-traditionalist Lord Nerven still stood, well into his seventies but so stubborn and irascible that he threatened to outlast them all. There was only one person of influence left in Suthdal who did not sit at that table: Garrett. He had come once as a concession, and would never be suffered to attend again.

'Quiet, my lords, quiet,' said Ruden, slapping one palm on the table, the other tugging at his great beard. 'Pray silence for Her Majesty.'

'To business,' said Aramilla. 'First, any word from the peace envoys I dispatched to the Black Lady?'

Bellamus looked down the table, taking note of the reactions. Most were looking around curiously, waiting for someone to reply. A few were staring at their own hands, not prepared to broach the topic. Eventually it was Sommers who answered this question.

'So eager were the envoys to do your bidding, Majesty, that they quite lost their heads.'

Aramilla turned to face the buffoon expressionless. 'What do you mean? They were executed?'

'I fear only their heads were returned, Your Majesty,' Bellamus put in. 'The Anakim evidently do not wish to talk.'

There was a moment's pause, and then Aramilla burst out laughing. 'Oh dear! I hadn't realised they had such spirit left in them.'

A ripple of relieved laughter swept the table and the tension dissipated.

Bellamus was not sure what would have happened if the envoys had reached the Anakim. He had not been prepared to find out.

'But that's absurd,' said Aramilla suddenly. 'You told me Lady Keturah was in the north, did you not Safinim?'

'Last I heard, Majesty.'

'Then she cannot possibly have heard of the envoys. Some lieutenant of hers rejected our olive branch.'

'I fear it was a waste of time, Majesty,' said Bellamus. 'The Black Kingdom does not take prisoners and does not negotiate.'

'Oh, hogwash,' the queen complained. 'You have always said this Black Lady is measured and intelligent. Why shouldn't we talk, one queen to another?'

Ruden raised his eyebrows. 'Do you truly wish to talk with these people, Majesty?'

Aramilla slapped a palm upon the table, and even Ruden paused. 'Yes I *do*! I am done with war: its poverty and restrictions and leaching. If our position is strong, they should be ready to negotiate.'

'Your Majesty—' Bellamus began, but the queen cut across.

'No more of your words, Safinim! For years we have trusted your interpretation of the Anakim, and where has it got us? A war with no end!'

The table had frozen. Even Ruden shifted uncomfortably, though a few of Bellamus's enemies were smirking into their own laps.

'Let them start responding to us. If they will not receive my envoys then I shall go over the lines myself.'

Bellamus took a breath, but knew she would not suffer a reply from him. He looked around the council, praying someone would object to this madness. Eventually the aged Lord Nerven did, but not with any kind of argument that would sway Aramilla.

'What has become of Blacklaw is no place for a queen, Majesty. Your safety—'

'Would be safeguarded by ten thousand soldiers,' the queen interrupted again. 'We can at last break this stalemate. I've been misled by you all!' she suddenly lashed out at the table, wiping away the last remaining grins. 'War suits you gentlemen, does it not? You strut about like roosters, your influence growing, your egos swelling and you send the bill for all this to your queen. Well, my patience has run out.'

'Fools!' Sommers shrieked gleefully. 'Trying to win a war by fighting. Ludicrous!'

That lifted some of the tension until Aramilla turned on Sommers with narrowed eyes. 'For another word like that, I will ruin you, Sommers.'

Sommers sank a little in his seat, hands clasped together as if praying the queen would swoop overhead. Ruden opened his mouth, but had not uttered a sound when the queen cut across him.

'No, enough . . . *Enough!* Be grateful I suffer any of you!' Aramilla climbed to her feet, face alive with rage and vengeance. Her councillors hastened up after her, Ruden rising only slowly, frowning at the queen as though disappointed.

'All attacks on Blacklaw – *all* of them – are to cease

immediately! I am going past the lines to speak with Lady Keturah, and fully expect greater wisdom from the mouth of that barbarian than I hear from this council.'

She strode to the door, a silence in the hall so profound her slippers slapping the stone floor made it ring. Then she was gone, a trail of ladies rustling after her and leaving the council standing in foolish silence.

'I thank you for coming, my lords,' said Bellamus. 'Her Majesty must bear a disproportionate burden in this conflict, and understandably wants it concluded. I'm sure she will soon be as considerate to your wishes as usual.'

Nobody responded. There came a few awkward gestures, shared helpless looks, some murmured words, a relieved laugh and the council dispersed.

'Lord Safinim . . .' Bellamus found himself gently turned around by Ruden, who put an arm over his shoulder and drew him away from the long table. 'I fear to go back to my master with an account of this day. As you know his generosity was rather contingent on us achieving something decisive over the Black Kingdom. A fragile peace, which emboldens the Ereboan Anakim and leaves the Black Kingdom as a force intact . . . well I fear it was not the use he had in mind for his troops.'

'Nor I, my lord.'

Ruden nodded sympathetically, but still Bellamus felt as though he were being crushed beneath the wheel of an immense wagon. 'Still less after that fiasco with the Anakim crossing, eh? It'll look as though we've panicked and sued for peace. My own feeling is that we should be launching our assault now. You have influence over Her Majesty, no one more. I can rely on you to bring her around?'

'I intend to try, my lord, but I do not pretend to control Her Majesty. I fear, too, my influence is not what it was.' No harm in admitting that: it was there for all to see.

'No,' said Ruden, giving Bellamus a grin. 'But you don't actually require her favour, do you? For example, I know you took care of those first envoys for us.'

Bellamus started, but Ruden's arm was consoling about his shoulders, and he was speaking so intimately that none of the rest of the council chattering behind them could hear. 'It had to be done, Safinim, we both know it had to be done. I assure you, no one else knows and nor shall they. I have conveyed to the Emperor you are a true friend of ours, however.'

Bellamus could not decide how he felt about Ruden. He was too powerful to like, too competent to despise, too suave to properly fear. Bellamus might simply have adored him, if he had not had such wild ambitions himself. He was like an undertow: innocuous until you looked back and realised you had been dragged miles from shore. You could expend all your energy thrashing and trying to fight him, but in some ways it was easiest just to be swept along.

'Generous of you, my Lord Ruden. I can rely on your assistance?'

'Oh, entirely, yes.'

'That is a great comfort, my lord.'

It might have been difficult to suspect Ruden of anything specific. But, he thought, as he watched the lord sweep from the hall, nodding affably to half a dozen councillors on his way, Bellamus would not have trusted him with a pair of shoes.

Bellamus usually interceded directly with the queen. But being out of favour, he needed allies to cajole and flatter and nod consolingly when the queen was in a more receptive mood, and convince her that invasion was preferable to peace.

Looking across the room he spied the Count of Gothland: a small bird-like figure; slender-boned, beak-nosed and proud, conversing with another lord in animated Occitese. Bellamus crossed the hall to hover next to them, waiting for a lull in conversation or some sign the count was ready to receive him. But both Gothland and his companion were failing to meet Bellamus's eye, jabbering away without giving him any recognition. Bellamus was on the verge of attempting to shift the language from Occitese, but then the two lords moved slightly, forming a V which left their backs facing the upstart lord. Bellamus was used to being scorned and stepped to their other side, offering a low bow and interrupting in Frankish: 'My Lord Gothland.'

Gothland, whom Bellamus had seen speak that language perfectly well, looked mystified and shrugged at Bellamus.

'I had the honour to fight beside some of your men-at-arms recently, my lord,' said Bellamus, but Gothland just shook his head blithely and shrugged.

'No understand, no understand,' he said in Saxon.

Struggling to hide his frustration, Bellamus turned to Gothland's companion. 'Perhaps you could translate for his lordship?' But this lord shrugged too and shook his head. The two observed him with a kind of blank incuriousness infinitely more wounding than active hostility. Bellamus gave up, bowing and turning away to look for somewhere else he might begin.

He spied Lord Sutton's pointed beard waggling in conversation and began to slide towards him, hoping to meet his eye. Sutton flashed the swiftest of glances towards the upstart, tapped his companion on the shoulder and gestured to the door. Together they began to stride from the room, heads determinedly angled towards one another to avoid interruption. Bellamus was not so easily defeated, and latched on to him. 'Might we speak, my lord?'

'Safinim,' said Sutton, blankly. 'These days you are chiefly a purveyor of servants, are you not?'

'The finest in Albion,' said Bellamus, mildly. 'As many of the lords in this hall would attest.'

Sutton shook Bellamus's arm from his sleeve. 'I have no need of servants.' He turned his back on Bellamus and left without another word. It was hard not to perceive his waning influence in how they treated him. When he was in favour with Aramilla, these lords swallowed their pride and dealt with him. Now the hall was draining rapidly, all moving carefully to avoid falling in with Bellamus.

Soon only the wild-looking Widukind remained, kneeling

before the table and head bent in prayer, filthy bare feet protruding beneath his robes. He finished and stood, gaze snagging on Bellamus. He inclined his head gravely in his direction. 'Lord Safinim. Be careful with Ruden. His master is a man of dark intentions.'

'I believe you, Lord Bishop,' said Bellamus. 'I know you don't speak without good cause.' He observed the bishop, one of the few whom Aramilla respected. It gave him an idea. 'Do you have any specific concerns over Lord Ruden?'

'Does one need specific concerns of a snake? Betrayal is in his nature.'

'Might you warn the queen, when you have a moment? I'd tell her myself, but it would be most effective from your own mouth.'

Widukind inclined his head once more. 'I shall. After mass.'

Bellamus thanked the bishop and left the hall thoughtfully. He went to Aramilla's chambers and there he hesitated. The queen was a master manipulator. She missed nothing when it came to people, even if she often chose to canter over what she observed. Could he deceive her? He was on the verge of talking himself out of it, but before he could, he raised his hand and knocked.

'What?' came a bellow in response.

'Majesty?' Bellamus peered around the door.

She spared him a cold glance.

'Majesty, there's something I feel you should know.'

'Out with it, Safinim.'

'I believe . . .' He looked behind him and slid inside as though worried he might be overheard. 'I believe there's a plot against your person.'

Aramilla narrowed her eyes. 'A plot? A plot to what?'

'To insert Emperor Karoli onto your throne.'

She raised her chin, eyeing him. 'Lord Ruden, you think?'

Bellamus nodded. 'I see you suspect him too, Majesty.' He should have stood before her until asked to be seated, but instead he slid onto a chair beside her as he had when they were close. 'I have for some while, but I've only recently received my first proof.'

She eyed his frame folded on the chair, and then looked him in the face. 'And?'

'My spies intercepted a letter,' Bellamus invented. 'From Ruden to Karoli.'

'Show me,' she said imperiously.

Bellamus shook his head. 'It would've aroused suspicion if the letter had vanished, Majesty, we could only delay it for a moment. Now the text was not conclusive: Lord Ruden is too careful a man for that. But there are references made to the "*weakening of Queen Aramilla's rule*" and "*encouraging the situation*" and "*taking advantage*".'

The queen's eyes were wet slits. '*Encouraging the situation?* What does that mean?'

Bellamus hesitated, for here was where his two ambitions collided. He needed to ignite the final push against the Anakim, *and* he needed to return to favour with the queen. He feared he could only manage one at a time. 'It's hard to be sure, but I believe he's hoping that if you invade Blacklaw, both you and they will be weakened enough that Karoli can move in and take what remains.'

'Ruden,' she repeated, looking at him dubiously.

'You must've noticed how the council now defers to him in almost all things, Majesty. It's only when you truly put your foot down that he is defied.'

A little of the doubt on her face lifted at that.

'We'll need more evidence of course,' Bellamus went on. 'We cannot move against him on the basis of that letter. But for now, your decision to cease invasion seems very wise.'

Aramilla scowled. 'How gracious of you to admit, Safinim.'

Bellamus bowed. He hated himself for his absurd desire to please her. He hated the obsequious, crouching figure he became, and the sweat that prickled his palms just to be in her presence. 'Rest assured, my men shall be watching Ruden very closely, Majesty.'

She gave him a sour look. 'May they be better at spying on our own side than they are on the Anakim.'

Bellamus withdrew. Once, he had thought himself her equal, and not even considered whether he would be equal to regaining her ear and doing away with this ugly peace she desired. Now, he was almost too frayed to act.

He dreamed sometimes, on these hot summer nights. He would awake clammy with sweat and gasping, the image of an empty town square fading from his mind's eye; a notched wooden block sitting at its centre.

31
The Thing in the Barrel

There came a knock at the door. 'Come,' barked Keturah.

Ormur crept around the door's edge, hair newly tied in the high ponytail of a Sacred Guardsman. His eyes travelled over the three men sitting on the floor with her, each occupying their own bearskin. 'Brother,' said Keturah, briefly. 'I see you're the guardsman you've long deserved to be, and you'll see I'm engaged. An hour, then we'll talk.'

'My lady,' murmured Ormur. 'My lords,' he added to the men sitting with her, and bowed his way outside. There he waited in silence with the bodyguards who escorted Keturah's guests. They all stood rigidly to attention, but presently Ormur slid onto the floor and began running his fingers in an endless pattern on the cold flagstones. It was not one hour but two before the door opened and the Anakim lords Keturah had been parlaying with began to file out. Strange men, strangely dressed and even strange-smelling, but all part of Keturah's new alliance.

'Come in, brother,' came Keturah's voice.

Ormur bent low to the passing lords, and then slid into the Black Lady's quarters. It looked much the same as it had when these rooms had been Roper's. On the wall hung the giant elk antlers Roper had hunted with Tekoa; in the corner his bed with its blankets still rough and woollen, Roper's wolfskin cloak hurled upon them, as if the great man had just returned from campaign and was merely seeing to his equipment somewhere out of sight. Keturah had made only two changes. The first was to remove the chairs, which she declared a Suthern extravagance. Chairs, she scoffed, were only necessary if one needed to write at a table. Of course the Anakim did not write, and Keturah was a popular leader, so many in the Black Kingdom had followed her lead and hacked their chairs into firewood.

The second change was the suit of armour, mounted on a stand in the corner. On top was Roper's famous Unthank-silver helmet, a sharp axe-blade on the crest at the front. And beneath was an eye-wateringly expensive cuirass: the first, Ormur believed, to have been made entirely of Unthank-silver. It was made to Roper's measurements: the suit Tekoa had commissioned in memory of his conquest of Lundenceaster. It had been completed shortly before Roper's assassination, though the Black Lord had never worn it.

But Keturah was not alone in the room. She stood with her back to him, deep in conversation with the broad-shouldered Virtanen. Her arm was on his shoulder, their heads leaned close together.

Virtanen spotted Ormur first and nodded at him, giving a wink. 'The young guardsman!' he declared.

Keturah turned and folded her arms, wryly observing Ormur's high guardsman's ponytail. 'Who's taken you for protégé then?'

'Captain Gray.'

'Ha!' Virtanen strode forward to embrace Ormur. 'So the old fellow's crumbled at last! I thought he'd keep putting it off, doubtless waiting for a special case to make an exception, eh?'

'I think the time was right,' said Ormur.

Virtanen regarded him fondly. 'Your lady's given me a job to do, I'll leave you two old souls to catch up. Congratulations again, Ormur.'

'Come back soon, Virtanen.'

Ormur showed the herald out, and when he turned back to Keturah, she was staring after him, wearing a smile which reminded him of how she had been before all this, when the responsibilities of the Stone Throne had not weighed on her. She sensed his eyes and gestured to a mat on the floor. 'Sit with me then, my guardsman, and bring that wine jug with you. We should mark this great honour of yours.'

She made no reference to the two hours he had been waiting.

Ormur fetched a pair of goblets and the earthenware jug indicated by the Keturah. The Black Lady rarely laughed as she had when they had first met. Her remarks were just as caustic, but much of the humour had gone from them. Keturah had never been particularly beautiful, but her manner, her confidence, her vitality and her striking green eyes had combined to make a compelling and appealing figure in her youth. That had gone somehow. She was stronger, colder, her face the same in repose but less capable of animation.

Ormur still loved her. Long before he had been a guardsman, long before she had been a queen, he had been at her command.

She poured the wine and raised her goblet to him. Hastily he took up his own.

'Congratulations, Ormur. A Prize of Valour and a spot in the Sacred Guard before you're twenty. I am proud of you.'

He sipped quickly to hide his embarrassment, but there was more to come.

'I spoke to the Battle Historian, you know. You are the youngest guardsman for six hundred years. Six hundred! Roper would've been proud too, and jealous. He always thought being a guardsman far more prestigious than occupying the Stone Throne.'

'What?' said Ormur. 'Jealous?'

'Certainly,' said Keturah, raising her eyebrows over her goblet as she took a sip. 'A Sacred Guardsman is the pinnacle of what a man may make himself. A Black Lord is born and therefore inferior, in some ways. But maybe you'll be both? You're famous. You have Chlodowich's royal blood. I'm endlessly hearing how popular you are, and that you should succeed the Stone Throne.'

Ormur was horrified. 'The throne is yours, my lady!'

'The throne is mine for now,' said Keturah. 'I keep it warm for Numa, when he is of age.'

'Numa must succeed, but you're the best,' said Ormur. 'Who could follow you?'

'I always tell them you'd reject it,' said Keturah wryly, 'when people say what a leader you'd be. They're right though, brother. Men would fight for you on the battlefield like it was their own son they were defending. You would be a wonderful Black Lord. A Sacred Guardsman, and still you blush like a maid,' she added.

Ormur did not know what to say. He had nearly finished the wine already and it was making him lightheaded. Light-headed, and perhaps a little bold. 'May I look at his armour?'

Keturah raised an eyebrow. 'Look at it, have it if you want. I've been thinking of getting rid of it, or at least sending it away.'

'My lady!' Ormur was horrified. 'How could you get rid of it?'

The smile faded from Keturah's eyes and she sat back a little, putting her goblet on the floor. 'It's a relic, Ormur. In the old days I liked to address that battered helmet and ask it what I should do. These days, I've been on the Stone Throne for three times longer than Roper ever was. If he were here, he'd be asking *me* for advice.' She turned her head and looked distantly at the burnished plates, smooth as glass. 'It tethers me to a past from which it is high time we all moved on, and you particularly. Try as we might, great man though he was, we can't get him back.'

'I could never wear that, my lady. I should not like people to think I compared myself to him.'

Keturah tutted. 'You put him on too much of a pedestal. I love him, of course. Still, I love him. He was brave, and energetic and kind and driven – driven like nothing I've seen before or since. He was a visionary. But he could also be prickly, stubborn, blinkered and tormented. Sometimes he was just a fool, and made plenty of mistakes. The situation we are in now, Ormur, is of his making, and it is not good. We are a shadow of our former selves. This society is in shock, and though we'd never surrender, I don't think we've got the strength to finish this either. Roper did that.'

To hear this from Keturah, of all people, rendered Ormur momentarily speechless. 'But . . . you supported him, did you not? When his campaign was conceived?'

She nodded. 'He convinced me. But we knew when we started that this might be impossible. It seems it might've been. He was still a great man, but you will be too, if you survive long enough. Don't torture yourself with an impossible image that never existed. Now let me not hear about him again.'

'Yes, my lady.'

'This fortress is at your disposal, Ormur! You should not be thinking of the dead. You are a Sacred Guardsman with a reputation peers would die for. You should be prowling the streets, showing off your scars and breaking girls' hearts. Anyone caught your eye?'

He could feel his face burning again. 'There was a girl who looked nice the other day,' he muttered.

'I shall summon her here and order her to wed you,' Keturah declared. 'That was a joke, Ormur,' she added in exasperation as he stirred desperately. 'What's her name?'

'I don't know. It was just in passing, she smiled at me.'

'Not exactly grounds for marriage,' said Keturah. 'But I have a command for you, my guardsman. Find her, impress her, and report back. See if this girl is worthy of your affections. Our country needs children, Ormur, we are fewer than we were. Many fewer. That is your solemn duty.' She glanced out of the window. 'I have business in the stables. I have been granted a request by King Drava, whom you just met. You'll recognise him: he was the one who had a raincloud trailing him around. Come with me, you may want to see.'

Keturah was already on her feet. Ormur collected their goblets, Keturah's barely touched, and set them aside before pursuing the Black Lady's retreating back. 'I scarcely dare believe what Drava is telling me, Ormur,' she was saying over her shoulder as he scurried after her. The last few months had been spent in endless marches, but still it was a struggle to match her pace. 'If he's reporting accurately then it'll be an historic matter. Frathi will be fascinated.'

'Where does King Drava rule, my lady?'

'Karantaji, the Alpine Kingdom, you know.'

'And why is he trailed everywhere by a raincloud?'

Keturah rolled her eyes. 'Whenever he enters a room the skies darken and I can feel myself ageing into a toothless crone. He harvests goodwill like a squirrel takes hazelnuts. Poor fellow has reason to be gloomy though. By all accounts, he's desperately unlucky. His palace has burned down twice, both his sons perished in an avalanche, his wife was killed by a bear, and I'm afraid that's only the start of his troubles. If something can go wrong for Old Drava, it will.'

'Sounds as though it would be better not to be a subject of his, my lady.'

'Oh, please, brother. You are a dog, which has very effectively disguised itself as a man. I mean that as the highest praise, as you know. If Drava was lucky enough to have you as a subject you'd be as loyal to him as you are to me.'

'Never, my lady.'

She shot him a glance of exasperation with those poisonous green eyes, and he beamed back at her. Nobody else, thought Ormur, could have done what she had done. Like the Sutherners, she had sent envoys and heralds to Anakim allies across the continent. She had won their trust, convinced them of her need and, most remarkable of all, found a way to get their soldiers to Albion when the Teuta had a stranglehold over the seas. She had abolished the auxiliary legions, liberating them from the task of subsistence and turning them all into full battle-legions (though there were still those who sneered that the auxiliaries were abolished in name only). And she had lowered the age of subjectcy, so that Ormur, who would ordinarily still have been an apprentice, had left education two years early and could now be a Sacred Guardsman. Many of these changes had been wildly unpopular in the conservative, insular Black Kingdom. They seemed desperate and unsustainable. But they had kept the Black Legionaries in command of Blacklaw, and the Teuta behind the Wylie Lines.

Keturah and Ormur swirled down the spiral staircase outside the Black Lady's quarters and into the foundations of the Central Keep. It smelt of hay and leather and dung, because this was where the war horses were kept. Huge destriers and lean coursers, chewing silage in the dim stone stalls that nestled among the arches.

'Zephyr!' Ormur blurted, for there he was. Lord Roper's steel-grey battle steed, alone in the largest stall, observing the pair of them with unblinking brown eyes. He might have been half as heavy again as the destrier in the next stable.

'We only keep him for breeding,' said Keturah briefly. 'Otherwise he'd make an excellent and extensive stew. Nobody can ride him any more.'

'Why?'

'Because he's a vicious bastard of a horse with ideas above his station,' declared Keturah, shooting Zephyr a black look. 'Half of his lineage is from the giant wild horses at Trawden. My father thought it a worthwhile experiment, and when Zephyr was young and malleable, it seemed to have worked. But his wild blood has shown itself and he'll suffer no man on his back.'

'But Lord Roper used to take him into battle, did he not?' asked Ormur.

'What did I tell you about that perfect image in your head, brother?'

'Isn't it true though, my lady?'

Keturah shrugged. 'He did. This way.' She was leading him to the edge of the stables. Ormur gave the horse one final look before he followed her through a low arched door into a chamber of such unfamiliar smells that it set Ormur's hair on end. The scent was damp and oily, and there was the kind of silence that is present only when something is listening intently. But the only contents of the room were a score of large barrels, and two men stood by them. They jumped at the sight of Keturah and bowed deeply, murmuring honorifics at the floor.

'Rise,' she said briefly. 'It seems I've come to the wrong place. I'm looking for the finest assassins in Erebos.'

The mountain men straightened together. 'No mistake, my lady,' said one in his lyrical dialect. Both were substantially shorter than Keturah and Ormur, and seemed strangely proportioned too. Their eyes were narrow, their arms short, their skin a richer hue than Ormur had seen before. They wore heavy boots and thick quilted tunics, belted at the waist and extending to their ankles. The one who had spoken indicated the barrel beside him. 'We keep them in here.' His accent was dense and barely penetrable to ears tuned in the Black Kingdom.

Keturah stepped forward and walked around the barrels, eyes boring into them. 'I remember these being carried off the boats, and I thought they were supplies. But there are *people* in there? Assassins?'

'Ancient people, yes. Who will work with a skilled negotiator.'

That made Keturah raise an eyebrow. Each barrel was no higher than her waist, and she crouched before one of them, looking it up and down. 'Show me.'

'If we extract it, my lady, we shall have to use it. They cannot be turned off so easily.'

'I have a use for it.'

The two men exchanged a burst in their Anakim dialect, too rapid for Ormur to comprehend, then shrugged at one another. One of them reached for a strange instrument propped against the wall, like a shepherd's crook with a wire noose on the end. The other began to unfasten the brass catches that held the lid on the nearest barrel.

As the first latch clicked open, the contents of the barrel stirred violently. There was a rasping noise, as though something scaled was scuffing the wooden staves.

Ormur took an involuntary pace backwards, and even Keturah straightened up suddenly, apparently in two minds over whether she should retreat. Ormur's hand strayed towards Warspite, the sword Keturah had given him seven years ago on a platform drenched in autumn sun.

'What is this, my lady?' He had no desire to see whatever was in that barrel. Its smell, something like dried fish, nearly made him squirm.

The first man had manoeuvred the crook over the barrel's top, and the second deftly removed the lid from beneath it. Ormur held his breath.

Nothing happened.

The barrel was still and the four of them waited, every eye fixed on the open top. A minute thumped by, then one of the mountain men began to speak. 'Sometimes—'

And it appeared.

Out of the barrel swarmed a creature the pale pink of dawn, with limitless joints and bones of rubber.

Keturah and Ormur both flinched. Whatever this was, it moved in rapid jerks like a spider, flashing forward almost too fast to see and then utterly still, calculating what next. But the noose had been positioned perfectly, and the creature – more like a skeletal child than anything else – had strayed right into it. It had frozen, perched on the edge of the barrel, noose tight about its neck.

It looked weak and frail, but was so alien that the blood was roaring in Ormur's ears.

It had no eyes. Or perhaps there were lumps beneath the translucent skin of its eyelids, but certainly it could not see. A delta of veins spread beneath its hairless, blue-tinged skin. Its mouth was huge, its arms very long, palms massive, fingers short and disproportionately thick, its ears tall and close to the side of its head. It was a deformed person, no doubt about that. A sickly, naked man that crouched and listened, held still by the noose about its neck.

Ormur did not know how to react to this thing, but Keturah was regarding it with satisfaction. 'You know what it is, Ormur?'

'No, my lady.'

'That is a *haefingar*. Ancient people of the deepest caves, not seen in Albion since the Sutherner arrived. The last chant from the Academy to reference one of these is twelve-thousand years old.'

'And what are they doing in these barrels?' asked Ormur, observing the thing warily.

'Tell us,' commanded Keturah. 'Why are they in the barrels?'

One of the mountain men turned to a larger barrel and produced what seemed to be a salted catfish. He held it out to the haefingar, which at first did not move. Ormur could not see how the blind creature would even know it was being offered a fish. Then its hand lashed out, snatching the fish and holding it close to its emaciated chest. Ormur saw that its short fingers had actually cut into the flesh of the fish, like claws. The mountain man hummed three deep, resonant notes as though beginning some profound chant. The creature did not react.

'We keep them where it is cool and cramped,' he explained to Keturah. 'That way they do not move, and need little food. They will wait in these barrels forever. Nothing is more patient than the *katata*.'

That was a new word to Ormur, a little reminiscent of the word for *song* in the Black Kingdom.

The mountain man hummed those three deep notes once again and very slowly, the haefingar – the *katata* – raised the fish to its mouth. In a horribly sluggish motion it swallowed the twelve-inch length of fins and scales whole, the tail disappearing so gradually that Ormur wondered it did not choke.

'What is that humming?' asked Keturah, leaning forward in fascination. Ormur knew she would discuss this later with the Chief Historian, and wanted to make a full report.

'The katata is conditioned to stir at those three notes. Now if we give it the scent of a man and sing another tune, it will begin to search for that man. Sometimes they will take years, which is the scale a katata thinks on. They are infinitely patient, they move perfectly in the dark, and with those two skills they can penetrate any defences. It will remember the smell we give it exactly. It will find the one who carries it, sometime in the dark, and it will strangle them.'

Ormur imagined waking up to the sound of that rough skin, rasping like sandstone as it scraped through his window. Or the feel of those short, sharp fingers.

'Does it always work? This katata . . . when you set it going, does it succeed?'

The mountain man shook his head. 'The training is not always successful. Or sometimes it can't locate the scent, or we make a mistake when showing it who to target. We do not think like the katata. Give it the scent of a shepherd and you may recover it when it has killed one of his sheep. We usually release three. Send three, and one should get through.'

'So to set it going, we need a scent,' said Keturah, watching the katata with glittering eyes. Ormur could not take his eyes off the hands, the fingers curved like the talons of a bird, the knuckles covered in a strange scaly pad on which the thing seemed to walk. 'Presumably it does not recognise names?'

'Only smells.'

'So just a scent, and then this thing is set going and will not stop.'

'Yes.'

'This scent . . . does it have to be fresh? Could it be years old?'

The two men looked at one another, and the one holding the

noose shrugged. 'It does not matter how old as long as it is strong enough.'

Keturah nodded slowly. 'Good. Ormur? I'd like you to go and find that girl of yours. Next time I see you, I want to hear her name. But there is one job I'd like you to do first. Please show these men to the house that once belonged to Vigtyr the Quick.'

32
The Wagon

The Black Kingdom was weak. Roper's Campaign and the subsequent wars to suppress and maintain the captured lands had eroded the legions to a mere forty thousand men. With the merging of full and auxiliary legions, the tasks of construction and food production had been largely delegated to the Suthern inhabitants of Blacklaw. As the Sutherners worked the lands and the quarries, it allowed the subjects of the Black Kingdom to dedicate more of their time to war. They were good at it: better than ever before, but tired. The brief rotations into the Black Kingdom to heal did not make up for the months spent at the Wylie Lines, for the mud, the constant raids, the gravedogs, the rotting feet, gangrenous wounds, alarm trumpets, bouts of plague and above all that alien feeling of kjardautha: crippling homesickness. The Suthern monocultures on which legionaries now subsisted rotted their teeth, sapped their energy and made them ill.

The Black Lady did the best she could. Better, perhaps, than anyone else could have. But there was a grim feeling in the Hindrunn. It was a nation in decline: once proud, now almost resigned to its own decay. It was obvious, even to those with a relatively short memory, how few of them were left compared to the thousands they had been. Fully a third of the houses in the Hindrunn now stood empty. There were not enough people to occupy them all, and so the dwelling that once belonged to Vigtyr the Quick had been left empty. The outside walls had fallen victim to the occasional hurled cobble, but inside it was unchanged enough that even Ormur could detect the cloying scent Vigtyr had employed. He showed the mountain men and their assassin inside, and then waited in the street.

When they emerged both handlers seemed confident. 'The impression was still very strong. Where is the man who carries the scent?'

'Behind the Wylie Lines, in the south,' said Ormur.

'Too far. The katata will need to be closer, or the target will die of old age before he has been found.'

Ormur found a wagon train laden with sacks of wool that was heading south, and offered them two iron ingots to take the handlers with them. The wagon driver glanced at the ingots, then the silver Prize of Valour about Ormur's wrist, then up at his high ponytail. 'No charge.' An escort already accompanied them as protection from the gravedogs who scrapped over Blacklaw quite as fiercely as the human armies. He saw the wagon train out of the gate, feeling a drop of horror at the thought of anyone in the grip of those uncanny, claw-like hands.

He thought briefly of Keturah's second order: to find the girl who had smiled at him. But he knew the encounter would be mortifying, and convinced himself he would do it later. Instead, he went to the Academy.

Though the silver eye that capped it was one of the three main landmarks he used to navigate his way around the Hindrunn, he had never actually crossed the waters surrounding it and set foot inside its great granite mouth. He found a small fire crackling within, and a hooded acolyte inviting him to share its warmth and some tea while he waited for the Chief Historian. Ormur thanked her and sat awkwardly, throwing regular glances at the two berserkers guarding the entrance, who stared back at him with frank scorn. Some berserkers liked to claim that their tradition was braver and more specialist than the Sacred Guard. Doubtless Ormur's youthful countenance would be taken as evidence of this.

'Is there some way I can assist you two?' he asked coldly.

'Maybe we can help you,' said one. 'The haskoli is about two hundred leagues that way.'

Ormur jumped to his feet, but before he could move there came an imperious voice behind him. 'Guardsman!' Frathi was striding from a corridor to the right of the antechamber and Ormur froze at once. Twice in his youth, the old historian had given him a withering dressing down. 'What can I do for you?'

'Message from the Black Lady,' said Ormur, almost stumbling over his words.

Frathi tutted. 'She doesn't want to discuss the island across the sea again, does she? I keep telling her, there's a chant might reference it from the tale of a lost traveller, but we've not yet had a muster to locate it.'

'No, my lady, not the island. She wanted you to know there was something you'd find exceedingly interesting in the stables beneath the Central Keep.'

'When did Lady Keturah become so coy?' asked the historian without a trace of a smile. 'Come now, you know what it is?'

'I do, lady.'

She left him half a heartbeat before she barked: 'Well then?'

Ormur hated the customs and complexities of this fortress. Life was far simpler in Blacklaw, where rules and principles were spare. 'One of our allies – King Drava – has brought with him some cave-dwelling people. They use them as assassins, but the Black Lady thought you would be particularly interested to see them in the flesh.'

Frathi had raised her eyebrows. 'Indeed? Well that truly is interesting, I shall certainly have to examine them. I am grateful to you, Guardsman.' She nodded to him and seemed about to turn away when she caught herself. 'You have another enquiry?'

Ormur had not been going to ask, but now put on the spot he could hardly back down. 'I was wondering, my lady, is the "Chant of the Kryptean Pact" recorded anywhere?'

'Certainly,' said Frathi. She scrutinised his face. 'Come closer, Guardsman, my eyes are not what they were.' He stepped forward a little. 'You are Lord Roper's brother, are you not? Ormur Kynortasson. I heard you'd been made a young guardsman, though you were famous before, of course. We shall include you in a chant.' Ormur's face burned and Frathi looked icily surprised. 'The historic version of you shall have to blush less easily.'

'Please, my lady, the chant?'

'Your curiosity shall make it in though. Guardsmen are often curious. Your leanness too – like a snake. Your trust – it is naïve, but endearing.' Frathi was well known for her character portraits. She could distil the essence of a person into a few details, not quite complete – you could never squeeze the full complexity of someone into a chant memorised by heart – but a faithful projection, nonetheless. 'Now then, this chant. Why do you want to know? It is relevant to your brother, I suppose.'

'I heard a portion a few days ago and it sounded . . . important.'

Frathi took a couple of paces towards the entrance, causing the berserkers to brace up as she squinted up at the sun. 'Is it past noon, do you suppose, Guardsman?'

'Not yet, my lady,' said Ormur.

'I have time. If you are curious on this subject I can take you to the proper cell. Come, come.'

The Chief Historian turned on her heel and swept into the Academy, carelessly beckoning him to follow. Ormur cast a last glance at the berserkers, then trotted after her, intensely curious to see the inside of the Academy. Chanting voices swirled through the stonework, and Ormur tried to take in the wall-carvings that flashed past. An immense bird, pulverising the ground with talons of lightning. What seemed to be a great ocean, boiling away to nothing. An earth with six moons crashing into one another and raining shards onto the people below.

They had wound up a spiral staircase onto the second level before Frathi came to a door and rapped on its boards, abruptly hushing the chanting that was ringing the walls. She leaned inside, murmured something to the historians, and then held the door open for Ormur.

'These peers will perform the "Chant of the Kryptean Pact" for you, Master Guardsman, and set that portion you heard in its proper context.'

He scuttled past her to find three robed historians kneeling together on a rush mat apiece, laid over a rough stone floor. The room smelt strongly of jasmine: one of the olfactory signatures used by the academy as memory aids.

Ormur looked back over his shoulder to thank the Chief Historian, but the old woman had gone. It was just him and the three historians in this jasmine-scented cell.

'Sit, sir,' said the central historian: a dark-eyed woman of middle-age with iron-streaked hair. 'It has been some while since we performed the chant you wish to hear; we may have to adjourn to its traditional cell where the memory is strongest.'

Ormur murmured that would be no problem.

The three historians shuffled in to face each other. The two on the periphery began to exchange rapid gasps, and the senior historian, after a moment to shut her eyes and compose herself, began to sing.

It was dusk by the time Ormur emerged from the Academy, startled by how dim it was outside. It was a clear, glorious night: the water before the Academy mirror-bright, reflecting skies the purple of deep water, pricked with stars. Either side of the doors stood the two berserkers, and as he passed, he heard one of them spit. Something wet splattered onto the back of his neck and there came the sound of laughter.

Ormur ground to a halt, trying to control his temper but

finding himself turning towards the men almost at once. They were looking for a fight, and fight he could.

'I will assume the spit on my neck was accidental drool as you attempted to muddle your way through a sentence,' he said. 'I will be pleased to accept an apology for your mistake.'

The laughter redoubled in the dark. 'Ho ho! A fighter. You're on your own here, little guardsman. No loving mentor or shiny armour to hide behind.'

They were bearing down on him, enjoying the showdown, but Ormur had always been impatient. And he was angrier than either realised.

They could not see clearly in the dark and maybe he would have been too fast anyway, but the man who had spat at him did not have a moment to react before Ormur smacked a palm into the bone plate overlying his liver. The berserker was solid as an oak, and Ormur did not wait to launch a vicious uppercut with his elbow, followed by a flail of hooks. Every blow connected hard and rocked his opponent back in increments, Ormur on the advance. Then something crashed into the side of his head so hard that he was spun around by the force of it. He had taken many punches in his short life and managed to keep his feet, straightening up as a second blow soared through the dark. He dodged on instinct, his impression of the world very hazy. One figure seemed to be on the retreat, another assaulting him, and he raised a knee hard into his attacker's stomach. Not waiting to see what impact it had, he latched two hands around his opponent's thick neck, driving his knees up again and again into the broad stomach. These men were so solid! It did not feel as though his attacks were having any impact whatsoever.

Another huge blow cracked his head just above the ear and knocked him flat. He was dazed, too dazed to stand quickly and a boot smashed into his face and burst his nose. He grabbed onto the boot before it could be withdrawn, trying to prevent any further kicks until he could get back to his feet. Another boot was slamming again and again into his body but the pulverising thumps seemed distant and he was able to haul himself half-upright. He launched a fist into the groin of the man who's leg he clutched, eliciting a satisfying howl of rage and pain. Ormur gave a little gurgle of laughter and then there came a final shattering blow on his head. He fell back, a torrent of stars swirling past his eyes. Boots were smashing down on his head again and again, and a voice was roaring for them to stop, *stop*!

The blows did stop. Ormur panted on the floor, blood raw in his mouth and making the breath through his nose bubble. 'How *dare* you!' the voice demanded. 'How dare you! Two on one, you cowards!'

'He punched me in the balls!' groaned another voice.

'I saw – you deserved worse. Now get out of my way. Out of my way! You want the Chief Historian to hear about this? You'll be flayed alive! Off with you, brutes!'

'I can't . . .' moaned a voice. It was the berserker Ormur had hit in the liver and the pain of it was catching up with him. Someone had done it to Ormur once, when he was just a boy. There had been a delay, then a crushing, all-consuming agony came over him which completely halted further resistance. It had been a weapon of his ever since.

'Shameful. Now get out of my way.' A hand began to pull Ormur upright and he responded, gripping tightly onto his rescuer's sleeve and allowing himself to be pulled into a sitting position. 'Ormur, are you all right?'

He recognised the voice at last and blinked several times, spitting blood and trying to stop the world from spinning. 'Sigrid,' he mumbled, feeling a rush of affection for Gray's wife.

'Good,' she said. She left him a precious moment while he heard the berserkers mumbling about their wounds. 'Can you stand?'

The world was coming back into focus in patches and bursts. 'Yes,' he decided.

Sigrid lent a hand, and he was on his feet all too swiftly. For a moment he was sure he would topple back to the floor, but

Sigrid manoeuvred her shoulder deftly behind him and held him steady.

'Thank you,' he mumbled. He took a pace forward, swayed, and cleared the blood gathering in his mouth again.

'Our house isn't far, we'll get you patched up, and you'll need some tea. Maybe wine. This way.'

'I . . .' Not wishing to impose, Ormur was about to make an excuse. But he could not even walk unaided. That, and he was starving. The mess would have closed and even tea would be welcome. 'Thank you,' he finished. Following her warm hand, he allowed himself to be guided over the stone needle crossing the lake and into the warren of streets at the far side.

'They attacked first, I suppose,' said Sigrid.

'Spat at me,' said Ormur, dribbling out a clot.

'Is that all? They're berserkers, Ormur, just pass them by.'

'No, my lady,' said Ormur, trying to keep his head very still so as not to worsen the nausea.

She was silent for a few moments. 'You do realise if you'd just told them your name, you'd have been left alone? You're wildly famous, even among berserkers.'

'That is no way to win a fight,' he replied.

Sigrid frowned. 'Gray seems out of practice as a mentor, I'm not sure your perspective is quite right.'

'The captain has tried to alter it,' said Ormur.

'What were you even doing here?'

'I'd just heard a fragment of a chant with the captain. I wanted to know more about it.'

'Oh? Which fragment?'

'From the Chant of the Kryptean Pact. The man quoting it seemed to suggest that Roper was in a private hell, but in context it seems to have been talking about something else.'

'I don't understand.'

It hurt to talk, and Ormur did not reply for a while. They walked quietly for a few paces, turning into a street smelling of raw dough as bakers left their wares to prove for the next day's trade.

'Well . . . the hell it was referencing was called the *kungargrav.* And I think it may once have been a real place. When the Kryptea didn't gain Almighty favour to kill a Black Lord, they sometimes used to imprison him in this kungargrav instead. It seems to be some sort of prison, but one very deep and very dark, and where they control all the information going in. So they tell the Black Lord that his family is dead, his name is used as an insult and means "coward", everything he cared about has failed and the kingdom has become the very worst thing he could imagine. Every day they pile on fresh news and insults, until life in a cell where you believe the world outside is not better, but worse, is no longer worth living. They torment their prisoners until they destroy themselves. The kungargrav is a place the Kryptea hold you and drip poison in your ear for years, until you rot to nothing.'

Sigrid pursed her lips. 'New tales of what that organisation did seem to reach us every day. It is like we are just emerging from a spell. The fear of them kept us compliant. Our lack of choice meant we tried to reason they were a force for good. But your brother did a very great thing when he defied that organisation. They were the work of a desperate imagination. You must be proud. It was an act of genuine self-sacrifice, to have done that.'

'I am proud.' He thought again about what Gray had said about death, and also found himself glad. It was better that Roper had died than go through that.

They had reached Sigrid's house. She showed him into the parlour, where Gray sat by a merry fire, using a piece of sandstone to polish the handle of a small task-knife. With only one hand, he had braced the sandstone between his knees while he worked the knife over it. He looked up at Ormur, took in his swollen lips, closing eye and busted nose, and rolled his eyes. 'You fool,' he said gently.

'It is serious,' said Sigrid sternly. 'Two berserkers, and he'd hurt them both. They might've beaten him to death if I hadn't arrived.'

'You see how you get me into trouble, my friend,' said Gray, gesturing at Sigrid with the stump of his hand. 'Will that persuade you not to fight?'

'I'll try, sir.'

Gray looked fondly at Ormur and then held out the knife he had been working on. 'What say you, my young protégé? I had Saskal the smith help me forge the blade. Walnut handle, still needs some finishing.'

While Sigrid disappeared from the parlour, Ormur took the knife and inspected it. He felt the edge, the flex, the pitting of the steel, the tightness of the handle upon the tang. It seemed indistinguishable to him from professional work.

'Terrible,' he said, handing it back to Gray.

The captain laughed. 'No tea for Ormur,' he declared to Sigrid, who had just returned with some linen strips, a copper bowl and dried herbs. He patted the chair next to him and Ormur sat. 'You haven't eaten, have you?'

'What makes you think that?'

'I was looking for you in the mess.'

'No,' he admitted. 'I haven't.'

'Why didn't you say,' said Sigrid sternly. She disappeared again, ignoring Ormur's protestations and returning with an earthenware jar containing two cold goose legs preserved in a pool of creamy fat. She left it by the fire to soften and began toasting the bread. The kettle was roaring steam and she pulled it off the fire to steep a spray of pine needles in a cup and then poured the remaining hot water into the copper bowl. She gave Ormur the tea and soaked the linen strips and herbs in the bowl.

'Where were you this evening then?' Gray asked.

Ormur explained. 'So I'm glad,' he finished, 'that Roper's not in some personal hell, and it might almost be for the best that he fell off that cliff, rather than having to suffer this kungargrav.'

Gray nodded slowly. 'It certainly sounds it. Many things about that moment were cruel at the time but I'm now grateful for. When it happened I was desperate for one last word or look, but in the end, he was too distant for any of that. So the last memory I have of his face is the smile he gave me as he was led away.'

'Oh,' said Ormur. 'That's not how I imagined it. Could you not see his face when he went over the edge?'

'Not clearly, fortunately.'

Sigrid began dabbing at the blood on his face, and the water in the copper washbowl was soon scarlet. Ormur screwed up his eyes as he waited for her to move away from his tender nose. 'How could you tell it was him?'

'Who else were the Kryptea pushing off a cliff, Ormur?'

'True.' He flinched as Sigrid brushed his nose, and she tutted.

'I saw you take punches better than that.'

Ormur grinned, and Sigrid's eyes widened as a cut on his cheek split open again. 'Don't smile!'

'Didn't you say the Kryptea used to murder people at random sometimes,' he mumbled as Sigrid worked around his mouth, 'just to put people on edge?'

'They did, yes. But we also found his body, didn't we?'

'But even that was barely identifiable, you said.'

Gray raised his eyebrows. 'The fish got to him before we did.'

Ormur was silent. Presently, he became aware of a strange feeling settling on him. It was as though a hand had reached through his navel and gripped the viscera behind. He ignored it for some time, trying not to look at Gray. When he did, the captain did not seem to be the man he had been. He looked old, and foolish. 'If the fish had mostly destroyed the body then . . .' He was struggling to keep the accusation from his voice. 'I'm trying to understand why you thought it was him?'

'His scabbard,' said Gray stiffly. 'Strapped to his side.'

'So . . . you saw someone fall, but we can't actually be sure if it was Roper.'

Gray set down the knife. 'It was him, Ormur.'

'I don't see how you can know that.'

Gray was shaking his head. 'You're flirting with the absurd and letting it get out of hand.'

'Or maybe you're protecting yourself from the possibility that you didn't actually see Lord Roper die.'

'I did see!' Gray's voice was suddenly that of the infantry captain, booming an order across the battlefield. He sat forward in his chair, eyes set on Ormur. 'You weren't there, and I was. Who do you think that body belonged to, if not Roper? Where has he been all these years if that wasn't him?'

'I don't know!' shouted Ormur. 'He could've been in this kungargrav for all we know!' He did not believe that, but nor would he back down in the face of Gray's fury.

The captain actually banged his fist on the arm of his chair. 'I've *told* you what we did to Jokul! We tortured him for *days*. He screamed and he babbled and he gushed everything! If Roper were still alive, if this kungargrav had even still been used by the Kryptea in the last few centuries, Jokul would have sung out long before we finally put him out of his misery!'

Sigrid had paused from tending Ormur's injuries and was observing her husband. 'Why so angry, my love?'

'Because it's possession,' said Gray, throwing himself back in his chair. 'Why am I having to dig this up again? There is *no* chance Roper is alive, and nothing but misery to be gained going down that road. We've lost him and we have to move on. Even after seven years, we talk about him too much. I'm sick of seeing the people around me waste their energy, lingering on a past that cannot be changed.' Gray looked as though he was going to say more, but held himself to a dismissive gesture with his remaining hand.

There fell a silence more uncomfortable than Ormur had ever known with his mentor. Sigrid was frowning in disapproval. 'Brace yourself,' she said, pressing a thumb on either side of his nose. Ormur had experienced this often enough, and shut his eyes as Sigrid straightened the bones. The pain was intense, but brief.

'Thank you.'

'The only one that might need stitches is your nose, but it's not exactly easy,' she said, washing her hands and packing away her things. 'It should be well, but come back to me if it doesn't close up on its own.'

The goose fat had melted and she poured it over the toast, beginning to fry it in an iron pan. Ormur was aware of his fuming mentor and knew he should leave, but could not drag himself away from the sight of the frying bread as Sigrid shredded the goose leg and piled it over the toast. The food was ready before Gray was.

Sigrid handed him a bowl and Ormur murmured his thanks. He ate in silence, trying to be as fast as possible so that he could abandon the uncomfortable silence in the parlour. He had got to his feet, still chewing his final mouthful and wiping his hands on his leggings, when Gray spoke.

'I do not mean to be angry,' he said stiffly. 'It is not a memory I care to relive, or be pressed upon.' He took a deep breath. 'I shouldn't have shouted.'

Ormur watched him, and swallowed his mouthful. 'Was this because I insulted your knife?'

Gray snorted and tried to look sour. 'You little shit.'

Ormur cleared his throat. 'I'm sorry too, sir,' he said quietly. 'Sorry to have pried.'

Gray shrugged. 'Forget it.'

The atmosphere had not quite recovered, and Ormur left without saying farewell. Sigrid showed him to the door, arresting him by the shoulder before he could leave. 'Ormur?'

He turned to face her.

'I've not seen my husband that angry for many years. I don't think he'd have reacted like that if there hadn't been something to what you were saying.'

Ormur waited, that sense of alien discomfort in his guts again.

'I think he's thought what you have.'

'You think he is worried that person he saw may not have been Roper?'

Sigrid shrugged. 'Not genuinely worried. I don't think he believes that. But, it seems worried enough that your news about the kungargrav has made him uncomfortable.'

'That's what I thought,' said Ormur. 'I don't believe it either. But from the answers I got, it felt as though we didn't truly know.'

They gazed at each other for a moment. 'Do you know where it is?' asked Sigrid, eventually. 'This kungargrav?'

'*Nether Temple stones . . . With walls for doors and windows of stone*,' recalled Ormur. 'So beneath the Holy Temple but concealed, by the sounds of things.'

'Well you have, what, two weeks leave left before you rotate south? And you've been struggling to fill your time, I think. Looking for this kungargrav seems a better use of it than the drinking that occupies most of your peers, or the fighting that seems to tempt you. If you can see it empty, it might help both you and the captain set your minds to rest. Go hunting, Ormur.'

33
The Darkness

The Queen of Suthdal was preparing to cross the lines. She had decided to do so with a show of force, and there was much of it at her command. 'What proportion of the army should you like to take, Majesty?' Bellamus had asked.

'Tens of thousands,' she replied imperiously. Bellamus remained politely silent, causing the queen to tut irritably. 'What is it, Safinim?'

'Simply that I fear that would not be wise, Majesty. While thousands would undoubtedly provide some deterrent against casual attack, it will be extremely tempting for the Anakim to try and wipe out a significant portion of the army – not to mention your royal person – while it is separated from the rest.'

'Well then, what do you recommend?' she asked testily.

'All of them,' said Bellamus. 'If we wish to cow our enemy and exact favourable terms, let us send all of them. That would also avoid the tactical blunder of splitting our forces and allowing them to be destroyed separately.'

The queen looked first reluctant, then pleased. 'See to it, Safinim.'

Bellamus bowed. He had been seeing to it for weeks. The first step to war was massing both armies in one location.

The supply lines were ready. An honour guard was assembled to ride ahead of the main army: the smartest and most alien units that they commanded, so the Anakim could see they had monsters of their own. Elephants. Cataphracts. Knights, pikes, halberds, wardogs, crossbowmen, even camels gathered from across Erebos, given by this prince or that, all whipped into a fervour by a corps of priests that they were doing God's work. In his greatest master-stroke, Bellamus had even secured a papal decree that any man who died beneath an Anakim sword had his place in heaven secured. Thus, while many of their soldiers fought beneath the banner of foreign kingdoms, many others carried no banner at all. Styled the Holy Ereboan Army, they tied white cloths about their upper arms and were under the command of the Bishop Widukind. Bellamus had doubts over the utility of these fanatical troops, many of whom did not wear shoes.

'You are taking more than enough soldiers to launch an attack, Majesty,' Lord Ruden observed to the queen in a quiet moment before council. He knelt before her, all charm and gentle persuasion as the other lords arrived in twos and threes. 'I feel that would be a wise place to start. It is not merely my own soldiers who are here to see battle with the Anakim.' He spread his hands helplessly. 'I fear the Holy Ereboan Army will not stay together long unless there is some prospect of battle occurring, and an early victory would do wonders for your negotiating position.'

It might not have been obvious to Ruden, who was largely addressing the queen's hand, which he had grasped between his two paws, but Bellamus saw the sudden flash of suspicion on her face at this proof of Ruden's treachery. She glanced at Bellamus, who remained impassive. He had played his hand already, and had to avoid the temptation to lay any further cards.

Aramilla withdrew from Ruden's grasp, a frostiness so palpable coming over her that it was as though she had turned to porcelain. 'Your preference for battle is noted, Lord Ruden,' she said.

The queen would now be suspicious of everyone, and Bellamus kept quiet during the council. He must seem to be the only one not trying to manipulate her, and he was gratified that when she swept from the hall, she barked over her shoulder: 'Lord Safinim. A word, please.'

Bellamus followed her piously, offering a helpless shrug to the frustrated council as he departed. In the royal chambers, the queen rustled back and forth in her stiff silken gown, resembling a chess piece gliding across the board. His piece.

'Bishop Widukind came to me yesterday and told me he suspected Ruden,' she greeted Bellamus. She gestured impatiently that he should shut the door. 'Though clearly there is history between the two . . . Have you made progress with your investigations?'

Bellamus had been prepared since their last encounter, and produced a square of folded parchment from a pouch at his belt. 'My men intercepted another letter today and were able to make a transcript.' He held it out.

The queen snatched it and scanned down the lines. He had filled the letter with platitudes, news from the court and esteemed nobles, but watched in satisfaction as her mouth formed the words *prepare for your arrival* and *resume hostilities*. She glanced up at him, her face beneath its porcelain mask once more. He felt a jolt as those eyes were fixed on him, scouring his person from top to bottom. She did not trust anyone, and he knew with a sudden certainty that she was having him watched, just as he was watching everyone else. 'It's hardly proof, is it?'

Bellamus sat beside her. 'I fear not, Majesty. Lord Ruden has often spoken of Karoli's desire to meet you, and it is no secret the Emperor's condition in loaning us his soldiers was the continued conquest of Blacklaw. If we were to turn against Ruden now, we would not only lose his men, but also alienate the rest of our alliance. Arresting him would merely make us look paranoid.'

'Enemies within and without,' she observed quietly. 'At

least when the Anakim try and take my throne, they have the decency to do it to my face. I need more information, my Lord Safinim. More proof, we need specifics – something for which we can arrest him.'

'My men are working to infiltrate his household as we speak, Majesty, and I intend to meet with him this evening and see if wine can loosen his tongue a little.'

He was dismissed, but did not altogether like the look she gave him as he left. It seemed a reappraisal: one much clearer-eyed than he would have liked.

That night, Ruden arrived at his house for supper. It was a residence Bellamus had constructed himself, on a hillside, straddling a chalk stream which tumbled down a waterfall and into a lake he had excavated in front. Brimstream, he had called it, after his old headquarters south of the Abus. The name meant *foaming waters*, and was too good not to use again.

He and Ruden dined beneath the stars in the early summer's warmth, on a platform overlooking the lake. Bellamus had laid on spiced quails' eggs, swan roasted in salt, and oysters with vinegar, while Ruden provided a fine Frankish wine.

'You are an impressive operator, Lord Safinim,' said Ruden warmly, surveying the lake sparkling below them in the moonlight. 'There are those who resist the rise of a commoner, but they cannot deny you get results. What's the trick?'

'Knowing people, my dear Ruden. I've an eye for talent, and stop at nothing to acquire it.'

'So I've heard. Half the court seems to have servants originally trained here – highly sought-after, I hear.'

Bellamus flicked a hand. 'Servants are the least of it. I'll send you one: Octric. Barely more than a lad, but exceptional. If you need anything in this town, Octric will fix it for you.'

Ruden took an oyster, drowned it in vinegar and threw it back. 'Wouldn't you want to keep such a man for yourself?'

Bellamus smiled. 'A waste. I can do everything he can already.'

'I suppose you can. It is the papal decree I am most impressed by. How did you secure that?'

'His Holiness does not fear the Anakim because he has never lived close to them,' said Bellamus, pretending to sip the wine. 'They were not a problem to him, not real. So I made them real.'

'How?'

'I sent him a preserved Anakim warrior, mummified in their custom and dressed in weapons and armour.' In fact it had been a dead hybrid, the biggest Bellamus could find, which he had mummified himself. It had taken five experimental attempts before he was satisfied he could preserve one properly, and he had tattooed its cheeks with the evil eye, its arms with serpents and its hands with crows to make it all the more shocking. The pope had been horrified by this heathen giant and the hideously scarred delegation Bellamus had sent with it, bursting with stories of Anakim atrocity. It did not matter that the tales were not accurate, or the body not fully Anakim. The picture Bellamus had painted to the pope was truer than true.

'If I ever receive a present from you, I shall open it with extreme caution,' said Ruden, amused.

Bellamus smiled. 'I shall have to find you something in repayment for this superb wine.'

'Sent by the Emperor, you know, so you can be sure of its distinction. Among his many other virtues, my master has wonderful taste in wine.'

'It may be good enough to arrest my developing preference for quantity rather than quality,' said Bellamus. 'Speaking of quantity, my spies have sent the clearest indication yet that the Anakim are on their last legs.'

Ruden fixed Bellamus with his brown eyes, hand beginning to sort through his beard, as it often did when he was thinking.

'We must end this talk of peace that Her Majesty is considering,' Bellamus went on. 'I will be blunt, my lord, it could scarcely have come at a worse time. One final push and we could extract far more from them than would ever be gained from negotiations. We have the manpower to finish them, all we lack is the will.'

Ruden shrugged expansively. 'As you know, I quite agree, my Lord Safinim. But you saw the response I got trying to broach that subject today. Push much harder and I shall only alienate her.'

'Oh, Her Majesty can be prickly,' said Bellamus dismissively. 'I assure you though, sir, I know how much she respects you. Your word counts for quite as much as anyone else's at present.'

'Oh, surely not,' said Ruden, though he looked pleased.

'Your troops give you some handsome leverage as well. And there's a good few lords who are ambitious enough to stand against her. Lord Hamwic, Lord Karnow, Lord Badon, Lord Nerven—'

'Nerven?' interrupted Ruden. 'That hide-bound moralist? Surely he'd never turn on his queen.'

Bellamus took a breath, inclined his head and lifted the cup to his mouth.

'What? Go on, Safinim.'

'Lord Nerven's properties are crumbling across Suthdal. He is in desperate need of cash to salvage his dignity, and that of his house. Get it to him in private, and you'd have a friend for life. None of these men will work with me, of course, they think I'm too close to the queen, they don't trust me. But they'll work with you, they respect your master.'

Ruden nodded thoughtfully. 'I could try, no harm in it.' Then he looked shrewd. 'But what will you do, Lord Safinim? You surely don't intend me and my friends to stand alone against the queen?'

Bellamus sat forward, putting down his cup. 'Well, nothing formal, you understand. As a low-born foreigner without army or friends, I cannot be as frank in my defiance as you. I owe too much to the queen. But I intend to ensure your words seem wiser and wiser to Her Majesty's ears.'

'You undersell your position, sir,' Ruden replied mildly. 'I number myself among your friends if no one else does. And if your Thingalith aren't some of the most intelligent and independent soldiers in Erebos then I'm not sure what they are. But I shall need more in the way of assurances before standing alone against the Queen of Albion.' His eyes twinkled at the name.

Bellamus nodded. 'Of course, my lord, but I operate best in the shadows. I will do what I do best – warmonger. I rely on you, don't think otherwise. But what I trade you is this: my skills, and a secret. You advocate against the peace, as tactfully as you think you need. And as indemnity I offer you the knowledge that the Thingalith have been working against this peace from the start. You are aware it was they who killed the queen's original envoys. But even now they are past the Lines, repeatedly kicking the wasps' nest.' He feigned a careful sip of wine. This felt an even greater risk than deceiving the queen. He was now utterly in Ruden's power: all the nobleman needed to do was relay this information to the queen, and Bellamus would be imprisoned, mutilated and executed.

'You don't say,' said Ruden, comfortably. 'You mean enraging the Anakim to such an extent that there is no hope of them agreeing to a peace?'

'They should be in a white-hot fury by the time the queen arrives,' said Bellamus flatly. 'Now, evidently this would not be well-received by Her Majesty.'

'Treason rarely is,' said Ruden helpfully.

'Quite. You see how I have placed myself utterly in your trust, my lord? I hope we have an accord. I will ensure there is no possibility of peace occurring with our enemies. You will influence Her Majesty and the council, so that when the time comes we are ready to break the Anakim completely.'

Ruden was looking greatly pleased. 'Well. That seems only fair.' He raised his cup and they drank to their agreement.

After a pause, Bellamus continued: 'Did I ever tell you the story of my first conversation with a subject of the Black Kingdom?'

'I must've missed it,' said Ruden pleasantly, refilling his goblet and offering some to Bellamus, who declined.

'It was a legionary we captured,' he explained. 'In those days I used to take the Thingalith raiding beyond the Abus to stir up some trouble, and learn what I could about the Black Kingdom, and practise my Anakim too. So the first time we sallied north, we saw a man running over the hills, moving very slowly. He looked exhausted, and as we approached he just stopped and waited for us to catch up with him. To this day I'm not sure I've ever seen anyone so weary, and it felt less like a capture than a rescue. He was soaked through, and thin, and when we'd given him food and water we asked where he'd come from. The man told us that he'd run from a place called Stjornava. I'd never heard of this outpost, and when I asked how far it was, he estimated three hundred and fifty miles. Seeing his exhaustion, I asked if he'd run the whole way and he said he had. What, I asked, could possibly have compelled him to come so far? He told me he'd been given a message by his captain, to take to another officer nearby. When he'd arrived with his message, he was told the officer had gone already. He was riding south, to the Hindrunn. So he went after him. He ran for three hundred and fifty miles to deliver that message without a backwards glance.'

'It must've been a terribly important message.'

Bellamus shrugged. 'It was to say one of the great trees of his estate had come down in a storm. A significant piece of news to an Anakim, if inconsequential. But the point was not the message. The point was that he'd been given an order by his captain, and having to travel an additional three hundred miles did not justify a reassessment of his situation. The point, Lord Ruden, is that the Anakim don't think about choice like you and I. They do not reach for it like we do: much of the time, they don't even see it. Lord Roper, whom they adored and trusted, gave them instructions to wipe out Suthdal and subdue Albion. Neither his death, nor their vastly weakened position, justify a reassessment of their task. The queen can negotiate with them until she's blue in the face. She can offer them the earth and the sea. It would be like trying to elicit water from a cow's udder. They won't do it. They can't.'

But Bellamus was distracted from the dregs of his story by something in the street that ran below them, up beside the wall of his grounds.

'What is it?' asked Ruden, following his gaze.

'It looks like . . . men. Armed men, walking up the hill.' Then he recognised the curved sheen of a helmet and the glitter of a halberd. 'Royal retainers.'

'Are there any other houses on this hill?'

Bellamus shook his head.

Ruden was quite calm as he asked, 'Well, Lord Safinim. Are they here for me, or for you?'

Earlier that evening, in the grounds of the Royal Court on the other side of Wiltun, an oil lamp flickered at the entrance to an insubstantial hut. Gathered around it as though it were a bonfire were two halberdiers, who guarded the door. They were bored, for nothing ever happened on these shifts. They were mostly there to prevent the occupant of the hut from escaping, though he had not tried to do that in seven years. They were also supposed to protect him from the townsfolk, who had long heard the rumours that a tame Anakim was kept at court, and might try to find and kill it, and so put an end to the bad luck it would bring. But so far, nobody had uncovered Vigtyr's whereabouts and the halberdiers were on the verge of sleep. One already sat with his back against the hut, head tilted back, while the other stared at the flame of the oil lamp, eyes drooping.

Within the hut, lying in bed but far more alert than either of his guards, was Vigtyr.

The bed felt boiling. Each louse bite from his mattress itched unbearably and his thoughts spun like the wheel of an upturned wagon. Of all the stages of his wretched life, this was the worst. Humiliated, imprisoned, disgraced. Vigtyr had never truly had friends, but there had always been the occasional woman prepared to listen to his troubles and offer him comfort when he sobbed his sorry heart out. Until they too grew tired, and he was forced to push them away before they could do the same to him. Now he did not even have that connection. He dreaded the hours of darkness spent lying alone in this bed, exhausted but unable to sleep, ill thoughts picking at him like dogs.

And for some reason tonight was his worst for months. He could not place what particularly troubled him. There was a strange smell in the room, or perhaps it was that Sommers had spent the day tormenting him again, or that the queen seemed indifferent to his suffering. Try as he might, sleep was nowhere near and he was sweating. He needed water and reached a hand out into the darkness for the jug beside his bed. But instead of the jug, his hand met something unexpected. Something warm and soft, like the flesh of over-ripe fruit.

'Shit!' He recoiled so violently that he toppled backwards out of the bed, landing on the cold stone floor, woollen blanket wrapped about his legs. 'What was that?'

There was no response from the black room. It had felt like bare flesh. It felt like there had been someone standing in the darkness, beside his bed.

Vigtyr was frozen, left hand tingling and crawling where it had touched whatever had been beside him. *Coward*, he thought. *There's no one in here.* He must have been nearer sleep than he had thought. It had been a hallucination, or some fabric he had left over the jug and forgotten. But still he dared not move. Still his left hand trembled like the wing of a tiny bird and he held his breath, ears straining into the dark.

And then he definitely heard something. The softest of creaks as a weight settled on the ropes of his vacant bed.

Vigtyr had to raise a hand to his mouth to stop himself crying out. There was something in here with him. Something that now lay between him and the door. A man? The hairless skin had felt strangely coarse and dry, but there was nothing else it could be.

He had to move. He had cried out from this spot and his imagination conjured monstrous forms groping through the darkness towards the sound. Mouth dry, eyes stretched open and blind, he took his blanket, balled it hastily and tossed it to the other side of the room with a soft *flump*.

There was silence. Vigtyr waited with his breath held, left hand still trembling violently, praying he had distracted whatever was in here, that it could not see in this gloom any better than he could. Then came another slight creak from the bed. He felt, rather than heard, something slide onto the floor and move in the direction of his blanket.

This darkness was filled with menace. He could barely hear through the roar in his ears and the heart hurling itself again and again against his chest. He was being hunted.

There were no weapons in this room. If he called for the guards, would they be able to get inside fast enough? He had no choice. The dark was silent now. Whatever was in here might have found the blanket and realised Vigtyr was not there. It might be right beside him. His every muscle was taut, ready to recoil from a hand reaching out towards him. He had to go. He had to go now.

Vigtyr moved. He lurched to his feet and lunged forward, trying to leap over his bed but stumbling and slamming into the wall beside the door. 'Help!' he screamed. 'Help! Help me! Hurry, hurry! Please! Please, god help me!'

He groped sideways across the wall, feeling the door and pounding it desperately, fists bouncing off the wooden boards. His back was crawling as there came the sense of something closing in on him, of invisible pincers preparing to grip his neck.

'Shut up in there!' bellowed a voice from outside.

'Help! Help! Help!' he screamed. 'There's something in here, help for god's sake help!'

And then a leather noose snapped taut around Vigtyr's

neck. His last protestations were cut off and he was dragged over backwards, an impossibly tight grip on his throat, squeezing the life from him. Then something moved into position on top of him. Something dry and alien that made his flesh creep. His hands flew to his throat and tried to prise off that grip but it was like iron, he made not the slightest impression on it.

The bolts of the door were shooting back and the faintest glow of light crept in the room. For the first time Vigtyr saw the shadow on top of him, skeletal and grotesquely proportioned. There came an exclamation from one of the guards and the tinkle of breaking china.

The light disappeared.

'There's something here!' came a voice, but it sounded distant. It sounded as though Vigtyr was underwater. The pressure was building in his skull, not the faintest sound coming out of his mouth, try as he might. The feel of those hands around his neck was fading. The terror and pressure in his skull were slipping away. All that was left was the sound of those voices, high, high above, and floating further away.

34
The Assassin

Ruden refilled Bellamus's goblet. 'Until it becomes clear which of us the queen wishes to see, I say we finish this fine wine and our good conversation.'

Bellamus took up the cup and toasted his guest. 'To the death of the Black Kingdom.' He took a proper sip this time and found the wine was indeed superb.

'There was one thing I'd wanted to ask you,' Ruden began.

He was halted by a distant thunder at the door. The royal retainers had arrived.

'Lord Safinim! Lord Safinim! Answer at once in the name of Her Majesty the Queen!'

Ruden began to get to his feet, but Bellamus waved him back down. 'Entitled royal retainers I'm afraid, my Lord Ruden. My household will see to them and if they require my attention, they'll come find me. You were saying?'

Ruden grinned as the front door sustained another volley. 'I've noticed you are the only one to call Grendel "Lord Roper". I'd heard you met him, years ago. I was wondering what you'd made of the great man.'

'Grendel,' said Bellamus thoughtfully. There had been a time when he had railed against that nickname: it seemed to hand the psychological edge too easily to Roper, but he supposed that did not matter now. 'Yes indeed. I was his prisoner for some months. He and I would talk often, and play chess. I do believe he was a great man.'

The two of them determinedly ignored the sound of one of Bellamus's household answering the door and the heated exchange which began at once.

'What makes you say so?'

'Who can articulate these things? It is something you sense instinctively, rather than dissect. What I mostly remember is his drive. He was simply relentless: sitting down looked like a terrible effort of will for him. But he was also a visionary, and a true leader. That's why his own side killed him. His name was branded onto the heart of every soldier under his command, and that made him too powerful. That's also why I didn't want the name Grendel to stick. I didn't want the Anakim hearts to read *Roper* while the pits of our stomachs read *Grendel*.'

'You observe the Anakim as you once did? What do they say of their new queen?'

'My spies focus more on our own side than the Anakim these days. But the new queen is adored in Anakim fashion. They respect her absolutely.'

There came a bang, scuffling noises and a yell. Boots stomped through the hall and Bellamus knocked back the last of his wine, winking at Ruden. Half a dozen royal guards burst onto the platform, pursued by an increasing number of Bellamus's household. The only men Bellamus kept in this house were Thingalith, and they all knew how to fight. They were arming themselves already, some carrying cudgels, some warming pans, or pokers. Diethaad was there clutching a side-table by the legs, and ill-will leapt between the Thingalith and the royal guards like hot spitting oil.

The Thingalith outnumbered the guards, and even armed with such makeshift weapons, Bellamus felt sure they would have the better of them. He got to his feet, dabbing his lips on a napkin as the Thingalith looked to him for instruction. For the briefest instant, he considered giving the order to murder the retainers. They would have to flee afterwards, of course, but better that than face imprisonment at the hands of this paranoid queen. But he had no idea where he could flee to. He was not as ready for life on the road as he had once been, and the prospect of leaving this comfortable house tired him.

'Her Majesty has summoned you immediately, Lord Safinim,' said one of the retainers, crouching beneath his helmet as though he could pull it over his body altogether like a turtle-shell.

'I am at Her Majesty's disposal,' said Bellamus calmly. He waved the Thingalith to stand down. 'It's all right boys. Diethaad, my cloak please.'

Lord Ruden had stood as well. 'Sadly it seems our evening is to be terminated early, my Lord Safinim. I should like to resume our conversation when Her Majesty is done with you.'

He bowed civilly and with a courteous nod and a smile at the retainers, extricated himself from the scene and disappeared through the house, just as Diethaad came the other way with Bellamus's cloak. Bellamus swept it over his shoulders and nodded to the retainers, following them in silence as he was escorted through his own home and out into the slumbering town. He could hear Diethaad muttering orders behind him, and knew he would be planning a rescue. The thought heartened him.

Clouds covered moon and stars, the only light to see by flickering and leaping from the torches clutched by four of the retainers. He kept thinking of that appraising look the queen had given him. Had she known that his letter was a forgery? Perhaps every word he'd said that afternoon had condemned him further for treason.

Not a word was said as he was led through a back gate into the royal grounds. At this, the hair on the back of his neck began to stand up. Why was he not being taken through the hall? Was he to be executed in outlaw fashion, without trial? In the darkness before him a swarm of torches bobbed like will-o-the-wisps, clustered around some wooden structure, which he could not at first discern. For one hideous moment he thought it was a gallows and actually stopped in his tracks, preparing to flee. Then he realised it was Vigtyr's hut. Forty royal guards had assembled around it, each holding a torch, and within their protective cordon, Bellamus found the queen looking unusually agitated.

'Lord Safinim,' she greeted him. 'We need your skills.' She took his hand and led him into Vigtyr's hut. This was the opposite greeting to the one Bellamus had expected, and he did not trust himself to speak until he had gathered his wits.

The hut was a hovel, fit only for Suthdal's meanest subjects and filled with the musty scent of a stable. Crouched against the far wall, his eyes bloodshot and his extremities trembling violently, was Vigtyr. He lurched upright as Bellamus and the queen entered, giving a jerky bow which the upstart did not see. The two halberdiers also standing in the room he did not register at all. His attention was captivated entirely by the figure on the floor.

In a pool of blood, so black that it looked almost like a bucket-sized ink spill in the torchlight, lay the body of something which Bellamus took at first for an emaciated youth. He recoiled, looking up at Vigtyr and then registering the two halberdiers and their bloodied weapons.

'What is this?' he breathed.

Nobody answered him. Even Aramilla was awaiting his guidance.

He crouched down and reached out a hand towards the corpse. It lay face down, the back reduced to crimson tatters and the bald crown of the head staved in completely. Only then did he register the huge ears protruding from the side of the skull and the unnatural shape of those hands, the huge calloused pads on the back of the fingers. To the touch, the body was cool and dry, the skin rough like a catfish. With one hand on the shoulder, he turned it over.

A horrible eyeless face, dripping blood, was revealed to

him. Its mouth was huge, its teeth pointed and small. Bellamus raised his eyebrows, fascinated in spite of the strangeness of the scene. 'You killed this thing?' Bellamus asked the halberdiers without looking away.

'Yes, lord.'

'You made quite a mess of it.'

'It wouldn't stop, lord. It had its hands around the Anakim's neck and nothing we did made it even turn its head. We had to smash its skull, nothing else worked.'

'What is it?' asked the queen, captivated and horrified. 'Safinim?'

Bellamus shook his head. 'Nothing I've seen before. But maybe something I've heard of. There were legends of these things, in the mountains. And rumours . . . rumours that they were used as assassins by the Karantaji Anakim. They are among those who have joined the Black Lady's alliance, incidentally.'

There was silence after this report.

'An assassin?' said Aramilla, her tone almost in awe.

'Perhaps,' said Bellamus. Gently, he let the creature fall back to the floor so that its face was obscured once more. He stood, eyes searching the room. 'Tell me everything.'

The three witnesses explained while Bellamus paced the hut, prodding at various bits of wall, noting the lack of windows in the cramped space, tapping his feet on the floorboards and exerting pressure on the beams of the roof. The only furniture was a bed with a chamber pot and water jug set on opposite sides. The sole piece of decoration was a brass mirror hung on the wall, its polished surface turned to face the boards. He turned it back the right way, having to stand on tiptoe to see his own countenance reflected back at him.

'Why was this mirror facing the wall?' He looked around for an answer.

'That was me, lord,' said Vigtyr.

Bellamus took a breath, and nodded, moving on swiftly.

'Why?' asked Aramilla.

Vigtyr shifted, glancing at her. 'I don't . . . I don't like mirrors.'

'Do the Anakim not like mirrors?' she asked, mystified.

'I think that is particular to this Anakim, Your Majesty,' murmured Bellamus.

Vigtyr blushed and Bellamus turned to one of the guards before the queen could enquire further. 'The door is locked every night from the outside?'

'Yes, lord.'

'What time?'

'Nine o'clock, lord.'

'And you two were on guard out there from that point onwards.'

'Yes, lord.'

'There were no breaks? No changes of the guard? No time when you both went to piss simultaneously?'

'No, lord.'

He looked directly at the pair of them. 'I must have the truth of this now, you shall not be punished. But I must know. Did you fall asleep?'

'No, lord,' said one immediately, the other shaking his head. Bellamus scrutinised them. They would know that if they admitted, in the presence of the queen, to sleeping on guard, they would be punished whatever Bellamus said.

'I sit down sometimes, lord,' one of them admitted. 'But when I do, it is always with my back against the door.'

He was asleep, then. 'Did you do that tonight?'

'Yes, lord.'

'The whole night? At every point you were sitting down, your back was against the door?'

'Yes, lord.'

'What I wish very much to know is this. Was there a single moment when the door to this hut was left unguarded? When something might have entered?'

The two halberdiers exchanged glances. 'No, lord. No, I would say not. But obviously it got in somehow.'

'The Anakim have magic, don't they?' breathed Aramilla, pupils huge. 'They could conjure this thing in here perhaps?'

'Not magic like that,' said Bellamus grimly. 'It got in somehow, but not necessarily tonight.' Vigtyr looked as though he was about to be sick.

'You think it could have been in here already when we locked the door, lord?' asked one of the guards.

'I cannot think of an alternative,' replied Bellamus.

He crouched down again beside the corpse, examining hands, elbows and horny feet. On the feet and the knuckles were sickly grass stains, no doubt acquired when this thing had come through the grounds. Bellamus shifted around to face Vigtyr's bed, wrinkling his nose at the smell. Then he rolled onto his back and slid beneath the bedframe, inspecting the underside of the mattress and the ropes which held it up.

'It was here,' he said. Barely visible on the frayed fabric of the mattress were faint green smudges, like traces of mould, where the grass pigment had rubbed off the assassin's skin.

He wriggled out from beneath the bed and sat up, pausing thoughtfully on the floor before he looked across at Vigtyr.

'When you lay down to sleep tonight, this thing was hidden beneath you.'

Even to Bellamus, who had only just arrived and possessed nothing if not a strong stomach, that thought was uniquely horrible. Vigtyr's face was in his hands and he was drawing deep, slow breaths.

Bellamus found the sense of pity for this man, who could not stand the sight of his own reflection, almost unbearable. He turned his attention back to the body lying next to him. He took a breath, thought better of what he was about to say, and then smiled at the halberdiers.

'Why don't you two go and have a drink on me?' He stood, fishing in a pouch at his belt for some coppers, which he handed to the halberdiers. 'Buy one for Vigtyr, here, as well. You've had a very shocking night and I'm afraid I'll need to question you again before it's over.' He chivvied them out of the door, saying he would come and find them later. Then he turned back to Aramilla. 'May I take the body, Majesty? It would be extremely illuminating to be able to study this thing.'

'Study it?'

'Vigtyr was exceptionally lucky,' said Bellamus. 'If he had not reached out for the water jug when he did, he would've been strangled before he could so much as cry out. We must know as much about whatever this thing is as possible. I fear very much this is just the first of many we shall see. Before you retire tonight, and every night for the foreseeable future, your chambers must be searched from top to bottom.'

'I should sooner come to that smart house of yours,' she said. 'I still have not seen it, and that is doubtless now the safest place in this city.'

Bellamus bowed low. 'You know that would be my honour, Majesty. And besides, I should imagine you would like to examine this thing too.'

She gave her magpie's laugh and latched onto his arm. 'You know me so well, Lord Upstart.'

Arms linked as they had not been in years, they walked back through the streets to Bellamus's house, six retainers clanking into position around them, two more following awkwardly with the assassin's body in a sack. The shock of the scene in Vigtyr's hut had quite driven Bellamus's fears of being arrested from his mind. So it was that when they encountered a gang of twenty Thingalith waiting for them in the streets led by Diethaad, Bellamus was at first too surprised to react.

'Ah . . . Diethaad . . .' There was an awkward pause. 'Just back from escorting Lord Ruden back home, I assume. Don't dawdle, back to Brimstream.'

'We'd wondered if you'd need protection to get back as well, lord,' said Diethaad innocently. 'You might not've had a royal escort to return with.'

'So many of you?' said Aramilla, amused. 'These streets must be more dangerous than I'd realised. Off with you then,' she added to her own retainers. 'We are more than sufficiently protected now.'

'Majesty,' began one of the retainers with a filthy look at Diethaad.

'Off with you,' repeated the queen dangerously, and with a last hostile glance at the Thingalith, the retainers slung down the body and returned to the hall.

They walked back up the hill and inside the house, the queen demanding a tour at once. 'Start in your chambers,' she suggested.

He knew it would bore her to insist on a search of the property first, but after what they had just seen he would have far preferred to scour each room with armed men before using it again.

'Diethaad, see to it that the assassin is laid out in my workshop. I'll be back to examine it later.'

He lit a pair of oil lamps, one for each of them, and took the queen to his chambers. Along the way he pointed out the various flourishes with which he had furnished his house. The skin of a huge cave bear, killed in the Black Kingdom as it had raided their supplies. A pair of giant chairs sitting either side of an equally enormous table. A tapestry depicting his triumph over Kynortas's forces on that floodplain. Another showing the jagged mountains like a row of teeth where he had first met an Anakim.

'And this one?' asked Aramilla, holding her lamp close to a rectangle of night hung above the fireplace in his room, broken by a vicious talon of lightning.

Bellamus was distracted, attempting a covert search of the room. 'That?' He paused for a moment, observing it with her. 'That was Lord Roper's cloak.'

The queen shuddered and held out a hand, fingering the lightning embroidery. 'Grendel wore this?'

'Wore it, gave it to me when I was released.'

She turned to face him. 'Were you fond of him, Lord Upstart?'

He paused again, then shrugged. 'I respected him. And yes. I suppose I was.'

But the queen had noticed something else. On his dresser, something was glinting blood red in the lamplight. She crossed to it and exchanged it for the lamp.

'You kept this,' she said, holding out the spider brooch she had once given him, a huge ruby set in its back.

He looked at her, feeling an unexpected swell of emotion. Her face was harsher, but that had always been the main source of her beauty and she was as striking as ever.

'Of course I did.'

She was suddenly standing very close to him in the shadowed room. He put his own lamp down and before he knew what had happened, they were kissing. He was lonely. It had been years since he had anything close to a confidant, anything resembling a lover. As he never had before, he returned the queen's kiss.

Hours later, he and Aramilla stood together in his workshop. He looked down at the supine corpse of the assassin, while she browsed the shelves behind him.

'Try not to touch anything, Majesty,' he said, not taking his eyes off the thing. 'Quite a bit of it is poisonous.'

She laughed, while Bellamus looked at the assassin's face. It was the lack of eyes that was troubling. There was certainly some structure beneath the skin of the lids, but they had long-since sealed shut. He wondered: at some different stage in this thing's life, had it been able to see? Delicately, he took a flint blade and used it to cut open one of the seamless eyelids. The organ he found beneath it did not look as though it could ever have been used for sight, and he supposed this thing had always been blind.

So how did it find Vigtyr?

Scent, seemed the most obvious answer. It scented him out like a dog. It was the only way.

'What have you found?' asked the queen, coming to stand by him.

'I think it must locate its target by smell,' said Bellamus. 'It is the only way I can think of. They must provide it with the scent of its target. Vigtyr, naturally, they were able to get at. They will still have artefacts of his, such as his tent, from the days he worked undercover with the legions. But I doubt they have anything of yours, Majesty, or most of our nobles. You are probably safe from this thing for now, but leave *nothing* lying around. If there are spies working for the Anakim among us, they must have no opportunity to take something that carries your scent.'

Am I safe, though? he wondered. It had been years, but was there anything he could have left behind when he was captured?

'Do you think the Anakim have spies working among us?'

'I don't know. Having seen what this nearly did to Vigtyr, though, I am prepared to be exceptionally cautious.'

'True. Poor Vigtyr. We must cheer him up.'

Bellamus did not bother to point out that the queen's primary entertainment came from tormenting him. 'Perhaps we should take him with us, Majesty, when we cross the lines. If you gave him the chance to be a warrior again, I believe he'd reward you.'

'Well we'll certainly do something. Shall we retire to your chambers, my upstart? We'll need rest if we're to leave for Blacklaw tomorrow.' She was already halfway out of the door.

'You plan to cross the lines tomorrow?' he asked, staring after her.

'Well I'm certainly not waiting around here for one of those assassins to come and find me. Are the men not ready to march?'

'I suppose they could be.'

'Then come, Lord Upstart. We shall need our rest.'

35
The Dead Legion

Ormur had spent more time at the Holy Temple than any other part of the Hindrunn, mostly so he could pay homage to the heroes preserved there. His favourite was Gunwor Iron-Wheel, who had fought in the days when a pair of Sacred Guardsmen would man a chariot together. On his belt were hung the shoes of his two favourite horses, Kalaha and Kighui, mares from a horrible upland lineage, now extinct. Iron-Wheel had earned his reputation for tearing through enemy ranks as a plough through a field.

There were scores of these heroes, some thousands of years old, equipped with ancient bronze swords and boiled leather armour; others so famous that even their earthly remains took Ormur's breath away. He circled the temple, wondering where to begin in his search for the kungargrav, apparently concealed beneath.

'Pardon me,' Ormur approached a temple guard moving from one mummy to the next and examining them for maintenance. The guard, who was small and stocky, peered out from beneath a stiff mane of tail-feathers and horsehair. 'Are there any structures beneath the temple?'

'It's built above a crypt,' the guard replied, as though this answer was so obvious Ormur must have meant something else.

'What's in the crypt?'

'Most of the Dead Legion, of course. Only a few at a time stand above ground, the vast majority are beneath the temple.'

'May I see?'

The guard took a breath, spotting the Prize of Valour on his wrist and glancing at his high ponytail. 'Are you Ormur Kynortasson?'

Ormur felt himself blush and nodded brusquely.

'Of course, lord. This way.'

The guard led Ormur into the shadow of the temple's granite dome, and down an aisle cut through concentric rings of rough slate pews. They were orientated towards a huge black stone in the temple's centre, worn into a firepit. It smouldered even now like a vast block of charcoal, attended by another four temple guards, the smoke escaping through a hole in the roof. Ormur followed the smoke column and saw that the stone ceiling was perforated with thousands of tiny holes, so that the roof was pricked with daylight, as though they were beneath a grey and stony night sky inlaid with great jewels of stars. The sides of this dome were open to the elements, and the air was sweet with the scent of the burning cherry logs.

When they reached the firepit, the guard pulled back a wooden hatch that lay before it to reveal a narrow stone staircase, descending into the dark. He lit a torch from the sacred flames and gestured down at the stairs. 'This way, lord.'

Ormur followed him, embarrassed by the temple guard's old-fashioned use of the word 'lord' for a Sacred Guardsman. They were soon swallowed beneath the temple, the daylight replaced by a ghostly blue glow which seemed to be emanating from bright shafts built into the stone wall.

'We hardly need the torch,' said Ormur. 'There's enough light.'

'It's to test the air, lord,' came the reply. 'There is earth down here, mined near the edge of the Otherworld and placed beneath the temple. It is not good for the living, but helps preserve the dead. It is their world beneath the temple, and we shall not be able to stay for long. If the torch goes out, the air has become too foul and we must leave.'

Ormur eyed the torch, which did indeed seem to be growing dimmer, and wondered if the light-headedness and shortness of breath he now felt were imagined. What a dreadful place this would be to face imprisonment.

Presently, the stairs brought them to a low chamber, lit the same ghostly blue.

It was filled with the dead.

Hundreds of mummies stood upright in two parallel lines, which stretched in a broad arc away from Ormur and his guide. They faced one another in a strange guard of honour, all of them backlit by that eerie blue glow.

'The Dead Legion,' said the temple guard reverently.

Ormur had expected to be awed by these heroes, but instead he was frightened. He could see little more than the silhouette of each, seeming to sway a little in that wavering sapphire light.

'Was there any warrior you particularly wished to see, lord?' The guide was eyeing his torch nervously, the flame now a fragile lilac.

'No thank you. Just the crypt.' Ormur's vision was clouding and he was definitely light-headed. 'Is it one large space?' he murmured. 'There are no side passages or chambers?'

The guard did not answer, for the torch had gone out. He glanced swiftly at Ormur. 'We must surface immediately, lord.'

Ormur needed no convincing, and together they hurried back the way they had come.

As soon as they began to climb, Ormur found he was panting. His legs felt heavy, his thoughts so foggy and his vision so blurred he seemed drunk. He tried to pause but the guard hurried him. 'Onwards, lord, you won't recover until you reach the surface.'

Each step was like a small mountain, but with every one his breathing became less laboured and by the time he could see daylight above, he felt a little stronger.

They passed back through the trap door and Ormur fell to his knees on the temple's stone floor to catch his breath. He waited for the nausea to subside while the temple guard fretted above him. 'I'm sorry we had to retreat so soon, lord, the air must need flushing through a little.'

Ormur waved a hand, still panting too hard and feeling too nauseous to reply.

No wonder the kungargrav resisted discovery: a search for a concealed entrance would be quite impossible. Surely too, no one could survive being imprisoned down there. Not unless their prison had a passage to the outside air.

'The crypt is just the one passage, lord, there are no side chambers.'

None that you know of, thought Ormur. He took a few minutes more to recover, before thanking the guard and walking back outside, considering.

If those shafts could funnel light down into the crypt, they must have an opening to the surface. Skirting the edge of the temple, he began looking for holes in the floor, or perhaps columns standing above the surface, conducting light down into the strange land of the dead beneath his feet. But though he did a full circuit of the grounds around the temple and attracted curious looks from the temple guards, he saw nothing.

Perhaps the shafts were built into the temple dome itself. He began another revolution, this time searching the pillars and archways that supported the roof. Almost immediately, he spotted a lozenge-shaped hole built into a granite pillar, just above head-height and with a rain-cowl fitted above. After a surreptitious check to ensure the temple guards were not watching, he gripped onto the edge of the opening and pulled himself up. Before he had even seen inside, he knew from the cold metal beneath his fingers that he had found what he was looking for. Past the opening was the beginning of a shaft lined in bright bluish metal, disappearing out of view. It must be one of those funnelling light to the crypt.

Ormur slid back to earth before he could be spotted and began walking again, rounding the temple and noting each time he saw one of the lozenge-shaped openings. There seemed to be about twenty of them, each of which would run directly down to the deathly air in the crypt. But if the kungargrav was concealed down there too, then it would need its own supply of fresh air. Might it be supplied by one of these shafts? If so, then the shaft to the kungargrav would have clean air, all the others bad.

To test this, Ormur would have to lower a flame down the shaft and see if it went out. He decided to return in darkness to test this theory, but if he was right and one shaft had good air, then he had a bright, shining passageway leading directly to the Kryptea's secret prison.

So bewitched was Ormur by his task, that the wait for darkness seemed intolerable. He diverted himself by running laps of the Hindrunn's outer track, where he kept passing Aalanders: those blond-haired people with a bar tattooed over their eyeline, whom Gray had informed him practised strange rituals.

'They eat Sutherners,' Leon told him brusquely, when Ormur had retired to the mess to wolf down some food. He chewed in silence and glanced at Hartvig, another old guardsman sitting opposite, who was watching Leon expressionless.

'You don't believe me, boy?'

Ormur swallowed his mouthful. 'I do,' he said doubtfully.

Black Legionaries underwent ritual purification after fighting Sutherners. The idea of *eating* them was more horrifying than he could grasp.

'After battle they have a feast of the men they've killed,' Leon went on. 'Good meat, they say, especially the chest: like rich pork, and there's certainly a lot of it going spare. It would've solved our food shortage back in Roper's Campaign. Though even an Aalander would turn his nose up at you,' he added, inspecting Ormur grimly. 'If your famous sword weren't so well balanced, doubt you'd even be able to pick it up.'

'I think Ormur would surprise you with a sword, Leon,' said Hartvig. 'Not sure I've seen reflexes like his before.'

Leon waved his hand dismissively. 'The Captain's been training harder than anyone for the past few years, and it shows. It's him I want to fight next. But you're ahead of me there, boy, I hear you managed to piss him off.'

Ormur blushed.

'Be gone, Leon,' said Hartvig mildly.

'Boy's got to learn,' said Leon. He stuffed a final lump of bread in his mouth, took a last gulp of water and stood still chewing. 'He's too soft,' he said thickly. He took up his mug, turned and disappeared from the mess.

Ormur waited alone in his room until past midnight, fretting that Gray must have spoken of their quarrel. When he finally stepped outside, there was a light mist of summer rain, which made it hard for Ormur to light the storm lamp he had brought, but kept the streets empty, and the temple guards huddled around their sacred flame. Using a length of smouldering fuse cord, he lit the lamp's oil-soaked wick, tying it to a length of twine and lowering it carefully down the first shaft. Hooking his elbows over the edge, he was able to watch the lamp descend, the twinkling light growing dimmer and dimmer in the foul, heavy air of the crypt, until finally it went out.

Feeling a little stab of excitement that his plan seemed to be working, he pulled it up, relit the wick and proceeded to the next shaft.

There, he witnessed the flame grow dimmer and dimmer once more, before finally going out. The same thing happened at the third shaft, and the fourth. Shivering from the rain which had soaked him through, he tested one after another, glancing repeatedly over his shoulder to check he was not being observed.

Each was the same until he approached the next shaft and spotted a rainbow sheen, glowing in the lamp light. Intrigued, he pressed a finger to it, sniffed, and found it to be oil. He was giddy with excitement. What did this mean?

Then he realised: it meant he had already been here. He had accidentally spilt the oil from his lamp over the outside of the shaft when withdrawing it. He had tested them all, and they all led to the foul air of the crypt.

He turned his back on the temple and leaned against it, sliding down the edge of the pillar until he sat at its base. None of them contained fresh air. None of them led to the kungargrav; not unless it had been out of use so long that it had been allowed to degenerate into a place more suitable for the dead than the living.

He could not think where to go from here. The crypt was too toxic to explore, and he wondered briefly if the kungargrav might not be a prison, but a means of execution. Perhaps the chant had meant that Black Lords were put down there to die in the foul air. It would certainly be uniquely horrible.

He was shivering badly now, which gave him the will to pick himself up and begin the walk back to his cot in the mess. At least he tried, he thought as he peeled off his sopping clothes and huddled into the rough woollen blanket. Heart aching with disappointment, he fell into a weary sleep.

'Ormur?' Someone was shaking him. 'Boy?'

'Don't call me boy,' he murmured instinctively.

'I'll call you whatever gets you out of bed. And you refer to me as "sir". Up! The Black Lady has asked for you.'

Ormur sat bolt upright. 'Lady Keturah?'

'You truly are a dog,' said Leon. 'That's right, your mistress has whistled. She's in the keep stables. Now wag your tail and off you go. What is this?' he added in disgust. He had trodden in Ormur's clothes, still soaking and lying where he had cast them on the floor. 'Slovenliness! Imagine not even hanging them out to dry.'

Ormur was already out of bed and pulling on his other tunic. 'Be gone, Leon,' he said.

Leon froze on his way out of the door. 'What did you call me?'

'Sir,' said Ormur dismissively, belting his tunic.

Leon glared at him. 'I will be gone, boy, because I'm going south. There is a march-out, and the Black Lady is taking the rest of the Guard with her.'

'What?' Ormur stopped and glanced up at Leon. 'The Black Lady's going to Blacklaw?'

'She is. You are to stay behind.' With a malicious smile at Ormur, he shut the door. Ormur stared at the closed door for a moment. Stay behind, when his monarch was going into Blacklaw? That could not be true.

He hastened outside, and saw immediately that Leon had been telling the truth. Men in armour and laden with packs and weapons milled about every barracks and mess. Two enormous dragon cannons, their barrels divided in half, were even being wheeled along the street by a team of engineers. Ormur saw Hanoverians, Aalanders, Onogurians, Karantaji and every other allied nation who had joined Keturah.

Supervising the departure were three figures on horseback, draped in eagle-feather cloaks. Ormur recognised the one in the centre. 'Lord Tekoa!' he called. 'My lord!'

Tekoa turned and regarded him. 'The young guardsman.' He surveyed his bruised face. 'You look like you've been catapulted at something.'

'Where is everyone going, lord?'

'The moon.'

'Guardsman Leon said you're going to Blacklaw.'

'He's right. Shall you not be joining us?'

'No, lord.'

'A shame, it's going to be fun. Some extremely violent negotiations are about to take place. There's a fight in the air, young Ormur. I'll try and hold it off until you come join us, eh?'

Tekoa was not really looking at Ormur. His eyes had slid off him, and back to the preparing soldiers. The two legates with him had not even acknowledged him. One was drumming his fingers on his saddle, the other sat with arms folded.

Ormur hurried on to the stables beneath the Central Keep. There, he found Keturah almost at once. She was in discussion with two Onogurians – cavalry specialists, Gray had once told him. The three of them were standing outside Zephyr's stall, gesticulating occasionally at the great destrier, he eyeing them balefully in return. Ormur waited politely out of earshot until with a shrug, the Onogurians were dismissed and bowed their way out of Keturah's presence. She turned and spied him. 'Brother,' she beckoned him close. 'I've been hoping our allies know some tricks for getting this beast to behave again. He's as stubborn as his old master.'

'A shame, my lady. I should like to see him ridden.'

'If anyone tried, what you would see is them being hurled out of the saddle. But who knows, he could probably pull a cannon by himself so may yet find a use as a pack animal.' She scrutinised the bruises on his face. 'You haven't been fighting again have you?'

'Leon said you're going to Blacklaw,' blurted Ormur. 'And I'm to be left behind.'

'Did he? Always tactful, Guardsman Leon. If there's ever a country I fall out with particularly, I'll make Leon my ambassador to them. They'll soon wish they'd stayed in my good graces.'

'My lady? Am I to be left behind?'

She raised an eyebrow. 'Of course you are to be left behind, brother. Your leave is not yet up.'

'I've only a week left and I'd far sooner—'

'No,' she cut him off. 'You are nineteen. You shouldn't be engaged in this dirty war at all, let alone as consumed by it as you are. There's no one I'd feel safer with by my side, but your time in this kingdom is sacred. Do not rush back to those lands south of the Abus. They're no place to live your life. Not yet.' She eyed him, apparently disturbed by what she saw. 'I worry what we've done to you. It sometimes seems . . . You don't think about yourself at all, do you? Have you known a moment's peace in your whole life?'

Ormur was lost. 'We are not at peace.'

'Exactly. Stay here, brother. Spend your last week learning to be still. Then you and Captain Gray can come and join me. I daresay you won't have missed much.' A legionary arrived, tugging the bridle of a fine black mare, which he held as Keturah put a foot in the stirrup and swung herself into the saddle.

'Legate Tekoa said there might be a battle,' said Ormur desperately.

Keturah shrugged. 'Queen Aramilla has crossed into Blacklaw with an army. A much larger army, I admit, than we knew they possessed, though keep that to yourself.'

She looked strained, regarding him from horseback. Ormur had a sudden foreboding. She was leaving him behind because she feared Aramilla's army. She was trying to protect him.

'An invasion?' he asked.

She tilted her head a little to indicate: *Partly.* 'They say she wants to talk, but there's certainly a lot of burning going on as well. She must have something terribly important to say if she's brought all those men. I'd better go and listen.' There was a taut moment, which only enhanced Ormur's certainty: Keturah was afraid. Whatever Aramilla had brought to Blacklaw with her, Keturah did not think they had the strength to turn it back. 'So this is goodbye, brother. At least until you can come and join us. Stay out of trouble, will you? Absolutely no fighting, and that's a command.'

He stared up at her unhappily and she looked back with something like pity in her eyes.

'How will you understand them?' he asked her. Famously, Keturah had refused to learn Saxon. She had even refused to allow it to be taught to Numa, being tutored in the northern haskoli. Saxon, she declared airily, would soon be a dead language, on which she had no need to waste her time.

She rolled her eyes. 'There will be a translator, Ormur.'

'And how many men will you take to meet the queen's army?'

Keturah appeared to consider this, then raised a hand to him and turned her horse away, trotting for the stable doors. 'All of them.'

36
Roper's Toe

Ormur knew Keturah had his safety in mind, but nothing could have more depressed him than being left behind while the glorious and sacred art of war was waged in the south. The only people that he knew still in the fortress were Gray and Sigrid, but he was uncertain of his reception there. Instead, he collapsed onto his cot in the now-empty guardsmen's mess and did not rise, even for food. The daylight drained through the window, the fortress falling silent but for the owls hooting as they reclaimed the streets. He did not even stir when there came a knock at the door. It felt entirely irrelevant.

But it came again, more insistent. Ormur stared at the door, but did not get up. He was ashamed to be seen like this, wallowing in his despair. He had no intention of answering, not until a familiar voice called from outside: 'Ormur!'

Ormur hesitated. 'Sir?' He half sat up, staring at the dark boards.

'Let me in, lad.'

He pulled back the bolt to find Gray on the other side. When Ormur said nothing, the captain smiled wryly. 'Am I allowed in?' He was not quite meeting Ormur's eye.

Ormur moved aside and Gray stepped past him, holding up

a basket. 'Sigrid sends her love. It's pitch-black, are there any candles?'

'Here.' Ormur fumbled at a tinderbox on one of the stone shelves which, apart from the bed, were the room's only furnishings. The guardsmen's mess was privileged with individual rooms, but they were as spartan as any other.

Ormur coaxed a pair of sputtering candles into life, and Gray produced several thick strips of dried venison from the basket, wrapped in linen and seasoned to make the mouth water.

'For you, from Sigrid,' he said, taking a seat on the bed and lying the venison next to him. 'She's worried you won't be eating.'

She was entirely correct, and he eyed the venison hungrily. Gray rolled his eyes and held out a piece to him, which Ormur took immediately. For a while, neither spoke while the younger man chewed relentlessly.

'I'm sorry you've been left behind, Ormur,' said Gray, staring at the wall rather than his protégé. 'I know how disappointed you'll be.'

Ormur tried to think of a reply that would not sound self-pitying. 'But why have we been left?' he burst out. 'We are Sacred Guardsmen and our lady is going to war! Why have we been left with the cripples and the children?'

'Lady Keturah is frightened,' said Gray. 'Whatever's about to happen, she fears that those nearby will not survive it. And she wants to spare you, my young friend, because she treasures you as much as her own son.'

Ormur dismissed this. 'Is that why you've been left behind too? To take care of me?'

Gray smiled and dipped his head towards the floor. 'Yes, Ormur.'

'But if there's to be a battle, I can't bear missing it—'

'You shan't,' said Gray, simply. 'It's a vain hope on her part. Battles do not just erupt spontaneously. There is angling for tactical advantage, posturing and negotiations to play out beforehand, which can take months. Even then, nobody wants to fight except as a last resort. Lord Roper was a bit different, he'd just wade straight in, but Lady Keturah is more measured, and Legate Tekoa is meticulous, and loves detail. You shan't miss anything. They're supposed to be attending a peace summit, anyway. There may be no battle at all. The war may end, Ormur.'

Ormur took a deep breath, not certain it was acceptable to voice what was in his heart: that he hoped not, for what would he do then?

'Which is another reason I believe she was right to leave you behind,' Gray went on sternly. 'You must learn peace, Ormur. We will not always be at war, and you must be able to live without it.'

'I have time for that if peace breaks out,' he replied. 'But for now I want to be helping, by my lady's side.'

Gray did not speak for a moment. He just stared at Ormur's wall, wearing no expression at all. 'You'll get your chance, Ormur. We all will.'

Ormur fell silent and looked at the floor, taking another bite of the venison.

'I've been thinking a lot about our conversation a few nights ago,' said Gray quietly. Ormur looked up. 'First, I wanted to say I'm sorry for shouting. I didn't mean that.'

'I'm sorry too, sir. I pushed too hard. I don't know what happened when Lord Roper was killed.'

Gray nodded. 'My reaction wasn't aimed at you. It was frustration at myself, because I knew there was truth to what you were saying. The revelation about the kungargrav . . . It left me very cold. I've been wondering if I made a terrible mistake.'

Ormur paused, looking up from the dried venison. 'Do you think that's possible?'

'I've been trying to find out,' murmured Gray.

Ormur hesitated. 'I tried . . . looking for the kungargrav, sir. Beneath the temple. But the air down there is so bad it's impossible to search.'

'That was never going to be successful I'm afraid. The kungargrav is not beneath the Holy Temple.'

'I think it is,' said Ormur. '"*Nether Temple stones . . . With walls for doors and windows of stone*." Where else could that be?'

'I'm not sure,' he allowed. 'But certainly not the Holy Temple. Sigrid has been doing some research. That chant Sakeus was quoting is nearly two thousand years old. And the Holy Temple, including its crypt, is only twelve-hundred years old. Clearly, it does not reference a structure that would not be built for another eight hundred years. It cannot be there.'

It took Ormur a moment to absorb this. If the kungargrav was not in the Holy Temple, then he did not need to contend with that foul air in the crypt. It might be somewhere altogether more accessible. 'So where?' he said, lured away from his shelf to sit on the bed beside Gray. 'What temple existed two thousand years ago?'

'Something long-since crumbled, most likely. But after the Academy, the Holy Temple is the oldest structure here: it predates the Hindrunn itself. Before that, our capital was the ancient fortress at Myrklettur.'

That name was familiar to Ormur. He had heard it once before. 'Myrklettur,' he murmured, trying the shape of it on his tongue. 'Where's that?'

'A few days to the east. Just ruins now, set on top of a plateau.'

It was the word *plateau* which sparked his memory. 'Ah!' he said suddenly, for not only had he placed the name, he realised he had actually been there. It was the fortress he and Keturah had passed through more than seven years ago, on their way to the Hindrunn. 'I know it. You think the kungargrav could be there?'

'I think there's no harm in looking.'

Ormur froze at that. 'Looking for what? Roper's dead.'

Gray was still staring at the wall. 'I'm not sure about that any more, Ormur.'

Ormur set down his venison. 'Why? Is there something you've remembered?'

Gray shook his head. 'Your words just kept ringing round my head. In all honesty, they've tortured me over the past few days. I had to check.'

'Check,' repeated Ormur. 'How could you check?'

'When we stormed Lundenceaster's breach, Roper lost a toe. The body we recovered from the sea: it had the same toe missing. It looked a little fresh, but the fish had been picking at it, like everything else. But now . . . now it's been seven years, and all we have left is bones. So I went to check the wound.'

Ormur was half horrified, half compelled. Gray had examined Roper's corpse. 'And? What did you find?'

'I looked with one of the surgeons. He said the bone looked unhealed. He *thought* it might have happened only recently before death. And Roper lost that toe months before he died.'

'You mean . . .' Ormur shook his head in disbelief. 'You mean . . . that is not Lord Roper's body?'

Gray wavered his head, chewing on his lip. Then he looked at his protégé for the first time, and Ormur saw the shock in his mentor's eyes.

'No,' he said finally. 'I don't believe it is.'

37
The Favour

The objective was peace, of course. That was what the queen had decreed and it was the obedient duty of her councillors to ensure that the Anakim were soothed, sweetened, and brought to the negotiating table. Lord Safinim, restored to his place at Her Majesty's right hand, was particularly fierce about it: on no account were the Anakim to be antagonised, and he had made it clear how serious he was by hanging half a dozen men who had ambushed and butchered a pair of Anakim scouts. Though the councillors still complained about pursuing peace when their forces were now so obviously superior, the united front of Queen Aramilla and her loyal upstart – spymaster, tactician and expert adviser – kept those complaints private. Even Lord Ruden's influence was waning as he argued for battle and was ignored.

It would have surprised them all to learn that he and Bellamus were in secret alliance. It would have surprised them still further to learn the instructions the spymaster had issued to the Thingalith. 'Wreak havoc boys. On no account can we allow peace to break out now. If the Black Lady does make it into the negotiating tent, she must do so not trusting a single word we say. You've done this often enough before, you know your business. But for God's sake, don't get caught.'

Afterwards, Diethaad had come to him privately. 'And what happens if we *are* caught, my lord? We're loyal to you, you know we are. But this seems a thankless task.'

'If there is anything less than concrete evidence against you, I'll get you off. We'll pin it on the Barleymen.' If there were rumours of trouble involving Garrett's men, it was a safe bet you had not heard the half of them. To cover their tracks, Bellamus had ensured the Barleymen and the Thingalith were operating in the same area. 'But *don't* get caught,' he said severely. 'If you are, I cannot protect you. And even more important, do not leave *anything* belonging to you behind. Before you drop anything, I want you to imagine whether a dog could find you from its scent. And if it could, then take it with you.'

Diethaad squinted at Bellamus. 'Why?'

Bellamus hesitated. 'The assassin that tried to kill Vigtyr. There have been more.'

Diethaad looked suspicious. 'More? I haven't heard.'

'Two more. I took the bodies and threatened and bribed the witnesses. But two have been discovered and slain over the past few days. I think they were trying to find their way to Vigtyr.'

Now Diethaad looked horrified. 'How many did they send after him?'

'I don't know, but the Anakim must have many to be so careless with them. There will be more. They must have nothing by which they can trace you.'

In five columns, extending across the Wylie Lines like the fingers of a groping hand, the army marched into Blacklaw. Bellamus rode in the central column with the queen. It was the first time she had seen this country since it had been under Suthern rule, and the memory was in stark contrast to what she saw before her. A million marching feet had churned green to brown. The rivers were stagnant, the trees burnt or torn or toppled, and all of it infested with animals of horrible and gratuitous savagery. The Anakim called them gravedogs, and that was the name that had stuck with the men. They roamed in foul packs a hundred strong or more, feasting on the carrion left behind by a thousand skirmishes, and multiplying rapidly. They savaged people in their sleep, overwhelmed parties of foragers, and tore the dead to scraps, laughing all the while.

Aramilla was appalled and, as ever, fascinated. 'Oh, they are *hateful*,' she said, giving a delicious shiver as they watched a dozen of them standing along a treeline, observing the army file past. 'Do they attack the living?'

'If they outnumber them,' said Bellamus. 'You'll see, Majesty, that these are not lands of particular value any more. They've been worn out: if we are to come to a meaningful settlement with the Anakim, we'll need more than the frontier.'

'I have no intention of settling for the frontier,' replied the queen. 'I want Lundenceaster back. Do you think they'll grant it?'

Bellamus paused a moment, and then surprised himself. 'Maybe.' He had thought for so long that the Anakim were resolute. But now, marching with this army and watching the scattered resistance withdraw without so much as a skirmish, he suddenly found his confidence in them waning. Why would they resist? It would be suicide, nothing less. If they were offered peace and the chance to keep some of the lands they had captured, they might well accept. His strategy for years had been to erode their forces, and he had not realised how successful he had been. Even with the Thingalith rampaging through the south, even after the years of hatred and mistrust, perhaps the Anakim would concede after all. 'The Black Lady is certainly playing the game.'

Word had come that morning that Keturah was mustering her forces and marching south to meet them. It seemed the two great queens of Albion would meet after all, and decide the fate of the island they so uneasily shared.

Walking towards the back of the royal retinue was Vigtyr. Bellamus had persuaded the queen that he might be helpful, and secured proper-sized footwear and armour for the giant. Even so, it was the first time Bellamus had seen him in open daylight in years. He looked sick. His face was frayed and pale, and he moved like a puppet whose joints have swollen stiff with damp. But what he had lived through might have broken any man, and an eyeless assassin haunted his nightmares.

Even Aramilla refused to sleep alone since it had appeared. Each evening, Bellamus was invited into her chambers as though the thought had only just occurred to her. She framed it as an act of affection, but betrayed herself by bringing up the assassin whenever they lay down. Whatever the reason, Bellamus was happy to oblige.

There were no houses they could use as billets in this part of Blacklaw, so when they finished the day's marching, a pavilion was unfurled and pegged out in the dusk. Around it blossomed the tents of the other lords, each magnificent but never daring to surpass Aramilla's.

A heavy summer rain had begun to fall, and rolled on the canvas as the candles were lit, their bed prepared and a dinner of roasted pheasant and shredded crab laid out. The queen's face was pink from the sun-drenched road and she fell into a chair, one hand covering her eyes.

'Sunstroke?' asked Bellamus.

She nodded. Without thinking, Bellamus took one of her embroidered handkerchiefs abandoned on the table beside her, dipped it in a pewter pitcher beaded with condensation, and held it to her forehead. She let out a murmur of thanks, and permitted him to hold it there as the servants set the table with linen and liquid-bright cutlery.

'I'd forgotten how I valued you, Lord Upstart,' she said, eyes still closed. 'Nobody is closer to my person.' Bellamus was too stunned to reply, and the queen opened her eyes. 'Shall we eat?'

Bellamus bowed his head. He pressed Aramilla's hand to the damp handkerchief to keep it in place on her brow, but she shook her head. 'Keep it. A token of favour. Sit before me.'

'Majesty.' He half expected one of her cruel jokes – perhaps she would whip away the handkerchief with her magpie's laugh and banish him for a night in the rain. Instead she simply directed him to the chair opposite.

Perhaps she had changed over the years. She wanted to hear about his childhood, about his family, about life in Safinim and the mountains and Iberia. He usually hated such focus on his own person, but for some reason, that evening he did not mind it. He crumbled before her interrogation, and they retired together to the bed hauled from Suthdal.

'Your saddlebag even accompanies us to bed, I see,' she noted, eyes resting on the dust-stained satchel that he carried everywhere. They lay open to the air, the evening too hot to be under the cotton sheets. 'What's in it?'

'Just letters,' said Bellamus, shrugging. 'Useful letters I'd sooner not lose.'

'Will you ever go back to Safinim?' She played one-handed with his hair and he considered her question.

'I'd never thought about it. So probably not.'

'You wouldn't want to see your parents again?'

'I doubt they're still alive.'

'But wouldn't you like to know?'

He shrugged. 'What would we talk about if they were? My life would be unrecognisable to them. There would be a gulf, and it would be embarrassing. Better those memories are left in the past.' The canvas flapped in a sudden breeze and he felt her stiffen. 'Probably an assassin,' he said gravely.

She laughed. 'You dodge my questions.'

'So many of them. It's unlike you.'

She thought about that. 'Maybe it's age. I want to play less. I seem to like calm and quiet more now.'

Bellamus was almost afraid to reply in case he brought the queen to her senses and ended this pleasant contemplation. 'Is that why you seek peace, Majesty?'

'I suppose.'

'We change over time. Put it down to old age and it starts to seem as though your preferences are out of your hands.'

She snorted. 'You are in denial, Lord Upstart. You age like everyone, and hide it better from yourself than the rest of us.'

Bellamus was suddenly uncomfortable. For years he had fought against his waning drive and the voice that told him to settle rather than advance. To have it voiced so dismissively by Aramilla was unsettling, and she laughed at him again. 'You didn't know? I've shocked you, I see. Let us sleep, Lord Upstart. We're old and weary.'

Bellamus was awake long after Aramilla's rhythmic breathing had filled the dark, strangely hot and uncomfortable. He was not sure when he drifted into sleep, but when he woke up, the Anakim had come.

Naturally they could not see all of them. Not wishing to reveal the extent of her forces, Keturah approached only with her Sacred Guard, and that under cover of darkness. The first the Sutherners knew of the Black Lady's presence was when dawn came, and a pair of watchmen spotted a tent perched on a hilltop which they were sure had been bald the evening before. Fluttering above the tent were two flags: one a large square of white linen, the other a lidless silver eye.

'That is lazy,' said Bellamus sharply to the watchman who brought him this news. 'You allowed the Sacred Guard within five hundred yards of our border. Thank whatever angel watches over you that they didn't want to attack.'

'Yes, lord.'

'They're here now, Lord Safinim,' said Aramilla coolly. 'Let's waste no more time. We should go and meet this savage queen.'

'Only one of us should go, Majesty,' said Bellamus. 'The Anakim revere you, and know me by reputation. I fear the pair of us in one tent may be too much of a temptation for them.'

'Hogwash,' said the queen, jabbing his flank. 'You flatter yourself, Safinim. And I'd sooner face the Anakim with you by my side.'

So they went together, a retinue of knights falling in behind them to match the Sacred Guard man for man. Lord Ruden joined them, mostly because Bellamus did not trust him unsupervised with the army.

'You were right about that servant you sent me,' he murmured to Bellamus as the pair of them followed Aramilla. The queen was climbing the hill on a throne carried by six bearers. 'Octric. He seems to know everything.'

'Think nothing of it,' said Bellamus. 'I've got more, if you need. Not many as good as him, but capable still.'

'Ever met the Black Lady?' asked Ruden. He was tugging at his beard and seemed more flustered than usual.

'A few times, but not for many years. She has a reputation now that she did not in those days.'

The tent above the hill was open-sided, with all but two of the Sacred Guard standing some thirty yards back. The remaining pair flanked a figure Bellamus barely recognised: tall and black-cloaked, with fierce eyes of poisonous green which glowered as they came near. Keturah was leaner and harsher, and the aura of malice that came off her was almost palpable.

Aramilla raised an eyebrow at the sight of her. 'She hasn't even brought a stool.'

'The Black Lady disdains chairs of every sort, Majesty,' Bellamus explained. 'She thinks them necessary only for people who write at tables. For us.'

Aramilla looked delighted. 'So she'll stand before me on my throne? How fitting.'

Keturah did not stand. As the queen's throne was carried into the tent and set before her, Keturah sat on a deerskin laid on the floor. It should have looked as though the Black Lady was the supplicant, Aramilla her gracious liege. But to Bellamus it looked as though they were setting Keturah's table, and Aramilla was the main dish. The Black Lady looked hungry: all vein and bone, so lean as to be almost gaunt.

Bellamus gestured that Ruden should take his place on Aramilla's left, while he took the spot on the right. Keturah was staring at him from the floor with an expression equal parts amused and hateful. 'It's a long time since we fought shoulder to shoulder, Spymaster,' she observed in Anakim. 'I do recall you swore to my husband your part in this war was over.'

'What's that?' demanded Aramilla, who had not understood the harsh speech of the Black Kingdom. 'Does this dirty animal not know that you address a queen first?' Keturah might not have spoken Saxon, but the guardsman on her left certainly did. At Aramilla's words he went chalk-white and his nostrils flared.

'I fear not, Majesty,' said Bellamus swiftly, though he was sure Keturah had given the offence deliberately. 'I shall ask her.' Bellamus wanted these negotiations to end in violence, but not here. He switched to Anakim and addressed their seated enemy. 'You do not speak Saxon, my lady?'

'It will be extinct too soon to be worth the bother of learning,' said Keturah. She gestured up at her furious guardsman. 'For the interim, I've brought a translator. Not that I don't trust you, Spymaster, though I note you've not answered my question. You had a pact with my husband.'

'My pacts are with the living, lady,' he answered as gently as he could.

Keturah blinked at that, the amusement vanishing from her face. She considered him and then raised a hand. The guardsman on her right stepped forward with two goblets of what smelt like elderberry wine, offering them to Bellamus and Aramilla.

'She means to poison us,' said Aramilla, not taking the proffered cup.

'I should accept if you want peace, Majesty,' said Bellamus, taking his own goblet with a bow. 'Shared drink is sacred to the Anakim. They would no sooner poison it than spit in the Almighty Eye.'

Aramilla took hers doubtfully and sniffed before taking a sip. Elderberry wine as the Anakim drank it was rich and dark, but astringent enough to make it feel that the teeth were being sucked from their gums. The queen looked ready to spit it out, but managed to swallow and set it on the arm of her throne with the air of someone returning a bear-cub to its mother.

Keturah looked at last to Aramilla, green eyes fixed on the queen over the rim of her goblet as she took a sip. 'I hear you've come to talk,' she said, words echoed in good Saxon by the guardsman at her shoulder. 'What could be important enough to bring you into my lands?'

Keturah put on a fine show, but there was a disparity of power here. It was clear to the Black Lady, to the guardsmen; even to the servants who had carried the throne and now stood against the tent wall. The Anakim army was a ruin. True, they still had the Unhieru, and their Ereboan allies. But Bellamus commanded elephants, and camels, and cataphracts, and lines of bristling pikes and all manner of war-machines that would test the strength of the Anakim alliance. Keturah was here as a supplicant, and Aramilla keen to play with her vulnerable opponent.

'I am referred to as "Majesty",' she announced.

'Majesty,' said Keturah abruptly, before her guardsman had even finished translating. 'Come, out with it.'

'I am not pleased with the way my country has been treated, Lady Keturah,' said Aramilla. 'The lands we have passed through were as fertile as any in the world before you got your hands on them.'

Keturah was nodding impatiently and making a hurrying gesture with her hand to bring Aramilla to her point. The queen was still talking when Keturah turned to her translator. 'You're garbling it. What's she actually saying?'

'I cannot invent substance where none exists, my lady,' said the guardsman, stony-faced.

'Well that isn't true, you told me you were a poet.'

The translator was trying to suppress a grin, and Aramilla paused in her opening address, gazing slack-mouthed at the pair of them.

'You surely aren't interrupting me, Lady Keturah?' she demanded, louder than before.

'What is it that you want, Majesty?' Keturah replied heavily, turning back to the queen.

'For now I want you to know how outfaced you are. I have brought with me four times the number you can muster. We have beasts you cannot imagine. We have—' Keturah was making her impatient hurrying gesture again and Aramilla gave a vicious smile. 'Very well then, as you are so keen to hear. I want peace. This conflict must tire you even more than it does me. We fight over lands you occupy, and you can afford it less. In return for peace, we demand the return of Lundenceaster, and all the lands in between.'

Keturah was nodding as her translator repeated the demands back to her, and then suddenly she froze. 'What?' She looked up at the guardsman. 'This is no time for jokes.'

'No joke, my lady.'

'Well if you don't know what she's saying, you can't just make it up.'

The interpreter was trying to explain, while Aramilla went on. 'And for each occasion you interrupt me, I will demand another city is returned. The price for peace is now Lundenceaster and Oxenaford.'

'You're serious,' said Keturah, as the guardsman relayed this. Her manner became abruptly furious. 'That's all she came here for? *Peace?* That's why she brought this army across the lines?'

'Yes, my lady.'

'I thought she'd come to discuss terms for battle! And she has the nerve to imagine we'd give her land for this arrangement?' The guardsman nodded again, and Keturah got suddenly to her feet, swearing under her breath. 'What a complete waste of my time.' She shot a withering glance at Bellamus, spared none at all for the queen, turned on her heel and swept through the canvas tent flap. A stunned silence was left in her wake, interrupted by her parting roar. 'Waste of my bloody time!'

Her two guardsmen exchanged a glance and then hastened after the Black Lady, turning their backs on Aramilla, who seemed genuinely confused.

'But where's she gone?' she demanded.

'I'm not exactly sure,' murmured Bellamus.

'Is she coming back, Safinim?' asked Ruden.

'She's coming back?' persisted Aramilla.

Nobody replied.

'She's coming back, yes?'

Bellamus cleared his throat. 'I don't think so, Majesty.'

'But there must've been a mistake,' Aramilla objected. 'My meaning was not properly conveyed, she cannot simply have rejected us out of hand.'

Bellamus was trying to suppress his glee. He should have known he could rely on Lady Keturah. 'It's as I've said I'm afraid, Majesty. They are simply not interested in negotiating. The sword is the only tool to end this war.'

Aramilla was speechless. 'That . . . heinous *bitch*. How dare she turn her back on me? How *dare* she? I come all this way into the lands she's torn apart, and from the goodness of my heart try to offer her a way out of this hell, and she turns her back!'

'Immensely disrespectful,' Ruden agreed.

'Well if she wants war, I'll bloody give her one. Lord Safinim: you have permission to do whatever you see fit to begin dismantling the Anakim war-machine.'

Bellamus could not contain his grin. 'I have been making preparations, Majesty, we are ready to begin at once.'

The queen stood, and with one more furious glance after the retreating figure of Keturah, she stalked back towards their own lines, waving away the throne-bearers who hurried after her. Ruden winked at Bellamus and joined the exodus.

Bellamus was left last in the tent. Half a dozen guardsmen had already advanced to loosen the guy lines and extract the pegs holding taut the canvas walls. They bustled around Bellamus, ignoring him standing frozen between them.

His hand was in his pocket. He was fingering the square of linen there, running his fingertips over the queen's initials embroidered into it. He looked around. Nobody seemed to be paying him the slightest attention. Then he withdrew the handkerchief and discreetly, he let it fall onto the floor.

He turned on his heel and was gone, hastening after Queen Aramilla.

38
Myrklettur

Gray and Ormur had decided to walk to Myrklettur. They could have ridden, but not knowing how they might proceed when they arrived, did not want the encumbrance of horses. And besides, walking felt a better way to discharge the frustration at being left behind. Five days they marched, each evening settling footsore on the needles beneath a pine. Sharing the glare of a fire with his master, steel stars glinting through the canopy and the fat of a roasted woodcock running down his fingers, Ormur nearly forgot that he was missing the war.

On the sixth day, they woke to the stirring of ten thousand leaves. The canopy above was swelling like the sea, and the first few drops of a summer storm leaking through to patter the leaflitter.

The pair of them observed the canopy drowsily for a few minutes. '*Thrumat*,' said Gray. The week of the Thunderbird. He sat up. 'Let's get going. Only three leagues to go, and we'll get cold if we aren't moving by the time this storm hits. We can breakfast while we walk.'

They had each slept wrapped in a cloak, and it was the work of a minute to stow these in their packs, press some earth over the slumbering fire and drop onto one of the winding

Anakim roads. Above the canopy they heard the colossal wingbeats of the Thunderbird rumbling as it flew overhead. Then a flash, as it reached through the clouds with one of its great lightning talons. In a boom that hit them as a physical shock, it snatched a thousand-year oak into fragments. The thunder roared again and Ormur imagined the monstrous bird having swooped so low it was nearly unshrouded, and now beating its wings and straining back upwards.

'Who will the Thunderbird side with?' asked Ormur. 'At the end. The Almighty or Catastrophe?'

'Whoever earns her. Sometimes she does what the Almighty asks, sometimes not. Maybe she'll switch between the two. If she's with the Almighty, Pryce will probably try to ride her into battle.'

Ormur liked the thought of that. 'Maybe Pryce will be the one to kill Catastrophe.'

'Did you not just see what I saw? We are just men. The greatest of us is no more significant to Catastrophe than the greatest dormouse.'

It was moments before they were both drenched. The canopy briefly held out against the storm, before freezing pea-sized drops began to pummel them both. They dipped their heads and struggled on, but before long the rain turned into hail. It brushed past the leaves and rattled off the stones, so thick and furious that Ormur could barely keep his eyes open.

'Call this summer?' he complained to his mentor. They had slowed to a crawl, struggling forward side by side.

So thick was the hail that it was painful on Ormur's head, and after a time he realised he could no longer see Gray. He stopped to cast about, but could see nothing through the haze. Nothing but the muddy trail, and ferns bowing beneath the deluge. 'Captain? Sir!' Then Gray emerged as if conjured from the chaos behind him. He had been just five yards away and quite invisible.

'Stay at my side, lad!' Gray had to lean close and shout into Ormur's ear to make himself heard. They kept a hand on one another to avoid being separated again. The lightning flashed, followed an instant later by an awesome roar. Ormur began to wonder if they should take some shelter. If they stopped moving they would get cold, but if they pressed on they might easily blunder off the road and tumble down a ledge.

He opened his mouth to shout this to Gray, and stumbled into something solid coming the other way.

He blinked, trying to force his eyes open to see what he had hit, and found himself face to face with an equally surprised man. The stranger was hooded, black-haired and careworn, with a pair of penetrating blue eyes that were fixed on Ormur. For a moment they just stared at one another and Ormur realised that this stranger was not just surprised, but uncomfortable. He stood wary, as though their meeting place was the middle of an arena. At the edge of his vision, he could see that Gray had run into another man, and that there was a third traveller with this group, standing a little behind.

The stranger in front of Ormur was wrapped in a waxed black cloak and had a bow and a quiver of arrows slung over his shoulder. There was something at his side and Ormur glanced down automatically, just in time to see the man's cloak twitch over the hilt of something hung at his belt. It could have been a long knife, but in the brief glimpse Ormur had, he thought it was a sword.

Ormur nodded his head in greeting at the man. 'Bleak day,' he called through the roar of hail. 'Are you all right? Can we help you?'

The man regarded Ormur watchfully and then shook his head. Two strangers meeting on the road might normally have stopped to swap news and opine on the state of the trail up ahead, but this encounter was unexpectedly charged. Ormur had the strong impression that the stranger was deliberating rapidly.

He gave the man no time to reach any conclusions, nodding to him and stepping aside. Gray did the same, and they skirted determinedly round the trio, walking on down the road.

Ormur felt Gray's hand on his shoulder and was dragged nearly into a trot.

'We need to find shelter,' said Gray, leaning close to his ear and words coming out slurred through cold lips. 'Quickly.'

They walked on another ten yards before Gray's grip tightened and he pulled Ormur into a run. For several yards they pounded recklessly through the hail, stiff-legged and panting until Gray caught hold of him again and dragged them left, climbing the hillside bordering the road.

Their packs bouncing on their backs, they slid and scrambled over the sodden leaflitter until they reached a thick bed of juniper bushes.

'Here,' said Gray, indicating the bushes. 'This'll do.'

'We'll freeze,' said Ormur, who had imagined they were looking for a rocky outcrop beneath which they could shelter from the rain and light a fire to dry by.

'Never mind the cold, get under there. Quickly!'

Chilled to the bone, it took Ormur a few heartbeats to realise it was not the weather that concerned Gray. 'The travellers?'

'Of course, get in.'

Ormur swung off his pack and tossed it beneath the bushes, scrambling after it. Gray was on his heels and after some manoeuvring, they were lodged in a small hollow beneath the bushes. Their eyeline was just above ground level, and they could see down the hill, to where the trees were swallowed in the haze. The road was completely obscured.

'What's going on?' asked Ormur.

'There's been a full call-up, Ormur,' said Gray peering into the haze. 'Those men are fighting age. What are they doing on this road?'

'Same thing as us? They may have leave.'

'A full call-up is an emergency. Leave is cancelled. The only reason ours wasn't is that Lady Keturah fears you'll be killed. But even if they had special dispensation to stay behind like us, the man opposite me was carrying a sword.'

'So was the one I ran into.'

'So why take a sword on a hunting trip? This reeks.'

'Maybe they were worried about bandits?' he suggested.

'You've lived too long in Blacklaw. There are no bandits in the Black Kingdom.'

Ormur imitated Gray and peered into the haze. 'Well, who were they then?'

'Bad news, my friend.'

They fell silent. The earth beneath them was prickly from shed juniper needles, but not as sodden as the rest of the forest. Even so, before long Ormur was trembling violently. He and Gray huddled together for warmth and shared some shards of hard cheese. It was all they had left: they had planned to walk up their supper on the journey and been prevented by the downpour. Still, the combined effect of the cheese, the shelter, and two cloaks cast over the pair of them was enough to prevent the cold becoming disabling. Presently the hail stopped, though the canopy continued to drip itself dry.

They lay still beneath the bushes for some while. Ormur stewed on the reminder that Keturah had left him behind to protect him. He felt belittled. He was a Sacred Guardsman: he should be defending her and fighting at the front. Not kept away from it all like a child.

He took a breath to ask if they could just head south, but before he could utter a word, felt his mentor's hand clamp over his mouth. Gray had stiffened beside him and Ormur listened into the forest. There was a constant drip of leaves. A wood pigeon calling throatily. And then Ormur heard a faint sound behind them: something moving on the hillside above their hide. Whatever it was, it was obscured by the bushes. It might have been a bear: something massive and deliberate picking over the leaf-litter. Then for just an instant, the footsteps separated and two or perhaps three distinct individuals emerged from the noise. It could only have been the strangers they had met on the road, just a yard or two away, on the other side of their frail juniper shelter. Ormur held his breath.

There came the sound of a slip and abruptly a boot crashed

through the roof of the bushes, catching on one of the exposed roots. Gray and Ormur were entirely rigid. A voice above them swore softly and the boot was jerked out of view again. 'All right?' breathed another voice. There was no audible reply, and the strangers continued, picking their way past and traversing the hillside. The noise of their footfalls grew steadily more distant, and it was some minutes after it had faded completely that Ormur finally felt Gray relax next to him.

'They've moved off the road,' he murmured. 'They don't want to be spotted again. Let's go then.'

'Where?'

'Hunting.'

Ormur was almost too cold to move. They unfolded stiff limbs and disentangled from one another, taking just bow, arrow and knives, and leaving their packs beneath the bushes. Then they stole after the travellers.

Tracking in these conditions was easy, especially across a hillside. Though the light was poor, the earth was soft and yielded easily to footfalls, and the strangers had slid occasionally as they moved, leaving long scars in the leaflitter. So fast were they able to move that Ormur accidentally caught sight of their quarry: three dark-cloaked figures, not fifty yards ahead. He rolled immediately behind the trunk of an oak. Gray had seen him and sank smoothly into the hillside, lying still against the ground.

Where are they going? Ormur mouthed.

Gray just shook his head.

They dirtied their faces and hands to stop them shining through the gloom, then unfolded from their hiding places and slid after the strangers like twin shadows. Overhead was a layer of cloud so dense that it felt like the coming night, drawing the world beneath the canopy in shades of charcoal. They ricocheted between the trees, lying still whenever their quarry looked back, waiting for them to hurry forward once more.

Finally, when the world had gone from grey to blue and night was nearly upon them, the strangers re-joined the road.

'Where are we?' Ormur breathed.

In answer Gray just pointed to the edge of the trees. Between the trunks, the dark face of Myrklettur's outer wall was just visible.

The two guardsmen paused at the treeline and watched the three travellers climb the causeway up to the ancient stone gatehouse. They were soon swallowed by the fortress.

'So who on earth are they,' Gray murmured.

'We should capture one,' said Ormur. 'Get some information out of him.'

'How do you propose?' said Gray. 'I doubt he'd just tell us.'

'Torture.'

'And have him screaming through the forest and bringing his companions down on us? I don't think so. Besides, I'm done with torturing. They'll talk more easily with each other. We're better off eavesdropping. At the very least we should watch until we know how many of them there may be.'

In the last of the light, they retraced their steps and collected their packs. There would be no supper that night, but if they did not light a fire they would freeze. They found a rocky alcove that faced away from the old fortress and soon had a pile of damp wood that steamed and hissed as flames began to chew at its base.

'I think they're just brigands,' said Ormur. Both were tired and hungry and it had been an irritable evening. 'They've come up from Blacklaw, why not?'

'We should watch,' said Gray firmly, turning over a sodden log. 'They don't know they're being observed, and that opportunity may not come again.'

'I say we just ask them.'

'I admire that about you. But in this instance, that's just mad.'

There was a pause, then they both burst into manic laughter.

Before first light, Gray had crept away to watch over the entrance to Myrklettur, while Ormur went hunting. Ormur was back at the alcove by mid-afternoon with a roe buck, which he skinned and butchered as he waited for Gray. The rain restarted and night had fallen before his mentor was back. At the sight of the deer he raised his hands to the sky in vehement thanks. 'Venison! Well done lad. Your day was more successful than mine, I see.'

'What did you see?'

'Nothing,' said Gray. 'I watched the entrance the whole morning, and when there was no sign, I scuttled into the fortress itself. I didn't go wandering around inside but I couldn't see anyone. Checked both entrances, and there were no fresh prints leaving. So either they know a way out that I don't, or they're still in there somewhere. I'll go back tomorrow.'

Ormur had created a hot-rock oven, setting a haunch of venison to roast beneath the ground before Gray's return. Together, they dug it out with a pair of sticks. The two of them managed to destroy the joint in its entirety, and several handfuls of cattail roots, set to bake alongside the meat and now soft and hot.

On the second day, Ormur and Gray both went to watch over the fortress, Gray taking one exit and Ormur the other. Still, they saw no one. Still, there were no tracks to indicate that anyone had passed in or out since they had seen the mysterious band go in.

'They must've gone straight through to the other exit on the first night,' said Ormur. 'Let's go inside tomorrow.'

'One more day's watching,' said Gray. 'Then if we haven't seen anything, we'll assume they've gone.'

'But they can't have been waiting inside all that time without a fire,' Ormur protested. 'We've seen no smoke, and they'd surely have run out of water by now.'

'Just one more day,' Gray insisted. 'Then we'll go inside for a poke around.'

'I think they've gone,' Ormur noted.

But he was wrong, because on the third day, they saw the strangers again. Gray was watching one exit, Ormur half-watching the other. He was fidgeting, and on the verge of defying Gray and walking through Myrklettur's western gate, when something dark and shifting caught his eye at the top of the wall. He froze, searching the wall's silhouetted upper edge. There was nothing. Then . . . There! A dark head slipped behind the battlements. It had been so swift that it might have belonged to an animal, but when three figures emerged onto the road, Ormur knew it had been a lookout. The party were dressed in the same fashion as the group they had encountered in the rain, with black cloaks, bows and the occasional glint of a sword hilt at their waists. But one of the figures was skeletal: so tall and thin that Ormur was sure that if he had seen him before, he would have remembered.

They took the road down from Myrklettur, arrows nocked to their bowstrings and walking silently into the wind. From this, Ormur knew they were hunting. From trunk to trunk, gully to outcrop and bush to bank, he shadowed the three of them. Every now and then, he caught a waft of their scent on the wind. Stale and damp: the smell of unkempt men, long missing hearth and home.

They soon departed the road, and Ormur let them disappear from view, content to follow their trail. Before he had caught up with them, a new smell met him on the breeze, rich and metallic: blood. He found them gathered around a fresh red deer carcass, the skeletal figure leaning over it, the other two standing back with their bows now slung over their shoulders. The slender figure straightened up, holding a dark clotted mass in his hands, his forearms painted scarlet. Another figure produced a knife and carved thick strips off the liver, which the three began to slurp down raw.

They settled by an alder, a few yards from a sharp bank cut by a stream and overhung by ferns. By using the stream bed, Ormur thought he could approach unseen and eavesdrop. Holding onto the hilt of Warspite to stop it rattling, he slid down the bank, the water beneath his feet trickling fast and loud. This concealed the sounds of his approach, but meant that he stood almost beneath them by the time his ears had attuned themselves to the conversation.

'Another fine gut-shot from you, Ira.'

There came laughter.

'My speciality.'

'He's very consistent. We should have rankings. Whoever's on top gets to lead the hunt, bottom stays on guard in the grav.'

There came a hushing noise. 'Quiet!'

'What? They haven't got ears in the trees.'

'Just don't.'

There came a long pause. Ormur had gone so rigid that his muscles ached. These men knew he and Gray had been watching them, and were wary even now. There suddenly seemed a high chance of being caught. Now was the time to leave.

One of them started murmuring that liver was not the same eaten raw, and disguised by the noise, Ormur reversed along the stream bed. That word they had used: *grav*. Could it have been an abbreviation of *kungargrav*? If it was, he surely knew who these men were. So occupied was he by these thoughts that by the time he noticed the figure standing in his path, it was just a few heartbeats too late.

Ormur halted in his tracks. Standing before him in the bed of the stream was a black-cloaked figure, a half-drawn bow raised so that the arrow was directed at Ormur's neck.

'Unbuckle your sword-belt, Guard Dog,' said a voice from above him. Ormur's eyes flicked right, where he saw another black-cloaked figure standing on the bank: this one with another bow trained at his head. And a slight crunching of twigs and leaflitter to his left told him there was a third bowman, and that he had stumbled into a trap. These were not the same men he had overheard by the deer carcass. This was another group, who had obviously stayed behind to stalk anyone who tried to follow their hunting party.

And then a knife was pressed to his throat, and a voice hissed hot and violent into his ear.

'He said drop the sword. Drop it or die.'

39

Cold Voice

A hand was fumbling at his belt-buckle. Ormur allowed his sword to be stripped and flung up onto the bank. 'Make a sound and I'll cut your scrawny neck.' Then a boot reduced him to his knees. He splashed into freezing water up to his mid-thigh, before a second boot rocked his head. Stunned, he tipped forward and plunged into the stream. He was entirely submerged, deaf and blind and horribly vulnerable to the attacker standing over him. A hand gripped the back of his tunic and hauled him up again, and he emerged gasping from the water. Choking and spluttering, he cast about and saw another three figures had appeared on the bank above. It was the hunting party he had been stalking, evidently attracted by the commotion and now looking down at him without a hint of surprise.

'Where's your companion?' hissed the voice in his ear. 'The other guardsman, where is he?'

Ormur gritted his teeth, breathing hard and meaning to say nothing. But he nearly cried out when pain burned through his ear. Slowly, the attacker was carving through the flesh with his knife.

'Tell me where, Guard Dog.'

'Kill me then,' said Ormur, not troubling to keep his voice

low. He could feel hot blood dribbling down the side of his neck. 'You'll get nothing from me.'

That elicited laughter, rattling into the air like startled crows.

'You can have no idea how bored we are, Guardsman,' said the bowman on the riverbank, grinning down at him. 'You are the best entertainment we have had in months, and you'll stay with us for the rest of your life. You think that when you've got no nails, no teeth, no balls, and no eyes, you'll still say nothing? First you'll resist. Then you'll lie and hope we believe it. And by the time you're a single raw nerve, you'll tell us the truth. Everyone does.' He laughed again.

Ormur looked up at the bowman, unable to keep the horror from his face. He knew that his only escape from that suffering – and worse, from betraying Gray – was death. But he was ashamed to discover that instead he was nearly overwhelmed by the impulse to comply, and keep pain at bay in the vain hope that Gray might find and rescue him.

But that must not be allowed to happen. Before he could reconsider, he filled his lungs.

'My captain! Run!'

A hard, smooth stone from the stream crashed down on his head, and he collapsed.

Ormur awoke in stages. In the first, he seemed to inhabit a hot, feverish world without time or light. There was pain, and noise, both of which reverberated through the blackness like echoes in a cave, washing over him again and again. In the second stage came fear, and nausea. He had the strongest impression of trying to run but being unable to move. His limbs were like heavy rolls of cloth, but he had to rise because there was something coming after him: a black, stocky figure, which stank of blood and clutched a strange knife he could not see, but could feel the wounds it was about to create in his back. Finally came the third stage: confused jolts and flashes of light. Murmured words without meaning, and some thickness in his mouth which he tried to spit out but would not budge.

Presently, he became aware it was a gag. He was being carried over someone's shoulder, nose pressed into a tunic which smelt of stale water.

Gray. I must warn Gray.

He tried to call out, but the gag was so tight that moving his tongue nearly choked him. He tried to cough, found he could not, and spent the next few minutes desperately heaving for breath.

'Is he awake? Looks like he's struggling to breathe.'

'Who cares.'

'He'd better not die.'

'He won't.'

Ormur spluttered, but could not make a sound or move; his wrists and ankles were tightly bound.

'I want to know where the other guardsman is.'

'I told you it was Captain Gray.'

'Saying *my captain* doesn't mean it was *the* captain.'

'I recognised him when we ran into him on the road.'

'Why would the captain of the Sacred Guard be here alone, when Keturah is in the south?'

'Well, this one's here, why not Gray?'

'Gray's her most faithful hound, he'd have gone with her. I don't believe either of them are guardsmen, this one is too young.'

'I tell you, I recognised him.'

Another voice, like a cold draught, cut into the argument. 'It doesn't matter who he is, it matters where. When he realises we've got this one, he'll get reinforcements. We'll be uncovered and burnt out, unless we can find him before he escapes. We needed both of them. You should have waited and followed him back to the other one.'

There was silence. 'He'd heard you talking. We couldn't let him escape.'

'Fool,' replied the voice like a cold draught. 'We'd said nothing. It would've been better to let him escape than take one without the other. Now we've got to find his mate before he realises what's happened and slips away.' The voice was oppressive, and extinguished the others.

There was nothing but the tramping of boots for some minutes before there came a new voice who had not yet spoken. 'I believe they're guardsmen,' it said. 'This is not an ordinary sword.'

'You know nothing about swords.'

'I recognise Sindri's mark.'

There came a pause, then the rasp of blade on scabbard. 'I actually think he's right,' said another voice, softly.

'That's one of Sindri's?'

'No, no wait . . . if the other was Gray, then this would be his new protégé.' The voice broke off to hoot in disbelief. 'You know who that is? It's Ormur Kynortasson. Roper's brother! He's got a Sindri sword, one of the best he ever made. Warspite.'

'No,' said another voice. 'Ormur Kynortasson? The one everyone's been clamouring to take the Stone Throne? This one's too young.'

'Ormur *is* young, one of the youngest guardsmen for centuries.'

'Look at his bloody wrist lads, he's got the Prize of Valour!'

Expostulations of glee and disbelief erupted around him.

'Can this *be*? This sack of bones is Roper's brother?'

'Careful with that sword, Alines, it's worth a bloody fortune.'

'Why fight with something worth as much as a house?'

'Well, well. We shall have to reserve some special suffering for the brother of the Black Lord.'

Ormur was still too drowsy to absorb the conversation. He just hung limp, his bearer pausing to heave him from one shoulder to the other.

'Think harder,' said Cold Voice. 'We can use him better than that. If this is really Ormur Kynortasson, it excuses your slip, Varnim. It changes everything.'

'We still need to kill Gray.'

'You're still not thinking. Imagine if we had both Gray and

Ormur alive. This is the most extraordinary piece of good fortune. More than we could've dared hope. Imagine our leverage. It changes *everything*.'

A blurry sort of vision was returning to Ormur. Shadows mostly, but he could make enough sense of them to distinguish five figures – six, including the one carrying him – moving between vast tree trunks. He recognised one by silhouette: the skeletal figure he had watched hunting that morning, and when the cold draught of a voice came a few moments later, it was from him. 'We're nearly back on the road. Alines, Stilna: keep an eye out.'

There came the sound of cracking twigs and rustling leaves as two of the party loped away. The rest of the party trooped on in silence, and presently Ormur became aware that they were passing beneath the gatehouse at Myrklettur. He stirred, struggling against his bonds, but someone slapped his head hard and he fell back, stunned. 'Still, boy.'

Boy! Even in his confused state Ormur writhed ineffectually. But he was ignored and borne on, through the gatehouse and out onto the plain of the ancient fortress. There they were rejoined by Alines and Stilna.

'Saw nothing,' reported one. 'I don't know where Gray is.'

'Fine. Inside then, quick.'

'Could we use this one as bait?' suggested one. 'If we want to catch Gray we should injure the boy and leave him somewhere for him to find.'

'We'll plan inside.'

The party was rushing now, Ormur bouncing painfully as they cantered over a green swell; all that remained of ancient streets and walls. It seemed he was being carried towards a dark blot in the side of a massive stone wall. An abyss that stood behind a collapsed archway that he had last seen seven years before.

He remembered standing before it with Keturah. The cool breath that had come from it, the strange spiky symbols that lined the walls, and the overwhelming sensation of a figure standing in the blackness, looking back at them. He had not the least desire to set foot in that place, but his head rang like an ice-capped mountain and resisting was beyond him.

The group was swallowed by the tunnel and darkness fell over them. Their panting magnified as it reverberated from the walls and their footsteps clattered on the flagstones. They were inside barely ten heartbeats, pushing against the draught that moaned down the passage, when someone swore. 'He's there! Back there! The captain!'

Ormur felt a swell of hope and stirred suddenly, trying to call out once more and subsiding again into silent choking convulsions against the gag.

'Bastard's waking up,' muttered his bearer.

'Get him, after Gray, now!'

'Don't go alone, fool!' said Cold Voice. 'You two with him! Run!'

Footsteps broke out in the passageway, racing back the way they had come. Ormur tried to call out again but only managed to trigger a coughing fit that had him retching, such pressure building in his head that he felt it might burst his eardrums. Harder than he had ever wished for anything in his life, he wanted Gray to escape. The captain would not abandon him to this fate. If he knew where Ormur was, he would get him back one way or another. It did not matter if this passage led to the underworld itself: Gray would get him back.

'He's gone,' someone called back.

'Then go after him,' said Cold Voice. 'One of you stand guard over each exit, the other two to search him out. He mustn't escape this plateau.'

Another set of footsteps pounded away to trap Gray in Myrklettur.

'Drop him and help me.' Cold Voice again.

Before he could raise his hands to protect his head, Ormur was tipped backwards, rattling off the stones like a bundle of dropped kindling. The two remaining men – Cold Voice, and

Ormur's bearer – were working at one of the stones in the floor. They were distracted for a moment, and Ormur seized it, rolling onto his front and squirming towards the light at the far end of the tunnel. He managed just a few feet before a hand latched onto his ankle and dragged him backwards.

'No, Son of Kynortas,' said an amused voice. 'Not out there. But I'm glad you got one last look at the daylight.'

Ormur twisted round to face his enemy, hands bound impotently in front of him. He could do no more than watch as a shadow, now concealed up to his waist in a shaft exposed beneath the flagstones, dragged him closer. Standing above them was the skeletal form of Cold Voice, holding up the edge of a flagstone that seemed to be mounted on a hinge so that it lifted like a trap door.

The man standing in the shaft beneath the floor still had Ormur by the ankle and dragged him intractably away from the light, away from Gray, away from all that was free and precious. Ormur thrashed and flailed, jarring and bumping over the stones until with a final heave, he was pulled over the lip of the hole and began to plummet. For a heartbeat he dropped, blood roaring in his ears before he crunched against angular stone. He was tumbling down a staircase, bouncing and hurtling until he finally jarred to a halt at the bottom.

There he lay, ears ringing like struck flint, every thought knocked from his skull.

'He'd better not die,' said Cold Voice from somewhere in the high distance.

The yellow light of a lamp filtered down to Ormur, warming the cavity in which he had come to rest. He lay exposed in the middle of a floor, a stone passageway arching overhead.

The heavy tread of a pair of boots began to thump deliberately down the stairs. Ormur contracted slowly into a knot. *No . . . please. Please, please, please.*

The footsteps came to a halt immediately behind his head, and there came the creak of leather as someone bent low over him.

'Welcome, Son of Kynortas.' It was Cold Voice. Ormur bit down on the gag, bracing himself.

Just do it. Whatever you're going to do, get it over with.

'It may surprise you to learn that you are now in a very privileged position. Very, very few have seen this place. Winners of the Prize of Valour number in multitudes compared to those who've seen these passages. Here,' he added suddenly.

Rough fingers groped at the back of Ormur's head and he flinched, trying to writhe away before he realised that his gag was being unknotted. It was pulled free, the sudden ease of his breathing a brief treasure.

'Sorry about that,' said Cold Voice. 'A necessary precaution I'm afraid. We didn't want your companion coming to find you. It is Captain Gray, isn't it? And you are his protégé, Ormur Kynortasson?' He waited for a response, but Ormur just lay still, his back to Cold Voice, tensed and waiting for another attack. 'Well, never mind. I expect you're tired.'

There came the sound of another pair of footsteps descending the stairs. Somebody gripped beneath his arms and lifted him, this time quite gently. He was not tossed over a shoulder but held in front of his captor like a babe in arms, as the skeletal figure of Cold Voice led them down the passageway, lamp in hand.

Ormur tried to focus on his surroundings. He had to know the way out if there was to be any hope of escape, but the walls were unadorned and seemed to slip by in a gleam of damp yellow. They came to a fork and turned left, then left again, right, left again . . . Or perhaps right. And then he had missed another turn, and he was utterly lost in a labyrinth of pitch-black.

'Here,' said Cold Voice presently. They had come to a low wooden door: thick oak, reinforced with heavy iron rivets. It was no more than waist height, Cold Voice reduced to hands and knees to accommodate his spindly frame. Ormur was posted gently through the entrance behind him. The chamber beyond was low and domed, like a bread oven. Between them, Cold Voice and The Other shuffled Ormur inside and helped him to sit up.

'There,' said Cold Voice, setting the lamp on the floor. 'You can rest here for a moment and we'll get you some water. Oh, I nearly forgot.' And he leaned forward and untied Ormur's hands. 'There. Is there anything else you need?' He waited for a moment, but Ormur did not reply. 'Never mind. There's just one more thing.'

And he lunged across the chamber, knocking Ormur onto his back. A knee crushed down on his chest, and fists hammered down again and again at Ormur's teeth, his nose, his eyes. His vision burst into stars, his nose crunched beneath the onslaught and the fourth blow knocked a tooth into the back of Ormur's throat. Cold Voice was wearing a feral snarl, making a strange, desperate whimpering that echoed around the chamber.

Just faint, Ormur thought. *Please, please lose consciousness.*

But he would not. His brain clung to the waves of agony sweeping the length of him. There was still that odd helpless whimpering, and Ormur realised with a shock that it was coming not from Cold Voice, but his own mouth.

There came a heartbeat's pause in the onslaught, Cold Voice lifting his knee from Ormur's chest. He dared hope it was over. Then the knee came back down, hard on his belly, then again on his groin.

Just die, thought Ormur. *Please, please let me die.*

He could not take the pain, the complete vulnerability, or the shame of being made to whimper like a child. The character he had spent his life building and aspiring towards was obliterated, and Ormur was left in shame. He doubted they could ever have made Gray wail like this, or Roper, or Pryce. He was broken, beaten down to the child he had tried so hard to leave behind, and it had taken mere hours.

Cold Voice took his left little finger then and wrenched it aside with a crack. At last, Ormur's awareness seemed to slip. He did not notice Cold Voice get off him, but he could feel himself trembling. He heard a noise of weak outrage escape his mouth, appalled and disbelieving that even enemies – whoever they were – should have reduced him to this.

Cold Voice was panting. 'This is the rest of your life, Guard Dog. I'm getting you water because it'll prolong your suffering. There is no end to it. There's nothing I want from you, nothing you can give me to stop it. Just know that this is it, until you give in and take the coward's way out.'

'Who . . .' Ormur tried to speak but the words came out in a thick mumble. 'Who are you? Why are you doing this?'

'You know all you need to. If I hear another noise from you that isn't a scream, I'll douse your clothes in oil and let you burn.'

Cold Voice had the lamp in his hand and held it over Ormur for a moment. Ormur stared up at his captor, trying for defiance but knowing only terror. The eyes of a predator stared down at him from Cold Voice's gaunt face. Then he gave a smirk of contempt and backed out of the chamber, taking with him the only source of light. The door slammed, and Ormur was swallowed by the darkness.

40
The Tomb

Ormur fell in and out of consciousness, though without light or sound, it was hard to know when he had been asleep and when he had not. The man Ormur thought of as The Other – the one who had borne him into this place – came to deliver a pitcher of water and then left without a word. Ormur tried to improve what he could, gulping down half the water at once and then using the rest to clean his wounds. When that distraction had passed, all he was left with was the memory of how easily they had broken him. Without other stimulus, those thoughts swooped nauseatingly about his head.

Time stretched.

When the outside locking bar clunked, Ormur felt a stab of terror. He felt like a rabbit flattened at the bottom of a warren, nets over each run and two slavering dogs waiting for him to break cover. A wedge of light cracked the dark and Cold Voice stooped through the door, taking a knee before Ormur, who had backed against the wall before he could stop himself.

Cold Voice looked him over with disdain and then inspected his water pitcher. 'Finished already? That was for the whole day, you've only been here three hours.'

Three hours? It had felt days.

'Never mind, we'll get you another. Just this once though.' Cold Voice wrinkled his nose and smiled horribly. 'And a pot to piss in, you animal. You couldn't hold on for three hours?'

Ormur flushed. 'Who are you?' he croaked. 'Why are you doing this?'

Cold Voice sighed and set the lamp on the floor. Then like a lunging snake, he latched onto Ormur's ankle and dragged him close. Ormur clamped his mouth shut, his first instinct to stop himself screaming. Cold Voice set upon him again and though Ormur tried to fight back, he was too feeble and shaking too badly, and his blows were dismissed by a ruthless tormentor. When he was finished and Ormur had surrendered, lying limp on the floor, Cold Voice picked up the lamp once more. He pinned Ormur's right arm beneath his knees and poured five drips of oil from the front of the lamp. Each caught as it passed the wick, so that five splashes of liquid fire landed on Ormur's arm. Ormur thrashed, screaming at last as a vicious constellation blazed on his skin.

'You know why I did that, Guard Dog? You know why you've just had that beating? I told you. I told you to make no noise that wasn't a scream. You don't get to ask questions. You are here as our guest, and I haven't brought you for your company. I've brought you to watch you suffer.' He lifted his knees from Ormur's arm, who was then able to clutch it to his chest and smother the last burning remnants of the oil.

'But I enjoyed that, Guard Dog. We'll be back soon.' Cold Voice smirked at him again, and backed out of the room. The Other was crouched in the doorway behind him and pushed in a pot and a fresh pitcher of water, before the light went out again.

The waiting began anew. At first Ormur was simply relieved to have been left alone, to curl up and regather himself. Then his thoughts began picking at him once more. If that had been just three hours, what an eternity would the rest of his life feel? Unbearable. And where was Gray? Had he abandoned him to this underground prison? Fled and saved himself?

Ormur would have died for the captain. Or he thought he would have. But now that he had seen his own reaction to this torture: his childish screams and struggles, he was not sure any more.

When Cold Voice next arrived, a wave of horrid despair such as Ormur had never known swept up him. But he was not beaten on this occasion. Cold Voice just sat and talked. He sneered at Ormur, he laughed at him, he expressed his astonishment that anyone so feeble could have won the Prize of Valour, that it must be his noble blood that led Keturah to give him this tin bauble undeserved, and appoint him to the Sacred Guard.

'Well, Ormur,' he said as he prepared to leave, 'you've nearly lasted a whole day here. I hope you've enjoyed it as much as I.'

Ormur shuddered involuntarily at that. Just one day. He was starving. He was broken and he felt a constant ticking dread worse than anything he had known before. And it was just one day.

'We'll get you some bread. I daresay you're hungry.' Cold Voice nodded and shuffled out. When the bread arrived, Ormur tried to resist. He wanted to die: it would be better than this. Anything was better than this. But he was too hungry and despising himself more than ever, he fell upon the bread and devoured it.

Cold Voice visited regularly the next day too. Sometimes he beat Ormur, sometimes not. But the third occasion was the worst. That hateful sound: the locking bar scraping back. The sliver of light which grew so slowly, and triggered nothing but terror. Then that skeletal figure, crouched in the doorway, leering at him.

'I have some news for you, Ormur. You're not our only prisoner any more.' He watched Ormur, nearly licking his lips at the horror he saw there. 'We've got Gray. Gave us the slip for a bit, but we caught him trying to skulk out of the fortress. Do you hear me? We've got him, and now he's going to suffer the same as you. I suppose you'll just be pleased that he'll be punished for trying to leave you in this mess. But now we have you both. The only person who knows what happened to you is trapped. We're doing to him what we've done to you, though he's resisting much better, I have to say.'

No, thought Ormur. He found he did not care that Gray had tried to save himself. All he cared was that his mentor was now suffering this hell too. He considered lunging at Cold Voice, trying to fight his way out. But he found he was frozen. No matter how hard he tried, there seemed to be some barrier between his thoughts and his actions.

Over just two days, he had learned helplessness. However he behaved, he was punished. If he acted, he would certainly be punished. If he did not, he sometimes escaped. He just desperately wanted to comply, even to please Cold Voice, who was smiling as Ormur folded in on himself.

'You will never see daylight again.'

Ormur stared, aghast. He wanted to ask again who these people were, why they were so cruel and seemed to despise all that he loved, but he now feared to say anything at all. He knew what would happen if he did.

'That was all I had to tell you.' Cold Voice set down fresh bread and left without another word. Ormur watched as the light crept from his cell and the door clunked shut.

41

Why?

The instant Bellamus had left the tent, the embroidered favour of a queen left behind him, he regretted it. He was not halfway down the hill before cold sweat was prickling his back and forehead. He turned to stare back at the tent, but the canvas roof was deflating already, efficient Black Legionaries whipping the supports away and the whole structure settling to earth. The die was cast and it was too late to turn back now.

But it had been in his pocket so long! What if his scent were stronger than hers? Bellamus felt sick to the point of retching. He feared it must show on his face, but if it did then Aramilla, when he found her, was too angry to notice.

'How *dare* she?' The queen was striding back and forth across her tent, shooting him an enraged look when he edged through the canvas. 'That poisonous bitch! How dare she! I entertain her as an equal, offering to preserve her rotten society, and she turns her back on me! Who is she to reject any offer I make? She should be thanking me on bended knee, that I gave her the opportunity to retain even half of the land she's wrecked!'

'Just so, Majesty,' said Bellamus.

'No respect,' the queen fumed, still pacing. 'From start to

finish, capable of displaying none of the deference due a queen, still less the sisterly conduct that is only right between fellow monarchs. Well now I know why. She is no queen! Just a barbarous war-woman: some pathetic savage chieftain who knows nothing of sense, of judgement, of propriety!' The queen was nearly out of words.

'I fear it is as I warned, Majesty,' said Bellamus. 'The Black Kingdom do not discuss peace, and they do not take prisoners. Compromise is not on their minds.'

'Yes, yes, you were right, Safinim,' she said, stopping in her tracks. 'Of course. I should not have doubted you. But did even you suspect she would be so *impudent*?'

'No, Majesty. I never knew her well, and by all accounts she has changed significantly.'

'What would you do, Safinim? From here, I mean.'

'As – excuse me –' his voice cracked and he coughed delicately, trying to suppress the turbulence in his stomach – 'As you have directed, Majesty, now is the chance to defeat them forever.'

'You will command the army?'

'I will do whatever serves Your Majesty.'

She gave him a wry look. 'Whatever?'

'Of course.'

'Then share my pavilion again tonight.'

Bellamus hesitated then. He wanted to be nowhere near the queen, or her scent.

'Tonight, Majesty? I fear . . . With your leave, I had not intended to sleep tonight. I must set an example to the men. Show them how seriously we must take the Anakim threat after the Sacred Guard crept up on us last night.'

The queen narrowed her eyes. 'Nonsense, Safinim. The men will be just fine. You will share my tent.'

Bellamus bowed: he could hardly refuse. He would probably be safe enough tonight – even if the handkerchief had been found, he doubted one of the blind assassins would locate Aramilla so fast. But he must be prepared for the next time she asked. 'I would be honoured, Your Majesty. Now if you'll excuse me, the time to harry the Anakim is now.'

'Go, Lord Safinim.'

To the blaring of trumpets, they marched.

As far as Bellamus was aware, this was the largest army ever assembled in Erebos; so large that many had said it would be too unwieldy to function. The narrow tracks in Blacklaw could not accommodate the surge of wagons, oxen, sheep and sundries that would be required to keep it supplied. The logistics of shifting such a huge column into motion might take a whole day, and severely limit its mobility. And so many men inhabiting the same land would surely succumb to disease in short order.

Bellamus's solution was to divide the army into three columns, each taking a different road. The northernmost was commanded by Widukind, the southernmost by Ruden, and the central one under Bellamus himself. Three columns allowed three different supply lines. It also made them faster, but their paths ran close enough together that if one were engaged, the others would soon be able to come to their aid.

The Anakim were badly outmatched. If they turned to face one of the Suthern columns, the other two would simply encircle their flanks and they would find themselves attacked from all sides. If Keturah wished to make a stand, she would have to find somewhere they could not be flanked. Riding at the van on the first day, all Bellamus saw of his vaunted enemy was the dust raised by their retreating boots.

'I suppose they don't much value this land anyway,' Diethaad observed gloomily. 'They can keep withdrawing until they find somewhere to make a stand.'

It was the day's end, the low sun warming their backs and casting long shadows from the trees that lined the road. He and Bellamus trotted together with a group of Thingalith, each peeling an orange sent forward by Aramilla.

'I've left them no choice,' said Bellamus. 'They have to

retreat, but I doubt they're happy about it. Legate Tekoa commands them, and he's used to operating with the scouts. He'll know exactly what I'm doing.'

'And what are you doing?'

Bellamus threw the orange-rind into a hedgerow and wiped a hand on his hose. 'Widukind, in the north, has the best road; one of the old paved ones that cuts straight through. His column is on the double, marching out in front of our column and Ruden's. In fact, they've been on the double since before we parlayed with the Black Lady . . .'

'Naughty,' said Diethaad.

'And they now block the Anakim road north. Tekoa's two choices are retreat south, or east. Go south, and we will block his supply lines coming from the north. If he keeps going east, he hits the Tywys. Unless he slows to cross it – and if he does I intend to ensure that ends in disaster – then he is even more comprehensively cut off from his main supply line. We'll keep harrying them until they've got their backs to the sea, where our fleet is unchallenged. We won't let them unspool so much as a fishing line. Let them find the site of their last stand; it'll be the place they starve.'

Diethaad made a face of frank agreement, nodding thoughtfully. 'So you'll weaken them before you fight them. But you told me once that the way to beat the enemy is to think: *What would I do, if I were them?* And then plan for that. So what would you do if you were Tekoa? How do they escape starvation?'

'I've been thinking about that,' said Bellamus, though all he had thought of that day was that abandoned handkerchief. 'Now that we've stolen a march on him, I think his only chance would be to launch an attack between two of our columns, most likely between ours and Widukind's. If he was quick, and spent some of the Unhieru, he could probably break through between us and reconnect with his supply lines. But I doubt he will. He'll keep retreating and hope he can bring us to battle before they run out of food.' Bellamus snorted. 'The

Anakim still think of us as amateurs on the battlefield. He'll believe if he can find a good position, they can beat us.'

'Can they?'

Bellamus thought about that for some time. The Anakim might be outnumbered, but their veteran core of Black Legionaries were better than ever: distilled into a peerless elite, each one of them worth ten or more raw recruits. Alongside them marched thousands of Ereboan Anakim; less disciplined and experienced perhaps, but still huge, savage and proud. And with them were eight thousand Unhieru. Bellamus would not trust a man who did not admit to fearing the Unhieru. But when he compared them against his own forces?

'No,' he said at last. 'We've too many aces.'

Bellamus returned to dine with the queen that evening, picking over a venison and rabbit pie while Aramilla probed him with questions about the Anakim. 'What is it, Safinim?' she asked eventually, tilting her head to regard him with narrowed eyes. 'Something is on your mind.'

'Nothing, Majesty. Truly, I'm just tired.'

'You jumped when the servant brought the wine,' she pressed, brown eyes inspecting him. How like her that was: the servant had appeared twenty minutes before, and Bellamus thought his start had gone unnoticed.

'I suppose it's the pressure,' Bellamus invented. 'We've never had a better chance to beat the Black Legions, and we need to make it into a victory.' In truth he was confident about that, but the queen seemed satisfied.

'Come then, Lord Upstart. Allow me to take your mind off it.'

They retired to her bed. Aramilla was soon asleep, breathing deep and slow, while Bellamus lay awake next to her, sweating in the cool air and staring up at the dim form of the canvas ceiling. There was a soft breeze, which caused the canvas to flap occasionally and Bellamus's heart to start pumping.

He became aware of a dark something in the corner of the tent. The breath caught in his chest and without so much as moving his eyes, he tried to assess it through peripheral vision. It had four legs, set down like a spider, and was very still. *Do I move fast, or slow and hope it doesn't hear me?* Fast, he decided. The horrible thing would surely hear him either way and if he was fast, he had a chance. He bellowed incoherently, sitting bolt upright and drawing up the blanket as a shield.

'What?' Aramilla was up in an instant, clutching his shoulder and staring around wildly. There was a rattling as in an instant, four royal retainers were in the chamber, halberds lowered and the light of a brazier outside flickering through the opened flap.

'What?' the queen demanded again.

Bellamus was silent.

It was just a chair: the very one on which he had sat that evening.

'Nothing,' he said. 'Sorry.'

Aramilla tutted, giving him a look of total disdain. 'Leave us,' she commanded the retainers. 'What is wrong with you, Safinim?' the queen complained as the retainers bowed from the chamber. 'You've never been like this before.'

'As you said, Majesty. Maybe age catching up with me.'

She rolled her eyes and lay back down, turning away from him.

His heart was still pumping and he slumped back beneath the covers, staring at the ceiling. He certainly felt fear that he was about to encounter one of the blind assassins, but the feeling that kept him awake was worse. It was guilt. Nauseating, rotting guilt.

He might have slept an hour or two, rising the instant dawn penetrated the walls and leaving Aramilla undisturbed. The only way he could think to avoid having to share her tent again was not to let her ask. If he were always busy at the front, he would not have to offend her by refusing an invitation.

When he journeyed on, he did so with his scouts, riding far past the main army and even setting eyes on the Anakim rearguard: the Black Cavalry Corps. The freedom of a horse, a plan and miles of open country seemed to clear his head. He knew now why he had dropped that handkerchief. Because he wanted the freedom to live like this.

Because he hated her, for shredding his confidence over the years.

Because when Vigtyr had turned his mirror to the wall, Bellamus had understood why immediately.

Because all that he ever had been, and taken pleasure in, and loved, had been lost to the Queen of Albion.

And he would burn anything to get it back.

42
The Crossroads

'It's working,' said Diethaad, impressed.

'They had no choice, really,' Bellamus observed.

Widukind's northern column had forced the Anakim to flee south. They would find a defensive position, backs to the sea, and meet Bellamus there. Or so they thought. Bellamus himself had no intention of attacking a desperate Anakim army: not until he had made them more desperate still.

Bellamus was impressed by how Widukind's column was performing. The bishop's fanatical zeal and his silent, strangely compelling Abbio had whipped his men into a fervour, and they were marching faster than Bellamus would have thought possible. They had cut the Anakim off, and were now wheeling round the outside edge of the Suthern army as it hinged like a door, pressing the Anakim against Albion's southern coast.

'You've not spent much time with the queen lately,' Diethaad noted.

'I've been busy.'

'You're always busy.'

'But no mistakes now. This isn't even a once-in-a-generation opportunity. It's once-an-epoch. Throw this away and history would never forgive me.'

'You don't give a shit about history,' said Diethaad suspiciously.

'It's hard not to, when it is so obviously watching, pen loaded, parchment blank.' Bellamus was nearly convincing himself.

Not Diethaad it seemed. 'But you've got men watching you sleep. Why?'

Bellamus did not reply.

'Are you worried you're going to be arrested?'

'That will do.'

Diethaad raised his eyebrows but left it there.

It was true, Bellamus did not care about history. But it was hard not to be compelled by this moment, when so many different roads burst from it. If it came to a fight, it would be the largest – and perhaps most significant – battle that Albion had ever seen. All of their enemies were in one place, and all of their leaders. There was no one left in the Black Kingdom who might take command if the Anakim were defeated. Albion would be theirs.

But the Anakim knew that. They knew that although they fought in alien lands, it was their home, their children, and their society that would be overwhelmed if they lost. They were cornered, and Bellamus feared that. It is not easy to destroy a people. He would rather watch them fade than try to stamp them out.

The queen did not send for him that day. Perhaps she had been irritated by his restlessness a few nights before, but whatever the reason Bellamus was glad of it. He wanted to be nowhere near her tent, or her scent. He had already scrubbed himself in a freezing stream, though the water had done nothing for the guilt chewing at him. It seemed he had some strange affection for her, and could not help but wonder whether he would have done this if he had still been close with Stepan. The knight had always trusted Bellamus to restrain himself at the proper moment, and Bellamus had even begun to believe that was who he was. Without Stepan, he seemed unmoored.

By the day's end, Widukind had done as asked and cut off the road supplying the Anakim. They were trapped.

Lying beneath the stars that night, head resting on the saddlebag that was now his most constant companion, Bellamus could not keep his mind on the campaign. The queen might die, in the most horrible circumstances imaginable. *He* might die – had not that handkerchief been in his pocket?

I could tell her, he thought, then dismissed the idea. Even if he claimed it were an accident, she would execute him as a traitor. But what if he pretended to have learned through one of his spies that the Anakim were targeting her? He could give her the warning without admitting his part in it. He could alleviate this guilt, which might otherwise drive him mad. If that handkerchief had been found, and made its way into the hands of one of the blind assassins, it might still be weeks before the queen fell victim. He could not stay distant from her for all that time.

He glanced at the Thingman, Agnolo, he had set to watch them sleep. He was fidgeting, looking vaguely over the camp. Bellamus hesitated one moment longer and then threw off his cloak, getting silently to his feet. The queen was some miles back and on a night without a moon, the journey would be slow. He belted his long dagger at his side and set off on foot, through the winding roads.

'Lord?' whispered Agnolo, getting to his feet.

Bellamus waved him back down and indicated he wanted to be alone.

The camp was silent. The hearths were burnt low but for the occasional ember, and the crunch of his boots seemed the only sound at all.

He passed hedgerows laden with sour blackberries, and was once stopped in his tracks by a heavy rustling from the bushes beside him. Then a badger scampered across the road and disappeared beneath the neighbouring hedge. He laughed softly, feeling some relief already from having taken a decision.

He set off again humming an aimless tune, rounding a

corner and thinking it might have been years since he had last seen a badger. He had slept too long in comfortable rooms, looking out over manicured lawns. It took him several paces to realise there was a massive shadow sitting by the roadside. He jolted to a halt, hand flying instinctively to his long dagger. The figure's silhouette shifted slightly as it turned its head towards him, but it made no other move. It took Bellamus a moment to make out the face.

'Sir Stepan!'

The knight nodded his head. 'Lord Safinim.'

Bellamus felt as though he had been caught doing something he ought not. But there was nothing inherently suspicious about walking these roads at night. Was he not delivering a message for the queen? Still he managed to sound defensive. 'What are you doing here?'

'I was enjoying the solitude.'

Bellamus ignored this dismissal. 'As recommended by Widukind.'

'Indeed.'

'You are an acolyte of his now, I hear.'

Stepan shrugged. 'For my part. And you? What are you doing here?'

'I have a message for the queen.'

'You ought to deliver it, lord. Her Majesty is certainly a higher priority than I.'

It was the closest contact Bellamus had had with his old friend for years, time during which he had convinced himself they had both moved on. But evidently the knight had not forgiven him, and neither had Bellamus forgotten their friendship. 'Stepan . . . it's seven years. It was a mistake. I'm sorry. Do you really intend to carry a grudge for the rest of your life?'

Stepan was shaking his head. 'It's not a grudge, my lord. But I'm under no obligations to like you.'

Bellamus was thrown by this. 'Of course not,' he managed.

'Then let me be.'

Nobody had spoken to Bellamus like this in years. He

suddenly felt reduced to the rank of peasant once more, facing the indifference and hatred of his noble superiors. But there seemed no way this encounter would end positively. Without another word, he began walking again. He could feel his face burning in the dark. That, he thought angrily, was why it was such a poor idea to rely on others. They were too volatile to place one's trust in. Imagine holding a grudge for seven years!

He strode on, silently fuming the whole way. *Damn him.* Perhaps in their time apart, Stepan had acquired the widespread distaste for his low birth. It was not clear why else he should remain so cold.

He encountered nobody else before he was able to make out the pale mass of the queen's tent. *An error*, he thought angrily. He should have been checked several times before now. There was a sense of malaise filling his every corner, and he steeled himself for this performance. *Majesty*, he would say, *I must apologise for waking you but I've received intelligence which could not wait. Your life is in terrible danger.* She would ask him where this intelligence had come from, and he would say he could not reveal, lest it compromise his source. She would not accept that, of course, so what would he say then?

He was approaching the tent from its southern aspect, and paused. Something was wrong. There were still no guards.

Then he saw a dark shape, lying full length at the base of the pavilion wall. And beside it, a loose corner of canvas, bellying gently in the breeze.

Bellamus ground to a halt and stared dumbly at this scene. He cast about, but could see nobody in the dark. Swiftly he crossed to the body. It was a royal retainer, still warm to the touch but eyes fixed and unblinking. Bellamus wiped the dead man's brow and inspected his fingertips, moist with the droplets of sweat which had beaded there. He could not have been dead for more than a few minutes.

There might still be time.

Bellamus straightened up and took a breath. He paused. Nobody had seen him come here – nobody except Stepan. He thought of Aramilla, likely sound asleep as the blind assassin slid closer, drawn in by her scent. He thought of her cruelty, her callousness, her fickle whims. Of being so beholden to her power and status that he had to tolerate all that. Of the way the court despised him, and how every last one of them looked at him as though he had spent the night in a sty.

The world seemed to be spinning. The possibilities and risk tumbling from this moment and this decision were limitless, and he had to decide now. It was not as simple as doing nothing and letting this situation take its course. He had to commit to whatever happened and the chaos that would undoubtedly result. If he let this happen, there would be a scramble for power. Everything would be thrown into jeopardy on the eve of battle with the Anakim.

He hesitated. Then he turned back the way he had come.

Part III
BELLAMUS

43
The Cell

Ormur dreamed, or he hallucinated. He saw Gray, twisted so profoundly that his limbs were stretched like oak branches. He lay in a corner of Ormur's cell like a discarded doll, arms and legs trailing out in front of him, a look of disappointment on his face every time he saw Ormur whimper during his beatings.

He saw Keturah laughing and drinking by a fire with Cold Voice. In his dream, they were visible through non-existent bars in his cell, and he waved frantically that he was here and needed help. Keturah spotted him, nudged Cold Voice and the two shared a sly joke before turning away. And in the darkness, it was becoming difficult to distinguish between dreams and memories. It was only when Cold Voice came to visit him next that he realised that human beings did not have limbs like tree branches, and his visions of Gray could not be real.

'Good morning, Ormur.' That familiar cold whisper through the door. Ormur could never hear his footsteps approaching, and at the sound of the locking bar clunking back, a wave of dread swept over him.

Morning? Ormur would never adjust to time in this place. That would make it only the third day he had been here, but it felt like weeks. There were endless hours in which his thoughts ran wild. He was always in pain from his beatings and burnings, and hungry, and thirsty, and worst of all, consumed by self-disgust that he had been broken so easily. He could not handle the uncertainty of the locking bar scraping back, and whether he should expect a beating, verbal evisceration, or that occasional kindness that he desperately wanted to latch onto but made the punishment so much worse. And the despair: the pure hopelessness of knowing this was the rest of his existence. That all the joy and pride and friendship in his life were behind him and the last thing he would know was agony.

The door opened and, as usual, the dazzling light of a single oil lamp preceded Cold Voice into the cell. Ormur threw up a hand to cover his eyes and backed against the wall. Any thoughts of ambushing him were gone completely. He was desperate for one of the occasions when Cold Voice spoke words of encouragement, deposited fresh water and left Ormur in the dark without burns, lacerations and bruises.

Cold Voice spied him in the corner and bared a smile sharp as a knife. 'You can relax. You won't be beaten this time.' He licked his lips. 'I've got something worse than that.'

Ormur steeled himself, but Cold Voice was in no hurry, just relishing the sight of him. He wanted to demand they got this over with. But the words would not come. He could not remember the last time he had uttered a noise with any meaning beyond despair.

Three days. How can it only have been three days?

Cold Voice was looking at him intently, and raised the lamp so that he was properly illuminated. 'You're a sorry sight. I don't think I've ever seen a prisoner collapse so completely.' He laughed. 'I actually pity you.' He lingered on Ormur, gazing at him. 'And you've not even heard the worst of it. There's been a battle, in Blacklaw. Keturah and Tekoa were being bullied back by the Teuta and tried a night-attack to break through. They got smashed. The Teuta are retaking land without opposition, and look certain to make it to Lundenceaster.

And Keturah's been injured. They're not sure she's going to live.' His news delivered, Cold Voice backed out, the door thudding shut behind him.

Ormur's thoughts began to churn. He saw Keturah, grim-faced and pale, limping past his cell with Suthern horsemen thundering after her, their lances lowered for the charge. He saw Tekoa surrounded, yelling and purple in the face with rage as he was cut down and hacked apart, but still expostulating indignantly long after his wounds should have killed him.

He did not care if these visions were real or not: they were the only thing he knew. They may as well have been real, and death was his only escape. But how? The only way was to force Cold Voice to deal a fatal blow. But every trace of resolve had been taken from Ormur, and he no longer had the strength to carry that through.

Ormur discovered he was screaming. He bellowed and sobbed as he lay in the darkness, desperate for this to end and knowing it never would.

But there was something else under his cries. Something soothing and sweet. He took a long while to realise that it was not his voice at all. He could hear something else. His howls died away and he listened into the cell. All he could hear was his own panting and sniffing. He was sure there had been something, maybe even words.

Then they came again through the door, clear as a flute.

'Is that you, my brother?'

44
The Captain

Ormur had stopped breathing. This might be another hallucination, but it was an exceptionally sweet one. He would live it, if he had to.

'Gray?' He croaked, feeling foolish to have even said that name. 'Sir?'

'Quiet, lad,' came the urgent whisper. 'Can you use a sword?'

'A sword . . .' Ormur was disoriented. 'How can you have a sword?'

'I have two. Can you use one of them?'

'But . . . you're here . . . they've captured you.'

'I am here, but it is I who has caught them,' said Gray. 'There's no time, brother, I'll explain later. Can you use a sword?'

Ormur could feel his heart pounding. This could not be real. It made no sense.

'Truly . . .'

It did not matter. He wanted to believe. Ormur flexed his fingers. The smallest digit on his left hand was excruciating, his ribs hurt with every breath, and he was so stiff and sore in each joint that he could barely move. But heavier than all of that was the fear and helplessness which smothered him.

Can you use a sword, Ormur? 'Yes,' he said. Anger was

rising, pushing back against the fear and he seized on it, using it to pull himself up.

The locking bar slid back. So strongly did Ormur associate that noise with suffering that he flinched away. Gray could not really be here: it was another hallucination.

The door creaked open. Still Ormur could see nothing: it was too dark.

Then a warm hand found his shoulder and gave that familiar squeeze. With it came a waft of the myrtle with which Gray and Sigrid washed their clothes. Ormur could not help himself: he wept. He leaned forward into Gray and sobbed silently, while the captain embraced him.

'It's all right, my brother. I'm sorry it took so long. I'm sorry.'

Ormur tried to speak but the sobs were too thick.

'Come on, lad. We've got no time and we need to move.'

Ormur shook his head. 'I'm dreaming!'

'You're not, lad. You didn't think I'd leave you here?'

Ormur was half in shock, the grief of his imprisonment flooding out. But it seemed beneath that was another half: one trained for years and acting now without input. Even as he sobbed, his hand was casting about in the dark. Gray found it and guided it towards the handle of a sword. Ormur shivered to feel the rough fish-skin grip.

'How many of them?' he asked.

'I've counted a dozen,' said Gray. 'And they have another prisoner besides you.'

'Who?'

Gray hesitated. 'I don't know.'

'Where is this place? And who are these men? Why are they doing this?'

'We haven't got time for all that, but you know the answers anyway.'

In his heart, he did. 'They are the Kryptea. And we are in the Kungargrav.'

'Yes.'

There was a silence. The sword hilt in his hand was as

heavy and comforting as the leash of a wolfhound. 'The other prisoner . . .'

'I don't know,' repeated Gray quickly. 'But obviously they're quite willing to abduct passers-by. Don't . . . don't presume anything.'

'But Gray—'

'Enough talking now, they pass through here often enough and we need to act.'

'Are we escaping?'

Again, Gray hesitated. 'The prisoner . . .' he said. 'The other one. We're going to free them.'

'Do you think we can?' Ormur hated himself for asking, but he half hoped Gray would agree it was too risky and they ought to leave at once.

'I think we should.'

Ormur gritted his teeth, saying nothing.

Gray's hand encircled his upper arm, feeling how wasted he was. 'You think you can fight? Truly?'

'Them. I can fight them.'

'Come, then. They don't know we're here. Poor souls only outnumber us six to one.'

A grin came to Ormur's face, invisible in the blackness. He heard Gray turn away and grabbed his arm. 'There's a tall thin one, lanky like a skeleton. I want him.'

'He's yours. Do you remember the way out?'

'No. I wasn't clear-headed when I came in. I've forgotten.'

'Anyone would've forgotten after two weeks.'

'Two weeks?' said Ormur numbly. 'No. It's been three days.' He thought. 'They said it was three days.'

'You believed them?'

'I didn't . . .'

That suddenly seemed absurdly foolish, but they had controlled everything. His reality was theirs to warp, and as their hold over time broke, a sort of sanity returned to him. They had never captured Gray. Keturah was not injured, the legions not defeated. And Ormur himself. He was not weak at all. He had survived two weeks of starvation, not struggled with three days of full rations. Perhaps he was not the weakest prisoner Cold Voice had ever seen after all. Perhaps what he had been asked to resist, alone, was impossible.

'Hold onto my tunic so you don't lose me.'

Ormur was gripping the tunic with one hand, the other clutching the sword equally fiercely.

'Come on. We have work to do.'

45
Name Him

Gray and Ormur shuffled through the dark. Gray navigated by touch, his hand only leaving the rough walls to cross invisible hallways and corridors.

'How did you find me?' whispered Ormur.

'Later,' Gray replied. 'We're nearly at the main hall and there's always someone on guard.'

Much later, Gray would relay how he had spent two days groping through this labyrinth. For now, there seemed to be light ahead: a faint aura of it, radiating up the passage. Soon walls were beginning to resolve in the gloom, and when they slipped round a last corner, they found a cavernous hall. There was a staircase leading down into its centre, and a crackling hearth set into one stone wall, beside which sat two sentries on three-legged stools.

Their backs were turned to Gray and Ormur, and neither turned as the two guardsmen drifted closer.

It is near impossible to kill a man in silence. The neck is full of stiff structures which will resist the progress of a knife, often giving the victim time to cry out. A blow over the head is more decisive, but must be exceedingly hard and creates its own thump. Perhaps the quietest option is also the slowest.

Gray and Ormur lingered behind the oblivious Krypteans. Gray held up three fingers, then two, then one. Both guardsmen lunged forward, wrapping a forearm about a Kryptean neck, the other arm clamping it into place. Almost in the same movement, they were dragging their victims backwards so they could not gain their feet. Both stools toppled over and rattled off the stone as the two Krypteans flailed.

Gray's man reached up at once to try and prise the arm free from his neck. His fingers were sharp and desperate, but Gray kept reversing and the man could not get a proper grip, nor exert any control on where they moved. There was the soft squeak of boots on stone, the flap of stiff clothes moving rapidly and the hard breathing of the guardsmen. Distant blows were hammering at Gray's arm and sides, but he would not relent.

It was over in a few heartbeats. His victim began to jerk and twitch, eyes fluttering closed and arms ticking down by his sides in degrees. Ormur and Gray bore their enemies to the floor, but still they kept a tight grip. Release now and they would recover almost at once. They held and held and held, until they were certain both had been extinguished.

'Well done,' whispered Gray. 'Hide them back here.'

They dragged the two bodies into one of the dark corridors, and then Gray beckoned down another ink-black passage. He saw Ormur's face as the firelight flashed briefly over it. His protégé was deathly pale, his eyes very wide as they slid into the gloom.

'Are you all right?'

Ormur did not reply, but kept walking steadily alongside him.

'At the end of this passage,' Gray murmured, 'is their mess. There's usually a few of them in there and weapons by the door. Get between them and the weapons and we'll be wolves in a sheep fold.'

They could hear voices now, echoing through the dark. There was distant laughter and jeers, and a pinprick of light visible in the distance: an open doorway at the end of a straight corridor. Through it they could see the small gestures of seated men. The guardsmen were quite exposed to the open doorway and the half-dozen figures lounging within, but the passage was gloomy, the Kryptean mess bright, and nobody was watching for approaching enemies.

'Sword,' hissed Gray, and he heard Ormur's weapon slide clear of the sheath. 'Don't hesitate, brother.'

Ormur did not, darting in front of him to be first through the door. The nearest Krypteans glanced around, faces comfortable and enquiring.

They saw what Gray saw: a gaunt figure, hollow-cheeked and angular, with three missing teeth exposed by a snarl. The sunken eyes were ringed with clouded purple, the hair matted with dried blood. Without even looking at the nearest man, Ormur cut his throat with a vicious back-slice.

The laughter perished, and there was silence but for the scrape of chairs and stumbling feet as the Krypteans recoiled. Ormur's first victim toppled over backwards and landed with a crash, choking and twisting onto his side to try and breathe.

Gray stepped out from behind his protégé and his predictions of a sheep fold were realised. It was pandemonium: shouts, swearing, flustered scrambling and drops of blood spattering the long central table. One man upset some wooden goblets from a side table, seizing it by the legs and swinging it wildly at Gray. He stepped aside, sword arcing down to cut off the man's right hand and then booting him to the floor. He stole a glance at Ormur and was, briefly, captivated.

It was a beautiful thing to watch the transformation when his protégé took up a sword. Day to day, he was an uncomfortable soul, seldom looking even his friends in the eye and edging into each room as though he had never seen such a crowd before. But when fighting, he was possessed by the focus and balance of an amber-eyed predator. His awkwardness became an awareness of his surroundings better than anyone Gray had seen. Each move was deliberate, each attack made in the certain knowledge that he had thought three steps ahead of his enemy. He was not one of those warriors like Pryce had been, or Leon, or Vigtyr, who delighted in the one-to-one duel as though stepping from the verses of a saga. Any of them would have smashed Ormur one-to-one, but with an enemy who outnumbered them, there was no one Gray would rather have had at his side. The boy saw everything.

The mess was cleared in heartbeats. The last man was left stranded in a corner, hands raised in quarter. 'Please!'

Gray was closer, but Ormur got there first, punching a blade through his guts, up beneath his bone armour and into his chest. The man coughed brokenly, blood spattering his lips, one hand jumping to where the sword pierced his belly, the other flattening over his chest. Then he slid aside, slipping off the wall and onto the floor.

Ormur withdrew his sword and cleaned it on one of the bodies, Gray watching him.

'I've seen you do that before,' he commented. 'In through the guts, up into the chest. Bypasses the bone armour, I suppose.'

Ormur shrugged. 'I find you glance off too often if you try to go through the bone.' He was trembling.

'All right?' Gray asked.

He shrugged again. 'Cold Voice wasn't here.'

'We'll find him.'

For the first time, they were able to absorb their surroundings. The room was lit by a crackling fire, with strips of venison smoking in the chimney. Spread over the long central table was the detritus of spare time: knuckle bones, a chessboard with pieces carved from antler, goblets and half-finished works of scrimshaw. In a neighbouring room they found mounds of neatly-split firewood and a dark well, an oily shimmer of water gleaming at its bottom.

'Four of them left that I know,' said Gray. 'Two of us. Dare we risk a little light?'

'I never want to go through that dark again,' said Ormur.

They took a lamp from the Kryptean mess, and leaving the bodies where they had fallen, turned back. A block of light kept pace with the lamp clutched in Ormur's left hand, glinting off the bloody swords held out before them.

'How will we find the last of them?' Ormur whispered as they re-entered the hall, fire still crackling unattended in the hearth.

'I wouldn't even bother looking. Let's find their other prisoner. If we run into them on the way then so be it. If not, we leave this place and pile stones over the exit. Let the bastards die down here.'

It was strange for Gray to be able to see this place which he had only navigated by touch: it did not look at all as he had expected. He led them down another passage to reveal another stairway, vanishing into shadow. It was steep, the steps eroded in the centre and blocks in the ceiling on the verge of falling out. 'Glad we took the lamp,' he whispered. 'This is a perilous descent without it.'

Moisture was beginning to leak in patches down the walls, some of the old stones near cut in half by the ceaseless trickle. The stairs were dark with damp, some written with footprints which told of several men going down, none coming up the other way. 'It seems we'll meet them anyway,' said Gray, indicating the prints.

There was soon so much water perfusing the walls that they could even hear it: a soft gurgle as it found the gaps in the ancient stonework and trickled down the stairs.

'If we go much deeper, we'll be underwater,' Gray whispered. Whispered, because he thought there might be light down below.

There was.

A few yards beneath, the staircase levelled out, illuminated by the dim sunset of another oil lamp. Gray heard Ormur pause behind him, but he gestured his protégé onwards. They should continue towards the light as though there was nothing wrong.

'Well?' called a voice that made Gray's hair stand on end.

Whoever was down here had evidently heard their footsteps. 'What is it?'

He could hear Ormur's breath whistling through the gaps in his teeth as they rounded the corner. Four Krypteans stood in the passage before them, craning towards the approaching light. Two clutched oil lamps, all had swords belted at their sides, and at the sight of the two guardsmen, all four recoiled. Towering above the group was a skeletal figure, glaring at Ormur with narrowed eyes.

'You?' he said in disbelief.

Then one of the others yelled and reached for a weapon. He managed to scrape a sword clear of its scabbard just in time to parry Gray's attack. Another lunged in from the side and Gray parried, white sparks springing from the two weapons and flashing over the gloom like lightning. Gray looked up at the man who had attacked him, just in time to see Ormur's sword drilling through the side of his head and clobbering him flat.

All three lamps were dropped in a tinkle of breaking earthenware. All three were extinguished, but one cracked open in a wash of oil, and either the wick was still hot, or a stray spark from the clashing swords caught the warm oil, and flames leapt up, conical and spirit-blue, casting the room in fluttering shadows. There were only outlines and flashes as blades met and burst apart.

Ormur had taken on two assailants, stepping left and right so that they got in each other's way and he could isolate them. Gray faced the skeleton, beating aside a near-invisible sword on instinct. It had been a wild parry and he could not recover in time, so he stepped close, inside his enemy's guard. He could feel the skeletal man's sword sawing at his side as he tried to pull it back far enough for a lunge, but he ignored it. Lacking a left hand, he hammered an elbow up into his enemy's jaw. He was rocked backwards but managed to keep his feet, and still they were too close for swords or kicks. Gray heaved a knee into his groin, doubling him over, then dropped Ramnea so he could hook both arms over the back of his bony neck, dragging it down and raising his knee again to split the nose of the man Ormur called Cold Voice. He collapsed.

Ormur was still holding off two, and Gray's hand found Ramnea's pale handle, gleaming like a beacon in the dark. He paused a heartbeat to make sense of the flitting shadows and vicious flashes, then skewered one of Ormur's opponents in the back. He screamed and arched away from the attack, while Ormur finished the other with his favoured back-slice to the neck.

The man Gray had stabbed in the back was bellowing frantically, a sudden feral energy on him as he tried to dislodge Ramnea, but he was stilled by a final back-slice from Ormur.

'All right, brother?'

Ormur nodded curtly. 'Thank you.'

'I wasn't going to leave you to finish them alone.'

Ormur indicated the spindly figure folded on the floor. 'I meant for him.'

There was just enough of the mountain-blue light cast by the pool of burning oil to make out Cold Voice's eyes, watching them from the stones.

'He tortured you?'

'And worse.'

'We should ask him some questions before you have your fun.'

'We'll do both at the same time. He'll answer faster.'

They salvaged the one oil lamp that had not cracked, and lit it from the last vaporous flames flickering on the floor. A yellow glow warmed the damp walls, and Cold Voice's face was revealed. Blood was streaming from his nose and his eyes flicked rapidly between the pair of them.

'How many of you are there?' Gray began.

'Ten in total,' said Cold Voice without hesitation.

The two guardsmen did not react for a moment. Then Ormur stepped forward and stamped on his face.

'A lie,' said Gray, as Cold Voice cried out. 'We know most of the answers we're asking you for. Now I ask you again. How many?'

'Twelve,' mumbled Cold Voice, spraying blood from a split lip.

That was probably true, and Gray let it pass. 'What is this place?'

Cold Voice shook his head. 'Just a prison.'

'A prison for who?'

'Traitors. We work as hard for the Black Kingdom as you do. Harder. We just disagree on what is good for it.'

'Why am I a traitor?' asked Ormur.

'You are a traitor by proximity,' said Cold Voice. 'By blood. You were brother to a Black Lord. You support the Stone Throne and a corrupt system of power.'

They ignored that.

'But it isn't just passing guardsmen you kidnap,' said Gray. 'What about all the others who've gone missing near this place?'

Cold Voice shook his head. 'Our work is sacred. I make no apology for protecting it from anyone who threatens it.'

There was a pause, when everyone's attention seemed drawn to the thing behind Cold Voice. Set into the wall was another low door, like the one from which Ormur had emerged. Another cell in which a prisoner waited, listening to the clash of swords outside without uttering a sound.

'Who is your prisoner?'

Cold Voice shrugged again. 'Someone like you.' Suddenly he lunged for one of the weapons on the floor. Gray raised his sword but before he could act, Ormur had stamped on his wrist, pinning it to the flagstones. 'You denied me the chance to kill myself,' he said, voice shaking a little. 'I burden you with that same restriction.'

Gray held a hand out in front of Ormur. 'Who's the other prisoner?' he asked again, quite calmly.

Cold Voice shook his head. 'I told you, someone like you. I don't know his name. We aren't told. Just someone dangerous.'

Gray lowered his sword slowly over Cold Voice, but it was Ormur who spoke next.

'You do know his name,' he said, the quake in his voice more pronounced now. Gray glanced at his protégé, who had raised the oil lamp over Cold Voice. The supine Kryptean was frozen, wrist pinned beneath Ormur's boot, eyes on the oil lamp tilted above him. 'That's why you captured me, instead of killing me. You were going to use me to get to him.'

'Ormur,' said Gray, raising the stump of his left hand. 'Careful.'

Ormur's whole body was vibrating, his shoulders heaving with some grief or rage he was trying to fight. 'Name him. You've tortured him for seven years.'

Cold Voice said nothing, just staring at the oil lamp trembling above him.

'Ormur,' said Gray again. 'We need him.'

'You snake!' shouted Ormur, almost sobbing now. 'You heinous bastards! Say it! Name him!' And he tipped the oil lamp sideways, emptying its full contents over Cold Voice's head and torso.

Gray dropped Ramnea with a clang, stepping forward and meaning to grab hold of Ormur's wrist, but he was not fast enough. Ormur flung the lamp and its flaming wick down at his tormentor. It hit him, bounced off and there was a moment when it looked as though the oil had not caught.

Then Cold Voice was engulfed.

Fire swept his body, so bright that Gray threw up an arm to shield himself from the flash. For two heartbeats, Cold Voice's only reaction was that his eyes went shockingly wide and white. Covered in fire, he simply froze, silent for far longer than Gray had anticipated.

Then he howled.

He wrenched at his wrist, trying to dislodge it from beneath Ormur's boot so he could roll and extinguish the flames. But Ormur simply stepped on his other wrist so that he was pinned half on his side. The flames were so fierce they must have been burning Ormur too, but he leaned down, looking Cold Voice in the face. 'Name him!'

Cold Voice screamed. It was an awful, sustained noise like tearing cloth which dragged on and on, fading into a quiet whistle, as though he could not get the air back into his lungs. Gray was standing back, biting his lip and looking down as flames ravaged Cold Voice, Ormur still stood above.

'Name him.'

46
The Queen is Dead

A battle of succession was about to take place, and if Bellamus wanted to play any role in it, he first had to contrive some means by which he could be present. He had distanced himself from the queen, and now the nobles of the realm, who had pitched their own pavilions as near Aramilla as possible, had a start on him. Their proximity would hand them an advantage when news of her death broke.

He had selected Agnolo to watch over him that night because he was particularly trusted by Bellamus. He was an agreeable rogue: happy, tousle-haired and loyal, though occasionally prone to bouts of apologetic armed robbery. Bellamus went to find him.

'Tonight,' he said, wrapping an arm around Agnolo's shoulders and steering him away from his post so they could talk together, 'you saw a creature which made you suspicious, moving through the undergrowth. You will report this to Diethaad, and as a result I will start a manhunt. Do you understand?'

'Not really, lord,' said Agnolo cheerfully.

'That's probably for the best, in the long run. Just stick to that story.'

'What kind of creature did I see?'

'You're not sure, but it looked like a crawling man.'

'It *did* look like a crawling man,' said Agnolo thoughtfully.

'And if you keep this deception to yourself,' Bellamus went on, 'entirely to yourself, and tell not another soul on this mortal plain, then I will make you the richest man in the county.'

'What deception, lord?'

'Good man. Now I want you to go and wake Diethaad and tell him what you saw.'

'Now, lord?'

'Now, please.'

Agnolo ambled off to find Diethaad, and Bellamus found a seat on the back of a wagon, where he occupied himself with the contents of his ever-present saddlebag. Stowed inside were half a dozen letters, puckered seals already broken. He counted through them quickly, confirmed the identities they had been addressed to, and then stowed them inside his jerkin. Then he lit a lamp beside him and, shuffling onto the bed of the wagon so that he sat against its side, knees drawn up as a table, began scratching out a letter to Widukind. He was barely halfway through when Diethaad came to him, bleary-eyed and irritable.

'Agnolo thinks he's seen something, lord.'

Bellamus looked up thoughtfully, sucking on the top of his quill as though not much interested, and the charade began.

It took half an hour of carefully escalated concern before every Thingalith was on horseback and poised to ride. Bellamus was mounted alongside Diethaad and Agnolo, and the urgent chatter of his men did much to cover Bellamus's own anxiety. The queen might not even be dead. Stepan might report that he had seen Bellamus walking the road to her pavilion, and he was now acting as though he had done no such thing. And others might have better-laid plans than his own. In a life which had turned a hundred times on such moments, it was his greatest gamble yet: his vast winnings to date, snatched up and laid on the table once more.

'Hush, boys!' he called, and his band was still just small enough that they could all hear if he shouted. 'Hush now! If the creature that Agnolo has seen is the one I fear, then its target will be Her Majesty. Fifty of you are to scour the countryside from the point it was last seen. You can't track from horseback, so you'll be doing it the slow way. Leave not a stone unturned, and *never* walk alone! The rest of you with me, we must safeguard the queen!' He pulled his horse about and felt the rumble as his men fell in behind.

'What makes you think it's going for Her Majesty?' asked Diethaad.

'Who would you go for, Diethaad?'

He shrugged as though the answer were obvious. 'I'd go for you.'

A rose dawn was blooming in the east and they galloped the path Bellamus had walked just a few hours before. The birds chorused their passage, and he could not help crane over the hedgerows to see if Stepan was still at the spot he had left him last night. But the big man was gone, and Bellamus turned his attention back to planning, considering his opponents' first, second and third moves and readying counters of his own.

They were nearly arrived when Bellamus turned to Agnolo. 'I'm taking a dozen men ahead. I want the rest of you to stay here, for now.'

'When should I come and join you, lord?'

Bellamus explained. 'But keep an eye open, and I think you'll see the moment.'

He rode on with a dozen of his best fighters. Diethaad was making efforts to catch his eye, which he ignored. When they spied the cluster of noble tents with the queen's pavilion at the centre, his heart sank.

'We're too late,' said Diethaad.

The place was in uproar.

Six sets of guards wearing six sets of livery over their armour were clustered outside the tents, all of them bellowing for sheer excitement. Sommers was there too, cackling like a demon watching the world ignite.

'Sommers!' Bellamus roared, dragging his horse to a dusty halt. 'What's this? What's happened?'

The buffoon turned on Bellamus, nearly writhing with glee. 'She's dead! The queen is strangled in her bed, the assassin nowhere to be seen!' He burst into hysterical laughter.

'Dear God,' said Bellamus, so feebly he flushed with sudden self-awareness. But no one seemed to notice. 'Six sets of livery here, Sommers. Where are their lords?'

'Inside! They flapped here for a bit, then the commotion boiled over and Sutton demanded to see her body. He's in there, Lord Upstart! The others followed him in.'

Bellamus was out of the saddle already. His guts were churning as the reality of this situation settled over him. He was about to try and take the throne. Everything he had fought for, and chanced; every inch he had scrambled, further than he had had any right to expect, was to be risked yet again.

'Diethaad!' he called over his shoulder.

'I know, lord, I know,' said his lieutenant calmly.

Bellamus left him behind and brushed into the pavilion's gloom. A maid was sobbing in a corner, being comforted by one of her peers. He ignored them, sweeping through another two flaps until he was in the queen's bedchamber. It was populated with six embroidered lords, all in various states of agitation, and another six royal retainers: Aramilla's household guard, and the only armed persons permitted within the pavilion. The space was dominated by a great four-poster, its bedclothes torn off and knotted about the figure lying at its edge. Nearest was Sutton, heaving with emotion, who glanced up as Bellamus entered.

'Safinim!' he exclaimed, seeming nearly pleased to see him. 'What are you doing here? Your mistress is dead, and you're nothing again. Get out of here, you low villain. Out! You've no royal protection any more!'

Bellamus raised his hands. 'Calm yourself, my lord. You're overexcited.'

Sutton rolled his eyes. 'Plans are in motion that don't involve you, Safinim, and thank your low luck that they don't. Leave now, while we let you.'

He would have said more, but Ruden entered, and the others fell silent at the sight of him.

'Gentlemen,' he said nodding civilly to them all. 'What a terrible day. May I see her?'

A relative calm came over the party. The royal retainers shuffled hastily out of his path and even Sutton stood aside so that Ruden could cross to the queen. He laid a hand on her shoulder and closed her eyes, holding them shut for a time. That was as long as the peace was permitted to last.

Lord Doronon bounced through the entrance, followed by the grey-haired Lord Nerven. 'What is *he* doing here?' asked the latter, looking askance at Bellamus.

Sutton took up the attack once more. 'As I said, your day is done, dog! Out! Out!'

But he was interrupted by more lords bursting into the chamber each moment, uttering expostulations of grief, expressions of outrage and anger, and beneath all that, was an excited murmur. Soon a score of them were convened, the atmosphere more like the end of a decades-long drought than the death of a queen. Here was an opportunity to make dynasties. And settle old scores.

Almost as one, they turned on Bellamus.

'Lord Safinim, as was,' said Nerven. 'A queen of Albion has just died. What business has a foreign commoner here? Be gone! Be gone!'

The assembled lords started jeering, faces turned towards Bellamus and alive with malice.

'Out! Out! Out!' began Sutton, and soon the rest had taken up the chant. Bellamus stood unmoved, but his placid confidence seemed to enrage them. The nearest lords, Doronon, Melcombe and Offring, began jostling him with hard shoves, hoping either to bully him out of the tent or escalate the shouts of the crowd to physical violence. The tent was brimming, an instant from boiling over.

It was at this point that Diethaad chose to enter.

He processed in at the head of a column of Thingalith, so silent and darkly garbed that at first they were ignored, as though they were the servants come to clear the wreckage of a feast. But as the numbers following Diethaad grew from ten, to twenty, to thirty men lining the walls, the noise died away. There was a collective settling as the lords eased away from Bellamus's person. Calmly he straightened his clothes. The six royal retainers had backed together, each clutching a halberd as though it were a talisman.

Sutton was the first to speak. 'Arrest them!' he commanded, pointing at the Thingalith. Then he blushed to hear his words ring absurdly through the chamber. The retainers made no move. Diethaad caught the eye of their captain and winked.

'Brought your thugs in I see, Safinim,' said Nerven. 'Appropriate for the death of a queen, d'you think?'

'They are merely here to ensure everyone is heard over the din,' said Bellamus curtly. 'Naturally there will be some upheaval when a monarch dies, and I feared there might be less decorum than would be proper for the moment.'

Everyone present knew these thirty men made Bellamus the most influential person in the room. They also knew that if it came to it, the army was largely loyal to Bellamus. But they were nobly born, unused to ceding power and derisive of the upstart's claims to it.

'We all have armed men, just on the other side of this canvas,' said Ruden, tapping the tent wall. 'You cannot think to get away with bringing these soldiers in here.'

'Not as armed as you left them, I'm afraid, my lord,' put in Diethaad apologetically.

Ruden glanced swiftly about the room, and Bellamus took note of who met his eyes.

'Ya!' jeered Sutton. 'So the upstart has come to value what

was only loaned to him, and now thinks he owns. You want in on the games of power, is that it, Safinim?'

'It is not power I seek, but justice,' said Bellamus calmly. 'I have always protected Her Majesty's interests. Her death does not change that. Quite the contrary.'

'Justice,' said Ruden thoughtfully, looking at Bellamus as though disappointed. 'I hope you have an exceptionally good reason for your actions today. Disarming the noblest men in the realm is not commonly excused by recourse to *justice*.'

'Not so, Lord Ruden,' Bellamus corrected pleasantly, 'if those men are guilty of high treason.'

There was a stunned silence. Then came uproar.

The spell cast by the Thingalith was broken and the nobility were once again spitting vile curses at Bellamus, pointing vicious fingers at him and swearing they would see him swing. Bellamus raised his hands and waited for the noise to subside, but it did not. Not until Diethaad drew his sword and held it loosely by his side. That bright flash of steel gave the assembly pause, and Bellamus spoke before the muttering had quite died away.

'I present the evidence for my charges,' he said clearly, drawing the sheaf of letters from his jerkin. He unfurled the first of them and held it out for examination. 'Is this your seal, my Lord Ruden?' he enquired, directing them to the great splash of wax. 'Are these your words?'

Ruden hesitated. Then he edged through the crowd, murmuring pardons until he was able to inspect the letter up close. 'What of it?'

'It very kindly offers me your full support in all my endeavours.'

Ruden's smile was slightly incredulous. 'I hadn't anticipated this day, I must admit, Safinim.'

The lords laughed, and Bellamus smiled back.

'Nevertheless, these are your words?'

Ruden shrugged. 'They were.'

'Thank you.' Bellamus inserted the letter back into his

jerkin and produced another. As he did so, Diethaad came closer to his side, sword still low and naked. 'This one came into my possession as part of the duties I performed for Her Majesty. It's not your seal, Lord Ruden, but you may recognise the writing. And the signature.'

Without letting it go, Bellamus held it out for the inspection of those nearest. As it passed by Sutton, he lashed out and tried to seize it. Bellamus snatched it away and took a pace back.

'Quite right, Lord Sutton,' he said pleasantly, 'it was addressed to you. I hope you won't mind if I read it out? It's rather important, but don't worry, we needn't hear all of it. This passage should suffice.' Bellamus cleared his throat. '*As ever it was your company which proved the greatest satisfaction, my Lord Sutton. I have tonight conveyed your desire to assist my Master's interests on these shores, and shall inform you the instant I have a reply. However you may rest assured he is famous for rewarding loyalty with the most extreme generosity.*'

There was a sickly silence in the room as Bellamus folded the letter and threw it down on the floor before him.

'Treason, I think you'll agree, my lords.'

'May I see that letter, Safinim?' said Offring coldly, taking a step forward.

'I see that it doesn't bear my seal,' said Ruden, glaring at Bellamus.

Bellamus was able to silence these objections with a single raised finger. 'My lords will note who protested before and now utters not a sound,' he said. 'There may be something in it. Lord Melcombe, you've gone silent. How wise.'

Bellamus tossed another letter down on top of the first, this one bearing Melcombe's title on the front. He had gone white, and stared at the letter in sickly quiet.

'Don't worry, my Lord Melcombe. You're in good company.' Bellamus withdrew a third letter and threw it upon the others. 'Lord Nerven.' Bellamus looked up to see the effect this had had. The assembly was thrown into a silence that deepened as each new letter went down, and each new name was spoken.

Lord Karnow.

Lord Hamwic.

Lord Badon.

Six lords were denounced in total, the room darkening as each name was read out. The rest examined guilty consciences and held their breath, fearing their own name next.

But Bellamus left it at those six. He looked around the room, waiting for a response.

'Forgeries,' declared Lord Nerven dispassionately.

'No, I'm afraid not, my lord,' said Bellamus. 'Your servant, Gunweard . . . Well I'm afraid he's really *my* servant, Gunweard. He obtained the letter from your own study.'

Ruden's hand was tugging at his beard. 'And I suppose the excellent Octric is still your man as well.'

Bellamus shrugged apologetically.

'You spied on us, you low person?' spat Sutton, anger breaking his silence.

'The *queen* spied on you,' said Bellamus. 'I was merely her instrument. And can you say she was wrong, Sutton? Six of you, I find, in collusion with a foreign power to assist his coming to the throne.'

'That's not what the letter said!' Sutton objected.

'Lord Sutton!' Bellamus had suddenly swollen, his chest puffing out and an aura radiating from him like a physical barrier so that the nearest lords seemed forced backward. 'Hold your tongue! We know what it said. We know who benefits from the death of the queen, and here she lies, murdered. What sort of servant to Her Majesty would I be if I did not arrest every last one of you?'

There was silence. The six lords named were some of the most powerful in the kingdom. With them taken down, there were precious few around which a coalition to defeat Bellamus might rally. Agnolo entered the room and tapped Bellamus on the shoulder, muttering into his ear. Bellamus nodded and dismissed his man with a wave.

'Safinim,' said Ruden raising his hands placatingly. 'You must hear us out. Her Majesty's death is a calamity, but surely this bears the hallmark of the Anakim assassin who tried to kill your man Vigtyr?'

'Indeed,' put in Nerven. 'Does anyone here truly doubt I would serve the queen until my last breath? I have *nothing* to do with this appalling scene.'

'How could these lords you accuse even have facilitated this?' asked Ruden.

'All too easily,' replied Bellamus. 'All that was needed was an item recently touched by Her Majesty. As all of you knew. As I warned you all.'

'Well, I admit I have difficulty imagining any of these men taking such unholy measures,' said Ruden. 'Collaborating with the Anakim – creatures spat from hell itself – to facilitate the death of our queen. But what now, Safinim? We are on the eve of battle. You surely don't believe we can fight so divided. Or are the Anakim to delay politely while we conduct our trial?'

'Any trial must wait,' said Bellamus. 'We have our enemy in a more perfect position than we could dare hope. To squander that would be an enormous crime.'

Ruden frowned. 'I think you'd struggle to control my soldiers, Safinim. Particularly if I were in a dungeon.'

Bellamus affected a look of surprise. 'But you were never a subject of Her Majesty. You've committed no treason. I shall greatly rely on your troops in the coming days.'

This proposal caused consternation among the six accused lords, who stirred suddenly, every eye swivelling to Ruden. He had been offered a way out. If he took it, their cause would be stripped of King Karoli's influence, who would not expend a moment's effort on exposed conspirators. A look of surprised delight was spreading over Ruden's broad features, as though he were watching a favoured child reveal prodigious musical talent.

'Generous, Lord Safinim,' he murmured. 'Very generous. And what is to happen to these six lords you accuse here?' He gestured at the condemned nobles.

'That will depend on their trial.'

'But are they being charged? Here and now?'

'Lord Ruden,' said Bellamus wearily. 'You can keep me talking for as long as you see fit. I enjoy your company. But if you're waiting for the relieving force of two hundred halberdiers who you commanded here, then I'm afraid they've been waylaid.'

Ruden raised his eyebrows. 'Waylaid?' he said innocently.

'My man Agnolo has just told me. There was no need for them here, of course, so my men told them not to bother.'

Ruden grinned ruefully. 'I had the same plan as you, Safinim. Make sure there was no unrest on this tragic occasion, eh? But I suppose you've beaten me to it.'

'So what in God's name happened in there?' Bellamus and Diethaad exited the royal pavilion, scuttling faster and faster, as though each carried half the crown jewels tucked beneath a jerkin.

'I just inherited the throne of Suthdal,' Bellamus replied, giddy with it.

'I spotted that,' said Diethaad crisply. 'Don't forget I helped. I'll be wanting a duchy.'

'Your fee is exorbitant.'

'That'd make me your superior would it not? You can't call yourself king just yet. The nobles will need to be put in their place first.'

'I quite agree. Lord Defender, I was thinking.'

'Lord Regent?'

'Too near the bone. Lord Guardian?'

'A bit pompous. Lord Warden, perhaps.'

'Lord Warden,' Bellamus repeated thoughtfully. 'A temporary role in these extraordinary circumstances.'

'And next year?'

'There's always extraordinary circumstances. It's just a question of narrative.'

It was a diamond morning, soaked in the dew of late summer and a fragile moon of eggshell blue persisting overhead. The ground beyond the tent swarmed with Thingalith, prowling ranks of kneeling retainers who had come to lend influence to each lord inside the tent, and been disarmed. It had occurred to many of them that warriors in this time and place would give one disproportionate power, and thus disproportionate claim to this throne which had no heir. But the other lords had warriors almost as noble as they were: each with squires, servants and ceremonial armour that took half a morning to apply. Bellamus's Thingalith had been ready to move first and in greatest numbers.

'But go on,' said Diethaad. 'What exactly happened? I understood some of it, but not all.'

They had come to a halt on the far side of the field and stood together watching as the six accused lords were led out of the pavilion, escorted by fifty Thingalith. They were now hostages, in case their people attempted a revolt. Another score of Thingalith were going back to camp to retrieve Bellamus's effects and bring them here. If he was to be in command, he must occupy the royal premises.

'Ruden was sent here with two missions,' said Bellamus. 'The first was to keep the Anakim from dominating Albion. Karoli has no desire for an unchallenged Black Kingdom immediately off his coastline, free to accrue power and frustrate his ambitions. He has sent us an army with the genuine intention of stopping that from happening. But Ruden had another, secret mission: to lay the ground for a Frankish invasion. Karoli spotted chaos, and opportunity. He thinks that with Albion riven by infighting, it is his chance to take over, and move a step closer to complete hegemony of Erebos. Ruden was sent to foment unrest and take advantage of it. He's a shark, and to expose his plans, all I needed was to bleed into the water a little.'

'How? You didn't know the queen was going to die, did you?'

'Of course not,' said Bellamus hurriedly. 'But I did plant ideas in his head and distort the news he received. I put my men in his house, and I as good as told him who to recruit to his plot: all men whose households were riddled with my people.'

'How did you select them? They're just the ones you knew would commit treason?'

'Yes.' *And the ones I wanted out of the way.*

'Then . . . If Ruden is trying to take over on Karoli's behalf, why have you let him remain? It's not safe having him around; he'll surely try again.'

'Because we need him. We might beat the Anakim without his men, but I'm not for taking the risk. We'll just have to keep a close eye on him.'

'That's the first time I've seen you shy away from risk.'

'Chance is a friend of mine,' said Bellamus reflexively. 'But haven't I risked enough today?'

There was a pause. And then they both howled with laughter. The extraordinary tension of the morning was released and they both wept with it. Bellamus had entered that tent, half-convinced he would never leave. The contrast between that, and his current prospects, was giddying.

Finally they stopped, wiping their eyes and trying to suppress that upspring of glee. There was work to do.

'Go and get Widukind, Diethaad. This evening we gather everyone together and stamp them with my seal. Tomorrow, we do the same to the Anakim.'

Diethaad bowed ironically and turned away. Bellamus watched him go. Then he reached inside his jerkin and removed a sheaf of another dozen letters, each bearing the name of a lord who had escaped the day with his reputation unsullied. Quietly he returned them to his leather saddlebag and buckled it shut.

47
The Thirteenth Man

Gray had pieced together a wick and the remains of another lamp with a splash of oil left in it which he lit from the flames sweeping Cold Voice. It would illuminate the passage for a few minutes, no more. 'Do you mind?' he asked quietly, picking Ramnea off the floor.

'Sorry,' muttered Ormur, stepping back from his tormentor. 'No, do it.'

The flames ravaging Cold Voice had died, but he had lingered past them. Gray finished him off, not taking his eyes off Ormur. There was an awkward silence, both aware of their short window of light.

'I can't imagine those two weeks, Ormur,' said Gray.

'I shouldn't . . . Sorry. I couldn't stop.'

'I understand,' said Gray. 'I'm sorry it took so long. Truly, I was as fast as I could be.'

'I know,' said Ormur, flatly.

They were forced on by their dwindling light, and turned to the low door. 'It could be anyone in there, Ormur,' said Gray, observing it.

'It's not,' said Ormur. 'You know who it is.'

'I saw him die.'

'You didn't. You couldn't.'

Gray knelt before the riveted door, reaching forward to pull back the bolts. Even when the door swung open, the prisoner within still made no sound. The light of their makeshift lamp did not extend into the cell, but both could sense someone inside. 'Your captors are dead,' said Gray, 'and we haven't much light left. Who's there?'

There was no response from the dark.

Ormur dropped onto one knee, grunting as the burnt skin touched stone. 'Lord Roper? We came for you, my lord. You're free.'

'You're free whoever you are,' said Gray. 'We are leaving this place. Your captors are dead and you're free to go.'

And a hoarse voice replied from the blackness. 'Not more cruelty . . . Please.'

That voice sent a chill up Ormur's spine. He had half expected it, but not really believed. It was different from how he remembered, as though rusted stiff. But still it was recognisable.

'It's me, my lord,' said Gray. He wore a look of near horror at this nightmare cavern where dead friends could speak from the gloom. 'It's Gray, I swear it. We came to find you.'

'Please. Just leave me alone,' murmured the voice. 'No more of this.'

Gray reached his hand forward. 'Take my hand, lord. It held you back at Harstathur. It helped you up in Lundenceaster's breech. You took it and led me on when everything seemed lost. Perhaps you'll believe that.'

Gray's hand was outstretched and trembling, Ormur watching the ghostly outline of his fingers, just visible in the shadow. He almost started when a hand reached back. Tentatively, it took Gray's fingers, just holding them by the tips.

'Truly, brother? After all this time?'

Gray's mouth was hanging open, his face appalled. Ormur knew how he felt: he feared to see whatever was left in that cell. He hung back while Gray shuffled forward on his knees, reaching into the dark and embracing a figure Ormur could barely see. There was a grunt of pain and Gray recoiled. 'You're hurt, lord.'

'Yes. Will you lead me out? I do not know the way.'

'It would be the greatest honour, lord.'

Gray drew back from the cell, holding onto a dark figure by the wrist. Ormur was transfixed as the captain pulled, and a shadow was hauled from the tomb, unfolding into a man. Like a black ritual in which a full-grown man was birthed from the stone, it took a few steps, trembling and stooped.

The man straightened: Lord Roper Kynortasson, released from his tomb.

It was not possible. From all Ormur had heard about his deeds and his death, he would have been no less shocked to see one of the ancient heroes at the Holy Temple stir and walk stiffly out from beneath its alcove. Even Gray had recoiled slightly, ashen-faced at the man before him.

Roper was luminously pale and thin, so terribly thin. He staggered slightly, prompting Gray to step forward once more and offer an arm on which he could steady himself. Then he glanced at Ormur, who nearly jumped as Roper looked at him. He bowed instinctively as Roper scowled. 'Shield the lamp, Guardsman.'

Ormur covered the dying flame with a hand. 'Yes, lord.'

'You can manage the stairs, lord?' asked Gray. 'There's a great many.'

'I will manage them, Gray. I will climb out of this place, or not leave at all.'

Ormur glanced at Gray. He had wanted this moment for so long and now that it was here, found he was disturbed. How was Roper alive? Had the Kryptea resurrected him somehow? And what had this apparition seen? He looked so fragile that Ormur half feared he might drift apart if exposed to the free air above ground. But he was also somehow intimidating: that he should have even this much life seemed uncanny.

'I'll need your arm,' Roper said to Gray. The captain gave it, and together they began the climb out of the kungargrav.

It took hours. The lamp went out almost at once, but the only way to go was up. Roper had to stop frequently, and Gray waited patiently until he was ready to go on. Ormur was desperate to surface, to feel the wind, and grass beneath his toes, and leave this nightmare pit.

When they finally reached the main hall, the fire in the grate was just a few smouldering embers, casting a blacksmith's glow over the walls. Roper was panting and drenched in sweat. He leaned against the wall and gazed about the room. His robust features did not look as old as his frame suggested: on the contrary they seemed perfectly preserved. 'They're all dead?' he croaked. 'All the guards?'

'We believe so, lord,' said Gray. 'A dozen we think.'

Roper shook his head. 'It is thirteen. I have counted. Always the same thirteen.'

Gray hesitated. 'Well we shall have to keep an eye out for the last. But twelve are dead.'

'You killed them with one hand?' Roper seemed to have just noticed the stump of Gray's left wrist.

'Ormur killed most of them,' said Gray, indicating the guardsman. Roper nodded but did not acknowledge his brother. He stared instead at the flight of stairs, steeling himself.

'One flight left, lord.'

There came a flurry in the dark. Footsteps pounded from a side passage as someone broke cover and hurtled for the stairs. 'The last guard!' hissed Gray. He was stuck supporting Roper, so Ormur gave chase. But he was slow. Too slow and too weak, and the Kryptean was well ahead as he pelted up the stairs. Ormur saw him heave past a stone trapdoor at the top. There the Kryptean turned, seized its edges and prepared to throw the door shut. Ormur lunged forward, thrusting his borrowed sword over the rim of the exit, just as the stone slab crashed down on top of it. The blade shattered, but chips of it were left trapped in the door, holding open that precious sliver of the outside world. On the far side, Ormur heard footsteps as the Kryptean sprinted away.

The trapdoor was a long, heavy flagstone, mounted on a mechanism visible only beneath. Ormur set his shoulder against it and heaved upward. The stone hinged open, swinging smoothly on its mechanism, and suddenly there was a draught on his skin.

It was cold, and carried with it the scent of the night: dew and grass and earth. And even sweeter: he could see a shaft of silver moonlight beaming into the entrance of the tunnel. The mechanism of the entrance held it open and Ormur crawled out; thin, sore and craving that light.

He stumbled from the tunnel, feet slapping on the bare stone, and when he came to the soft grass beyond, he dropped to his knees. He ran his fingers through each blade, skin so sensitive it was almost unbearable. Then he fell on his back to look up at the stars. The night sky was not black as he remembered: it was radiant blue, liberal with crystal fragments and presided over by a bone-white jewel. It was the sea at calm. It was a snow-mosaiced mountain. It was the canopy glimmering in the breeze and he had thought he would never see it again.

Behind him walked a Black Lord everyone thought was dead. Roper and Gray came to stand next to Ormur, who climbed to his feet in the presence of his lord but was too frightened to face him.

'Welcome back, my lord,' said Gray softly.

Myrklettur undulated before them in shades of steel, the planets blazing above the horizon and the Winter Road gouging the sky in two.

Ormur dared a glance at Roper, who wore a grimace as he clutched onto Gray.

'How long was I down there?'

'It's been seven years, my lord.'

'Seven years,' Roper repeated dully. 'Just seven years.'

'They told you it was more?'

'They said it was less. One year. I knew it was a lie.'

In the darkness, Ormur blushed.

'What's happened? Does any of Albion remains to us? Does Jokul still rule?'

'Keturah rules, lord. Jokul has been dead for years. Albion is much as you left her. We control Suthdal up to the Wylie Lines, but the Sutherners are on the march.'

Roper was silent for a long while. He looked exhausted, staring out at the night. 'Keturah,' he said at last. 'She lives? You're sure?'

'She was well four weeks ago, lord, when we bade her farewell as she marched south. I've heard nothing since.'

Roper was silent still.

'They told you she was dead,' Gray said gently.

Roper nodded curtly.

'And that Jokul took the throne, and Albion was nearly lost?'

Silence. When he did speak, the word came like the rustle of mice through leaflitter. 'Yes.'

'Well it isn't yet, my lord. Though we are not the strength we were. It is as you feared would happen; we have been eroded. We have allies from Erebos, but so do the Sutherners. They are marching against Keturah and the situation is bleak.'

'So the job is still to be done,' said Roper, flat as ice.

Gray shrugged helplessly. 'Ultimately,' he said. 'But you're back from the Underworld, lord. Breathe the free air again. Do not be too fast to burden yourself.'

'No, Gray,' said Roper. 'Dying in that cause is more than I ever thought to have again. It is all I want.'

Nobody said anything for a long while. Presently Ormur became aware that Roper was trembling. 'Here, lord,' he said, reaching for his arm and helping him down to sit on the grass. There the Black Lord sat, lips pursed, his form as rigid as if he were made from brick.

'We thought you were dead, my lord,' said Gray, uncomprehendingly. 'What *happened* to you?'

And Roper began to cry.

48
Roper's Tale

Roper wept a long time in harsh, desperate sobs. He leaned forward, face pressed to the earth, fingers wrapped in the grass, beating the ground with a fist as he howled into it. Ormur could see the bones of his shoulders and spine through the thin tunic over his back. They were helpless to comfort him, held back by the magnitude of what he had endured over seven years.

When he finally stopped he was gasping. He sat back and leaned on his hands like a man who has found the shore after days clutching at driftwood. There was something other than weariness in his face at last, and he cast about the sky with shining eyes, as though it burned to see it after all this time.

'They captured me, Gray,' he said at last. 'They staged my death and I have been a prisoner in the dark since that day.'

Gray took a seat next to Roper. He let out a long breath. 'But I saw you fall. How did you survive?'

'I didn't. It wasn't me. They had found a man weeks before who they said would look like me from afar. They threw him off the cliff so nobody could inspect the body.'

Gray thought back to that day, to the figure he had seen tumble over the edge and the Krytean agent he had dragged with him.

'He did not go willingly. Why not just kill you? They've done it often enough before.'

'To kill a Black Lord requires Almighty blessing. They have a token they cast – a silver coin. They are permitted to cast it after each infraction, as they see it, committed by a Black Lord. If they fail to gain approval three times, then they accept the Almighty is against the death and settle for life imprisonment.'

'And they told you all this?'

Roper nodded. 'The goal was to destroy me. If I kill myself, they are blameless for my death. They wanted me to know how hopeless my situation was: that I was trapped forever. That you were certain I was dead, and wouldn't even look for me.'

Gray shifted onto one knee and bowed his head to Roper. 'Forgive me, my lord,' he said quietly. 'If I'd known, I swear I'd have . . . I was certain it was you . . . And they told you Jokul had taken over?'

'They said he had the Stone Throne. That the Sacred Guard had been destroyed, Keturah and Tekoa put to death. That my son . . .' he glanced at Gray, hardly daring to speak. 'They said I'd had a son, and he had died with Keturah.'

Gray shook his head. 'You have a son, my lord, and he lives. A strong lad named Numa, now in the haskoli.'

Roper fell to renewed weeping. Ormur heard him mutter: 'A son,' a few times beneath his breath, and it was some while before he sat up once more.

'What else did they tell you?' asked Gray.

'They said you had abandoned your loyalty to me and now served Jokul—'

'I killed Jokul,' blurted Gray. 'You are my lord, and the greatest regret of my life is that I failed to preserve you.'

Roper glanced sidelong at the captain. 'It was inevitable. They only needed one chance. I couldn't hide from them forever, not without inhabiting a prison of my own construction.' He let out a long breath and wiped his eyes, looking steadier, though he still squinted as if the moon was too bright. 'It is done,' he said softly. 'Onwards.'

Ormur saw Gray shiver to hear that word, spoken again in that voice. 'Do not give yourself so little sympathy, my lord. You have spent seven years in hell.'

'It was agony,' said Roper, flat once more. 'They would stand outside my cell and enact the scene of your betrayal, or Keturah begging for her life. In the dark, without any stimulus . . . You forget what reality looks like. You cannot tell what is memory, what is fantasy, what is reality. They controlled my thoughts. I forgot what things looked like. I forgot how they sounded and smelt. I have lived in a nightmare from which I couldn't wake up.'

'They beat you, lord?' asked Ormur, quietly.

'At first. But that stopped a long time ago. There was always the threat of it, but they wanted my body intact. They have a room they took me to exercise, where I could smell the world outside and stand in a shaft of sunlight leading up to the surface.'

'What for?'

'Because it was the greatest agony of all, to have those free moments to compare against my imprisonment. Spend too long in the cell and you forget what you're missing. What you used to be. The smell of the outside brings it back.'

'And you didn't kill yourself, lord?' asked Ormur, before he could stop himself.

Roper looked at Ormur as if he had been impudent. Eventually he seemed to decide he would allow the question. 'I tried to. At first.'

'You stopped trying? What kept you going?'

Roper hesitated. 'The knowledge that the Almighty had preserved me. There must've been a reason. I have some purpose yet to fulfil. It is not for the Kryptea to decide how I spend myself. They controlled everything else, but I had that.' He eyed Ormur and then looked at Gray. 'How did you find me?' He sounded almost suspicious, as though guarding against the possibility that this might still be a Kryptean trick.

Gray began to explain why they had come. He reached the part where Ormur went missing and looked expectantly at his protégé.

'They captured me,' said Ormur. 'They knew we were watching them. They sent out a hunting party, and then followed it with another one in case we tried to track them. The second group caught me, knocked me unconscious and took me below.'

Gray nodded. 'I'd not seen anything and thought it was time to have a look inside Myrklettur, which is when I saw Ormur being carried into the tunnel. I was shocked, and I must admit, caught in indecision. I'd just decided to hide and try to creep in after Ormur, when they spotted me. They came after me, and blocked the exits to the fortress to trap me inside. They hunted me until nightfall gave me some advantage. I knew if I stayed in the fortress they'd get me eventually, so chanced climbing down one of the outer walls.'

Ormur knew how frightening his master, who had never liked heights and had only one hand, would have found that. He met Gray's eyes, who shrugged as if to say, *I had no choice*.

'I wondered about going back to the Hindrunn for help, but thought it would take too long. And besides, if I tried to take you back by force, they might hold you hostage. Stealth was my only option. I'd seen where they took you, but when I finally had a clear route in, after two days of waiting, the Krypteans seemed to have gone and I couldn't find any way into their lair. I had to wait deep in the tunnel until they next emerged so I could see where they came out of. It took three days before they chanced leaving once more. But once I'd seen it, I knew where the entrance was. I waited until they were all inside and went in after them. Then of course I found myself in the dark and had to grope around looking for you. I was lost, and not a little frightened. I cannot imagine how it would've been to be trapped there, at their mercy.

'But after feeling my way through the dark for a long while, I found a prison, and someone alone inside, talking to himself. You, my lord.' Gray broke off but Roper did not seem embarrassed. 'At first I thought it was my young protégé here – who else could they be keeping? But after a while I realised the voice was different. I wanted to keep surprise on my side, and went back up the stairs. That was when I spotted the man with the lamp, heading for your cell.' He nodded to Ormur. 'You know the rest.'

'Of all the people who should find me,' murmured Roper. 'This is no coincidence. And you say we still hold most of Suthdal?'

Gray nodded cautiously. 'Most of it, but it has become a wasteland, lord, churned over by marching feet and ravaged by feral animals. And our numbers are much reduced. The reliability of our allies is doubtful. We are under assault.'

'So that is why I have been set free,' said Roper. 'We must go south immediately. We need horses.'

'Can you walk, lord?'

'We shall ride.'

'What about this thirteenth man?' asked Ormur. 'The Kryptean agent?'

'Forget him,' said Roper.

'He is an assassin,' said Gray dubiously. 'He could make life extremely difficult for us.'

'He will,' said Roper shortly. 'The Kryptea have been working with Bellamus. That agent will have gone south to tell him I am now free, and when Bellamus finds out, he will try to stop us linking up with Keturah. The die is cast. We cannot stop that now. We must just try and join the army before Bellamus can find us.'

'You'll be fit for nothing without food, lord,' said Gray firmly. 'There was a lot of dried venison in the mess, I'll go and get it.' He squeezed Ormur's shoulder. 'You can light the fire?'

He turned back to the kungargrav, leaving Roper and Ormur

alone together. Ormur busied himself with the fire and soon had the flames roaring.

'What else can I do, lord?' asked Ormur.

Roper did not immediately reply. He was staring at the fire: his first, Ormur supposed, for seven years. The look on his face was one of such pleasure that it seemed to hurt. Then he looked at Ormur properly for the first time. It was deeply uncomfortable; an utterly dispassionate assessment such as one might receive from a goshawk.

'Sit down. You look tired.'

Ormur was grateful and sat beside Roper, who continued to observe him. 'You are a very young guardsman.'

'I am, lord.'

'You are . . . eighteen?'

'Nineteen, lord.'

'Nineteen,' said Roper, looking back at the fire. 'So you shouldn't even be a full legionary and yet you are in the Sacred Guard.'

'We were called early out of our training, my lord. There are fewer legionaries than there were.'

Roper's face twitched a little at that. 'At what age were you summoned to the battle-line?'

'Seventeen, lord. But I've not seen a full battle yet. Safinim avoids them. It's been skirmishes for years.'

'My father always said the legions were our greatest treasure. Without them we have neither standing nor influence. We must be weak indeed if we are promoting seventeen-year-olds to full peers.'

Ormur did not know what to say and was spared by the arrival of Gray. At his side hung Ormur's sword, Warspite, and he had slung a cloak over one shoulder, knotted into a bundle which he had filled with venison. Ormur fell upon the venison, but found he could hardly bite it because of his missing teeth, and had to chew it carefully with his molars. Roper ate like a termite; pacing himself with small bites, as though he intended to consume their entire supply.

Ormur stopped eating abruptly. Then he climbed unsteadily to his feet and hurried behind a crumbling wall to be sick.

'Overreached himself,' he heard Gray say, amused.

'That guardsman is a little overfamiliar,' Roper replied.

Ormur tried not to listen and retched once more.

'Don't you recognise him, lord?' There was a pause. 'He is your brother.'

49
Burn the Boats

They needed horses.

Walking was sore for Ormur at the start, but he loosened after an hour or so. For Roper it seemed agony. He tottered like an old man, baring his teeth and accepting a staff to prop himself on when Gray offered it. There was no hope of catching the Kryptean agent, and try as they might to stay at Roper's pace, Ormur and Gray often found themselves forty or fifty yards ahead before realising they had left him behind.

'What was Lord Roper saying when you found him?' asked Ormur as they waited for him to catch up. It was the day after their escape from the kungargrav, and they were descending the path from Myrklettur, thin autumn sunlight rinsing the treetops ahead and making the low mist glow. 'In the cell, you said you heard the prisoner talking to himself. What was he saying?'

Gray hesitated. 'That he was going to kill someone. He didn't say a name. Just called them *you*. "I'm going to kill you," over and over again.' Ormur frowned. 'I think it might've been Jokul,' Gray added.

'Or maybe Cold Voice. You haven't asked?'

'It wasn't meant to be heard,' said Gray. 'And I shouldn't have repeated it. Forget it.'

Ormur was frightened of Roper. He had been desperate for years to find his brother alive and dreamed of discovering him. But in none of those dreams had Roper not recognised him. In none of them had he endured seven years of the fate which had broken Ormur after two weeks. Ormur had woken that morning to find Roper sitting on a ruined wall above him, watching the sun rise. His face glowed orange, and he was completely silent and still but for the tears, running down his cheeks like tiny jewels. Ormur was frightened of the Black Lord and what he had seen.

'This is foolish,' said Roper, catching up with them. 'We can't keep on at this pace. Gray: go on ahead and find us some horses. Ormur and I will keep on this road towards the Hindrunn. That is where you will find us.'

'Neither of you is fit enough to defend yourselves, lord,' Gray demurred. 'And as we have discovered, these woods are not safe. I cannot leave you to travel alone.'

'If you don't, we will be too late. Bellamus will hear of my survival and will undoubtedly stop us.'

'But the battle will likely already have happened, lord,' said Gray, gently. 'It was four weeks ago that Keturah marched. There is no sense risking our lives for the opportunity to arrive a few days earlier.'

Roper was adamant. 'You surely cannot believe all this is luck? That it was you two who found me, that it happened just as the Sutherners are resurgent? This has the ring of fate. We will make it south, Gray, fortune smiles on the bold. But we must do it in time.' Gray did not move. 'You delay,' Roper added impatiently.

'I lost you once, my lord. I let you fall into a place worse than death. Please do not ask me to leave you again so soon, so weakened, on a road so dangerous.'

'I do ask you, Gray,' said Roper remorselessly. 'Ormur is here, and from your account he is hardly defenceless. Find us horses. Get me back to my legions.'

It took four days for Gray to return with the horses.

Abandoning his pack, he ran to the Hindrunn in two days. Without telling a soul why, he took the three best horses remaining and half-rode, half-dragged them back to his companions.

He found Roper rejuvenated. He was still painfully frail, but after days of full rations and leaf-filtered sunlight, he could now stand straight once again. His skin had lost its deathly pallor and walking no longer seemed such agony. He nodded as Gray returned with the horses, and then froze as he saw what else Gray had brought.

A suit of Unthank-silver armour.

'It's the set Tekoa had made for you, lord,' Gray explained. 'I thought you might need it, where we're going.'

Roper helped steady the nearest horse and hauled himself into the saddle immediately. 'Onwards,' was the first and last word he said that morning.

They charged south.

Even for Gray, the pace was gruelling, and he wondered that Roper could not merely sustain it, but drive it. After the second day in the saddle, he noted blood trickling down the inside of Roper's legs.

'Saddleworn, lord?' he asked.

Roper followed his gaze and seemed surprised at the blood running down his legs. 'I suppose so.'

This new Roper seemed to react to nothing, pain least of all. He had not acknowledged his failure to recognise Ormur, said nothing of his tiredness, and strangest of all, neither displayed nor responded to affection. He was unreachable.

That is, until they were below the Abus.

They crossed the dark river, horses and all, on a barge owned by a river-dwelling family. That night, making six leagues before dark, they set up camp beside a lake. It was perfectly still, the sun's last influence draining from the west, and the water beside them looking-glass smooth. Roper, hobbling the horses with his usual speed, paused briefly to look up. He dropped the hobbles and took a few paces to the water's edge.

Trees stitched the mirror lake to the shore. Late glow-worms shone from below, stars from above, all of it doubled in the water's surface. 'But isn't this what we've dreamed of?' he murmured. 'This is the Black Kingdom now.'

Ormur and Gray paused. To them this was Blacklaw: the grim place below the river, overturned and ravaged by war. But Roper was right. In this place, on this night, the lofty goal to which they had devoted their lives seemed near. At a rate too slow for human perception, Albion was being untamed.

'There has been talk . . .' Gray began.

Roper glanced at him. 'Speak.'

'With Blacklaw so fiercely contested, there was talk of expanding to unclaimed lands,' said Gray. 'There's an island, across the sea. Halfway to the Otherworld, they say. The sky glows at night, the sea freezes over and teems with monsters. But it's abandoned. I know Keturah has wondered if that might be the home we were seeking all along.'

Roper looked at him blankly.

'If the worst happens in the south. If it might make a refuge against Suthern reprisal.'

Roper stared back at the lake, his eyes narrowed. 'I was told once that whenever the Sutherners started a new colony, they would arrive in their ships and as soon as they got off, they would burn them. Only then would the colonists not look back. Only then would they commit to what was before them hard enough to make a success of it. While there is the option of escape, success is impossible.

'Nothing in this world comes easily, Gray. Nothing. If we want this land, we must fight for it like our boats have been burned. There can be no other.'

50
The Messenger

The night after taking control of the army, Bellamus organised a supper in his new pavilion. Diethaad had requisitioned the one belonging to Sutton, who was now imprisoned in a fortified wagon and had no need of it. His crest of an adder had been stitched over in record time by a patch bearing Bellamus's own arms of a spider. The room was festooned with enough candles to make the air swim with their fumes, and on the far side was a four-poster, familiar to anyone who had been in the queen's chamber the previous morning.

And near everyone invited, with the exception of Widukind, had been there to witness the struggle for power which had played out beside that bed. Bellamus watched closely as each one entered, their eyes drawn immediately to the queen's bed and betraying their astonishment. But they said not a word. They accepted his welcome, bowed to him and professed their honour to be there. Then they took their seats at the long table.

It was a show of power far greater than the morning's arrests. They all saw the bed, where the queen had lain. All were forced to dine in its presence and say not a word about this flagrant pretension to royalty. Bellamus might claim to be a regent, holding the throne during extraordinary times to preserve stability. But here was such an obvious sign that this was a lie, that not to acknowledge it was a humiliation of every man present. It did not matter what was obvious or true any more. What mattered was what Bellamus told them.

But the mood recovered swiftly enough. The Lord Warden sat at the head of the table, Ruden on his right, Widukind on his left. Ruden had supplied a cask of fine Frankish wine, and laid out before them was pheasant with wine and caraway, skinless veal sausages, poached eggs with vinegar, a root broth with currants and spices and, serendipitously, a swan caught on the river that morning and roasted with mustard.

Bellamus could hardly taste it. He had not slept, and had spent the day cascading letters down to all the senior officers of the army, ensuring that the news of Aramilla's death came out on his own terms, with his own armed soldiers present, and blame could be attributed to the proper quarter. But there was work left to do in this great confidence trick. Bellamus was acting as though the power was so assuredly his that bemusedly, the army was following his lead.

'First a toast, my lords,' Bellamus began the evening, raising a goblet and getting to his feet. At various speeds, the company followed suit. 'To Her Majesty. Were the circumstances not so exceptional, we should be in mourning. But we can do no greater honour to her memory than destroying the enemy that forced her from her home, and murdered her father and husband.'

They drank together.

It was not until after they had sat, and knives had started sawing at the many dishes, that Ruden put in, 'Exceptional, eh, Lord Warden? These circumstances, I mean. Seems to me the old enemy is dead and buried.'

'If that is true, it is exceptional indeed,' said Bellamus, carving some of the swan. He noted that Widukind was staring expressionless at the food, finally deciding one of the eggs might not be too much of an extravagance.

'They're done,' said Offring confidently. 'We outnumber them by an absurd margin. We've cut off their supply lines, and their options are to make a fight of it now, on unfavourable ground where we can easily surround them, or allow themselves to be pinned to the coast. What can they do?'

'Nothing to fear in that army,' said Doronon, dabbing his fingers in a water bowl littered with rose petals. 'The Black Legions are not the force they were.'

'The Unhieru—' began another.

'Will abandon the Anakim when confronted with the reality of the situation,' finished Offring.

Bellamus watched this in disapproval. 'This is complacent talk, my lords. Focus, focus. We have won an advantage, that is all. Now we need to turn it into a victory.'

'But it's your great line, Safinim,' countered Ruden, 'that eight-tenths of the battle is won before the fighting starts.'

Bellamus nodded, chewing on a mouthful of swan. It was rather stringy. He swallowed. 'Tell me, my lords,' he asked pleasantly. 'Who here has seen the Black Legions defeated in pitched battle?'

The pudding was brought out. Honeyed ginger, sweet cakes flavoured with rose, and bread pudding with almonds.

'The Eoten-Draefend couldn't make it, I assume,' said Ruden.

The table rippled with laughter.

'You know, Lord Warden, there were some strange rumours about you,' said Offring. 'I half expected us to be sharing the table with hybrids.'

'There've been rumours among the men,' said Ruden, swallowing a mouthful of ginger, 'that when this is over and we've taken the North, you intend to invite the Anakim nobility to rule alongside us.' The table laughed again. 'Try assimilation, rather than annihilation.'

Bellamus smiled politely.

'So what will you do, Lord Warden?' asked Wulfheard.

What indeed? In his mind this had been a wholly defensive exercise. They were retaking that which had been stolen from them. They would chase the Anakim to the Abus and then? They could not just stop and let the Anakim regather their strength. They had to end this. 'Well . . . what say you, my lords?'

'Do to them what they did to our people,' said Offring, as though it was obvious. 'Enslave them.'

'Enslave them? And be looking over our shoulder for an uprising every year?' put in Wulfheard. 'Eradicate them. They are *demons*! If any of us wishes to be a servant to God, it's hard to see what more we could do.'

'I quite agree.'

'End it. Once and for all. I don't understand why you'd do anything else.'

Bellamus said nothing. He just sipped his wine, wondering why he had not considered this question before. It was not like him to leave so large a point unresolved.

'And speaking of the condemned,' chanced Ruden, 'what happens to the conspirators?'

'Ah,' said Bellamus, making a face of regret. 'We shall find out when we've had time to conduct a trial. But there can only be one punishment for high treason.'

There was a long silence, which Bellamus felt appropriately ominous.

He took a breath, but held on to it as the flap into the chamber was swept aside and Diethaad entered. He crossed straight to Bellamus and bent to whisper in his ear. 'Beg pardon, lord. There's an Anakim outside for you.'

Bellamus plucked an almond off his plate. 'You'd better send him in.'

Diethaad turned slightly so that he had his back to the table of curious onlookers. 'In present company, my lord?'

'Of course.'

Still Diethaad hesitated. Then he turned for the entrance.

'You'll forgive me, gentlemen,' Bellamus said as Diethaad brushed past the canvas. 'Sometimes business must take priority.'

'Nothing less than we'd expect from you, my lord,' said Ruden reasonably. There was a murmur of agreement, then a sudden hush fell.

Diethaad had stepped back in, and at his back came a figure straight from a fever-dream. Pale and stooped, he still filled the doorway, clothes ragged, filth-spattered, hair midway down his chest, and the tallest man there by half a head. He stank of sweat, horse and stale water. Eyes shone out from his grime-covered face like twin chips of sapphire, unnaturally bright. From this, from his height, from the extreme composure of his stance and the first few paces he took into the room, it was clear this was no Sutherner.

The hush that descended was profound, the nobles looking in shock between Bellamus and this apparition. It was a visceral demonstration of the uncanny forces with which the Lord Warden consorted. Had he conjured a spirit before them, they would have been no more shocked.

Bellamus did not recognise this man, but he was likely a herald sent by Lady Keturah. So she was willing to talk after all? He waved him over without bothering to stand. 'You look very weary,' he said in staccato Anakim impenetrable to the rest of the table. 'Food? Wine?'

The apparition bared its teeth, and it took Bellamus a moment to realise it was an expression of revulsion. 'I have not come to break bread with you, Spymaster.' The table did not comprehend the reply, but they understood the tone. Two of those seated nearest the Anakim got to their feet and retreated several paces.

Bellamus dabbed his mouth, suddenly aware of the carnage a man like this might wreak in a tent where only Diethaad was armed.

'Then let us come to the point,' he replied, glancing at Diethaad. His lieutenant stood very close to the Anakim, hand wrapped around his sword hilt. 'Why have you come?'

'To warn you.' The messenger seemed to be having trouble remaining upright. He passed a hand over his eyes and then sank slowly to one knee, head tilted to the floor.

'You're quite sure you wouldn't like some wine,' said Bellamus.

The Anakim flicked his hand dismissively.

'If you insist. What is your warning?'

'I need your help,' said the man, now swaying slightly where he knelt. 'You need to stop him.'

'Who? Who are you talking about?'

'Lord Roper,' said the Anakim. 'He's free.'

51
The Abbio

'Grendel?' asked Bellamus, then he cursed himself for using the name. As one, the noble attention at the table sharpened. 'You mean . . . the old Black Lord? Roper Kynortasson?'

'Yes.' The Anakim was still staring down at the floor. Near obscured by grime, Bellamus made out the stylised image of a spread-winged cuckoo on his shoulder. So this man was Kryptean.

Still, he was baffled. 'Free? What do you mean, free?'

'He's been set loose,' replied the Anakim. 'We've had him imprisoned, for seven years.'

This account, coming from such a vagabond, did not seem credible. 'Who's your master?' tested Bellamus. 'Who leads the Kryptea?'

The man shook his head. 'No one. The Kryptea is finished. The few of us guarding the Black Lord were all that was left.'

'And before? When the Kryptea was a force in your kingdom? What was the name of the man who led it?'

'What does it matter?'

'Just answer.'

'Jokul.'

A dreadful cold was stealing over Bellamus. 'I was told that the Black Lord was dead,' he said.

The company sat in tense silence, none understanding the words but clear about the nature of the news borne by this strange messenger.

'Imprisoned,' repeated the man. 'In secret. But two Sacred Guardsmen discovered him. They stormed the prison and set him loose.'

'But why's he alive?' Bellamus was suddenly on his feet. 'Why didn't you kill him?'

'We couldn't,' said the Anakim. 'We didn't have permission.'

'Permission!' Bellamus scoffed. 'Whose permission do you ask to kill a king?'

The Anakim raised his head at last, eyes narrowed. 'Your god.'

'Where is he?'

'I don't know. Last I saw, he was north of the Abus. But he may be in Blacklaw by now. He may be trying to rendezvous with the army.'

'Could he be ahead of you?'

'No.'

'You're sure?'

'He's very weak. When I left him, he had no horse. I have not rested. He must be days behind.'

Bellamus was breathing heavily. Then he turned abruptly to the table. 'Leave us,' he commanded. 'Widukind, you stay.'

Nobody moved. Then Ruden opened his mouth. 'What's he—'

'Leave us!' he bellowed, still not looking away from the Anakim.

The nobles were startled to their feet. Stunned into silence, they filed from the pavilion, clustering absurdly far from the figure kneeling on the floor.

Widukind rose silently and waited for the room to drain. Finally it was just him, Bellamus, the Anakim and Diethaad. Bellamus was still glaring at the Kryptean agent, who had now toppled onto his side and was lying on the floor, eyes shut.

Bellamus opened his mouth to speak, then thought better. He crossed to the tent flap and ripped it back. Revealed behind were Lords Offring and Doronon, already scuttling for cover.

'Diethaad.' Bellamus jerked his head outside. 'Keep an eye out.'

Diethaad glanced at the Anakim laying on the floor. 'Shout if I'm needed.'

Bellamus did not reply, seeing Diethaad out and fastening two of the toggles behind him. 'I can count on your discretion, Bishop,' he said, turning back.

It was barely a question and Widukind did not deign to acknowledge it with so much as a nod, merely observing Bellamus with his dark-ringed eyes.

'This man,' he indicated the Kryptean agent now on his side, head resting limply on the floor, 'works for a faction within the Black Kingdom who are enemies of Grendel. It was they who claimed credit for his assassination. Unfortunately, it appears that was untrue. He was kept imprisoned – in secret – instead. And now, he tells me, the Black Lord has escaped.'

Privately, Bellamus marvelled at Widukind's self-control. He just returned Bellamus's gaze, expressionless.

'Well, you are our northern bulwark. The Abbio show you unusual loyalty. If what this man reports is true, then under no circumstances must Grendel be permitted to rejoin the Black Legions. You understand me, Bishop? We have them served for breakfast, and if their greatest lord is returned in their hour of need, I very much fear the resistance that might inspire. And almost equally important, none of our side must hear about this. Whether you tell the Abbio who you're looking for, I leave to you. But word must not reach the rest of the army. Can you do that, my lord?'

Widukind spoke at last. 'Count on me, Lord Safinim.'

52
Identity

With an Anakim eye for land, Keturah's army had chosen the site for its last stand. Bullied, harassed and chased to the coast, they had flung scouts out in all directions, seeking a location to make home. What they found was a vast ridge, the sea beating at a shingle beach just forty yards behind. Its left flank was secured by dense forest, while the right flattened out into a sprawling marshland. It was a formidable defensive position, set before a vast grass basin.

'I'd wondered last night whether we could get a message to the fleet,' said Tekoa. He, Keturah, Leon and Virtanen stood atop the ridge, a blustering wind stinging their cheeks. 'Perhaps there's some way of getting past the Teutan fleet and managing a night evacuation. I'd sooner fight this battle in the Black Kingdom.'

'The fleet is sheltering up in Stjornava,' said Keturah flatly.

Tekoa ground his teeth, for Stjornava was in the far northwest of Albion, and utterly out of reach. 'What the hell is it doing up there?'

'Staying well away from the Teuta,' said Keturah. 'But suffice it to say, by the time we could get a message there and the fleet back, it would be significantly too late to help those of us here.'

'And it would get smashed,' Virtanen added helpfully.

'Besides,' said Keturah. 'I like that we've got our back to the sea. There's nowhere to retreat. Our men know our one chance is to fight like demons.'

'If Safinim ever lets us fight,' grumbled Tekoa.

For seventeen days now, they had been kept to their ridge as they used up their meagre rations and starved. They were harried too, three or four small raids each night. Often they did not even kill anyone, just waking them, forcing them to sleep in their armour and keep weapons to hand. For weeks, they had lived with the threat of a battle which never quite materialised.

'The Chief Historian says this field appears in an old chant,' Keturah told her companions. 'Carved by an ancient ice river, apparently.' The ice river had now run dry, but the bed it had gouged in front of the ridge remained. On its other side was a warren of low hills, where they could just perceive the distant sentries of the Teutan army.

'And what happened in this chant?' asked Tekoa.

'Some ancient victory for the Sutherners.'

Tekoa shook his head in disbelief. 'Glad she brought that up. Another morale-booster from Frathi.'

Virtanen held up a hand suddenly.

'What?'

The herald appeared to be scrutinising the far hills, but the peaks and gullies looked much as they had the past few weeks. Then Keturah realised that what she had taken for her own heartbeat was the distant boom of a drum. It thudded rapidly, one-two, one-two, one-two; no idle beat but a call to action.

'That's a trick of ours, isn't it?' Keturah mused. 'They've never used drumming before.'

But there was an irresistible weight to it.

'Sounds like Safinim's preparing something,' said Virtanen.

'So he'd like us to think,' said Tekoa curtly.

But Virtanen was right. It took half an hour for the response to declare itself, but presently, and in perfect order, six columns crept from the largest gullies across the field. A dark flood streaming onto the ancient plain, driven forward by the relentless beat. At last: after skirmishes, deadlock, stalemate, marching and attrition; after seven years of waiting, the battle was upon them.

The Anakim ridge lurched wearily into action. Soldiers staggered upright and scattered in search of weapons and armour. Orders were bellowed, horses saddled and banners hoisted, while their enemy came into sharper resolution. They were pikemen: weapons bristling overhead, each ash shaft twelve feet in length and their bearers chanting like the crowd at a bear baiting.

In an act of synchrony so precise it raised even Leon's eyebrows, a blare of trumpets caused each of the six columns to split in two. Each half wheeled outwards, diverging so that they now marched parallel with the ridge.

'This is charming,' Keturah said. 'They've been practising their marching.'

But her companions were watching this precision in uneasy silence. Nearly miraculously, from six columns the pikemen were slotting into a vast battle-front, facing the ridge. And the pikemen, who must have outnumbered the Anakim forces on their own, were merely the vanguard of a horde. Deployed behind them in similarly ingenious and disciplined formations came cavalry, camelry, elephantry, siege weapons, bowmen, men-at-arms, halberdiers and more, much more: so much that Keturah kept expecting to have seen the last of them before yet another column emerged from the hills, and her heart sank lower.

It was not so much the numbers – they were always outnumbered against the Teuta – it was the discipline. They were marching with an order and complexity they had all believed beyond their enemy. Safinim was trying to frighten them, and from the silence of her companions, Keturah could tell he had succeeded.

She turned and almost gasped to see the legionaries who

had assembled silently on the ridge. Serried ranks of them, watching their enemy deploy. Her standard-bearer was there, holding the emblem of House Vidarr high above their position: a huge tree, the roots being devoured by a snake. She turned to Tekoa. 'The orders are yours to give, Father.'

Tekoa watched their enemy for a moment longer, and the scale of the task arrayed before them. Then he snapped his fingers so that an aide galloped to his side. 'My compliments to the legates,' he said. 'They are to commence the pre-battle rituals now.'

A drenching autumn fret blew in and the lictors began growling across the line. The legionaries knelt in ranks atop the ridge, the legates riding in front, each holding aloft an eye of woven holly leaves to inspect their courage for the battle to come. In their wake came lictors, choking out ancient prayers like roaring stags.

Heed me Mighty One,
My peers need feel no fear nor mercy this moment.
We greed prisoners not,
Freely bleed enemy flesh for thee,
Kneel and believe we prevail here beneath thy Eye.

When it was done, each warrior took up a handful of earth, raised it to their mouth and ate as though it were snow. This did not happen before every battle, or even most of them. Just the ones where they were prepared for burial.

Vigtyr came up onto the hill where the Lord Warden had stationed himself.

'My lord?'

Bellamus cast him a brief glance. 'Vigtyr. I'm very busy.'

Far from being unburdened by the death of Aramilla, the giant seemed yet more crushed than before. He was drawn, and his face heavy, as though he could not sleep for fear of his own assassin crawling through the dark.

'I understand, lord. I'd just wondered if I might join the battle-line. Please.' Bellamus looked at him more closely. He seemed to be in earnest. 'Please, Lord! It's the only thing I know. The only thing I was ever good at. I need . . .' He broke off, looking utterly hopeless. 'I need some pride now. Whatever the cost.'

Bellamus turned back to the battlefield. 'No, I'm sorry, Vigtyr. The men don't want to fight beside an Anakim today.' He raised his hand as Vigtyr tried to speak again, cutting him off. 'I've spoken.'

Bellamus ignored Vigtyr, regarding the deployment with satisfaction. He craned his head left and right, took a few paces forward and pondered it like a man observing the play of light on a new tapestry. His eyes flicked between the Teutan side of the field and the Anakim, drawing lines between each threat and counter-threat.

He turned, and found that the Abbio had removed their winged helmets and had their heads pressed to the earth, praying silently. Widukind knelt before them, hands knotted into the grass, lips moving wordlessly.

'Have we assembled the telegraph?' Bellamus asked an aide, his voice muted so as not to disturb the prayers.

'She's just being brought up, lord.'

'Good,' said Bellamus quietly. 'Good. The board is set.'

'And what shall you attack first, my lord?' asked Ruden.

Bellamus tapped a finger on his teeth. 'Identity,' he said thoughtfully. 'Send me Garrett.'

Beneath him, the priests had stepped out in front of the ranks to cry a mass. Many of the pikemen were already drunk, some to the point of vomiting. The pikeline did not require special skill: only the nerve to stand your ground before Black Legionaries, and nerve could be ingested.

The legionaries dressed ranks and raised their thousand banners: tapestries of liquid-bronze eagle feathers; a wheel of raptor-wings suspended from a pole; enormous rattles, twelve feet high and six feet wide, sewn with ten thousand fox-teeth and raven-beaks which rushed like the sea when they shook.

Alongside them were the noises of terror. Retching. Slow exhalations. Loud, quavering voices.

When the legions were aligned, there came the traditional reshuffling. Some of the legionaries were taken by the shoulders and steered forcefully back through the ranks. All protested, all were ignored and deposited in the rearmost rank. The wisdom of a ten-thousand year warrior tradition dictated that distracted men died more easily. If a legionary had recently lost a close friend, or had bad news from home, or was expecting a child, then he would be placed at the back by his peers so that he might be preserved for another day. While he was allowed to protest, it was his solemn duty to accept the judgement of his peers, and to return the favour when they faced their own distractions.

Keturah and Tekoa had positioned themselves in the centre of the line, she on a charcoal stallion, he a grey gelding. They watched as the men bent to smear dirt on their hands to improve their grip, or broke ranks again and again to piss a pathetic trickle. Talking a little way behind them were Leon and Hartvig, debating the ground, and which way the battle might fall.

'You are ready, Father?' she asked quietly.

'I have commanded men my entire life, Daughter. Today is no different.'

She reached across and gripped his hand. 'Is there anything I can do?'

'You know that best.'

She squeezed his hand and then broke away, turning her horse along the ranks of Ramnea's Own and looking over the men. Unusually, there was no cheer to greet her: the soldiers were watching their enemy.

She glared over the legions, stopping here and there to address a group. 'Will you men make me proud? I know you will, Larnir. I'm looking forward to seeing your tournament form on this field.' She rode on until she reached the Aalanders, on the far side of Ramnea's Own, engaged in their own rituals.

They had captured some Suthern scouts, kept alive for this moment, who were led out naked in front of the lines. Warlocks – their faces painted, heads and shoulders covered by eagle headdresses – produced a flint dagger each and cut their prisoners' throats in full view of the Teutan army. Their blood was caught in large bowls and passed along the kneeling ranks so that each man might take a sip and receive a blessing.

Garrett would not be summoned to the Lord Warden like an unruly hound, so Bellamus descended to see him with the Barleymen. They were obnoxiously drunk, brawling among themselves, posturing and jeering at the hated Anakim on the ridge. When they saw the human sacrifices on the far side of the plain, they began to roar, the noise so huge that Bellamus's horse stopped in its tracks and refused to approach. Their resentment of the Anakim was palpable.

Garrett seemed more sober than his men, but his eyes were still a little glazed as he approached Bellamus and his twenty Thingalith. 'Are you returning my men, Safinim?' He eyed Bellamus's bodyguard morosely, slurring his words a little.

'You have enough, my lord,' Bellamus replied. 'And they look ready to fight.'

'We are always ready to fight Black Legionaries.'

Bellamus nodded thoughtfully. 'I don't suppose . . . Can you beat them?'

None of the legionaries sat. The lines fibrillated with restless twitching. One man in five had a hand flat over his stomach as it boiled and churned. Equipment was checked, tightened, checked again. 'Bastards,' someone muttered. 'Won't they just get this over with?'

'We should take it to them. Why are we waiting? Let's just go.'

But nobody moved.

Some of the men were laughing manically. Others rocked where they stood as though mad, so highly animated their energy exceeded their bodies.

On the right flank, the Onogurians were braiding the manes and tails of their horses, and working charms and amulets into the hair. The mounts were groomed and dressed, and only when they were ready did their riders don antlered helmets and leap into the saddle. Then their feet were tied together beneath the horse. If the beast went down, so did the rider.

Keturah came riding back to Tekoa in the centre. 'Who do you think Safinim will send first?' she asked.

'Some dead men,' said Tekoa.

She took the place next to her father, glancing at Virtanen beside her. 'You look pale, my herald. Are you well?'

'I do not feel good, my lady,' he admitted. 'I've never found battles easy.'

Leon's lip curled. 'Well shut up about it,' he snapped. 'We're going to cut those bastards down like we've always done, and anything else is rot.'

Tekoa glanced at Leon, eyebrow raised. 'And how are you feeling, Leon?'

'Like I want to get this over with.'

'So also shitting yourself.'

'Yes,' he snapped, 'but I'm not bloody going on about it.'

'Obnoxious though he is, I'm afraid he's right Virtanen,' said Tekoa. 'Best to keep those things to yourself.'

'Here they come,' said Keturah, suddenly.

It was mid-morning, and Bellamus was making his move.

53
The First Day

A battle is a slow business. Even men who have trained for war their entire lives must feel their way into the horror, approaching step by step until the violence does not seem so impossible. Even then, all but a very few fight with half an eye on death: self-preservation uppermost in their minds, several rungs above killing the enemy. It takes a long time for two men to finish a private duel in the front rank, both fighting to defend, the victor usually the one who can focus longest and make fewest mistakes.

Battles are slow once they have begun, and slower to start. Generals will shuffle and watch and feint, knowing that once committed, their forces are nearly impossible to extract. The decision to use them will likely be one they can make just once. And that decision must usually be carried on a horse, often over miles, and still be relevant once it arrives. If you are to throw your precious soldiers into the maelstrom, you must be certain that that is where you want them, and still will be in half an hour's time. For soldiers and generals alike, the threshold for spilling blood is set very high.

Or so Tekoa thought. Safinim seemed to have drawn different conclusions. On top of the hill where the Lord Warden had stationed himself, some huge contraption had started to flap and mutate. The Anakim watched suspiciously as a series of wooden arms were raised, silhouetting flags against the grey sky. They were held up in one formation for a few heartbeats, then swung back down to be replaced by another bank. To the Anakim, who did not write, this display was at first impenetrable.

'A ritual?' suggested Virtanen. The herald seemed to be perspiring heavily, but his voice was steady as ever.

'Must be a blessing of some sort,' Randolph agreed.

'It's a signalling system,' said Tekoa. 'He's communicating with his generals. Clever, really,' he allowed, grudgingly.

There came a sickly moment as the Anakim absorbed the huge advantage this offered their enemy. Bellamus had developed a system of communication which let him send messages to any portion of this sprawling battlefield in the time it took to finish an apple. By contrast, the Anakim could send only the most basic orders by trumpet: *Charge, Retreat, Hold, Advance, Halt.* Everything else moved at the speed of a man on a horse.

And nor did Safinim have to be particular about where he used his multitudes. In reply to that whirring bank of flags, a block of infantry was advancing from the centre of the Teutan line. They stood a head taller than any other unit under Bellamus's command, and were so ready to charge that their ranks looked as precarious as stones on the verge of avalanche. They carried long two-handed spears and were armoured in drilled and linked Anakim bone plates.

'Barleymen,' said Virtanen.

'Good,' said Leon. 'Above all, I want to watch those bastards die.'

'Why's he advancing them alone?' wondered Keturah.

'It's a test,' said Tekoa. 'He's offering us a private duel in front of both armies. One of our units versus one of theirs.'

Garrett's hybrid legion lurched forward and began to howl. The noise blew across the battlefield like a gale, fierce and alien enough to set the hairs on Tekoa's neck standing on end.

'They want it,' Randolph observed mildly.

'Well they can bloody well have it,' said Tekoa. The Barley-men's ranks were already warping as they began to race each other forward, desperate for contact. 'If Safinim wants a show, we can rattle him. Advance the Ulpha. Let the world watch how warfare is done.'

The trumpet pealed out and the Ulpha, one of Keturah's reformed auxiliary legions, stepped down off the ridge to match the hybrids.

Tekoa knew of no finer sight on earth than the advance of a Black Legion. The snap of their movements set them apart on the battlefield. So well drilled were these soldiers that executing such basic manoeuvres as a march, an about-turn, or a dressing of the ranks, was an act of intimidation. Every individual moved like the fibres in a muscle, each cohort like the muscles in an arm, and the overall effect was so coherent and fluid as to make the skin crawl. Left foot then right took turns so precisely that their banners bounced side to side in perfect synchrony. Only Black Legionaries trained hard enough to march in step over rough ground. Only they could dress ranks while engaged, all conducted to the rhythm of whatever battle-hymn guided their movement. And on this occasion, it was the *Hymn of Advance* which began to moan from the ranks.

> *Do you recall my brothers dear,*
> *The toils we've run, the tales of yesteryear?*
> *Of charges 'gainst which all hope seemed lost,*
> *Of ocean, frost and forest winter-locked?*
> *March on! March on!*
> *Next year we'll talk about what we do here.*

The waiting legions left on the ridge roared their approval at this public duel, and joined in with the Ulpha, bellowing them on.

Do you recall the wolf-worn days before?
The moon burnt ash, the wind that whipped flesh raw?

We've seen the ice-grey dawn, you and I,
We've traversed bloody-footed, fate defied.
March on! March on!
Let angels match our breath and beat and stride.

Tekoa could have refused Bellamus's offer of a duel: let the Barleymen exhaust themselves climbing the ridge and break over his line. But both armies would be watching this engagement like herons, desperate for some omen of what was to come. It would not do to look frightened. The Teuta had to be reminded of their place.

One unit was warping and churning in its own eagerness, bunching together as they fixated on their Anakim targets, roaring in hatred. The other walked in mechanical order, drummers hammering at their back, singing a song they had known as children.

I cannot rest from struggle, my peers,
Let fire unleash, and darkness swell my fears,
And unblinking, drive forth, don't look back,
Though ghosts oppose, our hearts still will 'Attack!'
March on! March on!
Stand fast, take no wound to your back.

The Barleymen lost their shape completely. Half a dozen broke ranks and surged out in front of their comrades, howling as they charged alone for the Anakim ranks. The rest followed their lead almost at once and broke into a dead sprint, no longer a formation but a mob in fury.

There was the blurt of a trumpet and the Ulpha halted, swords rising in a glittering wave to take the charge. The 'Hymn of Advance' died away as the Anakim braced for impact, and the two lines met.

Across the battlefield, near a mile and a half from where contact was made, Tekoa felt the visceral thump of that impact; the pummelling of hybrid bodies, hurled rapid-fire into the

Ulphan line. They arrived more like a flood than any advance Tekoa had seen before, their primary weapon their flesh as they threw themselves at knees, chests and hips, their spears half-forgotten. They were drunk. They had no thoughts of self-preservation or even victory. They only wanted to wound; to make an impression on their aloof cousins, to hurt as they had been hurt.

The toll of that first hit upon the Ulpha was enormous. From the vantage point on the Anakim ridge, it seemed that the entire front rank was bowled over, the wind knocked from them, and the wave of Barleymen rolling on.

'Fools,' said Tekoa, for the Barleymen had fired their shot. An impetuous charge could inflict a devastating initial blow, which was often enough to unnerve a green opponent and seal victory. But against soldiers from the Black Kingdom, it was suicide. The Ulpha might have had their front rank buried beneath a hybrid avalanche, but now they were in lines and their enemies were not. They were ordered, while the Barleymen were clambering over a writhing mass of downed soldiers to reach them. The 'Hymn of Advance' moaned back into life and the Ulpha began to dress their ranks and push back against the Barleymen, swords flashing.

There came a moment, the two masses advancing into one another, neither prepared to cede an inch, when the front few ranks of Barleymen seemed to be picked off the floor. They reared up like a wave, held by pressure from behind and the advancing legion in front.

'They really want it,' said Randolph, glancing at Tekoa.

The colliding lines were not behaving as Tekoa had expected. The Barleymen were taking more casualties by far, but their hatred was blistering and they kept hurling themselves onto Anakim swords. The Ulpha were being rammed together, the front ranks trying to retreat to give themselves space; the rear ranks holding to the Anakim mindset that retreat was impossible. So tightly packed were they that a dozen legionaries in the rearmost rank even stumbled over backwards as the shock of another hybrid surge was transmitted back to them.

'Advance the Blackstone,' said Tekoa suddenly.

Keturah and Randolph gave him a sidelong glance.

Leon barked, 'What?'

They were watching an immortal legion at work: it had not occurred to any of them that the Ulpha might need help. 'This is a public challenge,' said Randolph. 'Send forward the Blackstones, and we admit the Ulpha have lost.'

'Do it now,' snapped Tekoa. The trumpet blared and Randolph's legion, the Blackstones, started forward. 'Saltcoats to plug the gap,' said Tekoa, causing another aide to gallop off to find the reserves and fill the gap the two legions had left in the Anakim line.

'I wouldn't have done that,' said Randolph. He sounded disappointed. 'It's a mark of shame for the Ulpha. They don't need help, regardless of how motivated the enemy. If it was my legion, I'd be furious.' Tekoa gave no sign that he had heard and Randolph became cold. 'Think of the five-thousand-man message you've just sent to the rest of the army. That far from showing the world how warfare is done, this is the time to panic, and you're worried the Ulpha won't finish the job.'

Tekoa still did not face Randolph. 'Better that than losing the legion.' He wished bitterly he had not engaged in Safinim's game.

The Ulpha had now bowed so much that their line was bulging, the ranks at their centre stretched apart. The Barleymen were climbing over a press of wounded soldiers before jumping onto the ranks of legionaries below. Hybrid bodies rained onto the Ulpha, flattening great holes in their ranks, which swarmed immediately with deranged spearmen. Then came a moment so shocking that Tekoa could not at first accept it.

There were Barleymen behind the Ulpha. It was a sight so unexpected that he had not paid close attention to how it had happened. It was only now, confronted with the reality of it, that he realised what he had just seen.

The ranks of the Ulpha had stretched so thin that a surge of charging Barleymen had piled right through them and sprawled out the other side. They lay on the ground in a heap, but there was no time to dispatch them before more were driving through. Like the first bean trickling through a frayed sack, the tiny hole they had created was suddenly rent wide. Dozens of hybrids poured through, and the Ulpha was ripped in two.

Tekoa felt his stomach turn. His companions watched in sickly silence as the two halves of the legion were driven apart, backing further and further away from their frenzied enemy. The singing of the legionaries on the ridge petered out, and in the quiet that followed they could hear the triumphant roars of Safinim's army.

'I don't believe it,' said Leon simply.

The Blackstones were still five hundred yards short of the engagement and would be too late to save the splintered legion. Divided in two, stumbling and tripping with all the momentum running against them, the Ulpha knew they had lost in front of both armies. They backed off, faster and faster until some turned for the safety of the advancing Blackstones, pelting away from the feverish contest.

The Anakim side of the battlefield had been silenced, and there was a collective settling across the ranks as their shoulders fell. Tekoa knew that his whole army would be feeling what he did: a sense of confidence deflating, an assumed superiority vanishing as the light flashed over it. He found he could not look at the Ulpha as their failure was laid out naked for all to see.

Keturah was actually blushing. Leon looked on the verge of vomiting, while Virtanen was even paler than before. They might be outnumbered and trapped, but on this, they had all thought they could depend: the quality of the legions. Man for man, they had believed they were better than any unit the Teuta had to offer.

The remnants of the Ulpha were streaming back towards the Blackstone. The Barleymen, like the drunkards they were, pursued baying for fifty yards and then let them go. They turned to embrace one another, laughing and hooting with a joy Tekoa had never imagined from these damaged, down-trodden men. They were the scum of Bellamus's army but in that moment, they were bathed in the roars of approval swelling from the Teutan ranks.

Tekoa took a steadying breath. The last thing he wanted now was to fight a battle. It seemed far better to slink away, regain some pride and wait for a more auspicious day. The thought even crossed his mind of sending a messenger to Safinim and seeing if he would treat with them. 'Sometimes,' he said, 'you just come up against a more motivated force. Nothing you can do about it.'

'But we didn't have to engage in Safinim's games at all,' said Randolph. 'That was pure arrogance.'

'Let's be honest,' said Hartvig quietly, 'we all thought the Ulpha would brush them aside.'

'I don't agree,' said Randolph heatedly.

'Enough, legate,' said Keturah in a voice that brooked no argument. Randolph fell silent.

'Bring the dragon cannons here.' Tekoa broke the silence. 'I want them set up on this rise.'

The Blackstone was still advancing, and began their own war-hymn. The refugees of the Ulpha latched onto the order of their immaculate ranks and tried to fall in, but the Blackstones would not have them. The Ulpha were sworn at, shoved aside and left to fend for themselves. They had run and were disgraced in the eyes of their peers. The Blackstones had to distance themselves from the thought that in their place, they might have done the same.

The recall sounded from the Teutan army. The Barleymen were still jeering, but clearly agreed their work was done. They butchered some injured legionaries, postured and shouted at the advancing Blackstones, and then began to edge back towards their own ranks, arm in arm, laughing raucously.

Safinim's great signalling machine had begun to clack and

whirr again, a bold and repetitive signal flashing up again and again. Trumpets blasted and echoed across the line, and with a cheer the entire Teutan front lurched forward. They had won their miniature public battle, and now Safinim wanted to test the ravaged Anakim morale.

'A general advance,' said Hartvig.

'Here we go,' muttered Leon.

'Blackstones back,' Tekoa ordered. 'Saltcoats next to them. The remainder of the Ulpha behind the line as reserves.'

Cheers were pealing out from the Teutan pikemen as they advanced, spears raised to heaven. It was eight years since they had clashed with them on Harstathur. Now they came again.

'We should set someone to watch that machine,' said Keturah. She was glaring at the telegraph gesturing above the prickled ranks, coordinating their advance. 'See if we can interpret what it's saying. It might give us an advantage.'

Tekoa shook his head. 'Better to destroy it. It'll slow them down.'

Behind him, the dragon cannons were being assembled. They had arrived on the field in two parts, which measured eighteen feet long when screwed together and levered onto a supporting frame. The firing chamber was bell-shaped, the muzzle tubular, both of them the shallow-water colour of weathered bronze. Their precious store of stone balls, each weighing the same as two fully armoured legionaries, was loaded onto a wheeled frame that could feed them directly into the muzzle. This had to sit upon a floor of freshly laid wooden boards so that the wheels did not gouge into the earth. At Keturah's behest, this was the first time they were being used away from the Hindrunn.

'We have forty shots,' she said. 'You think we can destroy that machine in forty?'

'I think we should try,' said Tekoa.

Randolph shook his head. 'Not accurate enough. Not at that

range. We should just fire into their ranks, then at least we'll hit something.'

'If all forty hit something, we'll be lucky to kill a hundred pikemen,' said Tekoa. 'Which is irrelevant. We aim at the machine. Destroy that machine, and even Safinim will struggle to coordinate an army this big.'

Keeping pace with the advancing pikemen on both flanks were heavy cavalry: knights on one side, cataphracts the other. The cataphracts were fearsome: armed with heavy steel lances and even their horses drenched in scale-mail from head to knee. But at the moment, they were lined up against the Unhieru on the Anakim right. 'I don't envy those cataphracts,' Tekoa said. 'Heavy armour will be nothing but a hindrance against Gogmagoc's villains.'

But no sooner had he spoken than the signalling machine began to twist once more, and the cataphracts wheeled in a sweeping of steel coats and cantered back from the Suthern left. 'He's got plans for the Unhieru,' said Randolph.

Tekoa folded his arms. 'Of course he does.'

In place of the cataphracts came what seemed from this distance to be a landslide of unaccountable momentum. Shambling into place came a unit which shimmered and glittered in the grey light, each one of them so vast as to make the formation appear strangely granular. 'Have they used these before?' said Keturah, watching the vast mass of flesh and armour take the vacant place on the Suthern right. 'I've not seen them.'

'*Aredamra*,' said Tekoa, softly.

Elephants.

The Unhieru were stirring; unmistakably restless at the opponents lining up against them. None of them had seen Unhieru bravery truly tested before, and now the gap between the two lines was just three hundred yards, and for the first time they were looking into the eyes of something bigger than themselves.

'*Aredamra*,' Keturah repeated. 'Describe them.'

'Beasts of war the size of a house. Tusks as long as a man,

sheathed in iron. Steeped in scale-mail, a turret of two bowmen mounted on the back, a driver sat in front.'

'Do they have a weakness?'

'Madness. Enrage them enough and the drivers lose control.'

'Might they turn against their own side?'

Tekoa raised an eyebrow and nodded at that. 'Certainly.' He turned to the dragon cannon crew, just preparing their first shot. 'The gun,' he said. 'Can you turn it?'

The firing captain, who was heating a steel wire in a basket of blazing charcoal, squinted at Tekoa and cupped a hand behind one ear. The Teutan pikeline had started to chant savagely, and it was getting harder to hear one another. There was unmistakable hunger in that noise, which Tekoa had never before experienced in their opponents.

'Can it be turned?' Tekoa bellowed, gesturing at the cannon.

The captain looked dubiously at the assembled weapon. 'No, lord,' he said, shaking his head.

'Why not?'

The captain shrugged. 'The frame is pointing the wrong way and it's too heavy to turn. We'd need to unload, disassemble barrel and firing chamber, take them off the frame, turn it, reassemble with new blocks to change the trajectory and then reload. It'd take . . . two hours?'

'But it's ready to fire now?'

The captain cupped a hand behind his ear again. Years as an artilleryman had evidently left him deaf.

Tekoa rolled his eyes. 'Can it fire now?'

The captain nodded. 'Yes, lord.'

'Then just turn the whole thing,' said Tekoa. 'It's not too heavy, you have a thousand men to shift it if you need.'

'Even if we could lift it,' the captain explained, 'the trajectory would still be wrong. We need to break off the securing bands, lever up the barrel, remove the blocks and brace the barrel to the frame again.'

'You have ten minutes.' Tekoa nodded at an aide. 'Get them men. Thirty should do it.'

'No, lord,' said the captain, watching in consternation as the aide wheeled and galloped to extract thirty men from the nearest legion; Ramnea's Own. 'We have to lash it back to the frame after we've changed trajectory. That can't be done in ten minutes.'

'And if you fire without strapping it down?'

The captain seemed at a loss for words. 'You can't. It'd be blown off the frame and probably crack.'

'But the shot would be accurate?'

'As accurate as she can be,' he allowed, 'but—'

'We'll risk it,' Tekoa interrupted, waving his hand. 'This shot is why you are here. You have to make it.'

Legionaries summoned from the line were running towards them, heavy armour bouncing up about their ears.

'But the size of the target,' the captain protested. 'It's too far; they're too close to the Unhieru. We might hit our own line.'

'You've done your duty by informing me of the dangers. Now, let's see how you are at following orders. Proceed, Captain.'

Thirty legionaries had clustered around the cannon and were looking expectantly at the dismayed firing-captain.

'We're going to try and turn this thing to face the *aredamra*,' he said helplessly. 'Everyone grab what they can.'

'Here!' Virtanen swung himself out of the saddle and took up a few of the thick beams brought to stabilise the firing platform. 'Put these beneath the gun,' he said, passing them out. 'It'll let more people lift together.'

They slid the beams beneath the gun to act as handles, taking twelve in all so that they stood in twelve pairs on either side, like oarsmen arranged on the deck of a galleon. There was still room for more and Leon, Hartvig and Randolph dismounted to join in with Virtanen, along with the six crewmen.

'It's on you, Captain!' Tekoa had to shout over the noise of the pikeline, now just two hundred yards away, growing louder and more vehement.

The firing captain shook his head in disbelief, staring at the gun. 'Ready?' he bellowed, and the men set themselves along their beams. 'Lift!'

They heaved, teeth bared, arms shaking and faces flushed, until there came a barely perceptible movement from the mass of bronze. Ponderously, the wooden feet of the frame were lifted clear of the deep gouges in the earth. It hovered a few inches off the ground, taking the collective efforts of all forty to keep it there. 'Right!' bellowed the captain. 'Right, right, right!'

Those at the front began to shuffle the muzzle towards the right, Virtanen emitting a roar of effort and pain, his arms trembling. Hartvig was spraying spit with each laboured breath as the muzzle came haltingly around. The captain alone was not lifting as he sighted down the barrel. 'There!' he said. 'Down!'

The gun dropped like a felled beech, its feet sinking six inches into the ground, the frame creaking and rocking with the sudden weight. The legionaries fell aside, gasping and clenching their sore hands, but Tekoa would allow them no rest. He levelled a finger at the captain. 'Is that it? Will it work?'

The captain was squinting along the barrel, head wobbling from side to side in a gesture of indifference. 'It'll do,' he said at last.

'Well done,' said Tekoa, turning back to the advancing pikemen. But the captain was addressing his back.

'I still need to change the trajectory.'

'Do it. Now. Quickly, quickly!'

They had moments. The pikeline was climbing like a tide up the slope to the ridge, roaring like a storm blowing through the canopy.

The crewmen began to hack at the cannon with axes, cutting the leather bands which bound wooden frame and bronze gun together. Others waited with handspikes, which they used to raise one end of the barrel and snatch out the quoins which set the firing angle. When they let it fall back into the frame, the angle was close to horizontal, reducing the range so that the ball did not simply fly over the top of the Teutan ranks.

The pikeline was deafening, and the legionaries responded by moaning their own battle-hymn, the drummers joining in with an urgent clatter.

On the right flank, there were barely a hundred and fifty yards between Unhieru and elephants, and the captain shook his head at the target. 'They're too close, lord. We have as good a chance of destroying Unhieru as we do *aredamra*.'

Tekoa let out a roar of frustration, turning on the captain. 'Just do it, Captain! Do it!' The two armies were bellowing at each other, and even screaming, Tekoa was hardly audible. 'Do it now!'

The captain threw up his hands, shaking his head as he bent to pick up a staff from the brazier. At the end was a wire which had been resting in the blazing charcoal and was now the yellow of the sun. 'Well back!' he warned his crew. 'Back! Further! She's going to jump off the frame!' The crew scrambled back and clamped their palms over their ears. Just in time, Virtanen, Hartvig, Keturah and Randolph did the same. Tekoa and Leon just watched. The captain lowered the wire to a small fuse protruding from the wide bronze back. He murmured something under his breath, hesitating for a heartbeat more.

'Now! Now! Now!'

Fuse and wire met and there was a spurt of white smoke.

Then the fabric of the world rippled. Tekoa felt that shock hit him like a visceral fist as the cannon erupted, spurting a gout of fire and smoke forty feet from the muzzle. He heard no boom; instead the roaring armies were silenced abruptly to be replaced by a distant whine. The body of the cannon leapt off its frame, still vomiting smoke, and tumbled to earth with a dirty clunk as the bronze cracked. Tekoa's horse started violently, and he sawed at the bridle to try and keep it still even as he searched the sky for some sign of the ball.

There: a thin trace of smoke arcing towards the Anakim right.

He stood in his stirrups, tracking the faint line drawn by the cannonball. In the air for just four heartbeats which felt like minutes, it began to descend, every eye following its progress as it dropped towards the Unhieru. It must have screamed over their heads by feet and instead came down at the very edge of the elephant formation.

One of the beasts was hit directly. The body, armour and all, was snatched to mist and tatters while the head was left spinning briefly before it thumped to ground. The ball hit the earth behind in a wave of soil, and the elephants stampeded.

They lurched away from that monstrous impact and began to charge, not towards their own line as Tekoa had hoped, but out into the hills to the north of the battlefield. He could see their drivers slapping and dragging at the beasts with hooked sticks, but they were ignored utterly as nearly half the formation disintegrated.

'A brilliant shot, Captain,' said Tekoa, nodding at him. 'It seems you delayed until just the right moment.'

'A fluke,' said the captain helplessly. He looked down at the cracked bronze. 'That won't fire again.'

'It's done enough.'

The Unhieru would still be fighting elephants, but their numbers had halved. They stood a chance.

'Almighty help us,' muttered Virtanen, for the rest of the elephants had lurched forward and now launched a fully armoured charge against the Unhieru. Tekoa pitied even the Unhieru fighting against such monsters, but there were more immediate concerns. The ringing was fading from his ears and the roaring of the pikeline rising, his skin crawling.

'Bows!' he bellowed. 'Rip them to tatters! Bows!'

Officers were roaring out and trumpets agreeing: the time had come to blaze through their limited stock of arrows. Ramnea's Own already held their great curved yew bows, nocked arrows, and with a creak, drew and shot as a single unit.

The range was murderous: just fifty yards from the pikemen, the force and density of the arrows was enough to stop the advance dead in its tracks. It seemed as though the entire first rank was poleaxed, hollowing out the formation they had carefully maintained over a mile of advance.

There was another scream from the officers of Ramnea's Own, another trumpet, another great sweeping as the bows were drawn. The pikeline was stuttering forward over the bodies of their first rank, and another volley drilled into them. The noise was like a waterfall; a white hammering as arrows punched through wood, steel, fabric and flesh and men fell backwards, pikes clattering to earth.

Leon and Hartvig were dismounting, forcing their way through the rear ranks of Ramnea's Own. There was a huge cheer as they reached the front and the two Sacred Guardsmen were recognised.

'Charge!' the officers were crying. Bows were hurled overhead to be collected by the apprentice legionaries, scampering over the main battle-line like ants.

'Charge!' The whole legion took a pace forward. Even Virtanen was leaning forward in the saddle, adding to the noise.

'Charge!'

54
Aredamra

Bellamus did not care about the rankers' duel. The noise of it coming from his right felt as though it was forcing his head over to one side: a cacophonous white wall which made his ears ring. But his pikemen would hold the legions, and he had gone where he was needed: on the left, to oversee the fight which would decide the rest. Elephants against Unhieru.

'Riding one of those things looks the safest place on the battlefield,' said Diethaad, watching beside him. 'You weren't tempted to mount yourself in a howdah?'

Bellamus raised his eyebrows, watching the scene carefully, fingers drumming a downpour on the saddle. 'Never.' He was on horseback, along with fifty Thingalith, all of them raised on an ancient burial mound so they could see over the dust cloud rising behind the elephants. They were close enough to the beasts to smell their strange honey-scent and hear the belching calls of the mahouts, their drivers, as they charged for the Unhieru.

The giants were more numerous, especially since the cannon-shot, which had caused Bellamus to close his eyes in despair as it routed half his most valuable soldiers, but the elephants were heavier, with a charge like a battering ram.

The Unhieru were not advancing but flinching away as the elephants lowered their heads, steel-sheathed tusks curving out in front, trunks lashing.

The two lines collided in a billow of dust, and the Unhieru ranks buckled immediately. Bellamus saw one hurled fifteen feet above the ranks, spinning through the air and shedding helmet and weapons before crashing at the feet of another rampaging elephant. He was trampled, the elephants crushing in, battering, trumpeting and bristling with fury. One Unhieru was gored so violently that the tusk skewered him through, dragging him backwards. He tried weakly to free himself while the elephant's head was pulled down and to the left by the weight of the giant. Some of the elephants had iron balls chained to their trunks, which they could wield with vicious accuracy, clanging off the Unhieru helmets like bells. The Unhieru pulled away from the bladed tusks and swinging trunks, and only then did the crews mounted on top release their first volley.

Strapped to each elephant was a howdah, but rather than the bowmen who would usually occupy it, Bellamus had fitted each with a siege bow and two-man crew. Like a giant crossbow, each siege bow could spit a two-pound bolt capable of penetrating the thick Unhieru chainmail. The charge had bunched the giants into easy targets, and as the elephants passed by, the siege bows were swivelled in their direction. Each unloaded with a snap that made the howdah jump, coughing a projectile so fast that it was only visible when it struck home in a puff of blood, the giants rippling with the shock of it.

Diethaad was laughing in sheer glee as each Unhieru was reduced to a chainmail heap. 'Nothing makes me happier than watching these bastards die,' he said.

Bellamus's men had learned to fear the Unhieru terribly, and he had to show they could be beaten.

The first of the rampaging elephants were now emerging from the back of the Unhieru formation, still just under the control of the mahouts. It was tempting to have them smash into the back of the Anakim line, and for a heartbeat, Bellamus considered sending a message up to the telegraph. But the pikemen were holding the Anakim, and if he could finish the Unhieru, the battle was as good as won. The giants were bunched together, or picking themselves off the floor, or reeling drunkenly after the battering they had taken, and now was the time to make sure. The mahouts turned their beasts, the crews cranking furiously at their siege bows to reload as the elephants came about for a second charge.

The Thingalith roared the elephants on as they lumbered up to speed once more.

'Crush them!' Diethaad was bellowing. 'Smash those stinking, feral bastards!'

But Bellamus was silent, his palms suddenly prickling with sweat.

The Unhieru were not scared. He could tell by the way they were setting out in a strange, trance-like procession towards the charging elephants. By the way their axes were coming up and they were beginning to spread out once more. It was not the walk of the frightened, but the vengeful. These giants were the unchallenged masters of valleys and mountains, and had developed no capacity to back down. They were perhaps the most tightly bonded people on this battlefield and had watched their family members knocked down in their hundreds. Now they were entering that strange state of possession, despised by the Anakim, embraced by the Barleymen and natural to the Unhieru, where they lost all memory, flushed deep red beneath their chainmail and turned to fiends.

The elephants lowered their heads once more, ears flaring threateningly, the crewmen on their backs staggering as the howdahs rocked from side to side. The beasts were trotting, the Unhieru walking and when they came together this time there was no dust-shrouded collision. The Unhieru were more spread out and stepped aside to make room, letting the elephants pass deep inside their ranks. The siege bowmen held off, needing a dense target to aim for from their unstable platforms, and for a curiously long period, Bellamus saw not a single casualty. The formations swarmed harmlessly past one another, until they were entirely enmeshed. And then the elephants faltered, uncertain, their mahouts grunting that they should charge on, but slowing in the face of eerily silent Unhieru.

Then the axes came down.

Without fanfare, the Unhieru began hacking artlessly at the hind-quarters of each elephant. Axes which had barely been used in the first charge now proved capable of parting the elephant scale-mail like thick cream. There was a discordant blare of distress as the elephants wheeled to face their tormentors, and succeeded only in exposing their hindquarters to another Unhieran axe.

And the melee erupted. The elephants began to twist and lash out at the Unhieru, who were swinging as mindlessly as though they had been tasked with felling a forest.

Bellamus was watching the duel nearest him, and saw an Unhieru sheer off an entire tusk with a single hack, causing the elephant to trumpet in pain. The Unhieru was drawing back to swing again when the howdah jumped with the force of the siege bow unleashing a bolt. It ricocheted off the thick helmet in a streak of sparks and rocked the Unhieru's head back. It was still staggering when the single-tusked elephant rampaged forward and threw it off its feet, beginning to trample deliberately on the supine warrior.

The elephant was evidently unaware of the second Unhieru approaching purposefully from its right. In a butcher's cut, the giant parted the main strap holding the howdah in place. The elephant was raging from one side to the other, and the rocking of the howdah became steadily more deranged until it slipped half off its back, dangling at an angle which nearly tipped the crew onto the ground. Instead they latched onto the howdah's uppermost edge, looking down in terror as the Unhieru reached up a ham-like hand. It clamped onto the lower edge and wrenched the howdah clean off so that it fell, crewmen and all, in a matchwood heap at his feet. The remaining strap had slipped down around the elephant's rear legs, and it now acted as an anchor. The enraged beast was tethered in place and the Unhieru closed in, taking it in turns to torment it to death.

Another elephant caught Bellamus's eye, for this one had an Unhieru crouched upon its back. The contents of the howdah had already been torn apart and the Unhieru was crawling unsteadily towards the mahout sat at the front, who kept glancing over his shoulder at the giant, but urged his steed on, aiming it for the tethered elephant with the missing tusk. He struck from the flank, catching four of the Unhieru by surprise and knocking them flying like splinters bursting from a split log. The elephant and its courageous driver charged out of view before Bellamus could see what happened to it.

But he did see crewmen vomiting over the sides of a howdah, sick with the extreme motion of the charging elephant and the complex task of reloading their siege bows. He saw an elephant collapse beneath a mass of enemies only for the Unhieru to continue hacking, totally indifferent to whether it was living or dead. He saw one Unhieru wielding a shattered tusk, using it to hook the crew from an elephant's back as though fishing for termites with a stick. Others seemed to be targeting the mahouts directly and were sweeping them off their elephants with such prejudice that when Bellamus started looking, he realised there were nearly as many without drivers as with them. And without their mahouts, the elephants panicked. They were lost, maddened by pain and noise, rampaging away from the fight with heads swinging and trunks lashing.

'And that is why I would never sit on an elephant in battle,' said Bellamus.

The Thingalith had stopped hollering, now watching uneasily as their best hope against the Unhieru began to flee. A stream of them were even breaking clear of the melee and rampaging towards the Teutan pikemen. Their mahouts – who were given an elephant from childhood to live and grow with – were drawing poisoned spikes to try and kill them before they ruined the Teutan left. Tears in their eyes, they begged the crazed beasts to obey once more, leaving it as late as they possibly could before putting them down.

Diethaad swore viciously. Like Bellamus, he recognised a moment of instability which might cost them this battle if they could not immediately control it. Unoccupied, the Unhieru would surely turn their attentions to the vulnerable flank of the pikeline and unravel the whole formation.

Bellamus snapped his fingers and one of the Thingalith trotted to his side. 'Camels. Bring them forward immediately.'

He had two units nearby who might avert catastrophe. There were the cataphracts, powerful enough to frighten even the Anakim, but whose horses were unnerved by the stench of the Unhieru, and often refused to charge home. And then there was his camelry.

They were quite as strange as the elephants, and Bellamus had saved the shock of them for just such a moment. As they came loping into position, he experienced the same reaction now as he had when he first laid eyes on them: a strange buzzing in his ears and crawling of his skin. Serpentine necks, limbs like willow-wands, tails like flat-bodied eels, faces like hideous street-mutts and humped bodies draped in tasselled caparisons: it was not one beast but several combined. Each carried a rider armed with a lance, their faces hidden by a screen of mail. The camels stank like rotting vegetation and if that did not make them uncanny enough, their temperament did. They spat, they kicked, they grunted and they bit. Bellamus thought that if a camel were a man, it would be a drunken poacher: violent, cynical, capable, with a haughty, ugly face that betrayed every day spent in the wilderness.

The last of the elephants were routed, and the Unhieru were now liberated to observe the camels lining up against them. They paused at the sight of the bizarre animals, evidently uncertain what to make of them. As Bellamus had hoped, it seemed enough to break their maddened trance.

'Sound the withdrawal,' he commanded.

Some of the Thingalith looked at him. 'For who, my lord?' asked one eventually. 'Our pikemen have the legionaries tamed.'

'Everyone,' Bellamus snapped. He was struggling to focus. He had drunk nothing today, knowing he needed a clear head, and the environment was abrasive. The pikemen on his right were grinding forward, pushing the Anakim back before their bristling multitudes, and the noise of it was enough to hurt his ears. His eyes were watering with dust, the sun glaring into his face, and every order had to be bellowed to be heard. He was too close, nearly too overwhelmed to think. 'General withdrawal, now,' he repeated, irritably. They had the briefest of moments, perhaps just long enough while the Unhieru were hesitating, to salvage the pikemen. He knew the Unhieru had a sense of smell more acute than his own, and his nose was wrinkling with the stench of the camels. *It might just give us long enough*, he thought, glancing along the pikeline.

A trumpet was pealing out, repeated in a chain up to the signalling machine, which echoed the order.

Withdraw! Withdraw!

For the pikemen, the order did not seem to register. They had no idea what was happening in this corner of the field: all they saw were the Anakim before them, who were being driven back through superior tactics and numbers.

A mounted messenger came galloping towards Bellamus, clods of mud flicking up behind until he slowed and reined in before them. 'Lord Arnuwanda's compliments my lord, and are the camelry to advance?'

'Under no circumstances,' replied Bellamus. 'Even if the Unhieru charge, I want them to stay where they are and react in no way.'

If they actually fought, the Unhieru would almost certainly prove the stronger. This was a bluff, reliant on the uncanny smell and appearance of the camels. Fear tended to evaporate when confronted, and Bellamus would let the Unhieran imaginations do the fighting for him.

The messenger hesitated, then nodded and galloped back.

Bellamus threw glances along the pikeline, willing it to respond. The camelry would not give them much longer, and they needed to pull back and reorder before the Unhieru got over the shock of their appearance. The trumpets were echoing the withdrawal again and again, and to his relief, he saw a gap developing between the two lines nearest to where he stood. The pikeline was peeling away, and the exhausted legionaries were letting them go.

'Pull them back until they're just in front of the siege weapons. Skirmishers to cover their retreat.'

While Unhieru fought elephants and the infantry ground together, the engineers had been busy. Behind the pikeline, what looked like skeletal towers of timber were assembling. Trebuchets; more siege bows set beside them, already loaded to cough a volley at the limping Anakim battle-line. They could pick vulture-like at their enemy from a range of three hundred yards, and turn the ridge from a haven to a nightmare.

Skirmishers were peppering the legions with arrows, and the Anakim were forced to turn and scuttle back up the ridge, heads ducked as the siege bolts whistled flat into the line. They left behind the debris of a costly stalemate: a tideline of tangled pikes and bodies, neither side cheering to claim the victory.

The Unhieru were left as the only forward unit of Keturah's coalition, still in their stand-off with the camelry. Unsupported and still uncertain about their enemy, they too began to withdraw.

Bellamus let out a deep breath and glanced at Diethaad, who looked equally relieved. The Unhieru left behind thousands of their own casualties, but he had fired his best shot. Even the elephants had failed against them. The legionaries were stubborn enemies, and though he did not believe they would break through his pikeline front-on, if they could hold on, the Unhieru might spoil it all by demolishing his left and then turning on the pikemen.

'Back up the hill,' said Bellamus, eyes still on the retreating giants. 'Come, we should be by the telegraph.' *And the wine.*

They began to climb, the Thingalith whooping and gossiping about the fight they had just witnessed. 'They know how to wield a mace, eh, those elephants?'

'Did you see the sack which had picked up a broken tusk? Like he was trying to put together a skewer for his supper.' Sack was what the men were calling the Unhieru, after their shapeless chainmail armour. There was also something homely and unthreatening about a sack. It did not suggest the feral reek, the round-eyed helmets or the vengeful rage that accompanied the word *Unhieru*.

Bellamus left them to their conversation. He was surprised to find himself thinking not of the Unhieru, but of the Anakim legion breaking before the Barleymen. That was a victory he had never thought to see, but it had been accompanied by a feeling so unexpected that he had not recognised it until now.

Disappointment. So even Black Legionaries ran.

The hilltop, when he reached it, did not seem such a good place after all. There were several trenches gouged three feet into the soil where cannonballs had struck close to the telegraph. One of the enormous stone balls had broken in half and come to rest on the hilltop. For the benefit of his men, Bellamus sat upon it as though it were a stool. 'Bring a table, wine, ink and parchment,' he commanded. 'And Widukind, if you can find him.'

There he sat, a cannonball for a chair, scratching out orders and advice for his commanders while a projectile duel took place on the field below. The trebuchets and siege bows ceaselessly pelted the Anakim line, which could only reply with their remaining cannon. Bellamus kept glancing up, wondering if the unequal fight would tempt them off the ridge and onto the waiting pikemen.

His attention was wandering from the letter he was writing, which he was not sure how to finish. He was not sure he would even send it.

I believe the Thingalith would tolerate your presence. They are a band of outsiders, as you know, and used to strange circumstances. I believe the time has come, Vigtyr, for you to redeem yourself upon the field.

Distantly, he was aware of a faint rushing noise. He kept scratching, intending to finish his sentence before allowing himself to be distracted, when a shuddering boom from right in front made him jump. Earth sprayed over him and his desk, the grit stinging his cheeks as a cannonball, which had struck the ground twelve feet in front, bounced, and wailed just a yard over his head. His clothes were ruffled by a hot draught, as though the angel of death had swooped low to inspect and then passed him by like he was not worth the bother. He sat frozen, shocked by how near obliteration he had just come, and blinked foolishly down at the parchment before him, now scattered with sandy topsoil.

'Saves you blotting it, Lord Safinim,' said a solemn voice behind him. It was Widukind, barefoot as ever, drifting up the hill towards him. He came to a halt before Bellamus, who spotted another figure walking immediately behind him. Stepan, dressed in the robes of an Abbio.

Bellamus blinked, momentarily distracted by Stepan's presence. 'Thank you for coming, Bishop,' he said, shaking his head a little. 'Did you have a vantage point to observe the battle?'

Widukind nodded.

'What did you make of it?'

He considered. 'The Unhieru are a problem. You were wise to pull back when you did. We have days to finish the Anakim, if needed.'

Bellamus nodded. 'I'm glad you share my assessment. A problem indeed. They are proving extremely difficult to contain, and that makes the whole army vulnerable. If they win the fight on the left, they can turn on the pikeline and I fear we won't be able to stop them. I need someone who can keep them busy.'

Widukind said nothing, just fixing him with that light grey gaze, made almost hypnotic by the dark rings about his eyes.

'I wondered how you thought the zeal of the Holy Ereboan Army might stand up against the Unhieru?'

'Fleetingly.'

Bellamus raised his eyebrows at that. The bishop had an unshakeable belief in the power of faith, and that was a more clear-eyed assessment than he had anticipated. 'Then . . . might the Abbio stand against them? Treat the Unhieru as cavalry, to be contained with cavalry.'

'They would stand,' said Widukind. 'The horses would not. I would think spearmen our best chance.'

That was probably true, thought Bellamus. 'Maybe I'll ask Ruden's halberdiers.'

'Offer them the title Men Without Fear,' Widukind advised. 'It may motivate them.'

Bellamus nodded. 'I'll support them with the camelry too. I thank you for your advice, Lord Bishop.'

Widukind bowed. 'If martyrdom is required, speak the word, Lord Safinim.'

'Selfishly, I'd prefer to keep you alive.'

Widukind bowed again and as he turned back down the hill, Bellamus called, 'Sir Stepan? A word, please.'

'I am no knight, Lord Warden,' said Stepan, taking an unwilling pace towards Bellamus. 'The Abbio renounce all titles.'

Bellamus watched Widukind disappear down the hill. 'You're no Abbio,' he said.

'You've no idea what I am.'

'But you know what I am, is that it?' Bellamus felt himself become heated. 'I tried to help you, all those years ago. I didn't have to give you men to go and find your wife. Still you blame me for her death. Well it wasn't my fault! There is no reason to the universe, we have to live with the hand it deals us, and yours has been better than most. Blame ill becomes anyone, let alone apportioned so long after the event.'

Stepan watched this tirade without reacting. When Bellamus had burned himself out, he replied quietly. 'I do know what you are. And I'm sorry to see it. There was a time, years ago, when I'd forgiven you for what happened. But I'd heard too much else by then. You are not the man I was friends with.'

'I thought you knew better than to believe the rumours,' said Bellamus, curtly.

'Rumours . . .' repeated Stepan. 'In your own words then, Lord Warden, what happened to the queen?'

Bellamus froze. 'Again, you seem to attribute our enemy's actions to me.' But it was too late. Stepan had seen his shock.

He nodded. 'There's no more I can say without risking execution. By your leave, my lord.' He gave a derisive bow and turned away, marching back down the hill.

Bellamus nearly shouted after him. He did shout for two Thingalith with the intention of ordering them to bring Stepan back and forcing him into contrition. But by the time they had arrived, he had changed his mind. 'Lord?'

He sealed the letter angrily and held it out. 'Take that to Vigtyr.' He could not look at the letter as it was taken to the turncoat. Instead, he turned back to the ridge.

Below him, the Anakim were lying down.

55
The Cannon

Keturah and Virtanen had been talking on the ridge when the pikemen started to withdraw. 'Thank the ocean,' said Virtanen. 'I thought he had us there.'

'So did I,' said Keturah, eyeing the retreating lines. 'So why's he pulled back?'

The sun had burned off the fret, and it was turning into a bright, damp day. Legionaries were beginning to clamber back up the ridge, Leon striding among them: battered, irascible and spitting blood. 'Hartvig's dead,' he said as he drew within earshot. 'What the fuck happened? We were getting battered out there. Why's he withdrawn?'

'No!' said Keturah. 'Hartvig? How?'

'Like a bloody hero.' Leon dropped to the floor and began tugging at his left boot. 'Good man. Good guardsman.' He succeeded in pulling off the boot, which came away in a dribble of dark blood. He found some strips of cloth and began binding a long wound in his calf. 'Watch out,' he added, redundantly.

A siege bolt had just thumped into the grass a foot to the right of Keturah's boot. She started and Virtanen gripped her shoulders instinctively. She looked back to the battlefield and saw the battery of siege weapons revealed by the retreating pikeline. Another siege bolt cracked overhead like lightning, and then a boulder was lobbed into a pack of retreating legionaries nearby, flattening one and knocking another to the floor.

'Get them up the ridge!'

Keturah heard the shout and looked right to see her father on horseback, urging legionaries up the slope.

'Now, now!' The femur-trumpets were insisting but the legionaries had no more speed in them. They trudged and limped back up to the crest, siege bolts whistling flat into the slope.

Tekoa arrived in a thudding of hooves, eagle-feather cloak rippling behind him. 'That was damned lucky,' he said.

'Why's Safinim pulling back?' asked Keturah.

'Because he lost the battle on the right. The Unhieru – and the cannon – defeated his elephants and that left his pikemen vulnerable. So he had to pull them back.'

'So Gogmagoc came through for us,' said Virtanen. The herald was still very pale, but he flashed a wink at Keturah, who had often complained that the Unhieru alliance was more trouble than it was worth.

'Not like him,' she said. 'He must be drunk.'

Tekoa ignored Virtanen's chuckle. 'Safinim has still won the morning,' he insisted. 'After that fight and what happened to the Ulpha, the momentum's all with him. He won't leave us be for long, he'll want to finish it before dark.'

'He can do that without advancing,' said Leon, nodding at the siege weapons still spitting at their lines. Even standing on top of the ridge, the legions were well within range.

'March the battle-line backwards and have them lie down,' said Keturah. 'At least then we'll be hidden from the siege bows.' The trumpets sounded and the message was passed down the line. In a tattered wave, the men pulled back, jogging, limping and half-carried. Leon ignored the orders, tending to his injuries in full view of the siege weapons. Keturah and Tekoa too stood their ground to set an example. 'You should go back, Virtanen,' said Keturah. The herald was trembling with fear, and jumped every time a siege bolt hit the ground nearby.

'I stay with you, my lady,' he insisted.

'There's no sense you risking yourself here. Go back with the men.'

'I didn't have to stand in the battle-line,' he said. 'Showing some face here is the very least I can do.'

The four of them and the cannon crew were left the only figures on top of the ridge, the rest sheltering behind its crest, pressed to the ground like rabbits as a buzzard circles overhead. The crewmen worked relentlessly, discharging the huge gun once every half an hour, still aiming for the signalling machine on top of its distant hill. The ridge defended the legionaries from the flat siege bolts, but the trebuchets could still bowl their fifty-pound stones over the crest, dropping them in from a high arc and obliterating anyone beneath. Safinim had scores, working constantly with their crews on a relay, churning projectiles at the Anakim.

'Well I'm damned well not standing around for Safinim to finish his lunch,' said Keturah tartly. 'Virtanen, a walk?'

'A pleasure, my lady.'

They set off east, walking in front of the legionaries lying still in formation, just back from the crest of the ridge. To their right, out past the marram grass dunes behind the ridge, the sea was breaking softly over the beach and making the shingle rattle. To their left lay the battlefield, gulls and foxes squabbling over the morning's dead; the siege weapons arrayed in a line parallel to their ridge, and discharging constantly. It would need to be a lucky shot to catch either of them, but they were obvious targets, and each kept half an eye out.

'I've been thinking about that island, across the sea,' said Virtanen.

Keturah laughed briefly. 'You think of little else.'

The herald let out a shaky breath. 'Almighty, what I'd give to see it again. I truly thought our boat must've gone down during the night and slipped into the Otherworld. The sun scarcely slept while we were there, and there were mountains which smoked like lit charcoal mounds.'

'And empty, you said?'

'Not a soul.'

'Food?'

'Well . . . It was a barren sort of place, but the seas were the richest I'd ever seen. Stuffed with fish and huge smooth beasts like the slick pebbles you find on the shore. Just one of those would feed an army.'

'I must say, Virtanen,' said Keturah, amused, 'when you made me that offer all those years ago, of fleeing the Hindrunn with you and sailing to that island, I hadn't realised we'd be hunting sea-monsters for our supper.'

He looked at her sidelong, twinkling. 'You remember that still?'

'Of course.'

'Well let's not rule it out,' he said reasonably.

She laughed. They walked in silence for a moment, and Keturah became suddenly aware of a siege bolt, hurtling towards them from the left. She clutched at Virtanen, preparing to push him one way or another, not having the words at hand to warn him in time. Then it rushed over her head, she ducking entirely too late, but the bolt missing anyway. Her heart was fluttering, and Virtanen placed a palm over her hand, holding her arm on his. 'This is his plan, I suppose,' he said, nodding at the heavy weapons below them. 'Safinim doesn't actually need to engage us. He'll just wither us away with his siege engines.'

Keturah pursed her lips. 'Indeed.'

'I'm sorry, my lady,' he said, patting her arm and leading her on. 'I don't mean to be defeatist. But I suppose I'd feel better if I could see a path to victory. The Sutherners outnumbers us, so we need to kill two or three times as many men as he does to have a hope. But against the pikeline, we were losing more than him.'

Keturah shrugged, as if to say that it did not matter. 'Father will think of something. Hold out till night, and things will look different tomorrow. We'll get through this, and you'll get to explore your island across the sea once more.'

'I hope to have the honour to show you round it, my lady,' he said gravely. 'If it does indeed prove uninhabited, I shall name it Keturahsmark.'

She laughed again.

They turned around and retraced their steps along the ridge-line. By the time they passed the cannon crew again, their deaf captain had been killed, and the ground was deeply scarred on either side by trebuchet-strike. Doggedly, they were preparing their next shot, not even reacting as a siege bolt shrieked off the bronze barrel in a trail of sparks. Keturah made sure not to hurry past so that she shared at least briefly in their danger. 'You are magnificent,' she told them, and they grinned back through powder-blackened faces and scorched eyebrows.

They reached Tekoa, who looked pointedly at the pair of them, raising an eyebrow. Keturah realised they were still walking arm in arm, and pulled her hand away swiftly. 'I don't like this lying down,' he growled, gesturing at the legionaries.

'It's saving lives.'

'It's getting us used to prostrating ourselves. You have to square up to an enemy. You can't imagine you're just going to stand up when the moment is right and defeat them toe to toe. By then you've already lost.'

'The time to stand may be upon us,' said Keturah, nodding over Tekoa's shoulder. The shadows were growing long, and on the crest of the far hill, the signalling machine had started to whirr. Safinim had withered them long enough, and was about to unleash his next wave.

Boom.

As if its crew had been waiting for the machine to resume, the cannon roared. Keturah jumped, turning on her heel to search the sky for the speck of the cannonball. It was a heart-beat before she spotted a faint trace of smoke, hurtling over the Teutan army and towards the signalling machine. She craned forward, hand flying to her mouth. 'Oh!'

'Go on!' cried Tekoa.

The ball hit the ground a few feet beneath the crest of the hill, heaving a wave of earth out before it which swept over the signalling machine. It did not look like much, but there must have been more power in that wave than there appeared, because the contraption was torn to pieces. Wooden beams were flung out to either side, flags left falling raggedly to earth and several crewmen catapulted away from the shockwave.

'Yes!' bellowed Tekoa. 'Yes!' Along the ridge there came cheers from the guncrew, who were embracing wildly.

Keturah beckoned an aide behind them, who crawled along the grass until he lay by her feet. She rolled her eyes. 'Get up, you're not a ferret. My compliments to the crew on a fine shot; a ration of wine for them all in reward.'

The aide stood, bowing very low and never quite straightening as he scurried away.

Tekoa let out a vengeful noise. 'That might've been a prayer answered,' he said. 'I'm not sure Safinim will be able to coordinate another large advance without the machine. Not before nightfall.'

'Perhaps better than that,' said Virtanen, squinting at the hilltop. 'Do you suppose that's Safinim himself?' A commotion had assembled about the wreckage of the machine, a dozen figures scurrying around a single downed figure.

Keturah and Tekoa leaned towards it, Keturah scarcely daring to hope. 'If it is, I'm upgrading the guncrew's extra ration to a barrel. They can spend the rest of the battle getting drunk as far as I'm concerned.'

'I think . . .' said Tekoa, eyes narrowed. 'I think it could be.'

'It's his banner,' said Keturah, noting the distant flag of a black spider on a red background. 'He must be up there.' She exchanged a gleeful look with her father.

'I'd say that calls for a drink all round,' said Virtanen breezily.

Without saying a word, Leon held forward a small corked skin which had been hanging at his belt.

'Oh no,' said Keturah. 'Great heavens, Leon, what is that?'

'Drink.'

'For cleaning wounds?' asked Tekoa suspiciously.

The guardsman shrugged.

Tekoa took the skin with a little cackle. 'Could do worse, I suppose.' He uncorked it and raised it in the direction of the Teutan army. 'Death to Safinim,' he toasted, taking a sip. Eyes watering, he passed it to Keturah.

'To the guncrew,' said she, raising it to her lips. There was nothing pleasant about the liquid, which was bitter as dandelion leaves and made her mouth burn like vinegar, but she swallowed without spluttering and passed the brew to Virtanen.

'To Hartvig,' said the herald, taking his own sip as though it were the finest grape-wine. He passed it on to Leon, who stowed it back at his belt without drinking.

'Well,' said Virtanen, smacking his lips, 'I—'

He was interrupted by the siege bolt which none of them had spotted. It sped into the herald's low chest, picking him off his feet and bowling him down the back of the ridge. Keturah screamed, and even Tekoa yelled in shock. Virtanen himself had made not a sound.

All three of them sprinted down the back of the ridge, Keturah's feet slipping on the grass. By the time she reached the herald, the ground around him was saturated in blood. His eyes were closed, and did not open as Keturah raised his warm head and cradled it in her lap. His breathing was very slow, his face strangely serene. Keturah asked him where he thought he was going, and had he forgotten about that island he wanted to explore across the sea?

He died in her arms.

56
The Pass Beneath the Cliffs

Ormur, Gray and Roper's journey south through Albion had felt like travelling through a vast and recently abandoned temple. The country was eerily quiet, but with an atmosphere imprinted into its very foundations, strong enough to send shivers down the spine. Roper had been heartened. 'If there's no one here it means everyone's condensed in one place. We haven't missed the battle yet.'

They walked nearly directly south, but soon ran into the vigilant Abbio, and were forced to divert west. They decided to skirt around the Teuta, and link up with Keturah's forces via the coast, avoiding Abbio whenever they saw them and taking it as evidence they needed to go further west. They found a single shepherd whom they questioned for news, but the only other occupants of Blacklaw seemed to be the grave-dogs who gurgled raucously in the evenings.

'Do they ever attack?' asked Roper, staring into the dark as another surge of agonised laughter rang out. They had managed twenty-two miles that day and now sat footsore together by a fire. They had bolted their meagre rations, and it was Ormur's turn to scrape out their one cooking pot.

'Sometimes,' said Gray. 'They are terrors. Hard to drive off if they get started. They play and worry and gnaw until you're vulnerable, then the whole lot descend and rip you to pieces.'

'Sir,' said Ormur warningly. He had looked up from the blackened pot and now raised his hand to point at three pairs of glowing green eyes, hovering in the dark not twenty feet from where they sat. Heavily, the three Anakim shuffled closer together and pulled out their swords.

'Back to back,' said Gray. 'Don't show them a vulnerable side.'

They could stand if it came to it, but were too weary just now. They edged around so they sat braced against one another, each facing a separate angle of the night. The laughter died away and the eyes watched them in silence for a time, occasionally changing height and drifting a few yards as one of them changed position. Ormur was facing three, and when he looked over his shoulder to check for more, his mouth fell open. Facing Roper were half a dozen, yet the Black Lord had said nothing. Some had crept into the fire's light, heads held low, but they seemed to recognise the drawn sword resting on Roper's legs and dared not come within range.

'Be still,' said Gray, calmly. 'If you can skewer one, do, but under no circumstances move from this position. They'll tear you down.'

Ormur did not need telling. He kept his gaze on the green eyes before him. Occasionally they would move, one creeping close enough that he could see the flames shining off its wet nose. But they were patient, and just watched.

The fire was suddenly burned low. Ormur started, and looked around, but the gravedogs were gone. There was a faint grey light in the east, and it took some while to realise he must have fallen asleep. He was still propped against Roper and Gray, and looking carefully over his shoulder, he saw that they were both asleep too, chins resting on their chests.

The gravedogs had left them alone.

Ormur could not stir without waking his comrades, who needed sleep above all else. So he just sat and watched the dawn. Birds squeaked and trickled. A fox ran across the field before them, a gosling held by the neck in its jaws. Butterflies shook off the dew and fluttered on hinged wings. The last thing he wanted to do was start moving again, but it was not long before he felt Roper stiffen at his back. The tension returned to his brother like a bow under draw until suddenly it was as though Ormur were sitting against a wall.

'They've gone,' Roper said.

'Yes.'

Gray was next to announce his wakefulness. 'I fell asleep while they were still watching.'

Ormur agreed he had as well.

Gray snorted. 'Surrounded by gravedogs and every one of us falls asleep. Well that's a fair sign of the amount of jeopardy that now seems normal.'

'Or of how much we need sleep,' said Ormur.

The fire was out, so they gulped down their oats cold before Roper led them on. 'Come. I can smell the sea.'

It took no more than an hour to reach, footsore and blistered though they were. They crossed a rise and suddenly it was there beneath their feet. A great white cliff, the sun blazing off it like freshly shed snow, and furious waves crashing against its base. The noise: the blank noise of it, soothed Ormur like a balm.

'Keturah can't be far now,' said Roper. 'If we walk through the night, we should have reached the army by morning.' He hitched the pack over his shoulder and set off east. Gray and Ormur looked at one another, and then fell into line behind him.

They had progressed less than a league when Gray remarked: 'You know where this is, my lord?'

'No.'

'This is the cliff we believed you'd died on. I saw a Kryptean prisoner flung off here and thought he was you.'

Roper did not seem much interested. 'You didn't go after the body?'

'We found the body. Cheeks, eyes and ears gone, picked at by fish and the scabbard of Cold-Edge strapped to its side. We thought it was you.' They walked on in silence, the wind tearing at their clothes. Spume was scudding across the base of the cliffs in great clouds, and salt-spray stung their skin. 'I'm sorry, my lord. Nothing I do will ever atone for that mistake.'

Roper looked sidelong at Gray. 'I'm sorry you think so.'

'But it was dreadful. It was cowardice, no more. I did not want to inspect your corpse as closely as I needed.'

'You torture yourself, Captain. No man is defined by a single action, still less an accidental one. Set against your lifetime, it is nothing.'

In the far distance, there came a profound rumble. The three Anakim halted, staring at the horizon. 'That was a cannon,' said Gray.

'Does Keturah have cannon?' asked Roper.

'A couple.'

'So the battle has started.' Roper shrugged, rearranging the pack and armoured plates on his shoulders. 'We must hurry. Onwards.'

They heard the rumble several times that day, each time a little clearer. Every step was agony now to Ormur, whose boots had been filled with blood clots the last two times he had removed them. They marched on with the cliff on their right, stopping just twice to refill their water-skins before the sun was casting tall shadows before them.

Suddenly, Gray's hand was on Ormur's shoulder. 'Down!' he hissed. The three dropped to the floor like sacks of rubble. Ormur, blustered by the wind, his clothes stiff and salt-stained from the sea spray, took some time to raise his head and see what had caused Gray's alarm.

Two hundred yards in front were five mounted figures, washed rose and gold by the low sun and each with a distinctive halo of white feathers.

Abbio.

Ormur's head sank back to the earth. The cannon had gone

off just a few minutes before: the battle was still going, but the will to reach it was now beyond him.

'How do we get through?' he heard Gray whisper. 'They guard the passage as far south as the cliffs.'

Ormur twisted half-about and saw Roper was crawling to the cliff edge to peer over. 'Down there,' he said. 'I saw a way down a mile or so west. Wait for low tide and slip past tonight.'

They crept back the way they had come until they found a slope where a stream had eroded a shallower incline in the cliff face. They scrambled down to the stony beach, and waited there for the sea to retreat.

'I'm not sure about this, lord,' said Gray. 'We don't know where the next path up onto the clifftop is. We may get trapped beneath it with the tide coming in.'

'We'll have to be fast,' said Roper simply. 'This is our best chance, and we should eat the last of our food now. There's nothing to save it for.'

The three of them ate in silence, humbled between sky, sea and cliff; the stars coming down like snowfall. The night was quiet but for the rhythmic boom as the sea thudded onto the beach, and the rattle of scrambling shingle as each wave retreated.

'Let's go,' said Roper.

There was just enough light to pick out a narrow corridor of shingle between the sea and the cliffs. Even so it was more by sound that they navigated: by the crunch of stone underfoot and the occasional splash as they placed a boot into the waves. They set off with the tide still on its way out, and their path steadily widened until the three of them could walk abreast. There was no indication of when they might encounter a path back up from the shore, or how far away were the Anakim lines, and they walked as fast as heavy legs would permit.

'How long do you suppose we have?' asked Ormur, when they had been marching for several hours. He was eyeing the tide, now beginning to encroach on their passage once more.

'Still an hour or two,' said Gray, pointing at seaweed stuck to the cliffs above his head. 'This path will be eight feet under at high tide.'

There came a shout from up above. Ormur looked up and saw a distant head, silhouetted against the faint lightness from the sky.

'Against the cliff,' said Roper, grabbing Ormur's arm and dragging him close to the chalk. Gray reversed after them and the three froze, bodies pressed against the cliff, voices calling above them.

'The Abbio?' murmured Gray.

'Must be,' said Roper.

Ormur saw a light overhead. It looked like a distant candle, sputtering in the night and then seeming to grow rapidly to a fireball. Just in time, he realised it was falling towards him and leapt aside.

With a thump, a flaming torch landed exactly where he had been standing. It bounced off the stones like a tiny meteorite, flames bursting from the point of impact and momentarily dazzling the three of them as they were cast in orange light.

From the cliffs above there came a roar.

'Run!' shouted Roper.

They fled, pelting past the torch and along the beach. They slipped into the darkness and for a moment it seemed they had left their pursuers behind. Then there came a crack like lightning from right behind Ormur. Something sharp stung the back of his neck and he flung a look over his shoulder, but saw nothing. But he could smell the gunpowder stench of pulverised flint.

There came another deafening crack from just ahead and he saw an orange bloom of sparks as a lump of flint hit the shingle and burst into shards and powder. Gray stumbled and swore viciously. Ormur grabbed his shoulder. 'Captain!'

'Just got my foot, forget it, run!'

They limped on together as another three torches were tossed down from the clifftop, splashing a carpet of burning pitch from the site of impact on each occasion. Now their route for the next hundred yards was illuminated and they could see the blocks of flint hurtling down from above.

'They must know who we are!' shouted Gray. 'The Kryptea tipped off Safinim!'

He was probably right, and the stones pummelling their route were getting more accurate as the torches betrayed their progress. 'Shit, shit, shit,' Ormur was chanting, eyes narrowed against the fragments of razor flint filling the air. Many were hitting the cliffside on the way down and dislodging a tumble of chalk fragments that rattled off Ormur's skull, light and soft enough to draw blood without knocking him senseless.

And now the torches were illuminating a narrowing of the path: the advancing sea washing at the base of the cliff so that they had to splash into the surf, sinking up to their ankles, water flooding Ormur's worn boots almost at once. Just ahead, a block of flint clipped Roper's shoulder. His armour finally proved its worth, preserving his shoulder, but still he staggered. Before he could fall, Ormur had half picked him up and set him back on his feet.

The sea had slowed them to a wade and peppered their clothes with splashes from the plummeting stones, but it had also reinstated the darkness. Every torch that thumped down now hissed into the water and went out. The shattering blocks of flint diverged wildly as the Abbio overhead were rendered blind.

Still they ran, arms over their heads, clothes soaked by the spray thrown up by their boots. Something struck Ormur's shoulder hard, and for a second he thought there was hot blood streaming from the wound. Then he realised it was fire: he was burning. One of the torches had hit him directly and splashed him with burning pitch. He dropped into the water at once, quenching the fire, and was followed by three titanic cracks smashing down around him: a flint bombardment attracted by the light flickering on his shoulder.

Gray had him beneath the armpit and dragged him to his feet. 'Come on!'

Ormur resisted. 'We should freeze!' he hissed. 'They're listening to us splashing about, that's how they're aiming.'

'We can't, lad, the tide, we're out of time.'

Gray was right: the water was now up to Ormur's knees. They waded on, fortunate that their passage was no longer illuminated as the water reached mid-thigh and they slowed to a dead crawl. The occasional block of flint still rocketed into the waves, but too far off to be any risk. And then the barrage stopped altogether.

'Why've they stopped?' Ormur wondered, teeth chattering as the water reached his waist. Though the tide was coming in, this seemed a lower portion of the coastline and they were descending into the water as much as it was rising.

'They've run out of space to chase us,' Roper called over his shoulder. 'Somewhere above us will be Anakim forces.'

'You think so?'

'Count on it,' said Roper. 'We just need to survive this tide.'

They had not yet encountered a single passable route up the cliff, and the water was getting deeper. It was now up to Ormur's navel and the rhythmic heave of the ocean was nearly enough to pull him off his feet. Anakim could not swim, and if it reached much higher, there would be little any of them could do but sink beneath the waves.

'Perhaps we should turn back,' said Ormur.

'Too late for that,' replied Gray. 'The tide will swallow us up on the way back. We either find a way up soon or we die.'

At those words, Ormur felt a swell of dread. The water was black, turbulent and rising. With each surge, his boots slid on the shingle beneath and he was nearly sucked off his feet. None of them knew where there might be a path up from the beach, and the cliffs were too sheer and too soft to consider climbing. They had no choice but to press on, the water soon up to Ormur's chest.

'At least we're not being pelted by stones any more,' Gray observed grimly.

Ormur could not laugh: a wave had just gone over his head

for the first time and he was near panic. He was the shortest of the three, and the other two seemed to be pulling away from him. He wanted to shout that they should wait. If Gray had been within reach, he would have lashed out and grabbed him to hold him back. He did not want to drown.

Then Gray turned around and beamed at him. 'Cold, lad?'

Ormur made a noise of desperate assent. He had wanted to shout for Gray to wait, but the smile satisfied him for a moment.

'Best hope there's a path up soon, eh?' He turned back with a cheery laugh and started wading forward again. By now the water was above Ormur's shoulders, and each minor heave of it lifted his feet off the ground.

Well panic be damned, he thought. Roper was not panicking, Gray was not panicking and he would not let them down by panicking either. He thrashed after Gray, desperately slow, clawing at the water, feet dragging over the shingle. His head was tilted towards the sky but even so he kept spluttering as his mouth filled with water.

And then a wave washed over his head. He was blind, he was deaf. His mouth was flooded with brine and his ears thumped with a pounding heart as he begged every angel he could remember for the waters to retreat. His face broke the surface again and he gasped down precious lungfuls of air, casting after his companions.

He could just see Roper's matte head against the oily gleam of the water, some ten yards ahead, Gray labouring just behind him. They both slipped beneath a wave which heaved towards Ormur. Moments later he was submerged again. It looked the same as the one that had come before, but seemed to somehow contain four times the power. It struck him in the face like a sack of earth and knocked him off his feet.

He was lost in darkness. All was silent but for the bubbles rattling past his ears as his body was racked and twisted by the currents. He did not know which way was up, or when he might be released. He kept praying for it to end, but he was rolled and tumbled, his breath growing short, his limbs weak, desperate for the world above the water.

At last, his tumbling had placed shingle beneath his boots and he pushed himself upwards, rushing through the water, praying he was not too deep to stand. His face broke the surface and he gasped for air. 'There he is!' shouted a voice. 'Ormur! Ormur!'

It was Gray, but it was too dark, and Ormur's eyes too filled with water, to see where he might be. He struggled towards the sound of his voice, just able to keep his face above the water if he stood on the tips of his boots. He crept forward until another wave engulfed him and he was sucked back what felt like yards. But he stayed upright and fought his way towards Gray's voice, still calling his name. 'Ormur! This way lad! Come on! Come on, you're nearly there!'

He clawed towards his mentor, his captain, his most treasured companion, who sounded so close. Then Ormur's fingers caught on something firm in the water. He latched onto it and it clung on back: Gray's hand, pulling him forward. The ground seemed to be rising, and he could stand on the flats of his feet once more. Gray tugged, Ormur scrabbled and suddenly his shoulders were clear of the water's jaws. The ground was sloping up, and wiping his eyes, he could just make out a beach before them, gloriously dry and solid.

He stumbled out of the sea, shocked at his own weight, and dropped to his knees, still in a foot of water. Roper was there, he and Gray helping him up, the three of them staggering onto the shingle and collapsing together in a sodden heap. Ormur was trembling violently, fingers digging into the stones just to feel their solidity. His body was so heavy that even breathing felt an effort.

Then Gray started to laugh.

'That wasn't funny,' said Ormur, before he capitulated too. They howled together into the beach, Ormur so past control that he was drooling into shingle, his head pressed into the beach. 'Almighty. Almighty One. God that was close.'

'Truly, that was horrible,' said Gray.

'I thought you were relaxed,' said Ormur.

'You idiot,' Gray said. 'I nearly drowned.'

Ormur raised his head from the shingle to see Roper, who was not laughing. He was sitting up, trembling like Ormur and glittering tears on his cheeks. 'Are you all right, my lord?' he asked.

Roper nodded. 'Yes. Yes I am. Come,' he said, climbing to his feet. He was still trembling, but clearly itched to be moving. 'We're nearly there.'

Above the beach were dunes bristling with marram grass, and there they found the first sentries of Keturah's army, huddled beside a driftwood fire. 'Who's that?' one of them called when the three half-drowned pilgrims were nearly on top of them. Beside him, Ormur felt rather than saw Roper hoist his hood and pull the sodden cloak over his bright armour.

'A little late for that,' said Gray. 'Luckily for you, we're friends.'

'Watchword,' demanded the sentry.

'I don't know it,' Gray admitted. 'But do you not recognise me?'

The sentries, two Saltcoat legionaries silhouetted by the popping fire, squinted at Gray.

'I know your voice,' said one. 'That isn't Captain Gray? My lord? I heard you were in the north.'

'I have been,' said Gray. 'I've come back.'

There was so little curiosity from these sentries that Ormur found it strange. They just waved them past, pointing Gray east along the coast where they said the Black Lady had set up a pavilion.

'Not like her,' Gray commented as they left the sentries behind. 'She hates tents.'

Roper walked in silence, shrouded in his cloak. They passed dozens of hearths, each surrounded by silent legionaries, showing as little curiosity for the new arrivals as had the sentries. It was long past the hour for sleep, but most seemed to be staring listlessly into the flames.

It was an army more exhausted than any Ormur had seen.

One could sense the lost hope on the air, the lack of ambition. The sensation in the camp was eerie, a feeling of decline stealing over Ormur.

'There,' said Roper softly. He nodded ahead, where a bonfire was illuminating the front of a tent. The slit in the entrance was unfastened and stirring in the breeze, its inner edges glowing with candlelight, and gentle voices coming from within.

Ormur heard Roper take a deep breath as they approached. He had dropped to the back, and Gray led them inside. Within, a dozen smoky candles lit a parlay of seven or eight lords and three legates, along with Keturah and Tekoa. All were seated on animal skins, and silence fell as they turned towards the new arrivals. For Ormur, just seeing Keturah alive and well was a tonic, though she looked different in some way. She seemed a blunted version of her former self, like a sword that had been left to rust, or a door overcome with ivy so that it is half concealed.

'Captain,' she said. At the sight of Gray, a tiny flare of hope entered that mask-like face. 'Welcome. Welcome indeed. Your skills are in particular need this night.' Then she spotted Ormur, and there was rueful pleasure there. 'My guardsman. I'd hoped to spare you our current situation, but I can't deny it is a comfort to have you both here. By the earth,' she said, invested with sudden animation, 'how did you make it through? You found an unguarded path?' She glanced at Roper, who had lowered his hood but still stood behind Ormur, half in shadow, and her gaze slid off him.

'Peers,' said Tekoa, eyes glittering. 'Don't apologise for being late, you've not missed anything.'

'It was a challenging journey, legate,' said Gray mildly.

'Oh, stop complaining.'

Keturah hushed her father irritably. 'Come and sit with us,' she ordered Gray and Ormur, gesturing at an empty skin beside her. She glanced back at Roper as though she had been troubled by her first appraisal, and the colour drained from her face as though bitten by a poisonous snake. 'Captain . . .' she said. Abruptly she was on her feet, eyes interrogating Roper from top to bottom and leaning slightly away from him, as though wary he would lash out. 'Who is this?'

Tekoa, too, was staring at Roper, an expression of deep suspicion on his face. The rest of the tent, lords and kings, only one of whom Ormur recognised distantly as King Drava, were watching this scene in mild interest. None of them had ever seen the Black Lord. They did not recognise the tall, skeletal man who stood in the entrance.

Ormur chanced a glance at Roper and found him staring back at Keturah with a face half of weariness, half of longing. 'Don't you recognise me?' he said.

Keturah raised a hand to her mouth. Still she said nothing. It was left to Gray to break the impasse.

'Lady Keturah,' he said formally, 'the Black Lord Roper Kynortasson is returned to us.'

The reaction was not at all as Ormur had anticipated. Every occupant of the tent was suddenly appalled. They could not have been more shocked had they dragged the remains of Roper's carcass in with them.

Tekoa stood, eyes narrowed and staring at Roper. 'You?' he said, uncomprehending.

'Me,' said Roper, eyes still fastened on Keturah.

'So what is this?' she demanded suddenly, her voice quivering. 'You are dead. You are dead! What am I seeing here?'

For the first time since they had freed him, Roper seemed uncertain.

'I can explain, my lady,' said Gray, as though worried she would turn on him. 'If you've time, we can tell the whole story.'

'The story?' demanded Keturah, and she sounded furious now. 'You brought me his body, and I buried it beneath the temple! It's been seven years! You watched him die, Captain!'

'So I thought, my lady,' Gray murmured. 'Lord Roper has been gracious enough to pardon me that terrible mistake.'

'And what of my pardon?' Keturah barked.

Gray knelt before her. 'In vain hope, my lady, and with no expectation, I beg it.'

Keturah ignored him and turned on Roper. She looked undecided what to do with him, and for a moment Ormur thought she might step forward and embrace him. 'And where in the name of every angel have you been?' she demanded finally. 'Seven years! Seven years we've struggled, and toiled, and despaired in the world you left us! Where were you?'

It looked as though Roper wanted to close the distance between them, but Keturah was still leaning away, almost on the far side of the tent, and it was some while before he managed an answer. 'Trapped,' he said, quiet as a moth. 'Sustained only by thoughts of this moment. Returning to this army, and its great task. Returning to you.'

Keturah let out a noise of exasperation, casting around the assembled company who were looking on quietly. 'You assume a great deal,' she said, almost gently. It seemed to Ormur that she only continued so she could erase the look on Roper's face. 'The battle is begun, and you don't know the first thing about our alliance, or the enemy we now face, or what has come before.' She paused. 'I can't . . . Things cannot simply go back to how they were.'

Gray, still on one knee, cleared his throat. 'I believe this could be a great boost for our men, my lady,' he said. 'If the legions had Lord Roper leading them into battle—'

Keturah silenced him with a hand, turning a face of disbelief and rage on Gray. 'What is this?' She looked back to Roper, cast one withering glance at Ormur which made him blush furiously, and then settled on Gray once more. 'Have you brought him to replace me?'

'Never, my lady—'

'But you surely considered this,' she interrupted. 'You knew when you brought the Black Lord here that it as good as whips the throne out from beneath me.' She glared down at him. 'Of the people I expected treason from, Captain, it was you least of all.'

Gray held his hands out. 'I thought I would be doing your will, my lady. I developed suspicions that Lord Roper was alive, and thought it was my duty to pursue them.'

'In short you acted as one of *his* guardsmen, rather than one of mine.'

Gray did not seem equal to that accusation. He just bowed his head. 'If you feel I have betrayed you, my lady, I will submit to whatever punishment you see fit.'

Ormur too dropped to his knees, while Roper just watched.

'That won't be necessary,' said Tekoa, stepping forward. 'There's no doubt the situation presents an unfortunate conflict, but it is an opportunity.'

Keturah turned to him. 'What are you suggesting?'

Even Tekoa paused at her tone. 'If Lord Roper feels able to lead us on the field, perhaps he is the lift we need.'

Keturah looked as though she had been slapped. 'I can't do this without you, Father.'

Tekoa took a step towards her. 'You have me, Daughter. Always. But this is a fight tailor-made for the leader who stands in that entrance.'

Keturah appealed to the legates behind her, still seated on the floor. 'You, peers, have fought beneath me and my father for years. We have built an alliance that held back the Teuta in impossible circumstances. Something real, which exists in the here and now. You surely don't support surrendering that to . . . to a memory?'

She looked to Randolph, to Skallagrim, to Stonax, and not one of them could hold her eye. They looked down at the floor, and said nothing.

'You are all determined that he should take over?' she went on, more quietly. 'After what he left us? You choose him?'

'If . . . the Black Lord is truly returned to us, my lady,' ventured Randolph. 'Then it has been his throne all along. The army is his to command.'

'That is what the men will say,' said Stonax calmly. 'They would follow Lord Roper over anyone.'

Keturah recoiled into the side of the tent. She looked at Roper again, and the expression on her face made Ormur ashamed. 'I'll move aside then, my lord,' she said calmly.

'Lord Roper can command, on the field, just for now,' said Tekoa gently. 'Anything else can be settled later.'

Keturah shrugged. 'Whatever role you peers see fit. I haven't the influence to decree otherwise. My lords,' she turned to the foreign allies, watching from the tent floor. 'We'll resume tomorrow. If you have any queries, direct them to the Black Lord here.' She waved a hand at Roper, already moving to the tent flap. Without another word she ducked past the canvas and hurried into the night.

Gray's bowed head sank slowly into his hands. Tekoa was staring at the tent flap through which his daughter had departed, and Roper had slumped like a rotten birch tree, the bark crushed to reveal nothing but disintegrating pulp beneath. It took some time for anyone to move, but finally King Drava led the exodus, edging from the tent. He was followed immediately by the other lords, each murmuring their excuses until it was just the three new arrivals and Tekoa.

'I don't know how this has happened, Lord Roper,' Tekoa murmured, 'but it's good to have you back.' He did not look at him as he too began moving for the exit. 'I'll see to it you get some sustenance. When this is all over, you owe me a drink and a story.'

57
Zephyr

Ormur left the tent in search of Keturah. It did not take long to find her. She had walked the short distance downhill to the beach, and now stood just beyond the reach of the waves, staring out over the dark gleam of the water.

'My lady,' he announced his presence behind her.

She turned, hardly visible in such dark. 'My guardsman,' she said stiffly.

'I'm sorry for what we did, my lady.'

Keturah sighed and turned back to the sea. 'You didn't do wrong, Ormur. You are a Sacred Guardsman, and you found your lord. In the old days, when the Black Lord died, so did his guard. The new Black Lord would select his own generation of guardsmen. One of those ancient laws we thought unnecessary, but perhaps we have discovered its purpose.'

He hesitated. 'I have always been your guardsman, my lady.'

She still did not face him, and presently she asked: 'Is . . . that really him?'

Ormur came to stand beside her. 'It is, my lady.'

'Where did you find him?'

'A prison, my lady, run by the remains of the Kryptea. Deep under the old fortress at Myrklettur.'

'Myrklettur,' she repeated. 'What a journey you've had. I

look forward to the story.' The shingle clattered as it was set scrambling by the incoming tide. 'The Stone Throne has not been a comfortable seat, Ormur,' she said quietly. 'I've had this sense of doom, resting on my shoulders, getting heavier with each year that passes. I have been given the helm of a ship bound inexorably for the rocks. No matter what I do, or how hard I work, every soul in the Black Kingdom – our traditions and history and culture – all of it seems destined for destruction. Things that I love dearly, and took the age of the earth to build, and once they are gone can never be restored. How do you live with that knowledge? That has sat on my shoulders, and I blame him. He got us here, in this unsalvageable situation. I've poured everything into reversing this. I've ruled three times longer than him, and all of it is to be forgotten now the legionaries' hero has returned home.'

'I can't imagine, my lady,' said Ormur. 'The responsibility.'

'No,' said Keturah. She took a deep breath. 'You did no wrong, Ormur. I've dreamed of him returning myself, passing that tiller over so I could relinquish this horrible burden and let someone else fix it. But in that tent, all I felt was resentment.' She went silent again for a moment. 'And I lost someone very precious to me today,' she said, quieter than ever. 'Perhaps I'm not at my best.'

'That would be more than understandable, my lady.'

'You always say you understand, Ormur. Whether understandable or not, it is where I find myself. It is good news for our men, I suppose. He certainly has a legend now even greater than when he left. Roper the Daring,' she said bitterly. 'We can use that. Who knows? It may be enough to put some spark back into them.'

'Our men love you no less, my lady. People say you are a great Black Lady. That we'd have succumbed long ago without you to lead us.'

'And all that counts for nothing next to the legend of a dead man,' she replied. 'Ah, Ormur. It is what it is. Well . . . we'll use what advantages the Almighty grants us, and Roper is certainly one of them. I have no talent for command, I've left that to Father. If he wishes, the Black Lord can take the legions into battle. If the legions are happy, when we show them tomorrow.'

'I believe our men would need nothing more than to see Lord Roper returned to them,' said Ormur.

'We'll see, Ormur. I slightly fear that if we spring this on them, they'll think the dead have risen and Catastrophe is about to rear out of the sea. Their reaction may be even less favourable than my own. I'll need to introduce him. We'll put him on Zephyr: see if the big lump still remembers his old master. Then maybe the men will believe.'

Ormur thrilled to hear this. Roper in command once again, in the grand battle to decide the fate of Albion. 'The Wylie Lines are undefended, my lady. We passed them on the way here. Barely a soul mans the defences.'

'That's no good to us now, Ormur. If we could be anywhere but here, we would be. But we're trapped.'

Ormur thought about that. 'But if we win, if the battle goes in our favour, we could take the rest of Suthdal.'

Keturah went quite still. Ormur thought she would not respond until she murmured: 'We can't win, Ormur. Safinim has us by the throat, pinned to the wall. All that's left is to give a good account of ourselves.' She faced him again then, placing a hand on his shoulder. She tutted. 'You're soaked. Go and find a fire at once and dry out. There's armour and weapons befitting your status. We've lost a few of your comrades recently, I fear. We'll show Roper to the legionaries tomorrow. And until then, I need some time alone. I'll see you in the morning.'

Ormur bowed. *Goodnight, my queen.*

The sun rose the next day over a sight horrifying and awesome beyond Ormur's imagination. Their huge ridge, backed against the sea, had been gouged to shreds by the mechanical onslaught of the previous day. Upon it swarmed more people than he had conceived in the whole of Albion: a multitude in armour, close as flies about a carcass.

And that was just his own side. Across the vast grass basin, interrupted by a wash of corpses and sleeping siege weapons standing above like wading birds, lay their enemy. Unmasked in its full power, the Teutan horde stirred like an inland sea. Most frightening of all was the noise: an expectant murmuring, a sighing like a full forest of willows shivering in the breeze.

When Ormur had imagined a battle, what he had really seen was himself and one opponent set on the grandest stage of all. The scale of this was more humbling and impersonal than anything he had expected. He could not fathom how they could defeat the forces massed against them, or how his contribution to such a battle would make even the slightest difference.

'Morning, lad.' Gray had come to find him. 'Did you sleep?'

'I must've done,' he said, grateful for the distraction, 'because I remember some strange dreams.'

Gray raised his eyebrows, taking a sip of nettle tea. 'Me too. And I've just seen Leon, he's reporting the same.'

'Does that often happen before battle?'

Gray shrugged. 'Not that I've recalled before. Maybe it's this place.'

'What were yours about?'

Gray did not answer, instead nodding over Ormur's shoulder. He turned and saw Tekoa approaching, bearing bread and dried venison: a veritable feast with food in such short supply. 'After this you'll be on starvation rations with the rest of us,' he warned. 'Better make the most of it.'

The pair of them found a wagon bed on top of the ridge and sat there together, wolfing their rations and gazing out over the field. They soon discovered that Keturah had sent out a summons, for while each was gnawing at a heel of dried bread, officers from every legion began to assemble on the slope of the ridge beneath them. Their backs faced the Teutan army so that all could see up slope, and though they barely talked, there was a restless stirring until Keturah rode out above the expectant crowd, mounted on a satin-black courser.

Gray and Ormur looked on, still chewing, as she raised a hand to quell the murmuring. 'Peers,' she called. 'Peers. I have news. But first, let me just say before you now, assembled officers and representatives of your legions: thank you. Thank you for coming. Thank you for your service. Thank you for being the staunchest of soldiers in the most testing of times. They grow yet more extraordinary. Three of our own men slipped past the Suthern blockade and joined our side last night.'

'Fools!' cried a voice from the crowd. There was a ripple of dark laughter.

Keturah observed this stony-faced. 'They should all be known to you. Lord Gray Konrathson and Lord Ormur Kynortasson of the Sacred Guard.' She gestured to the wagon and the pair of them saluted with their bread crusts. This was met with a roar of approval. Ormur felt himself grinning as the assembled crowd thumped their feet and bellowed in welcome. Keturah allowed these celebrations for a moment before silencing them with another impatient hand. 'It is no surprise when two such men brave a hostile country to fulfil their duty. Our third recruit is less expected, but shows resolve greater even than these two.'

Ormur could hear massive hoof beats pounding the ridge as a monstrous horse rode up behind Keturah. He could not resist turning his head to see Zephyr ridden again at last.

'Peers, our plight has not gone unnoticed. Resolve does not go unrewarded, and bravery is never in vain. The Almighty has accepted the self-sacrifice made yesterday on this field, and returned one of our great heroes to us. Tell me this is not his work! The Black Lord, Roper Kynortasson, is restored!'

Keturah pulled her horse aside so that the figure behind her was now visible to the whole assembly, and a hush blew over the crowd like wind on water.

Roper was mounted on Zephyr, the huge horse at just an amble, but its head lowered as though about to charge, an eighteen-inch spike protruding from his champron and each measured hoof heavy enough to break stone. Roper's Unthank-silver armour had been polished overnight so that it shone like moonlight. Only those up close could see the layers of cloud and shadow, as though looking through the mirrored surface of a lake to the stones beneath. A black cloak hung over his shoulders, lightning-riddled from top to bottom, and his helmet covered his eyes. His reputation had already fermented to a potency not afforded the living, and added to that now came the shock of his return.

There came a fierce muttering at the sight of him, and Ormur could feel the dread coming off the crowd: the same he had felt at the first sound of that voice in the kungargrav. They might revere Roper, but to see him in the flesh was an insult to the natural order.

'It's a trick!' someone shouted into the silence. 'Roper is dead!'

Before anyone else could react to this, Roper pulled back his helmet. 'This is no trick!' he called. 'I have come back to you.'

There was a pause, and Ormur saw a moment perched on a knife-edge. The crowd was aghast to see Roper, and had Keturah not introduced him in such positive terms, that might already have progressed to horror and a riot. That shock could yet be harnessed, but it would take a master to bring the crowd there willingly.

'I have come back,' Roper repeated, voice carrying over the wide eyes and wide mouths. 'From the world which has trapped me for seven years. A prison designed by malice, constructed of illusions, just one dream keeping me alive. The image of this moment, where I stand before you once again.'

Roper paused and there came a silence more intense than any Ormur had before witnessed. Nearly a thousand watched spellbound, the shape of the ridge affording all of them a clear view of the returning Black Lord. Every one craned forward, only the few of them as close as Ormur able to see Roper's jaw trembling.

'Peers,' he said, voice cracking. He cleared his throat and tried again. 'Peers. I thank the Almighty that I have come back to witness this moment. Since our island was young, those old days when men were giants, when the first words were spoken and crackled like lightning, and angels showed us how to make fire, we have been at war. Our forebears – warriors whose names have become bywords for courage and honour – fought an enemy that does not diminish, and has taken slow bites from our kingdom; the same enemy we fight today. And we find ourselves with a chance our ancestors never had. As dark as things look, as hopeless as they seem, hold on to one thing.' He tilted back his head, and Ormur could see the relief as he finally gave voice to the thought which had possessed him. 'We can finish this here. On the way to join this army, I saw the Wylie Lines left bare. Break them on this battlefield, and the path to Suthdal is open to us. You have an opportunity for which your forebears would have given their right hands: the chance to defeat our enemy forever.'

Ormur could feel his hair standing on end with the force of Roper's belief. The only emotion coming off his brother was desperation: a fevered desire that they should all understand.

'Our enemy outnumbers us. They've brought their allies from Autaria, Frankia, Skaane, Iberia, Hatusa and more. A dozen nations: a continent in arms has pinned our backs to the sea and cut off our supplies. Well so be it. This is our hand, and the greater the challenge, the greater the opportunity. Pity the man that lives without that, who never gets that moment to find out what he's made of. Pity the man who has never seen the world in colour; who doesn't know what terror feels like, or that when stripped to their core, his friends are heroes who'd stand beside him against a multitude! Pity the man who's never seen a battlefield like this one, and drifts through life, a breeze that barely rustles the leaves.'

The crowd were in an intense and silent fever. They were desperate to believe with him. They wanted his words to unknot their stomachs and still their trembling limbs. 'Well, we are the men of the Black Kingdom, and we choose the hard road. Every last one of you will need to struggle like a cornered polecat! You'll need to work the skin off your palms, and hold out your hand to pick your peers off the floor again and again and again! But do that, and your deeds will echo down the ages. Do that, and we avert the worst fate imaginable: that we should live to see the day that the light of the Black Kingdom goes out! That the forests fall, our families live in Suthern shackles, and the last cell in the Academy echoes quiet. I ask you all – does that happen on our watch?'

'No!' roared the legions.

'We are not like the Sutherners, who sacrifice things! We are not like our allies the Aalanders, who sacrifice their enemies! We are a warrior nation who sacrifice ourselves, and that's what I ask from all of you: to bleed for each other! I ask you to bleed for family and home! I ask you to die here, in your prime, in an historic hour that shall be more closely scrutinised than any other, before fear and age can take that chance from you. I ask that you die here, or else that when you march back home, you can look your children in the eye and tell them you did not run. You fought, you endured, you suffered, so that they could have the time that you had, so that the things you believe in might live on, and the world you see in your dreams grows nearer and not further.

'It will be the hardest thing we have ever done, but if we are not equal to it, then who? Who better than us, a warrior nation of equals and brothers, to finish this great task? Who will draw the line and say we have sacrificed too much of ourselves to merely survive? You want to know where I've been for seven years? I've been in a nightmare! I've seen what the world becomes when you've sacrificed everything except survival! Please! Please! Do not let fear reduce you to that! Love your suffering – embrace it all, surrender to nothing and just keep going. Be born again on the other side and revisit calm and wild and the grip of your loved ones with renewed eyes and heart. Take that chance, hold it close and die if you must. And I ask you again! If your loved ones need it from you, what will you do?'

'Die!' they bellowed, and Gray roared it with them.

'What will you do?'

'Die!' The blood was roaring in Ormur's ears.

'Who are you going to die for? Tell me who!'

The army bellowed, reeling off the names of their dear and their beloved.

'You are about to make this earth sacred!' Roper howled. 'This is the earth that will remember the greatest battle ever fought, and you were here! You got that chance! This is your Winter Road!

'This is the most important thing you've ever done, but think what you've accomplished already! By the work of your hands, we occupy land our enemy has held for the ages! Eight years you've toiled for this! Eight years of campaigning, of mud and swords and *kjardautha* to get to this moment, and before that, a lifetime of training! The entire Black Kingdom has bent towards this battlefield. Generations of history and struggle got us near! You have fought the final inches, and now there is one inch more!'

The crowd was boiling. It was stirring and swarming like a plague of locusts working itself up to fly, and now they roared Roper on with every word.

'We've been preparing for this all our lives! It's not us that's cornered! It's them! Are we going to let this moment go?'

'No!' came the roar.

'Do we lay the Black Kingdom to rest this day?'

'No!' they howled.

'Who leaves this field first?'

'Them!'

'They do!' Roper hollered back. 'We fight! We rage! We boil and storm! We suffer, or everyone you love dies! We are desperate! They are trying to take everything from us! If there is ever a moment to do your very worst, this is it!'

The army was in a paroxysm, and Roper was most demented of all.

'We can defeat them forever! We have this one chance, I beg you! I beg you! Take it! Take it, and let nothing take it back!'

58
The Silver Wolf

'I like the bandage, my lord,' said Diethaad.

Bellamus had been standing by the telegraph machine when it was destroyed, and the shockwave had knocked him off his feet. He now sported a fresh cotton bandage around his forehead, which kept slipping down over his eyes. 'Just a splinter,' he said. 'Thrown off by one of the beams.'

'Chance is a friend of yours, eh?'

Bellamus was not listening. There was some commotion unfolding on the Anakim side of the field. He sipped a mug of hot broth and watched through narrowed eyes. Some hundreds of the enemy were arrayed on the slope, but facing away from the Teutan army, towards a mounted figure standing over them. Their distant roars were carrying over the plain, fierce and defiant.

'What is going on over there?' asked Diethaad.

Bellamus did not immediately reply. He poured the steaming broth on the floor, shaking out the cup. 'Send me Widukind.'

'Lord Warden,' said a sombre voice in reply. Bellamus turned and saw Widukind already approaching, eyes boring into him.

'Bishop. I trust nobody's made it past your cordon?'

Widukind stopped before him, that familiar waft of cold coming off his clothes. 'Three men may have done.'

'May have?'

'They were seen passing under the cliffs at low tide, but the passage is treacherous. They may not have survived.'

'Three men,' said Diethaad. He was staring at Bellamus, who would not meet his eye. 'Two guardsmen found Grendel, didn't they?'

Bellamus raised a finger. 'Do not call him Grendel.' He glanced at Widukind. 'Well, Bishop? Who were they?'

Widukind gave the tiniest shrug. 'There are already rumours circulating among the men. They're saying that the Black Lord has returned.'

Bellamus gritted his teeth. 'Your Abbio have talked.'

'They said nothing.'

'Where else could those rumours have come from?'

For answer, Widukind pointed across the plain.

Bellamus turned back to the Anakim ridge and inspected the mass of cheering men. Behind the central mounted figure, he saw a banner; one familiar from rain-battered, iron-flecked days.

The howling Silver Wolf of the Jormunrekur.

'Last flown seven years ago, I understand,' said Widukind calmly.

The battlefield suddenly looked different to Bellamus. It seemed to be painted in squares of black and white, like a chess board. His own warriors armoured in ivory, the Anakim in sheets of black slate. And there was that figure, mounted on a monstrous horse, shining cuirass gleaming like a star.

Still, he did not believe.

'My horse,' said Bellamus quietly. 'Let's allow the Anakim no room in our imaginations. We should go and see with our own eyes.'

He had not meant to parlay. He had thought to keep the Anakim at arm's length, batter them from range, ignore any heralds they might send. But he found himself beneath a white flag, riding past the frozen trebuchets, over the carnage of the day before, aiming for the shockingly familiar banner of the Silver Wolf.

He took fifty Thingalith, Vigtyr among them, and riding out from the Anakim side came just five. He did not recognise the young guardsman clutching the Silver Wolf banner, but the rest he knew.

Gray Konrathson, Captain of the Sacred Guard.

Leon Kaldison, Earl Northwic's killer.

Tekoa Urielson, their foremost general of the past seven years.

And at the centre of them all, he was there. The Unthank-silver helmet of the Black Lord in place above his jutting jaw. A moonlight cuirass clamped around his chest. His huge horse, shaped like an oversized wild boar. In flesh as solid as ever: his worst and oldest enemy, Roper Kynortasson.

The two parties drew to a halt before one another, and for the first ten or fifteen heartbeats, each side just stared at the other. Bellamus inspected every inch of his old adversary, settling last on the eye slits of his helmet. 'I'd thought you were dead.'

Roper reached up and pulled the helmet off his head, revealing the upper part of his face. He looked gaunt, his countenance bonier, his nose perhaps twisted by an old break. But there was no doubting it was him. 'You must've come to surrender, Safinim.'

Bellamus shook his head. 'I just wanted to see. Though I didn't believe you'd died. Not at first.'

'No more than I believed those dreams you once told me, of a farm, and a woman, and a quiet life.'

Bellamus had quite forgotten that. 'You told me you were going to displace my entire people. I would never have let that happen.'

Roper shook his head. 'You can't stop me. You may think the advantage is with you this day, but this is exactly where I want to be. Reaching this moment is all I have ever wanted.' He looked across the Thingalith arrayed behind Bellamus, his gaze snagging on Vigtyr. He recoiled a little, unsettled for the first time. Then he spoke again, eyes still set on Vigtyr. 'I have nothing else to say to you.'

'You needn't die here, Lord—'

Bellamus had been going to offer Roper his life, but the Black Lord overrode him, pointing at Vigtyr. 'And I'll look for you on the field,' he said. He pulled his helmet back down and turned Zephyr around, his companions falling in behind.

Bellamus watched him go, struck dumb.

Ruden was waiting for them as they came clattering back into the lines, chewing on the end of a pipe he had yet to light. 'Safinim! I can't believe what I hear. They say you've been parlaying with a resurrected Grendel.'

Bellamus opened his mouth to reply, but was interrupted by Vigtyr. 'It wasn't him,' said the Anakim curtly. Ruden raised his eyebrows to be so addressed, but Vigtyr did not seem abashed. 'His brother, who looks like him. That's why they've put up the banner of the Jormunrekur. Just his brother.'

Ruden looked at Bellamus, who in turn watched Vigtyr in some surprise. Then he nodded. 'Indeed. Just a desperate attempt to intimidate us, but Grendel remains dead and buried.'

'It did seem rather unlikely,' said Ruden comfortably. He beckoned an aide, who fumbled in a tinderbox to light his pipe. 'Steady lad, steady,' said Ruden, beaming at him. 'I'll not bite.'

'Vigtyr,' said Bellamus, regarding the Anakim. 'You and Roper's brother have some unfinished business, do you not?'

'Oh yes, lord. I've thought of it for years.'

'I daresay he won't be able to resist joining the battle-line. Any chance you could find him and finish him today?'

'Easier than a bear,' said Vigtyr quietly.

59

The Second Day

'Where the bloody hell did he come from?' asked Randolph. 'It can't actually be him.'

'It is,' said Ormur.

'Where's he been then?'

'Held captive by the Kryptea.'

'The Kryptea don't exist any more.'

'So we thought,' said Gray, mildly.

An impromptu parlay had gathered behind the ridge. Half a dozen legates and a few guardsmen stood about a cooking hearth, though neither Roper nor Keturah was present. Their position offered some shelter from the siege weapons, which had started firing again almost as soon as Safinim had returned to the Teutan lines. Projectiles whooshed incessantly overhead, often accompanied by a boom as they hit the ridge and bounced over them, shedding flecks of grit. One of them – a boulder the size of a boar's head – lost so much momentum after striking the ridge that it dropped right in the middle of their group, nearly flattening Randolph and making all of them start. The cannon no longer replied: it was stone cold, having run out of ammunition the night before and now abandoned on the ridge.

'Does it matter where he came from?' asked Randolph, shaken by his narrow escape. 'What can even Roper achieve from here? If we advance, we lose the ridge and get stabbed to bits by the pikeline. We stay here and they'll just blast us to ribbons.'

'We're lucky they withdrew when they did yesterday,' said Skallagrim, legate of the Gillamoor. 'We were losing that fight, just slowly.'

'Not that slowly in the centre,' said Leon.

'That wasn't confined to the centre, we were bleeding everywhere. They outnumbered us already, and we were still dying faster than them. We can't sustain another fight like that.'

'We'd break,' said Randolph simply.

'We're losing men as we speak,' agreed another legate.

'And not just from trebuchets,' growled Tekoa. 'The Skiritai caught nearly a hundred deserters last night.'

There was a shocked silence at this.

'From the allies?' ventured Randolph.

Tekoa exhaled noisily. 'Mostly.'

That elicited a gasp. 'Black Legionaries deserting?'

There was no place in the Black Kingdom for a legionary who had deserted. Their home would be taken, their subjectcy forfeit and everyone they loved obliged to distance themselves publicly. For most, the disgrace of running away was worse than risking death in battle. If Black Legionaries were leaving the field, it suggested they thought the kingdom itself was doomed.

'There's a path beneath the cliffs, to the east,' said Tekoa. 'Not the side from which Lord Roper arrived, the other. At low tide, it seems you can skirt around the Suthern scouts, and escape. Word of it has spread.'

There was a pause. 'If it came to it,' began Skallagrim, hesitantly, 'could we use it to retreat?'

'No. A couple of hundred could make it at most, the rest would be caught by the tide. Hasn't stopped men trying, though.'

'Well who can blame them,' said Randolph bleakly. 'Let's be

realistic: there isn't the honour attached to being a legionary which there used to be. A legion fled the field yesterday. The shame! And against hybrids.'

'Never felt so sick.'

'Safinim has out-manoeuvred us at every turn.'

'Warfare has moved on,' said Randolph. 'We've known for years that Safinim was finding ways to fight us. Pikemen were the answer. We got lucky the last time we fought them properly, on Harstathur.' He shrugged. 'I think the day of the swordsman is at an end. He can match legionaries who've trained their whole lives for war with cheaply armed and armoured pikemen, given just weeks of training.'

Ormur was caught between disapproval and hopelessness. He wished Keturah were here. He did not think they would dare speak like this in her presence, but she was soothing the allied generals who had taken fright at the events of the day before.

Yet these men were legates, used to covering their doubt and fear for the benefit of those they commanded. For the conversation to carry this note of panic, they must still be blinded to the possibility of victory or survival. The Ulpha had run, and with them had gone the battered confidence and identity of a civilisation. The momentum was with their enemies, and that was everything in war. Their day was done, and the time of a younger and hungrier civilisation had arrived.

'This is possession, peers,' said Gray, voice still mild. 'Now is not the time to lose faith.'

'Well, let's be frank,' said Tekoa, 'blind faith in our own side is what got us here. We've been traditionalists for centuries and sneered at innovation. We thought that was for our enemies. Let them try every trick under the sun, the fact remained they could not surpass the quality of the legionaries. Whatever they did was just noise. And now, in our darkest hour, Safinim has managed it. If we'd been a little less superior for the past few decades, we might have foreseen this moment.'

Then the conversation died away, for Roper had arrived.

He appeared gnawing on a strip of dried venison, moving to an empty spot by the hearth in the untroubled slink of a lion. There, he settled comfortably on the ground, half-reclined and entirely focused on the thick twist of venison in his fist. He considered it, seeming to decide some new angle of attack was required, and inserted it experimentally onto a back molar, working at it with an expression half of puzzlement. Every eye about the fire watched as he succeeded in tearing off a strip, and looking pleasantly surprised, sat back again to chew. His eyes travelled up from this problem, as though becoming vaguely aware of the heavy silence and the weight of each gaze resting on him. He met a few eyes, chewing slowly, and swallowed. 'Peers,' he acknowledged, before turning his attention back to the morsel in his hand.

With this simple entrance, the atmosphere had lurched to calm. There was something about how Roper moved, how he sounded, even the air around him, which made everyone about the fire suddenly aware of how foolish it was to be stood restlessly on their feet as though about to begin a dance. The silence had a different note, the despair of the moments before suddenly ludicrous.

Roper picked the final scraps of flesh off a thick ligament, smacking his lips and inspecting to ensure there was not a shred left. Then he tossed it over his shoulder and looked up at them all expectantly. 'Shall we?'

They stood there like a flock of geese, awaiting his lead. Roper stood, wiping his hands on his thighs and looking thoughtful. 'So, he wants a hammer-blow this morning. He knows that our morale is restored, and he wants to prove we'll still be crushed beneath his boot. You did exceptionally to destroy the signalling-machine yesterday, and it'll take him a long while to coordinate an advance, so he'll need to get started soon. He'll deploy the Barleymen in the pikeline, most likely on the left flank so they can hold off the Unhieru if he can't control them again. We'll leave them to the Greyhazel, eh? Sacred Guard and Ramnea's Own with me in the centre. We'll break through there.'

Tekoa cleared his throat. 'My lord,' he began. 'I firmly believe we should deploy Ramnea's Own against the Barleymen. If they break another legion—'

'Break another legion?' Roper interrupted, sounding politely confused. 'Are you worried they might?'

'Well yesterday—'

'Yesterday was the product of emotion. It happens. But it's a double-edged sword because now they've exhausted themselves. They have fired their shot and it won't happen again. Isn't that right, Stonax?'

The legate of the Greyhazel blinked to be so suddenly addressed. 'Count on us, my lord.'

'I do,' said Roper. 'On all of you. Today I'll ask you to fight without your bows as well.'

There came a shocked murmur at this. 'What?'

'My lord!'

'The bows were the only thing that had any impact yesterday,' growled Tekoa.

Roper nodded. 'But we're short on arrows. We'll stockpile them in Ramnea's Own. We'll break through there, and you must simply hold on until we do.'

There was a fraught silence.

'You are thinking,' Roper surmised quietly, 'how selfish of him to have taken our most effective weapon and hoarded it for his part of the battle-line, leaving us to face the pikes with just our swords.' He raised his eyebrows and looked around at them. 'Isn't that right?' The silence answered his question. 'I can promise you that by the end of this day, you will not envy those of us in the centre.' He nodded at them, as though that had settled it. And it had. 'To your legions. Godspeed.'

Stunned, hesitant, obedient, the legates dispersed. Ormur and Gray exchanged a bemused glance, and Roper enquired whether there might be any more food. He was ravenous.

But they had no time, because distant horns were crying out on the far side of the ridge. Roper beckoned them to follow and they climbed up its rearward side so that they could look over the battlefield. The Teuta were reshuffling: a battle-line emerging, bristling with pikes once again and, as Roper had predicted, its left flank capped by the Barleymen.

'How did you know?' asked Ormur before he could stop himself.

'Isn't it what you'd have done?' said Roper, shrugging.

No, thought Ormur. He would not have had the first idea where to begin deploying an army. He looked over the pikemen, who had started chanting distantly. It reminded him of that windswept day with Gray, where they had cleared a rise and the sea had been laid out before him. At the time he had never seen anything so furious, but the sight before him now exceeded even that. The pikeline was clawed, seething, and so vast that it seemed not to march over the plain but to swamp it. Whatever they were chanting, the line was too big to sustain a single rhythm and the tune swelled and collapsed, billowing like a tempest.

Roper seemed not to feel the fear making Ormur's breath short. He called for a horse, and when a courser was brought, he rode in front of Ramnea's Own, disdaining the churning trebuchets and siege bolts still thudding into the ridge. 'Up, my peers, up! We get another crack at our enemy today and we should be on our feet to receive them.'

The Anakim line rose unevenly to its feet, banners sitting up in their thousands and confronting the pikemen with a tapestry of eyes, skins, rattles and totems. 'Drums!' shouted Roper, and they clattered into an urgent volley. The trumpets blared, and Ormur felt his fear surge nearly to the point of vomiting. Beside him, Gray took a deep breath and began to sing. It was not the *Hymn of Advance*, which would for evermore be inauspicious after the previous day's events, but the more percussive 'Ramnea's Hymn', which spread swiftly over the ranks, pealing out and clashing with the howling pikemen.

Ormur tried to join in but stopped at the feeble sound of his own voice. *Nemandis* – apprentice legionaries – were running forward and distributing quivers stuffed with arrows to each legionary, and then pelting back to get more. Roper was riding in front of the men, bellowing over the singing. 'We'll hold off until they're close! Have them nice and far from their reserves! The closer we let them get, the better!'

The pikemen were a hundred yards away, well in range of the bows.

'They're nearly upon us,' Ormur muttered to Gray. 'Should we not be firing now?'

'Trust him,' said Gray. 'There's more time than you think.'

Ormur tried to believe Gray, but it seemed to him that not only should they be firing, but Roper should retreat, lest he get trapped between the two forces. 'Just remember we've got to be quick!' he was bellowing. 'Your brothers rely on you! Spend your arrows, and then give them hell!'

There was so much noise! The drums clattered like a hail of rubble. The trumpets soared in such numbers and synchrony that Ormur could feel the vibrations ringing through his lungs. The earth was rumbling beneath his feet from the marching multitudes, and over all that; ominous, furious, awesome, was the singing of his own side and the chanting of the pikeline.

This was a battlefield, then. He was assaulted by it, nearly paralysed by the sheer intensity of it. He looked to his right and saw that they had been joined by Tekoa and Leon, whose footsteps he had not heard in the din.

Ormur looked back, just in time to see Roper go down. A siege bolt thudded into his horse and knocked it flat, the Black Lord hurled from his saddle and disappearing from view behind the ranks of Ramnea's Own.

'Oh hell,' said Tekoa, the four of them leaning forward to try and see the downed Roper. The singing faltered and there came a vicious roar as the pikeline claimed an early triumph. But moments later, Roper was back on his feet and bellowing. Ormur could not hear what he was saying, but a trumpeter in the front rank began blaring the advance, which was echoed along the legion. Stung to anger by the sight of their lord knocked to the ground, Ramnea's Own cheered and began their uncanny mechanical march down the forward slope of the ridge.

Tekoa leaned towards Ormur and yelled in his ear. 'And that is why you save your best destrier for the moments which matter!'

The legion was marching away from them, towards the pikemen, and Roper emerged from the rear ranks, men clutching at his cloak and shoulders to prove to themselves that he was solid, and absorb some of the good fortune they were sure he must carry. An aide hurried forward with another horse, and Roper reared up on the saddle, bellowing the halt.

Ramnea's Own was now arranged on the forward-face of the slope below them, each rank at a different height so that all could see over the heads of the men in front, to the enemy ranks fifty yards away.

It also gave Ormur, left on the crest of the ridge, a perfect overview of the two forces. He could distinguish individuals in the pikeline now, their faces alive with malice as they screamed murder at the Anakim. Their long weapons, still pointed up at the sky, bounced and clattered in such numbers it sounded like the swarming of bees. He could even smell their enemy; alcohol, sweat, grease and the sour scent of agriculture oozing through their skin. 'Now destroy them!' He could hear Roper begging distantly. 'Destroy them!'

The pikeline was thirty yards away, their weapons lowering in a dreadful thicket, when there came a sound like a vast intake of breath. It was the combined rustling and creaking of five thousand bows bending, and five thousand arrows being loaded with a hundredweight of tension. And just for an instant in the face of all that poised energy, the chanting of the pikemen faltered. They almost paused.

The volley hit like a hot blast of gunpowder. With a *whoomp* like avalanching snow, it seemed all of the Teutan front rank, and half the second, were knocked to the earth by the mass of arrows. An entire layer of pikes clattered down in front of them, and just audible beneath this was the profound hum of five thousand vibrating bowstrings.

The pikemen had heartbeats to absorb that volley, and had only just begun staggering forward over the bodies of their first rank when the second wave hit. They were armoured only in padded leather, and relied on their massed and vicious weapons for defence. But the arrows threaded between the pike shafts, the second wave doing nearly as much damage as the first.

Ramnea's Own was still singing as they drew and fired mindlessly, spitting one arrow every five heartbeats. They could go faster, but their quivers were full, their bowstrings heavy, and they were pacing themselves. By lining up on the forward slope of the ridge, Roper had deployed the legion so everyone could fire into the pikeline with a flat trajectory, hollowing out their formation like sand before a stream of water.

Roper was possessed. 'Again!' he was screaming. 'Again! Again! Again!'

The bowstrings tore off fingernails, the shock of each shot reverberating up the arm, the fletching slicing the hand. Siege bolts still whistled into the ranks and a drizzle of returning arrows was coming from the longbowmen positioned behind the pikemen. Still, Ramnea's Own stood their ground and fired.

'Kill them!' Tekoa was bellowing. Leon was screaming too, while Gray was calmly checking Ramnea moved easily in her sheath. Ormur knew why, knew what was coming, and was desperate for just a little longer.

But time was up. Even with the pooled arrows of the whole army, the legion blazed through them in just under three minutes. They had drilled more than one hundred and fifty thousand arrows into this portion of the pikeline, at a range where their leather jerkins held like paper. The formation had nearly collapsed.

Roper held his reins out to an aide, who fumbled to take

them. 'It's yours, Tekoa,' he said, swinging himself out of the saddle.

'And if you fall?' asked Tekoa pointedly.

'He won't,' said Leon, hand resting on his sword. He, Gray and Ormur were to defend the Black Lord, with the rest of the guard held back in reserve, and Roper turned towards Ramnea's Own, beckoning his companions to follow. Ormur felt sick with fear. His legs trembled beneath him and he could hardly bear the thought of joining that battle-line, spitting yet another volley at the pikemen. If he had not been so frightened of being left alone in this place, he could not say with any certainty that he would have followed Gray into the legion's ranks. Roper was in the lead, gouging a path through to the front and roaring 'Bows down! Bows down!' The bows were tossed backwards to be gathered up by the apprentice legionaries.

Ormur pushed after Roper's shining form, stumbling into the front rank with him and accidentally finding himself at the Black Lord's shoulder, standing between him and Leon. And then he forgot about that, because revealed before him, fifty feet away, was the seething mass of the pikeline. They were swarming over their fallen peers with weapons lowered, boots crunching on the thousands of arrowshafts, mouths working furiously as they chanted and spat. He was trembling so violently he was not sure how he could walk. How was anyone expected to fight like this?

Then Roper was spotted in the front rank, unmistakable with his moonlit armour and escort of guardsmen. A roar erupted from Ramnea's Own, sweeping over Ormur and standing his hair on end. Roper raised his sword and there came another cheer. Ormur felt a swell of strength from sheer proximity to the Black Lord, to the heroes Leon and Gray, and found he was panting. He knew what came next; they would charge into that nest of spears. He was so frightened he could hardly see, his vision narrowed to a single beam in front of him. But he could feel a swell of motivation now too. Now that he was part of it, this huge, horrendous noise, it had become compelling.

There was a hand on his shoulder and he turned to find it was Roper's. Ormur met his eye for a brief moment, and again found it like the pitiless gaze of a goshawk. 'I am proud of you,' he said. Then he raised his head to the sky. 'Now!' he roared, the reveille echoing along the legion, which drew swords in a rasp like dull iron scraping over slate. It had not even occurred to Ormur that he had a sword, and he snatched it from the scabbard. 'Now!' Roper was bawling. 'Now! Now! Now!'

The charge did not start at a sprint. No man wanted to be first out of the line and be left alone facing an army. It had to build its own momentum, and commenced at a shuffle, led by Roper taking a few stuttered paces forward. Ormur stepped after him, immediately feeling a wave of cold fear as he left the safety of the line and stood naked before the pikemen. Were they really about to do this? Leon had stepped after him, Roper took another pace and Ormur half-stumbled forward, puffing each breath through pursed lips as though he might blow off the fear. Then Roper was trotting, and Ormur knew he had to run with him or not advance at all. He could not look at the tattered pikeline, reassembling as the legionaries began to sprint, and fixed his eyes somewhere over their heads.

'For our dead! For the dead!' Roper was howling, he and Ormur accelerating faster and faster.

'The *dead*!' went the roar.

The thicket of pikes had been thinned to a threadbare remnant of its former self, but still Ormur's eyes shrank from the blades. Feet were braced, pikes levelled to meet them. The Teuta were bellowing, the legionaries roaring, Ormur deaf to it all as the two lines collided.

The storm of arrows had done its job. Ormur could beat aside the first weapon, dodge a second and sprint straight through to the pikeline where he charged a man to the floor with a lowered shoulder. There came a streak of sparks on his left as a pike grated off Roper's cuirass, the Black Lord knocking another blade aside with a swing of Cold-Edge. The man before Ormur was retreating, still clutching his pike which was useless with the guardsman so close, and Ormur cut his throat with a back-swing, aware all the time of his brother. The Black Lord was half-ignoring the enemy in his determination to shatter the pikeline and his armour was already taking a battering. Another pike was reaching towards him from the rear ranks, and Ormur deflected it, finding himself in a bubble of relative calm as Roper attracted all the surrounding fury.

Roper was a battering ram, ploughing deep into the pikeline, and Ormur knew his job was to keep his brother alive. He barged to his side, aware of Gray at his other shoulder, and Leon on Ormur's right, furiously chopping the heads of pike shafts like daffodils. Another pike was heaved towards Ormur, who knocked it aside and seized the shaft with his free left hand. He used its long bulk, still attached to its wriggling owner at the far end, to hold off another weapon, staggering past them both so that he and Roper were beyond their lethal tips. They were being propelled deeper into the pikeline by the weight of men pushing from behind, and Ormur found himself before another enemy who dropped his pike with a hollow *thunk*, eyes wide with terror. He was halfway through drawing a sword when Ormur cut his head off. The Teuta nearest recoiled from that blow. Ormur could see the shock on their faces, saw the half-heartbeat of hesitation it brought him to step over the decapitated body and poleaxe another with his favoured back-slice. His victim fell away, revealing a pikeman further back, gathering himself to heave a blow at Roper. Ormur stepped in front of the blade. It hit him in the guts and knocked the breath from him, but was at an angle, and gouged the steel of his cuirass without breaking through.

They were nearly racing through their shaken enemy, who stumbled and slipped back. Pikes were clattering to earth all around as the Teuta panicked, dropping their unwieldy weapons in favour of the short-swords they carried as a last resort. But without a pike, and without a formation, the pikemen stood no chance against heavily armoured legionaries. Their swords were cheap, their armour padded leather, and their experience of fighting man on man completely inadequate against Black Legionaries. Ramnea's Own were advancing so swiftly that it was foolhardy. Ormur kept losing his footing, and there was a constant sensation of near-misses as weapons he had not even seen missed him by inches. But momentum was everything, and higher up the slope, to either side of Ramnea's Own, the rest of the battle-line were facing fully ordered pikemen.

A pike-shaft, swung like a log, smashed into Ormur's helmet and nearly knocked him flat. But that was lucky, because it saved him from another thrust which had been aimed at his neck and ended up sweeping past his ear by less than an inch. Fear vanquished by fury, Ormur made eye contact with the man responsible, but he was twelve feet back through the ranks, and Ormur's lungs were heaving like a bellows. Sweat was pouring off his brow and he glanced at Roper, hoping he would pull back and let someone else lead the charge. But the Black Lord was staggering towards a pocket of pikemen as though they were a feast. All Ormur could do was defend, trying to catch his breath and using his body to shield Roper's right. Beside him, Leon had picked up a short-sword and was using it to dismiss pike-thrusts while he wielded Silence, his war-blade, right-handed like a meat-cleaver.

In between Ormur and Leon pushed one of Ramnea's Own, screaming as he aimed a huge swing at a Suthern helmet. It crashed right through the centre with a tin thud, killing its target immediately. The legionary was in the process of trying to tug the blade free when a pike threaded through the ranks and skewered his shoulder. He was thrown to the floor, yelling. He abandoned his sword and reached instead for the blood blossoming from the wound. 'I die!' he gasped. 'Tell Lord Roper I do it for him.'

Leon looked down at him pitilessly. 'You live!' he snapped. 'Tell him yourself.'

Ormur would have laughed aloud at that, had there been enough breath in his lungs. He met Leon's eye for a brief moment, and could have sworn the lictor was wearing the ghost of an evil smile. Then Leon's face changed horribly, his features dissolving into agony and neck whiplashing with the force of the pike that had found him. It pierced the plates of his cuirass, clipped his bone armour and slid deep into his lungs.

'Leon!' Ormur staggered towards him but was hit in the upper arm by another blade which knocked him onto one knee. Leon toppled down beside him, a fleck of blood falling down his chin. He dropped the short-sword and reached his free hand round to the wound in his side, inspecting the blood-smeared palm with a scowl, as though irritated.

Ormur climbed back to his feet and hooked Leon beneath one armpit, another legionary taking the other, hauling him back between them. They pulled him ten yards clear of the lines and laid the lictor on his back. Ormur met his eye once more and was horrified by the change there. Leon was white as drifted snow and panting.

'Leon.' Ormur tried to kneel next to him but was pushed away.

'What are you—' Leon began to cough wretchedly. Ormur tried to move closer again and again was pushed away. 'What are you doing?' Leon managed before succumbing to racking coughs once more, bringing up thick gobbets of blood which slid down his breastplate. 'Protect Roper, boy.' He hauled in a bubbling breath. 'Protect the Black Lord!' His coughing looked like torment, the blood around his lips stark against the chalk skin. Leon grimaced and leaned forward, trying to alleviate some agonising pain.

That was the position he died in; sat forward, slumped over his breastplate and fingers only now loosening about his sword. Ormur blinked down at the corpse, too shocked and numb to comprehend. Leon could not be dead. The roar of battle had dimmed as Ormur felt something he had never thought to while looking at Leon: pity. He could not be dead.

The legionary who had helped drag his body back grimaced at Ormur and then turned back to the fight, stumbling towards the pikemen once more. Ormur could not just abandon his body, but it seemed the only thing he could do was honour the lictor's last wishes. He had to protect Roper. He bent to unstrap Leon's scabbard, taking up Silence and buckling it on his waist alongside Warspite. 'Sorry,' he muttered, still panting. 'I'm sorry, Leon.'

He looked down at the guardsman's slumped body once more, and then turned away. The advance had left him behind: the pikeline was collapsing at speed, the ground chewed to mud in its wake, slick with blood and piss, strewn with flattened bodies, discarded weapons and the wailing injured. The noise had lessened as the drummers abandoned their instruments and hurled their mass behind into the advance, and what remained were the sounds of effort: the grunting, coughing and raw panting. The knock and clatter as weapons smashed together and then agonised screams as they hit vulnerable skin.

Ormur broke into a trot, finding he was still so weary that running made him lightheaded and settling instead for a fast walk. It seemed the pikeline here in the centre was near broken, but from the vantage of the slope, Ormur could see a block of reserves approaching at speed. Safinim must have seen at once what they were doing and hurled in reinforcements to hold the centre.

Ormur broke into a run again, unable to absorb what was happening. *Leon*. The guardsman's name reverberated through his head like echoes in a cave. He could not be dead.

He soon caught up with the rear of Ramnea's Own. To find Roper, all he had to do was burrow towards the fiercest of the fighting. The last of the pikemen were disintegrating, but pushing past them were Safinim's reserves: the Thingalith.

Hermit-Crabs, the legionaries called them, after their habit of armouring themselves in Anakim bone plates, and they were Safinim's very best. Alongside them came a corps of dismounted knights, the nobles of Erebos, radiant in plate armour. They waded into the back of the pikeline, bellowing and slapping fleeing pikemen with the butts of their spears. And angling in from the right, buffeting retreating pikemen, an enormous figure was veering towards them.

Vigtyr.

His toothless mouth was open, his face horribly scarred and his eyes set unflinchingly on the silver-armoured Roper, to Ormur's left. Roper and Gray stood flank-to-flank, nearly black with blood and the filth that had gummed on to it, gritted teeth shining through the grime. Roper was barely defending himself now, his armour pocked and twisted but still intact and still keeping him alive. Both he and Gray were gasping for breath, trying to regain some energy before the Thingalith hit. Neither had noticed Vigtyr, who had started to run, mouth drawn back in an empty snarl, sword coming up in a lunge intended to break the Unthank cuirass.

Vigtyr was swerving across the ranks, eyes so fiercely set on Roper that he did not see Ormur step out to intercept him, driving a shoulder into his chest that nearly knocked the traitor off his feet. His head whiplashed and he stumbled back a few paces, eyes wild for whoever had stopped him. He saw Ormur and narrowed his eyes. 'Do you not know who I am, boy?'

'I know you,' said Ormur. The fear was gone: even his exhaustion seemed to have given way to rage. 'You killed one of my brothers. You'll not get to the other.'

Vigtyr blinked, glancing at the still distracted Roper. 'Ormur Kynortasson? You offer me the chance to destroy the House of the Wolf entirely? Then step forward, boy, I accept.'

Roper had finally seen Vigtyr. He emitted an ear-splitting roar, and hurled himself forward, but Ormur thrust him aside, snarling that the Black Lord would have to wait his bloody turn. Roper was sufficiently shocked to be still, and stared at Ormur as though he had gone mad. 'I've dreamed of this for years,' he said, blankly.

'So have I,' spat Ormur. 'He killed Numa. He's mine!'

'You'll both have your turn,' said Vigtyr, probing Ormur's guard with an inquisitive sword. Ormur tried to beat it aside, but the blade was whipped away before Warspite was anywhere near making contact. Instead, Vigtyr's sword was now sliding almost lazily towards Ormur's extended forearm. The guardsman was fast – fast enough to jerk his arm out of the way on instinct – but that left his sword far past his body, and Vigtyr's well inside his guard.

The traitor could have stepped forward and finished him then and there. Instead, he just lowered the tip of his blade and looked across at Roper to make sure he had seen how carelessly he had opened Ormur's defences. 'Are you watching closely, my lord? I'll keep it quick. I don't want you so distracted you can't fight.'

There were smashes to Ormur's left and right as Hermit-Crabs and legionaries collided, and the fighting began to escalate once more. But Ormur and Vigtyr were left a dance-floor by the men on both sides.

'Destroy him, Ormur. Please!' Roper was almost begging. Something in his tone made Ormur glance at his brother. His eyes were very wide and full of fear, and it was clear there was something he wanted Ormur to comprehend. 'Don't duel him. Destroy him!'

Ormur tried for a half-beat to understand, before he turned and lunged at Vigtyr in one movement, trying to catch him unawares. Vigtyr seemed in no hurry at all. His feet moved with such parsimony that he had stepped past Ormur's attack without effort, his own blade coming up to thump against Ormur's breastplate and jar him to a halt. It could just as easily have been his neck.

'Careless, careless,' Vigtyr said, tutting.

'Ormur . . .'

He flashed a glance over his shoulder and saw Gray now standing behind him. He and Roper were half clutched on to one another, both leaning forward, their faces agony as they watched his contest with Vigtyr.

'You've an audience, young guardsman,' said Vigtyr. 'Don't let them down.'

Ormur tried to put them from his mind and lunged again, but this time Vigtyr did not even bother to step aside. He was so tall, his reach so far, that all he had to do was extend his own sword so that it grated off Ormur's shoulder plate. Ormur's ill-judged lunge was disturbed and, over-extended and off-balance, he was knocked sideways into the mud.

Vigtyr was not even watching him. 'Up, lad, up,' he said, prowling about the edge of the circle of onlookers. Ormur scrambled upright, horribly aware of Gray and Roper watching Vigtyr toy with him. The Hermit-Crabs were cheering and slapping Vigtyr's shoulder as he passed, laughing as Ormur staggered up once more, covered in mud.

Ormur was furious. He was desperate to destroy this enemy who had taken from him the most precious companion he would ever have, but knew he stood no chance of winning this duel. Vigtyr was too skilled, he too angry. *But I'm not letting him get to Roper, or Gray. I'm going to kill him.*

Vigtyr was still pacing, eyes fastened on Ormur's and drinking in the fury there. He smiled and beckoned him forward with a careless right hand. 'Come, Kynortasson, come, we'll try that again shall we?'

Ormur did as Vigtyr asked, starting towards him, sword held low. *Destroy him, Ormur.*

Vigtyr left his reaction late. Ormur was just walking forward, his sword not even raised, and for a fighter like Vigtyr, there was all the time in the world. His sword whipped up, the tip placed to grate into Ormur's breastplate once more and stop him dead. Then his eyes widened in shock.

Ormur had hurled himself onto Vigtyr's sword. Shifting just enough so that it missed his chest, he drove forward hard so that the tip lodged in his shoulder. He kept going, driving onto the weapon until it emerged more than a foot through his flesh.

Vigtyr's feet were suddenly scrambling as he tried to work back and extricate the blade, but he bundled into the watching Thingalith. He could not move, his sword was stuck in Ormur's shoulder, and Ormur had a fleeting glimpse of his mouth forming a curse as he jammed Warspite two-handed into Vigtyr's belly. The tip crashed through his armour and burst out of his back.

He could hear Roper and Gray hollering with shock, could feel the sword through his shoulder wriggling as Vigtyr thrashed to retrieve it, and the Thingalith scrambling to get out of Vigtyr's way and give him some room. But Ormur had eyes only for that point where Warspite's blade disappeared through the ugly metal lips in Vigtyr's armour, and into his belly. He regripped the handle and twisted.

Somewhere above his head, he heard Vigtyr's gasp. He stepped back, trying to pull Warspite clear, but the weapon was stuck. He could feel the sword in his shoulder being worked free and had to abandon Warspite in Vigtyr's belly, snatching Silence from his side. Vigtyr had at last pulled his sword from Ormur's shoulder, and the guardsman just had time to bat it aside.

The Thingalith had finally cleared some space for their champion and Vigtyr, who had been held up by their presence behind him, stumbled back and crashed onto one side. His sword was still clutched loosely in his left hand, but his right went to the blade protruding from his armour, and the hot blood leaking from either side. Then he looked up at Ormur in disbelief.

'I'm not going to finish you,' said the guardsman, panting. 'Find someone to do it for you. Or face the agony, if you haven't enough friends.'

The pain was splashed across Vigtyr's pale face. He groaned, trying to pull the blade out, but succeeded only in making himself retch.

And around the two duellers, chaos erupted.

The Thingalith lost patience and rushed forward, one of them with eyes set hungrily on the bleeding Ormur. But before the Thingman had even made it within six feet, Roper knocked him to the floor with an elbow-charge. Ormur lost sight of Vigtyr behind Roper, who was scrapping like a hound. Gray was next to him, bellowing 'The Wolf! The Wolf! The Wolf! The Wolf!' and the other legionaries took it up, ready to unleash their counter-charge against the Thingalith.

Ormur barged in beside Gray but was rocked back immediately by a strike on his breastplate, so hard that it punctured the steel and stopped only at the bone armour. The previous blows had not hurt, but this one stung appallingly. He found he was too exhausted to even strike back, his wounded left arm held in at his side, body lacking the energy of his mind.

Roper was tired too, his movements growing clumsy and the sweat dripping off his face. Gray was stepping back, all of them regrouping, too weary in the face of this renewed onslaught.

But then a man brushed past Ormur in the armour of a Sacred Guardsman, sword drawn back for a huge swing which he heaved down on the ranks before him. That one blow put down two Thingalith, and the guardsman did not pause, bringing his knee up into the midriff of the next man who let out a great *'Oof!'* and bent double. This hero, whose name Ormur would never learn, kneed again, connected with the bridge of a nose, and threw his enemy aside. Then another guardsman was digging into the gap alongside him, and another had pushed in front of Ormur and begun slashing like a harvester.

Tekoa had thrown in the reserves. The Sacred Guard had arrived, and to Ormur they looked like battle-angels.

'With them!' Roper was nearly bent double, scarcely able to talk for panting, but still he staggered after the avenging guardsmen, hunting the Thingalith who were battered backwards.

The dark-armoured guardsmen were experienced enough to recognise an opportunity that would not repeat itself, and began digging into the exposed edges of the pikeline, upending the ranks so fast that they began to disintegrate. A wave of fleeing men swept along the battle-line, and like a single woollen strand plucked from the centre of a garment, the legions tugged and tugged until the pikeline was unravelling at speed, the centre dissolving to a shapeless mass.

It was not as Ormur had supposed, at the start of the day. He had thought on a field of this scale, a single individual was shrunk to nothing. Even a unit such as the Sacred Guard was dwarfed by the forces they opposed. But battle, he was coming to learn, was a question of momentum. One man could infect others with it. Three hundred men, in the right place at the right time, could turn it from one side to another. And if you claimed it completely enough at one location, it was inexorable.

The pikemen were impregnable in formation, their flanks defended, and equally vulnerable when that order crumpled. The Anakim may have lost the first day, but they had never broken formation, which is when the vast majority of casualties occur. By doing that to their enemies, they had claimed the second day as their own.

The low sun of the early evening found the pikeline's atomised survivors pelting for the safety of the Teutan reserves, their weapons discarded, and the shadow of antler-helmeted cavalry drawing up behind.

60
With Me

When the Onogurian cavalry went past, Ormur and his rank-mates slumped to the ground as though leaning on their enemies was all that had kept them upright. Ormur was on elbows and knees, trembling with fatigue, the armour on his back nearly too heavy to breathe. Some men had simply collapsed, lying on top of bodies, tongues lolling like a dog in midsummer heat. There were no reserves to come down from the ridge with skins of water and a helping hand. Every one of them had been in that silk-fine line, holding back the pikemen.

A distant trumpet was pealing out, summoning the legions back to the ridge, but it elicited barely a stir from the crumpled ranks. When Ormur tried to move, there was pain everywhere. He seemed to have sustained half a dozen injuries he had not even noticed. The elbows he leaned on were so inflamed that they creaked and burned when he tried to lift Leon's sword. His left shoulder, stabbed through by Vigtyr, rendered that arm near useless with pain, though the bleeding had slowed. And when he finally tried to get to his feet, it took two goes as pain shot through his right sole. Looking down, it seemed to have been lanced through, with blood welling out of a puncture in his boot.

His only feeling was that of being overwhelmed. Leon was dead. But so was Vigtyr. The day was theirs, though they had lost the one before. He was numb to it all. Even now, the Onogurians and Black Cavalry Corps were turning the rankers' victory into a slaughter and evening the disparity between Teutan and Anakim forces. The Teuta had enough troops held back to regather themselves, but this was a blow from which they would struggle to recover.

Labouring up the slope of the ridge, Ormur came across Roper. The Black Lord had strained his lower back so badly that he could hardly stand, and kept falling back to hands and knees. When Ormur took his left arm and tried to hook it over his shoulder, it felt unnaturally mobile in his grasp. Roper groaned and pulled himself away. Ormur paused a moment, barely able to see through the white shadows of exhaustion blotting his vision. 'It feels dislocated.'

Roper was still panting, right elbow propped on right knee, staring at the floor. 'Maybe,' he said, gesturing at his limp left arm. 'Help me.'

With much heaving and grunting from Roper, the shoulder finally gave a very soft pop. Roper groaned again and let out a long exhalation, closing his eyes.

'How long was it out?'

Roper shrugged asymmetrically. 'Just after your fight with Vigtyr.'

'You've been fighting for an hour with a dislocated shoulder?'

The Black Lord did not reply. 'Where's Leon?' he asked instead. 'He was next to you, wasn't he?'

'Leon's dead,' said Ormur.

Roper just continued panting at the ground. 'A good death?' he asked eventually.

Ormur hesitated. 'A brave one.'

Together they staggered back up to the ridge. Gray was there, lying on his side, cradling his right hand and grimacing. Tekoa was there too, and as the least injured of them, it was he who cleaned Ormur's shoulder. The legate had still been shot through the forearm by a Teutan longbowman, the arrow passing through the wound, which was bleeding freely.

'How did you get this?' he asked, rubbing at Ormur's shoulder with a vinegar-soaked rag.

The sting was breathtaking, and Ormur tried to ignore it. 'Vigtyr did it.'

Tekoa froze. 'You saw him?'

'I killed him.'

Tekoa glanced around, meeting Gray's eye. The captain nodded, and Tekoa leapt to his feet, crowing in triumph. 'Ha! The old bastard got what he deserved, eh? Even after all these years, the Almighty is not mocked! How did you do it?'

Ormur relayed what he could remember, which was not much. The memory seemed lost in fog.

'It was lunacy,' Gray intervened, managing to prop himself up on one knee and winking at Ormur. 'But it might've been the only way to beat Vigtyr. He was just toying with you, and that last move came out of nowhere. You shocked him.' He gave a fuller account of the story, while Tekoa smiled evilly to himself.

'This is pleasing indeed. There was more good news, did you hear what happened to the Barleymen?'

'No?' said Gray.

Tekoa nodded in satisfaction, still scrubbing at Ormur with the wretched vinegar rag. 'They caught the Ulpha cold yesterday, but the Greyhazel were ready for them today, and it was their turn for a little emotion. Let's just say Vigtyr wasn't the only score that was settled.'

'Did they break them?'

'Like an old chamber pot.' There was blood running down the legate's forearm which splattered onto Ormur, causing him to jerk away instinctively. Tekoa scowled. 'I do apologise, Guardsman,' he said nastily. 'Has my injury inconvenienced you?'

Ormur snorted.

'It's inconvenienced me, Tekoa,' said Gray, waving at Keturah and Randolph, who had just arrived. 'You've not shut up about it since.' When the captain revealed his right hand Ormur saw he had lost the outer two fingers, in addition to a catalogue of slashes running up his forearms. With his missing left hand, he now had a total of three fingers remaining to him.

'I look forward to your many injuries being cleansed in vinegar, Captain,' Tekoa advised. 'You'll not say a word I assume.'

Keturah and Randolph had each brought half a dozen sopping water-skins, freshly swollen from a spring running off the ridge.

'The Black Lady fetching water?' asked Gray.

'As good a thing as any to do just now,' she replied, tossing them on the ground between them. Ormur fell upon a skin, drinking until he was nearly sick. It was suddenly cold on the ridge. The sun was not as strong as it had been, and his sweat-soaked tunic was stuck to his back. He manoeuvred himself onto one side and began working at his pierced boot.

Keturah had not sat down, and was staring instead at Ormur's waist. 'Is that Leon's sword?' she asked, quietly.

Not wanting to deliver the news again, Ormur nodded, still working at his boot which seemed stuck in place.

'Dead?' asked Gray, after a time.

'Yes. He was brave, and it was quick.'

There was a silence. Ormur looked up and found Tekoa looking at Keturah, she glancing at Gray, all wearing expressions of sadness and rueful fondness. 'Well . . .' said Gray, and he held his waterskin aloft. 'Leon Kaldison.'

The others raised their skins as well, and drank.

'And Hartvig Uxison,' added Tekoa, and they drank again.

'Virtanen,' finished Gray. He was smiling sadly at Keturah, who raised her skin again swiftly, nodding at the captain. 'I wish I could've heard Leon's dream,' Gray went on. 'This morning, we all said we'd had some strange ones. For Leon to bring that up it must've been unusual indeed.'

I wish I'd made peace with him before he died, thought Ormur.

'Didn't know he had dreams,' said Tekoa. 'It was probably about eating Sutherners for supper or something, doubt you missed much.'

'Perhaps . . . Ormur, do you think you'd know where his body was?'

'Maybe.'

'Perhaps if there's time we could try and retrieve it. If Safinim doesn't attack again this evening.'

'He won't,' said Roper. 'Without his signalling machine, he won't have time to coordinate a new advance before dark.'

'Thank god,' said Tekoa faintly.

'Tiring, was it?' said Randolph sympathetically. 'Riding around on that horse all day?'

Tekoa looked on the verge of saying something scathing, but the moment was broken when Ormur finally succeeded in tugging off his boot. From the neck was released a spinning clot the size of a sheep's liver which threw off drips of blood before splattering on the grass by Tekoa's cloak.

'Bloody hell!' roared Tekoa, snatching at his cloak and leaping to his feet, away from the offending clot.

'Sorry, Legate,' said Ormur. 'I hope my injury hasn't inconvenienced you.'

Gray and Randolph cheered at this rejoinder and Keturah clapped her hands in glee. Even Roper smiled. Ormur bent to inspect his foot, rust-red and punctured neatly on top with a triangular-shaped wound. 'That's a proper job, Ormur,' said Gray. 'You'll need some help. Maybe someone with more fingers could take a look at it?'

It was Keturah who treated his wound, taking it tenderly in her lap and producing the leather medical roll which she still carried, despite her lofty rank.

'I can't believe we broke them,' said Gray softly. He was looking out over the field at a felled forest of the dead. Gulls were crying overhead as they circled the carrion, the skuas already on the ground squabbling over the easiest pickings. The Onogurians and Black Cavalry corps had been turned back by the well-ordered Teutan reserves and a screen of approaching camels, but they had exacted a dreadful toll on the pikemen in the time they had been allowed. 'We could do this,' he went on. 'In spite of everything, it's us who've stood our ground, not them.'

'It's made what happened yesterday feel like part of a victory,' said Keturah.

'Exactly!' Gray nodded. 'Beat them back tomorrow and... we can break them. If we turn their battle-line again and we keep advancing, and get the Unhieru and cavalry forward too, their reserves won't stand.'

The tone of this encounter was so different from any other since Ormur had arrived at his battlefield. For the first time, there was a belief that they might prevail. They had lost so much already, and now that seemed a source of shared identity.

Perhaps that was what persuaded Roper to speak. 'I'd wondered,' he said calmly, looking at Keturah, 'whether you might tell me of our son.'

Keturah looked back at Roper with a little sympathy for the first time. 'Numa is seven years old, and he thrives. He loves the owls in the Hindrunn, and runs everywhere. Or he did, last I saw. When he gets back from the haskoli, he will be someone new.'

Roper looked back at the ground, smiling foolishly to himself.

Tekoa spoke suddenly. 'What's that?'

There came a creaking as everyone craned about to observe some distant spectacle, invisible to Ormur, who still lay on his back, foot in Keturah's lap.

'Bellamus?' said Gray.

'Must be,' murmured Keturah.

'What is it?' asked Ormur, looking at her face. She was staring into the far distance.

'Horsemen with a white flag,' she said, not looking at him. 'A wagon behind them.'

'He's panicking!' exclaimed Randolph, rubbing his hands together. 'He wants to talk!'

There was a long silence as they all observed the distant envoy.

'But not with us,' said Keturah bleakly.

Unable to help himself, Ormur rolled onto his front and looked out across the plain. The sun had cast the whole scene in gold, with the brightest spot the distant white flag fluttering above a group of horsemen who were disturbing a trail of gulls as they cantered over the bodies. Behind them was a sleek wagon, pulled by a team of four horses, and Keturah seemed to be right. They were not making for the Anakim part of the ridge, but the Unhieru.

'Why would Bellamus want to speak to Gogmagoc?' Tekoa spoke for the group, and the silence answered. It could mean nothing good.

'Well, they're not speaking alone,' said Roper. Using his sheathed sword as a walking stick, he staggered to his feet. 'Horse! Bring me a horse!'

Ormur glanced at Gray, who nodded at him that they should follow. 'Wait,' Keturah commanded. She deftly wound linen strips around Ormur's foot, finishing it with a flat plaited knot that would not catch when he put his boot back on. 'Go,' she said shortly, releasing him.

Roper was already being helped into Zephyr's saddle, and Gray was waiting with a pair of coursers. Ormur hobbled to join them, Roper bawling out orders. 'Every legate to their legions! Assume this wretched day has one last fight left in it and make certain your men are ready for it.'

'We can't fight again,' murmured Randolph, but too softly for Roper to hear.

'I shudder to ask,' Tekoa agreed quietly.

Roper and Gray had already charged off, and Tekoa had started riding for the Skiritai. Ormur hauled himself into the saddle with one arm, and only now he was mounted did he realise he had left his sword – or rather Leon's sword – on the ground. But Keturah had already picked it up, and held it out to him. 'Thank you, my lady,' he said, bowing and taking Silence and sheathing it. 'You're staying?'

'If the men are to fight again, they'll need preparing,' she said. 'Go,' and she gave the rump of his horse a hard smack. It lunged forward, almost jerking out from beneath him.

Left arm tight to his side, he kicked back his heels and tore after Roper and Gray. They were at a full gallop, riding directly along the line of the ridge, but Ormur could see already that the Suthern delegation would reach the Unhieru first. Ormur could not think what they might discuss, but the fear of his senior officers was enough to rattle him. It suddenly felt as though they were riding to save the army.

Roper, despite his injured shoulder and back, was stretching ahead of Gray. Ormur managed to catch the captain and together the two guardsmen laboured behind their lord, always twenty feet in front.

A quarter of a mile on, a score of Sutherners had met five Unhieru.

'It's Bellamus!' They heard Roper's shout as they drew within a hundred yards. Ormur had never seen Lord Safinim before, but one figure stood out from the others. A man in early middle-age, grey-haired, a patch over one eye and an expensively dyed cloak of ocean blue about his shoulders. He was the most decorated human being that Ormur had ever beheld. His every edge seemed trimmed with gold, fur or colours that Ormur did not know cloth could carry, and the effect was not gaudy, but uncanny. Safinim, with his mobile face and charming demeanour, was so different from anyone Ormur had seen before that he was frightening.

It was he who was positioned at the front, surrounded by a score of Hermit-Crabs, all of them battered, their bone plates chipped from the day's fighting. He was talking to Gogmagoc in terms of utmost civility. The giant king had come forward with four companions, all of them female, and had removed his helmet for the occasion. His dark mane was revealed, rattling with vertebrae and bronze trinkets, and he had leaned his huge butcher's tool of an axe against his legs. His golden eyes were fixed steadily on Safinim, who glanced at the three Anakim horsemen as they reined in beside the parlay, sweating and panting.

'Ah. This parlay is between myself and King Gogmagoc, Lord Roper,' said Bellamus in pleasant Anakim. 'You needn't have troubled yourself, riding all this way.'

Gogmagoc's eyes had not left Safinim.

'Bellamus,' said Roper, chest rising rapidly. 'This is not worthy.'

'We'll let King Gogmagoc decide that, shall we? I was just making my offer.'

The negotiations were up to Roper, and Ormur focused instead on their enemy. None of the Anakim carried a white flag, and so were not protected by the ancient custom. Against them were twenty of Safinim's household guard, and behind them that wagon, pulled by a team of four horses. The driver had positioned it twenty yards back so that it faced away from the parlay, as if ready to leave at a moment's notice. And lying in the bed of the wagon was a bound figure as large as an Anakim, identifiable by a shock of bright-blond hair.

Garrett.

Like a cold wave slapping him in the face, Ormur suddenly understood Safinim's offer.

'We should not have individual parlays with the enemy, Lord King,' said Roper, beckoning Gogmagoc away. 'Not in an alliance of equals. If there are things we wish to discuss, we can send envoys to the Sutherners later.'

Gogmagoc gave a growl like distant thunder. 'No. We talk now.'

'I quite agree,' said Bellamus.

'Is this what you are, Safinim?' demanded Roper. 'No more than—'

'Silence!' Gogmagoc spoke like cracking glacial ice, facing

Roper at last. Beneath that bronze glare, even the Black Lord fell quiet.

Bellamus carried a look of ill-suppressed excitement, but spoke quite mildly, as though his offer might be of no interest at all to Gogmagoc. 'Over there, in the bed of that wagon, you will find the man who killed your son. Garrett Eoten-Draefend of Eskanceaster. For his crimes against you, Lord King, he has been bound and gagged. The offer I make you could hardly be more favourable.'

'Nor more dishonourable,' Roper interjected harshly.

Bellamus continued as if he had not spoken. 'If you are prepared to ally yourself with our side, I will turn him over to you as a gesture of goodwill. Do as you see fit with him: dispense whatever justice the codes of your people demand. And all I ask in return is a friendship that liberates you from Lord Roper's doomed army.'

'If we are indeed doomed, Lord Safinim,' snarled Roper, 'then why would you be here, making such a desperate offer?'

Bellamus did not react. He did not need to, for Gogmagoc had lashed out at Roper with a massive paw. It struck him in the midriff and knocked him clean off Zephyr. Roper crashed to the ground without an utterance, too winded to speak. Gogmagoc shifted slightly towards the downed Black Lord, but Gray and Ormur blocked his path immediately, putting their mounts between the two kings. 'Easy now,' said Gray quite calmly. He had not even moved his hand to his sword, and nor did he advance. He just returned Gogmagoc's golden glare.

'We had a deal, Gogmagoc,' Roper gasped from the ground. Dazed, he was trying to clamber back to his feet. He tried twice, stumbled back to the floor and spoke from there. 'We armed and . . .' Roper drew a laboured breath, '. . . armoured your people.' He stopped, talking, clearly in considerable pain. 'We promised you Garrett.'

'Years ago!' rumbled Gogmagoc. 'Years ago! And used my desire of him to direct me like a hound. And still I do not have him!'

'Take him now,' said Bellamus. 'Turn on the Anakim, we will attack at the same time. We will destroy them together, and you get the Eoten-Draefend.'

'Done,' said Gogmagoc immediately.

'No,' moaned Roper. He tried to rise again, and this time succeeded by pulling himself up on his stirrup.

'Done,' Gogmagoc repeated greedily, holding a hand out towards Garrett. 'Give him to me.'

'He's yours when we have finished the Anakim,' said Bellamus firmly.

'He's mine when I say!' roared Gogmagoc suddenly, spit flying from his mouth and making Bellamus's horse start. 'And I take him now! The River-King has it right. You would not make this offer unless you feared to lose. Give him to me now, no more waiting. Now, or I give you nothing.'

Bellamus hesitated. 'You swear that once payment is made, you will turn on the Anakim?'

'I swear it. Now give him to me!'

'Don't!' coughed Roper, still leaning against his horse and fighting for breath. 'You don't have to . . . When we win this battle together, you'll get Eoten-Draefend.'

'No!' Gogmagoc shook his head, braids rattling and tongue protruding as though he had tasted something vile. 'No more waiting!' he sneered. 'No more! With him, we cannot lose. And I want to take my people home. I like his offer better, River-King.' Gogmagoc's wives had begun to babble in their strange language.

'Very good,' said Bellamus. 'I'm so pleased we could reach an arrangement.' He beckoned over his shoulder without turning round. 'Bring the Eoten-Draefend here.' The wagon-master cracked his whip and coaxed his horses about, making soothing noises as they tossed and faltered at the sight of the five Unhieru.

Gray spoke quietly, looking up at Gogmagoc. 'Lord King. In our culture, fighting alongside someone makes you brothers. We have done that for eight years. Will you truly turn against us?'

Gogmagoc was panting, eyes never leaving the prize being dragged towards him. 'Eight years of fighting your war! Of being tricked into doing your bidding. We have paid for our armour. Now I want my reward. I want revenge, and I want my people to survive, River-Man.'

'There was no trick, Lord King,' Gray began. He stopped abruptly when Gogmagoc snatched up the huge axe that had been leaning against his legs and turned on him.

'Liar!' he howled, raising the weapon. There was so much force and violence in that word that Gray's mount backed away instinctively, reversing out of range and tossing nervously. 'Liar!' Gogmagoc roared again, pacing after him. Ormur's horse and even Zephyr began to retreat as well. 'Liar!'

Roper looked as though he were about to try and force Zephyr forward to confront Gogmagoc, but Gray seized his left arm, making Roper grunt in pain and forcing him to look round. 'We have to go, lord,' said Gray. 'We have to prepare the army.'

Ormur, horse still reversing of its own accord, was watching the wagon carrying Garrett. It reached Gogmagoc and slewed around. Its bound contents were presented like a centrepiece at a feast, and the giant king was distracted. Garrett looked up wide-eyed at the face of nightmarish intensity set upon him, and he began to thrash violently against his bonds. He seemed to be attempting to reach his bastardised spear, Heofonfyr, which lay in the wagon-bed alongside him.

'We must go, lord,' Gray urged, pulling Roper backwards. 'We can do no more here. The army must be prepared immediately.'

Roper allowed himself to be dragged back but still would not turn away. Ormur could not blame him, for he was watching his life's work annihilated. There was longing in his face, and unutterable grief, as Gogmagoc set down his axe and took up Heofonfyr.

'Gogmagoc!' Roper bellowed. 'Gogmagoc!' The giant king barely spared him a glance as his wives rumbled forward gleefully and seized Garrett, twisting him around and repositioning him so that he lay prone, head protruding over the edge of the wagon. Bellamus was observing with fascination as the hybrid was held still.

'No,' moaned Roper softly.

They stayed just long enough to see Garrett decapitated. Gogmagoc had flushed maroon and was near trembling with rage and joy as he slashed Heofonfyr in a grey arc which removed not just the hybrid's head, but part of a shoulder as well.

Roper was shaking his head disbelievingly. 'Gogmagoc! You faithless backstabber! I will kill you! Do you hear me? I am going to kill you for this! If you are to destroy my people, I will do the same to yours! I promise you! I promise you!'

Gogmagoc did not seem to have registered these threats. Roper stared after him, such fury in his face that Ormur thought he might attack then and there. Then he turned away and kicked Zephyr into a gallop. Ormur and Gray fell in behind him.

If the Unhieru turned on them, this battle was finished. They would attack from the flank; from the front would come the Sutherners, and their depleted force would be crushed.

'Maybe he won't go through with it,' said Gray. 'Take Garrett and ignore the rest of Safinim's offer.'

Ormur doubted that. Why would he? Bellamus was offering Gogmagoc survival. He and Gogmagoc together would easily defeat the Anakim.

Ormur twisted in his saddle and looked over his shoulder, to see Safinim and his Hermit-Crabs riding back to the Suthern lines. Behind them, a huge figure was parading through the Unhieru, holding aloft a head impaled on a long spear. The figure was roaring, and in reply the whole mass of them were turning to face their Anakim allies.

The sun was dropping and they rode as hard as they could for the legions. The army still had no idea what had happened. They did not know the Unhieru were now enemies. And riding out to meet them, silhouetted against the evening sky, was Tekoa, flanked by half a dozen Skiritai officers.

'What's going on?' he called as they drew close. 'Why is Gogmagoc redeploying? What's happened?'

They reined in before one another, Tekoa looking from Roper, to Gray, to Ormur and reading the shock transparent on each of them.

'Gogmagoc's turned on us,' said Roper, blankly.

Tekoa looked stunned, then appalled. 'What?' he demanded. 'How? He's sided with Safinim?'

'Never mind how,' said Roper. 'They're attacking, and we need someone to hold them while we redeploy.' He met Tekoa's eyes, and at first the legate looked a little confused. 'The Skiritai are closest,' Roper said brutally.

There was still a moment when Tekoa did not realise what Roper was asking. Then he recoiled, eyes still set on Roper's, stunned and hurt. He looked to Gray and Ormur once more, as though hoping they would betray this for a joke. But they stared back with such obvious pity that it seemed to settle the issue. 'I suppose they are,' Tekoa agreed.

What time there was, Tekoa was about to buy. Roper evidently did not intend to waste a moment of it. He nodded brusquely. 'Brave of you.' Then he spurred on, riding towards the line, leaving the others hovering in his wake. Tekoa and the Skiritai officers looked thunderstruck. Tekoa's gaze slid off Ormur and Gray and went to the distance, and the massing Unhieru. They were still swirling about that vast central figure, and a distant bellowing was rising from the ranks. At this range the Unhieru fury was rendered something like a mustering colony of bees: an ominous throb which set Ormur's hair on end.

He wanted to say something, but there was nothing he could express which did not seem utterly inadequate. 'We should follow,' murmured Gray, nodding at Roper's retreating form.

'He wants us to stop the Unhieru?' blurted a Skiritai lieutenant, his eyes wild at the absurdity of this task.

'He didn't say stop,' said another. 'He said hold.'

Tekoa did not seem to hear any of this. He was still staring at the Unhieru.

'How are we supposed to hold them?' demanded the lieutenant. 'We're skirmishers, not rankers, we have no stopping power. It'll barely take them five minutes to blast us aside. You can't reorganise an army in that time, it's a waste. I'm not throwing away my life for that.'

Gray cleared his throat. 'You were given an order,' he observed.

'But it's mad!' exclaimed the Skiritai.

'And yet,' said Gray a little spikily, 'it's yours to obey.'

'But he's right,' said the second officer. 'It's nothing but a waste, the rankers should hold them off.'

'Absolutely,' agreed a third.

Ormur felt himself bristle, half in contempt at their naked panic, but before he could say anything Tekoa barked over the top of the hubbub. 'Shut up!' he snarled, snapping a withering gaze on his lieutenant. 'You melt-brained bastard! Shut up all of you! Our master has given us an order, and until he says otherwise, we hold back those fat stinking beasts.' He glanced around at the appalled faces and then exploded: 'Well? What more do you want? I'm not a fucking orator. Yes: by the end of this, we'll all be dead, but our traditions will live on! We suffer naught to fate, compromise for nothing and yield to nobody. Not even the bloody Unhieru. Captain,' he turned to Gray. 'Piss off. They'll need you on that ridge. The rest of you bastards, with me! With me now! With me! Ha!' He raked back his heels and his black stallion lurched forward. Tekoa's face was set in a grim sneer as he charged away, his officers falling in dumbly behind.

The last Ormur saw of Tekoa Urielson was his retreating shoulders, black hair bouncing with the gait of his horse, the declining sun stretching a long shadow before him.

61

Gogmagoc

Even immediately after the fight against the Unhieru, Ormur struggled to recall it in anything more than fragments. They had redeployed on the ridge, trusting to the bravery of the Skiritai for the time they needed to form a second front to receive the giants, and constantly aware of the Teutan ranks churning across the plain as they prepared an attack of their own. Gray had promised they would face the Unhieru together, and been at his side when they ran into the thick of it.

It was those moments which Ormur recalled better than the fighting. The leaders, who it now became clear this army had possessed in abundance, bringing out the best from those around them with the right word and the right manner. Those who stood still as their peers took a pace backwards, and stubbornly refused to indulge in the complaints of their rank-mates. Who endured until the moment came to throw their lot in with another, and turn a lone madman into a counter-attack, and a tiny victory. Most of them not born, but grown from a hundred conflicts into soldiers who had time to think beyond their own panic, and make the small conscious gestures which their drowning peers latched onto: a joke, or casual remark on what they would do once the battle was won. And the legions had not hundreds of these warriors, but thousands. Their experience did not always translate into beating an enemy one on one: battles are too chaotic for such justice. But it made for an army which endured, listened and acted when asked.

As for the fighting, Ormur remembered defeating an eight-footer with the help of an Aalander, one of them assaulting the beast from either side. Then how he had looked around for Gray and realised he had lost the captain. He remembered getting crushed when a marauding female fell on top of him, and the certainty that it was where he would die.

He was saved by two Sacred Guardsmen, who rolled her off him and then limped off without another word to continue the fight. And he remembered staggering to his feet, gasping for breath and looking around. He saw Anakim being knocked to the floor, where a surprising number of dead Unhieru lay like felled oak trees. Banners being used to blind the giants as they were stabbed again and again. Many were not bothering with weapons against the thick chainmail but just seizing Unhieru legs in an effort to topple their enemies over. Once on the floor it seemed their armour was too heavy for them to rise easily, and the Anakim swarmed on them like terriers. Shattered weapons lay everywhere.

But the clearest memory had come when Ormur straightened, preparing to fight once more, and seeing something which sent energy surging through his limbs.

Gray alone. He was walking quite deliberately towards a single vast Unhieru; bigger than any of the others, who had singled out the Captain of the Guard for destruction. The Unhieru held a familiar long-bladed spear by his side, blood-stained and glittering like a savage icicle.

It was Gogmagoc.

'Gray!'

The sense of dread radiating from the giant king was so much that the air throbbed with it. He was not charging like the others, but prowling with horrible intention, Heofonfyr rising overhead like a scorpion's tail. Gray advanced with equal purpose, neither prepared to be moved as they walked out to meet each other.

'Gray! Hold on!'

They were nearly toe to toe, Gogmagoc ready to gore the captain through, when Gray surged forward, and ducked low. The shaft of the spear, spat like the bolt from a crossbow, passed over his head, and Gray swarmed beneath it, ripping his sword up beneath the giant's chainmail sark, aiming for the arteries at the groin. But it was a blind thrust beneath the mail, and the blade came to an abrupt halt while it was still at the level of Gogmagoc's knee. Then a hand like a leg of beef thumped into his side and knocked him full length.

'Gogmagoc!' Ormur was heartbeats away, hurtling towards the giant king and trying to distract him. 'Here, you backstabbing oaf! You traitorous, shapeless sack of shit!'

Gray was stirring, trying to get to his feet, but another glancing blow sent him tumbling in a huff of dust. Gogmagoc pressed a foot down on his chest and raised Heofonfyr, harpoon-like above him.

Ormur struck home. With Silence held level, all his bodyweight behind it like a lance, he drove it into Gogmagoc's heel. He felt it penetrate the thick leather, the skin, and then jar against granite bone. Then the sword came loose and Ormur had fallen onto his front. He regripped the hilt and pushed himself onto all fours just as Gogmagoc swung round, looming over Ormur. The giant king had not uttered a sound.

Ormur could see Gray between Gogmagoc's legs, still down, surely unconscious, and resolved to keep Gogmagoc distracted. He scrambled back, raising Silence before him and realising only then that the sword was broken. The top third of it had lodged in Gogmagoc's heel and snapped off, leaving Ormur without a point. The giant king was reaching a hand towards him, and he stabbed at it. The blow bounced off his gauntlet and was ignored by Gogmagoc, who seized his ankle and jerked him off his feet. Ormur was dragged on his back towards Gogmagoc, and lifted upside down into the air, a bass rhythm like a profound drum pounding in his ears, louder and louder.

And then all he could see was dust.

He was cartwheeling through the air as an almighty smash rang through his head. He seemed to spin for an impossible time, eventually thudding to earth with enough violence to knock the sense from him.

What had happened and why Gogmagoc had released him, he could not conceive. His face was pressed into the dirt, and even coordinating a movement as simple as lifting his head took three attempts. When he managed it, he found a strange scene before him.

Gogmagoc was lying on the ground, stirring groggily. A jagged metal shard protruded beneath his armpit, blood trickling around the sides as though it were a spigot. Entangled with him was an armoured beast even larger than the giant king, tossing its metal mane and snorting as it tried to clear its head.

It was Zephyr.

The horse was trying to rise but slowed by the weight of its armour. The saddle was empty, and the unicorn's spike on its head snapped off just an inch from the champron, with the rest buried deep in Gogmagoc's side. Then Ormur saw Roper, also trying to climb to his feet on Gogmagoc's far side. He had charged his immense horse directly into Gogmagoc, putting so much weight behind that huge spike that it penetrated even the thick Unhieru chainmail. How he had persuaded Zephyr to charge home into such an enemy, Ormur could not imagine.

There was a two-foot iron spike in his chest, but still Gogmagoc was not defeated.

He had climbed to his knees, one arm reaching towards Zephyr, the other groping for Heofonfyr. Zephyr was half upright too, and stiffened as Gogmagoc's fingers closed about his leg.

The horse's other hoof snapped back.

It struck Gogmagoc on his chain-mailed shoulder, which buckled horribly beneath the blow. Gogmagoc slewed around with the power of it, half falling back to his side. Somehow though he had kept hold of Zephyr's leg with his right hand and the horse toppled over with him.

Gogmagoc's left arm was broken. It hung loose by his side, catching on the broken spike protruding from the wall of his chest. Still he held onto Zephyr, drool swinging from his chin, leering over the horse and using his mass to hold it down. Zephyr thrashed and whinnied furiously, teeth drawn back and trying to rise. But Gogmagoc was clever as well as savage and would not let the beast get its hooves beneath it. Using his one good arm he half crawled, half dragged himself on top of the horse, pinning it to the mud with his chest. His right hand began groping across the mud, settling on a huge rock.

Zephyr still screamed and thrashed as Gogmagoc tugged the rock closer. It was so huge that he could only lift it when held in close at his body, and even then he only managed at a swing. In a momentous arc he brought it hurtling round to crash on the horse's head.

Ormur tried to get to his feet but staggered over at once, his legs like rope. Gray was stirring groggily, but could not stand. Then Ormur saw Roper. The Black Lord was on his feet and limping towards Gogmagoc, propped on the giant's abandoned spear and using it like a staff. Garrett's spear: Heofonfyr. His eyes were set upon the giant as he took another swing with the rock and finally silenced Zephyr.

Gogmagoc stared down at his handiwork for a moment, panting and wheezing past the spike buried in his chest. Then, satisfied that the horse was dead, he dropped the stone. He had not seen Roper approaching from his right-hand side, but the Black Lord called to him.

'Gogmagoc!'

The noise filtered through Ormur's skull as though he were underwater.

'Gogmagoc!'

The giant king turned his head and saw Roper at last. He tried to lurch to his feet but he was injured, bleeding and slow.

'I told you, traitor,' said Roper, sounding as though he were on the verge of tears. 'I told you!' Gogmagoc was halfway up when Roper, face set in a vicious grimace, heaved Heofonfyr at his head.

The blade struck the underside of Gogmagoc's jaw and sank nearly a full foot into his head. Half upright, one leg still trailing over Zephyr, Gogmagoc froze. His eyes were suddenly glassy. His fingers fibrillated minutely. Then he dropped to his knees so that he and Roper were at eye level. 'I told you,' hissed Roper, his teeth gritted in hatred. 'You broke faith with my people. The last thing I do will be to destroy yours.'

Gogmagoc had not heard. Falling to his knees had jammed the butt-spike of Heofonfyr into the mud so that it propped him upright. He knelt before Roper, entirely still and quite dead.

Roper panted, staring into his face with loathing for a time. Then he walked round Gogmagoc and gave him a shove so that he slumped onto his right-hand side. He seized the shaft of Heofonfyr, still protruding from his jaw, and tried to pull it clear. It took three attempts before he was able to lever it out. Then he toppled over, stumbling against Gogmagoc's bulk and panting, his face very pale.

'Are you all right, lord?' Ormur had managed to stand and staggered over to Roper. They seemed to occupy an odd vacuum in the battle. Fierce fighting still raged to either side, but the nearest Unhieru was fifty yards away.

Roper nodded curtly.

'How did you get Zephyr to charge into Gogmagoc? I thought he'd have shied away.'

Roper was panting and closed his eyes for a moment. 'Covered his eyes.' He gestured at a sword lying in the mud, and Ormur recognised Cold-Edge. 'With that. He couldn't see what he was about to hit.'

Gray, recognising their voices, began crawling towards

them. They sheltered together behind the twin bulks of Gogmagoc and Zephyr as though in refuge from a storm. 'Where's Safinim?' asked Gray, head leaning on Zephyr's motionless leg. 'Where are the Sutherners?'

Ormur seemed the only one able to stand, and clambered up onto Gogmagoc's body for a vantage point. The sun had set, and the moon was the brightest thing in the sky. Gentle blue light lit the field, and it seemed this patch of calm was not so unusual. So many were now dead from each side that the warriors were scraped over the ridge. Over the heads of weary legionaries and waning Unhieru, he could see the Teuta in the far distance.

They had not moved. They had simply watched as their two enemies hacked themselves apart.

'He's betrayed them,' said Ormur bleakly. 'Safinim.'

'Of course,' said Roper. The Teutan muster they had witnessed had been a feint to coax the Unhieru into committing. Now they just stood off, watching as their enemies destroyed each other. Bellamus had left Gogmagoc to fight alone.

Some of the Unhieru were beginning to run now. They had realised no help would come to finish off the Anakim. Isolated, dispersed and heat-exhausted, they were beginning to fall more easily. They tired faster than the Anakim and some were loping clear of the fight while they still had the strength. Soon there was a steady stream of them wading clear of the ridge.

The Anakim could not pursue. They wilted to the ground like settling leaves. Not one that Ormur could see took a single step towards company, food or water. They just fell where they stood. Banners were toppling as their bearers lost the strength to hold them up, spears sagged from vertical to horizontal and before Ormur's eyes, what was left of their grand army sank to the earth.

The Teuta were still not moving. It was nearly dark, and it seemed they intended to finish the wretched fragments of the Anakim in the morning. They occupied the field in name only; a shadow of the force which had arrived.

Ormur slid off Gogmagoc's body and fell down beside Roper, his legs trembling. A slight breeze was drying the sweat that soaked his tunic, and he was very cold. There was nothing to say. Roper stared at his own feet, head nearly slumped into his chest. Gray lay stretched in the mud, head resting on the dead horse, gazing at the moon low on the horizon.

Ormur watched the pair of them. His hands stung with a half-dozen raw blisters, his foot was agony and even when cramp overtook his calf, he found he was too stiff and weary to alleviate it. From the distant shore came the soft boom of waves and there were gulls crowing over the limitless feast laid out beneath them.

There were faint hoof beats too: a single horse, drawing steadily nearer. He had no curiosity as to who it might be, even when it became clear the rider was approaching the three of them. The horse drew up, snorting and wheezing just a few yards away. 'Thank the Almighty,' said a familiar voice. He tilted his head a fraction so that he could just see the rider looming over him, plated in mother-of-pearl by the moonlight.

Keturah.

She was chalk-white, staring down at them with horror. 'I saw the Skiritai go in first,' she said, her voice wavering.

There was a long silence which no one had the strength to break. Ormur glanced at Roper, who had not acknowledged Keturah. Then Gray shifted minutely. 'Oh, my lady,' he murmured. With a grunt he propped himself up, glancing at Roper as though this news was his to break. But obstinately Roper was still not looking at any of them. 'Yes. The Skiritai went in first.' He paused. 'I haven't seen Tekoa.'

Keturah swayed in the saddle. Then she dismounted gracelessly, half falling from the horse and ending up sitting next to Gray. She drew her knees up to her chest and held her head in her hands. The sound of her gentle sobbing filled the dark, unbearable to Ormur. He crawled towards it and swung an arm over her shoulder. She leaned into his chest and howled like a wounded wolf. He held onto her, still with that feeling of numbness. It seemed certain now: everyone he loved was either dead, or would be tomorrow.

'Hear those waves?' asked Gray distantly. They were still booming softly against the beach. 'I think we should go down to the sea.'

It was such an odd thing to say that Ormur nearly rebuked Gray for insensitivity. But he found he wanted the same. Keturah had stopped crying. 'Yes,' she agreed. She picked up her head and wiped her eyes. 'That's a good idea, Captain.'

She stood first, holding out a hand to pull Ormur to his feet. They helped Gray up between them, though the captain seemed hardly able to stand and had to hook an arm over Keturah's shoulder for support. Ormur looked to Roper who nodded and murmured that he would catch them up. He did not want company, and Ormur left with Keturah and Gray, aware of the Black Lord following at a distance.

They were not the only ones heading for the beach. A trickle of injured warriors were limping in twos and threes down the back of the ridge, towards the saltwater smell of the sea. The shingle crunched beneath their boots, which were the first things Ormur shed. His breastplate clanked onto the stones, his helmet, his broken sword. Gray and Keturah shed footwear and clothes in a trail, never fully coming to a halt. Ormur was stopped in his tracks by the dreadful wounds revealed on Gray's pale torso. He still needed Keturah's help to walk and they splashed into the cold waves together.

It seemed the whole army was following now. In eerie silence they stripped and waded into the waves, which took the weight from their injured limbs. So thick was the blood and grime washed off that the clear water ran dark in the moonlight.

The waves glittered, the gulls cried, and they washed together.

62
Across the Sea

'I had more of those dreams on the beach,' said Ormur.

He, Gray and Randolph were back on the ridge, sitting beside a driftwood fire. After washing in the sea, they had crawled back onto the beach and, too weary even to set a watch, they had fallen asleep on the shingle. Bellamus could have killed what was left of the Anakim army with a hundred quiet men. When Ormur had finally woken, he had been trembling bitterly, and so cold he could barely pick up his sword.

'So did I,' said Gray.

'I did as well,' murmured Randolph. 'What is going on?'

'What was yours, Ormur?' asked Gray.

'A forest,' said Ormur, sunk immediately into that other world. 'A moon as bright as the sun, and leaves made of silver glass. Between the trees was a stag, which I knew I had to keep up with, but it moved like mercury. I only caught flashes of it, and once I saw it had pine branches for antlers. But even though the dream was different, it felt the same as the others I've had since I got here. They all seemed like *days*. And when I woke up, I felt calm.'

Gray nodded, perhaps recognising the description.

'What about you then, Captain?' asked Randolph. 'You've been silent on yours. Are you going to tell us now?'

Gray paused, and then shrugged. 'I dreamed of Pryce.'

Ormur hesitated. 'What happened? Did you speak to him?'

'No. I couldn't. We stood on opposite banks of a river of lightning. I must admit, it was terrifying. It crackled and singed the grass on either side and the whole air smelt . . . burnt, I suppose. I couldn't imagine how to get across. It was terrifying, but when I woke I felt comforted, like you Ormur.'

Ormur considered this. 'What was he doing? Pryce?'

Gray was staring into the flames. He seemed not to have heard.

'Captain? What was he doing?'

Gray shrugged. 'Waiting.'

Footsteps thumped in the dark, and Keturah came to settle by the fire, wrapped in a fur. Half a pace behind her came Frathi, and they murmured a greeting.

'Anything, my lady?' asked Ormur. Keturah had gone looking for Tekoa's body.

She shook her head.

'He was very brave,' said Gray. 'His officers were panicking, and he'd hear none of it.'

She looked up at him, half wistful, half desolate. 'What did he say?'

'"I'm not a fucking orator," I believe.'

She laughed suddenly. 'Sounds like him. Then what?'

'Just Tekoa as he lived. *Yield to no one, compromise for nothing*, I remember. He accepted they were going to die, and wanted it done by our own principles.'

She took up a skin by her side, raised it to the night and drank. She offered it to Frathi, who wrinkled her nose, and passed it to Ormur, who found it was a potent elderberry wine, tart and strengthening. 'Try and piece together the rest of it,' said Keturah. 'It'll go in the Academy.'

'The hour is late for that, Lady Keturah,' said Frathi. 'We'll all be dead by lunchtime tomorrow. The story will not survive us.'

This proclamation threw the fire into silence, which stretched as other guardsmen and legionaries traipsed in from the beach and sat with them. Last came Roper, limping heavily and leaning on what Ormur first took for a staff, and then realised was Heofonfyr.

'You got it back, lord,' said Gray, wryly. 'At last.'

The blade had been in Roper's father's scabbard the day he died, taken by Bellamus and bastardised into this spear.

Roper nodded. He slid haltingly down the handle to half sit, half kneel beside Gray.

'Are there any left on the beach?' Gray pressed.

Roper nodded. 'Hundreds.'

'They must be freezing.'

'Stone cold.'

Bleeding inside and out, exhausted beyond measure, crawling down to the sea had been the final act of many of them.

All of them were in shock, but the night seemed to weigh most heavily on Roper. He had set them on this path, and under his command, they had failed to win the day.

This was not lost on any of them. Even now, Ormur could see resentful looks directed at him from several about the fire. He himself felt a strange disappointment at the sight of Roper, half like homesickness. He had been so sure Roper would deliver them.

'We're all sorry it has come to this,' said Keturah. 'But I wanted to say: that was the bravest thing I've ever seen.' She nodded at them all. 'After fighting for a whole day, after being betrayed. You just defeated the Unhieru.'

'And the story dies here with us,' said a guardsman heavily. 'Not a man leaves this battlefield.'

'The Sutherners will store it in their papers,' said another.

The first guardsman snorted contemptuously. 'Their ability to store the skeleton of a tale has cost them the ability to keep it alive. It is but the shadow of one which passes ear to ear.'

They fell into silence again. Though no one seemed to have the appetite for this conversation, Ormur could not stop thinking. 'But why should we all die?' he ventured. 'It's dark, and

Tekoa spoke this morning about a passage beneath the cliff, used by some deserters. As long as enough of us remain, some could escape before dawn without being pursued. Those who stay could keep them busy. Make sure they're distracted and don't notice a hundred or so escaping.'

'Who'd bear that shame?' said one legionary.

'You would, I suppose,' said another, acidly. He was glaring at Ormur. 'Your question betrays you.'

Ormur was about to make a heated reply, but Gray exploded before he got his chance. 'Hold your tongue fool! This is Ormur Kynortasson. I'd beg him to leave if I thought there was even the faintest chance he'd listen.'

The legionary stared at Gray in sullen defiance.

'But he should,' said Keturah. She sat with her furs wrapped close around her neck, staring down at the spiking shadows thrown by the fire. Silence fell to hear what she had to say. 'I've heard of an uninhabited island, across the sea. A land of ice and black glass. My thoughts keep coming back to it. Perhaps that's our salvation. Unclaimed territory. Maybe sea will separate us from the Sutherners after all.'

'The one your herald was so bewitched by,' said Frathi. 'What do we preserve by moving our people there? Take it from one who is old. There comes a time to die. This is ours.'

'Why?' asked Keturah, frowning. 'Why should it? We can rebuild.'

'How horrible has the *kjardautha* been these past years in Suthdal?' said the historian. 'And that was just crossing a river. Imagine crossing a sea. All of us uprooted, and for what? To scratch out a living on some island of jagged rock.'

'But our children would not feel that,' said Keturah. 'To them it would be home. We could give them that. And we would have our soul – our history. The Academy is flesh, not stone. We can move it all and restart.'

Frathi observed Keturah fiercely. 'I shall not be part of this. How could we just leave the Black Kingdom to die? Shame! She shall not survive without us, nor we without her. We grew around one another. Take either away, and it shall be the death of the other.'

'We are both dead anyway if we don't try this,' said Keturah dismissively.

'Another experiment, just like your husband's, which will cause untold suffering before we perish. We should go now. Go with honour and without betraying the great kingdom which kept us alive.'

Keturah shook her head and turned pointedly away from Frathi. 'So we'll need a leader to take people into a new land,' she went on. 'Someone who preserves Chlodowich's blood, and commands their loyalty.'

'Lord Roper,' said Ormur immediately.

'I die here,' said Roper, so quickly it seemed he feared the silence that might follow this utterance. 'I brought us to this place. Above all, I must see it through.'

Nobody argued. Roper was so entangled with this task that it seemed impossible he could survive. And even Ormur could see that people would not follow him now as they once had.

'It was you I was thinking of, Ormur,' said Keturah.

Ormur was dumbstruck. Then he knew what to say at once. 'Never. I couldn't, my lady. It should be you.'

There was a murmur of agreement. Gray reached a hand over to Roper and placed it on his shoulder. 'This is the leader I would die with,' he said. 'But Lady Keturah is the one I would live under. You should go, my lady. If there's anyone to lead our people in that alien land, it is you.'

Keturah smiled wearily. 'Oh yes? And you all think I could just ride away from here?'

'I do believe so, my lady,' he replied. 'Because although you are proud and brave, when it has come to it, you've always sacrificed your pride for what best serves our people.'

'It sounds like you're telling me my duty, Captain,' she said, a warning note in her voice.

'I think he's right,' said Roper, softly. 'You were always the better ruler. Having you die here is a waste.'

'It would give the rest of us something to fight for tomorrow,' said Gray. 'Someone must lead what's left, and that is unquestionably you. You have the vision of how it could be done. You are divorced from the warrior's code and can leave without the shame the rest of us would carry.'

Keturah had gone white. 'I would be ashamed whether you said so or not,' she said scathingly.

'But you believe in this,' said Roper. 'And who'll lead our people if not you?' He met her eye. 'Please live. Please.' They looked long at one another across the hearth, Ormur strangely frozen as he waited for one of them to break the moment. 'Please don't let me be responsible for your death,' he said extremely quietly.

'I don't owe you anything,' she said.

Roper took a moment to recover from that blow. 'I know,' he said, voice tinged with heartache.

'Who else should go?' asked Gray, as though it had been settled that the Black Lady would lead an exodus from Albion. Ormur was heartened to see that she did not immediately object. 'You'll not have the time or the ships to take everyone. The historians must go, and the young from the freyi and haskoli.'

'The Chief Historian,' suggested one. 'The Academy must survive.'

'Your plan sacrifices too much to be of interest to me,' said Frathi. 'I'd rather die than see it come to pass.'

'Frathi can be replaced,' said Keturah. 'The young men cannot. A new society will need children, and its boys will need role models.' She met Ormur's eye. 'You told me you'd find a wife, brother. You've not kept that promise yet.'

Ormur looked away from her, hoping that was as directly as she would ask.

'You remember our pact, brother?' she pressed. 'That day I took you from the haskoli?'

'I will never forget,' he said, still not looking at her.

'Well?'

He took a heavy breath. 'You told me from that moment on we stood back to back, until the world overturned.'

'There is nobody I'd rather the young men of our kingdom emulate than you, my guardsman. So will you come?' She watched him. 'Or shall your last gesture to me be to break our pact?'

Ormur said nothing. He felt sick, knowing every moment this silence stretched wounded the woman he admired and loved above anyone else. And there were so many witnesses to it about this oppressive fire, watching him frozen. *Are you a coward, Ormur?*

Heavily he got to his feet, requiring two attempts before his limbs would unfold, joints creaking like ropes hauled through a pulley. Eyes still lowered, he crossed the space around the fire to kneel before Keturah and bowed his head. 'My lady. I will do whatever you ask of me, whenever you ask. If you so direct, I will come north with you to that new land. But what would accompany you there would be my shell. My greater part could not leave my friends here, to fight and die alone. I would be no role model to those young men if I could not stand the sight of my own reflection.'

His eyes remained weighted to the floor. He could not bear to look at her face and see the disappointment there.

'Well . . .' she said after some time. 'I thank you for your honesty. That makes it clear. Preserving your empty body for my benefit is not something I'd ask of anyone.'

He looked up, searching her face for some sign that she understood, and was horrified not to find the disappointment he had expected, but confusion and hurt. 'I'd come if you asked,' he repeated, hoping to make it better.

'I don't ask,' she said simply. 'Sit down, Ormur.'

'Perhaps none of us should go,' said Randolph, as Ormur shuffled back to his seat. 'Maybe the Chief Historian is right. All good things come to an end, and we should end them together.'

Nobody replied to that for a long while.

'And what? Just doom those left in the Black Kingdom to slavery?' said Gray at last. He raised his eyebrows. 'That's what Safinim will do, when he swamps the walls of the Hindrunn. That or worse. Everyone who'll go should be evacuated. It will take a leader to persuade all those people to abandon their homes. One who's seen the army which will cross the Abus. Lady Keturah could do it.' He shrugged helplessly, looking around at them all. 'If I knew I was fighting tomorrow to give her the chance to lead some survivors north, I'd die happy. It would give me great comfort to know my wife stood a chance at a new life.'

Ormur looked up and caught the glance between Roper and Keturah, just a heartbeat before the former looked away.

'Agreed,' said Randolph. 'Lady Keturah is the one to save those left in the north. The historians will survive, and we should send with her the youngest men left here. Those without children.'

'Two hundred of those left at most?' hazarded Gray. 'I fear they've paid a disproportionate price in this battle. It is mostly the veterans who have survived. There's enough of us left to occupy the Sutherners while Keturah leads the young men on the road.'

'Excepting the Sacred Guard,' said Ormur. 'They die with the Black Lord.'

Gray hesitated. Then he inclined his head. 'Yes. The Sacred Guard dies with the Black Lord.'

'Low tide will be an hour before dawn, we'll need to have the escapees in position before then,' said Roper. 'So what are we waiting for?'

63
The Third Day

'If you want to send a message to anyone back home, then pass them on to the historians now,' said Keturah. 'They'll tell whoever needs to hear, but you've not got long.'

Those historians present had trained memories that surpassed all others, and would be able to relay, word for word, the last testament of those that remained. For those leaving, the very least they needed for the road north had been packed. There were enough supplies for them to eat well on the journey: those that remained would not need them. There was the faintest hint of dawn in the east, and they had to go.

Cautiously, Gray approached Keturah. 'I wondered if you might carry my message, Lady Keturah,' he said. 'I know it would mean more to Sigrid if she got it from you.'

'Captain,' said Keturah, laying a fond hand on his shoulder. 'Of course. What do you want to say?'

'Tell my beloved wife . . . we had the measure of the Teuta, but the Unhieru did for us. Tell her we struggled to the end, and have nothing to regret. Though these are small things. My love for her is forever. Tell her all is well.'

Tears splashed silently down Keturah's cheeks. 'I'll tell her. I admire you more than I can say, Captain.'

'And I you, my queen.'

They embraced. 'I'll see you again,' said Keturah vehemently.

'But not for many years, I hope,' said Gray. 'Save your stories for me.'

Keturah beamed. They broke apart, hands holding together for one last time, Keturah giving his remaining fingers a final squeeze before they parted.

Queues were forming before the historians, who would take each man's name, a keepsake to give over with his message and with which to stir the memory, and then listen carefully to the words he wanted recalled. Those who had no one to send a message to busied themselves determinedly with sharpening their swords, or digging a broken iron tip from their boots, or any other job that might disguise their failure to participate in this moment.

Ormur was one of them. All those he loved were dead already, or staying here with him. Except, of course, Keturah. He hovered nearby, wanting to make some form of farewell, unsure of his reception or what he should say. Keturah was taking a stern instruction from the Chief Historian when her eye finally caught his.

She did the smallest of double-takes, and then gave a rueful smile. Frathi was giving grudging instruction on starting a new society, declaring that the secret to settling a contentious issue was to side with the status quo, and that there must be a grand narrative to tie the nation together. Keturah nodded placatingly at this, keeping an eye on Ormur. She eventually excused herself without ever looking back to the old historian. They drifted together, oblivious to the heartfelt messages being passed around them.

Ormur had thought to apologise and seek forgiveness for disappointing her. He was desperately aware of the need to make things right between them, this last time. But as he stood before Keturah, she every inch as tall as him, all harsh face and poisonous eyes and hair the black gloss of a raven's wings, he found he did not need to say anything at all. She did not speak either.

They just shared a look. A long moment of comprehension and satisfaction. She seemed a little amused, and sorrowful, and proud. They bowed to one another, then stepped forward and embraced. She smelt of woodsmoke, and that aromatic juniper from the Academy which seemed to uniquely imprint her clothes. He felt he would choke at the prospect of losing something so precious. He suddenly remembered something she had told him, years and years before. He had asked how you knew you loved someone. And she had replied if they seem to loom larger, the closer to them you get.

They broke apart, and both backed away, holding that look. And the last he saw of Keturah was the sad smile she gave him before they turned away.

The young men she was leading had formed up, equal parts relieved to be spared and nervous that the remaining veterans would scorn their retreat. But there was no stand-off between condemned and spared.

One veteran approached an unfamiliar lad in the front rank, a youth who in normal times would still be in the berjasti rather than on a battlefield. 'Remember us. Take care of our people.'

This seemed to be the greatest desire of those left behind: that they should be remembered. They pressed charms and tokens on the departing, or a few words which came to them. Many approached the Battle Historian to plead for an epic chant to commemorate this moment. 'Rest assured,' she told them on the fifth time she received this request, 'the chant made of this moment will be burned deep into the memory of whatever survives the Black Kingdom. This is a gesture on which the identity of a people can be built.' Reassured, they dispersed.

Ormur gave away Leon's sword, Silence. He had no attachment to it, and even broken, the famous blade was valuable. It seemed better that it become part of that new society than have its legend lost when he fell. It would not be difficult to find a spare: they littered the floor. But as he handed it over, he realised with a shock that he was giving it to a lad his own age. He seemed comically young to be on a battlefield: face fresh as a mountain spring and fraught with nerves as the famous Ormur Kynortasson passed over this legendary weapon. Ormur was the same age as most of those who were to be spared, but he did not feel like one of them.

'Thank you, lord,' said the lad.

Lord. It sounded so strange. 'See if his wife wants it first, but I doubt she will. She hated him.'

'Give them hell, Lord Ormur,' said another lad with a wink. Dimly, Ormur recognised him as someone he had been at the haskoli with.

'Maybe ask if they'll surrender, lord?' said another. 'It's worth a shot.'

'Godspeed, my lord.'

Ormur did not know what to say to any of them. He just nodded, turning back to the veterans, who were forming a tunnel to see off Keturah's band of refugees. They mounted up on the few remaining horses, and because they could not call out a farewell and risk alerting the Sutherners to their departure, they clinked past in silence. Keturah had already gone past when Ormur joined the line: he could tell by the way the veterans were getting off their knees. He joined them in patting the horses as they filed past and touching hands with their riders. One of the riders rode stiffly, not touching hands with any of those remaining, helmet covering his eyes. Ormur looked at him curiously and realised that the rider was older than the others: perhaps forty. A stowaway who had found a horse and hoped to slip away without being noticed. Ormur said nothing, watching the man sadly.

Someone further down the line noticed, as Ormur had known they would, and there came a shout of protest. A legionary leapt at his horse, pulling himself up on the saddle and reaching up to yank off the stowaway's helmet. As his face was revealed there came a cry of derision and disgust at this cowardice. 'I recognise you Vidjor Hallison!' shrieked a voice. 'Four sons you had, and trying to slip away with the no-sires!'

'Shame!' roared the veterans. 'Shame! Shame!' They began reaching out to tug him from the saddle, the man's horse skittering violently as he was tugged this way and that. Vidjor clutched his saddle and hacked back with his heels to try and spur his way clear, but his horse was being held.

'Leave him!' roared a voice. 'Unhand him!' It was Roper, striding into the fray and yanking back one of the legionaries trying to pull the deserter from his horse. 'Silence, all of you! We must not be heard. Let go. Let him go!' The veterans relinquished their grip on Vidjor, who sat up and straightened his armour, shrinking from the withering attention focused on his person. 'You want him punished?' demanded Roper, looking around at them all, one hand gripping a corner of Vidjor's breastplate. There came a low growl of agreement. By now the procession had halted as the no-sires waited for their path to clear. 'Which of you did not consider this, as the spared mounted up? Which of you had not a single thought of trying to leave this place, and save your own skin this night, or each of the five nights before?' Silence. 'Still you want him punished?'

'Yes!' cried a voice. 'Because we didn't do it!'

There came a rumble of agreement.

'But how would you punish him?' demanded Roper. 'Which of you envies his position now? Would any one of you trade places with this man? Speak! I'm sure he'd swap with you in an instant.' Nobody spoke. 'If you want him punished, then let him go,' said Roper, releasing the deserter. He shook his head and shrugged. 'Let him have the years on earth he craves, and the infamy that'll come with them. I wouldn't wish that on any man.' Roper stood back and gestured for Vidjor to ride onwards.

'I'm sorry, lord,' he murmured. 'It was a moment of weakness and I wish to stay.' He tried to dismount, but Roper stuck out an arm and kept him in the saddle.

'It's too late now, Vidjor. I would not die beside you. Go and do whatever you see fit. Live if you can bear your shame. Die alone if you can't. But we won't have you here.'

Vidjor protested but the veterans, understanding Roper now, joined in. Even when the deserter was fighting to get off his horse, they kept him in the saddle and some even began to lead it on, away from the army. Ormur watched the legionary go, head held in his hands, the most piteous sight he had seen on this battlefield.

The rest of the spared followed him. There were perhaps two hundred of them, chosen mostly for youth, and it did not take long for them to clink past and fade into the darkness.

Ormur found himself standing next to Frathi. True to her word, she was staying. She had given up her dark stallion to one of the young men going north, and stood watching wrapped in a black cloak, hair flecked with feathers, apparently unmoved by the departure. She appeared to be unarmed.

'Can I offer you a weapon, my lady?' he asked. 'I doubt the Sutherners will show you the respect you deserve.'

She gave her one-shouldered shrug. 'I am an old woman. I have a knife if they try to take me alive. But my years are advanced for swords and axes.'

The spared left behind a sense of dreadful bereavement, and Roper, ten yards or so along the line, gathered the nearest men into a huddle. There was no distinction now between guardsmen, legion or nation: just a random collection of thirty or so, with representatives from six different Anakim allies. Even so, Ormur, Gray and Roper all found themselves standing in the same huddle.

'Thank you all for coming with me this far,' began Roper, so softly it would have been a struggle to hear him had the atmosphere been less fraught. 'It has been an honour, and there is just a little further to go. The prowess of the legions is our identity, and our link with our ancestors. They handed us a warrior tradition that means everything. Yesterday, some of us ran on the battlefield. There is just one way that I know of to atone for that mistake. Those of you here will help me settle that debt.' He looked around the circle. 'Does anyone have anything they wish to say?'

There came a pause. 'The historians will survive,' said one guardsman Ormur recognised but did not know by name. 'Our soul survives. And people will know. They carry proof of what happened here.'

'And of the name Vidjor Hallison,' growled one.

'Forget him,' said Roper. 'It is punishment enough that he wasn't here, with us. This is the only company I wish to keep.'

At Roper's words, the legionary next to Ormur glanced around the circle, and then noticed the young guardsman beside him. He gave a flash of recognition. 'Ormur Kynortasson. I believe you dropped something,' he said, grinning. He was holding out Ormur's sword, Warspite. It was filthy, the blade still covered with blood but as profiled and balanced as it ever had been.

'Ah!' Ormur took it, hand and hilt embracing, his wrist rejoicing in that familiar balance. He swung it, savouring the feeling of having it back: an old and trusted friend, and a gift from Keturah, the last remnant of her in this place. He ran his hand up the familiar silhouette: it needed a good sharpen.

It took some while to realise that much of the sweetness at this reunion had been imaginary. It felt a little hollow, in this place. The only bright colours seemed to be the people standing here with him. Everything else had dimmed, and being reunited with his sword now seemed neither here nor there.

He thought for a moment, then turned to the man on his other side: an alpine warrior whose face he had never seen before. He touched his arm to get his attention and nodded at him. 'This is Warspite,' he said self-consciously, aware that the rest of the circle was still in silence and now watching this exchange. 'Made by our greatest smith, Sindri, gifted to me by the Black Lady, my dearest possession and most faultless tool.' He turned it around, holding out the handle to the man. 'I'd be honoured if you might have it.'

The man looked startled, glancing around at the many onlookers. Then he grinned sheepishly, taking it gently from Ormur as though the offer might at any moment be retracted. He admired it for a moment and then, fumbling slightly, he drew his own sword and held it out in return, shrugging apologetically. Ormur bowed and took the weapon: a well-worn steel blade, deeply nicked but sharpened to a feather's edge. The two of them smiled foolishly at one another, the alpine warrior running a finger along Warspite's blunt edge and tutting at Ormur. He laughed and the two turned aside awkwardly, each inspecting their new weapon.

This was observed in fascinated silence by the rest of the circle. Then Gray turned to the man next to him, an Ulphan legionary, and offered him Ramnea. 'I was given this sword by a man who meant a great deal to me, in his final moments. Since I find myself in a similar position, perhaps you would take it?'

The legionary did. He knew Ramnea: one of the Black Kingdom's most famous blades, held by a full roll-call of historic figures and legendary warriors, now his. He took it, gawping, unable to make any response at all.

'You'll probably need to give yours to the captain, or he'll be fighting with his fingernails,' said the guardsman next to Ormur. Everyone laughed and blushing, the legionary pulled out his own sword and gave it over to Gray, following it with an embrace, though he was still too stunned to talk.

In ones and twos, the rest followed suit.

They swapped weapons, breastplates, helmets and cloaks. The marks that had separated a Sacred Guardsman, or Ramnea's Own Legionary from an Ulphan, or Black Legionaries from allied Anakim, were dispersed, intermixed, shared. The sword Gray swapped for Ramnea was called Smoke. Roper gave away Cold-Edge and received Forlorn-Hope in its place. Ormur passed his treasured guardsman's helmet to an Autarian man who had none, and received his shield instead. By the end, they were a single harlequin band.

There was laughter as Roper offered his silver breastplate to a legionary, who recoiled in horror from its distinctive shade.

'I'm not wearing that, it's a death sentence!'

'That sentence has been long-since handed down, friend,' said Roper. Eventually the legionary relented, grinning stupidly as Roper strapped the battered cuirass into place.

'That's handsome,' said Gray. 'The cuirass of the Black Lord.'

'Here, Gray,' said Roper, pulling off his Unthank-silver helmet with the axe blade at its prow and tossing it to the captain. 'That one's for you.'

'The Black Lord's gone undercover,' said a guardsman. 'He's hoping Safinim doesn't notice he's still here.'

Everyone laughed except Roper, who smiled down at the floor and said nothing. *He's already decided he won't be taken alive,* thought Ormur. He observed Roper, feeling not his usual mixture of awe and fear, but deep affection and pity.

Hardly aware of what he was doing, he crossed the circle to meet the Black Lord. The observers fell silent as he hauled at the Prize of Valour around his wrist, bending it open so that it came off. Without asking permission, he took Roper's wrist in his hands. 'You couldn't win it yourself,' he said, bending the silver band into place on his brother. 'But I'd have given you one.'

Roper snatched his hand away as though stung. He looked at Ormur, shocked, the only unguarded moment that Ormur had ever seen on that face. And then, try as he might to hold them back, tears were spilling down Roper's cheeks. Ormur looked on, a new understanding of his brother kindling. Was this all he had ever wanted? Then he found himself being pulled into an embrace, in which for the first time, he did not feel the younger.

The fires were burning low, their crimson being drowned by dawn's deep-water glow. Ormur was released and returned to his place in the circle, only now able to see his companions clearly. They were a wretched crew: mud-smeared, blood-crusted, wounded and hobbling. Their armour and weapons were mismatched, battered and ill-fitting. They looked more like deserters, militia or mutineers than the remnants of the Black Legions.

'My peers,' said Roper. He wiped his eyes and hooked his arms about the men on either side. The circle linked arms and leaned together. 'Thank you all for staying. I'm honoured beyond words to be in such company. I need hardly tell you, but we are not here to merely throw away our lives. The longer we survive, the harder we resist, the more of a distraction we are. The more time Keturah has to get those two hundred out of range, and perhaps salvage a nation. Sell your lives dearly. Though victory may be out of reach, I still want to confound our enemy. Let them remember today as their worst yet. Let them stand last on this battlefield and wish they'd been on the other side. This may be the last major action of the Anakim in this ancient land, but we shall haunt it long after we're gone. Make no mistake, what we do now is how we'll be remembered. A thousand years from now, let men and women say they don't make warriors like these any more. Let them say this was the best of us.'

There was a murmur of agreement. Some called for Gray to speak, and he just beamed about the circle. 'Just savour it. It's the last thing any of us have left. Savour this place, savour these people.' He nodded at them. 'I'll see you all out there.'

The circle dispersed. Many of the other groups had swapped their weapons and armour too. Everyone whose eye caught Ormur's became an embrace. 'A bit young to be staying, aren't you?' said a legionary, observing Ormur sternly. The man was scowling from beneath a horrible injury: part of his skull seemed to be missing, and he surely had no more than hours left in him.

'It doesn't feel that way,' said Ormur shrugging.

'You've got children?' pressed the man.

Ormur blushed and shook his head.

The legionary tutted, and he and Ormur gripped each other's shoulders. 'Good luck, brother.'

'See you on the other side.'

Ormur spotted Roper and Gray hobbling along the ridge, arm in arm as they would have been years before, the sun's first rays gilding the hills behind. He tried not to listen, but could not help but overhear. 'I remember your ambition, old friend,' Roper was saying. 'Tell me: are you ready to die?'

Gray did not hesitate. 'Yes, lord. I'm ready to die and meet my god.'

'Your goal always inspired me, to do it without fear. You wanted to feel gladness alone that you could lay down your life.'

'I said so, didn't I?' said Gray. 'I'm still petrified. But now I am here, I don't think the point was ever to truly achieve that lofty goal. It was something to hold on to. Something to strive for, and keep me going through the horror. But what a life it has been. I am frightened, but this does not feel unjust. I am the most fortunate of men, that I can do this alongside my friends.'

They spotted Ormur, and Gray raised an arm in welcome. Across the battlefield, the Sutherners were massing. 'We should probably adopt some kind of formation,' Gray observed.

'That's why I've got this,' said Roper, raising a femur trumpet hung at his side. He blew on it, drawing the dregs of them together.

Together, they lined up.

It was a pathetic formation: seven or eight thousand of them left at the most, while across the field, dawn was breaking over a multitude. It seemed they had barely dented their opponents. The Teuta were not bothering to chant any more. Instead, from the smoke of cooking fires rising from the front rank, it seemed they were concluding a leisurely breakfast before they finished off their enemy.

'I miss Tekoa,' said Gray.

'I miss Leon,' said Roper. 'He was the man to have at your shoulder in a fight.'

Ormur was surprised to hear himself agree.

'Let's just try and get Keturah out.'

'Agreed. I want Sigrid to have her, where they're going,' said Gray.

Almost casually, the Sutherners were drifting into line. There seemed to be no hurry, indeed a positive reluctance. This fight was so nearly over, and it would be a dreadful shame to lose your life when you had so nearly survived the great clash of the age. Bellamus had clearly decided to overwhelm them: the line forming now was three times as long as the Anakim formation and twice as deep.

'We're up against the Hermit-Crabs,' noted Ormur, observing the centre of the line.

From somewhere further down the line, the 'Hymn for the Departed' was moaning out. Randolph was first to take it up, the rest of them joining in. With a heavy dread, they watched the Sutherners begin their advance, their death creeping across the field.

'Who's that behind the Hermit-Crabs?' asked Roper, squinting.

'Longbowmen,' said Ormur softly. There were thousands of them, far outnumbering the Anakim scraps. They were yet out of range, but it was only a matter of time.

'They're going to try not even engaging us,' said Randolph.

'We're not giving them a choice,' said Roper. He raised the femur trumpet to his lips and blew out a lonely couplet. He repeated it without taking a breath, then again, and again until one had joined, then another and a dozen and a score. Soon a hundred trumpets were blaring out and Ormur closed his eyes. Roper stopped for breath, and Ormur saw that the longbowmen had halted. 'Again!' cried Roper, and the trumpets pealed out. 'Again!' he bellowed, and another glorious couplet soared out. 'Again!'

The trumpets were still ringing as they plunged off the ridge. The longbowmen were preparing their first volley, a screen of infantry between them and the Anakim survivors. Ormur had never been subject to concentrated volley-fire before. It was a noise to chill the marrow: a profound buzzing, like the fury of distant wasps. There was a rattling too as shafts and tips jostled mid-flight, and beneath all that, the purposeful soaring of ten thousand wingtips.

Ormur had his traded shield and raised it between him and Gray, running on his left. Before the volley hit, there was a moment of terrible apprehension when it seemed to shriek and Ormur could feel something elemental bearing down on their tattered band. There was a drumming: a tin clatter and a punching as the arrows grated off armour, punched through, or hit bare flesh with a thump. The air seemed so dense with fury and steel tips that every inch of Ormur's skin bristled with the knowledge that it was about to be parted by a barb. Two arrows bounced off his shield like blacksmith's blows, making his arm ring. Randolph, on his other side, dropped without making a sound, and looking back, Ormur saw the arrow-struck ranks parting around his prone body.

Another trumpet called out. Ormur raised his head, picking out the Thingalith he would aim for, eighty yards ahead. He kept his eyes set on that man. His left ear was for Gray, tracking his panting. His right was for Roper, muttering 'Come on, *come on*!' But his eyes never left the Thingalith in that front rank. The man stopped. He lowered his spear.

They suffered another volley. It felt suddenly as though the three were running alone.

Another trumpet blast.

'Pryce!' Gray was bellowing. 'Pryce!'

Roper was howling Tekoa's name.

Nobody else would choose Leon, so Ormur took it up. 'Leon! Leon!'

'Pryce!'

'Charge!'

64
Framskular

So there it was.

After these long years, decades spent battling the Anakim across a continent, Bellamus laid eyes for the first time on their greatest stronghold. On the horizon, swimming in the haze of late summer warmth, was the squat mass of the Hindrunn.

'How . . .?' said Diethaad. 'How can the civilisation which built that have been defeated?' Still the walls bristled with weapons, their granite faces blankly horrible: a smooth wave of stone, mountainous in its scale, regal and imperious. The king of fortresses on which an aggressor could but look and despair. What a place this would have been when manned by those legionaries left in the south.

'Hubris,' Bellamus answered. 'Grendel overreached them, tormented by a memory of what they used to be.'

'He's Grendel again, I see.'

'No harm in adding to his legend now I've defeated him. It adds to my legend as well. He's dead.'

'Let's hope he doesn't come back this time.'

'He won't.'

Bellamus had seen him fall.

They rode together at the head of a mounted column,

followed by Thingalith, Abbio and knights. The quality of the light that day spoke unmistakably of autumn. Summer's glare was diluted, and there was a sense of the year turning. Finches flickered by, whistling plaintively to one another, and hares bounded away from their hoof beats.

They had only come to lay eyes on the Hindrunn and see what it might take to seize it, but as they drew nearer Diethaad pointed suddenly. 'The gates are open.' Bellamus squinted and had to agree he was right. He could see daylight through the gatehouse. 'A trap?' Diethaad wondered.

Bellamus knew it was no trap from the profound and unexpected ache rooted somewhere behind his naval. 'No trap. They'd need twenty thousand to man a place like this. They've abandoned it.'

There were no men on the walls and they had not seen a human being since entering the Black Kingdom. Even so, Bellamus's confidence that it had been abandoned was tested when they passed through the colossal gatehouse. The tunnelled passage behind was so long that the patch of daylight at its terminus was no larger than an apple held at arm's length. The roof was riddled with charred holes, the walls rough as though hewn into a mountain and reverberating with the ring of their horseshoes. Bellamus could not escape the vision of the gates closing at both ends and sticky-fire flooding the passage.

They passed through in complete silence, the open street at the tunnel's far end exceptionally bare and welcome after the dark of the passage. 'Ah!' said Bellamus as they rode blinking into the light. 'We meet again.'

Stood before him in a stone niche, brittle flowers and sun-bleached antlers lying at its feet, was an embalmed and armoured figure. Bellamus stopped to admire it. 'This, Diethaad, is Pryce the Wild. Manifest proof of what was everything to this society. He had no wealth beyond a common ranker and was promoted only to the rank of lictor – an infantry sergeant. But embalming is the highest honour they bestow. The only way to the Anakim heart is through actions. Here in the Black Kingdom, one builds character, not wealth.'

'Pryce the Wild. Did he kill Earl William?'

'Well remembered. Made a fool of his bodyguard and cut his head off in front of both armies. And it was he who blinded Vigtyr's eye and broke his teeth.' Bellamus shook his head, marvelling to finally see one of these embalmed figures.

'He wasn't popular, Old Vigtyr,' said Diethaad. The traitor had been found only in fragments.

They rode on, Bellamus drumming his fingers on the saddle as he gazed around. He had longed to walk these streets, even imagined them in his mind's eye, certain it would illuminate things about these people he had never dreamed. But although there was much that was fascinating – he had never stopped to consider how scaled up it would all be to accommodate the larger Anakim proportions – he should have realised that this was a culture defined by verbs, not nouns. He had seen their actions in their final hours, which said more than he would ever learn from this granite skeleton.

So invested had he been in the last deeds of Roper's men that watching had proved nearly impossible. What if, in their last moments they proved fallible, and the ideals by which they lived came to nothing? He could not bear to see them humiliated like the Ulpha. He needed what they brought to the world: the belief that a man – a strange, alien being from a distant culture, but a man nonetheless – could overcome fear.

He crossed one of the streams that ran through the streets, a tiny marvel set in an artificial stone bed. The fortress was full of such touches: the low buildings and their gaping windows, the wide streets and light flooding everything. The houses, half-eaten by bushes and creepers. The air thick with the smell of flowers. The niches built into high walls and occupied by sleeping owls, who would occasionally open a bright orange eye, scour Bellamus and then shutter it dismissively. It was a reluctant fortress built with one eye cast longingly at the wild.

'Clean, isn't it?' noted Diethaad with a faint tone of disapproval. 'Imagine all that work.'

They passed frozen water-mills, silent smithies, empty sties. Bellamus was trying to ignore that discomfort behind his navel, but it grew stubbornly. He forgot it when they came to the Holy Temple, and the embalmed corpses standing guard around it. There was an atmosphere to this place: an imprint left by centuries of ritual and significance, and a faint odour of fragranced smoke. 'Bodies,' Diethaad said in disgust. 'What a way to treat your kings.'

'These aren't kings.'

'Just commoners? How do they honour royalty then?'

'I think you saw that with your own eyes.'

It had been two weeks since they had watched a king die.

The Anakim had swapped weapons and armour, but even so it was not hard to recognise Roper. Bellamus had seen him bowled off his feet by a mad Thingalith, knocked onto his back with a spitting villain on top of him, plunging a dagger wildly into the Black Lord. Half a dozen spearmen had piled in after him, digging at his body, and that had seemed to be the last of him.

But four Anakim warriors battled through to his side. They were too injured and mismatched to be identifiable, but Bellamus was sure they would be Sacred Guardsmen. They fought like guardsmen, putting down the Thingalith in such quick succession that Bellamus had no time to assimilate it. The spearmen fought back fiercely, a sudden blaze igniting in the centre of the ranks as they scrapped and brawled over Roper's body.

The Black Lord had been nothing like the monarchs Bellamus had known. Osbert. Aramilla. The prince who had ruled over Bellamus's homeland, Safinim, when he had been a boy. They paid for loyalty with gold and land, and sometimes enforced it with fear. Roper's currencies were blood and sweat, shed beside his men. He took more responsibility than glory. He slept in the open, a saddle for his pillow, exposed for the army's inspection. He was their servant. Compared to the other kings Bellamus had known, Roper lived in poverty. He had no gold and not so much as a bronze circlet on his unhelmeted head. He travelled without entourage, held no great lands, and suffered the protests and influences of the senior factions in the Black Kingdom.

In the fight for his body, it was the Anakim who prevailed briefly, two hauling back Roper's remains while two others, both hacking with broken swords, held off the Thingalith. It was around that body that they rallied for the last time, a plaintive trumpet calling out again and again that this was the territory they had chosen to die on. Bellamus had no more fear that they might betray themselves and run. The fighting intensified yet further, broken swords and shivered spears spitting from the brawl.

That was a king.

Diethaad was becoming impatient. 'Let's find the strongroom, lord,' he said. 'They must have some treasure.'

Bellamus wanted to dismount and explore the temple's interior, but that was a moment to savour when he was alone. So he turned away with Diethaad, riding through another district, pretending that they were making for the Central Keep when his eye was set on the great stone pyramid that lay beyond it.

They passed through curtain walls and enclosed courtyards surrounded by fire-throwers, which made Bellamus yet gladder the fortress was abandoned. When they came to the tall Central Keep, Diethaad made to turn his horse up the broad main staircase.

'You go,' said Bellamus. 'If the strongroom's anywhere, it'll be in there. I'm going to have a look at the pyramid.'

'Take some Thingalith, lord. What if you run into survivors?'

Bellamus waved a hand dismissively, the warning lost on him.

'Well, this is more like it,' he said under his breath as he reached the Academy. He had not expected the vast lake it sat on, the water clear as a harpstring plucked by a master. The huge silver eye flashed at its apex, and he decided that would be the place to take in the fortress. He left his horse tied to a torch bracket, and trod the narrow bridge over the waters. If any building could manifest Anakim society, it was this one. Their love of memory and natural form. Their piety, their confidence and faith in narrative to bind a stone colony and a nation without letters.

There was just one passage, which spiralled inward like a snail's shell. The crude but painstaking carvings on the walls. The empty cells, each with its own distinctive scent. The unique wood of every door. That sense of discomfort in his belly was now strong enough to make him nauseous.

It took a long time to wind his way to the uppermost level, where he found a cell that smelt of rosemary, and closed the door softly behind him. The room was bare, but opposite was a broad window looking out over the concentric walls of the Hindrunn. He stared down at the houses in the outermost residential district, wondering if one had been home to the Captain of the Sacred Guard.

Gray Konrathson, the last Anakim alive whom he had recognised, and one of those who had retrieved Roper's corpse. He had lost his helmet, and though his hair was matted stiff with blood, Bellamus recognised him, standing still, clutching a trumpet in the three fingers that remained to him. He pressed it to his lips, calling out again and again in the moments left to him. The score of them left about Roper's corpse gathered close, Gray continuing the rally until he was forced to hurl the trumpet at a spearman and stoop for a shattered sword on the ground.

Next to him was a young warrior with no helmet and no sword, just a shield with the edges hewn off. This he wielded as a weapon, ramming it again and again at the Thingalith. It finally broke under a double-handed spear thrust which cracked it apart like pottery, going through the wooden boards to impale the warrior's forearm. Pinioned, he tried to use his free arm to rip a spear free from one of the Thingalith. He was still wrenching at the ash shaft when he died. A longbowman shot him in the chest at point-blank range, his heart bursting beneath its steel point.

Gray had reacted only by wriggling to his right so that he could stand over the body, guarding it from any further assault. The captain held on with his shattered sword, keeping Thingalith spearmen at bay for more than a minute, and even knocking one down. Bellamus thought every moment a blow must fell him, and every time Gray dodged or deflected or just took the shot, giving out as good as he was dealt with a labouring fist and two elbows. So enraged were the Thingalith by his defiance that when he was finally blasted off his feet by a charging spearman, he was set upon as he lay on the ground for a long while after his death.

They did not fall like heroes, but like friends, in naked grief as each of their comrades went down, fighting to do right by each other's memory. A solitary wound, no matter how grievous, no longer seemed enough to put them down. They had to be disassembled, piece by piece, and still they spat and snarled defiance.

Standing last of all was a warrior Bellamus did not know, holding the banner of the Almighty Eye. It had been passed from hand to hand, held onto even though it attracted the worst of enemy attention, kept up until that final moment. When the standard-bearer went down, he would still not let go of the banner. It tilted only slowly, haltingly, appearing to stand unsupported before coming gently to rest.

Bellamus had dreamed of that halting movement every night since. It was encapsulated in a jar of precious oil, which he wanted to save but seemed doomed to watch fall, over and over again. It tottered on the edge of a high table, rolling around its base, fighting for balance, hovering for a moment on one edge. Finally it tipped. It pitched to the floor, falling strangely like that Anakim banner, until it touched the ground and burst in an instant, the precious contents gushing over the stone. And Bellamus would awake with that same discomfort he had now, looking out over these deserted streets.

There was a word for it in Anakim: *framskular.* The feeling of something good drawing to a close.

Epilogue

Keturah stood on a beach of black sand, looking out over a charcoal sea. Waves were heaving onto the beach with a soft boom, carrying with them large chunks of ice; tumbled smooth as droplets of steel, and marbled by streaks of grey and blue and white. And in the offing lay a Suthern ship: one of the broad-sided dogfish. It had been revealed by the dawn, anchored some way offshore, flying a banner so long that it near trailed into the cold waters. On the banner was a spider, and dispatched from the great ship was a rowing boat, even now hauling through the surf.

'Where are those whales when you need them?' Keturah asked irritably.

Sigrid, stood next to her in the black robes of the Chief Historian, laughed.

When they had tried to land on this beach months before, the waters had been heaving with monstrous black backs, rising and falling in such numbers that they had threatened to crack the boats in which they sheltered like eggshells.

The day was grey, as so often here; volleys of gannets plunging into the waters, and a first hint of snow stinging Keturah's cheeks. On the distant rowboat, she recognised the uncanny finery of Lord Safinim, though he seemed to be wearing a gold circlet around his grey hair – King Safinim, was he now?

'Is there no corner of the earth safe from this wretched man?'

The rowboat carried six oarsmen and a dozen Hermit-Crabs alongside Safinim, and the two women waited to receive them alone. They had little in the way of an army, and there was no point pretending otherwise. When the boat finally scraped into the black sands, the Hermit-Crabs leapt out with their spears, advancing on Keturah and Sigrid. The two watched them with enough indifference to stop them in their tracks, Keturah just waiting as Safinim was helped over the gunwale and onto the beach. He was more decorated than ever, holding an immaculate cloak of ice blue carefully above the surf. His jacket was blood red, trimmed with black fur, and his eye-patch now carried an image which appeared to be the Almighty Eye, sewn elaborately in gold thread. Keturah stared at this, while Safinim bowed before her.

'My lady,' he said politely. 'I'm very pleased to see you well.'

'I can't say the same, Safinim. What brings you here?'

He hesitated, eye roving over the huge stone building-site behind Keturah, where they had begun constructing their new Academy. It would take years to recreate, but Keturah was determined they should not forget a single chant. The precious narrative it preserved: the austere code passed from one generation to the next of what it meant to be a subject of the Black Kingdom, had to be sheltered against the wind which raged against this coast.

Safinim was still studying their new settlement, enthralled by the low stone buildings they had built to resist the wind, and the high, snow-capped mountains behind.

'If this is a reconnaissance mission, Safinim, it's an obvious one,' said Keturah pointedly.

He looked back at her and grinned apologetically. 'I came to give you something,' he said. He snapped his fingers, and one of the Hermit-Crabs staggered forward over the soft sands, holding what seemed to be a staff, wrapped in velvet. Safinim took it and held it out to Keturah.

She eyed him for a moment, and then took the object, removing the velvet cover from one end to reveal the marbled-cream handle of Cold-Edge.

Roper's sword.

She looked back up at Safinim, and then removed it from the velvet, which she discarded on the ground. The winds whipped it into the waves almost at once.

'Your new home is beautiful, my lady,' said Safinim, looking once more over her shoulder. 'And cold too, which I know you will enjoy. Do you have forests, I wonder?'

'Not worth the name,' she said. 'But we have always built in stone. Are we safe here, Safinim? We have travelled so far that we seem to have one foot in the Otherworld. We see lights moving in the night sky. Some of our rivers run hot, and thunder rumbles beneath our feet, yet you have pursued us all this way. I doubt you came just to present me with this sword.'

Safinim pursed his lips. 'You're quite right, my lady,' he said, quietly. 'I'd wondered if you might permit me to tell you how Lord Roper died.'

Keturah shook her head. 'I know how he died.'

Safinim raised his eyebrows. 'You heard?'

'I don't need to.'

Safinim hesitated, then bowed once more. 'Then I have come to say you are safe here. As long as I rule in Albion, your people shall not be troubled. And we will trade with you, when you are ready.'

'Then I hope you have need of fish,' said Keturah acidly.

Safinim smiled. 'I think your people have greater treasures to offer.'

'Is this why you now wear our Almighty Eye, in place of your own?' she asked, scrutinising his eyepatch.

Safinim nodded thoughtfully. 'Exactly that.'

'And what have you done with the Black Kingdom?'

'I've walked it. Awake and asleep, it possesses me, and has

done since I first set foot there. Your people are gone, but I hear strange music between the trees.' He paused, studying Keturah's face as though hoping she would tell him that was not a sign of madness. 'I've followed it up your crystal mountains, and heard birds calling like phantoms. And despite the bears and the wolves and the aurochs, I know peace there like I never have below the Abus. I want to learn to inhabit those trees as your people did.'

Keturah regarded him coolly. 'Then you will need generations. Thousands of them.'

Safinim inclined his head. 'But you have that knowledge already. And I would trade for it, handsomely.'

'You've nothing to offer us, Safinim.'

'What about the people you left behind in the Black Kingdom?' suggested Bellamus. 'I could send them here, as a sign of goodwill.'

'They would not come,' said Keturah. 'We had space on our boats for more, but the thought of abandoning their homes was unthinkable for most. The people who I love – those of them left alive – are here. The first children who will call this place home have been born. We have food, and shelter, and identity. I cannot think what you might contribute.'

The wind was biting, and Safinim had begun to shiver. He wrapped his cloak tight about himself, and gave her a look of regret. 'Very well. I did not expect to be offered hospitality here, though my cartographers shall map your coast now that we have made the voyage. Should you reconsider, of course, I shall be pleased to receive your envoys. I simply wished to say that Albion shall not forget you.'

Keturah said nothing. Her poisonous green eyes were levelled at Safinim, who hesitated, then bowed politely once more, turning to lead his men back onto the rowboat. The little vessel was pushed clear of the shore, and after riding the breakers carefully for a few minutes, began to pull away across the waves.

'You are more resolute than I, my love,' said Sigrid as they watched the oars heave. 'You didn't want to hear what became of Lord Roper?'

Keturah looked down at the sword. 'He and I said what we needed to. Safinim can add no more.'

There had been a final meeting, and she had carried his last words with her like a torch in this cold land. It had taken place after that parlay by the fireside where it had been decided she was to live, and he to die. Amid the farewells, final words, swapped tokens and tears, Keturah had excused herself. 'Forgive me, I've a couple of things left to throw on my horse. I'll not be a moment.'

Gray looked as though he were about to ask a question or offer his help, but before he could do anything of the sort, he lifted his chin in sudden comprehension. 'Absolutely, my lady. I'll make sure nobody disturbs you, shall I?'

'Would you, Captain?' She backed away from him, smiling fondly and then turned for her horse, waiting some fifty yards through the dark. There was nothing left to burden it with: it was harnessed, saddled and packed with every possession that seemed important. She just checked the straps once more, and did not have to wait long before there came a voice behind her.

'I don't want to disturb you.'

'You're not disturbing.' She turned to face Roper. They had shared a look across the fire, and had both known to allow time for this moment. Even so, Roper was hesitant, evidently wary of her harsh words before.

'Thank you,' he murmured. 'For going.'

'I didn't do it for you.'

'No.' He seemed to realise how timidly he stood, and straightened. 'I'd want you with me, you know . . . But it brings me comfort to think you'll survive. And our boy.'

'We might,' she said. 'It's a long road and if they realise we've escaped then they'll undoubtedly catch us. Then after that, we have an ocean to cross.'

'Yes. Well I also wanted to say . . . for what it's worth . . . that

I'm sorry.' He shrugged helplessly. She just glared as he struggled on in a suppressed voice. 'For bringing us to this point. And what you'll have to inherit. And for . . . leaving you to do it all alone.'

She shrugged. 'Sorry's no use now. It's happened. Nothing either of us can do about that.'

'No. But time is very short, and I wanted to say it.'

They looked at each other a long time. There was so much she wanted to say, and so much he seemed to as well. She felt nearly paralysed by anger, but he was right, time was short. Here would be her only chance to settle things.

'We both knew this might be the end,' she said. 'When we talked about this, all those years ago. We both knew this was a roll of the dice, and the only one worth taking. You got us close. At least you gave us a chance.'

Roper's mouth was slightly open. 'That's what I try and tell myself,' he murmured.

She hesitated. Then she reached out a hand and took his in her own. 'It's a brave thing you're doing. I admire you for it. I always have. I always will.' His hand was nearly crushing her own. She met his eyes, and found that they were blurring before her. 'Please be quick,' she said, resolve suddenly wavering. 'I've already had to do this once. I resented that you weren't there, but it's harder now that you are.'

His cool hand rested on her cheek. 'I'm sorry I left you alone,' he said. 'And that I'm going to do it again. But it's everything that you will survive. You are symmetry to me. My piece of the sublime. My star.'

Keturah clutched at his hand on her cheek. She could smell him, the same after all the years apart and all he had endured. But Roper was backing away, gently disentangling her hands, leaving her reaching after him. He kept reversing, neither wanting to take their eyes off the other, until finally he turned. He faced away from her for a moment, standing perfectly still. Then he began his march back to the condemned, high ponytail swinging behind him.

'And now you'll just walk away?' she called after him. 'Leave me to linger on here, alone with the ruins of our world?'

Roper stopped in his tracks once more. 'Wherever you go,' he said quietly. He did not turn back to her. 'Whatever great deeds you perform, whatever you become . . . I beg you, don't forget that you alone shall consume the thoughts of a dying man.'

Roll of Black Legions

Full Legions:
Ramnea's Own Legion
Blackstone Legion
Pendeen Legion
Greyhazel Legion
Skiritai Legion

Auxilliary Legions:
Gillamoor Legion
Saltcoat Legion
Dunoon Legion
Fair Island Legion
Ulpha Legion
Soay Legion
Ancrum Legion

Houses and Major Characters of the Black Kingdom

Major Houses and Their Banners:

Jormunrekur – *The Silver Wolf*
Roper Kynortasson *m.* Keturah Tekoasdottir (House Vidarr)
Numa Roperson
Ormur Kynortasson

Lothbrok – *The Wildcat*
Uvoren Ymerson (deceased) *m.* Hafdis Reykdalsdottir (House Algauti)
Tore Sturnerson
Unndor Uvorenson
Urthr Uvorenson
Leon Kaldison
Sakeus Ketilson

Vidarr – *Catastrophe and the Tree*
Tekoa Urielson *m.* Skathi Hafnisdottir (House Atropa)

Pryce Rubenson (deceased)
Skallagrim Safirson

Baltasar – *The Split Battle-Helm*
Vigtyr Forraederson
Harald Galirson

Alba – *The Rampant Unicorn*
Gray Konrathson *m.* Sigrid Jureksdottir

Oris – *The Rising Sun*
Jokul Krakison

Algauti – *The Angel of Madness*
Randolph Reykdalson

Kinada – *The Frost Tree*
Vinjar Kristvinson *m.* Sigurasta Sakariasdottir

Neantur – *The Skinned Lion*
Hartvig Uxison

Rattatak – *The Ice Bear*
Frathi Akisdottir
Talva Radburnsdottir

Tiazem – *The Dark Mountain*
Virtanen Lanterison

Denisarta – *The Rain of Stars*
Sindri Steinnson

Nadoddur – *The Snatching Hawk*
Kaiho Larikkasdottir

Other Houses and Their Banners:

Indisar – *The Dying Sun*
Eris – *The Mother Aurochs*
Atropa – *The Stone Knife*
Kangur – *The Angel of Divine Vengeance*
Alupali – *The Eagle's Talon*
Keitser – *The Almighty Spear*
Brigaltis – *The Angel of Fear*
Tiazem – *The Dark Mountain*
Horbolis – *The Headless Man*
Denisarta – *The Rain of Stars*
Hybaris – *The Mammoth*
Mothgis – *The Angel of Courage*

Acknowledgements

This was a harder book to write than I'd thought (and not just because it has ended up being enormous). It was started in my final year of medical school, which was originally supposed to finish with several relaxed months of elective, graduation and summer holiday, during which I would have abundant time to finish off a first draft. That was early 2020 and as it happens, things didn't work out as planned. All those nice things were cancelled, and we were called up straight after our final exams to a radically expanded intensive care unit to help with the Covid effort. That didn't leave much time for writing a book, and life hasn't really calmed down since. My first thank you is therefore to you, the reader, for persevering, and waiting for yet another fantasy author to finish their overdue project. The messages of support, and the degree to which people have invested in this world, have always blown me away.

Chief among the others waiting patiently for this book were the splendid staff at Wildfire, and in particular my editor Serena, who was a delight to work with, and remarkably forgiving every time I sheepishly requested another extension. I am grateful to Patrick Insole for yet another wonderful cover design, and Tim Peters for updating and adding his splendid artistic flourishes to the maps contained within. My copy editor Julia was sensitive, thorough and accommodating in taking not one but two passes at the manuscript, and probably knows the story better than I do at this point. Very many thanks too to my agent Felicity for her usual sage input.

I am grateful to have any family and friends remaining to me after being so aloof for so long. Those particularly in need of recognition are my mother, always trusted with first reading my manuscripts (no small task when this one came out close to a quarter of a million words) and my siblings, to whom this book is dedicated.

Author Bio

Leo Carew is a graduate of biological anthropology and medicine, currently writing alongside work as an army doctor. Apart from storytelling, his real passion is exploration, which led him to spend a year living in a tent in the High Arctic. It was here that he started writing *The Wolf*, the first book in the Under the Northern Sky trilogy. *The Spider* and *The Cuckoo* make up the rest of the captivating trilogy.